MOLL FLANDERS

Defoe, Daniel
　　The fortunes and misfortunes of the
　　famous Moll Flanders, etc.
　　Bibl.
　　ISBN 0-19-281194-0
　　1. Title 2. Starr, George Alexander.
　　823'.5　　　　　PR 3404.M6

DANIEL DEFOE

THE
FORTUNES
AND
MISFORTUNES
Of the FAMOUS

Moll Flanders, &c.

Who was Born in NEWGATE,
and during a Life of continu'd Variety for
Threescore Years, besides her Childhood,
was Twelve Year a *Whore*, five times a *Wife*
(whercof once to her own Brother) Twelve Year a *Thief*,
Eight Year a Transported *Felon* in *Virginia*,
at last grew *Rich*, liv'd *Honest*,
and died a *Penitent*,

Written from her own MEMORANDUMS.

EDITED WITH AN INTRODUCTION BY
G. A. STARR

OXFORD UNIVERSITY PRESS
LONDON   OXFORD
1976

Oxford University Press, Walton Street, Oxford, OX2 6DP

OXFORD LONDON GLASGOW NEW YORK
TORONTO MELBOURNE WELLINGTON CAPE TOWN
IBADAN NAIROBI DAR ES SALAAM LUSAKA ADDIS ABABA
KUALA LUMPUR SINGAPORE JAKARTA HONG KONG TOKYO
DELHI BOMBAY CALCUTTA MADRAS KARACHI

ISBN 0 19 281194 0

Introduction, Notes, Bibliography, and Chronology
© *Oxford University Press 1971*

First published in the OXFORD ENGLISH NOVELS *series*
by Oxford University Press, London, 1971
First issued as an Oxford University Press paperback 1976

Printed in Great Britain
at the University Press, Oxford
by Vivian Ridler
Printer to the University

CONTENTS

INTRODUCTION

I

Robinson Crusoe has often been referred to as a romance, but *Moll Flanders*, which followed it by three years, is widely taught and written about as the first English novel. Few other works of fiction have been the subject of so much critical debate in recent years; most widely canvassed has been the question of Defoe's artistic control. Are the numerous contradictions in the words, actions, and total character of Moll Flanders the result of deliberate authorial strategy, of unresolved ambivalences in Defoe's conception of his heroine, or perhaps merely of hasty and unrevised composition by a wonderfully gifted yet somewhat primitive writer? Is Moll the object of Defoe's sustained conscious irony, or do we as readers perceive ironies which Defoe did not intend, and in which his own values are gravely implicated? Criticism preoccupied with the problem of irony has called attention to many inconsistencies that might otherwise have gone unnoticed in Moll's narrative; considerable research into the moral, economic, social, and literary background of *Moll Flanders* has been brought to bear on the discussion, and although such information has not settled the debate over irony,[1] it too has fostered a sense of the book's complexities. At the same time, an unstated premise of much of the debate has been that Defoe's artistry is vindicated if inconsistencies can be shown to have been deliberate. This view is not confined to critics of Defoe—works of all kinds are prized today for containing paradoxes, untrustworthy *personae*, and other forms of calculated ambiguity—nor is it groundless; but it may shed less light

---

[1] The main contentions are summarized in Watt, 'Recent Critical Fortunes of *M.F.*'; for fuller references to works cited in this Introduction see Bibliography, *infra*.

on what is distinctive and valuable in Defoe than on the
achievements of certain of his contemporaries, such as Swift
and Pope. At all events, criticism that puts a premium on
calculated ambiguity tends to conceive of both the creative
process and the reading experience in highly intellectual
terms, and although a predilection for subtlety and complexity
is not the sole explanation of recent critical interest in *Moll
Flanders*, one suspects that it does account for the com-
parative critical neglect of *Robinson Crusoe*, a greater work
the chief merits of which lie elsewhere.

But so, I would maintain, do those of *Moll Flanders*. It
may be that insofar as this book is what we should ordinarily
describe as a novel, it is abundantly and deliberately ironic.
Yet within the novel is a romance, which gives the story
much of its emotional force, and from which irony is absent.
We cannot solve critical problems, of course, simply by
manipulating generic labels, but whatever term we choose,
we should recognize that *Moll Flanders* is akin to tales of
obsession by Hogg or Hawthorne or Melville as well as to
the traditional English novel. We are drawn into the quest
of a heroine who in some degree escapes the bounds of
everyday moral, social, and psychological laws. To be sure,
much of Defoe's celebrated realism consists in his submitting
Moll to such laws. She is in part the product of her environ-
ment—many of her actions as orphan, widow, and criminal
are traced to the pressures of society on those who are its
victims—and when she likens herself as an unattached
female to 'a Bag of Money or a Jewel dropp'd on the
Highway, which is a Prey to the next comer', her image of
the plight of women is firmly rooted in the facts of contemporary life. Yet this picture is belied by a great deal in
Moll's own story. Far from being predatory in the manner
of Richardson's Lovelace, the men she has to do with tend
to be timid and solicitous towards her, and the roles of
initiative and passivity assigned to male and female in the
account of her first seduction are virtually reversed in most
later episodes. In fact, Moll is curiously immune to the

influences of her sex and milieu: although she engages in frequent self-reproach, she distinguishes her admittedly sinful and criminal outward behaviour from her essential self, which remains untainted by her background, her associates, and even her own actions. Nor do her actions have the effect on others that we should normally expect; just as she herself does not become embittered or brutalized, so others stay strangely attached to her, despite her neglect or exploitation of them. So if Moll is in some ways the product of sociological and psychological conditioning, in other ways she is quite untouched by experience, a free spirit whom no pitch can defile. In this sense she leads a charmed life: she is not spared vicissitudes, but spared their ordinary consequences.

Judged by standards of novelistic realism, this aspect of *Moll Flanders* makes for implausibility, as in the reunion scene between Moll and her son Humphry towards the end of the book.[1] But such scenes can also be regarded as obeying formal demands of a different kind, for they follow a pattern which runs through nearly all Defoe's imaginative works. Although his major narratives are usually associated with a variety of distinct genres, such as voyage literature and criminal biography, they are no less closely linked to one another by the quest which is their common theme. Most of Defoe's heroes and heroines are actual or virtual orphans, victims either of abandonment (Colonel Jack), of kidnapping (Captain Singleton), or of their own willful relinquishment of paternal protection, through early mis-marriage (Roxana), or flight (Robinson Crusoe). All are motivated not only by the social and economic aspirations discussed by recent critics, but by regret for a kind of lost paradise, and despite their far-flung wanderings, all long for family reunions, and show as remarkable an aptitude for acquiring surrogate parents and children as for accumulating other kinds of security-yielding property. This pattern extends to such conduct manuals as *The Family Instructor* and *Religious Courtship* as well as the better-known first-person

[1] On this point see Watt, *The Rise of the Novel*, pp. 110–4.

narratives; in all these books, attachments between the sexes tend to be weaker than familial or quasi-familial ones involving the dominance of one party—parent, master, mentor, governess, or God—and the submission of the other. Love is mentioned, but guilt and anxiety are the prevailing emotions, and give a sombre undertone to many otherwise cheerful or sedate passages. Crusoe's elaborate self-enclosure is only the most graphic version of a task that preoccupies most of Defoe's characters, that of achieving impregnability; each seeks a 'safe Harbour' from poverty and other external threats, but also from the painful sense of his own isolation, which is more or less explicitly regarded as a punishment for his own or his parents' misdeeds. The Defoe hero fears betrayal, and to lessen his risks he tries not to get 'entangled with the dull Measures of other People', as Moll puts it, yet he yearns for a perfect community, more often represented in terms of parent-child than of husband-wife relationships. His dream of familial paradise comes true when he manages to find extraordinary exemplars of parental or filial loyalty, who echo God's assurance to Crusoe: 'I will never, never leave thee, nor forsake thee'.

In *Moll Flanders*, this quest-pattern emerges most clearly in the heroine's recurring attachments to older women, each of whom she 'learn'd to call Mother'—the 'good motherly Nurse' in Colchester, the midwife-governess at the Sign of the Cradle, and the mother-in-law who turns out to be her real mother; 'trick'd once by *that Cheat* call'd LOVE', Moll is less intimate with any of the men in her adult life than with this series of maternal figures. It is as if she were intent on demonstrating that she would have been an ideal daughter had she had a proper mother. But one 'mother' leaves her in the lurch by dying, another countenances incest, a third proposes abortion and later leads her 'as it were by the Hand' into a labyrinth of crime: none proves quite equal to Moll's filial longings. Near the end of the book, however, positions are reversed. Hitherto frustrated in the search for an ideal mother, Moll seizes on an alternative possibility, and the reunion with her son Humphry serves as a testimonial that she herself, favoured with a proper child, would make an ideal mother. This latterly-assumed role may also help to explain Moll's satisfaction with her last husband, the ex-highwayman Jemy, who is helpless both in Newgate and Virginia, but who trustingly submits to Moll's maternal care.[1]

Such themes are not as prominent in *Moll Flanders* as in *Robinson Crusoe*, nor does Moll's quest yield any sanctuary to compare in dramatic effectiveness with Crusoe's island 'castle', any parental figure to compare with Crusoe's God, or any filial figure to compare with Crusoe's Friday. And although Moll is in a sense no less alone within society than Crusoe on his island, her story lacks the mythical starkness of Crusoe's solitary encounters with natural and supernatural forces. Nevertheless, within the framework of a realistic novel *Moll Flanders* contains various elements of fantasy, and as we are caught up in the heroine's quest, we find a compelling logic—if such patterns can be called logical—in certain scenes which no doubt fall short of (or exceed) our 'realistic' expectations. In any case, an important source of the book's continuing appeal is its power to involve us imaginatively in Moll's quest; and without denying that amused detachment is a legitimate response to much of the story, one can regard some of Defoe's intermittent irony at Moll's expense as a means rather than an end; that is to say, as a device enabling the reader—and possibly the author as well—to escape the self-reproach which complicity in such activities as Moll's might otherwise cause him.[2]

[1] The idyllic relationship between Colonel Jack and his final wife appears to have a similar basis: after suffering sexual betrayal at the hands of various women, Jack finds security at last with a woman who masterfully shelters and directs him.

[2] The heroine is not the sole object of irony in Moll Flanders; respectable society also comes in for its share, in the course of Moll's casuistical attempts at self-justification. When it succeeds, such irony tends to strengthen her hold on the reader rather than distancing him, for it suggests that the difference in their behaviour is owing mainly to the difference in their circumstances; that the reader too would be driven to crime by poverty and the other pressures which Moll faces; and (more boldly) that bad as she acknowledges herself to be, her values are essentially the same as those of contemporary society at large.

Moll's search for a lost familial paradise takes place, however, alongside other pursuits, and there is no question that yearnings for wealth and gentility play just as conspicuous a part in her narrative. Moll also seeks spiritual salvation; less consistently, perhaps, than her other goals, but at certain moments no less intently. One's opinion as to which of these aspects of *Moll Flanders* is most fundamental will probably depend less on the book itself than on one's personal convictions about the relative weight of psychological, economic, social, and religious 'explanations' of human behaviour. Defoe was clearly fascinated by the complex and overlapping roles of economic, social, and religious motivation as springs of conduct, and it would be wrong to represent him as reducing all such promptings to rationalizations of unconscious urges on the part of his heroes and heroines. My intention in dwelling on psychological themes has not been to assert their primacy, but to point out a significant dimension of Defoe's fictional works, including *Moll Flanders*, which has been neglected by critics. What should be emphasized, though, is the relatedness of these four themes. As recent scholarship has shown, *Moll Flanders* merits the serious attention of students of English economic, social, and religious thought. But however great their historical or theoretical interest, these topics probably possess fictional vitality only insofar as Moll permeates them with her anxiety, and makes money, gentility, and salvation obsessive goals complementary to (and partly interchangeable with) the familial security she also seeks.

II

The first modern editor of *Moll Flanders* surmised that the book was based on the life of a real criminal, and thought it 'quite possible that the person's name will some day be traced'; other scholars have predicted that 'journalistic and biographic sources shall be eventually found for all of Defoe's great narratives'; and in a recent article entitled

'Who Was Moll Flanders?', Gerald Howson proposes
Moll King, alias Mary Godson or Golstone, as the pick-
pocket who served as the model for Defoe's heroine.[1] Few
as they are, the correspondences between this actual Moll
and the fictional Moll are quite suggestive. In 1718 Moll
King had been sentenced to seven years' transportation for
stealing a gold watch from a gentlewoman in St. Anne's
Church, Soho; six months prior to the appearance of *Moll
Flanders* she was condemned to death at the Old Bailey for
returning illegally from America, and although she was soon
given a reprieve from execution, she remained throughout
the autumn of 1721 in Newgate, where Defoe may have met
her. Moll King's vicissitudes were reported in the news-
papers of the day,[2] and *Moll Flanders* may represent Defoe's
attempt to gratify public curiosity by writing at length about
someone whose adventures had been treated only briefly in
journals and pamphlets. But to say that Moll King 'was'
Moll Flanders suggests an identity where there may be a
relation at best fleetingly, sketchily allusive; it suggests that,
even if Defoe did not set out to write what we should call a
biography, he derived the *Fortunes and Misfortunes Of the
Famous Moll Flanders* from those of his real-life 'subject',
who may in fact have furnished little more than an occasion
for writing about a female criminal late in 1721. In short, it
may be misleading to imply that *Moll Flanders* is to any
significant degree about Moll King, for the book is even less
her history than *Robinson Crusoe* is Alexander Selkirk's. The

[1] G. A. Aitken, Introduction to *M. F.* in *Rom. & Narr.*, vii, ix; E. Bernbaum,
Mary Carleton Narratives (1914), p. 87; cf. William Minto, *Daniel Defoe* (1902),
p. 136; Thomas Wright, *Life of Daniel Defoe*, second edn. (1931), pp. 89, 138;
Howson, *TLS*, 18 Jan. 1968, pp. 63–4.

[2] Mr. Howson pieced together her career from court records, but other contemporary writings attest to her notoriety. See e.g. *Life of Mr. John Stanley* (1723),
pp. 10–11, in *Works of Thomas Purney*, ed. H. O. White (1933), pp. 100–101, where
she is associated with St. Anne's Church, said to be 'well known for her Dexterity
in borrowing Gold Watches, or Snuff Boxes, from Ladies', and reported to have
been 'apprehended for privately taking Things, (as I remember from a Mercer) . . .
convicted at the *Old Bailey*, afterwards transported, etc.'. Cf. Defoe's reference to
'M-ll K-ng' in *Life & Actions of Jonathan Wild, Rom. & Narr.*, xvi, 264–5.

heroine's varied criminal exploits have been assembled from diverse sources. One ruse is called 'an old Bite', and several others recall the 'Tricks' and 'Pranks' of traditional rogue literature, but on the whole her career owes less to such semi-fictional narratives than to accounts of actual thefts, which were available to Defoe in newspaper reward-advertisements, in the published proceedings of Old Bailey trials, and in conversation with friends. The image of Defoe hobnobbing with criminals in Newgate has appealed greatly to his biographers, and to those critics who regard his novels as essentially journalistic achievements. He may have come by some information in this way, yet his closest lifelong associations were not with Moll King and her fellows but with the mercantile class on whom they mainly preyed, and Defoe could have obtained as much of his underworld lore from victims, in bourgeois coffee-houses and shops, as from actual thieves in Newgate. If so, his ability to portray crime vividly and sympathetically from the criminal's point of view is all the more noteworthy. It may be that few if any of the thieving exploits in *Moll Flanders* are purely imaginary, but to acknowledge this is quite different from identifying the heroine with one or another criminal of the day.

That Defoe was working from any single model appears even more unlikely if we turn from the criminal section to the other three-quarters of the book. Molly Bloom's conception of her namesake—'the one from Flanders a whore always shoplifting anything she could cloth and stuff and yards of it'—takes into account only a fraction, after all, of the earlier heroine's *Life of continu'd Variety*. Many of the non-criminal scenes have precedents in earlier literature and close analogues elsewhere in Defoe's writings; for instance, various passages reflect his long-standing concern over the callousness of society towards the unprotected and the un-productive—orphans, debtors, criminals, single women without trades, and other marginal types. A similar interest in borderline cases characterizes Defoe's presentation of moral problems: certain of Moll's dilemmas can be traced to

cases of conscience which had been discussed in the casuistical literature of the seventeenth century, in John Dunton's
question-and-answer periodical, *The Athenian Mercury*
(1691–7), and in Defoe's own *Review* and conduct manuals.
And there are several scenes, such as Moll's exchange of
rhymes with the Virginia planter, in which Defoe may be
indebted to earlier writings that have not been traced. The
notes to the present edition indicate the background of some
of Defoe's material, but his 'bookishness' should not be
exaggerated. If (as I believe) some commentators on *Moll
Flanders* have attached undue importance to Defoe's hypothetical interviews with Newgate prisoners, it would nevertheless be a mistake to regard the work as entirely derivative,
the product of literary eclecticism rather than first-hand
journalism. The truth probably lies somewhere between
these extremes, and the remarkable thing is that passages
evidently based on traditional materials should seem no less
lifelike than those drawn from contemporary events.

In this connection it is perhaps worth stressing that Defoe
does not use traditional materials to represent an earlier
period. Some investigators of the sources of *Moll Flanders*
have been led astray by its last five words, 'Written in the
Year 1683'. Once or twice, it is true, places and customs are
referred to as no longer existing, but no attempt is made to
recreate seventeenth-century life from the vantage point of
1721, let alone of 1683. Insofar as the story can be dated, it is
almost entirely contemporary, both in its materials and its
perspective; as my notes indicate, it touches on many
subjects of immediately topical rather than historical interest.
Indeed, some events and practices to which Defoe alludes
were so recent that we should have to judge Moll's retro-
spective mention of them anachronistic, if ordinary chronology were at all crucial to her narrative. But it is not. The
only past that concerns her is her own; the passage of time
may furnish the chief organizing principle of her recollections,
but the tale she tells ultimately eludes calendars and clocks,
and hovers in a timeless fictional once-upon-a-time.

III

Who read *Moll Flanders*? What makes this a question of more than antiquarian interest is the difficulty of determining, behind the voice of the first-person narrator, what Defoe's intentions are. Some critics have supposed that his attitude towards Moll can be deduced from views expressed elsewhere in his writings; others have maintained that the identification of his original reading public can shed similar light on the meaning of the book, since Defoe presumably catered, as a thoroughly professional man of letters, for the tastes and expectations of his audience. Whether either assumption is inherently valid is too large a critical problem to be dealt with here; in practice, however, both indirect approaches to the text of *Moll Flanders* have been beset with difficulties. On many moot points in the book Defoe did express himself elsewhere—abundantly, emphatically, yet inconsistently; and even if his pronouncements in other contexts were altogether uniform, one might hesitate to regard them as decisive prescriptions as to how *Moll Flanders* should be read. One might similarly question the legitimacy of basing interpretations of the book on information about its original readers, even if the evidence were abundant and consistent. In fact, it is neither. That Defoe addressed himself to a petty-bourgeois audience, prizing respectability yet craving adventure, has been inferred from Defoe's own background and from the tone of the novel itself; that many readers were drawn from a class which had only recently achieved literacy has been inferred retroactively from mid-eighteenth-century data about the growth of the reading public; and allusions by enemies and rivals to Defoe's popularity among 'low' readers have been accepted as sociologically and critically revealing. Reprints, piracies, and 'continuations' by other hands indicate that *Moll Flanders* was an immediate success, but we do not really know very much about who its readers were, or what they thought of the book. One contemporary distich—'Down in the kitchen, honest Dick and Doll / Are studying Colonel Jack and Flanders Moll'—certainly points to a lower-class audience, as does the remark in a novel of 1727 that *Gulliver's Travels* have entertained 'the Superiour Class of Mankind', while 'Robinson Crusoe, Moll Flanders, and Colonel Jack have had their Admirers among the lower Rank of Readers'.[1] But as another contemporary observed, an interest in low subject matter is not necessarily confined to lowly readers. Objecting to 'the fabulous Adventures and Memoirs of Pirates, Whores, and Pickpockets, wherewith for some time past the Press has so prodigiously swarmed', this critic cites 'your *Robinson Crusoe*'s, *Moll Flanders*'s, *Sally Salisbury*'s, and *John Shepard*'s' as instances of 'how indulgent we are to the *Biographers* of *Newgate*, who have been as greedily read by People of the better Sort, as the Compilers of *Last Speeches* and *Dying Words* by the rabble'.[2] The price of *Moll Flanders* probably put it beyond the means of 'the rabble', and internal evidence also suggests that Defoe anticipated readers 'of the better Sort': Moll's frequent pleas for sympathy are addressed to people who are securely, complacently respectable, not to those whose precarious, shady existence more nearly resembles her own. We know from Spence's *Anecdotes* that Pope read and thought well of several of Defoe's works, particularly *Robinson Crusoe*, and the scarcity of published discussion by Pope's social and intellectual peers may not mean that they failed to read such books as *Moll Flanders*; it may merely indicate that the emerging novel was not felt to call for critical comment on other than moral grounds, owing to the commonness of its subject matter and the remoteness of its formal and stylistic properties from those of the established genres.

Another point frequently made about the original readers

[1] *The Flying Post: or Weekly Medley*, 1 Mar. 1729, quoted in Sutherland, *Defoe*, p. 236; *The Hermit, or, the . . . Adventures of Mr. Philip Quarll*, Preface.

[2] [James Arbuckle], *Hibernicus's Letters*, No. 9, 29 May 1725. Arbuckle's main complaint—that such works tend 'to corrupt the Taste of the more young and unwary sort of Readers'—is the burden of most contemporary notices of Newgate biography; cf. *The Plain Dealer*, No. 80, 25 Dec. 1724.

of *Moll Flanders* (as well as its author and heroine) is that
they were vestigial Puritans, rechannelling the otherworldly
aspiration of their forefathers into more mundane enter-
prises, which they pursued with comparable zeal. *Moll
Flanders* does seem to translate into secular terms some of the
religious intensity of an earlier era, for its heroine brings to
her worldly self-seeking the same sense of mission with which
the generation of Cromwell and Milton had gone about its
preparations for the millenium. Moreover, Moll has stronger
promptings of faith and hope than of charity, stronger
impulses to acquire than to enjoy, and a stronger sense of her
unfulfilled destiny than of her actual identity. Add to this
that her residual moral fervour largely takes the form of
censoriousness, and one might suppose that the picture of a
latter-day Puritan was complete. Used figuratively, to
designate a type of personality, the label is no doubt appropriate to Defoe's heroine, or at least to one side of her
nature; but alleged as a historical influence on the values of
the book, its author, or its original readers, the accuracy of
the term becomes somewhat more problematic. If the word
'Puritanism' were intended to suggest merely tonal rather
than substantive departures from English Protestantism at
large, its application to eighteenth-century writers such as
Defoe and Richardson might seem less strained, although
few scholars seem content to restrict its meaning in this way.
Yet Defoe denied throughout his life that his religious
beliefs differed on any essential point from the teachings of
the Church of England, and to the limited extent that *Moll
Flanders* touches on doctrinal questions, it bears out his
claim. Among its explicitly religious motifs are the heroine's
allusions to Satan, Providence, and 'Spirits', all of which
take an interest in her affairs, and the charting of her
spiritual career in terms of gradual hardening of heart,
periodic imperfect repentances, and a genuine if belated
conversion. On each of these topics, Defoe's remarks can be
duplicated from the writings of orthodox Anglican divines
as well as from those of his fellow Dissenters. Still, by

venturing to introduce such topics in 'the fabulous Adventures and Memoirs of Pirates, Whores, and Pickpockets', Defoe was guilty, in the eyes of some contemporary and modern readers, of a characteristically Puritan indecorousness. It must be acknowledged, however, that scholarly opinion is nearly unanimous in ascribing the religious elements of *Moll Flanders* to a Puritan tradition shared by Defoe and his readers; disagreement has centred instead on the question— which is part of the larger debate over irony—of whether Defoe himself takes Moll's religiosity seriously, or deploys it to show up the shallow Pharisaism of his heroine. A case can be made for either possibility; my point here is that the question has not been settled, nor perhaps can it be, by producing testimony from Defoe's other writings or evidence about the book's initial readers. That such information can have considerable value seems to me beyond doubt, and is implicitly asserted by various notes to the present edition: that it provides a solution to any of the more enigmatic features of *Moll Flanders* is far less certain.

One fact about his readers Defoe clearly does take for granted: that they are Londoners, who share his own intimate knowledge of local topography and customs. Some scenes in *Moll Flanders* are of course deliberately exotic— not only the remote American ones, but those set in the Mint, in Mother Midnight's lying-in home, or in Newgate, close at hand but outside the direct experience of most law-abiding Londoners. Nevertheless, much of the book assumes a thorough familiarity with London places and practices. When a pickpocket is seized and 'deliver'd up to the Rage of the Street', Moll calls his fate 'a Cruelty I need not describe', and she often avoids spelling out what would be obvious to her fellow-townsmen. More generally, the action of the book is peripatetic but revolves around London, and if Moll's course is often geographically centrifugal, it has a strong centripetal tendency as well. Not only does she return to Newgate to be reborn, or in any case to venture forth once more into a new world, but after various provincial and colonial forays she gravitates back to town, and although London as a whole often seems as chaotic and inhospitable as Newgate itself, Moll draws some of her Antaeus-like resilience from her contact with it.

IV

Except in the Newgate scene, however, our sense of Moll's surroundings depends less on direct description than on her habit of itemizing each step in her itinerary; we seize on place-names as fixed points in an otherwise fluid landscape, and the very fact that its features lack definition gives a special potency to proper names, such as they possess on old maps of newly-discovered regions. But this paucity of visual detail cannot be ascribed simply to Defoe's assumption of a London audience, since it extends to his treatment of other places and of Moll's entire physical setting. He presents the external world chiefly as it is experienced and interpreted by the heroine herself. This is not to say that what matters is only the counting, weighing, measuring, and pricing of things in terms of their economic and social value, and that the physical texture of life is unimportant.[1] It is rather that Moll is less concerned with people, places, and things in themselves than with their bearing on what she does and undergoes: we are given more adverbial than adjectival information, told more about how, when, and where things impinge on her than about what they intrinsically are. Defoe uses active verbs where another writer might use copulatives, favours subordinate over co-ordinate clauses, and relies heavily on participial constructions; the resulting narrative style slights pictorial effects but conveys well the sensations of bodies and minds in restless, obsessive motion—particularly the heroine's:

WANDRING thus about I knew not whither, I pass'd by an Apothecary's Shop in *Leadenhall-street*, where I saw lye on a Stool just before the Counter a little Bundle wrapt in a white Cloth; beyond it,

---

[1] See Van Ghent, *English Novel*, p. 35; Schorer, Introduction, *passim*.

stood a Maid Servant with her Back to it, looking up towards the
top of the Shop, where the Apothecary's Apprentice, as I suppose,
was standing up on the Counter, with his Back also to the Door,
and a Candle in his Hand, looking and reaching up to the upper
Shelf for something he wanted, so that both were engag'd mighty
earnestly, and no body else in the Shop.[1]

These brief stage-directions for Moll's first theft form a kind
of tableau, yet what makes them vivid is not information
about the surfaces of things—the size or colour of the
bundle—but the apprentice's animated absorption in his
task, the maidservant's misplaced attentiveness, and the
speed with which Moll scans the scene and grasps its
momentary pattern. She does not lack a good eye, but can
seldom afford to linger over outward appearances with a
static, painterly gaze. In her more contemplative periods her
attention is directed inwards; she is at pains to specify the
exact hue of moral and psychological predicaments, not of
objects outside herself:

. . . now I repented heartily my easiness with the eldest Brother,
not from any Reflection of Conscience, but from a View of the
Happiness I might have enjoy'd, and had now made impossible;
for tho' I had no great Scruples of Conscience *as I have said* to
struggle with, yet I could not think of being a Whore to one
Brother, and a Wife to the other; but then it came into my
Thoughts, that the first Brother had promis'd to make me his
Wife, when he came to his Estate; but I presently remember'd
what I had often thought of, that he had never spoken a Word of
having me for a Wife, after he had Conquer'd me for a Mistress;
and indeed till now, tho' I said I thought of it often, yet it gave
me no Disturbance at all, for . . .[2]

This passage is typical of Moll's musings: their order is
mainly chronological, but parallels and antitheses, marked
off by conjunctions, introduce an element of logical pattern-
ing into the temporal sequence linked together by adverbs.
Her reflections retain a good deal of the pace and vigour of
her narrative manner, but the greater formality of sentence

[1] p. 191, ll. 24–33.   [2] p. 31, ll. 9–22.

structure, with its balancing of alternatives and modifying of positive assertions, creates an impression of probity and candour. In many such passages, however, Moll's situation is complicated rather than clarified by the welter of qualifications and disclaimers, and her seeming effort to put things precisely is often at odds with the effect she actually achieves, which is to perplex and unsettle. Paradoxes tend to be multiplied rather than resolved. Clauses beginning with 'but', 'yet', 'however', and 'nevertheless', which purport to narrow the scope of an initial proposition, are in fact used to amplify it, and although their logical role is to negate part or all of an earlier statement, their rhetorical function in *Moll Flanders* frequently turns out to be inclusive rather than exclusive. One is ordinarily married or single; in Moll's world one may have 'a Husband and no Husband'. One's words are ordinarily truths or falsehoods; in Moll's world they are often both. Moll's world is one in which things are not good *or* evil, but characteristically good *and yet* evil. This kind of double vision extends from the structure of individual sentences and paragraphs to the ethos of the book as a whole, and affects not only Moll's own attitude towards life but our response to her, which is at once critical and sympathetic.

G. S.

NOTE ON THE TEXT

Moll Flanders was first published 27 January 1722 by W. Chetwood and T. 'Edling' (for Edlin).[1] In July of the same year appeared 'The Second Edition Corrected' bearing the imprint of T. Edlin, W. Chetwood, W. Mears, J. Brotherton, C. King, and J. 'Stags' (for Stagg);[2] another issue of 'The Second Edition, Corrected' was published by J. Brotherton alone:[3] apart from the title-page, the 'Second Edition' copies I have examined are identical. At the end of the year there was one 'Third Edition, Corrected' published by J. Brotherton alone, and another with the names of W. Chetwood, T. Edlin, W. Mears, J. Brotherton, C. King, and J. Stagg on the title-page.[4] Although this 'Third Edition' has been the basis of most modern reprints, it is merely the second edition with a new title-page: in effect, then, there is a first edition and four issues of the second.[5] To pursue this discovery by establishing

1. Since I have had to rely on xerox copies, which fail to indicate the presence of conjugate blank leaves, cancels, stubs, etc., the collations in this note and the next are offered with some diffidence. First-edition signatures: A7, B–Dd8, Ee4; pagination: title-page, [Ar]; blank, [Av]; Preface, A2–[A7r], pp. [iii]–xiii; blank, [A7v]; Text, B–[Ee4v], pp. 1–424. The William Andrews Clark Memorial Library copy, corresponding with No. 446 in John Robert Moore's *Checklist of the Writings of Daniel Defoe* (Bloomington, 1960), and with No. 128 in William H. McBurney's *A Check List of English Prose Fiction 1700–1739* (Cambridge, Mass., 1960).

2. Second-edition signatures: A3, B–Z8, Aa7; pagination: title-page, unsigned; blank, title-page verso; Preface, A–[A3v], pp. [i]–vi; Text, B–[Aa7v], pp. [1]–366. The Cornell University Library copy; this issue not recorded in McBurney's *Check List*.

3. For collation, see preceding note. The Indiana University Library copy, corresponding with No. 128a in McBurney's *Check List*.

4. Collations as in n. 2 *supra*; the Newberry Library and Yale University Library copies of No. 128b in McBurney's *Check List*, the British Museum copy of No. 128c.

5. McBurney states that the third edition was reissued by W. Chetwood in 1723 (*Check List*, No. 128d), but he does not locate a copy, nor have I succeeded in doing so. He also mentions two further versions for which Defoe was evidently not re-

the exact relations between the four second-edition issues was beyond the scope of the present edition, and variants between them have not been recorded in the textual apparatus.[6]

The second edition introduces numerous textual changes: 'the alterations', Herbert Davis observes, 'consist mostly of elimination of epithets, simplification of sentence structure, which sometimes spoils the sense, deletion of phrases which often removes a vivid detail, and in general a shortened, neater, but less flowing narrative'.[7] The key word here is 'shortened', for compression seems to have been the chief objective in revising. This is to say that economic considerations on the part of the publishers, rather than aesthetic considerations on Defoe's part, probably dictated the preparation of a 'Corrected' second edition: by reducing 27 1/2 octavo gatherings to 24 1/2, enough was presumably saved in paper-costs to offset the expense of completely resetting the type, and of engaging someone other than the compositor to prune the text.[8] Much of the compression, however, is clearly the work of the compositor, who has chosen smaller type for the preface, run

sponsible: *The Life and Actions of Moll Flanders ... Adorn'd with Cuts suitable to each Chapter*, 1723 (No. 128e, 'An abridgment [of 188 12mo pp.], with additional material describing the death of Moll Flanders (Elizabeth Atkins)'); *Fortune's Fickle Distribution: In Three Parts. Containing, First, The Life and Death of Moll Flanders ... Part II. The Life of Jane Hackabout, her Governess ... Part III. The Life of James Mac-Faul, Moll Flanders' Lancashire Husband*, 1730 (No. 128f; 124 12mo pp.).

6. Whether the 'Third Edition' issues were reprinted from standing type of the second edition, or consist merely of unsold second-edition sheets bound up with new title-pages, remains to be determined. Occasional press variants occur—e.g. the letters 've' in 'very' at the end of l. 27, p. 34 of the Cornell and Indiana copies of the 'Second Edition' issues have dropped out in the Newberry copy yet not in the Yale copy of the Brotherton 'Third Edition'—but to assess their significance, one would have to compare multiple copies of each of the four issues of the second edition, which has not been attempted here.

7. 'Note on the Text' for the World's Classics edition, a modernized reprinting of the first edition (1961).

8. That the compositor worked from a corrected copy of the first edition, rather than making all the changes himself, is indicated by such passages as the following: where first-edition 'you were fully satisfy'd that' (p. 221) becomes second-edition 'you were fully satisfy'd sure that' (p. 187), one surmises that the words 'fully satisfy'd' had been marked for deletion, but were mistakenly retained along with the word 'sure' which had been inserted to replace them (this edn., p. 181 l. 18).

paragraphs together, and used other space-saving devices.[9]
The crucial question is whether Defoe was responsible for
altering the text itself: in my opinion he probably had no
hand in the revisions.

The editors of the 1738 edition of Defoe's *Complete English
Tradesman* say of his writings, '. . . generally speaking they
are too verbose and circumlocutory; insomuch that it has been
well observed of them, That to have a complete work come
out of his hands, it was necessary to give him so much *per*
sheet to write it in his own way; and half as much afterwards
to lop off its excrescences, or abstract it; And then, especially
if it were on a trading subject, no Author of his time could
produce a more finished performance'.[10] These remarks are
the only external 'evidence' we have of Defoe's role in revising
his own writings; it is hard to know how much credit they
deserve, and in any case they seem to refer to the pre-publica-
tion abridgment of manuscripts rather than the condensing of
works already printed. But if Defoe was indeed willing to
lop to order even his economic writings, in which he took
particular pride, it is not likely that aesthetic scruples
would have prevented him from submitting his fictional
writings to the same operation; and if he was in fact paid
half as much to revise a book as to write it in the first place,
pruning *Moll Flanders* might well have seemed to him a
reasonably remunerative and undemanding piece of work.
Gossip of 1738, evidently introduced to justify further cutting
of the *Complete English Tradesman*, proves nothing as to
Defoe's role in revising *Moll Flanders*, but it does suggest that
the possibility should not be ruled out merely because many
of the changes are perfunctory deletions.

Moreover, the title-page claim that the later edition has been

9. Professor William Hagestad, who is engaged in a detailed bibliographical
analysis of *Moll Flanders*, estimates that actual cuts in the text reduce the length of
the book by approximately one gathering (16 pp.), so that twice as much shortening
is achieved by typographical means.

10. On this passage see Bonamy Dobrée, 'Some Aspects of Defoe's Prose', in
Pope and His Contemporaries: Essays Presented to George Sherburn, ed. J. L. Clifford
and L. A. Landa (1949), pp. 173–4.

'Corrected' is not altogether specious. The original manuscript does not survive, but there are various reasons to suppose that it was as full of abbreviations as the manuscript of *The Compleat English Gentleman* now in the British Museum.[11] If Defoe were being paid 'so much *per* sheet to write it in his own way', abbreviations would increase the speed and volume of his output; *Due Preparations for the Plague, Religious Courtship, A Journal of the Plague Year*, and *Colonel Jack* were all published the same year as *Moll Flanders*, which would suggest that Defoe was writing at an extraordinary pace late in 1721; and from the 'inordinate number of cracks' in the plot of *Moll Flanders* itself, critics have inferred that Defoe 'worked piecemeal, very rapidly, and without any subsequent revision'.[12] More direct evidence is afforded by the first-edition text: a number of words which make no sense in their contexts represent obvious compositorial misreading of Defoe's abbreviations.[13] In a few instances, the second edition restores what was almost certainly Defoe's original intention; more often the entire phrase is deleted, so that the crux is evaded rather than solved.

Although the great majority of substantive changes involve either simple cutting or the replacement of long words and phrases by shorter ones, there are occasional substitutions of

11. 'The MS. [of *Comp. Eng. Gent.*] is well preserved, but the close and hurried writing, the indistinct characters, which may very often mean different letters, the great number of emendations, additions, and deleted passages, the extensive use of contractions and of shorthand and other abbreviations, and the uncommon, irregular, and often curious and faulty spelling make it difficult and sometimes perplexing to read. ... Defoe scarcely puts any commas, and only very rarely puts a full stop or other mark; ... he puts [capitals] quite at random' (Karl D. Bülbring's Foreword, 1890, pp. xvii, xix; on Defoe's abbreviations, cf. also G. H. Healey's Preface to the *Letters* (1955), pp. vii–viii).

12. Watt, *Rise of the Novel*, pp. 100, 99. Watt's view is interestingly borne out by Defoe's tendency to repeat the same word two or three times in as many lines; the second edition, striving for elegant variation, changes 'propose' to 'mention' (p. 139 l. 22), 'obtain' to 'get' (p. 140 l. 20), 'Countenances' to 'Faces' (p. 34 l. 2), 'Gentlewoman's' to 'Lady's' (p. 13 l. 5), etc., when the former term has been used in immediately preceding phrases.

13. Particularly important is first-edition 'which' for 'with' (ms. 'wth'?), p. 278 l. 18; two notable misreadings corrected in the second edition are 'diversion' to 'Direction', p. 339 l. 37; 'sigh'd' to 'high', p. 146 l. 3.

equivalent length and even a few additions.[14] Most of the inter-
polations are in keeping with the spirit of the original text, and
in some cases could be said to 'improve' the first-edition
reading; such changes suggest that the revision was done
with intelligence and care, but do not seem to me distinctive
enough either in substance or style to be claimed as un-
mistakably Defoe's own. Furthermore, some of the second-
edition 'corrections' tend to garble perfectly intelligible
passages. During a game of hazard, when Moll has accumu-
lated 'a good handful of Guineas in [her] Lap', she says, 'I
would have told [i.e. counted] them to see how much I had
got' (first edn., p. 321); the second edition alters this to 'I
would have him to have seen how much I had got' (p. 275;
see present edn., p. 261). This is not only a change for the
worse but is evidently prompted by a failure to understand
Defoe's idiom, which suggests that someone other than Defoe
is responsible. By the same token, certain errors and ob-
scurities have been allowed to remain in the second edition
which one supposes Defoe would have removed, had he indeed
had a hand in the revision.

I therefore think it possible but on the whole rather unlikely
that the second-edition revisions are authorial, and have
adopted the first edition as copy-text. I had hoped to record
all the second-edition substantive variants (some 3,000), but
considerations of space and economy have dictated otherwise. In the Textual Notes (p. 344 below) I have selected
approximately a third of that total to give readers a fairly
good idea of the scope and nature of the substitutions and
deletions. Second-edition changes have been incorporated
in the text only when, as in the instances listed in n. 13 above,
they correct obvious first-edition misreadings, and only when
the latter make no sense.[15]

14. E.g. among the inmates of Newgate on execution day, 'some huzza'd' says
the first edition (p. 359), 'some Brutishly huzza'd' says the second (p. 308; present
edn., p. 291); cf. the important nine-word addition recorded in textual n. to p. 17
l. 23, and discussed in explanatory note.

15. E.g. first-edition 'and the like' (p. 329) makes sense and has been retained,

G. H. Healey's edition of the *Letters* shows that Defoe's manuscripts were lightly punctuated and erratically capitalized, even when addressed to distinguished correspondents, and Karl Bülbring's edition of *The Compleat English Gentleman* indicates that both tendencies—along with the use of abbreviations mentioned earlier—were especially pronounced when Defoe was composing rapidly and in quantity for the press. In the case of *Moll Flanders*, one suspects that the first-edition punctuation was almost entirely the compositor's doing, not Defoe's,[16] but the present edition proceeds as if it were Defoe's: it has been altered only when it actively distorts or obscures the sense of a passage, and in such cases second-edition readings have with few exceptions been adopted. Similarly, first-edition misspellings that reflect known Defoean usage (e.g. 'peice') or *OED*-recorded seventeenth- or eighteenth-century usage (e.g. 'usuage') have been retained, even when they are 'corrected' in the second edition; but misspellings that can safely be ascribed to typographical error are replaced by second-edition readings, and the (probably Defoean) 'whether' and 'then' have been replaced by second-edition 'whither' and 'than' wherever we should now use the latter forms. Although the second-edition accidentals retain

---

although second-edition 'an you like' (p. 282) makes better sense and may have been what Defoe wrote; see p. 267 l. 12 in present edition.

The only other substantive departures from the first-edition text involve accidentally transposed words and phrases: thus where the first edition reads 'and to whole peices also make up' (p. 421), the second-edition correction 'and whole Pieces also, to make up' (p. 363) has been adopted (present edition, p. 340). A more significant instance occurs at p. 281. The first-edition reading, 'the harden'd wretch'd boldness of Spirit, which I had acquir'd, abated, and conscious in the Prison Guilt began to flow' (p. 347), is clearly defective; the second edition merely deletes 'in the Prison' (p. 298) but on the assumption that these three words were Defoe's and simply got misplaced, the present edition emends to '. . . acquir'd in the Prison abated, and conscious Guilt . . .' (see textual note).

16. Certain problems in the printing history remain unsolved (see n. 6 above), and thus make further bibliographical research on *Moll Flanders* desirable. But if most of the first-edition punctuation was supplied by the compositor, and represents an early interpretation of what Defoe intended rather than a transcription of what he actually wrote, then a definitive edition prepared according to the principles of modern textual scholarship might be scarcely more authoritative *with respect to accidentals* than an intelligently modernized text.

numerous first-edition errors and introduce many new ones, there are also many points at which they offer better (or at least more modern) forms; but wherever the first edition is comprehensible it has been preserved, and no departures from it have been made for the sake of 'improving' already intelligible passages.

SELECT BIBLIOGRAPHY

JOHN Robert Moore's *Checklist of the Writings of Daniel Defoe* (1960) lists 547 distinct titles; University Microfilms Ltd. has reproduced all items which can be located, except certain periodicals with only minor contributions by Defoe. The major fictional works and a few social and economic tracts are conveniently reprinted in George A. Aitken's edition of *Romances and Narratives*, 16 vols. (1895), and in the Shakespeare Head Press *Novels and Selected Writings*, 14 vols. (1927–8). Defoe's *Review* has been edited in facsimile by Arthur W. Secord, 22 vols. (1938), with a useful index volume by William L. Payne (1948). Some of Defoe's contributions to other periodicals are reprinted in William Lee's *Daniel Defoe: His Life and Recently Discovered Writings*, 3 vols. (1869). Defoe's *Tour thro' the Whole Island of Great Britain* is available in an Everyman edition, ed. G. D. H. Cole and D. C. Browning, 2 vols. (1962). Defoe's *Letters* have been edited by George H. Healey (1955). The standard biography remains James Sutherland's *Defoe* (1937; 2nd edn., 1950); much additional information is assembled in John Robert Moore's *Daniel Defoe: Citizen of the Modern World* (1958). Among earlier studies of Defoe's life and writings, the most important are Paul Dottin's *Daniel De Foe et ses Romans* (1924) and Arthur W. Secord's *Studies in the Narrative Method of Defoe* (1924). Defoe is discussed at length in various histories of the early English novel; Ian Watt's *The Rise of the Novel* (1957) and Alan D. McKillop's *Early Masters of English Fiction* (1956) are particularly valuable.

A helpful survey and critique of modern studies of *Moll Flanders* is to be found in Watt's 'Afterword' to the Fawcett paperback edition of the book (1967); this essay appeared originally as 'The Recent Critical Fortunes of *Moll Flanders*', *Eighteenth-Century Studies*, i (1967), 109–26. Much critical debate has grown out of Mark Schorer's Introduction to the Modern Library edition (1950), Dorothy Van Ghent's chapter 'On *Moll Flanders*' in *The English Novel: Form and Function* (1953), pp. 33–43, and Watt's chapter on 'Defoe as Novelist: *Moll Flanders*' in *The Rise of the*

Novel, pp. 93–134. Among articles dealing entirely with *Moll Flanders* during the past decade, the following are of special interest: Terence Martin, 'The Unity of *Moll Flanders*', *Modern Language Quarterly*, xxii (1961), 115–24; Robert R. Columbus, 'Conscious Artistry *in Moll Flanders*', *Studies in English Literature*, iii (1963), 415–32; Howard L. Koonce, 'Moll's Muddle: Defoe's Use of Irony in *Moll Flanders*', *English Literary History*, xxx (1963), 377–94; Denis Donoghue, 'The Values of *Moll Flanders*', *Sewanee Review*, lxxi (1963), 287–303; Arnold Kettle, 'In Defence of *Moll Flanders*', in *Of Books and Humankind: Essays and Poems Presented to Bonamy Dobrée*, ed. John Butt (1964), pp. 55–67; Maximillian E. Novak, 'Conscious Irony in *Moll Flanders*', *College English*, xxvi (1964), 198–204; Douglas Brooks, '*Moll Flanders*: An Interpretation', *Essays in Criticism*, xix (1969), 46–59. Other useful discussions of *Moll Flanders* may be found in Novak's *Defoe and the Nature of Man* (1963); Martin Price's *To the Palace of Wisdom* (1964); Robert Alter's *Rogue's Progress: Studies in the Picaresque Novel* (1964); and the present editor's forthcoming *Defoe and Casuistry*. A number of these essays are reprinted in *Twentieth-Century Interpretations of Moll Flanders*, ed. Robert C. Elliott (1970).

The following studies deal only in part with *Moll Flanders*, but have significant bearing on one or another aspect of the novel: Hans H. Andersen, 'The Paradox of Trade and Morality in Defoe', *Modern Philology*, xxxix (1941), 23–46; Jonathan Bishop, 'Knowledge, Action, and Interpretation in Defoe's Novels', *Journal of the History of Ideas*, xiii (1951), 3–16; Benjamin Boyce, 'The Question of Emotion in Defoe', *Studies in Philology*, l (1953), 45–58; James T. Boulton, 'Daniel Defoe: His Language and Rhetoric', Introduction to *Daniel Defoe* (1965), pp. 1–22.

A CHRONOLOGY OF
DANIEL DEFOE

THIS is based mainly on the detailed 'Chronological Outline' in John Robert Moore's *Daniel Defoe: Citizen of the Modern World* (1958), pp. 345–55.

THE PREFACE

THE World is so taken up of late with Novels and Romances, that it will be hard for a private History[1] to be taken for Genuine, where the Names and other Circumstances of the Person arc concealed, and on this Account we must be content to leave the Reader to pass his own Opinion upon the ensuing Sheets, and take it just as he pleases.

THE Author is here suppos'd to be writing her own History, and in the very beginning of her Account, she gives the Reasons why she thinks fit to conceal her true Name, after which there is no Occasion to say any more about that.

IT is true, that the original of this Story is put into new Words, and the Stile of the famous Lady we here speak of is a little alter'd, particularly she is made to tell her own Tale in modester Words than she told it at first; the Copy which came first to Hand, having been written in Language, more like one still in *Newgate*, than one grown Penitent and Humble, as she afterwards pretends[2] to be.

THE Pen employ'd in finishing her Story, and making it what you now see it to be, has had no little difficulty to put it into a Dress fit to be seen, and to make it speak Language fit to be read: When a Woman debauch'd from her Youth, nay, even being the Off-spring of Debauchery and Vice, comes to give an Account of all her vicious Practises, and even to descend to the particular Occasions and Circumstances, by which she first became wicked, and of all the progression of Crime which she run through in threescore Year, an Author must be hard put to it to wrap it up so clean, as not to give room, especially for vitious Readers[3] to turn it to his Disadvantage.

ALL possible Care however has been taken to give no leud

Ideas, no immodest Turns in the new dressing up this Story,
no not to the worst parts of her Expressions; to this Purpose
some of the vicious part of her Life, which cou'd not be
modestly told, is quite left out, and several other Parts, are
very much shortn'd; what is left 'tis hop'd will not offend
the chastest Reader, or the modestest Hearer;[1] and as the
best use is made even of the worst Story, the Moral 'tis
hop'd will keep the Reader serious, even where the Story
might incline him to be otherwise: To give the History of a
wicked Life repented of, necessarily requires that the wicked
Part should be made as wicked, as the real History of it will
bear; to illustrate and give a Beauty to the Penitent part,
which is certainly the best and brightest, if related with
equal Spirit and Life.

IT is suggested there cannot be the same Life, the same
Brightness and Beauty, in relating the penitent Part, as is in
the criminal Part: If there is any Truth in that Suggestion, I
must be allow'd to say, 'tis because there is not the same
taste and relish in the Reading,[2] and indeed it is too true
that the difference lyes not in the real worth of the Subject
so much as in the Gust and Palate of the Reader.[3]

BUT as this Work is chiefly recommended to those who
know how to Read it, and how to make the good Uses of it,
which the Story all along recommends to them; so it is to
be hop'd that such Readers will be much more pleas'd with
the Moral, than the Fable; with the Application,[4] than with
the Relation, and with the End of the Writer, than with the
Life of the Person written of.

THERE is in this Story abundance of delightful Incidents,
and all of them usefully apply'd. There is an agreeable turn
Artfully given them in the relating, that naturally Instructs
the Reader, either one way, or other. The first part of her
leud Life with the young Gentleman at *Colchester*, has so
many happy Turns given it to expose the Crime, and warn
all whose Circumstances are adapted to it, of the ruinous
End of such things, and the foolish Thoughtless and abhorr'd Conduct of both the Parties, that it abundantly

attones for all the lively Discription she gives of her Folly and Wickedness.

THE Repentance of her Lover at the *Bath*, and how brought by the just alarm of his fit of Sickness to abandon her; the just Caution given there against even the lawful Intimacies of the dearest Friends, and how unable they are to preserve the most solemn Resolutions of Vertue without divine Assistance; these are Parts, which to a just Discernment will appear to have more real Beauty in them, than all the amorous Chain of Story, which introduces it.

IN a Word, as the whole Relation is carefully garbl'd[1] of all the Levity, and Looseness that was in it: So it is all applied, and with the utmost care to vertuous and religious Uses. None can without being guilty of manifest Injustice, cast any Reproach upon it, or upon our Design in publishing it.

THE Advocates for the Stage,[2] have in all Ages made this the great Argument to persuade People that their Plays are useful, and that they ought to be allow'd in the most civiliz'd, and in the most religious Government; Namely, That they are applyed to vertuous Purposes, and that by the most lively Representations, they fail not to recommend Vertue, and generous Principles, and to discourage and expose all sorts of Vice and Corruption of Manners; and were it true that they did so, and that they constantly adhered to that Rule, as the Test of their acting on the *Theatre*, much might be said in their Favour.

THROUGHOUT the infinite variety of this Book, this Fundamental is most strictly adhered to; there is not a wicked Action in any Part of it, but is first or last rendered Unhappy and Unfortunate: There is not a superlative Villain brought upon the Stage, but either he is brought to an unhappy End, or brought to be a Penitent: There is not an ill thing mention'd, but it is condemn'd, even in the Relation, nor a vertuous just Thing, but it carries its Praise along with it: What can more exactly answer the Rule laid down, to recommend, even those Representations of things which have so many other just Objections lying against them? Namely, of Example, of bad Company, obscene Language, and the like.

UPON this Foundation this Book is recommended to the Reader, as a Work from every part of which something may be learned, and some just and religious Inference is drawn, by which the Reader will have something of Instruction, if he pleases to make use of it.

ALL the Exploits of this Lady of Fame, in her Depredations upon Mankind stand as so many warnings to honest People to beware[1] of them, intimating to them by what Methods innocent People are drawn in, plunder'd and robb'd, and by Consequence how to avoid them. Her robbing a little innocent Child, dress'd fine by the vanity of the Mother, to go to the Dancing-School, is a good Memento to such People hereafter; as is likewise her picking the Gold-Watch from the young Ladies side in the *Park*.

HER getting a parcel from a hair-brained Wench at the Coaches in St. *John-street*; her Booty made at the Fire, and again at *Harwich*; all give us excellent Warnings in such Cases to be more present to ourselves in sudden Surprizes of every Sort.

HER application to a sober Life, and industrious Management at last in *Virginia*, with her Transported Spouse, is a Story fruitful of Instruction, to all the unfortunate Creatures who are oblig'd to seek their Re-establishment abroad; whether by the Misery of Transportation, or other Disaster; letting them know, that Diligence and Application have their due Encouragement, even in the remotest Parts of the World, and that no Case can be so low, so despicable,[2] or so empty of Prospect, but that an unwearied Industry will go a great way to deliver us from it, will in time raise the meanest Creature to appear again in the World, and give him a new Cast for his Life.[3]

THESE are a few of the serious Inferences which we are led by the Hand to in this Book, and these are fully sufficient to Justifie any Man in recommending it to the World, and much more to Justifie the Publication of it.

THERE are two of the most beautiful Parts still behind, which this Story gives some idea of, and lets us into the Parts of them, but they are either of them too long to be brought into the same Volume; and indeed are, *as I may call them* whole Volumes of themselves, (*viz.*) I. The Life of her Governess, as she calls her, who had run thro', it seems in a few Years all the eminent degrees of a Gentlewoman, a Whore, and a Bawd; a Midwife, and a Midwife-keeper,[1] as *they are call'd*, a Pawn-broker, a Child-taker, a Receiver of Thieves, and of Thieves purchase, that is to say, of stolen Goods; and in a Word, her self a Thief, a Breeder up of Thieves, and the like, and yet at last a Penitent.

THE second is the Life of her Transported Husband, a Highway-man; who it seems liv'd a twelve Years Life of successful Villany upon the Road, and even at last came off so well, as to be a Voluntier Transport, not a Convict; and in whose Life there is an incredible Variety.

BUT as I have said, these are things too long to bring in here, so neither can I make a Promise of their coming out by themselves.

WE cannot say indeed, that this History is carried on quite to the End of the Life of this famous *Moll Flanders*, as she calls her self, for no Body can write their own Life to the full End of it, unless they can write it after they are dead; but her Husband's Life being written by a third Hand, gives a full Account of them both, how long they liv'd together in that Country, and how they came both to *England* again, after about eight Year, in which time they were grown very Rich, and where she liv'd it seems, to be very old; but was not so extraordinary a Penitent, as she was at first; it seems only that indeed she always spoke with abhorence of her former Life, and of every Part of it.

IN her last Scene at *Maryland*, and *Virginia*, many pleasant things happen'd, which makes that part of her Life very agreeable, but they are not told with the same Elegancy as those accounted for by herself; so it is still to the more Advantage that we break off here.

THE
HISTORY
AND
MISFORTUNES

Of the FAMOUS
Moll Flanders, &c.

MY True Name is so well known in the Records, or Registers at *Newgate*, and in the *Old-Baily*,[1] and there are some things of such Consequence still depending there, relating to my particular Conduct, that it is not to be expected I should set my Name, or the Account of my Family to this Work; perhaps, after my Death it may be better known, at present it would not be proper, no, not tho' a general Pardon should be issued, even without Exceptions and reserve of Persons or Crimes.

IT is enough to tell you, that as some of my worst Comrades, who are out of the Way of doing me Harm, having gone out of the World by the Steps and the String, as I often expected to go, knew me by the Name of *Moll Flanders*; so you may give me leave to speak of myself, under that Name till I dare own who I have been, as well as who I am.

I HAVE been told, that in one of our Neighbour Nations, whether it be in *France*, or where else, I know not;[2] they have an Order from the King, that when any Criminal is condemn'd, either to Die, or to the Gallies, or to be Transported, if they leave any Children, as such are generally unprovided for, by the Poverty or Forfeiture of their

Parents; so they are immediately taken into the Care of the
Government, and put into an Hospital call'd the *House* of
Orphans, where they are Bred up, Cloath'd, Fed, Taught,
and when fit to go out, are plac'd out to Trades, or to
Services, so as to be well able to provide for themselves by
an honest industrious Behaviour.

HAD this been the Custom in our Country, I had not been
left a poor desolate Girl without Friends, without Cloaths,
without Help or Helper in the World, as was my Fate; and
by which, I was not only expos'd to very great Distresses,
even before I was capable, either of Understanding my Case,
or how to Amend it, nor brought into a Course of Life,
which was not only scandalous in itself, but which in its
ordinary Course, tended to the swift Destruction both of
Soul and Body.

BUT the Case was otherwise here, my Mother was convicted of Felony for a certain petty Theft, scarce worth
naming, (*viz.*) Having an opportunity of borrowing three
Pieces of fine *Holland*,[1] of a certain Draper in *Cheapside*:
The Circumstances are too long to repeat, and I have heard
them related so many Ways, that I can scarce be certain,
which is the right Account.

HOWEVER it was, this they all agree in, that my Mother
pleaded her Belly,[2] and being found quick with Child, she
was respited for about seven Months, in which time having
brought me into the World, and being about again, she was
call'd Down, as they term it, to her former Judgment, but
obtain'd the Favour of being Transported to the Plantations,
and left me about Half a Year old; and in bad Hands you
may be sure.

THIS is too near the first Hours of my Life, for me to
relate any thing of myself, but by hear say, 'tis enough to
mention, that as I was born in such an unhappy Place, I had
no Parish to have Recourse to[3] for my Nourishment in my
Infancy, nor can I give the least Account how I was kept
alive; other, than that as I have been told, some Relation of
my Mothers took me away for a while as a Nurse, but at

whose Expence, or by whose Direction I know nothing at all of it.

THE first account that I can Recollect, or could ever learn of myself, was, that I had wandred among a Crew of those People they call *Gypsies*, or *Egyptians*; but I believe it was but a very little while that I had been among them, for I had not had my Skin discolour'd, or blacken'd,[1] as they do very young to all the Children they carry about with them, nor can I tell how I came among them, or how I got from them.

IT was at *Colchester* in *Essex*, that those People left me; and I have a Notion in my Head, that I left them there, (that is, that I hid myself and wou'd not go any farther with them) but I am not able to be particular in that Account; only this I remember, that being taken up by some of the Parish Officers of *Colchester*, I gave an Account, that I came into the Town with the *Gypsies*, but that I would not go any farther with them, and that so they had left me, but whither they were gone that I knew not, nor could they expect it of me; for tho' they sent round the Country to enquire after them, it seems they could not be found.

I WAS now in a Way to be provided for; for tho' I was not a Parish Charge upon this, or that part of the Town by Law; yet as my Case came to be known, and that I was too young to do any Work, being not above three Years old, Compassion mov'd the Magistrates of the Town to order some Care to be taken of me, and I became one of their own, as much as if I had been born in the Place.

IN the Provision they made for me, it was my good hap to be put to Nurse, as they call it, to a Woman who was indeed Poor, but had been in better Circumstances, and who got a little Livelihood by taking such as I was suppos'd to be; and keeping them with all Necessaries, till they were at a certain Age, in which it might be suppos'd they might go to Service, or get their own Bread.

THIS Woman had also a little School, which she kept to teach Children to Read and to Work; and having, as I have said, liv'd before that in good Fashion, she bred up the

Children she took with a great deal of Art, as well as with a great deal of Care.

BUT that which was worth all the rest, she bred them up very Religiously, being herself a very sober pious Woman. (2.) Very Housewifly and Clean, and, (3.) Very Mannerly, and with good Behaviour: So that in a Word, excepting a plain Diet, course Lodging, and mean Cloths, we were brought up as Mannerly and as Genteely, as if we had been at the Dancing School.

I WAS continu'd here till I was eight years Old, when I was terrified with News, that the Magistrates, as I think they call'd them, had order'd that I should go to Service;[1] I was able to do but very little Service where ever I was to go, except it was to run of Errands, and be a Druge to some Cook-Maid, and this they told me of often, which put me into a great Fright; for I had a thorough Aversion to going to Service, as they call'd it, that is to be a Servant, tho' I was so young; and I told my Nurse, as we call'd her, that I believ'd I could get my Living without going to Service[2] if she pleas'd to let me; for she had Taught me to Work with my Needle, and Spin Worsted, which is the chief Trade of that City,[3] and I told her that if she wou'd keep me, I wou'd Work for her, and I would Work very hard.

I talk'd to her almost every Day of Working hard; And in short, I did nothing but Work and Cry all Day, which griev'd the good kind Woman so much, that at last she began to be concern'd for me, for she lov'd me very well.

ONE Day after this, as she came into the Room, where all we poor Children were at Work, she sat down just over against me, not in her usual Place as Mistress, but as if she set herself on purpose to observe me, and see me Work: I was doing something she had set me to, as I remember, it was Marking some Shirts, which she had taken to Make, and after a while she began to Talk to me: Thou foolish Child, says she, thou art always Crying; (for I was Crying then) prethee, What doest Cry for? because they will take me away, *says I*, and put me to Service, and I can't Work House-Work;

well Child, says she, but tho' you can't Work House-Work,
as you call it, you will learn it in time, and they won't put
you to hard Things at first; yes they will, says I, and if I
can't do it, they will Beat me, and the Maids will Beat me to
make me do great Work, and I am but a little Girl, and I
can't do it, and then I cry'd again, till I could not speak any
more to her.

THIS mov'd my good Motherly Nurse, so that she from
that time resolv'd I should not go to Service yet, so she bid
me not Cry, and she wou'd speak to Mr. *Mayor*, and I
should not go to Service till I was bigger.

WELL, this did not Satisfie me, for to think of going to
Service, was such a frightful Thing to me, that if she had
assur'd me I should not have gone till I was 20 years old, it
wou'd have been the same to me, I shou'd have cry'd, I
believe all the time, with the very Apprehension of its being
to be so at last.

WHEN she saw that I was not pacify'd yet, she began to be
angry with me, and what wou'd you have? *says she*, don't I
tell you that you shall not go to Service till you are bigger?
Ay, says I, but then I must go at last, why, what? said she,
is the Girl mad? what, would you be a Gentlewoman?[1] Yes
says I, and cry'd heartily, till I roar'd out again.

THIS set the old Gentlewoman a Laughing at me, as you
may be sure it would: Well, Madam forsooth, says she,
Gibing at me, you would be a Gentlewoman, and pray how
will you come to be a Gentlewoman? what, will you do it by
your Fingers Ends?

YES, *says I again*, very innocently.

WHY, what can you Earn, *says she*, what can you get at
your Work?

THREE-Pence, *said I*, when I Spin,[2] and 4*d*. when I Work
plain Work.[3]

ALAS! poor Gentlewoman, *said she again*, Laughing, what
will that do for thee?

IT will keep me, *says I*, if you will let me live with you;
and this *I said*, in such a poor petitioning Tone, that it made

the poor Womans Heart yearn to me, as she told me afterwards.

BUT, *says she*, that will not keep you, and buy you Cloths too; and who must buy the little Gentlewoman Cloths, *says she*, and smil'd all the while at me.

I will Work Harder then, *says I*, and you shall have it all.

POOR Child! it won't keep you, *says she*, it will hardly keep you in Victuals.

THEN I will have no Victuals, *says I*, again very Innocently, let me but live with you.

WHY, can you live without Victuals? *says she*, yes, *again says I*, very much like a Child, you may be sure, and still I cry'd heartily.

I HAD no Policy in all this, you may easily see it was all Nature, but it was joyn'd with so much Innocence, and so much Passion, That in short, it set the good Motherly Creature a weeping too, and she cry'd at last as fast as I did, and then took me, and led me out of the teaching Room; come *says she*, you shan't go to Service, you shall live with me, and this pacify'd me for the present.

SOMETIME after this, she going to wait on the *Mayor*, and talking of such things as belong'd to her Business, at last my Story came up, and my good Nurse told Mr. *Mayor* the whole Tale: He was so pleas'd with it, that he would call his Lady, and his two Daughters to hear it, and it made Mirth enough among them, you may be sure.

HOWEVER, not a Week had pass'd over, but on a suddain comes Mrs. *Mayoress*, and her two Daughters to the House to see my old Nurse, and to see her School and the Children: When they had look'd about them a little: Well, Mrs. ———— says the *Mayoress* to my Nurse; and pray which is the little Lass that intends to be a Gentlewoman? I heard her, and I was terrible frighted at first, tho' I did not know why neither; but Mrs. *Mayoress* comes up to me, Well Miss says she, And what are you at Work upon? The Word Miss was a Language that had hardly been heard of in our School, and I wondred what sad[1] Name it was she call'd me; However, I stood up, made a Curtsy, and she took my Work out of my Hand, look'd on it, and said it was very well; then she took up one of my Hands, nay, says she, the Child may come to be a Gentlewoman for ought any body knows, she has a Gentlewoman's Hand, says she; this pleas'd me mightily you may be sure, but Mrs. *Mayoress* did not stop there, but giving me my Work again, she put her Hand in her Pocket, gave me a Shilling, and bid me mind my Work, and learn to Work well, and I might be a Gentlewoman for ought she knew.

Now all this while, my good old Nurse, Mrs. *Mayoress*, and all the rest of them did not understand me at all, for they meant one Sort of thing, by the Word Gentlewoman, and I meant quite another; for alas, all I understood by being a Gentlewoman, was to be able to Work for myself, and get enough to keep me without that terrible Bug-bear *going to Service*, whereas they meant to live Great, Rich, and High, and I know not what.

WELL, after Mrs. *Mayoress* was gone, her two Daughters came in, and they call'd for the Gentlewoman too, and they talk'd a long while to me, and I answer'd them in my Innocent way; but always if they ask'd me whether I resolv'd to be a Gentlewoman, I answer'd YES: At last one of them ask'd me, what a Gentlewoman was? that puzzel'd me much; but however, I explain'd myself negatively, that it was one that did not go to Service, to do House-Work; they were pleas'd to be familiar [with] me, and lik'd my little Prattle to them, which it seems was agreeable enough to them, and they gave me Money too.

As for my Money I gave it all to my Mistress Nurse, as I call'd her, and told her she should have all I got for myself when I was a Gentlewoman, as well as now; by this and some other of my talk, my old Tutress began to understand me, about what I meant by being a Gentlewoman; and that I understood by it no more, than to be able to get my Bread by my own Work, and at last, she ask'd me whether it was not so.

I told her *yes*, and insisted on it, that to do so, was to be a Gentlewoman; for says I, there is such a one, naming a Woman that mended Lace, and wash'd the Ladies Lac'd-heads,[1] she, *says I*, is a Gentlewoman, and they call her Madam.

POOR Child, says my good old Nurse, you may soon be such a Gentlewoman as that, for she is a Person of ill Fame, and has had two or three Bastards.

I DID not understand any thing of that; but I answer'd, I am sure they call her Madam, and she does not go to Service, nor do House-Work, and therefore I insisted that she was a Gentlewoman, and I would be such a Gentlewoman as that.

THE Ladies were told all this again to be sure, and they made themselves Merry with it, and every now and then the young Ladies, Mr. *Mayor's* Daughters would come and see me, and ask where the little Gentlewoman was, which made me not a little Proud of myself.

THIS held a great while, and I was often visited by these young Ladies, and sometimes they brought others with them; so that I was known by it, almost all over the Town.

I WAS now about ten Years old, and began to look a little Womanish, for I was mighty Grave and Humble; very Mannerly, and as I had often heard the Ladies say I was Pretty, and would be a very handsome Woman, so you may be sure, that hearing them say so, made me not a little Proud; however, that Pride had no ill effect upon me yet, only as they often gave me Money, and I gave it my old Nurse, she *honest Woman*, was so just to me, as to lay it all out again for me, and gave me Head-Dresses, and Linnen, and Gloves and Ribbons, and I went very Neat, and always Clean; for that I would do, and if I had Rags on, I would always be Clean, or else I would dabble them in Water myself; but *I say*, my good Nurse, when I had Money given me, very honestly laid it out for me, and would always tell the Ladies, this, or that, was brought with their Money; and this made them oftentimes give me more; Till at last, I was indeed call'd upon by the Magistrates as I understood it, to go out to Service; but then I was come to be so good a Work-woman myself, and the Ladies were so kind to me, that it was plain I could maintain myself, that is to say, I could Earn as much for my Nurse as she was able by it to keep me; so she told them, that if they would give her leave, she would keep the Gentlewoman as she call'd me, to be her Assistant, and teach the Children, which I was very well able to do; for I was very nimble at my Work, and had a good Hand with my Needle, though I was yet very young.

But the kindness of the Ladies of the Town did not End here, for when they came to understand that I was no more maintain'd by the publick Allowance, as before, they gave me Money oftner than formerly; and as I grew up, they brought me Work to do for them; such as Linnen to Make, and Laces to Mend, and Heads to Dress up, and not only paid me for doing them, but even taught me how to do them; so that now I was a Gentlewoman indeed, as I understood that Word, and as I desir'd to be, for by that time, I was twelve Years old, I not only found myself Cloaths, and paid my Nurse for my keeping, but got Money in my Pocket too before-hand.

The Ladies also gave me Cloaths frequently of their own, or their Childrens, some Stockings, some Petticoats, some Gowns, some one thing, some another, and these my old Woman Managed for me like a meer Mother,[1] and kept them for me, oblig'd me to Mend them, and turn them and twist them to the best Advantage, for she was a rare House-Wife.

At last one of the Ladies took so much Fancy to me, that she would have me Home to her House, for a Month she said, to be among her Daughters.

Now tho' this was exceeding kind in her, yet as my old good Woman said to her, unless she resolv'd to keep me for good and all, she would do the little Gentlewoman more harm than good: Well, says the Lady, that's true, and therefore I'll only take her Home for a Week then, that I may see how my Daughters and she agree together, and how I like her Temper, and then I'll tell you more; and in the mean

time, if any Body comes to see her as they us'd to do, you
may only tell them, you have sent her out to my House.

THIS was prudently manag'd enough, and I went to the
Ladies House, but I was so pleas'd there with the young
Ladies, and they so pleas'd with me, that I had enough to
do to come away, and they were as unwilling to part with me.

HOWEVER, I did come away, and liv'd almost a Year more
with my honest old Woman, and began now to be very
helpful to her; for I was almost fourteen Years old, was tall
of my Age, and look'd a little Womanish; but I had such a
Tast of Genteel living at the Ladies House, that I was not
so easie in my old Quarters as I us'd to be, and I thought it
was fine to be a Gentlewoman indeed, for I had quite other
Notions of a Gentlewoman now, than I had before; and as I
thought, I say, that it was fine to be a Gentlewoman, so I
lov'd to be among Gentlewomen, and therefore I long'd to
be there again.

ABOUT the Time that I was fourteen Years and a quarter
Old, my good old Nurse, Mother I ought rather to call her,
fell Sick and Dyed; I was then in a sad Condition indeed, for
as there is no great Bustle in putting an end to a Poor bodies
Family, when once they are carried to the Grave; so the poor
good Woman being Buried, the Parish Children she kept
were immediately remov'd by the Church-Wardens; the
School was at an End, and the Children of it had no more to
do but just stay at Home, till they were sent some where else;
and as for what she left, her Daughter a married Woman with
six or seven Children, came and swept it all away at once,
and removing the Goods, they had no more to say to me,
than to Jest with me, and tell me, that the little Gentlewoman might set up for her self if she pleas'd.

I was frighted out of my Wits almost, and knew not what
to do, for I was, as it were, turn'd out of Doors to the wide
World, and that which was still worse, the old honest
Woman had two and twenty Shillings of mine in her Hand,
which was all the Estate the little Gentlewoman had in the
World; and when I ask'd the Daughter for it, she huft me

and laught at me, and told me, she had nothing to do with it.

IT was true, the good poor Woman had told her Daughter of it, and that it lay in such a Place, that it was the Child's Money, and had call'd once or twice for me, to give it me, but I was unhappily out of the way, some where or other; and when I came back she was past being in a Condition to speak of it: However, the Daughter was so Honest afterward as to give it me, tho' at first she us'd me Cruelly about it.

NOW was I a poor Gentlewoman indeed, and I was just that very Night to be turn'd into the wide World; for the Daughter remov'd all the Goods, and I had not so much as a Lodging to go to, or a bit of Bread to Eat: But it seems some of the Neighbours who had known my Circumstances, took so much Compassion of me, as to acquaint the Lady in whose Family I had been a Week, as I mention'd above; and immediately she sent her Maid to fetch me away, and two of her Daughters came with the Maid tho' unsent; so I went with them Bag and Baggage, and with a glad Heart you may be sure: The fright of my Condition had made such an Impression upon me, that I did not want now to be a Gentlewoman, but was very willing to be a Servant, and that any kind of Servant they thought fit to have me be.

BUT my new generous Mistress, for she[1] exceeded the good Woman I was with before, in every Thing, as well as in the matter of Estate; I say in every Thing except Honesty; and for that, tho' this was a Lady most exactly Just, yet I must not forget to say on all Occasions, that the First tho' Poor, was as uprightly Honest as it was possible for any One to be.

I was no sooner carried away as I have said by this good Gentlewoman, but the first Lady, *that is to say*, the *Mayoress* that was, sent her two Daughters to take Care of me; and another Family which had taken Notice of me, when I was the little Gentlewoman, and had given me Work to do, sent for me after her, so that I was mightily made of, as we say; nay, and they were not a little Angry, especially, Madam the *Mayoress*, that her Friend had taken me away

from her as she call'd it; for as she said, I was Hers by
Right, she having been the first that took any Notice of me;
but they that had me, wou'd not part with me; and as for
me, tho' I shou'd have been very well Treated with any of
the other, yet I could not be better than where I was.

HERE I continu'd till I was between 17 and 18 Years old,
and here I had all the Advantages for my Education that
could be imagin'd; the Lady had Masters home to the
House to teach her Daughters to Dance, and to speak
French, and to Write, and others to teach them Musick; and
as I was always with them, I learn'd as fast as they; and tho'
the Masters were not appointed to teach me, yet I learn'd by
Imitation and enquiry, all that they learn'd by Instruction
and Direction. So that in short, I learn'd to Dance, and
speak *French* as well as any of them, and to Sing much
better,[1] for I had a better Voice than any of them; I could
not so readily come at playing on the Harpsicord or Spinnet,
because I had no Instrument of my own to Practice on, and
could only come at theirs in the intervals, when they left it,
which was uncertain, but yet I learn'd tollerably well too,
and the young Ladies at length got two Instruments, that is
to say, a Harpsicord, and a Spinnet too, and then they
Taught me themselves; But as to Dancing they could
hardly help my learning Country Dances, because they
always wanted me to make up even Number; and on the
other Hand, they were as heartily willing to learn me every
thing that they had been Taught themselves, as I could be
to take the Learning.

BY this Means I had, as I have said above, all the Advantages of Education[2] that I could have had, if I had been as
much a Gentlewoman as they were, with whom I liv'd, and
in some things, I had the Advantage of my Ladies, tho' they
were my Superiors; but they were all the Gifts of Nature,
and which all their Fortunes could not furnish. First, I was
apparently Handsomer than any of them. Secondly, I was
better shap'd, and Thirdly, I Sung better, by which I mean,
I had a better Voice; in all which you will I hope allow me to

say, I do not speak my own Conceit of myself, but the Opinion of all that knew the Family.

I HAD with all these the common Vanity of my Sex (*viz.*) That being really taken for very Handsome, or if you please for a great Beauty, I very well knew it, and had as good an Opinion of myself, as any body else could have of me; and particularly I lov'd to hear any body speak of it, which could not but happen to me sometimes, and was a great Satisfaction to me.

THUS far I have had a smooth Story to tell of myself, and in all this Part of my Life, I not only had the Reputation of living in a very good Family, and a Family Noted and Respected every where, for Vertue and Sobriety, and for every valluable Thing; but I had the Character too of a very sober, modest, and vertuous young Woman, and such I had always been; neither had I yet any occasion to think of any thing else, or to know what a Temptation to Wickedness meant.

BUT that which I was too vain of, was my Ruin, or rather my vanity was the Cause of it. The lady in the House where I was, had two Sons, young Gentlemen of very promising Parts, and of extraordinary Behaviour; and it was my Misfortune to be very well with them both, but they manag'd themselves with me in a quite different Manner.

THE eldest a gay Gentleman that knew the Town, as well as the Country, and tho' he had Levity enough to do an ill natur'd thing, yet had too much Judgment of things to pay too dear for his Pleasures; he began with that unhappy Snare to all Women, (*viz.*) taking Notice upon all Occasions how pretty I was, as he call'd it; how agreeable, how well Carriaged, and the like; and this he contriv'd so subtilly, as if he had known as well, how to catch a Woman in his Net, as a Patridge when he went a Setting; for he wou'd contrive to be talking this to his Sisters when tho' I was not by, yet when he knew I was not so far off, but that I should be sure to hear him: His Sisters would return softly to him, Hush Brother, she will hear you, she is but in the next Room;

then he would put it off, and Talk softlier, as if he had not known it, and begun to acknowledge he was Wrong; and then as if he had forgot himself, he would speak aloud again, and I that was so well pleas'd to hear it, was sure to Lissen for it upon all Occasions.

AFTER he had thus baited his Hook,[1] and found easily enough the Method how to lay it in my Way, he play'd an opener Game; and one Day going by his Sister's Chamber when I was there, doing something about Dressing her, he comes in with an Air of gayty, O! Mrs. *Betty*,[2] said he to me, How do you do Mrs. *Betty*? don't your Cheeks burn, Mrs. *Betty*? I made a Curtsy, and blush'd, but said nothing; What makes you talk so Brother, *says the Lady*; Why, says he, we have been talking of her below Stairs this half Hour; *Well says his Sister*, you can say no Harm of her, that I am sure, so 'tis no matter what you have been talking about; nay, *says he*, 'tis so far from talking Harm of her, that we have been talking a great deal of good, and a great many fine Things have been said of Mrs. *Betty*, I assure you; and particularly, that she is the Handsomest young Woman in *Colchester*; and, in short, they begin to Toast her Health in the Town.

I wonder at you Brother, *says the Sister*; *Betty* wants but one Thing, but she had as good want every Thing, for the Market is against our Sex just now; and if a young Woman have Beauty, Birth, Breeding, Wit, Sense, Manners, Modesty, and all these to an Extream; yet if she have not Money, she's no Body, she had as good want them all, for nothing but Money now recommends a Woman;[3] the Men play the Game all into their own Hands.

HER younger Brother, who was by, cry'd *Hold Sister*, you run too fast, I am an Exception to your Rule; I assure you, if I find a Woman so Accomplish'd as you Talk of, *I say*, I assure you, I would not trouble myself about the Money.

O, says the Sister, but you will take Care not to Fancy one then, without the Money.

YOU don't know that neither, *says the Brother*.

But why Sister, (*says the elder Brother*) why do you exclaim so at the Men, for aiming so much at the Fortune? you are none of them that want a Fortune, what ever else you want.

I understand you Brother, (*replies the Lady very smartly,*) you suppose I have the Money, and want the Beauty; but as Times go now, the first will do without the last, so I have the better of my Neighbours.

Well, *says the younger Brother*, but your Neighbours, as you call them may be even with you; for Beauty will steal a Husband sometimes in spight of Money; and when the Maid chances to be Handsomer than the Mistress, she oftentimes makes as good a Market, and rides in a Coach before her.

I thought it was time for me to withdraw, and leave them, and I did so; but not so far, but that I heard all their Discourse, in which I heard abundance of fine things said of myself, which serv'd to prompt my Vanity; but as I soon found, was not the way to encrease my Interest in the Family; for the Sister, and the younger Brother fell grieviously out about it; and as he said some very disobliging things to her, upon my Account, so I could easily see that she Resented them, by her future Conduct to me; which indeed was very unjust to me, for I had never had the least thought of what she suspected, as to her younger Brother: Indeed the elder Brother in his distant remote Way, had said a great many things, as in Jest, which I had the folly to believe were in earnest, or to flatter myself, with the hopes of what I ought to have suppos'd he never intended, and perhaps never thought of.

It happen'd one Day that he came running up Stairs, towards the Room where his Sisters us'd to sit and Work, as he often us'd to do; and calling to them before he came in, as was his way too, I being there alone, step'd to the Door, and said, Sir, the Ladies are not here, they are Walk'd down the Garden; as I step'd forward, to say this towards the Door, he was just got to the Door, and clasping me in his Arms, as if it had been by Chance, O! Mrs. *Betty, says he,* are you here? that's better still; I want to speak with you, more than I do with them, and then having me in his Arms he Kiss'd me three or four times.

I struggl'd to get away, and yet did it but faintly neither, and he held me fast, and still Kiss'd me, till he was almost out of Breath, and then sitting down, says, *dear Betty* I am in Love with you.

HIS Words I must confess fir'd my Blood; all my Spirits flew about my Heart, and put me into Disorder enough, which he might easily have seen in my Face: He repeated it afterwards several times, that he was in Love with me, and my Heart spoke as plain as a Voice, that I lik'd it; nay, when ever he said, I am in Love with you, my Blushes plainly reply'd, *wou'd you were* Sir.

HOWEVER nothing else pass'd at that time; it was but a Surprise, and when he was gone, I soon recover'd myself again. He had stay'd longer with me, but he happen'd to look out at the Window, and see his Sisters coming up the Garden, so he took his leave, Kiss'd me again, told me he was very serious, and I should hear more of him very quickly, and away he went leaving me infinitely pleas'd tho' surpris'd, and had there not been one Misfortune in it, I had been in the Right, but the Mistake lay here, that Mrs. *Betty* was in Earnest, and the Gentleman was not.

FROM this time my Head run upon strange Things, and I may truly say, I was not myself; to have such a Gentleman talk to me of being in Love with me, and of my being such a charming Creature, as he told me I was, these were things I knew not how to bear, my vanity was elevated to the last Degree: It is true, I had my Head full of Pride, but knowing nothing of the Wickedness of the times, I had not one Thought of my own Safety, or of my Vertue about me; and had my young Master offer'd it at first Sight, he might have taken any Liberty he thought fit with me; but he did not see his Advantage, which was my happiness for that time.

AFTER this Attack, it was not long, but he found an opportunity to catch me again, and almost in the same

posture, indeed it had more of Design in it on his Part, tho'
not on my Part; *it was thus*; the young Ladies were all gone
a Visiting with their Mother; his Brother was out of Town;
and as for his Father, he had been at *London* for a Week
before; he had so well watched me, that he knew where I
was, tho' I did not so much as know that he was in the
House; and he briskly comes up the Stairs, and seeing me
at Work comes into the Room to me directly, and began
just as he did before with taking me in his Arms, and
Kissing me for almost a quarter of an Hour together.

IT was his younger Sisters Chamber, that I was in, and as
there was no Body in the House, but the Maids below Stairs,
he was it may be the ruder: In short, he began to be in
Earnest with me indeed; perhaps he found me a little too
easie, for God knows I made no Resistance to him while he
only held me in his Arms and Kiss'd me, indeed I was too
well pleas'd with it, to resist him much.

HOWEVER as it were, tir'd with that kind of Work, we sat
down, and there he talk'd with me a great while; *he said*, he
was charm'd with me, and that he could not rest Night, or
Day till he had told me how he was in Love with me; and if
I was able to Love him again, and would make him happy, I
should be the saving of his Life; and many such fine things.
I said little to him again, but easily discover'd that I was a
Fool,[1] and that I did not in the least perceive what he meant.

THEN he walk'd about the Room, and taking me by the
Hand, I walk'd with him; and by and by, taking his Advantage, he threw me down upon the Bed, and Kiss'd me there
most violently; but to give him his Due, offer'd no manner
of Rudeness to me, only Kiss'd me a great while; after this
he thought he had heard some Body come up Stairs, so he
got off from the Bed, lifted me up, professing a great deal of
Love for me, but told me it was all an honest Affection, and
that he meant no ill to me; and with that he put five Guineas
into my Hand, and went away down Stairs.

I WAS more confounded with the Money than I was
before with the Love; and began to be so elevated, that I

scarse knew the Ground I stood on: I am the more particular in this part, that if my Story comes to be read by any innocent young Body, they may learn from it to Guard themselves against the Mischiefs which attend an early Knowledge of their own Beauty; if a young Woman once thinks herself Handsome, she never doubts the Truth of any Man, that tells her he is in Love with her; for if she believes herself Charming enough to Captivate him, tis natural to expect the Effects of it.

THIS young Gentleman had fir'd his Inclination, as much as he had my vanity, and as if he had found that he had an opportunity, and was sorry he did not take hold of it, he comes up again in half an Hour, or thereabouts, and falls to Work with me again as before, only with a little less Introduction.

AND, First, when he enter'd the Room, he turn'd about, and shut the Door. Mrs. *Betty*, said he, I fancy'd before, some Body was coming up Stairs, but it was not so; however, *adds he*, if they find me in the Room with you, they shan't catch me a Kissing of you; I told him I did not know who should be coming up Stairs, for I believ'd there was no Body in the House, but the Cook, and the other Maid, and they never came up those Stairs; well my Dear, *says he*, 'tis.good to be sure however, and so he sits down and we began to Talk; and now, tho' I was still all on fire with his first visit, and said little, he did as it were put Words in my Mouth, telling me how passionately he lov'd me, and that tho' he could not mention such a thing, till he came to his Estate, yet he was resolv'd to make me happy then, and himself too; *that is to say*, *to Marry me*, and abundance of such fine things, which I poor Fool did not understand the drift of, but acted as if there was no such thing as any kind of Love, but that which tended to Matrimony; and if he had spoke of that, I had no Room, as well as no Power to have said No; but we were not come that length yet.

WE had not sat long, but he got up, and stoping my very Breath with Kisses, threw me upon the Bed again, but then being both well warm'd, he went farther with me than Decency permits me to mention, nor had it been in my power to have deny'd him at that Moment, had he offer'd much more than he did.

HOWEVER, tho' he took these Freedoms with me, it did not go to that, which they call the last Favour, which, to do him Justice, he did not attempt; and he made that self denial of his a Plea for all his Freedoms with me upon other Occasions after this: When this was over, he stay'd but a little while, but he put almost a Handful of Gold in my Hand, and left me; making a thousand Protestations of his Passion for me, and of his loving me above all the Women in the World.

IT will not be strange, if I now began to think, but alas! it was but with very little solid Reflection: I had a most unbounded Stock of Vanity and Pride, and but a very little Stock of Vertue; I did indeed cast sometimes with myself what my young Master aim'd at, but thought of nothing, but the fine Words, and the Gold; whether he intended to Marry me, or not to Marry me, seem'd a Matter of no great Consequence to me; nor did my Thoughts so much as suggest to me the Necessity of making any Capitulation[1] for myself, till he came to make a kind of formal Proposal to me, as you shall hear presently.

THUS I gave up myself to a readiness of being ruined without the least concern, and am a fair *Memento* to all young Women, whose Vanity prevails over their Vertue: Nothing was ever so stupid on both Sides, had I acted as became me, and resisted as Vertue and Honour requir'd, this Gentleman had either Desisted his Attacks, finding no room to expect the Accomplishment of his Design, or had made fair, and honourable Proposals of Marriage; in which Case, whoever had blam'd him, no Body could have blam'd me. In short, if he had known me, and how easy the Trifle he aim'd at, was to be had, he would have troubled his Head no farther, but have given me four or five Guineas, and have lain with me the next time he had come at me; and if I had known his

Thoughts, and how hard he thought I would be to be gain'd, I might have made my own Terms with him; and if I had not Capitulated for an immediate Marriage, I might for a Maintenance till Marriage, and might have had what I would; for he was already Rich to Excess, besides what he had in Expectation; but I seem'd wholly to have abandoned all such Thoughts as these, and was taken up Onely with the Pride of my Beauty, and of being belov'd by such a Gentleman; as for the Gold I spent whole Hours in looking upon it; I told the Guineas over and over a thousand times a Day: Never poor vain Creature was so wrapt up with every part of the Story, as I was, not Considering what was before me, and how near my Ruin was at the Door; indeed I think, I rather wish'd for that Ruin, than studied to avoid it.

IN the mean time however, I was cunning enough, not to give the least room to any in the Family to suspect me, or to imagine that I had the least Correspondence with this young Gentleman; I scarce ever look'd towards him in publick, or Answer'd if he spoke to me, if any Body was near us; but for all that, we had every now and then a little Encounter, where we had room for a Word or two, and now and then a Kiss; but no fair opportunity for the Mischief intended; and especially considering that he made more Circumlocution, than if he had known my Thoughts he had occasion for, and the Work appearing Difficult to him, he really made it so.

BUT as the Devil is an unwearied Tempter, so he never fails to find opportunity for that Wickedness he invites to: It was one Evening that I was in the Garden, with his two younger Sisters, and himself, and all very innocently Merry, when he found Means to convey a Note into my Hand, by which he Directed me to understand, that he would to Morrow desire me publickly to go of an Errand for him into the Town, and that I should see him somewhere by the Way.

ACCORDINGLY after Dinner, he very gravely says to me, his Sisters being all by, Mrs. *Betty*, I must ask a Favour of you: What's that? *says his second Sister*; nay, Sister *says he*, very gravely, if you can't spare Mrs. *Betty* to Day, any other time will do; *yes they said*, they could spare her well enough, and the Sister beg'd Pardon for asking; which she did but of meer Course, without any Meaning; Well, but Brother, says the eldest Sister, you must tell Mrs. *Betty* what it is; if it be any private Business, that we must not hear, you may call her out, there she is: Why Sister, says the Gentleman, very gravely, What do you mean? *I* only desire her to go into the *High-street*, (and then he pulls out a Turn-Over)[1] to such a Shop, and then he tells them a long Story of two fine Neck-cloths he had bid Money for, and he wanted to have me go and make an Errand to buy a Neck to the Turn-Over that he showed, to see if they would take my Money for the Neck-cloths; to bid a Shilling more, and Haggle with them; and then he made more Errands, and so continued to have such petty Business to do, that *I* should be sure to stay a good while.

WHEN he had given me my Errands, he told them a long Story of a Visit he was going to make to a Family they all knew, and where was to be such and such Gentlemen, and how Merry they were to be; and very formally asks his Sisters to go with him, and they as formally excus'd them-selves, because of Company that they had Notice was to come and Visit them that Afternoon, which by the Way he had contriv'd on purpose.

HE had scarce done speaking to them, and giving me my Errand, but his Man came up to tell him that Sir *W*———— *H*————*s* Coach stop'd at the Door; so he runs down, and comes up again immediately, alas! *says he*, aloud, there's all my Mirth spoil'd at once; Sir *W*———— has sent his Coach for me, and desires to speak with me upon some earnest Business: It seems this Sir *W*———— was a Gentleman, who liv'd about three Miles out of Town, to whom he had spoken on purpose the Day before, to lend him his Charriot for a particular occasion; and had appointed it to call for him, as it did about three a Clock.

IMMEDIATELY he calls for his best Wig, Hat and Sword, and ordering his Man to go to the other Place to make his

Excuse, that was to say, he made an Excuse to send his Man
away; he prepares to go into the Coach: As he was going, he
stop'd a while, and speaks mighty earnestly to me about his
Business, and finds an Opportunity to say very softly to me,
come away my Dear as soon as ever you can. I said nothing, but
made a Curtsy, as if I had done so to what he said in publick;
in about a Quarter of an Hour I went out too, I had no Dress,
other than before, except that I had a Hood, a Mask, a Fan
and a pair of Gloves in my Pocket; so that there was not the
least Suspicion in the House: He waited for me in the Coach
in a back *Lane*, which he knew *I* must pass by; and had
directed the Coachman whither to go, which was to a certain
Place, call'd *Mile-End*,[1] where lived a Confident of his,
where we went in, and where was all the Convenience in the
World to be as Wicked as we pleas'd.

WHEN we were together, he began to Talk very Gravely
to me; and to tell me, he did not bring me there to betray
me; that his Passion for me, would not suffer him to Abuse
me; that he resolv'd to Marry me as soon as he came to his
Estate,[2] that in the mean time, if *I* would grant his Request,
he would Maintain me very Honourably, and made me a
thousand Protestations of his Sincerity, and of his Affection
to me; and That he would never abandon me, and as *I* may
say, made a thousand more Preambles than he need to have
done.

HOWEVER as he press'd me to speak, I told him, I had no
Reason to question the Sincerity of his Love to me, after so
many Protestations, But —— and there I stopp'd, as if I
left him to Guess the rest; BUT WHAT my Dear? *says he*, I
guess what you mean; what if you should be with Child, is
not that it? Why then, *says he*, I'll take Care of you, and
Provide for you, and the Child too, and that you may see I
am not in Jest, *says he*, here's an Earnest for you; and with
that he pulls out a silk Purse, with an Hundred Guineas in
it, and gave it me; and I'll give you such another, *says he*,
every Year till I Marry you.

MY Colour came, and went, at the Sight of the Purse, and

with the fire of his Proposal together; so that I could not say
a Word, and he easily perceiv'd it; so putting the Purse into
my Bosom, I made no more Resistance to him, but let him
do just what he pleas'd; and as often as he pleas'd; and thus
I finish'd my own Destruction at once, for from this Day,
being forsaken of my Vertue, and my Modesty, I had nothing
of Value left to recommend me, either to God's Blessing, or
Man's Assistance.

BUT things did not End here, I went back to the Town,
did the Business he publickly directed me to, and was at
Home before any Body thought me long; as for my Gentleman, he staid out as he told me he would, till late at Night,
and there was not the least Suspicion in the Family, either
on his Account or on mine.

WE had after this, frequent Opportunities to repeat our
Crime; chiefly by his contrivance; especially at home; when
his Mother and the young Ladies went Abroad a Visiting,
which he watch'd so narrowly, as never to miss; knowing
always before-hand when they went out; and then fail'd not
to catch me all alone, and securely enough; so that we took
our fill of our wicked Pleasure for near half a Year; and yet,
which was the most to my Satisfaction, I was not with Child.

BUT before this half Year was expir'd, his younger
Brother, of whom I have made some mention in the beginning of the Story, falls to work with me; and he finding me
alone in the Garden one Evening, begins a Story of the same
Kind to me, made good honest Professions of being in Love
with me; and in short, proposes fairly and Honourably to
Marry me, and that before he made any other Offer to me
at all.

I was now confounded and driven to such an Extremity,
as the like was never known; at least not to me; I resisted the
Proposal with Obstinancy; and now I began to Arm my self
with Arguments: I laid before him the inequallity of the
Match, the Treatment I should meet with in the Family; the
Ingratitude it wou'd be to his good Father and Mother, who
had taken me into their House upon such generous Prin-

ciples, and when I was in such a low Condition; and in short, I said every thing to dissuade him from his Design that I could imagine, except telling him the Truth, which wou'd indeed have put an end to it all, but that I durst not think of mentioning.

But here happen'd a Circumstance that I did not expect indeed, which put me to my Shifts; for this young Gentleman as he was plain and Honest, so he pretended to nothing with me, but what was so too; and knowing his own Innocence, he was not so careful to make his having a Kindness for Mrs. *Betty*, a Secret in the House, as his Brother was; and tho' he did not let them know that he had talk'd to me about it, yet he said enough to let his Sisters perceive he Lov'd me, and his Mother saw it too, which tho' they took no Notice of it to me, yet they did to him, and immediately I found their Carriage to me alter'd, more than ever before.

I saw the Cloud, tho' I did not foresee the Storm;[1] it was easie, *I say*, to see that their Carriage to me was alter'd, and that it grew worse and worse every Day; till at last I got Information among the Servants, that I shou'd, in a very little while, be desir'd to remove.

I was not alarm'd at the News, having a full Satisfaction that I should be otherwise provided for; and especially, considering that I had Reason every Day to expect I should be with Child, and that then I should be oblig'd to remove without any Pretences for it.

After some time, the younger Gentleman took an Opportunity to tell me, that the Kindness he had for me, had got vent[2] in the Family; he did not Charge me with it, *he said*, for he knew well enough which way it came out; he told me his plain way of Talking had been the Occasion of it, for that he did not make his respect for me so much a Secret as he might have done, and the Reason was, that he was at a Point;[3] that if I would consent to have him, he would tell them all openly that he lov'd me, and that he intended to Marry me: That it was true his Father and Mother might Resent it, and

be unkind, but that he was now in a Way to live, being bred
to the Law, and he did not fear Maintaining me, agreeable
to what I should expect; and that in short, as he believed I
would not be asham'd of him, so he was resolv'd not to be
asham'd of me, and that he scorn'd to be afraid to own me
now, who he resolv'd to own after I was his Wife, and
therefore I had nothing to do but to give him my Hand, and
he would Answer for all the rest.

I was now in a dreadful Condition indeed, and now I
repented heartily my easiness with the eldest Brother, not
from any Reflection of Conscience, but from a View of the
Happiness I might have enjoy'd, and had now made impossible; for tho' I had no great Scruples of Conscience *as I
have said* to struggle with, yet I could not think of being a
Whore to one Brother, and a Wife to the other; but then it
came into my Thoughts, that the first Brother had promis'd
to make me his Wife, when he came to his Estate; but I
presently remember'd what I had often thought of, that he
had never spoken a Word of having me for a Wife, after he
had Conquer'd me for a Mistress; and indeed till now, tho'
I said I thought of it often, yet it gave me no Disturbance at
all, for as he did not seem in the least to lessen his Affection
to me, so neither did he lessen his Bounty, tho' he had the
Discretion himself to desire me not to lay out a Penny of
what he gave me in Cloaths, or to make the least show
Extraordinary, because it would necessarily give Jealousie in
the Family, since every Body knew I could come at such
things no manner of ordinary Way; but by some private
Friendship, which they would presently have suspected.

BUT I was now in a great strait, and really knew not what
to do; the main Difficulty was this, the younger Brother not
only laid close Siege to me, but suffered it to be seen; he
would come into his Sisters Room, and his Mothers Room,
and sit down, and Talk a Thousand kind things of me, and
to me, even before their Faces, and when they were all there:
This grew so Publick, that the whole House talk'd of it, and
his Mother reprov'd him for it, and their Carriage to me

appear'd quite Altered: In short, his Mother had let fall some Speeches, as if she intended to put me out of the Family, that is in *English*, to turn me out of Doors. Now, I was sure this could not be a Secret to his Brother, only that he might not think as indeed no Body else yet did, that the youngest Brother had made any Proposal to me about it; But as I easily cou'd see that it would go farther, so I saw likewise there was an absolute Necessity to speak of it to him, or that he would speak of it to me, and which to do first I knew not; that is, whether I should break it to him, or let it alone till he should break it to me.

UPON serious Consideration, for indeed now I began to Consider things very seriously, and never till now: I say, upon serious Consideration, I resolv'd to tell him of it first, and it was not long before I had an Opportunity, for the very next Day his Brother went to *London* upon some Business, and the Family being out a Visiting, just as it had happen'd before, and as indeed was often the Case, he came according to his Custom to spend an Hour or Two with Mrs. *Betty*.

WHEN he came and had sate down a while, he easily perceiv'd there was an alteration in my Countenance, that I was not so free and pleasant with him, as I us'd to be, and particularly, that I had been a Crying; he was not long before he took notice of it, and ask'd me in very kind Terms what was the Matter, and if any thing Troubl'd me: I wou'd have put it off if I could, but it was not to be Conceal'd; so after suffering many Importunities to draw that out of me, which I long'd as much as possible to Disclose; I told him that it was true, something did Trouble me, and something of such a Nature, that I could not Conceal from him, and yet, that I could not tell how to tell him of it neither; that it was a thing that not only Surpriz'd me, but greatly perplex'd me, and that I knew not what Course to take, unless he would Direct me: He told me with great Tenderness, that let it be what it wou'd, I should not let it Trouble me, for he would Protect me from all the World.

I then begun at a Distance, and told him I was afraid the

Ladies had got some secret Information of our Correspondence; for that it was easie to see, that their Conduct was very much chang'd towards me for a great while, and that now it was come to that pass, that they frequently found Fault with me, and sometimes fell quite out with me, tho' I never gave them the least Occasion: That whereas, I us'd always to lye with the Eldest Sister, I was lately put to lye by my self, or with one of the Maids; and that I had overheard them several times talking very Unkindly about me; but that which confirm'd it all, was, that one of the Servants had told me, that she had heard I was to be Turn'd out, and that it was not safe for the Family, that I should be any longer in the House.

He smil'd when he heard all this, and I ask'd him, how he could make so light of it, when he must needs know, that if there was any Discovery, I was Undone for ever? and that even it would hurt him, tho' not Ruin him, as it would me: I upbraided him, that he was like all the rest of the Sex, that when they had the Character and Honour of a Woman at their Mercy, often times made it their Jest, and at least look'd upon it as a Trifle, and counted the Ruin of those, they had had their Will of, as a thing of no value.

He saw me Warm and Serious, and he chang'd his Stile immediately; *he told me*, he was sorry I should have such a thought of him; that he had never given me the least Occasion for it, but had been as tender of my Reputation, as he could be of his own; that he was sure our Correspondence had been manag'd with so much Address, that not one Creature in the Family had so much as a Suspicion of it; that if he smil'd when I told him my Thoughts, it was at the Assurance he lately receiv'd, that our understanding one another, was not so much as known or guess'd at; and that when he had told me, how much Reason he had to be Easie, I should Smile as he did, for he was very certain, it would give me a full Satisfaction.

This is a Mystery I cannot understand, *says I*, or how it should be to my Satisfaction, that I am to be turn'd out of

Doors; for if our Correspondence is not discover'd, I know not what else I have done to change the Countenances of the whole Family to me, or to have them Treat me as they do now, who formerly used me with so much Tenderness, as if I had been one of their own Children.

WHY look you Child, *says he*, that they are Uneasie about you, that is true; but that they have the least Suspicion of the Case as it is, and as it respects you and I, is so far from being True, that they suspect my Brother *Robin*; and in short, they are fully persuaded he makes Love to you: Nay, the Fool has put it into their Heads too himself, for he is continually Bantring them about it, and making a Jest of himself; I confess, I think he is wrong to do so, because he can not but see it vexes them, and makes them Unkind to you; but 'tis a Satisfaction to me, because of the Assurance it gives me, that they do not suspect me in the least, and I hope this will be to your Satisfaction too.

So it is, *says I*, one way, but this does not reach my Case at all, nor is this the chief Thing that Troubles me, tho' I have been concern'd about that too: What is it then, *says he*? With which, I fell into Tears, and could say nothing to him at all: He strove to pacifie me all he could, but began at last to be very pressing upon me, to tell what it was; at last *I answer'd*, that I thought I ought to tell him too, and that he had some right to know it, besides, that I wanted his Direction in the Case, for I was in such Perplexity, that I knew not what Course to take, and then I related the whole Affair to him: *I told him*, how imprudently his Brother had manag'd himself, in making himself so Publick; for that if he had kept it a Secret, as such a Thing ought to have been, I could but have Denied him Positively, without giving any Reason for it, and he would in Time have ceas'd his Sollicitations; but that he had the Vanity, first, to depend upon it that I would not Deny him, and then had taken the Freedom to tell his Resolution of having me, to the whole House.

I *told him* how far I had resisted him, and *told him* how Sincere and Honourable his Offers were, but *says I*, my

Case will be doubly hard; for as they carry it Ill to me now, because he desires to have me, they'll carry it worse when they shall find I have Deny'd him; and they will presently say, there's something else in it, and then out it comes, that I am Marry'd already to somebody else, or else that I would never refuse a Match so much above me as this was.

THIS Discourse surpriz'd him indeed very much: He *told me*, that it was a critical Point indeed for me to Manage, and he did not see which way I should get out of it; but he would consider of it, and let me know next time we met, what Resolution he was come to about it; and in the mean time, desir'd I would not give my Consent to his Brother, nor yet give him a flat Denial, but that I would hold him in Suspence a while.

I seem'd to start at his saying, I should not give him my Consent; I *told him*, he knew very well, I had no Consent to give; that he had Engag'd himself to Marry me, and that my Consent was at the same time Engag'd to him; that he had all along told me, I was his Wife, and I look'd upon my self as effectually so, as if the Ceremony had pass'd; and that it was from his own Mouth that I did so, he having all along persuaded me to call myself his Wife.

WELL, my Dear *says he*, don't be Concern'd at that now, if I am not your Husband, I'll be as good as a Husband to you, and do not let those things Trouble you now, but let me look a little farther into this Affair, and I shall be able to say more next time we meet.

HE pacify'd me as well as he could with this, but I found he was very Thoughtful, and that tho' he was very kind to me, and kiss'd me a thousand Times, and more I believe, and gave me Money too, yet he offer'd no more all the while we were together, which was above two Hours, and which I much wonder'd at, indeed at that Time, considering how it us'd to be, and what Opportunity we had.

HIS Brother did not come from *London*, for five or six Days, and it was two Days more, before he got an Opportunity to talk with him; but then getting him by himself, he

began to talk very Close to him about it; and the same
Evening got an Opportunity, (for we had a long Conference
together) to repeat all their Discourse to me, which as near
as I can remember, was to the purpose following. He *told
him* he heard strange News of him since he went, (*viz.*) that
he made Love to Mrs. *Betty*: Well, *says his* Brother, a little
Angrily, and so *I do*, And what then? What has any body to
do with that? Nay, *says his* Brother, don't be Angry *Robin*, I
don't pretend to have any thing to do with it; nor do I
pretend to be Angry with you about it: But I find they do
concern themselves about it, and that they have used the
poor Girl Ill about it, which I should take as done to my self;
Who do you mean by THEY? *says* Robin, I mean my
Mother, and the Girls, *says the* elder Brother.

BUT hark ye, *says his* Brother, are you in Earnest, do you
really Love the Girl, you may be free with me you know?
Why then *says* Robin, I will be free with you, I do Love her
above all the Women in the World, and I will have Her, let
them say, and do what they will, I believe the Girl will not
Deny me.

IT stuck me to the Heart when he *told me* this, for tho' it
was most rational to think I would not Deny him, yet I
knew in my own Conscience, I must Deny him, and I saw
my Ruin in my being oblig'd to do so; but I knew it was my
business to Talk otherwise then, so I interrupted him in his
Story thus.

AY! *said I*, does he think I can not Deny him? but he shall
find I can Deny him, for all that.

WELL my dear *says he*, but let me give you the whole
Story as it went on between us, and then say what you will.

THEN he went on and *told me*, that he reply'd thus: But
Brother, you know She has nothing, and you may have
several Ladies with good Fortunes: 'Tis no matter for that,
said Robin, I Love the Girl; and I will never please my
Pocket in Marrying, and not please my Fancy; and so my
Dear *adds he*, there is no Opposing him.

YES, yes, *says I*, you shall see I can Oppose him, I have

learnt to say NO now, tho' I had not learnt it before; if the best Lord in the Land offer'd me Marriage now, I could very chearfully say NO to him.

WELL, but my Dear *says he*, What can you say to him? You know, as you said when we talk'd of it before, he will ask you many Questions about it, and all the House will wonder what the meaning of it should be.

WHY *says I* smiling, I can stop all their Mouths at one Clap, by telling him and them too, that I am Married already to his elder Brother.

HE smil'd a little too at the Word, but I could see it Startled him, and he could not hide the disorder it put him into; however, he return'd, Why tho' that may be true in some Sense, yet I suppose you are but in Jest, when you talk of giving such an Answer as that, it may not be Convenient on many Accounts.

No, no, *says I* pleasantly, I am not so fond of letting that Secret come out, without your Consent.

BUT what then can you say to him, or to them, *says he*, when they find you positive against a Match, which would be apparently so much to your Advantage?

WHY, *says I*, should I be at a loss? First of all, I am not oblig'd to give them any Reason at all, on the other hand, I may tell them, I am Married already, and stop there, and that will be a full Stop too to him, for he can have no Reason to ask one Question after it.

AY, *says he*, but the whole House will teize you about that, even to Father and Mother, and if you deny them positively, they will be Disoblig'd at you, and Suspicious besides.

WHY, *says I*, What can I do? What would you have me do? I was in strait enough before, and as I *told you*, I was in Perplexity before, and acquainted you with the Circumstances, that I might have your Advice.

MY dear *says he*, I have been considering very much upon it, you may be sure, and tho' it is a piece of Advice, that has a great many Mortifications in it to me, and may at first seem Strange to you, yet all Things consider'd, I see no better way for you, than to let him go on; and if you find him hearty and in Earnest, Marry him.

I gave him a look full of Horror at those Words, and turning Pale as Death, was at the very point of sinking down out of the Chair I sat in: When giving a start, my Dear, *says he* aloud, What's the matter with you? Where are you a going? and a great many such things; and with joging and calling to me, fetch'd me a little to my self, tho' it was a good while before I fully recover'd my Senses, and was not able to speak for several Minutes more.

WHEN I was fully recover'd he began again; My dear *says he*, What made you so Surpriz'd at what I said, I would have you consider Seriously of it? you may see plainly how the Family stand in this Case, and they would be stark Mad if it was my Case, as it is my Brothers, and for ought I see, it would be my Ruin and yours too.

AY! *says I*, still speaking angrily; are all your Protestations and Vows to be shaken by the dislike of the Family? Did I not always object that to you, and you made a light thing of it, as what you were above, and would not Value; and is it come to this now? *Said I*, is this your Faith and Honour, your Love, and the Solidity of your Promises?

HE continued perfectly Calm, notwithstanding all my Reproaches, and I was not sparing of them at all; but *he reply'd* at last, My Dear, I have not broken one Promise with you yet; I did tell you I would Marry you when I was come to my Estate; but you see my Father is a hail healthy Man, and may live these thirty Years still, and not be Older than several are round us in the Town; and you never propos'd my Marrying you sooner, because you know it might be my Ruin; and as to all the rest, I have not fail'd you in any thing, you have wanted for nothing.

I could not deny a Word of this, and had nothing to say to it in general; but why then, *says I*, can you perswade me to such a horrid step, as leaving you, since you have not left me? Will you allow no Affection, no Love on my Side, where there has been so much on your Side? Have I made you no Returns? Have I given no Testimony of my Sincerity, and of my Passion? are the Sacrifices I have made of Honour and Modesty to you, no Proof of my being ty'd to you in Bonds too strong to be broken?

BUT here my Dear, *says he*, you may come into a safe Station, and appear with Honour, and with splendor at once, and the Remembrance of what we have done, may be wrapt up in an eternal Silence, as if it had never happen'd; you shall always have my Respect, and my sincere Affection, only then it shall be Honest, and perfectly Just to my Brother, you shall be my Dear Sister, as now you are my Dear ———— and there he stop'd.

YOUR Dear whore, *says I*, you would have said, if you had gone on; and you might as well have said it; but I understand you: However, I desire you to remember the long Discourses you have had with me, and the many Hours pains you have taken to perswade me to believe myself an honest Woman; that I was your Wife intentionally, tho' not in the Eye of the World; and that it was as effectual a Marriage that had pass'd between us, as if we had been publickly Wedded[1] by the Parson of the Parish; you know and cannot but remember, that these have been your own Words to me.

I found this was a little too close upon him, but I made it up in what follows; he stood stock still for a while, and said nothing, and I went on thus; you cannot, *says I*, without the highest injustice believe that I yielded upon all these Perswasions without a Love not to be questioned, not to be shaken again by any thing that could happen afterward: If you have such dishonourable Thoughts of me, I must ask you what Foundation in any of my Behaviour have I given for such a Suggestion.

IF then I have yielded to the Importunities of my Affection; and if I have been perswaded to believe that I am really, and in the Essence of the Thing your Wife, shall I now give the Lye to all those Arguments, and call myself your Whore, or Mistress, which is the same thing? And will you Transfer me to your Brother? Can you Transfer my Affection? Can you bid me cease loving you, and bid me love him? is it in my Power think you to make such a Change at Demand? No Sir, *said I*, depend upon it 'tis impossible, and whatever the Change of your Side may be, I will ever be True; and I had much rather, since it is come that unhappy Length, be your Whore than your Brothers Wife.

HE appear'd pleas'd, and touch'd with the impression of this last Discourse, and told me that he stood where he did before; that he had not been Unfaithful to me in any one Promise he had ever made yet, but that there were so many terrible things presented themselves to his View in the Affair before me, and that on my Account in particular, that he had thought of the other as a Remedy so effectual, as nothing could come up to it: That he thought this would not be an entire parting us, but we might love as Friends all our Days, and perhaps with more Satisfaction, than we should in the Station we were now in, as things might happen: That he durst say, I could not apprehend any thing from him, as to betraying a Secret, which could not but be the Destruction of us both, if it came out: That he had but one Question to ask of me, that could lye in the way of it, and if that Question was answer'd in the Negative, he could not but think still it was the only Step I could take.

I guess'd at his Question presently, namely, Whether I was sure I was not with Child? As to that, *I told him*, he need not be concern'd about it, for I was not with Child; why then my Dear, *says he*, we have no time to Talk farther now; consider of it, and think closely about it, I cannot but be of the Opinion still, that it will be the best Course you can take; and with this, he took his Leave, and the more hastily too, his Mother and Sisters Ringing at the Gate, just at the Moment that he had risen up to go.

HE left me in the utmost Confusion of Thought; and he easily perceiv'd it the next Day, and all the rest of the Week, for it was but *Tuesday* Evening when we talked; but he had no Opportunity to come at me all that Week, till the *Sunday* after, when I being indispos'd did not go to Church, and he making some Excuse for the like, stay'd at Home.

AND now he had me an Hour and a Half again by myself, and we fell into the same Arguments all over again, or at least so near the same, as it would be to no purpose to repeat them; at last, *I ask'd him* warmly what Opinion he must have of my Modesty, that he could suppose, I should so much as Entertain a thought of lying with two Brothers? And assur'd him it could never be: *I added* if he was to tell me that he would never see me more, than which nothing but Death could be more Terrible, yet I could never entertain a thought so Dishonourable to my self, and so Base to him; and therefore, I entreated him if he had one Grain of Respect or Affection left for me, that he would speak no more of it to me, or that he would pull his Sword out and Kill me. He appear'd surpriz'd at my Obstinancy as he call'd it, *told me* I was unkind to my self, and unkind to him in it; that it was a Crisis unlook'd for upon us both, and impossible for either of us to foresee; but that he did not see any other way to save us both from Ruin, and therefore he thought it the more Unkind; but that if he must say no more of it to me, he added with an unusual Coldness, that he did not know any thing else we had to talk of; and so he rose up to take his leave; I rose up too, as if with the same Indifference, but when he came to give me as it were a parting Kiss, I burst out into such a Passion of Crying, that tho' I would have spoke, I could not, and only pressing his Hand, seem'd to give him the Adieu, but cry'd vehemently.

HE was sensibly mov'd with this; so he sat down again, and said a great many kind things to me, to abate the excess of my Passion; but still urg'd the necessity of what he had proposed; all the while insisting, that if I did refuse, he would notwithstanding provide for me; but letting me plainly see, that he would decline me in the main Point; nay, even as a Mistress; making it a point of Honour not to lye with the Woman, that for ought he knew, might come to be his Brothers Wife.

THE bare loss of him as a Gallant was not so much my

Affliction, as the loss of his Person, whom indeed I Lov'd to
Distraction; and the loss of all the Expectations I had, and
which I always had built my Hopes upon, of having him one
Day for my Husband: These things oppress'd my Mind so
much, that in short, I fell very ill, the agonies of my Mind,
in a word, threw me into a high Feaver, and long it was, that
none in the Family expected my Life.

I was reduc'd very low indeed, and was often Delirious
and light Headed; but nothing lay so near me, as the fear,
that when I was light Headed, I should say something or
other to his Prejudice; I was distress'd in my Mind also to
see him, and so he was to see me, for he really Lov'd me
most passionately; but it could not be; there was not the
least Room to desire it, on one side, or other, or so much as
to make it Decent.

IT was near five Weeks that I kept my Bed, and tho' the
violence of my Feaver abated in three Weeks, yet it several
times Return'd; and the Physicians said two or three times,
they could do no more for me, but that they must leave
Nature and the Distemper to fight it Out; only strengthening
the first with Cordials to maintain the Strugle: After the end
of five Weeks I grew better, but was so Weak, so Alter'd, so
Mellancholly, and recover'd so Slowly, that the Physicians
apprehended I should go into a Consumption; and which
vex'd me most, they gave it as their Opinion, that my Mind
was Oppress'd, that something Troubl'd me, and in short,
that I was IN LOVE; upon this, the whole House was set
upon me to Examine me, and to press me to tell, whether I
was in Love or not, and with who? but as I well might, I
deny'd my being in Love at all.

THEY had on this Occasion a Squable one Day about me
at Table, that had like to have put the whole Family in an
Uproar, and for sometime did so; they happen'd to be all
at Table, but the Father; as for me I was Ill, and in my
Chamber: At the beginning of the Talk, which was just as
they had finish'd their Dinner, the old Gentlewoman who had
sent me somewhat to Eat, call'd her Maid to go up, and ask

me if I would have any more; but the Maid brought down Word, I had not Eaten half what she had sent me already.

ALAS, *says the* old Lady, that poor Girl; I am afraid she will never be well.

WELL! *says the* elder Brother, How should Mrs. *Betty* be well, *they say* she is in Love?

I believe nothing of it *says the* old Gentlewoman.

I don't know *says the* eldest Sister, what to say to it, they have made such a rout[1] about her being so Handsome, and so Charming, and I know not what, and that in her hearing too, that has turn'd the Creatures Head I believe, and who knows what possessions may follow such Doings? for my Part I don't know what to make of it.

WHY Sister, you must acknowledge she is very Handsome, *says the* elder Brother.

AY, and a great deal Handsomer than you Sister, *says* Robin, and that's your Mortification.

WELL, well, that is not the Question, *says his* Sister, the Girl is well enough, and she knows it well enough; she need not be told of it to make her Vain.

WE are not a talking of her being Vain, *says the* elder Brother, but of her being in Love; it may be she is in Love with herself, it seems my Sisters think so.

I would she was in Love with me, *says* Robin, I'd quickly put her out of her Pain.

WHAT d' ye mean by that Son, *says the* old Lady, How can you talk so?

WHY Madam, *says* Robin again, very honestly, Do you think I'd let the poor Girl Die for Love, and of one that is near at hand to be had too.

FYE Brother, *says the* second Sister, how can you talk so? would you take a Creature that has not a Groat in the World?

PRETHEE Child *says* Robin, Beauties a Portion, and good Humour with it, is a double Portion;[2] I wish thou hadst half her Stock of both for thy Portion: So there was her Mouth stopp'd.

I find, *says the* eldest Sister, if *Betty* is not in Love, my Brother is; I wonder he has not broke his Mind to *Betty*, I warrant she won't say NO.

THEY that yield when they're ask'd *says* Robin, are one step before them that were never ask'd to yield, Sister, and two Steps before them that yield before they are ask'd: And that's an Answer to you Sister.

THIS fir'd the Sister, and she flew into a Passion, and said, things were come to that pass, that it was time the Wench, *meaning me*, was out of the Family; and but that she was not fit to be turn'd out, she hop'd her Father and Mother would consider of it, as soon as she could be remov'd.

Robin reply'd, That was business for the Master and Mistress of the Family, who were not to be taught by One, that had so little Judgment as his eldest Sister.

IT run up a great deal farther; the Sister Scolded, *Robin* Rally'd and Banter'd, but poor *Betty* lost Ground by it extreamly in the Family: I heard of it, and I cry'd heartily, and the old Lady came up to me, some body having told her that I was so much concern'd about it: I complain'd to her, that it was very hard the Doctors should pass such a Censure upon me, for which they had no Ground; and that it was still harder, considering the Circumstances I was under in the Family; that I hop'd I had done nothing to lessen her Esteem for me, or given any Occasion for the Bickering between her Sons and Daughters; and I had more need to think of a Coffin, than of being in Love, and beg'd she would not let me suffer in her Opinion for any bodies Mistakes, but my own.

SHE was sensible of the Justice of what I said, but *told me*, since there had been such a Clamour among them, and that her younger Son Talk'd after such a rattling way as he did; she desir'd I would be so Faithful to her, as to Answer her but one Question sincerely; I told her I would with all my heart, and with the utmost plainess and Sincerity: Why then the Question was, Whether there was any thing between her Son *Robert* and me? I told her with all the Protestations of

Sincerity that I was able to make, and as I might well do, that there was not, nor ever had been; I *told her*, that Mr. *Robert* had rattled and jested,f as she knew it was his way, and that I took it always as I suppos'd he meant it, to be a wild airy way of Discourse that had no Signification in it: And again assured her, that there was not the least tittle of what she understood by it between us; and that those who had Suggested it, had done me a great deal of Wrong, and Mr. *Robert* no Service at all.

THE old Lady was fully satisfy'd, and kiss'd me, spoke chearfully to me, and bid me take care of my Health, and want for nothing, and so took her leave: But when she came down, she found the Brother and all his Sisters together by the Ears; they were Angry even to Passion, at his upbraiding them with their being Homely, and having never had any Sweet-heart, never having been ask'd the Question, and their being so forward as almost to ask first: He rallied them upon the Subject of Mrs. *Betty*; how Pretty, how good Humour'd, how she Sung better than they did, and Danc'd better, and how much Handsomer she was; and in doing this, he omitted no Ill-natur'd Thing that could vex them, and indeed, push'd too hard upon them: The old Lady came down in the height of it, and to put a stop to it, told them all the Discourse she had had with me, and how I answer'd, that there was nothing between Mr. *Robert* and I.

SHE'S wrong there, *says* Robin, for if there was not a great deal between us, we should be closer together than we are: I told her I Lov'd her hugely, *says he*, but I could never make the Jade believe I was in Earnest; I do not know how you should *says his* Mother, no body in their Senses could believe you were in Earnest, to Talk so to a poor Girl, whose Circumstances you know so well.

BUT prethee Son *adds she*, since you tell me that you could not make her believe you were in Earnest, what must we believe about it? for you ramble so in your Discourse, that no body knows whether you are in Earnest or in Jest: But as I find the Girl by your own Confession has answer'd truely, I wish you would do so too, and tell me seriously, so that I may depend upon it; Is there any thing in it or no? Are you in Earnest or no? Are you Distracted indeed, or are you not? 'Tis a weighty Question, and I wish you would make us easie about it.

BY my Faith Madam, *says* Robin, 'tis in vain to mince the Matter, or tell any more Lyes about it, I am in Earnest, as much as a Man is, that's going to be Hang'd. If Mrs. *Betty* would say she Lov'd me, and that she would Marry me, I'd have her to morrow Morning fasting; and say, *To have, and to hold*, instead of eating my Breakfast.

WELL, *says the Mother*, then there's one Son lost; and she said it in a very mournful Tone, as one greatly concern'd at it.

I hope not Madam, *says* Robin, no Man is lost, when a good Wife has found him.

WHY but Child, *says the* old Lady, she is a Beggar.

WHY then Madam, she has the more need of Charity *says* Robin; I'll take her off of the hands of the Parish, and she and I'll Beg together.

ITS bad Jesting with such things, *says the Mother*.

I don't Jest Madam, *says* Robin: We'll come and beg your Pardon Madam; and your Blessing Madam, and my Fathers.

THIS is all out of the way Son, *says the Mother*, if you are in Earnest you are Undone.

I am afraid not *says he*, for I am really afraid she won't have me, after all my Sisters huffing and blustring; I believe I shall never be able to persuade her to it.

THAT'S a fine Tale indeed, she is not so far out of her Senses neither; Mrs. *Betty* is no Fool, *says the youngest Sister*, Do you think she has learnt to say NO, any more than other People?

No Mrs. *Mirth-Wit* says ROBIN, Mrs. *Betty's* no Fool; but Mrs. *Betty* may be Engag'd some other way, And what then?

NAY, *says the eldest Sister*, we can say nothing to that, Who must it be to then? She is never out of the Doors, it must be between you.

I have nothing to say to that *says* Robin, I have been Examin'd enough; there's my Brother, if it must be *between us*, go to Work with him.

THIS stung *the elder Brother* to the Quick, and he concluded that *Robin* had discover'd something: However, he kept himself from appearing disturb'd; Prethee *says he*, don't go to shamf your Stories off upon me, I tell you, I deal in no such Ware; I have nothing to say to Mrs. *Betty*, nor to any of the *Miss Betty*'s in the Parish; and with that he rose up and brush'd off.t

No, *says the eldest Sister*, I dare answer for my Brother, he knows the World better.

THUS the Discourse ended; but it left *the elder Brother* quite confounded: He concluded his Brother had made a full Discovery, and he began to doubt, whether I had been concern'd in it, or not; but with all his Management, he could not bring it about to get at me; at last, he was so perplex'd, that he was quite Desperate, and resolv'd he wou'd come into my Chamber and see me, whatever came of it: In order to this, he contriv'd it so; that one Day after Dinner, watching *his eldest Sister*, till he could see her go up Stairs, he runs after her, *Hark ye Sister*, *says he*, Where is this sick Woman? may not a body see her? *YES*, *says the Sister*, I believe you may, but let me go first a little, and I'll tell you; so she run up to the Door, and gave me notice; and presently call'd to him again: BROTHER, *says she*, you may come if you please; so in he came, just in the same kind of Rant: Well, *says he*, at the Door *as he came in*, Where is this sick Body that's in Love? How do ye do Mrs. *Betty*? I would have got up out of my Chair, but was so Weak I could not for a good while; and he saw it and his Sister too, and she said, *Come do not strive to stand up*, my Brother desires no Ceremony, especially, now you are so Weak. No, No, Mrs. *Betty*, pray sit still *says he*, and so sits himself down in a Chair over-against me, and appear'd as if he was mighty Merry.

HE talk'd a deal of rambling Stuff to his Sister, and to me;

sometimes of one thing, sometimes of another, on purpose to Amuse his Sister;f and every now and then, would turn it upon the old Story, directing it to me: Poor Mrs. *Betty*, *says he*, it is a sad thing to be in Love, why it has reduced you sadly; at last I spoke a little, I am glad to see you so merry, Sir, *says I*, but I think the Doctor might have found some thing better to do, than to make his Game at his Patients: If I had been Ill of no other Distemper, I know the Proverb too well to have let him come to me: What Proverb *says he*? O! I remember it now: What,

> "*Where Love is the Case*,
> "*The* Doctor's *an Ass*.[2]

Is not that it Mrs. *Betty*? I smil'd, and said nothing: Nay, *says he*, I think the effect has prov'd it to be Love; for it seems the Doctor has been able to do you but little Service, you mend very slowly they say, I doubt there's somewhat in it Mrs. *Betty*, I doubt you are Sick of the Incureables, and that is Love; I smil'd and said, No, *indeed Sir*, that's none of my Distemper.

WE had a deal of such Discourse, and sometimes others that signify'd as little; by and by He ask'd me to Sing them a Song; at which I smil'd, and said, my singing Days were over: At last he ask'd me, if he should Play upon his Flute to me; his Sister said, she believ'd it wou'd hurt me, and that my Head could not bear it; I bow'd and said, No, it would not hurt me: And pray Madam, *said I*, do not hinder it, I love the Musick of the Flute very much; then his Sister said, well do then Brother; with that he pull'd out the Key of his Closet, Dear Sister, *says he*, I am very Lazy, do step to my Closet and fetch my Flute, it lies in *such a Drawer*, naming a Place where he was sure it was not, that she might be a little while a looking for it.

As soon as she was gone, he related the whole Story to me, of the Discourse his Brother had about me, and of his pushing it at him, and his concern about it, which was the Reason of his contriving this Visit to me: I assur'd him, I had never open'd my Mouth either to his Brother, or to any

Body else: I told him the dreadful Exigence I was in; that my Love to him, and his offering to have me forget that Affection, and remove it to another, had thrown me down; and that I had a thousand Times wish'd I might Die, rather than Recover, and to have the same Circumstances to strugle with as I had before; and that this backwardness to Life, had been the great Reason of the slowness of my Recovering: I added, that I foresaw, that as soon as I was well, I must quit the Family; and that as for Marrying his *Brother*, I abhor'd the thoughts of it, after what had been my Case with him, and that he might depend upon it, I would never see his Brother again upon that Subject: That if he would break all his Vows and Oaths, and Engagements with me, be that between his Conscience and his Honour, and himself: But he should never be able to say, that I who he had persuaded to call my self his Wife, and who had given him the Liberty to use me as a Wife, was not as Faithful to him as a Wife ought to be, what ever he might be to me.

HE was going to reply, and had said, That he was sorry I could not be persuaded, and was a going to say more, but he heard his Sister a coming, and so did I; and yet I forc'd out these few Words as a reply, That I could never be persuaded to Love one Brother, and Marry another: He shook his Head and said, *Then I am Ruin'd*, meaning himself; and that Moment his Sister enter'd the Room, and told him she could not find the Flute; Well, *says he* merrily, this Laziness won't do, so he gets up, and goes himself to go to look for it, but comes back without too; not but that he could have found it, but because his Mind was a little Disturb'd, and he had no mind to Play; and besides, the Errand he sent his Sister of, was answer'd another way; for he only wanted an Opportunity to speak to me, which he gain'd, tho' not much to his Satisfaction.

I had however, a great deal of Satisfaction in having spoken my Mind to him with Freedom, and with such an honest Plainess, as I have related; and tho' it did not at all Work that way, I desir'd, *that is to say*, to oblige the Person to me the more; yet it took from him all possibility of quiting me, but by a down right breach of Honour, and giving up all the Faith of a Gentleman to me, which he had so often engaged by, never to abandon me, but to make me his Wife as soon as he came to his Estate.

IT was not many Weeks after this, before I was about the House again, and began to grow well; but I continu'd Melancholly, silent, dull, and retir'd, which amaz'd the whole Family, except he that knew the Reason of it; yet it was a great while before he took any Notice of it, and I *as backward to speak, as he*, carried respectfully to him, but never offer'd to speak a Word to him, that was particular of any kind whatsoever; and this continu'd for sixteen or seventeen Weeks, so that as I expected every Day to be dismiss'd the Family, on Account of what Distaste they had taken another Way, in which I had no Guilt; so I expected to hear no more of this Gentleman, after all his solemn Vows, and Protestations, but to be ruin'd and abandon'd.

AT last I broke the way myself in the Family, for my Removing; for being talking seriously with the old Lady one Day, about my own Circumstances in the World, and how my Distemper had left a heaviness upon my Spirits, that I was not the same thing I was before: The old Lady said, I am afraid *Betty*, what I have said to you, about my Son, has had some Influence upon you, and that you are Melancholly on his Account; Pray will you let me know how the Matter stands with you both? if it may not be improper, for as for *Robin*, he does nothing but Rally and Banter when I speak of it to him: Why truly Madam, *said I*, that Matter stands as I wish it did not, and I shall be very sincere with you in it, what ever befalls me for it, Mr. *Robert* has several times propos'd Marriage to me, which is what I had no Reason to expect, my poor Circumstances consider'd; but I have always resisted him, and that perhaps in Terms more positive than became me, considering the Regard that I ought to have for every Branch of your Family: But *said I*, Madam, I could never so far forget my Obligations to you, and all your House, to offer to Consent to a Thing, which I know must needs be Disobliging to you, and this I have made my Argument to him, and have possitively told him, that I would never entertain a Thought of that kind, unless I had your Consent, and his Fathers also, to whom I was bound by so many invincible Obligations.

AND is this possible Mrs. *Betty*, says the old Lady? then you have been much Juster to us, than we have been to you; for we have all look'd upon you as a kind of a Snare to my Son; and I had a Proposal to make to you, for your Removing, for fear of it; but I had not yet mention'd it to you, because I thought you were not thorough Well, and I was afraid of grieving you too much, least it should thro' you down again, for we have all a Respect for you still, tho' not so much, as to have it be the Ruin of my Son; but if it be as you say, we have all wrong'd you very much.

As to the Truth of what I say, Madam, *said I*, I refer you to your Son himself, if he will do me any Justice, he must tell you the Story just as I have told it.

AWAY goes the old Lady to her Daughters, and tells them the whole Story, just as I had told it her, and they were surpris'd at it, you may be sure, as I believ'd they would be; one *said*, she could never have thought it; another said, *Robin* was a Fool, a *Third* said, she would not believe a Word of it, and she would warrant that *Robin* would tell the Story another way; but the old Gentlewoman, who was resolv'd to go to the bottom of it, before I could have the least Opportunity of Acquainting her Son, with what had pass'd, resolv'd too, that she would Talk with her Son immediately, and to that purpose sent for him, for he was gone but to a Lawyers House in the Town, upon some petty Business of his own, and upon her sending, he return'd immediately.

UPON his coming up to them, for they were all still together; sit down *Robin, says the old Lady*, I must have some talk with you; with all my Heart, Madam, *says Robin, looking very Merry*; I hope it is about a good Wife, for I am at a great loss in that Affair: How can that be, *says his* *Mother*, did not you say, you resolved to have Mrs. *Betty*? Ay Madam, says *Robin*; but there is one has *forbid the Banns*: Forbid the Banns! *says his Mother*, who can that be? Even Mrs. *Betty* herself, says *Robin*. How so, *says his Mother*; Have you ask'd her the Question then? *Yes, indeed Madam*, says Robin; I have attack'd her in Form, five times since she was Sick, and am beaten off; the Jade is so stout, she won't Capitulate, nor yield upon any Terms, except such as I cannot effectually Grant: Explain your self, *says the Mother*, for I am surpris'd, I do not understand you, I hope you are not in Earnest.

WHY, Madam, *says he*, the Case is plain enough upon me, it explains itself; she wont have me, *she says*; is not that plain enough? I think 'tis plain, and pretty rough too; well but *says the Mother*, you talk of Conditions, that you cannot Grant, what, does she want a Settlement? her Jointure ought to be according to her Portion;[1] but what Fortune does she bring you? Nay, as to Fortune, *says Robin*, she is rich enough; I am satisfy'd in that Point; but *'tis I* that am not able to come up to her Terms, and she is positive she will not have me without.

HERE the Sisters put in, Madam, *says the second Sister*, 'tis impossible to be serious with him; he will never give a direct Answer to any thing; you had better let him alone, and talk no more of it to him; you know how to dispose of her out of his way, if you thought there was any thing in it; *Robin* was a little warm'd with his Sisters rudeness, but he was even with her; and yet with good Manners too: There are two sorts of People, Madam, *says he, turning to his Mother*, that there is no contending with, that is a wise Body and a Fool,[2] 'tis a little hard I should engage with both of them together.

THE younger Sister then put in, we must be Fools indeed, *says she*, in my Brother's Opinion, that he should think we can believe, he has seriously ask'd Mrs. *Betty* to Marry him, and that she has refus'd him.

Answer, and *Answer not*,[1] says *Solomon*, *replyed her Brother*: When your Brother had said to your Mother, that he had ask'd her no less than five Times, and that it was so, that she positively Denied him; methinks a younger Sister need not question the Truth of it, when her Mother did not: My Mother you see did not understand it, *says the second Sister*: There's some difference *says* Robin, between desiring me to Explain it, and telling me she did not believe it.

WELL but Son, *says the old Lady*, if you are dispos'd to let us into the Mystery of it, What were these hard Conditions? Yes Madam *says* Robin, I had done it before now, if the *Teazers* here had not worried me by way of Interruption: The Conditions are, that I bring my Father and you to Consent to it, and without that, she protests she will never see me more upon that Head; and these Conditions *as I said*, I suppose I shall never be able to Grant; I hope my warm Sisters will be Answer'd now, and Blush a little; if not, I have no more to say till I hear farther.

THIS Answer was surprizing to them all, tho' less to the Mother, because of what I had said to her; as to the Daughters they stood Mute a great while; but the Mother said with some Passion, WELL, I had heard this before, *but I cou'd not believe it*; but if it is so, then we have all done *BETTY* wrong, and she has behav'd better than I ever expected: Nay, *says the eldest Sister*, if it is so, she has acted Handsomely indeed: I confess *says the Mother*, it was none of her Fault, if he was Fool enough to take a Fancy to her; but to give such an Answer to him, shews more Respect to your Father and me, than I can tell how to Express; I shall value the Girl the better for it, as long as I know her. But I shall not *says* Robin, unless you will give your Consent: I'll consider of that a while *says the Mother*; I assure you, if there were not some other Objections in the way, this Conduct of hers would go a great way to bring me to Consent: I wish it would go quite thro' with it, *says* Robin; if you had as much thought about making me Easie, as you have about making me Rich, you would soon Consent to it.

WHY *Robin, says the Mother again*, Are you really in Earnest? Would you so fain have her as you pretend? Really Madam *says* Robin, I think 'tis hard you should Question me upon that Head, after all I have said: I won't say that I will have her, how can I resolve that point, when you see I cannot have her without your Consent? besides I am not bound to Marry at all: But this I will say, I am in Earnest in, that I will never have any body else, if I can help it; so you may Determine for me, *Betty*, or no Body, is the Word; and the Question which of the Two shall be in your Breast to decide Madam; provided only, that *my good humour'd Sisters here, may have no Vote in it.*

ALL this was dreadful to me, for the Mother began to yield, and *Robin* press'd her Home in it: On the other hand, she advised with the eldest Son, and he used all the Arguments in the World to persuade her to Consent; alledging his Brothers passionate Love for me, and my generous Regard to the Family, in refusing my own Advantages, upon such a nice point of Honour, and a thousand such Things: And as to the Father, he was a Man in a hurry of publick Affairs, and getting Money, seldom at Home, thoughtful of the main Chance; but left all those Things to his Wife.

YOU may easily believe, that when the Plot was thus, as *they thought* broke out, and that every one thought they knew how Things were carried: it was not so Difficult, or so Dangerous, for the elder Brother, who no body suspected of any thing, to have a freer Access to me than before: Nay the Mother, *which was just as he wish'd*, Propos'd it to him to Talk with Mrs. *Betty*; for it may be Son *said she*, you may see farther into the Thing than I; and see if you think she has been so Positive as *Robin* says she has been, or no. This was as well as he could wish, and he as it were yielding to Talk with me at his Mother's Request, She brought me to him into her own Chamber; told me her Son had some Business with me at her Request, and desir'd me to be very Sincere with him; and then she left us together, and he went and shut the Door after her.

HE came back to me, and took me in his Arms and kiss'd me very Tenderly; but told me, he had a long Discourse to hold with me, and it was now come to that Crisis, that I should make my self Happy or Miserable, as long as I Liv'd: That the Thing was now gone so far, that if I could not comply with his Desire, we should be both Ruin'd: Then he told me the whole Story between *Robin*, as he call'd him, and his Mother, and Sisters, and himself; as it is above: And now dear Child, *says he*, consider what it will be to Marry a Gentleman of a good Family, in good Circumstances, and with the Consent of the whole House, and to enjoy all that the World can give you: And what on the other Hand, to be sunk into the dark Circumstances of a Woman that has lost her Reputation; and that tho' I shall be a private Friend to you while I live, yet as I shall be suspected always; so you will be afraid to see me, and I shall be afraid to own you.

HE gave me no time to Reply, but went on with me thus: What has happen'd between us Child, so long as we both agree to do so, may be buried and forgotten: I shall always be your sincere Friend, without any Inclination to nearer Intimacy, when you become my Sister; and we shall have all the honest part of Conversation without any Reproaches between us, of having done amiss: I beg of you to consider it, and do not stand in the way of your own Safety and Prosperity; and to satisfie you that I am Sincere, *added he*, I here offer you 500 *l*. in Money, to make you some Amends for the Freedoms I have taken with you, which we shall look upon as some of the Follies of our Lives, which 'tis hop'd we may Repent of.

HE spoke this in so much more moving Terms than it is possible for me to Express, and with so much greater force of Argument than I can repeat, that I only recommend it to those who Read the Story, to suppose, that as he held me above an Hour and Half in that Discourse, so he answer'd all my Objections, and fortified his Discourse with all the Arguments, that humane Wit and Art could Devise.

I cannot say however, that any thing he said, made Impression enough upon me, so as to give me any thought of the Matter; till he told me at last very plainly, that if I refus'd, he was sorry to add, that he could never go on with me in that Station as we stood before; that tho' he Lov'd me as well as ever, and that I was as agreeable to him, as ever; yet, Sense of Vertue had not so far forsaken him, as to suffer him to lye with a Woman, that his Brother Courted to make his Wife; and if he took his leave of me, with a denial in this Affair; whatever he might do for me in the Point of support, grounded on his first Engagement of maintaining me, yet he would not have me be surpriz'd, that he was oblig'd to tell me, he could not allow himself to see me any more; and that indeed I could not expect it of him.

I receiv'd this last part with some tokens of Surprize and Disorder, and had much a do, to avoid sinking down, for indeed I lov'd him to an Extravagance, not easie to imagine; but he perceiv'd my Disorder, he entreated me to consider seriously of it, assur'd me that it was the only way to Preserve our mutual Affection, that in this Station we might love as Friends, with the utmost Passion, and with a love of Relation untainted, free from our just Reproaches, and free from other Peoples Suspicions; that he should ever acknowledge his happiness owing to me; that he would be Debtor to me as long as he liv'd, and would be paying that Debt as long as he had Breath; Thus he wrought me up, in short, to a kind of Hesitation in the Matter; having the Dangers on one Side represented in lively Figures, and indeed heightn'd by my Imagination of being turn'd out to the wide World, a meer cast off Whore, *for it was no less*, and perhaps expos'd as such; with little to provide for myself; with no Friend, no Acquaintance in the whole World, *out of that Town*, and there I could not pretend to Stay; all this terrify'd me to the last Degree, and he took care upon all Occasions to lay it home to me, in the worst Colours that it could be possible to be drawn in; on the other Hand, he fail'd not to set forth the easy prosperous Life, which I was going to live.

HE answer'd all that I could object from Affection, and from former Engagements, with telling me the Necessity that was before us of taking other Measures now; and as to his Promises of Marriage, the nature of things *he said*, had put an End to that, by the probability of my being his Brothers Wife, before the time to which his Promises all referr'd.

THUS in a Word, I may say, he Reason'd me out of my Reason; he conquer'd all my Arguments, and I began to see a Danger that I was in, which I had not consider'd of before, and that was of being drop'd by both of them, and left alone in the World to shift for myself.

THIS, and his perswasion, at length Prevail'd with me to Consent, tho' with so much Reluctance, that it was easie to see I should go to Church, like a Bear to the Stake;[1] I had some little Apprehensions about me too, least my new Spouse, who by the way, I had not the least Affection for, should be skilful enough to Challenge me on another Account, upon our first coming to Bed together; but whether he did it with Design, or not, I know not; but his elder Brother took care to make him very much Fuddled before he went to Bed; so that I had the Satisfaction of a drunken Bedfellow the first Night: How he did it I know not, but I concluded that he certainly contriv'd it, that his Brother might be able to make no Judgment of the difference between a Maid and a married Woman; nor did he ever Entertain any Notions of it, or disturb his Thoughts about it.

I should go back a little here, to where I left off; the elder Brother, having thus manag'd me, his next business was to Manage his Mother, and he never left till he had brought her to acquiesce, and be passive in the thing; Even without acquainting the Father, other than by Post Letters: So that she consented to our Marrying privately, and leaving her to manage the Father afterwards.

THEN he Cajol'd with his Brother, and perswaded him what Service he had done him, and how he had brought his Mother to Consent, which *tho' True*, was not indeed done to serve him, but to serve himself; but thus diligently did he cheat him, and had the Thanks of a faithful Friend for shifting off his Whore into his Brothers Arms for a Wife. So certainly does Interest banish all manner of Affection, and so naturally do Men give up Honour and Justice, Humanity, and even Christianity, to secure themselves.

I must now come back to Brother *Robin*, as we always call'd him; who having got his Mother's Consent *as above*, came big with the News to me, and told me the whole Story of it, with a Sincerity so visible, that I must confess it griev'd me, that I must be the Instrument to abuse so honest a Gentleman; but there was no Remedy, he would have me, and I was not oblig'd to tell him, that I was his Brother's Whore,[1] tho' I had no other way to put him off; so I came gradually into it, to his Satisfaction, and behold, we were Married.

MODESTY forbids me to reveal the Secrets of the Marriage Bed, but nothing could have happen'd more suitable to my Circumstances than that, *as above*, my Husband was so Fuddled when he came to Bed, that he could not remember in the Morning, whether he had had any Conversation with me or no, and I was oblig'd to tell him *he had*, tho' in reallity *he had not*, that I might be sure he could make no enquiry about any thing else.

IT concerns the Story in hand very little, to enter into the farther particulars of the Family, or of myself, for the five Years that I liv'd with this Husband; only to observe that I had two Children by him, and that at the end of five Year he Died: He had been really a very good Husband to me, and we liv'd very agreeably together; But as he had not receiv'd much from them, and had in the little time he liv'd acquir'd no great Matters, so my Circumstances were not great; nor was I much mended by the Match: Indeed I had preserv'd the elder Brother's Bonds to me, to pay me 500 *l.* which he offer'd me for my Consent to Marry his Brother; and this with what I had saved of the Money he formerly gave me, and about as much more by my Husband, left me a Widow with about 1200 *l.* in my Pocket.

My two Children were indeed taken happily off of my Hands, by my Husband's Father and Mother, and that by the way was all they got by Mrs. *Betty*.

I confess I was not suitably affected with the loss of my Husband; nor indeed can I say, that I ever Lov'd him as I ought to have done, or as was proportionable to the good Usage I had from him, for he was a tender, kind, good humour'd Man as any Woman could desire; but his Brother being so always in my sight, *at least*, while we were in the Country, was a continual Snare to me; and I never was in Bed with my Husband, but I wish'd my self in the Arms of his Brother; and tho' his Brother never offer'd me the least Kindness that way, after our Marriage, but carried it just as a Brother ought to do; yet, it was impossible for me to do so to him: In short, I committed Adultery and Incest with him every Day in my Desires, which without doubt, was as effectually Criminal in the Nature of the Guilt, as if I had actually done it.[1]

Before my Husband Died, his elder Brother was Married, and we being then remov'd to *London*, were written to by the old Lady to come, and be at the Wedding; my Husband went, but I pretended Indisposition, and that I could not possibly Travel, so I staid behind; for in short, I could not bear the sight of his being given to another Woman, tho' I knew I was never to have him my self.

I was now *as above*, left loose to the World, and being still Young and Handsome, as every body said of me, *and I assure you*, *I thought my self so*, and with a tollerable Fortune in my Pocket, I put no small value upon my self: I was Courted by several very considerable Tradesmen; and particularly, very warmly by one, a *Linnen-Draper*, at whose House after my Husband's Death I took a Lodging, his Sister being my Acquaintance; here I had all the Liberty, and all the Opportunity to be Gay, and appear in Company that I could desire; my Landlord's Sister being one of the Madest, Gayest things alive, and not so much Mistress of her Vertue, as I thought at first she had been: She brought me into a World of wild Company, and even brought home several Persons, *such as she lik'd well enough to Gratifie*, to see her pretty Widow, *so she was pleas'd to call me*, and that Name I got in a little time in Publick; now as Fame and Fools make an Assembly, I was here wonderfully Caress'd; had abundance of Admirers, and such as call'd themselves *Lovers*; but I found not one fair Proposal among them all; as for their common Design, that I understood too well to be drawn into any more Snares of that Kind: The Case was alter'd with me, I had Money in my Pocket, and had nothing to say to them: I had been trick'd once by *that Cheat call'd* LOVE, but the Game was over; I was resolv'd now to be Married, or Nothing, and to be well Married, or not at all.

I lov'd the Company indeed of Men of Mirth and Wit, Men of Gallantry and Figure, and was often entertain'd with such, as I was also with others; but I found by just Observation, that the brightest Men came upon the dullest Errand, *that is to say*, the Dullest, as to what I aim'd at; on the other Hand, those who came with the best Proposals, were the Dullest and most disagreeable Part of the World: I was not averse to a Tradesman, but then I would have a Tradesman forsooth, that was something of a Gentleman too; that when my Husband had a mind to carry me to the Court, or to the Play, he might become a Sword, and look as like a Gentleman, as another Man; and not be one that had the mark of his Apron-strings upon his Coat, or the mark of his Hat upon his Perriwig; that should look as if he was set on to his Sword, when his Sword was put on to him, and that carried his Trade in his Countenance.

WELL, at last I found this amphibious Creature, this *Land-water-thing*, call'd, *a Gentleman-Tradesman*;[1] and as a just Plague upon my Folly, I was catch'd in the very Snare, which *as I might say*, I laid for my self;[2] *I say laid for my self*, for I was not Trepan'd[3] I confess, but I betray'd my self.

THIS was a *Draper* too,[4] for tho' my Comrade would have brought me to a Bargain with her Brother; yet when it came to the Point, it was it seems for a Mistress, not a Wife, and

I kept true to this Notion, that a Woman should never be kept for a Mistress, that had Money to keep her self.

THUS my Pride, not my Principle, my Money, not my Vertue, kept me Honest; tho' as it prov'd, I found I had much better have been Sold by my *She Comrade* to her Brother, than have Sold my self as I did to a Tradesman, that was Rake, Gentleman, Shop keeper, and Beggar all together.

BUT I was hurried on (by my Fancy to a Gentleman) to Ruin my self[1] in the grossest Manner that ever Woman did; for my new Husband coming to a lump of Money at once, fell into such a profusion of Expence, that all I had, and all he had before, if he had any thing worth mentioning, would not have held it out above one Year.

HE was very fond of me for about a quarter of a Year, and what I got by that, was, that I had the pleasure of seeing a great deal of my Money spent upon my self, and as I may say, had some of the spending it too: Come, my dear, *says he to me one Day*, Shall we go and take a turn into the Country for about a Week? Ay, my Dear, *says I*, Whither would you go? I care not whither *says he*, but I have a mind to look like Quality for a Week; we'll go to OXFORD *says he*: How *says I*, shall we go, I am no Horse Woman, and 'tis too far for a Coach; too far *says he*, no Place is too far for a Coach and Six: If I carry you out, you shall Travel like a Dutchess; hum *says I*, my Dear 'tis a Frolick, but if you have a mind to it I don't care. Well the time was appointed, we had a rich Coach, very good Horses, a Coachman, Postilion, and two Footmen in very good Liveries; a Gentleman on Horseback, and a Page with a Feather in his Hat upon another Horse; The Servants all call'd him my Lord, and the Inn-Keepers you may be sure did the like, and I was *her Honour*, the Countess; and thus we Travel'd to OXFORD, and a very pleasant Journey we had; for, give him his due, not a Beggar alive knew better how to be a Lord than my Husband: We saw all the Rareties at OXFORD, talk'd with two or three Fellows of Colleges, about putting out a young Nephew, that was left to his Lordship's Care to the University, and of their being his Tutors; we diverted our selves with bantering several other poor Scholars, with hopes of being at least his Lordship's Chaplains and putting on a Scarf;[1] and thus having liv'd like Quality indeed, as to Expence; we went away for *Northampton*, and in a word, in about twelve Days ramble came Home again, to the Tune of about 93 *l.* Expence.

VANITY is the perfection of a Fop;[2] my Husband had this Excellence, that he valued nothing of Expence, and as his History you may be sure, has very little weight in it; 'tis enough to tell you, that in about two Years and a Quarter he Broke, and was not so happy to get over into the *Mint*,[3] but got into a *Spunging-House*,[4] being Arrested in an Action too heavy for him to give Bail to, so he sent for me to come to him.

IT was no surprize to me, for I had foreseen *sometime*, that all was going to Wreck, and had been taking care to reserve something if I could, *tho' it was not much* for myself:[5] But when he sent for me, he behav'd much better than I expected, and told me plainly, he had plaid the Fool and suffer'd himself to be Surpriz'd which he might have prevented; that now he foresaw he could not stand it, and therefore he would have me go Home, and in the Night take away every thing I had in the House of any Value and secure it;[6] and after that, he told me, that if I could get away 100 *l.* or 200 *l.* in Goods out of the Shop, I should do it, only *says he*, let me know nothing of it, neither what you take, or whither you carry it; for as for me *says he*, I am resolv'd to get out of this House and be gone; and if you never hear of me more, my Dear, *says he*, I wish you well; I am only sorry for the Injury I have done you: He said some very handsome Things to me indeed at Parting; for *I told you* he was a *Gentleman*, and that was all the benefit I had of his being so; that he used me very handsomely, and with good Manners upon all Occasions, even to the last, only spent all I had, and left me to Rob the Creditors for something to Subsist on.

HOWEVER, I did as he bad me, *that you may be sure*, and having thus taken my leave of him, I never saw him more;

for he found means to break out of the Bailiff's House that Night, or the next, and got over into *France*;[1] and for the rest, the Creditors scrambl'd for it as well as they could: How I knew not, for I could come at no Knowledge of any thing, more than this; that he came Home about three a Clock in the Morning, caus'd the rest of his Goods to be remov'd into the *Mint*,[2] and the Shop to be shut up; and having rais'd what Money he could get together, he got over as I said to *France*, from whence I had one or two Letters from him, and no more.

I did not see him when he came Home, for he having given me such Instructions as above, and I having made the best of my Time; I had no more Business back again at the House, not knowing but I might have been stop'd there by the Creditors;[3] for a *Commission of Bankrupt*, being soon after Issued, they might have stop'd me by Orders from the *Commissioners*: But my Husband having so dextrously got out of the Bailiff's House by letting himself down in a most desperate Manner, from almost the top of the House, to the top of another Building, and leaping from thence which was almost two Stories, and which was enough indeed to have broken his Neck: He came home and got away his Goods, before the Creditors could come to Seize, *that is to say*, before they could get out the Commission,[4] and be ready to send their Officers to take Possession.

MY Husband was so civil to me, *for still I say, he was much of a Gentleman*, that in the first Letter he wrote me from *France*, he let me know where he had Pawn'd 20 Pieces of fine *Holland* for 30 *l.* which were really worth above 90 *l.* and enclos'd me the Token, and an order for the taking them up, paying the Money, which I did, and made in time above 100 *l.* of them, having Leisure to cut them and sell them, some and some,[5] to private Families, as opportunity offer'd.

HOWEVER with all this, and all that I had secur'd before, I found upon casting things up, my Case was very much alter'd, and my Fortune much lessen'd, for including the Hollands, and a parcel of fine Muslins, which I carry'd off

before, and some Plate, and other things; I found I could
hardly muster up 500 *l.* and my Condition was very odd, for
tho' I had no Child, (*I had had one by my Gentleman* Draper,
but it was buried,) yet I was a Widow bewitch'd,[1] I had a
Husband, and no Husband,[2] and I could not pretend to
Marry again, tho' I knew well enough my Husband would
never see *England* any more, if he liv'd fifty Years: *Thus I
say,* I was limitted from Marriage,[3] what Offer soever might
be made me: and I had not one Friend to advise with, in the
Condition I was in, at least not one I durst Trust the Secret
of my Circumstances to, for if the Commissioners were to
have been inform'd where I was, I should have been fetch'd
up, and examin'd upon Oath, and all I had sav'd be taken
away from me.

UPON these Apprehensions the first thing I did, was to go
quite out of my Knowledge,[4] and go by another Name: This
I did effectually, for I went into the *Mint* too, took Lodgings
in a very private Place, drest me up in the Habit of a Widow,
and call'd myself Mrs. *Flanders.*

HERE, however I conceal'd myself, and tho' my new
Acquaintances knew nothing of me, yet I soon got a great
deal of Company about me; and whether it be that Women
are scarce among the Sorts of People that generally are to be
found there; or that some Consolation in the Miseries of the
Place, are more Requisite than on other Occasions; I soon
found an agreeable Woman was exceedingly valuable among
the Sons of Affliction[5] there; and that those that wanted
Money to pay Half a Crown in the Pound to their Creditors,
and that run in Debt at the Sign of the *Bull*[6] for their
Dinners, would yet find Money for a Supper, if they lik'd
the Woman.

HOWEVER, I kept myself Safe yet, tho' I began like my
Lord *Rochester's* Mistress,[7] that lov'd his Company, but
would not admit him farther, to have the Scandal of a Whore,
without the Joy; and upon this score tir'd with the Place and
indeed with the Company too, I began to think of Removing.

IT was indeed a Subject of strange Reflection to me, to see

Men who were overwhelm'd in perplex'd Circumstances; who were reduc'd some Degrees below being Ruin'd; whose Families were Objects of their own Terror and other Peoples Charity; yet while a Penny lasted, nay, even beyond it, endeavouring to drown their Sorrow in their Wickedness;[1] heaping up more Guilt upon themselves, labouring to forget former things, which now it was the proper time to remember, making more Work for Repentance, and Sinning on, as a Remedy for Sin past.

BUT it is none of my Talent to preach; these Men were too wicked, even for me; there was something horrid and absurd in their way of Sinning, for it was all a Force even upon themselves; they did not only act against Conscience, but against Nature; they put a Rape upon their Temper to drown the Reflections, which their Circumstances continually gave them; and nothing was more easie than to see how Sighs would interrupt their Songs,[2] and paleness, and anguish sit upon their Brows, in spight of the forc'd Smiles they put on; nay, sometimes it would break out at their very Mouths, when they had parted with their Money for a lewd Treat, or a wicked Embrace; I have heard them, turning about, fetch a deep Sigh, and cry *what a Dog am I!* Well *Betty*, my Dear, I'll drink thy Health tho', *meaning the Honest Wife*, that perhaps had not a Half a Crown for herself, and three or four Children: The next Morning they are at their Penitentials again, and perhaps the poor weeping Wife comes over to him, either brings him some Account of what his Creditors are doing, and how she and the Children are turn'd out of Doors, or some other dreadful News; and this adds to his self Reproaches; but when he has Thought and Por'd on it till he is almost Mad, having no Principles to Support him, nothing within him, or above him, to Comfort him; but finding it all Darkness on every Side, he flyes to the same Relief again, (*viz.*) to Drink it away, Debauch it away, and falling into Company of Men in just the same Condition with himself, he repeats the Crime, and thus he goes every Day one Step onward of his way to Destruction.[3]

I was not wicked enough for such Fellows as these *yet*; on the contrary, I began to consider here *very seriously* what I had to do; how things stood with me, and what Course I ought to take: I knew I had no Friends, no not one Friend, or Relation in the World; and that little I had left apparently wasted, which when it was gone, I saw nothing but Misery and Starving was before me: Upon these Considerations, I say, and fill'd with Horror at the Place I was in, and the dreadful Objects, which I had always before me, *I resolv'd to be gone*.

I had made an Acquaintance with a very sober good sort of a Woman, who was a Widow too like me, but in better Circumstances; her Husband had been a Captain of a Merchant Ship, and having had the Misfortune to be Cast away coming Home on a Voyage from the *West-Indies*, which would have been very profitable, if he had come safe; was so reduc'd by the Loss, that tho' he had saved his Life then, it broke his Heart, and kill'd him afterwards, and his Widow being persued by the Creditors was forc'd to take Shelter in the *Mint*: She soon made things up with the help of Friends, and was at Liberty again; and finding that I rather was there to be conceal'd, than by any particular Prosecutions, and finding also that I agreed with her, *or rather she with me* in a just Abhorrence of the Place, and of the Company; she invited me to go Home with her, till I could put myself in some posture of settling in the World to my Mind; withal telling me, that it was ten to one, but some good Captain of a Ship might take a Fancy to me, and Court me, in that part of the Town where she liv'd.

I accepted her Offer, and was with her Half a Year, and should have been longer; but in that interval what she propos'd to me happen'd to herself, and she marry'd very much to her Advantage; but whose Fortune soever was upon the Encrease, mine seem'd to be upon the Wane, and I found nothing present, except two or three Boatswains, or such Fellows, but as for the Commanders they were generally of two Sorts. 1. Such as having good Business, *that is to say,* a good Ship, resolv'd not to Marry, but with Advantage, that is, with a good Fortune. 2. Such as being out of Employ, wanted a Wife to help them to a Ship, I mean. (1.) A Wife, who having some Money could enable them to hold, as they call it, a good part of a Ship themselves, so to encourage Owners to come in; Or. (2.) A Wife who if she had not Money, had Friends who were concern'd in Shipping, and so could help to put the young Man into a good Ship, which to them is as good as a Portion, and neither of these was my Case; so I look'd like one that was to *lye on Hand*.

THIS Knowledge I soon learnt by Experience, (*viz.*) That the State of things was altered, as to Matrimony, and that I was not to expect at *London*, what I had found in the Country; that Marriages were here the Consequences of politick Schemes, for forming Interests, and carrying on Business,[1] and that LOVE had no Share, or but very little in the Matter.

THAT, as my Sister in Law, at *Colchester* had said; Beauty, Wit, Manners, Sence, good Humour, good Behaviour, Education, Vertue, Piety, or any other Qualification, whether of Body or Mind, had no power to recomend: That Money only made a Woman agreeable:[2] That Men chose Mistresses indeed by the gust of their Affection, and it was requisite to a Whore to be Handsome, well shap'd, have a good Mein, and a graceful Behaviour; but that for a Wife, no Deformity would shock the Fancy, no ill Qualities, the Judgement; the Money was the thing; the Portion was neither crooked, or Monstrous, but the Money was always agreeable, whatever the Wife was.

ON the other Hand, as the Market run very Unhappily on the Mens side,[3] I found the Women had lost the Privilege of saying NO, that it was a Favour now for a Woman to have THE QUESTION ask'd, and if any young Lady had so much Arrogance as to Counterfeit a Negative, she never had the Opportunity given her of denying twice; much less of Recovering that false Step, and accepting what she had but seem'd to decline: The Men had such Choice every where, that the Case of the Women was very unhappy; for they seem'd to Plie at every Door, and if the Man was by great Chance refus'd at one House, he was sure to be receiv'd at the next.

BESIDES this, I observ'd that the Men made no scruple to set themselves out, and to go a Fortune Hunting, *as they call it*, when they had really no Fortune themselves to Demand it, or Merit to deserve it; and That they carry'd it so high, that a Woman was scarce allow'd to enquire after the Character, or Estate of the Person that pretended to her. This, I had an Example of, in a young Lady at the next House to me, and with whom I had Contracted an intimacy; she was Courted by a young Captain, and though she had near 2000 *l.* to her Fortune, she did but enquire of some of his Neighbours about his Character, his Morals, or Substance; and he took Occasion at the next Visit to let her know, truly, that he took it very ill, and that he should not give her the Trouble of his Visits any more: I heard of it, and as I had begun my Acquaintance with her, I went to see her upon it: She enter'd into a close Conversation with me about it, and unbosom'd herself very freely; I perceiv'd presently that tho' she thought herself very ill us'd, yet she had no power to resent it, and was exceedingly Piqu'd that she had lost him, and particularly that another of less Fortune had gain'd him.

I fortify'd her Mind against such a Meanness, *as I call'd it*; I told her, that as low as I was in the World, I would have despis'd a Man that should think I ought to take him upon his own Recommendation only, without having the liberty to inform myself of his Fortune, and of his Character; also *I told her*, that as she had a good Fortune, she had no need to stoop to the Dissaster of the times; that it was enough that the Men could insult us that had but little Money to recommend us; but if she suffer'd such an Affront to pass upon her without Resenting it, she would be render'd low-priz'd upon all Occasions, and would be the Contempt of all the Women in that part of the Town; that a Woman can never want an

Opportunity to be Reveng'd of a Man that has us'd her ill, and that there were ways enough to humble such a Fellow as that, or else certainly Women were the most unhappy Creatures in the World.

I found she was very well pleas'd with the Discourse, and she told me seriously that she would be very glad to make him sensible of her just Resentment, and either to bring him on again, or have the Satisfaction of her Revenge being as publick as possible.

I told her, that if she would take my Advice, I would tell her how she should obtain her Wishes in both those things; and that I would engage I would bring the Man to her Door again, and make him beg to be let in: *She smil'd at that*, and soon let me see, that if he came to her Door, her Resentment was not so great as to give her leave to let him stand long there.

HOWEVER, she lissened very willingly to my offer of Advice; so *I told her*, that the first thing she ought to do, was a piece of Justice to herself; namely, that whereas she had been told by several People, that he had reported among the Ladies, that he had left her, and pretended to give the Advantage of the Negative to himself; she should take care to have it well spread among the Women, which she could not fail of an Opportunity to do in a Neighbourhood, so addicted to Family News, as that she liv'd in was; that she had enquired into his Circumstances, and found he was not the Man as to Estate he pretended to be: Let them be told Madam, *said I*, that you had been well inform'd that he was not the Man that you expected, and that you thought it was not safe to meddle with him, that you heard he was of an ill Temper, and that he boasted how he had us'd the Women ill upon many Occasions, and that particularly he was Debauch'd in his Morals, &c. The last of which indeed had some Truth in it; but at the same time, I did not find that she seem'd to like him much the worse for that part.

As I had put this into her Head, she came most readily into it; immediately she went to Work to find Instruments, and she had very little difficulty in the Search; for telling her Story in general to a Couple of Gossips in the Neighbourhood, it was the Chat of the Tea Table all over that part of the Town, and I met with it where ever I visited: Also, as it was known that I was Acquainted with the young Lady herself, my Opinion was ask'd very often, and I confirm'd it with all the necessary Aggravations, and set out his Character in the blackest Colours; but then as a piece of secret Intelligence, I added, as what the other Gossips knew nothing of (*viz.*) That I had heard he was in very bad Circumstances; that he was under a Necessity of a Fortune to support his Interest with the Owners of the Ship he Commanded: That his own Part was not paid for, and if it was not paid quickly his Owners would put him out of the Ship, and his Chief Mate was likely to Command it, who offer'd to buy that Part which the Captain had promis'd to take.

I added, for I confess I was heartily piqu'd at the Rogue, *as I call'd him*, that I had heard a Rumour too, that he had a Wife alive at *Plymouth*, and another in the *West Indies*, a thing which they all knew was not very uncommon for such kind of Gentlemen.

THIS work'd as we both desir'd it, for presently the young Lady at next Door, *who had a Father and Mother that Govern'd*, *both her*, *and her Fortune*, was shut up, and her Father forbid him the House: Also in one Place more where he went, the Woman had the Courage, *however strange it was*, to say No, and he could try no where but he was Reproached with his Pride, and that he pretended not to give the Women leave to enquire into his Character, *and the like*.

WELL, by this time he began to be sensible of his mistake, and having allarm'd all the Women on that side the Water, he went over to *Ratcliff*, and got access to some of the Ladies there; but tho' the young Women there too, were according to the Fate of the Day, pretty willing to be ask'd, yet such was his ill luck, that his Character follow'd him over the Water, and his good Name was much the same there, as it was on our side; so that tho' he might have had Wives enough, yet it did not happen among the Women that had good Fortunes, which was what he wanted.

BUT this was not all, she very ingeniously manag'd another thing her self, for she got a young Gentleman, who was a Relation, and was indeed a marry'd Man, to come and visit her Two or Three times a Week in a very fine Chariot and good Liveries, and her Two Agents and I also, presently spread a Report all over, that this Gentleman came to Court her; that he was a Gentleman of a Thousand Pounds a Year, and that he was fallen in Love with her, and that she was going to her Aunt's in the City, because it was inconvenient for the Gentleman to come to her with his Coach in *Redriff*,[1] the Streets being so narrow and difficult.

THIS took immediately, the Captain was laugh'd at in all Companies, and was ready to hang himself; he tryed all the ways possible to come at her again, and wrote the most passionate Letters to her in the World, excusing his former Rashness, and in short, by great Application, obtained leave to wait on her again, *as he said*, to clear his Reputation.

AT this meeting she had her full Revenge of him; for *she told him* she wondred what he took her to be, that she should admit any Man to a Treaty of so much Consequence, as that of Marriage, without enquiring very well into his Circumstances; that if he thought she was to be huff'd into Wedlock, and that she was in the same Circumstances which her Neighbours might be in, (*viz.*) to take up with the first good Christian that came, he was mistaken; that in a word his Character was really bad, or he was very ill beholding to his Neighbours; and that unless he could clear up some Points, in which she had justly been Prejudiced, she had no more to say to him, but to do herself Justice, and give him the Satisfaction of knowing, that she was not afraid to say NO, either to him, or any Man else.

WITH that she told him what she had heard, *or rather rais'd herself by my means, of his Character;* his not having paid for the Part he pretended to Own of the Ship he Commanded; of the Resolution of his Owners to put him out of the Command, and to put his Mate in his stead; and of the Scandal rais'd on his Morals; his having been reproach'd with such and such Women; and his having a Wife at *Plymouth* and in the *West-Indies, and the like*; and she ask'd him, whether he could deny that she had good Reason, if these things were not clear'd up, to refuse him, and in the mean time to insist upon having Satisfaction in Points so significant as they were?

HE was so confounded at her Discourse that he could not answer a word, and she almost began to believe that all was true, by his disorder, tho' at the same time she knew that she had been the raiser of all those Reports herself.

AFTER some time he recover'd himself a little, and from that time became the most humble, the most modest, and the most importunate Man alive in his Courtship.

SHE carried her jest on a great way, she ask'd him, if he thought she was so at her last shift, that she could or ought to bear such Treatment, and if he did not see that she did not want those who thought it worth their while to come farther to her than he did, meaning the Gentleman who she had brought to visit her by way of sham.

SHE brought him by these tricks to submit to all possible measures to satisfie her, as well of his Circumstances, as of his Behaviour. He brought her undeniable Evidence of his having paid for his part of the Ship; he brought her Certificates from his Owners, that the Report of their intending to remove him from the Command of the Ship, and put his chief Mate in, was false and groundless; in short, he was quite the reverse of what he was before.

THUS I convinc'd her, that if the Men made their Advantage of our Sex in the Affair of Marriage, upon the supposition of there being such Choice to be had, and of the Women being so easie; it was only owing to this, that the Women wanted Courage to maintain their Ground, and to play their Part; and that according to my Lord *Rochester*,[1]

"*A Woman's ne'er so ruin'd but she can*
"*Revenge herself on her undoer, Man.*

AFTER these things, this young Lady plaid her part so well, that tho' she resolved to have him, and that indeed having him was the main bent of her design, yet she made his obtaining her be TO HIM the most difficult thing in the World; and this she did, not by a haughty Reserv'd Carriage, but by a just Policy, turning the Tables upon him, and playing back upon him his own Game; for as he pretended by a kind of lofty Carriage, to place himself above the occasion of a Character,[1] and to make enquiring into his Character a kind of an affront to him; she broke with him upon that Subject; and at the same time that she made him submit to all possible enquiry after his Affairs, she apparently shut the Door against his looking into her own.

IT was enough to him to obtain her for a Wife, as to what she had, she told him plainly, that as he knew her Circumstances, it was but just she should know his; and tho' at the same time he had only known her Circumstances by common Fame, yet he had made so many Protestations of his Passion for her, that he could ask no more but her Hand to his grand Request, *and the like ramble*[2] *according to the Custom of Lovers*: In short, he left himself no room to ask any more questions about her Estate, and she took the advantage of it like a prudent Woman, for she plac'd part of her Fortune so in Trustees, without letting him know any thing of it, that it was quite out of his reach, and made him be very well content with the rest.

IT is true she was pretty well besides, that is to say, she had about 1400 *l.* in Money, which she gave him, and the other, after some time, she brought to light, as a perquisite to her self; which he was to accept as a mighty Favour, seeing though it was not to be his, it might ease him in the Article of her particular Expences; and I must add, that by this Conduct the Gentleman himself became not only the more humble in his Applications to her to obtain her, but also was much the more an obliging Husband to her when he had her: I cannot but remind the Ladies here how much they place themselves below the common Station of a Wife, which if I may be allow'd not to be Partial is low enough already; *I say* they place themselves below their common Station, and prepare their own Mortifications, by their submitting so to be insulted by the Men before-hand, which I confess I see no Necessity of.

THIS Relation may serve therefore to let the Ladies see, that the Advantage is not so much on the other Side, as the Men think it is; and tho' it may be true, that the Men have but too much Choice among us; and that some Women may be found, who will dishonour themselves, be Cheap, and Easy to come at, and will scarce wait to be ask'd; yet if they will have Women, *as I may say*, worth having, they may find them as uncomatable[1] as ever; and that those that are otherwise, are a Sort of People that have such Defficiencies, *when had*, as rather recommend the Ladies that are Difficult than encourage the Men to go on with their easie Courtship, and expect Wives equally valluable that will come at first call.

NOTHING is more certain, than that the Ladies always gain of the Men, by keeping their Ground, and letting their pretended Lovers see they can Resent being slighted, and that they are not affraid of saying No. They, I observe insult us mightily, with telling us of the Number of Women; that the Wars and the Sea, and Trade, and other Incidents have carried the Men so much away,[2] that there is no Proportion between the Numbers of the Sexes; and therefore the Women have the Disadvantage; but I am far from Granting that the Number of the Women is so great, or the Number of the Men so small; but if they will have me tell the Truth, the Disadvantage of the Women, is a terrible Scandal upon the Men, and it lyes here, and here only; *Namely*, that the Age is so Wicked, and the Sex so Debauch'd, that in short the Number of such Men, as an honest Woman ought to meddle with, is small indeed, and it is but here and there that a Man is to be found who is fit for a Woman to venture upon.

BUT the Consequence even of that too amounts to no more than this; that Women ought to be the more Nice; For

how do we know the just Character of the Man that makes
the offer? To say, that the Woman should be the more easie
on this Occasion, is to say, we should be the forwarder to
venture, because of the greatness of the Danger; which in
my way of Reasoning is very absurd.

ON the contrary, the Women have ten Thousand times
the more Reason to be wary, and backward, by how much
the hazard of being betray'd is the greater; and would the
Ladies consider this, and act the wary Part, they would
discover every Cheat that offer'd; for, *in short*, the Lives of
very few Men now a-Days will bear a Character; and if the
Ladies do but make a little Enquiry, they will soon be able
to distinguish the Men, and deliver themselves: As for
Women that do not think their own Safety worth their
Thought, that impatient of their present State, resolve *as
they call it* to take the first good Christian that comes; that
run into Matrimony, as a Horse rushes into the Battle;[1] I
can say nothing to them, but this, that they are a Sort of
Ladies that are to be pray'd for among the rest of distemper'd People; and to me they look like People that
venture their whole Estates in a Lottery where there is a
Hundred Thousand Blanks to one Prize.

No Man of common Sense will value a Woman the less,
for not giving up herself at the first Attack, or for not
accepting his Proposal without enquiring into his Person or
Character; on the contrary, he must think her the weakest
of all Creatures in the World, as the Rate of Men now goes;
In short, he must have a very contemptible Opinion of her
Capacities, nay, even of her Understanding, that having but
one Cast for her Life, shall cast that Life away at once, and
make Matrimony like Death, be *a Leap in the Dark*.

I would fain have the Conduct of my Sex a little Regulated
in this particular, which is the Thing, in which of all the
parts of Life, I think at this Time we suffer most in: 'Tis
nothing but lack of Courage, the fear of not being Marry'd
at all, and of that frightful State of Life, call'd *an old Maid*;
of which I have a Story to tell by itself: This I say, is the

Woman's Snare; but would the Ladies once but get above that Fear, and manage rightly, they would more certainly avoid it by standing their Ground, in a Case so absolutely Necessary to their Felicity, than by exposing themselves as they do; and if they did not Marry so soon as they may do otherwise, they would make themselves amends by Marrying safer; she is always Married too soon, who gets a bad Husband, and she is never Married too late, who gets a good one: In a Word, there is no Woman, *Deformity, or lost Reputation excepted*, but if she manages well, may be Marry'd safely one time or other; but if she precipitates herself, it is ten Thousand to one but she is undone.

BUT I come now to my own Case, in which there was at this time no little Nicety. The Circumstances I was in, made the offer of a good Husband, the most necessary Thing in the World to me; but I found soon that to be made Cheap, and Easy, was not the way: It soon began to be found that the Widow had no Fortune, and to say this, was to say all that was Ill of me; for I began to be dropt in all the Discourses of Matrimony: Being well Bred, Handsome, Witty, Modest and agreeable; all which I had allowed to my Character, whether justly, or no, is not to the Purpose; I say, all these would not do without the Dross, which was now become more valuable than Virtue itself. In short, *the Widow*, they said, *had no Money*.

I resolv'd therefore, as to the State of my present Circumstances; that it was absolutely Necessary to change my Station, and make a new Appearance in some other Place where I was not known, and even to pass by another Name if I found Occasion.

I Communicated my Thoughts to my intimate Friend the Captain's Lady; who I had so faithfully serv'd in her Case with the Captain; and who was as ready to serve me in the same kind as I could desire: I made no scruple to lay my Circumstances open to her, my Stock was but low, for I had made but about 540 *l.* at the Close of my last Affair, and I had wasted some of that; However, I had about 460 *l.* left, a

great many very rich Cloaths, a gold Watch, and some Jewels,
tho' of no extraordinary value, and about 30 or 40 *l.* left in
Linnen not dispos'd of.

MY Dear and faithful Friend, the Captain's Wife was so
sensible of the Service I had done her in the Affair above,
that she was not only a steddy Friend to me, but knowing my
Circumstances, she frequently made me Presents as Money
came into her Hands; such as fully amounted to a Maintenance; so that I spent none of my own; and at last she
made this unhappy Proposal to me (*viz.*) that as we had
observ'd, *as above*, how the Men made no scruple to set
themselves out as Persons meriting a Woman of Fortune,
when they had really no Fortune of their own; it was but
just to deal with them in their own way, and if it was
possible, to Deceive the Deceiver.[1]

THE Captain's Lady, in short put this Project into my
Head, and told me if I would be rul'd by her I should
certainly get a Husband of Fortune, without leaving him any
room to Reproach me with want of my own; I told her as I
had Reason to do, That I would give up myself wholly to her
Directions, and that I would have neither Tongue to speak,
or Feet to step, in that Affair, but as she should direct me;
depending that she would Extricate one out of every
Difficulty that she brought me into, which she said she
would Answer for.

THE first step she put me upon, was to call her Cousin,
and go to a Relations House of hers in the Country, where
she directed me; and where she brought her Husband to
visit me, and calling me Cousin, she work'd Matters so
about, that her Husband and she together Invited me most
passionately to come to Town and be with them, for they
now liv'd in a quite different Place from where they were
before. In the next Place she tells her Husband, that I had
at least 1500 *l.* Fortune, and that after some of my Relations
I was like to have a great deal more.

IT was enough to tell her Husband this, there needed
nothing on my Side; I was but to sit still and wait the Event,

for it presently went all over the Neighbourhood that the young Widow at Captain ———s was a Fortune, that she had at least 1500 *l.* and perhaps a great deal more, and *that the Captain said so*; and if the Captain was ask'd at any time about me, he made no scruple to affirm it, tho' he knew not one Word of the Matter, other than that his Wife had told him so; and in this he thought no Harm, for he really believ'd it to be so, because he had it from his Wife; so slender a Foundation will those Fellows build upon, if they do but think there is a Fortune in the Game: With the Reputation of this Fortune, I presently found myself bless'd with admirers enough, and that I had my Choice of Men, as scarce as they said they were, *which by the way confirms what I was saying before*: This being my Case, I who had a subtile Game to play, had nothing now to do but to single out from them all, the properest Man that might be for my Purpose; *that is to say*, the Man who was most likely to depend upon the *hear say* of a Fortune, and not enquire too far into the particulars; and unless I did this, *I did nothing*, for my Case would not bear much Enquiry.

I Pick'd out my Man without much difficulty, by the judgement I made of his way of Courting me; I had let him run on with his Protestations and Oaths that he lov'd me above all the World; that if I would make him happy, that was enough; all which I knew was upon Supposition, nay, it was upon a full Satisfaction, that I was very Rich, tho' I never told him a Word of it myself.

THIS was my Man, but I was to try him to the bottom, and indeed in that consisted my Safety; for if he baulk'd, I knew I was undone, as surely as he was undone if he took me; and if I did not make some scruple about his Fortune, it was the way to lead him to raise some about mine; and first therefore, I pretended on all occasions to doubt his Sincerity, and told him, perhaps he only courted me for my Fortune; he stop'd my Mouth in that part, with the Thunder of his Protestations, *as above*, but still I pretended to doubt.

ONE Morning he pulls off his Diamond Ring, and writes

upon the Glass[1] of the Sash in my Chamber this Line,
  You I Love, and you alone.
I read it, and ask'd him to lend me his Ring, with which I
wrote under it thus,
  And so in Love says every one.
He takes his Ring again, and writes another Line thus,
  Virtue alone is an Estate.
I borrow'd it again, and I wrote under it,
  But Money's Vertue; Gold is Fate.
He colour'd as red as Fire to see me turn so quick upon him,
and in a kind of a Rage told me he would Conquer me, and
writes again *thus*,
  I scorn your Gold, and yet I Love.
I ventur'd all upon the last cast of Poetry, as you'll see, for I
wrote boldly under his last,
  I'm Poor : Let's see how kind you'll prove.
This was a sad Truth to me, whether he believ'd me or no
I cou'd not tell; I supposed then that he did not. However
he flew to me, took me in his Arms, and kissing me very
eagerly, and with the greatest Passion imaginable he held me
fast till he call'd for a Pen and Ink, and then *told me* he could
not wait the tedious writing on the Glass, but pulling out a
piece of Paper, he began and wrote again,
  Be mine, with all your Poverty.
I took his Pen and follow'd him immediately thus,
  Yet secretly you hope I lie.
HE told me that was unkind, because it was not just, and
that I put him upon contradicting me, which did not consist
with good Manners, any more than with his Affection; and
therefore since I had insensibly drawn him into this poetical
scribble, he beg'd I would not oblige him to break it off, so
he writes again,
  Let Love alone be our Debate.
I wrote again,
  She Loves enough, that does not hate.
This he took for a favour, and so laid down the Cudgels, that
is to say the Pen; I say he took it for a favour, and a mighty

one it was, if he had known all: However he took it as I
meant it, that is, to let him think I was inclin'd to go on with
him, as indeed I had all the Reason in the World to do, for
he was the best humoured merry sort of a Fellow that I ever
met with; and I often reflected on my self, how doubly
criminal it was to deceive such a Man; but that Necessity,
which prcss'd me to a Settlement suitable to my Condition,
was my Authority for it, and certainly his Affection to me,
and the Goodness of his Temper, however they might argue
against using him ill, yet they strongly argued to me, that he
would better take the Disappointment, than some fiery tem-
pered Wretch, who might have nothing to recommend him
but those Passions which would serve only to make a Woman
miserable all her Days.

BESIDES, tho' I had jested with him, as he suppos'd it, so
often about my Poverty, yet, when he found it to be true, he
had fore-closed all manner of objection, seeing whether he
was in jest or in earnest, he had declar'd he took me without
any regard to my Portion, and whether I was in jest or in
earnest, I had declar'd my self to be very Poor, so that *in a
word*, I had him fast both ways; and tho' he might say
afterwards he was cheated, yet he could never say that I had
cheated him.

HE persued me close after this, and as I saw there was no
need to fear losing him, I play'd the indifferent part with him
longer than Prudence might otherwise have dictated to me:
But I considered how much this caution and indifference
would give me the advantage over him, when I should come
to be under the Necessity of owning my own Circumstances
to him; and I manag'd it the more warily, because I found
he inferr'd from thence, as indeed he ought to do, that I
either had the more Money, or the more Judgment, and
would not venture at all.

I TOOK the freedom one Day, after we had talk'd pretty
close to the Subject, to tell him, that it was true I had
receiv'd the Compliment of a Lover from him; namely, that
he would take me without enquiring into my Fortune, and

I would make him a suitable return in this, (*viz.*) that I would make as little enquiry into his as consisted with Reason, but I hoped he would allow me to ask a few Questions, which he should answer or not as he thought fit; and that I would not be offended if he did not answer me at all; one of these Questions related to our manner of living, and the place where, because I had heard he had a great Plantation in *Virginia*, and that he had talk'd of going to live there, and I told him I did not care to be Transported.[1]

HE began from this Discourse to let me voluntarily into all his Affairs, and to tell me in a frank open way, all his Circumstances, by which I found he was very well to pass in the World; but that great part of his Estate consisted of three Plantations, which he had in *Virginia*, which brought him in a very good Income, generally speaking, to the tune of 300 *l.* a Year; but that if he was to live upon them, would bring him in four times as much; very well, thought I, you shall carry me thither as soon as you please, tho' I won't tell you so before-hand.

I JESTED with him extremely about the Figure he would make in *Virginia*; but I found he would do any thing I desired, tho' he did not seem glad to have me undervalue his Plantations, so I turn'd my Tale; I told him I had good reason not to desire to go there to live, because if his Plantations were worth so much there, I had not a Fortune suitable to a Gentleman of 1200 *l.* Year, as he said his Estate would be.

HE reply'd generously, he did not ask what my Fortune was, he had told me from the beginning he would not, and he would be as good as his word; But whatever it was, he assur'd me he would never desire me to go to *Virginia* with him, or go thither himself without me, unless I was perfectly willing, and made it my Choice.

ALL this, you may be sure, was as I wish'd, and indeed nothing could have happen'd more perfectly agreeable; I carried it on as far as this with a sort of indifferency, that he often wondred at, more than at first, But which was the only support of his Courtship; and I mention it the rather to intimate again to the Ladies, that nothing but want of Courage for such an Indifferency, makes our Sex so cheap, and prepares them to be ill us'd as they are; would they venture the loss of a pretending Fop now and then, who carries it high upon the point of his own Merit, they would certainly be slighted less, and courted more; had I discovered really and truly what my great Fortune was, and that in all I had not full 500 *l.* when he expected 1500 *l.* yet I had hook'd him so fast, and play'd him so long, that I was satisfied he would have had me in my worst Circumstances; and indeed it was less a surprize to him when he learnt the Truth, than it would have been, because having not the least blame to lay on me, who had carried it with an air of indifference to the last, he could not say one word, except that indeed he thought it had been more, but that if it had been less he did not repent his bargain; only that he should not be able to maintain me so well as he intended.

IN short, we were married, and very happily married on my side I assure you, *as to the Man*; for he was the best humour'd Man that ever Woman had, but his Circumstances were not so good as I imagined, as on the other hand he had not bettered himself by marrying so much as he expected.

WHEN we were married I was shrewdly put to it[1] to bring him that little Stock I had, and to let him see it was no more; but there was a necessity for it, so I took my opportunity one Day when we were alone, to enter into a short Dialogue with him about it; MY DEAR, *said I*, we have been married a Fortnight, is it not time to let you know whether you have got a Wife with something, or with nothing? Your own time for that, my Dear, *says he*, I am satisfied that I have got the Wife I love, I have not troubled you much, *says he*, with my enquiry after it.

THAT'S true, *said I*, but I have a great difficulty upon me about it, which I scarce know how to manage.

WHAT'S that, my Dear, *says he*?

WHY, *says I*, 'tis a little hard upon me, and 'tis harder

upon you; I am told that Captain ——— (meaning my Friend's Husband) has told you I had a great deal more Money than I ever pretended to have, and I am sure I never employ'd him to do so.

WELL, *says he*, Captain ——— may have told me so, but what then, if you have not so much that may lye at his Door, but you never told me what you had, so I have no reason to blame you if you have nothing at all.

THAT is so just, *said I*, and so generous, that it makes my having but a little a double Affliction to me.

THE less you have, *my Dear*, *says he*, the worse for us both; but I hope your Affliction you speak of, is not caus'd for fear I should be unkind to you, for want of a Portion, No No, if you have nothing tell me plainly, and at once; I may perhaps tell the Captain he has cheated me, but I can never say you have cheated me, for did you not give it under your Hand that you were Poor, and so I ought to expect you to be.

WELL, said I, *my Dear*, I am glad I have not been concern'd in deceiving you before Marriage, if I deceive you since, 'tis ne'er the worse; *that I am Poor* is too true, but not so Poor as to have nothing neither; so I pull'd out some Bank Bills, and gave him about a Hundred and Sixty Pounds, there's something, my Dear, *says I*, and not quite all neither.

I HAD brought him so near to expecting nothing, by what I had said before, that the Money, tho' the Sum was small in it self, was doubly welcome to him; he own'd it was more than he look'd for, and that he did not question by my Discourse to him, but that my fine Cloths, Gold Watch, and a Diamond Ring or two had been all my Fortune.

I LET him please himself with that 160 *l.* two or three Days, and then having been abroad that Day, and as if I had been to fetch it, I brought him a Hundred Pounds more home in Gold, and told him there was a little more Portion for him; and in short, in about a Week more I brought him 180 *l.* more, and about 60 *l.* in Linnen, which I made him believe I had been oblig'd to take with the 100 *l.* which I gave him in Gold, as a Composition for a Debt[1] of 600 *l.*

being little more than Five Shilling in the Pound, and overvalued too.

And now, MY DEAR, *says I to him*, I am very sorry to tell you, that there is all, and that I have given you my whole Fortune; I added, that if the Person who had my 600 *l.* had not abus'd me, I had been worth a Thousand Pound to him, but that as it was, I had been faithful to him, and reserv'd nothing to my self, but if it had been more he should have had it.

HE was so oblig'd by the Manner, and so pleas'd with the Sum, for he had been in a terrible fright least it had been nothing at all, that he accepted it very thankfully: And thus I got over the Fraud of *passing for a Fortune without Money*, and cheating a Man into Marrying me on pretence of a Fortune; which, *by the way*, I take to be one of the most dangerous Steps a Woman can take, and in which she runs the most hazard of being ill us'd afterwards.

My Husband, *to give him his due*, was a Man of infinite good Nature, but he was no Fool; and finding his Income not suited to the manner of Living which he had intended, if I had brought him what he expected, and being under a Disappointment in his return of his Plantations in *Virginia*, he discover'd many times his inclination of going over to *Virginia* to live upon his own; and often would be magnifying the way of living there, how cheap, how plentiful, how pleasant, *and the like*.

I BEGAN presently to understand his meaning, and I took him up very plainly one Morning, and told him that I did so; that I found his Estate turn'd to no account at this distance, compar'd to what it would do if he liv'd upon the spot, and that I found he had a mind to go and live there; and I added, that I was sensible he had been disappointed in a Wife, and that finding his Expectations not answer'd that way, I could do no less to make him amends than tell him, that I was very willing to go over to *Virginia* with him and live there.

HE said a thousand kind things to me upon the subject of

my making such a Proposal to him: He told me, that however he was disappointed in his Expectations of a Fortune, he was not disappointed in a Wife; and that I was all to him that a Wife could be, and he was more than satisfied in the whole when the particulars were put together; but that this offer was so kind, that it was more than he could express.

To bring the story short, we agreed to go; *he told me*, that he had a very good House there, that it was well Furnish'd, that his Mother was alive and liv'd in it, and one Sister, which was all the Relations he had; that as soon as he came there, his Mother would remove to another House which was her own for life, and his after her Decease; so that I should have all the House to my self; and I found all this to be exactly as he had said.

To make this part of the story short, we put on board the Ship *which we went in*, a large quantity of good Furniture for our House, with stores of Linnen and other Necessaries, and a good Cargoe for Sale, and away we went.

To give an account of the manner of our Voyage, which was long and full of Dangers, is out of my way, I kept no Journal, neither did my Husband; all that I can say is, that after a terrible passage, frighted twice with dreadful Storms, and once with what was still more terrible, I mean a Pyrate, who came on board and took away almost all our Provisions; and which would have been beyond all to me, they had once taken my Husband to go along with them but by entreaties were prevail'd with to leave him: I say, after all these terrible things, we arriv'd in *York River* in *Virginia*, and coming to our Plantation, we were receiv'd with all the Demonstrations of Tenderness and Affection (by my Husband's Mother) that were possible to be express'd.

WE liv'd here all together, my Mother-in-law, *at my entreaty*, continuing in the House, for she was too kind a Mother to be parted with; my Husband likewise continued the same as at first, and I thought my self the happiest Creature alive; when an odd and surprizing Event put an end to all that Felicity in a moment, and rendred my Condition the most uncomfortable, if not the most miserable, in the World.

MY Mother was a mighty chearful good humour'd old Woman, I may call her old Woman, for her Son was above Thirty; I say she was very pleasant, good Company, and us'd to entertain *me, in particular*, with abundance of Stories to divert me, as well of the Country we were in, as of the People.[1]

AMONG the rest, she often told me how the greatest part of the Inhabitants of the Colony came thither in very indifferent Circumstances from *England*; that, generally speaking, they were of two sorts, either (1.) such as were brought over by Masters of Ships to be sold as Servants, *such we call them*, my Dear, *says she*, but they are more properly call'd *Slaves*.[2] Or, (2.) Such as are Transported from *Newgate* and other Prisons, after having been found guilty of Felony and other Crimes punishable with Death.

WHEN they come here, *says she*, we make no difference, the Planters buy them, and they work together in the Field till their time is out; when 'tis expir'd, *said she*, they have Encouragement given them to Plant for themselves; for they have a certain number of Acres of Land allotted them by the Country,[3] and they go to work to Clear and Cure the Land,[4] and then to Plant it with Tobacco and Corn for their own use; and as the Tradesmen and Merchants will trust them with Tools, and Cloaths, and other Necessaries, upon the Credit of their Crop before it is grown, so they again Plant every Year a little more than the Year before, and so buy whatever they want with the Crop that is before them.

HENCE Child, *says she*, many a *Newgate* Bird becomes a great Man, and we have, *continued she*, several Justices of the Peace, Officers of the Train Bands,[5] and Magistrates of the Towns they live in, that have been burnt in the Hand.[6]

SHE was going on with that part of the Story, when her own part in it interrupted her, and with a great deal of good-humour'd Confidence she told me, she was one of the second sort of Inhabitants herself; that she came away openly, having ventur'd too far in a particular Case, so that she was become a Criminal, and here's the Mark of it, CHILD, *says she*, and pulling off her Glove, look ye here, *says she*, turning up the Palm of her Hand, and shewed me a very fine white Arm and Hand, but branded in the inside of the Hand, as in such cases it must be.

THIS Story was very moving to me, but my Mother (smiling) said, you need not think such a thing strange, *Daughter*, for as I told you, some of the best Men in this Country are burnt in the Hand, and they are not asham'd to own it; there's Major ———— *says she*, he was an Eminent Pickpocket; there's Justice *Ba——r* was a Shoplifter, and both of them were burnt in the Hand, and I could name you several, such as they are.

WE had frequent Discourses of this kind, and abundance of instances she gave me of the like; after some time, as she was telling some Stories of one that was Transported but a few Weeks ago, I began in an intimate kind of way to ask her to tell me something of her own Story, which she did with the utmost plainness and Sincerity; how she had fallen into very ill Company in *London* in her young Days, occasion'd by her Mother sending her frequently to carry Victuals and other Relief to a Kinswoman of hers who was a Prisoner in *Newgate*, and who lay in a miserable starving Condition, was afterwards Condemned to be Hang'd, but having got Respite by pleading her Belly, dyed afterwards in the Prison.

HERE my Mother-in-Law ran out in a long account of the wicked practices in that dreadful Place, and how it ruin'd more young People than all the Town besides; and Child, *says my Mother*, perhaps you may know little of it, or it may be have heard nothing about it, but depend upon it, *says she*, we all know here, that there are more Thieves and Rogues made by that one Prison of *Newgate*, than by all the Clubs and Societies of Villains in the Nation; 'tis that cursed Place, *says my Mother*, that half Peoples this Colony.[1]

HERE she went on with her own Story so long, and in so particular a manner, that I began to be very uneasy, but coming to one Particular that requir'd telling her Name, I thought I should have sunk down in the place; she perceived I was out of order, and asked me if I was not well, and what ail'd me? I told her I was so affected with the melancholy Story she had told, and the terrible things she had gone thro', that it had overcome me; and I beg'd of her to talk no more of it: *Why*, my Dear, *says she*, *very kindly*, what need these things trouble you? These Passages were long before your time, and they give me no trouble at all now, nay I look back on them with a particular Satisfaction, as they have been a means to bring me to this place. Then she went on to tell me how she very luckily fell into a good Family, where behaving herself well, and her Mistress dying, her Master married her,[1] by whom she had my Husband and his Sister, and that by her Diligence and good Management after her Husband's Death, she had improv'd the Plantations to such a degree as they then were, so that most of the Estate was of her getting, not her Husband's, for she had been a Widow upwards of sixteen Year.

I HEARD this part of the Story with very little attention, because I wanted much to retire and give vent to my Passions, which I did soon after; and let any one judge what must be the Anguish of my Mind, when I came to reflect, that this was certainly no more or less *than my own Mother*, and I had now had two Children, and was big with another by my own Brother, and lay with him still every Night.

I WAS now the most unhappy of all Women in the World: O had the Story never been told me, all had been well; it had been no Crime to have lain with my Husband, since as to his being my Relation, I had known nothing of it.

I HAD now such a load on my Mind that it kept me perpetually waking; to reveal it, *which would have been some ease to me*, I cou'd not find wou'd be to any purpose, and yet to conceal it wou'd be next to impossible; nay, I did not doubt but I should talk of it in my sleep, and tell my Husband of it whether I would or no:[2] If I discover'd it, the least thing I could expect was to lose my Husband, for he was too nice and too honest a Man to have continued my Husband after he had known I had been his Sister, so that I was perplex'd to the last degree.

I LEAVE it to any Man to judge what Difficulties presented to my view,[1] I was away from my native Country at a distance prodigious, and the return to me unpassable; I liv'd very well, but in a Circumstance unsufferable in it self; if I had discover'd my self to my Mother, it might be difficult to convince her of the Particulars, and I had no way to prove them: *On the other hand*, if she had question'd or doubted me, I had been undone, for the bare Suggestion would have immediately separated me from my Husband, without gaining my Mother or him, who would have been neither a Husband or a Brother; so that between the surprise on one hand, and the uncertainty on the other, I had been sure to be undone.

IN the mean time, as I was but too sure of the Fact, I liv'd therefore in open avowed Incest and Whoredom, and all under the appearance of an honest Wife; and tho' I was not much touched with the Crime of it, yet the Action had something in it shocking to Nature, and made my Husband, *as he thought himself*, even nauseous to me.

HOWEVER, upon the most sedate Consideration, I resolv'd, that it was absolutely necessary to conceal it all, and not make the least Discovery of it either to Mother or Husband; and thus I liv'd with the greatest Pressure imaginable for three Year more, but had no more Children.

DURING this time my Mother used to be frequently telling me old Stories of her former Adventures, which however were no ways pleasant to me; for by it, tho' she did not tell it me in plain terms, yet I could easily understand joyn'd with what I had heard my self, of my first Tutors, that in her younger Days she had been both WHORE and THIEF; but I verily believe she had lived to repent sincerely of both, and that she was then a very Pious sober and religious Woman.

WELL, let her Life have been what it would then, it was certain that my Life was very uneasie to me; for I liv'd, as I have said, but in the worst sort of Whoredom, and as I cou'd expect no Good of it, so really no good Issue came of it, and all my seeming Prosperity wore off and ended in Misery and Destruction; it was some time indeed before it came to this, for, but I know not by what ill Fate guided, every thing went wrong with us afterwards, and that which was worse, my Husband grew strangely alter'd; froward, jealous, and unkind, and I was as impatient of bearing his Carriage, as the Carriage was unreasonable and unjust: These things proceeded so far, that we came at last to be in such ill Terms with one another, that I claim'd a promise of him which he entered willingly into with me, when I consented to come from *England* with him (*viz.*) that if I found the Country not to agree with me, or that I did not like to live there, I should come away to *England* again when I pleas'd, giving him a Year's warning to settle his Affairs.

I SAY *I now claim'd this promise of him*, and I must confess I did it not in the most obliging Terms that could be in the World neither; but I insisted that he treated me ill, that I was remote from my Friends, and could do my self no Justice, and that he was Jealous without cause, my Conversation having been unblameable, and he having no pretence for it, and that to remove to *England*, would take away all Occasion from him.

I INSISTED so peremptorily upon it, that he could not avoid coming to a point, either to keep his word with me or to break it; and this notwithstanding he used all the skill he was master of, and employ'd his Mother and other Agents to prevail with me to alter my Resolutions; indeed the bottom of the thing lay at my Heart, and that made all his Endeavours fruitless, for my Heart was alienated from him, *as a Husband*; I loathed the Thoughts of Bedding with him, and used a thousand Pretences of Illness and Humour to prevent his touching me, fearing nothing more than to be with Child again by him, which to be sure would have prevented, or at least delay'd my going over to *England*.

HOWEVER, at last I put him so out of Humour, that he

took up a rash and fatal Resolution. In short I should not go to *England*; and tho' he had promis'd me, yet it was an unreasonable thing for me to desire it, that it would be ruinous to his Affairs, would Unhinge his whole Family, and be next to an Undoing him in the World; That therefore I ought not to desire it of him, and that no Wife in the World that valu'd her Family and her Husbands prosperity would insist upon such a thing.

THIS plung'd[1] me again, for when I considered the thing calmly, and took my Husband as he really was, a diligent careful Man in the main Work of laying up an Estate for his Children, and that he knew nothing of the dreadful Circumstances that he was in; I could not but confess to myself that my Proposal was very unreasonable, and what no Wife that had the good of her Family at Heart wou'd have desir'd.

BUT my Discontents were of an another Nature; I look'd upon him no longer as a Husband, but as a near Relation the Son of my own Mother, and I resolv'd some how or other to be clear of him, but which way I did not know, nor did it seem possible.

IT is said *by the ill-natured World* of our Sex, that if we are set on a thing, it is impossible to turn us from our Resolutions: *In short*, I never ceas'd poreing upon the Means to bring to pass my Voyage, and came that length with my Husband at last, as to propose going without him. This provok'd him to the last degree, and he call'd me not only an unkind Wife, but an unnatural Mother, and ask'd me how I could entertain such a Thought without horror as that of leaving my two Children (for one was dead) without a Mother, and to be brought up by Strangers, and never to see them more? *It was true*, had things been right, I should not have done it, but now, *it was* my real desire never to see them, or him either any more; and as to the Charge of unnatural I could easily answer it to myself, while I knew that the whole Relation was Unnatural in the highest degree in the World.

HOWEVER, it was plain there was no bringing my Husband

to any thing; he would neither go with me, or let me go without him, and it was quite out of my Power to stir without his Consent,[1] as any one that knows the Constitution of the Country I was in, knows very well.

WE had many Family quarrels about it, and they began (in time) to grow up to a dangerous Height, for as I was quite Estrang'd from my Husband (*as he was call'd*) in Affection, so I took no heed to my Words, but sometimes gave him Language that was provoking: And, *in short*, strove all I could to bring him to a parting with me, which was what above all things in the World I desir'd most.

HE took my Carriage very ill, and indeed he might well do so, for at last I refus'd to Bed with him, and carrying on the Breach upon all occasions to extremity he told me once he thought I was Mad, and if I did not alter my Conduct, he would put me under Cure; *that is to say, into a Mad-House*: I told him he should find I was far enough from Mad, and that it was not in his power, or any other Villains to Murther me; I Confess at the same time I was heartily frighted at his Thoughts of putting me into a *Mad-House*, which would at once have destroy'd all the possibility of breaking the Truth out, whatever the occasion might be; for that then, no one would have given Credit to a word of it.

THIS therefore brought me to a Resolution, *whatever came of it* to lay open my whole Case; but which way to do it, or to whom, was an inextricable Difficulty, and took me up many Months to Resolve; *in the mean time*, another Quarrel with my Husband happen'd, which came up to such a mad Extream as almost push'd me on to tell it him all to his Face; but tho' I kept it in so as not to come to the particulars, I spoke so much as put him into the utmost Confusion, and in the End brought out the whole Story.

HE began with a calm Expostulation upon my being so resolute to go to *England*; I defended it; and one hard Word bringing on another as is usual in all Family strife, *he told me*, I did not Treat him as if he was my Husband, or talk of my Children, as if I was a Mother; and *in short*, that I did

not deserve to be us'd as a Wife: That he had us'd all the
fair Means possible with me; that he had Argu'd with all the
kindness and calmness, that a Husband or a Christian ought
to do, and that I made him such a vile return, that I Treated
him rather like a Dog than a Man, and rather like the most
contemptible Stranger than a Husband: That he was very
loth to use Violence with me, but that *in short*, he saw a
Necessity of it now, and that for the future he should be
oblig'd to take such Measures as should reduce me to my
Duty.

My blood was now fir'd to the utmost, *tho' I knew what
he had said was very true*, and nothing could appear more
provok'd; I told him for his fair means and his foul they were
equally contemn'd by me; that for my going to *England*, I
was resolv'd on it, come what would; and that as to treating
him not like a Husband, and not showing my self a Mother
to my Children, there might be something more in it than he
understood at present; but, for his farther consideration, I
thought fit to tell him thus much, that he neither was my
lawful Husband, nor they lawful Children, and that I had
reason to regard neither of them more than I did.

I Confess I was mov'd to pity him when I spoke it, for he
turn'd pale as Death, and stood mute as one Thunder
struck, and once or twice I thought he would have fainted;
in short, it put him in a Fit something like an Apoplex; he
trembl'd, a Sweat or Dew ran off his Face, and yet he was
cold as a Clod, so that I was forced to run and fetch something for him to keep Life in him; when he recover'd of that,
he grew sick and vomited, and in a little after was put to Bed,
and in the next Morning was, as he had been indeed all
Night, in a violent Fever.

However it went off again, and he recovered tho' but
slowly, and when he came to be a little better, he told me, I
had given him a mortal Wound with my Tongue, and he had
only one thing to ask before he desir'd an Explanation; I
interrupted him, and told him I was sorry I had gone so far,
since I saw what disorder it put him into, but I desir'd him

not to talk to me of Explanations, for that would but make things worse.

THIS heighten'd his impatience, and indeed perplex'd him beyond all bearing; for now he began to suspect that there was some Mystery yet unfolded, but could not make the least guess at the real Particulars of it; all that run in his Brain was, that I had another Husband alive, which I could not say in fact might not be true; but I assur'd him however, there was not the least of that in it; and indeed as to my other Husband he was effectually dead in Law to me, and had told me I should look on him as such, so I had not the least uneasiness on that score.

BUT now I found the thing too far gone to conceal it much longer, and my Husband himself gave me an opportunity to ease my self of the Secret much to my Satisfaction; he had laboured with me three or four Weeks, *but to no purpose*, only to tell him, whether I had spoken those words only as the effect of my Passion, to put him in a Passion? Or whether there was anything of Truth in the bottom of them? But I continued inflexible, and would explain nothing, unless he would first consent to my going to *England*, which he would never do, *he said*, while he liv'd; on the other hand I said it was in my power to make him willing when I pleas'd, NAY to make him entreat me to go; and this increased his Curiosity, and made him importunate to the highest degree, *but it was all to no purpose*.

AT length he tells all this Story to his Mother, and sets her upon me to get the main Secret out of me, and she us'd her utmost Skill with me indeed; but I put her to a full stop at once, *by telling her* that the Reason and Mystery of the whole matter lay in herself; and that it was my Respect to her that had made me conceal it, and that in short I could go no farther, and therefore conjur'd her not to insist upon it.

SHE was struck dumb at this Suggestion, and could not tell what to say or to think; but laying aside the supposition as a Policy of mine, continued her importunity on account of her Son, and if possible to make up the breach between us two; as to that, *I told her*, that it was indeed a good design in her, but that it was impossible to be done; and that if I should reveal to her the Truth of what she desir'd, she would grant it to be impossible, and cease to desire it: At last I seem'd to be prevail'd on by her importunity, and told her I dar'd trust her with a Secret of the greatest Importance, and she would soon see that this was so, and that I would consent to lodge it in her Breast, if she would engage solemnly not to acquaint her Son with it without my consent.

SHE was long in promising this part, but rather than not come at the main Secret she agreed to that too, and after a great many other Preliminaries, I began and told her the whole Story: First I told her how much she was concern'd in all the unhappy breach which had happen'd between her Son and me, by telling me her own Story, and her *London* Name; and that the surprize she see I was in, was upon that Occasion: Then I told her my own Story and my Name, and assur'd her by such other Tokens as she could not deny that I was no other, nor more or less than her own Child, *her Daughter* born of her Body in *Newgate*; the same that had sav'd her from the Gallows by being in her Belly, and the same that she left in such and such Hands when she was Transported.

IT is impossible to express the Astonishment she was in; she was not inclin'd to believe the Story, or to remember the Particulars; for she immediately foresaw the Confusions that must follow in the Family upon it; but every thing concurr'd so exactly with the Stories she had told me of her self, and which if she had not told me, she would perhaps have been content to have denied, that she had stop'd her own Mouth, and she had nothing to do but to take me about the Neck and kiss me, and cry most vehemently over me, without speaking one word for a long time together; at last she broke out, *Unhappy Child*! *says she*, what miserable chance could bring thee hither? And in the Arms of my own Son too! *Dreadful Girl*! says she, *why we are all undone*! Married to thy own Brother! Three Children, and two alive, all of the

same Flesh and Blood! My Son and my Daughter lying
together as Husband and Wife! All Confusion and Des-
traction for ever! *miserable Family*! what will become of us?
what is to be said? what is to be done? and thus she run on for
a great while, nor had I any power to speak, or if I had, did
I know what to say, for every word wounded me to the Soul:
With this kind of Amasement on our Thoughts we parted
for the first time, tho' my Mother was more surpriz'd than I
was, because it was more News to her than to me: However,
she promis'd again to me at parting, that she would say
nothing of it to her Son, till we had talk'd of it again.

IT was not long, you may be sure, before we had a second
Conference upon the same Subject; when, as if she had been
willing to forget the Story she had told me of herself, or to
suppose that I had forgot some of the Particulars, she began
to tell them with Alterations and Omissions; but I refresh'd
her Memory, and set her to rights in many things which I
supposed she had forgot, and then came in so opportunely
with the whole History, that it was impossible for her to go
from it; and then she fell into her Rhapsodies[1] again, and
Exclamations at the Severity of her Misfortunes: When these
things were a little over with her we fell into a close Debate
about what should be first done before we gave an account of
the matter to my Husband, but to what purpose could be all
our Consultations? we could neither of us see our way thro'
it, nor see how it could be safe to open such a Scene to him;
it was impossible to make any judgment, or give any guess
at what Temper he would receive it in, or what Measures he
would take upon it; and if he should have so little Government of himself, as to make it publick, we easily foresaw that
it would be the ruin of the whole Family, and expose my
Mother and me to the last degree; and if at last he should
take the Advantage the Law would give him, he might put
me away with disdain, and leave me to Sue for the little
Portion that I had, and perhaps wast it all in the Suit, and
then be a Beggar; the Children would be ruin'd too, having no
legal Claim[2] to any of his Effects; and thus I should see him

perhaps in the Arms of another Wife in a few Months, and be my self the most miserable Creature alive.

My Mother was as sensible of this as I; and upon the whole, we knew not what to do; after some time, we came to more sober Resolutions, but then it was with this Misfortune too, that my Mother's Opinion and mine were quite different from one another, and indeed inconsistent with one another; for my Mother's Opinion was, that I should bury the whole thing entirely, and continue to live with him as my Husband, till some other Event should make the discovery of it more convenient; and that in the mean time she would endeavour to reconcile us together again, and restore our mutual Comfort and Family Peace, that we might lie as we us'd to do together, and so let the whole matter remain a secret as close as Death, for Child, *says she*, we are both undone if it comes out.

To encourage me to this, she promis'd to make me easy in my Circumstances as far as she was able, and to leave me what she could at her Death, secur'd for me separately from my Husband; so that if it should come out afterwards, I should not be left destitute, but be able to stand on my own Feet, and procure Justice from him.

This Proposal did not agree at all with my Judgment of the thing, tho' it was very fair and kind in my Mother, but my Thoughts run quite another way.

As to keeping the thing in our own Breasts, and letting it all remain as it was, I told her it was impossible; and I ask'd her how she cou'd think I cou'd bear the thoughts of lying with my own Brother? In the next place I told her that her being alive was the only support of the Discovery, and that while she own'd me for her Child, and saw reason to be satisfyed that I was so, no body else would doubt it; but that if she should die before the Discovery, I should be taken for an impudent Creature that had forg'd such a thing to go away from my Husband, or should be counted Craz'd and Distracted: Then I told her how he had threaten'd already to put me into a Mad-house, and what concern I had been in about it, and how that was the thing that drove me to the necessity of discovering it to her as I had done.

FROM all which I told her, that I had on the most serious Reflections I was able to make in the Case, come to this Resolution, which I hop'd she would like, as a medium between both, (*viz.*) that she should use her endeavours with her Son to give me leave to go for *England*, as I had desired, and to furnish me with a sufficient Sum of Money, either in Goods along with me, or in Bills for my Support there, all along suggesting, that he might one time or other think it proper to come over to me.

THAT when I was gone she should then in cold Blood, and after first obliging him in the solemnest manner possible to Secresie, discover the Case to him; doing it gradually, and as her own Discretion should guide her, so that he might not be surpriz'd with it, and fly out into any Passions and Excesses on my account, or on hers; and that she should concern herself to prevent his slighting the Children, or Marrying again, unless he had a certain account of my being Dead.

THIS was my Scheme, and my Reasons were good; I was really alienated from him in the Consequence of these things; indeed I mortally hated him as a Husband, and it was impossible to remove that riveted Aversion I had to him; *at the same time* it being an unlawful incestuous living added to that Aversion; and tho' I had no great concern about it in point of Conscience, yet every thing added to make Cohabiting with him the most nauseous thing to me in the World; and I think verily it was come to such a height, that I could almost as willingly have embrac'd a Dog, as have let him offer any thing of that kind to me, for which Reason I could not bear the thoughts of coming between the Sheets with him; I cannot say that I was right in point of Policy in carrying it such a length, while at the same time I did not resolve to discover the thing to him; but I am giving an account of what was, not of what ought or ought not to be.

IN this directly opposite Opinion to one another my

Mother and I continued a long time, and it was impossible to reconcile our Judgments; many Disputes we had about it, but we could never either of us yield our own, or bring over the other.

I INSISTED on my Aversion to lying with my own Brother; and she insisted upon its being impossible to bring him to consent to my going from him to England; and in this uncertainty we continued, not differing so as to quarrel, or any thing like it; but so as not to be able to resolve what we should do to make up that terrible breach that was before us.

AT last I resolv'd on a desperate course, and *told my Mother* my Resolution, (*viz.*) that in short, I would tell him of it my self; my Mother was frighted to the last degree at the very thoughts of it; but *I bid her be easie*, told her I would do it gradually and softly, and with all the Art and good Humour I was Mistress of, and time it also as well as I could, taking him in good Humour too: *I told her* I did not question but if I cou'd be Hypocrite enough to feign more Affection to him than I really had, I should succeed in all my Design, and we might part by Consent, and with a good Agreement, for I might love him well enough for a Brother, tho' I could not for a Husband.

ALL this while he lay at my Mother to find out, if possible, what was the meaning of that dreadful Expression of mine, as he call'd it, which I mention'd before; namely, *That I was not his lawful Wife, nor my Children his legal Children*: My Mother put him off, told him she could bring me to no Explanations, but found there was something that disturb'd me very much, and she hop'd she should get it out of me in time, and in the mean time recommended to him earnestly to use me more tenderly, and win me with his usual good Carriage; *told him* of his terrifying and affrighting me with his Threats of sending me to a Mad-house, and the like, and advis'd him not to make a Woman Desperate on any account whatever.

HE promis'd her to soften his Behaviour, and bid her assure me that he lov'd me as well as ever, and that he had no such design as that of sending me to a Mad-house, whatever he might say in his Passion; also he desir'd my Mother to use the same Perswasions to me too, that our Affections might be renew'd, and we might live together in a good understanding as we us'd to do.

I FOUND the Effects of this Treaty presently; my Husband's Conduct was immediately alter'd, and he was quite another Man to me; nothing could be kinder and more obliging than he was to me upon all Occasions; and I could do no less than make some return to it, *which I did as well as I cou'd*; but it was but in an awkward manner at best, for nothing was more frightful to me than his Caresses, and the Apprehensions of being with Child again by him, was ready to throw me into Fits; and this made me see that there was an absolute necessity of breaking the Case to him without any more delay, which however I did with all the caution and reserve imaginable.

HE had continued his alter'd Carriage to me near a Month, and we began to live a new kind of Life with one another; and could I have satisfied my self to have gone on with it, I believe it might have continued as long as we had continued alive together. One Evening as we were sitting and talking very friendly together under a little Auning, which serv'd as an Arbour at the entrance from our House into the Garden, he was in a very pleasant agreeable Humour, and said abundance of kind things to me, relating to the Pleasure of our present good Agreement, and the Disorders of our past breach, and what a Satisfaction it was to him, that we had room to hope we should never have any more of it.

I FETCH'D a deep Sigh, and told him there was no Body in the World could be more delighted than I was, in the good Agreement we had always kept up, or more afflicted with the Breach of it, and should be so still, but I was sorry to tell him that there was an unhappy Circumstance in our Case, which lay too close to my Heart, and which I knew not how to break to him, that rendred my part of it very miserable, and took from me all the Comfort of the rest.

HE importun'd me to tell him what it was; I told him I could not tell how to do it, that while it was conceal'd from him, I alone was unhappy; but if he knew it also, we should be both so, and that therefore to keep him in the dark about it was the kindest thing that I could do, and it was on that account alone that I kept a secret from him, the very keeping of which I thought would first or last be my Destruction.

IT is impossible to express his Surprize at this Relation, and the double importunity which he used with me to discover it to him: He told me I could not be call'd kind to him, nay, I could not be faithful to him if I conceal'd it from him; I told him I thought so too, and yet I could not do it. He went back to what I had said before to him, and told me he hoped it did not relate to what I had said in my Passion; and that he had resolv'd to forget all that, as the Effect of a rash provok'd Spirit; I told him I wish'd I could forget it all too, but that it was not to be done, the Impression was too deep, and I cou'd not do it, it was impossible.

HE then told me he was resolved not to differ with me in any thing, and that therefore he would importune me no more about it, resolving to acquiesce in whatever I did or said; only begg'd I would then agree, that whatever it was, it should no more interrupt our quiet and our mutual kindness.

THIS was the most provoking thing he could have said to me, for I really wanted his farther importunities, that I might be prevail'd with to bring out that which indeed it was like Death to me to conceal; so I answer'd him plainly, that I could not say I was glad not to be importuned, tho' I could not tell how to comply; but come, *my Dear*, *said I*, what Conditions will you make with me upon the opening this Affair to you?

ANY Conditions in the World, *said he*, that you can in reason desire of me; well, *said I*, come, give it me under your Hand, that if you do not find I am in any fault, or that I am willingly concern'd in the Causes of the Misfortune that is to follow, you will not blame me, use me the worse, do me any Injury, or make me be the Sufferer for that which is not my fault.

'THAT, *says he*, is the most reasonable demand in the World; not to blame you for that which is not your fault; give me a Pen and Ink, *says he*, so I ran in and fetch'd a Pen, Ink, and Paper, and he wrote the Condition down in the very words I had proposed it, and sign'd it with his Name; well, says he, *what is next*, my Dear?

WHY, *says I*, the next is, that you will not blame me for not discovering the Secret of it to you before I knew it.

VERY just again, *says he*, with all my Heart; so he wrote down that also and sign'd it.

WELL, *my Dear*, says I, then I have but one Condition more to make with you, and that is, that as there is no body concern'd in it but you and I, you shall not discover it to any Person in the World, except your own Mother; and that in all the Measures you shall take upon the discovery, as I am equally concern'd in it with you, *tho' as innocent as your self*, you shall do nothing in a Passion, nothing to my Prejudice, or to your Mother's Prejudice, without my knowledge and consent.

THIS a little amaz'd him, and he wrote down the words distinctly, but read them over and over before he Sign'd them, hesitating at them several times, and repeating them; *my Mother*'s Prejudice! *and your Prejudice*! what mysterious thing can this be? however, at last he Sign'd it.

WELL, *says I*, my Dear, I'll ask you no more under your Hand, but as you are to bear the most unexpected and surprizing thing that perhaps ever befel any Family in the World, I beg you to promise me you will receive it with Composure and a Presence of Mind suitable to a Man of Sense.

I'LL do my utmost, *says he*, upon Condition you will keep me no longer in suspence, for you Terrify me with all these Preliminaries.

WELL then, *says I*, it is this, as I told you before in a Heat, that I was not your lawful Wife, and that our Children were not legal Children; so I must let you know now in calmness, and in kindness, but with Affliction enough that *I am* your own Sister, *and you* my own Brother, and that we are both the Children of our Mother now alive, and in the House, who is convinc'd of the Truth of it, in a manner not to be denied or contradicted.

I SAW him turn pale, and look wild, and I said, now remember your Promise, and receive it with Presence of mind; for who cou'd have said more to prepare you for it, than I have done? However I call'd a Servant, and got him a little Glass of Rum, which is the usual Dram of the Country,[1] for he was just fainting away.

WHEN he was a little recover'd, *I said to him*, this Story you may be sure requires a long Explanation, and therefore have patience and compose your Mind to hear it out, and I'll make it as short as I can, and with this, I told him what I thought was needful of the Fact, and particularly how my Mother came to discover it to me, as above; and now my Dear, *says I*, you will see Reason for my Capitulations, and that I neither have been the Cause of this Matter, nor could be so, and that I could know nothing of it before now.

I AM fully satisfy'd of that, *says he*, but 'tis a dreadful Surprize to me; however, I know a Remedy for it all, and a Remedy that shall put an End to all your Difficulties, without your going to *England*; That would be strange, *said I*, as all the rest; No, No, *says he*, I'll make it easie, there's no Body in the way of it all, but myself: He look'd a little disorder'd, when he said this, but I did not apprehend any thing from it at that time, believing as it us'd to be said, that they who do those things never talk of them; or that they who talk of such things never do them.[2]

BUT things were not come their height with him, and I observ'd he became Pensive and Melancholly; and in a Word, as I thought a little Distemper'd in his Head; I endeavour'd to talk him into Temper, and to Reason him into a kind of Scheme for our Government in the Affair, and sometimes he would be well, and talk with some Courage about it; but the Weight of it lay too heavy upon his Thoughts, and in short, it went so far that he made two attempts upon himself, and in one of them had actually strangled himself, and had not his Mother come into the Room in the very Moment, he had died; but with the help of a *Negro* Servant, she cut him down and recover'd him.

THINGS were now come to a lamentable height in the Family: My pity for him now began to revive that Affection, which at first I really had for him, and I endeavour'd sincerely by all the kind Carriage I could to make up the Breach; but in short, it had gotten too great a Head, it prey'd upon his Spirits, and it threw him into a long ling'ring Consumption, tho' it happen'd not to be Mortal. In this Distress I did not know what to do, as his Life was apparently declining, and I might perhaps have Marry'd again there, very much to my Advantage, it had been certainly my Business to have staid in the Country; but my Mind was restless too, and uneasie; I hanker'd after coming to *England*, and nothing would satisfie me without it.

IN short, by an unwearied importunity my Husband who was apparently decaying, as I observ'd, was at last prevail'd with, and so *my own Fate pushing me on*, the way was made clear for me, and *my Mother concurring*, I obtain'd a very good Cargo for my coming to *England*.

WHEN I parted with my Brother, for such I am now to call him; we agreed that after I arriv'd he should pretend to have an Account that I was Dead in *England*, and so might Marry again when he would; he promis'd, and engag'd to me to Correspond with me as a Sister, and to Assist and Support me as long as I liv'd; and that if he dy'd before me, he would leave sufficient to his Mother to take Care of me still, in the Name of a Sister, and he was in some respect Careful of me, when he heard of me; but it was so oddly mannag'd that I felt the Disappointments very sensibly afterwards, as you shall hear in its time.

I CAME away for *England* in the Month of *August*, after I had been Eight Years in that Country, and now a new Scene of Misfortunes attended me, which perhaps few Women have gone thro' the like of.

WE had an indifferent good Voyage, till we came just upon the Coast of *England*, and where we arriv'd in two and thirty Days, but were then Ruffled with two or three Storms, one of which drove us away to the Coast of *Ireland*, and we put in at *Kinsale*: We remain'd there about thirteen Days, got some Refreshment on Shore, and put to Sea again, tho' we met with very bad Weather again in which the Ship sprung her Main-mast,[1] *as they call'd it, for I knew not what they meant*: But we got at last into *Milford Haven* in *Wales*, where tho' it was remote from our Port; yet having my Foot safe upon the firm Ground of my Native Country the Isle of *Britain*, I resolv'd to venture it no more upon the Waters, which had been so terrible to me; so getting my Cloths, and Money on Shore with my Bills of Loading, and other Papers, I resolv'd to come for *London*, and leave the Ship to get to her Port as she could; the Port whither she was bound, was to *Bristol*, where my Brothers chief Correspondent liv'd.[2]

I GOT to *London*, in about three Weeks, where I heard a little while after that the Ship was arriv'd in *Bristol*; but at the same time had the Misfortune to know that by the violent Weather she had been in, and the breaking of her Mainmast; she had great damage on board, and that a great part of her Cargo was spoil'd.

I HAD now a new Scene of Life upon my Hands, and a dreadful Appearance it had; I was come away with a kind of final Farewel; what I brought with me, was indeed considerable, had it come safe, and by the help of it I might have married again tollerably well; but as it was, I was reduc'd to between two or three Hundred Pounds in the whole, and this without any hope of Recruit:[3] I was entirely without Friends, nay, even so much as without Acquaintance, for I found it was absolutely necessary not to revive former Acquaintances; and as for my subtle Friend that set me up formerly for a Fortune she was Dead, and her Husband also; as I was inform'd upon sending a Person unknown to enquire.

THE looking after my Cargo of Goods soon after oblig'd
me to take a Journey to *Bristol*, and during my attendance
upon that Affair, I took the Diversion of going to the *Bath*,
for as I was still far from being old, so my Humour, which
was always Gay, continu'd so to an Extream; and being now,
as it were, a Woman of Fortune, tho' I was a Woman without
a Fortune, I expected something, or other might happen in
my way, that might mend my Circumstances as had been
my Case before.

THE *Bath* is a Place of Gallantry enough; Expensive, and
full of Snares; I went thither indeed in the view of taking
any thing that might offer; but I must do myself that Justice,
as to protest I knew nothing amiss, I meant nothing but in
an honest way; nor had I any Thoughts about me at first
that look'd the way, which afterwards I suffered them to be
guided.

HERE I stay'd the whole latter Season, *as it is call'd there*,
and Contracted some unhappy Acquaintance, which rather
prompted the Follies, I fell afterwards into, than fortify'd me
against them: I liv'd pleasantly enough, kept good Company,
that is to say, gay fine Company;[1] but had the Discourage-
ment to find this way of Living sunk me exceedingly, and
that as I had no settl'd Income, so spending upon the main
Stock was but a certain kind of *bleeding to Death*; and this
gave me many sad Reflections in the Intervals of my other
Thoughts: However I shook them off, and still flatter'd
myself that something or other might offer for my Advantage.

BUT I was in the wrong Place for it; I was not now at
Redriff, where If I had set myself tollerably up, some honest
Sea Captain or other might have talk'd with me upon the
honourable terms of Matrimony; but I was at the *Bath*
where Men find a Mistress sometimes, but very rarely look
for a Wife;[2] and Consequently all the particular Acquaintances a Woman can Expect to make there, must have some
Tendency that way.

I HAD spent the first Season well enough, for tho' I had
Contracted some Acquaintance with a Gentleman, who came

to the *Bath* for his Diversion, yet I had enter'd into no *felonious Treaty*, as it might be call'd: I had resisted some Casual offers of Gallantry, and had manag'd that way well enough; I was not wicked enough to come into the Crime for the meer Vice of it, and I had no extraordinary Offers made me that tempted me with the main thing which I wanted.

HOWEVER I went this length the first Season, (*viz.*) I contracted an Acquaintance with a Woman in whose House I Lodg'd, who tho' she did not keep an ill House, *as we call it*, yet had none of the best Principles in herself: I had on all Occasions behav'd myself so well as not to get the least Slur upon my Reputation[1] on any Account whatever, and all the Men that I had Convers'd with, were of so good Reputation that I had not given the least Reflection[2] by Conversing with them; nor did any of them seem to think there was room for a wicked Correspondence, if they had any of them offered it; yet there was one Gentleman, *as above*, who always singl'd me out for the Diversion of my Company, as he call'd it, which *as he was pleas'd to say* was very agreeable to him, but at that time there was no more in it.

I HAD many melancholly Hours at the *Bath* after all the Company was gone, for tho' I went to *Bristol* sometimes for the disposing my Effects, and for Recruits of Money, yet I chose to come back to *Bath* for my Residence, because being on good Terms with the Woman in whose House I lodg'd in the Summer, I found that during the Winter I liv'd rather cheaper there than I could do any where else; here, *I say*, I pass'd the Winter as heavily[3] as I had pass'd the Autumn chearfully; But having contracted a nearer intimacy with the said Woman, in whose House I Lodg'd, I could not avoid communicating to her something of what lay hardest upon my Mind, and particularly the narrowness of my Circumstances, and the loss of my Fortune by the Damage of my Goods by Sea: I told her also that I had a Mother and a Brother in *Virginia* in good Circumstances, and as I had really written back to my Mother in particular to represent my Condition, and the great Loss I had receiv'd, which indeed came to almost 500 *l.* so I did not fail to let my new Friend know, that I expected a Supply from thence, and so indeed I did; and as the Ships went from *Bristol* to *York* River in *Virginia*, and back again generally in less time than from *London*, and that my Brother Corresponded chiefly at *Bristol*, I thought it was much better for me to wait here for my Returns, than to go to *London*, where also I had not the least Acquaintance.

MY new Friend appear'd sensibly affected with my Condition, and indeed was so very kind, as to reduce the Rate of my living with her to so low a Price during the Winter, that she convinced me she got nothing by me; and as for Lodging during the Winter, I paid nothing at all.

WHEN the Spring Season came on, she continu'd to be as kind to me as she could, and I lodg'd with her for a time, till it was found necessary to do otherwise; she had some Persons of Character that frequently lodg'd in her House, and in particular the Gentleman who, as I said, singl'd me out for his Companion the Winter before; and he came down again with another Gentleman in his Company and two Servants, and lodg'd in the same House: I suspected that my Landlady had invited him thither, letting him know that I was still with her, but she deny'd it, and protested to me that she did not, and he said the same.

IN a Word, this Gentleman came down and continu'd to single me out for his peculiar Confidence as well as Conversation; he was a compleat Gentleman, *that must be confess'd*, and his Company was very agreeable to me, as mine, *if I might believe him*, was to him; he made no Professions to me but of an extraordinary Respect, and he had such an Opinion of my Virtue, that *as he often profess'd*, he believ'd if he should offer any thing else, I should reject him with Contempt; he soon understood from me that I was a Widow, that I had arriv'd at *Bristol* from *Virginia* by the last Ships; and that I waited at *Bath* till the next *Virginia Fleet* should arrive, by which I expected considerable Effects;

I understood by him, and by others of him, that he had a
Wife, but that the Lady was distemper'd in her Head, and
was under the Conduct of her own Relations, which he
consented to, to avoid any Reflections that might, *as was not
unusual in such Cases*, be cast on him for mismanaging her
Cure; and in the mean time he came to the *Bath* to divert
his Thoughts from the Disturbance of such a melancholy
Circumstance as that was.

MY Landlady, who of her own accord encourag'd the
Correspondence on all Occasions, gave me an advantageous
Character of him, as of a Man of Honour and of Virtue, as
well as of a great Estate; and indeed I had a great deal of
Reason to say so of him too; for tho' we lodg'd both on a
Floor, and he had frequently come into my Chamber, even
when I was in Bed;[1] and I also into his when he was in Bed,
yet he never offered any thing to me farther than a kiss, or
so much as solicited me to any thing till long after, as you
shall hear.

I FREQUENTLY took notice to my Landlady of his exceeding
Modesty, and she again used to tell me, she believ'd it was
so from the beginning; however she used to tell me that she
thought I ought to expect some Gratification from him for
my Company, for indeed he did, as it were, engross me, and
I was seldom from him; *I told her* I had not given him the
least occasion to think I wanted it, or that I would accept of
it from him; *she told me* she would take that part upon her,
and she did so, and manag'd it so dextrously, that the first
time we were together alone, after she had talk'd with him,
he began to enquire a little into my Circumstances, as how
I had subsisted my self since I came on shore? and whether
I did not want Money? I stood off very boldly, I told him
that tho' my Cargo of Tobacco was damag'd, yet that it was
not quite lost; that the Merchant I had been consign'd to,
had so honestly manag'd for me that I had not wanted; and
that I hop'd, with frugal Management, I should make it hold
out till more would come, which I expected by the next
Fleet; that in the mean time I had retrench'd my Expences,

and whereas I kept a Maid last Season, now I liv'd without; and whereas I had a Chamber and a Dining-room then on the first Floor, *as he knew*, I now had but one Room two pair of Stairs, *and the like*; but I live *said I*, as well satisfy'd now as I did then; *adding*, that his Company had been a means to make me live much more chearfully than otherwise I should have done, for which I was much oblig'd to him; and so I put off all room for any offer for the present: However, it was not long before he attack'd me again, and told me he found that I was backward to trust him with the Secret of my Circumstances, *which he was sorry for*; assuring me that he enquir'd into it with no design to satisfie his own Curiosity, but meerly to assist me, if there was any occasion; but since I would not own my self to stand in need of any assistance, he had but one thing more to desire of me, and that was, that I would promise him that when I was any way streighten'd, or like to be so, I would frankly tell him of it, and that I would make use of him with the same freedom that he made the offer, *adding*, that I should always find I had a true Friend, tho' perhaps I was afraid to trust him.

I OMITTED nothing *that was fit to be said by one infinitely oblig'd*, to let him know, that I had a due Sense of his Kindness; and indeed from that time, I did not appear so much reserv'd to him as I had done before, tho' still within the Bounds of the strictest Virtue on both sides; but how free soever our Conversation was, I cou'd not arrive to that sort of Freedom which he desir'd, (*viz.*) to tell him I wanted Money, tho' I was secretly very glad of his offer.

SOME Weeks pass'd after this, and still I never ask'd him for Money; when my Landlady, a cunning Creature, who had often press'd me to it, but found that I cou'd not do it, makes a Story of her own inventing, and comes in bluntly to me when we were together, O Widow, *says she*, I have bad News to tell you this Morning; What is that, said I, are the *Virginia* Ships taken by the *French*? *for that was my fear*. No, no, *says she*, but the Man you sent to *Bristol* Yesterday for Money is come back, and says he has brought none.

Now I could by no means like her Project; I thought it look'd too much like prompting him, which indeed he did not want, and I saw clearly that I should lose nothing by being backward to ask, so I took her up short; I can't imagine why he should say so to you, *said I*, for I assure you he brought me all the Money I sent him for, and here it is *said I*, (pulling out my Purse with about 12 Guineas in it) and added, I intend you shall have most of it by and by.

HE seem'd distasted a little at her talking as she did at first, as well as I, taking it as I fancied he would as something forward of her; but when he saw me give such an Answer, he came immediately to himself again: The next Morning we talk'd of it again, when I found he was fully satisfy'd; and smiling said, he hop'd I would not want Money and not tell him of it, and that I had promis'd him otherwise: I told him I had been very much dissatisfy'd at my Landladies talking so publickly the Day before of what she had nothing to do with; but I suppos'd she wanted what I ow'd her, which was about Eight Guineas, which I had resolv'd to give her, and had accordingly given it her the same Night she talk'd so foolishly.

HE was in a mighty good Humour, when he heard me say, *I had paid her*, and it went off into some other Discourse at that time; but the next Morning he having heard me up about my Room before him, he call'd to me, *and I answering*, he ask'd me to come into his Chamber; he was in bed when I came in, and he made me come and sit down on his Bed side, *for he said*, he had something to say to me, which was of some Moment: After some very kind Expressions he ask'd me, if I would be very honest to him, and give a sincere Answer to one thing he would desire of me? after some little Cavil with him at the word *Sincere*, and asking him if I had ever given him any Answers which were not Sincere, I promis'd him I would; why then his Request was, *he said*, to let him see my Purse; I immediately put my Hand into my Pocket, *and Laughing at him*, pull'd it out, and there was in it three Guineas and a Half; *then he ask'd me*, if there was all the Money I had? I told him no, *Laughing again*, not by a great deal.

WELL then, *he said*, he would have me promise to go and fetch him all the Money I had every Farthing: *I told him I would*, and I went into my Chamber, and fetch'd him a little private Drawer, where I had about six Guineas more, and some Silver, and threw it all down upon the Bed, and told him there was all my Wealth, honestly to a Shilling: He look'd a little at it, but did not tell it, and Huddled it all into the Drawer again,[1] and then reaching his Pocket, pull'd out a Key, and bad me open a little Walnuttree box, he had upon the Table, and bring him such a Drawer, which I did, in which Drawer, there was a great deal of Money in Gold, I believe near 200 Guineas, but I knew not how much: He took the Drawer, and taking my Hand, made me put it in, and take a whole handful; I was backward at that, but he held my Hand hard in his Hand, and put it into the Drawer, and made me take out as many Guineas almost as I could well take up at once.

WHEN I had done so, he made me put them into my Lap, and took my little Drawer, and pour'd out all my own Money among his, and bad me get me gone, and carry it all Home into my own Chamber.

I RELATE this Story the more particularly because of the good Humour there was in it, and to show the temper with which we Convers'd: It was not long after this, but he began every Day to find fault with my Cloths, with my Laces, and Head-dresses; and in a Word, press'd me to buy better, which by the way I was willing enough to do, tho' I did not seem to be so; for I lov'd nothing in the World better than fine Clothes, I told him I must Housewife the Money he had lent me, or else I should not be able to pay him again. He then told me in a few Words, that as he had a sincere Respect for me, and knew my Circumstances, he had not Lent me that Money, but given it me, and that he thought I had merited it from him, by giving him my Company so intirely as I had done: After this, he made me take a Maid, and keep House, and his Friend that came with him to *Bath*, being gone, he oblig'd me to Dyet him, which I did very willingly, believeing *as it appear'd*, that I should lose nothing by it, nor did the Woman of the House fail to find her Account in it too.

WE had liv'd thus near three Months, when the Company beginning to wear away at the *Bath*, he talk'd of going away, and fain he would have me to go to *London* with him: I was not very easie in that Proposal, not knowing what Posture I was to live in there, or how he might use me: But while this was in Debate he fell very Sick; he had gone out to a place in *Somersetshire* called *Shepton*, where he had some Business, and was there taken very ill, and so ill that he could not Travel, so he sent his Man back to *Bath* to beg me that I would hire a Coach and come over to him. Before he went, he had left all his Money and other things of Value with me, and what to do with them I did not know, but I secur'd them as well as I could, and Lock'd up the Lodgings and went to him, where I found him very ill indeed; however, I perswaded him to be carry'd in a Litter to the *Bath*, where there was more help and better advice to be had.

HE consented, and I brought him to the *Bath*, which was about fifteen Miles, *as I remember*: here he continued very ill of a Fever, and kept his Bed five Weeks, all which time I nurs'd him and tended him my self, as much and as carefully as if I had been his Wife; indeed if I had been his Wife I could not have done more; I sat up with him so much and so often, that at last indeed he would not let me sit up any longer, and then I got a Pallate Bed into his Room, and lay in it just at his Bed's Feet.

I WAS indeed sensibly affected with his Condition, and with the Apprehension of losing such a Friend as he was, and was like to be to me, and I us'd to sit and Cry by him many Hours together: However at last he grew Better, and gave hopes that he would recover, as indeed he did, tho' very slowly.

WERE it otherwise than what I am going to say, I should

not be backward to disclose it, as it is apparent I have done in other Cases in this Account; but I affirm, that thro' all this Conversation, abating the freedom of coming into the Chamber when I or he was in Bed, and abating the necessary Offices of attending him Night and Day when he was Sick, there had not pass'd the least immodest Word or Action between us. O! that it had been so to the last.

AFTER some time he gathered Strength, and grew well apace, and I would have remov'd my Palate Bed, but he would not let me till he was able to venture himself without any Body to sit up with him, and then I remov'd to my own Chamber.

HE took many Occasions to express his Sense of my Tenderness and Concern for him; and when he grew quite well, he made me a Present of Fifty Guineas for my Care, and, as he call'd it, for hazarding my Life to save his.

AND now he made deep Protestations of a sincere inviolable Affection for me, but all along attested it to be with the utmost reserve for my Virtue, and his own: I told him I was fully satisfyed of it; he carried it that length that he protested to me, that if he was naked in Bed with me, he would as sacredly preserve my Virtue, as he would defend it if I was assaulted by a Ravisher; I believ'd him, and told him I did so; but this did not satisfie him, he would, *he said*, wait for some opportunity to give me an undoubted Testimony of it.

IT was a great while after this that I had Occasion, on my own Business, to go to *Bristol*, upon which he hir'd me a Coach, and would go with me, and did so; and now indeed our intimacy increas'd: From *Bristol* he carry'd me to *Gloucester*, which was meerly a Journey of Pleasure to take the Air; and here it was our hap to have no Lodging in the Inn but in one large Chamber with two Beds in it: The Master of the House going up with us to show his Rooms, and coming into that Room, said very frankly to him, Sir, *It is none of my business to enquire whether the Lady be your Spouse or no*, but if not, *you may lie as honestly in these two*

Beds as if you were in two Chambers, and with that he pulls a great Curtain which drew quite cross the Room, and effectually divided the Beds; well, *says my Friend*, very readily, these Beds will do, and as for the rest, we are too near a kin to lye together, tho' we may Lodge near one another; and this put an honest Face on the thing too. When we came to go to Bed he decently went out of the Room till I was in Bed, and then went to Bed in the Bed on his own side of the Room, but lay there talking to me a great while.

AT last repeating his usual saying, that he could lye in the naked Bed with me and not offer me the least Injury, he starts out of his Bed, and now, *my Dear, says he*, you shall see how just I will be to you, and that I can keep my word, and away he comes to my Bed.[1]

I resisted a little, but I must confess I should not have resisted him much, if he had not made those Promises at all; so after a little struggle, *as I said*, I lay still and let him come to Bed; when he was there he took me in his Arms, and so I lay all Night with him, but he had no more to do with me, or offer'd any thing to me other than embracing me, as I say, in his Arms, no not the whole Night, but rose up and dress'd him in the Morning, and left me as innocent for him as I was the Day I was born,

THIS was a surprizing thing to me, and perhaps may be so to others who know how the Laws of Nature work; for he was a strong vigorous brisk Person; nor did he act thus on a principle of Religion at all, *but of meer Affection*; insisting on it, that tho' I was to him the most agreeable Woman in the World, yet because he lov'd me he cou'd not injure me.

I OWN it was a noble Principle, but as it was what I never understood before, so it was to me perfectly amazing. We Travel'd the rest of the Journey as we did before, and came back to the *Bath*, where, as he had opportunity to come to me when he would, he often repeated the Moderation, and I frequently lay with him, and he with me, and altho' all the familiarities between Man and Wife were common to us, yet he never once offered to go any farther, and he valued himself much upon it; I do not say that I was so wholly pleas'd with it as he thought I was: For I own I was much wickeder than he, *as you shall hear presently*.

WE liv'd thus near two Year, only with this exception, that he went three times to *London* in that time, and once he continued there four Months, but, to do him Justice, he always supply'd me with Money to subsist me very handsomly.

HAD we continued thus, I confess we had had much to boast of; but as wise Men say, it is ill venturing too near the brink of a Command,[1] so we found it; and here again I must do him the Justice to own, that the first Breach was not on his part: It was one Night that we were in Bed together warm and merry, and having drank, I think, a little more Wine that Night, both of us, than usual, tho' not in the least to disorder either of us, when after some other follies which I cannot name, and being clasp'd close in his Arms, *I told him,* (*I repeat it with shame and horror of Soul*) that I cou'd find in my Heart to discharge him of his Engagement for one Night and no more.

HE took me at my word immediately, and after that, there was no resisting him; neither indeed had I any mind to resist him any more, let what would come of it.

THUS the Government of our Virtue was broken, and I exchang'd the Place of Friend, for that unmusical harsh-sounding Title of WHORE. In the Morning we were both at our Penitentials,[2] I cried very heartily, he express'd himself very sorry; but that was all either of us could do at that time; and the way being thus clear'd, and the bars of Virtue and Conscience thus removed, we had the less difficulty afterwards to struggle with.

IT was but a dull kind of Conversation that we had together for all the rest of that Week, I look'd on him with Blushes; and every now and then started that melancholy Objection, *what if I should be with Child now? What will become of me then?* He encourag'd me by telling me, that as long as I was true to him he would be so to me; and since it was gone such a length, (which indeed he never intended) yet if I was with Child, he would take care of that, and of me too: This harden'd us both; I assur'd him if I was with Child, I would die for want of a Midwife rather than Name him as the Father of it; and he assur'd me I should never want if I should be with Child: These mutual assurances harden'd us in the thing; and after this we repeated the Crime as often as we pleas'd, till at length, as I had fear'd, so it came to pass, and I was indeed with Child.

AFTER I was sure it was so, and I had satisfied him of it too, we began to think of taking measures for the managing it, and I propos'd trusting the Secret to my Landlady, and asking her Advice, which he agreed to: My Landlady, a Woman (as I found) us'd to such things, made light of it; she said she knew it would come to that at last, and made us very merry about it: As I said above, we found her an Experienc'd old Lady at such Work; she undertook every thing, engag'd to procure a Midwife and a Nurse, to satisfie all Enquiries, and bring us off with Reputation, and she did so very dexterously indeed.

WHEN I grew near my time, she desir'd my Gentleman to go away to *London*, or make as if he did so; when he was gone, she acquainted the Parish Officers that there was a Lady ready to lye in at her House, but that she knew her Husband very well, and gave them, as she pretended, an account of his Name, which she called Sir *Walter Cleave*;[1] telling them, he was a very worthy Gentleman, and that she would answer for all Enquiries, and the like: This satisfied the Parish Officers[2] presently, and I lay INN with as much Credit as I could have done if I had really been my Lady *Cleave*; and was assisted in my Travel[3] by three or four of the best Citizens Wives of *Bath*, who liv'd in the Neighbourhood, which however made me a little the more expensive to him, I often expressed my concern to him about it, but he bid me not be concern'd at it.

As he had furnish'd me very sufficiently with Money for the extraordinary Expences of my Lying Inn, I had every thing very handsome about me; but did not affect to be Gay or Extravagant neither; besides, knowing my own Circumstances, and knowing the World as I had done, and that such kind of things do not often last long, I took care to lay up as much Money as I could for a wet Day, as I call'd it; making him believe it was all spent upon the extraordinary appearance of things in my Lying Inn.

BY this means, and including what he had given me as above, I had at the end of my Lying Inn about 200 Guineas by me, including also what was left of my own.

I WAS brought to Bed of a fine Boy indeed, and a charming Child it was; and when he heard of it he wrote me a very kind obliging Letter about it, and then told me, he thought it would look better for me to come away for *London* as soon as I was up and well, that he had provided Appartments for me at *Hammersmith* as if I came thither only from *London*, and that after a little while I should go back to the *Bath*, and he would go with me.

I LIK'D this offer very well, and accordingly hir'd a Coach on purpose, and taking my Child and a Wet-Nurse to Tend and Suckle it, and a Maid Servant with me, away I went for *London*.

HE met me at *Reading* in his own Chariot,[1] and taking me into that, left the Servant and the Child in the hir'd Coach, and so he brought me to my new Lodgings at *Hammersmith*; with which I had abundance of Reason to be very well pleas'd, for they were very handsome Rooms, and I was very well accommodated.

AND now I was indeed in the height of what I might call my Prosperity, and I wanted nothing but to be a Wife, which however could not be in this Case, there was no room for it; and therefore on all Occasions I study'd to save what I could, as I have said above, against a time of scarcity; knowing well enough that such things as these do not always continue, that Men that keep Mistresses often change them, grow weary of them, or Jealous of them, or something or other happens to make them withdraw their Bounty; and sometimes the Ladies that are thus well us'd, are not careful by a prudent Conduct to preserve the Esteem of their Persons, or the nice Article of their Fidelity, and then they are justly cast off with Contempt.

BUT I was secur'd in this Point, for as I had no Inclination to change, so I had no manner of Acquaintance in the whole House, and so no Temptation to look any farther; I kept no Company but in the Family where I Lodg'd, and with a Clergyman's Lady at next Door; so that when he was absent I visited no Body, nor did he ever find me out of my Chamber or Parlor whenever he came down, if I went any where to take the Air it was always with him.

THE living in this manner with him, and his with me, was certainly the most undesigned thing in the World; he often protested to me, that when he became first acquainted with me, and even to the very Night when we first broke in upon our Rules, he never had the least Design of lying with me; that he always had a sincere Affection for me, but not the least real inclination to do what he had done; I assur'd him I never suspected him, that if I had, I should not so easily have yielded to the freedoms which brought it on, but that it was all a surprize, and was owing to the Accident of our having yielded too far to our mutual Inclinations that Night; and indeed I have often observ'd since, and leave it as a caution to the Readers of this Story; that we ought to be cautious of gratifying our Inclinations in loose and lewd Freedoms, least we find our Resolutions of Virtue fail us in the juncture when their Assistance should be most necessary.

IT is true, *and I have confess'd it before*, that from the first hour I began to converse with him, I resolv'd to let him lye with me, if he offer'd it; but it was because I wanted his help and assistance, and I knew no other way of securing him than that: But when we were that Night together, and, as I have said, had gone such a length, I found my Weakness, the Inclination was not to be resisted,[1] but I was oblig'd to yield up all even before he ask'd it.

HOWEVER he was so just to me that he never upbraided me

with that; nor did he ever express the least dislike of my
Conduct on any other Occasion, but always protested he was
as much delighted with my Company as he was the first
Hour we came together, I mean came together as Bedfellows.

IT is true that he had no Wife, that is to say, she was as no
Wife to him, and so I was in no Danger that way, but the
just Reflections of Conscience oftentimes snatch a Man,
especially a Man of Sense, from the Arms of a Mistress, as it
did him at last, tho' on another Occasion.

ON the other hand, tho' I was not without secret
Reproaches of my own Conscience for the Life I led, and
that even in the greatest height of the Satisfaction I ever
took, yet I had the terrible prospect of Poverty and Starving
which lay on me as a frightful Spectre, so that there was no
looking behind me: But as Poverty brought me into it, so
fear of Poverty kept me in it, and I frequently resolv'd to
leave it quite off, if I could but come to lay up Money
enough to maintain me: But these were Thoughts of no
weight, and whenever he came to me they vanish'd; for his
Company was so delightful, that there was no being melancholly when he was there, the Reflections were all the
Subject of those Hours when I was alone.

I LIV'D six Year in this happy but unhappy Condition, in
which time I brought him three Children, but only the first
of them liv'd; and tho' I remov'd twice in those six Years,
yet I came back the sixth Year to my first Lodgings at
Hammersmith: Here it was that I was one Morning surpriz'd
with a kind, but melancholy Letter from my Gentleman;
intimating, that he was very ill, and was afraid he should
have another fit of Sickness, but that his Wife's Relations
being in the House with him, it would not be practicable to
have me with him, which however he express'd his great
Dissatisfaction in, and that he wish'd I cou'd be allowed to
Tend and Nurse him as I did before.

I WAS very much concern'd at this Account, and was very
impatient to know how it was with him; I waited a Fortnight
or thereabouts, and heard nothing, which surpriz'd me, and

I began to be very uneasy indeed; I think I may say, that for the next Fortnight I was near to distracted: It was my particular difficulty, that I did not know directly where he was; for I understood at first he was in the Lodgings of his Wife's Mother; but having remov'd my self to *London*, I soon found by the help of the Direction I had for writing my Letters to him, how to enquire after him, and there I found that he was at a House in *Bloomsbury*, whither he had, a little before he fell Sick, remov'd his whole Family; and that his Wife and Wife's Mother were in the same House, tho' the Wife was not suffered to know that she was in the same House with her Husband.

HERE I also soon understood that he was at the last Extremity, which made me almost at the last Extremity too, to have a true account: One Night I had the Curiosity to disguise my self like a Servant Maid in a Round Cap and Straw Hat, and went to the Door, as sent by a Lady of his Neighbourhood, where he liv'd before, and giving Master and Mistresses Service, I said I was sent to know how Mr. ——— did, and how he had rested that Night; in delivering this Message I got the opportunity I desir'd, for speaking with one of the Maids, I held a long Gossips Tale with her, and had all the Particulars of his Illness, which I found was a Pleurisie attended with a Cough and a Fever; she told me also who was in the House, and how his Wife was, who, by her Relation, they were in some hopes might Recover her Understanding; but as to the Gentleman himself, *in short* she told me the Doctors said there was very little hopes of him, that in the Morning they thought he had been dying, and that he was but little better then, for they did not expect that he could live over the next Night.

THIS was heavy News for me, and I began now to see an end of my Prosperity, and to see also that it was very well I had play'd the good Housewife, and secur'd or saved something while he was alive, for that now I had no view of *my own living* before me.

IT lay very heavy upon my Mind too, that I had a Son, a

fine lovely Boy, above five Years old, and no Provision made
for it, at least that I knew of; with these Considerations, and
a sad Heart, I went home that Evening, and began to cast
with my self how I should live, and in what manner to
bestow my self, for the residue of my Life.

You may be sure I could not rest without enquiring again
very quickly what was become of him; and not venturing to
go my self, I sent several sham Messengers, till after a
Fortnights waiting longer, I found that there was hopes of
his Life, tho' he was still very ill; then I abated my sending
any more to the House, and in some time after I learnt in
the Neighbourhood that he was about House, and then
that he was Abroad again.

I MADE no doubt then but that I shou'd soon hear of him,
and began to comfort my self with my Circumstances being,
as I thought, recovered; I waited a Week, and two Weeks,
and with much surprize and amazement I waited near two
Months and heard nothing, but that being recover'd he was
gone into the Country for the Air, and for the better Recovery
after his Distemper; after this it was yet two Months more,
and then I understood he was come to his City-House again,
but still I heard nothing from him.

I HAD written several Letters for him, and Directed them
as usual, and found two or three of them had been call'd for,
but not the rest: I wrote again in a more pressing manner
than ever, and in one of them let him know, that I must be
forc'd to wait on him myself, Representing my Circumstances, the Rent of Lodgings to pay, and the Provision for
the Child wanting, and my own deplorable Condition,
destitute of Subsistence after his most solemn Engagement,
to take Care of, and Provide for me; I took a Copy of this
Letter, and finding it lay at the House, near a Month, and
was not call'd for, I found means to have the Copy of it, put
into his own Hands at a Coffee-House, where I had by
Enquiry found he us'd to go.

THIS Letter forc'd an Answer from him, by which, tho' I
found I was to be abandon'd, yet I found he had sent a

Letter to me sometime before, desiring me to go down *to the Bath again*, its Contents I shall come to presently.

IT is True that Sick Beds are the times, when such Correspondences as this are look'd on with different Countenance, and seen with other Eyes than we saw them with, or than they appear'd with before: My Lover had been at the Gates of Death, and at the very brink of Eternity; and it seems had been strook with a due remorse, and with sad Reflections upon his past Life of Gallantry, and Levity; and among the rest, this criminal Correspondence with me, which was neither more or less, than a long continu'd Life of Adultery had represented it self, as it really was, not as it had been formerly thought by him to be, and he look'd upon it now with a just, and a religious Abhorrence.

I cannot but observe also, and leave it for the Direction of my Sex in such Cases of Pleasure, that when ever sincere Repentance succeeds such a Crime as this, there never fails to attend a Hatred of the Object; and the more the Affection might seem to be before, the Hatred will be the more in Proportion:[1] It will always be so, indeed it can be no otherwise; for there cannot be a true and sincere Abhorrence of the Offence, and the Love to the Cause of it remain, there will with an Abhorrence of the Sin be found a detestation of the fellow Sinner; you can expect no other.

I found it so here, tho' good Manners, and Justice in this Gentleman, kept him from carrying it on to any extream; but the short History of his Part in this Affair, was thus; he perceiv'd by my last Letter, and by all the rest, which he went for after, that I was not gone to the *Bath*, that his first Letter had not come to my Hand, upon which he writes me this following,

Madam,

"I AM surpriz'd that my Letter Dated the 8th of last Month "did not come to your Hand, I give you my Word it was "deliver'd at your Lodgings, and to the Hands of your Maid.

"I NEED not acquaint you with what has been my Con-"dition for sometime past; and how having been at the Edge

"of the Grave, I am by the unexpected and undeserv'd
"Mercy of Heaven restor'd again: In the Condition I have
"been in, it cannot be strange to you that our unhappy
"Correspondence has not been the least of the Burthens
"which lay upon my Conscience; I need say no more, those
"things that must be repented of, must be also reform'd.

"I WISH you would think of going back to the *Bath*, I
"enclose you here a Bill for 50 *l.* for clearing your self at
"your Lodgings, and carrying you down, and hope it will be
"no surprize to you to add, that on this account only, and
"not for any Offence given me on your side, I can SEE YOU
"NO MORE; I will take due care of the Child, leave him where
"he is, or take him with you, as you please; I wish you the
"like Reflections, and that they may be to your Advantage.
"I am, &*c*.

I WAS struck with this Letter as with a thousand Wounds,
such as I cannot describe; the Reproaches of my own Conscience were such as I cannot express, for I was not blind to
my own Crime: and I reflected that I might with less Offence
have continued with my Brother, and liv'd with him as a
Wife, since there was no Crime in our Marriage on that
score, neither of us knowing it.

BUT I never once reflected that I was all this while a
marry'd Woman, a Wife to Mr. ———— the Linnen
Draper, who tho' he had left me by the Necessity of his
Circumstances, had no power to Discharge me from the
Marriage Contract which was between us, or to give me a
legal liberty to marry again; so that I had been no less than
a Whore and an Adultress all this while: I then reproach'd
my self with the Liberties I had taken, and how I had been
a Snare to this Gentleman, and that indeed I was principal
in the Crime; that now he was mercifully snatch'd out of the
Gulph by a convincing Work[1] upon his Mind, but that I was
left as if I was forsaken of God's Grace, and abandon'd by
Heaven to a continuing in my wickedness.

UNDER these Reflections I continu'd very pensive and sad
for near a Month, and did not go down to the *Bath*, having

no inclination to be with the Woman who I was with before; least, as I thought, she should prompt me to some wicked course of Life again, as she had done; and besides, I was very loth she should know I was cast off as above.

AND now I was greatly perplex'd about my little Boy; it was Death to me to part with the Child, and yet when I consider'd the Danger of being one time or other left with him to keep without a Maintenance to support him, I then resolv'd to leave him where he was; but then I concluded also to be near him my self too, that I might have the satisfaction of seeing him, without the Care of providing for him.

I sent my Gentleman a short Letter therefore, that I had obey'd his Orders in all things, but that of going back to the *Bath*, which I cou'd not think of for many Reasons; that however parting from him was a Wound to me that I could never recover, yet that I was fully satisfied his Reflections were just, and would be very far from desiring to obstruct his Reformation or Repentance.

THEN I represented my own Circumstances to him in the most moving Terms that I was able: I told him that those unhappy Distresses which first mov'd him to a generous and an honest Friendship for me, would, I hope, move him to a little concern for me now; tho' the Criminal part of our Correspondence, which I believed neither of us intended to fall into at that time, was broken off; that I desir'd to Repent as sincerely as he had done, but entreated him to put me in some Condition, that I might not be expos'd to the Temptations which the Devil never fails to excite us to from the frightful prospect of Poverty and Distress; and if he had the least Apprehensions of my being troublesome to him, I beg'd he would put me in a Posture to go back to my Mother in *Virginia*, from whence he knew I came, and that would put an end to all his Fears on that account; I concluded, that if he would send me 50 *l.* more to facilitate my going away, I would send him back a general Release, and would promise never to disturb him more with any Importunities; unless it

was to hear of the well-doing of the Child, who if I found my
Mother living, and my Circumstances able, I would send for
to come over to me, and take him also effectually off of his
Hands.

THIS was indeed all a Cheat thus far, *viz.* that I had no
intention to go to *Virginia*, as the Account of my former
Affairs there may convince any Body of; but the business
was to get this last Fifty Pounds of him, if possible, knowing
well enough it would be the last Penny I was ever to expect.

HOWEVER, the Argument I us'd, namely, of giving him a
general Release, and never troubling him any more, prevail'd effectually with him, and he sent me a Bill for the
Money by a Person who brought with him a general Release
for me to sign, and which I frankly[1] sign'd, and receiv'd the
Money; and thus, tho' full sore against my will, a final End
was put to this Affair.

AND here I cannot but reflect upon the unhappy Consequence of too great Freedoms between Persons stated as
we were, upon the pretence of innocent intentions, Love of
Friendship, *and the like*; for the Flesh has generally so great
a share in those Friendships, that it is great odds but inclination prevails at last over the most solemn Resolutions; and
that Vice breaks in at the breaches of Decency, which really
innocent Friendship ought to preserve with the greatest
strictness; but I leave the Readers of these things to their
own just Reflections, which they will be more able to make
effectual than I, who so soon forgot my self, and am therefore
but a very indifferent Monitor.

I WAS now a single Person again, *as I may call my self*, I
was loos'd from all the Obligations either of Wedlock or
Mistressship in the World; except my Husband the Linnen
Draper, who I having not now heard from in almost Fifteen
Year, no Body could blame me for thinking my self entirely
freed from; seeing also he had at his going away told me,
that if I did not hear frequently from him, I should conclude
he was dead, and I might freely marry again to whom I
pleas'd.

I Now began to cast up my Accounts; I had by many Letters, and much Importunity, and with the Intercession of my Mother too, had a second return of some Goods from my Brother, *as I now call him*, in *Virginia*, to make up the Damage of the Cargo I brought away with me, and this too was upon the Condition of my sealing a general Release to him, and to send it him by his Correspondent at *Bristol*, which though I thought hard of, yet I was oblig'd to promise to do: However, I manag'd so well in this case, that I got my Goods away before the Release was sign'd, and then I always found something or other to say to evade the thing, and to put off the signing it at all; till *at length* I pretended I must write to my Brother, and have his Answer, before I could do it.

INCLUDING this Recruit, and before I got the last 50 *l*. I found my strength to amount, put all together, to about 400 *l*. so that with that I had above 450 *l*. I had sav'd above 100 *l*. more, but I met with a Disaster with that, which was this; that a Goldsmith[1] in whose Hands I had trusted it, broke, so I lost 70 *l*. of my Money, the Man's Composition not making above 30 *l*. out of his 100 *l*. I had a little Plate, but not much, and was well enough stock'd with Cloaths and Linnen.

WITH this Stock I had the World to begin again; but you are to consider, that I was not now the same Woman as when I liv'd at *Redriff*; for first of all I was near 20 Years older, and did not look the better for my Age, nor for my Rambles to *Virginia* and back again; and tho' I omitted nothing that might set me out to Advantage, except Painting, for that I never stoop'd to, and had Pride enough to think I did not want it, yet there would always be some difference seen between Five and Twenty, and Two and Forty.

I cast about innumerable ways for my future State of Life and began to consider very seriously what I should do, *but nothing offer'd*; I took care to make the World take me for something more than I was, and had it given out that I was a Fortune, and that my Estate was in my own Hands, the last

of which was very true, the first of it was as above: I had no
Acquaintance, which was one of my worst Misfortunes, and
the Consequence of that was, I had no adviser, at least who
cou'd advise and assist together; and above all, I had no
Body to whom I could in confidence commit the Secret of
my Circumstances to, and could depend upon for their
Secresie and Fidelity; and I found by experience, that to be
Friendless is the worst Condition, next to being in want, that
a Woman can be reduc'd to: *I say a Woman*, because 'tis
evident Men can be their own Advisers, and their own
Directors, and know how to work themselves out of Diffi-
culties and into Business better than Women; but if a
Woman has no Friend to Communicate her Affairs to, and
to advise and assist her, 'tis ten to one but she is undone;
nay, and the more Money she has, the more Danger she is in
of being wrong'd and deceiv'd; and this was my Case in the
Affair of the Hundred Pound which I left in the Hand of the
Goldsmith, *as above*, whose Credit, it seems, was upon the
Ebb before, but I that had no knowledge of things, and no
Body to consult with, knew nothing of it, and so lost my
Money.

IN the next place, when a Woman is thus left desolate and
void of Council,[1] she is just like a Bag of Money, or a Jewel
dropt on the Highway, which is a Prey to the next Comer; if
a Man of Virtue and upright Principles happens to find it,
he will have it cried,[2] and the Owner may come to hear of it
again; but how many times shall such a thing fall into Hands
that will make no scruple of seizing it for their own, to once
that it shall come into good Hands.

THIS was evidently my Case, for I was now a loose un-
guided Creature, and had no Help, no Assistance, no Guide
for my Conduct: I knew what I aim'd at, and what I wanted,
but knew nothing how to pursue the End by direct means;
I wanted to be plac'd in a settled State of Living, and had I
happen'd to meet with a sober good Husband, I should have
been as faithful and true a Wife to him as Virtue it self could
have form'd: If I had been otherwise, the Vice came in

always at the Door of Necessity, not at the Door of Inclination;[1] and I understood too well, by the want of it, what the value of a settl'd Life was, to do any thing to forfeit the felicity of it; nay, I should have made the better Wife for all the Difficulties I had pass'd thro', by a great deal; nor did I in any of the Times that I had been a Wife, give my Husbands the least uneasiness on account of my Behaviour.

BUT all this was nothing; I found no encouraging Prospect; I waited, I liv'd regularly, and with as much frugality as became my Circumstances, but nothing offer'd; nothing presented, and the main Stock wasted apace; what to do I knew not, the Terror of approaching Poverty lay hard upon my Spirits: I had some Money, but where to place it I knew not, nor would the Interest of it maintain me, at least not in *London*.

AT length a new Scene open'd: There was in the House, where I Lodg'd, a North Country Woman that went for a Gentlewoman, and nothing was more frequent in her Discourse, than her account of the cheapness of Provisions, and the easie way of living in her County; how plentiful and how cheap every thing was, what good Company they kept, and the like; till at last I told her she almost tempted me to go and live in her County; for I that was a Widow, tho' I had sufficient to live on, yet had no way of encreasing it, and that *London* was an expensive and extravagant Place; that I found I could not live here under a Hundred Pound a Year, unless I kept no Company, no Servant, made no Appearance, and buried my self in Privacy, as if I was oblig'd to it by Necessity.

I SHOULD have observ'd, that she was always made to believe, as every Body else was, that I was a great Fortune, or at least that I had Three or Four Thousand Pounds, if not more, and all in my own Hands; and she was mighty sweet upon me when she thought me inclin'd in the least to go into her Country; she said she had a Sister liv'd near *Liverpool*, that her Brother was a considerable Gentleman there, and had a great Estate also in *Ireland*; that she would go down there in about two Months, and if I would give her my

Company thither, I should be as welcome as her self for a
Month or more as I pleas'd, till I should see how I lik'd the
Country; and if I thought fit to live there, she would under-
take they would take care, tho' they did not entertain
Lodgers themselves, they would recommend me to some
agreeable Family, where I shou'd be plac'd to my content.

IF this Woman had known my real Circumstances, she
would never have laid so many Snares, and taken so many
weary steps to catch a poor desolate Creature that was good
for little when it was caught; and indeed I, whose case was
almost desperate, and thought I cou'd not be much worse,
was not very anxious about what might befall me, provided
they did me no personal Injury; so I suffered my self, tho'
not without a great deal of Invitation, and great Professions
of sincere Friendship and real Kindness, *I say* I suffer'd my
self to be prevail'd upon to go with her, and accordingly I
pack'd up my Baggage, and put my self in a Posture for a
Journey, tho' I did not absolutely know whither I was to go.

AND now I found my self in great Distress; what little I
had in the World was all in Money, except as before, a little
Plate, some Linnen, and my Cloaths; as for Houshold stuff
I had little or none, for I had liv'd always in Lodgings; but
I had not one Friend in the World with whom to trust that
little I had, or to direct me how to dispose of it, and this
perplex'd me Night and Day; I thought of the Bank, and of
the other Companies in *London*, but I had no Friend to
commit the Management of it to, and to keep and carry
about with me Bank Bills, Talleys,[1] Orders, and such things,
I look'd upon it as unsafe; that if they were lost my Money
was lost, and then I was undone; and on the other hand I
might be robb'd, and perhaps murder'd in a strange place
for them; this perplex'd me strangely, and what to do I knew
not.

IT came in my Thoughts one Morning that I would go to
the *Bank* my self, where I had often been to receive the
Interest of some Bills I had, which had Interest payable on
them, and where I had found the Clark, to whom I applyed

my self, very Honest and Just to me, and particularly so fair one time, that when I had miss-told my Money, and taken less than my due, and was coming away, he set me to rights and gave me the rest, which he might have put into his own Pocket.

I WENT to him, and represented my Case very plainly, *and ask'd if he would trouble himself to be my Adviser, who was a poor friendless Widow, and knew not what to do: He told me*, if I desir'd his Opinion of any thing within the reach of his Business, he would do his Endeavour that I should not be wrong'd, but that he would also help me to a good sober Person who was a grave Man of his Acquaintance, who was a Clark in such business too, tho' not in their House, whose Judgment was good, and whose Honesty I might depend upon, *for*, added he, *I will answer for him, and for every step he takes; if he wrongs you*, Madam, *of one Farthing, it shall lye at my door, I will make it good*; and he delights to assist People in such Cases, he does it as an act of Charity.

I WAS a little at a stand at this Discourse, but after some pause I told him, I had rather have depended upon him because I had found him honest, but if that cou'd not be, I would take his Recommendation sooner than any ones else; *I dare say*, Madam, says he, *that you will be as well satisfied with my Friend as with me, and he is thoroughly able to assist you, which I am not*; it seems he had his Hands full of the Business of the Bank, and had engag'd to meddle with no other Business than that of his Office, which I heard afterwards, but did not understand then: He added, that his Friend should take nothing of me for his Advice or Assistance, and this indeed encourag'd me very much.

HE appointed the same Evening after the Bank was shut, and Business over, for me to meet him and his Friend; and indeed as soon as I saw his Friend, and he began but to talk of the Affair, I was fully satisfied that I had a very honest Man to deal with, his Countenance spoke it, and his Character, as I heard afterwards, was every where so good, that I had no room for any more doubts upon me.

AFTER the first meeting, in which I only said what I had
said before, we parted, and he appointed me to come the
next Day to him, *telling me*, I might in the mean time satisfie
my self of him by enquiry, which however I knew not how
well to do, having no Acquaintance my self.

ACCORDINGLY I met him the next Day, when I entered
more freely with him into my Case, *I told him* my Circumstances at large, that *I was a Widow* come over from *America*,
perfectly desolate and friendless; that I had a little Money,
and but a little, and was almost distracted for fear of losing
it, having no Friend in the World to trust with the management of it; that I was going into the North of *England* to live
cheap, that my stock might not waste; that I would willingly
Lodge my Money in the Bank, but that I durst not carry the
Bills about me, and the like, as above; and how to Correspond
about it, or with who, I knew not.

HE told me I might lodge the Money in the Bank as an
Account, and its being entred in the Books would entitle me
to the Money at any time, and if I was in the North I might
draw Bills on the Cashire and receive it when I would; but
that then it would be esteem'd as running Cash, and the
Bank would give no Interest for it; that I might buy Stock
with it, and so it would lye in store for me, but that then if I
wanted to dispose of it, I must come up to Town on purpose
to Transfer it, and even it would be with some difficulty I
should receive the half yearly Dividend, unless I was here in
Person, or had some Friend I could trust with having the
Stock in his Name to do it for me, and that would have the
same difficulty in it as before; and with that he look'd hard
at me *and smil'd a little*; at last, *says he*, why do you not get a
head Steward, Madam, that may take you and your Money
together into keeping, and then you would have the trouble
taken off of your Hands? Ay, Sir, and the Money too it may
be, *said I*, for truly *I find the hazard that way is as much as*
'tis t'other way; but I remember, *I said*, secretly to my self,
I wish you would ask me the Question fairly, I would consider very seriously on it before I said NO.

HE went on a good way with me, and I thought once or twice he was in earnest, but to my real Affliction, I found at last he had a Wife; but when he own'd he had a Wife he shook his Head, and said with some concern, that indeed he had *a Wife*, and *no Wife*: I began to think he had been in the Condition of my late Lover, and that his Wife had been Distemper'd or Lunatick, or some such thing: However, we had not much more Discourse at that time, but he told me he was in too much hurry of business then, but that if I would come home to his House after their Business was over, he would by that time consider what might be done for me, to put my Affairs in a Posture of Security: I told him I would come, and desir'd to know where he liv'd: He gave me a Direction in Writing, and when he gave it me he read it to me, and said, there 'tis, Madam, if you dare trust your self with me: Yes, Sir, *said I*, I believe I may venture to trust you with my self, for you have a Wife you say, and I don't want a Husband; besides, I dare trust you with my Money, which is all I have in the World, and if that were gone, I may trust my self any where.

HE said some things in Jest that were very handsome and mannerly, and would have pleas'd me very well if they had been in earnest; *but that pass'd over*, I took the Directions, and appointed to attend him at his House at seven a Clock the same Evening.

WHEN I came he made several Proposals for my placing my Money in the Bank, in order to my having Interest for it; but still some difficulty or other came in the way, which he objected as not safe; and I found such a sincere dis-interested Honesty in him, that I began to muse with my self, that I had certainly found the honest Man I wanted; and that I could never put my self into better Hands; so I told him with a great deal of frankness that I had never met with Man or Woman yet that I could trust, or in whom I cou'd think my self safe, but that I saw he was so dis-interestedly concern'd for my safety, that *I said* I would freely trust him with the management of that little I had, if he would accept to be Steward for a poor Widow that could give him no Salary.

HE smil'd, and standing up with great Respect saluted me; he told me he could not but take it very kindly that I had so good an Opinion of him; that he would not deceive me, that he would do any thing in his Power to serve me and expect no Sallary; but that he cou'd not by any means accept of a Trust, that it might bring him to be suspected of Self-interest, and that if I should die he might have Disputes with my Executors, which he should be very loth to encumber himself with.

I TOLD him if those were all his Objections I would soon remove them, and convince him, that there was not the least room for any difficulty; for that *first* as for suspecting him, if ever I should do it now was the time to suspect him, and not put the Trust into his Hands, and whenever I did suspect him, he could but throw it up then and refuse to go any farther; *Then* as to Executors, I assur'd him I had no Heirs, nor any Relations in *England*, and I would have neither Heirs or Executors but himself, unless I should alter my Condition before I died, and then his Trust and Trouble should cease together, which however I had no prospect of yet; but I told him if I died as I was, it should be all his own, and he would deserve it by being so faithful to me as I was satisfied he would be.

HE chang'd his Countenance at this Discourse, and ask'd me, how I came to have so much good will for him? and looking very much pleas'd, said, he might very lawfully wish he was a single Man for my sake; I smil'd and told him, that as he was not, my offer could have no design upon him in it, and to wish, as he did, was not to be allow'd, 'twas Criminal to his Wife.

HE told me I was wrong; for, *says he*, Madam, as I said before, I have a Wife and no Wife, and 'twould be no Sin to me to wish her hang'd, if that were all; I know nothing of your Circumstances that way, Sir, *said I*; but it cannot be innocent to wish your Wife dead; I tell you, *says he again*, she is a Wife and no Wife; you don't know what I am, or what she is.

THAT'S true, *said I*, Sir, I do not know what you are, but I believe you to be an honest Man, and that's the cause of all my Confidence in you.

WELL, well, *says he*, and so I am, *I hope*, too, but I am something else too, Madam; for, *says he*, to be plain with you, I am a *Cuckold*, and she is a *Whore*; he spoke it in a kind of Jest, but it was with such an awkward smile, that I perceiv'd it was what stuck very close to him, and he look'd dismally when he said it.

THAT alters the case indeed, Sir, *said I*, as to that part you were speaking of; but *a Cuckold* you know may be an honest Man, it does not alter that Case at all; besides I think, *said I*, since your Wife is so dishonest to you, you are too honest to her, to own her for your Wife; but that, *said I*, is what I have nothing to do with.

NAY, *says he*, I do think to clear my Hands of her, for to be plain with you, Madam, *added he*, I am no contented Cuckold neither: *On the other hand*, I assure you it provokes me to the highest degree, but I can't help my self, she that will be *a Whore*, will be a *Whore*.

I WAV'D the Discourse, and began to talk of my Business, but I found he could not have done with it, so I let him alone, and he went on to tell me all the Circumstances of his Case, too long to relate here, particularly, that having been out of *England* some time before he came to the Post he was in, she had had two Children in the mean time by an Officer of the Army; and that when he came to *England*, and, upon her Submission, took her again, and maintain'd her very well, yet she run away from him with a Linnen-Draper's Apprentice; robb'd him of what she could come at, and continued to live from him still; so that, Madam, *says he*, she is a Whore not by Necessity, which is the common Bait of your Sex, but by Inclination, and for the sake of the Vice.

WELL, I pitied him and wish'd him well rid of her, and still would have talk'd of my Business, but it would not do;

at last he looks steadily at me, *look you*, Madam, *says he*, you came to ask Advice of me, and I will serve you as faithfully as if you were my own Sister; but I must turn the Tables, since you oblige me to do it, and are so friendly to me, and I think I must ask advice of you; *tell me what must a poor abus'd Fellow do with* a Whore? *what can I do* to do my self Justice *upon her*?

ALAS, *Sir*, *says I*, 'tis a Case too nice for me to advise in, but it seems she has run away from you, so you are rid of her fairly; what can you desire more? Ay she is gone indeed, *said he*, but I am not clear of her for all that.

THAT'S true, *says I*, she may indeed run you into Debt, but the Law has furnish'd you with Methods to prevent that also, you may Cry her down,[1] *as they call it*.

No, no, *says he*, that is not the Case neither, I have taken care of all that; 'tis not that part that I speak of, but I would be rid of her so that I might marry again.

WELL, Sir, *says I*, then you must Divorce her; if you can prove what you say, you may certainly get that done, and then, I suppose, you are free.

THAT'S very tedious and expensive,[2] *says he*.

WHY, *says I*, if you can get any Woman you like to take your word, I suppose your Wife would not dispute the Liberty with you that she takes herself.

AY, *says he*, but 'twou'd be hard to bring an honest Woman to do that; and for the other sort, *says he*, I have had enough of her to meddle with any more Whores.

IT occurr'd to me presently, I would have taken your word with all my Heart, if you had but ask'd me the Question, but that was to my self; *to him I reply'd*, why you shut the Door against any honest Woman accepting you, for you condemn all that should venture upon you at once, and conclude, that really a Woman that takes you now, can't be honest.

WHY, *says he*, I wish you would satisfie me that an honest Woman would take me, I'd venture it, and then turns short upon me, *will you take me*, Madam?

THAT'S not a fair Question, *says I*, after what you have

said; however, least you should think I wait only for a Recantation of it, I shall answer you plainly NO *not I*; my Business is of another kind with you, and I did not expect you would have turn'd my serious Application to you in my own distracted Case, into a Comedy.

WHY, Madam, *says he*, my Case is as distracted as yours can be, and I stand in as much need of Advice as you do, for I think if I have not Relief some where, I shall be mad my self, and I know not what course to take, I protest to you.

WHY, Sir, *says I*, 'tis easie to give Advice in your Case, much easier than it is in mine; speak then, *says he*, I beg of you, for now you encourage me.

Why, *says I*, if your Case is so plain as you say it is, you may be legally Divorc'd, and then you may find honest Women enough to ask the Question of fairly, the Sex is not so scarce that you can want a Wife.

WELL then, *said he*, I am in earnest, I'll take your Advice, but shall I ask you one Question seriously before hand?

ANY Question, *said I*, but that you did before.

No, that Answer will not do, *said he*, for, in short, that is the Question I shall ask.

You may ask what Questions you please, but you have my Answer to that already, *said I*; besides Sir, *said I*, can you think so Ill of me as that I would give any Answer to such a Question beforehand? Can any Woman alive believe you in earnest, or think you design any thing but to banter her?

WELL, well, *says he*, I do not banter you, I am in earnest, consider of it.

But, SIR, *says I*, *a little gravely*, I came to you about my own Business, I beg of you let me know, what you will advise me to do?

I WILL be prepar'd, *says he*, against you come again.

NAY, *says I*, you have forbid my coming any more.

WHY so, *said he*, and look'd a little surpriz'd?

BECAUSE, *said I*, you can't expect I should visit you on the account you talk of.

WELL, *says he*, you shall promise me to come again

however, and I will not say any more of it till I have gotten
the Divorce, but I desire you will prepare to be better condition'd when that's done, for you shall be the Woman, or I
will not be Divorc'd at all: Why I owe it to your unlooked
for kindness, if it were to nothing else, but I have other
Reasons too.

HE could not have said any thing in the World that pleas'd
me better; however, I knew that the way to secure him was
to stand off while the thing was so remote, as it appear'd to
be, and that it was time enough to accept of it when he was
able to perform it; so I said very respectfully to him, it was
time enough to consider of these things, when he was in a
Condition to talk of them; in the mean time I told him, I
was going a great way from him, and he would find Objects
enough to please him better: We broke off here for the
present, and he made me promise him to come again the
next Day, for his Resolutions upon my own Business, which
after some pressing I did; tho' had he seen farther into me,
I wanted no pressing on that Account.

I CAME the next Evening accordingly, and brought my
Maid with me, *to let him see* that I kept a Maid, but I sent
her away, as soon as I was gone in: He would have had me
let the Maid have staid, but I would not, but order'd her
aloud to come for me again about Nine a-Clock, but he
forbid that, and told me he would see me safe Home, which
by the way I was not very well pleas'd with, supposing he
might do that to know where I liv'd, and enquire into my
Character, and Circumstances: However, I ventur'd that,
for all that the People there, or thereabout knew of me, was
to my Advantage; and all the Character he had of me, after
he had enquir'd, was, *that I was a Woman of Fortune*, and
that I was a very modest sober Body; which whether true or
not in the Main, yet you may see how necessary it is, for all
Women who expect any thing in the World, to preserve the
Character of their Virtue, even when perhaps they may have
sacrific'd the Thing itself.

I FOUND, *and was not a little pleas'd with it*, that he had provided a Supper for me: I found also he liv'd very hand-somely, and had a House very handsomely furnish'd, all which I was rejoyc'd at indeed, for I look'd upon it as all my own.

WE had now a second Conference upon the Subject matter of the last Conference: He laid his business very Home indeed; he protested his Affection to me, and indeed I had no room to doubt it; he declar'd that it began from the first Moment I talk'd with him, and long before I had mention'd leaving my Effects with him; 'tis no matter when it begun, *thought I*, if it will but hold, 'twill be well enough: *He then told me*, how much the offer I had made of trusting him with my Effects, and leaving them to him, had engag'd him; so I intended it should, *thought I*, but then I thought you had been a single Man too: After we had Supp'd, I observ'd he press'd me very hard to drink two or three Glasses of Wine, which however I declin'd; but Drank one Glass or two: He then told he had a Proposal to make to me, which I should promise him I would not take ill, if I should not grant it: I told him I hop'd he would make no dishonourable Proposal to me, especially in his own House, and that if it was such, I desir'd he would not propose it, that I might not be oblig'd to offer any Resentment to him, that did not become the respect I profess'd for him, and the Trust I had plac'd in him, in coming to his House; and beg'd of him he would give me leave to go away, and accordingly began to put on my Gloves, and prepare to be gone, tho' at the same time I no more intended it, than he intended to let me.

WELL, he importun'd me not to talk of going, he assur'd me he had no dishonourable thing in his Thoughts about me, and was very far from offering any thing to me that was dishonourable and if I thought so, he would chuse to say no more of it.

THAT part I did not relish at all; I told him, I was ready to hear any thing that he had to say, depending that he would say nothing unworthy of himself, or unfit for me to hear; upon this, he told me his Proposal was this, That I would

Marry him, tho' he had not yet obtain'd the Divorce from the Whore his Wife; and to satisfie me that he meant honourably, he would promise not to desire me to live with him, or go to Bed to him till the Divorce was obtain'd: My Heart said yes to this offer at first Word, but it was necessary to Play the Hypocrite a little more with him; so I seem'd to decline the Motion with some warmth, and besides a little Condemning the thing as unfair, told him, that such a Proposal could be of no Signification, but to entangle us both in great Difficulties; for if he should not at last obtain the Divorce, yet we could not dissolve the Marriage, neither could we proceed in it; so that if he was disappointed in the Divorce, I left him to consider what a Condition we should both be in.

IN SHORT, I carried on the Argument against this so far, that I convinc'd him, it was not a Proposal that had any Sense in it: WELL then he went from it to another, and that was, that I would Sign and Seal a Contract with him, Conditioning to Marry him as soon as the Divorce was obtain'd,[1] and to be void if he could not obtain it.

I TOLD him such a thing was more Rational than the other; but as this was the first time that ever I could imagine him weak enough to be in earnest in this Affair, I did not use to say YES at first asking, I would consider of it.

I PLAY'D with this Lover, as an Angler does with a Trout: I found I had him fast on the Hook, so I jested with his new Proposal; and put him off: I told him he knew little of me, and bad him enquire about me; I let him also go Home with me to my Lodging, tho' I would not ask him to go in, for I told him it was not Decent.

IN SHORT, I ventur'd to avoid Signing a Contract of Marriage, and the Reason why I did it, was because the Lady that had invited me so earnestly to go with her into *Lancashire* insisted so possitively upon it, and promised me such great Fortunes, and such fine things there, that I was tempted to go and try; perhaps, *said I*, I may mend myself very much, and then I made no scruple in my Thoughts, of quitting my

honest Citizen, who I was not so much in Love with, as not
to leave him for a Richer.

IN a Word I avoided a Contract; but told him I would go
into the *North*, that he should know where to write to me by
the Consequence of the Business I had entrusted with him,
that I would give him a sufficient Pledge of my Respect for
him; for I would leave almost all I had in the World in his
Hands; and I would thus far give him my Word, that as soon
as he had su'd out a Divorce from his first Wife, if he would
send me an Account of it, I would come up to *London*, and
that then we would talk seriously of the Matter.

IT was a base Design I went with, *that I must confess*, tho'
I was invited thither with a Design much worse than mine
was, as the Sequel will discover; well I went with my
Friend, *as I call'd her*, into *Lancashire*; all the way we went
she Caressed me with the utmost appearance of a sincere
undissembled Affection; treated me, except my Coach hire
all the way; and her Brother brought a Gentleman's Coach
to *Warrington*, to receive us, and we were carried from thence
to *Liverpool* with as much Ceremony as I could desire: We
were also entertain'd at a Merchant's House in *Liverpool*
three or four Days very handsomely: I forbear to tell his
Name, because of what follow'd; then she told me she would
carry me to an Uncles House of hers, where we should be
nobly entertain'd; she did so, her Uncle as she call'd him,
sent a Coach and four Horses for us, and we were carried
near forty Miles, I know not whither.

WE came however to a Gentleman's Seat, where was a
numerous Family, a large Park, extraordinary Company
indeed, and where she was call'd Cousin; I told her if she
had resolv'd to bring me into such Company as this, she
should have let me have prepar'd my self, and have furnish'd
my self with better Cloths; the Ladies took notice of that,
and told me very genteely, they did not value People in their
Country so much by their Cloths, as they did in *London*;
that their Cousin had fully inform'd them of my Quality,
and that I did not want Cloths to set me off; in short, they

entertain'd me not like what I was, but like what they thought I had been, Namely, a Widow Lady of a great Fortune.

THE first Discovery I made here was, that the Family were all *Roman Catholicks*,[1] and the Cousin too, who I call'd my Friend; however, *I must say*, that nothing in the World could behave better to me; and I had all the Civility shown me that I could have had, if I had been of their Opinion: The Truth is, I had not so much Principle of any kind, as to be Nice in Point of Religion; and I presently learn'd to speak favourably of the *Romish Church*; particularly I told them I saw little, but the prejudice of Education in all the Differences that were among Christians about Religion,[2] and if it had so happen'd that my Father had been a *Roman Catholick*, I doubted not but I should have been as well pleas'd with their Religion as my own.

THIS oblig'd them in the highest Degree, and as I was besieg'd Day and Night with good Company, and pleasant Discourse, so I had two or three old Ladies that lay at me upon the Subject of Religion too; I was so Complaisant that tho' I would not compleatly engage, yet I made no scruple to be present at their Mass, and to conform to all their Gestures as they shew'd me the Pattern, but I would not come too cheap; so that I only in the main encourag'd them to expect that I would turn *Roman Catholick*, if I was instructed in the *Catholick Doctrine* as they call'd it, and so the matter rested.

I STAY'D here about six Weeks; and then my Conducter led me back to a Country Village, about six Miles from *Liverpool*, where her Brother, (as she call'd him) came to Visit me in his own Chariot, and in a very good Figure, with two Footmen in a good Livery; and the next thing was to make Love to me: As it had happen'd to me, one would think I could not have been cheated, and indeed I thought so myself, having a safe Card at home,[3] which I resolv'd not to quit, unless, I could mend myself very much: However in all appearance this Brother was a Match worth my lissening to, and the least his Estate was valued at, was a 1000 *l.* a

Year, but the Sister said it was worth 1500 *l.* a Year, and lay most of it in *Ireland.*

I THAT was a great Fortune, and pass'd for such, was above being ask'd how much my Estate was; and my false Friend taking it upon a foolish hearsay had rais'd it from 500 *l.* to 5000 *l.* and by the time she came into the Country she call'd it 15000 *l.* The *Irishman,*[1] for such I understood him to be, was stark Mad at this Bait: In short, he Courted me, made me Presents, and run in Debt like a mad Man for the Expences of his Equipage, and of his Courtship: He had to give him his due, the Appearance of an extraordinary fine Gentleman; he was Tall, well Shap'd, and had an extraordinary Address; talk'd as naturally of his Park, and his Stables; of his Horses, his Game-Keepers, his Woods, his Tenants, and his Servants, as if we had been in the Mansion-House, and I had seen them all about me.

HE never so much as ask'd me about my Fortune, or Estate; but assur'd me that when we came to *Dublin* he would Joynture me in 600 *l.* a Year good Land; and that he would enter into a Deed of Settlement, or Contract here, for the performance of it.

THIS was such Language indeed as I had not been us'd to, and I was here beaten out of all my Measures; I had a she Devil in my Bosom, every Hour telling me how great her Brother liv'd: One time she would come for my Orders, how I would have my Coaches painted, and how lin'd; and another time what Cloths my Page should wear: In short, my Eyes were dazl'd, I had now lost my Power of saying No, and to cut the Story short, I consented to be married; but to be the more private we were carried farther into the Country, and married by a Romish Clergyman, which I was assur'd would marry us as effectually as a Church of *England* Parson.[2]

I CANNOT say, but I had some Reflections in this Affair, upon the dishonourable forsaking my faithful Citizen; who lov'd me sincerely, and who was endeavouring to quit himself of a scandalous Whore, by whom he had been indeed barbarously us'd, and promis'd himself infinite Happiness in his new choice; which choice was now giving up her self to another in a manner almost as scandalous as hers could be.

But the glittering show of a great Estate, and of fine Things, which the deceived Creature that was now my Deceiver represented every Hour to my Imagination, hurried me away, and gave me no time to think of *London*, or of any thing there, much less of the Obligation I had to a Person of infinitely more real Merit than what was now before me.

But the thing was done, I was now in the Arms of my new Spouse, who appear'd still the same as before; great even to Magnificence, and nothing less than a Thousand Pound a Year could support the ordinary Equipage he appear'd in.

After we had been marry'd about a Month, he began to talk of my going to *West-chester* in order to embark for *Ireland*. However, he did not hurry me, for we staid near three Weeks longer, and then he sent to *Chester* for a Coach to meet us at the *Black Rock*, as they call it, over-against *Liverpool*: Thither we went in a fine Boat they call a Pinnace with Six Oars, his Servants, and Horses, and Baggage going in the Ferry Boat. He made his excuse to me, that he had no Acquaintance at *Chester*, but he would go before and get some handsome Apartment for me at a private House; I ask'd him how long we should stay at *Chester*? he said not at all, any longer than one Night or two, but he would immediately hire a Coach to go to *Holyhead*; then I told him he should by no means give himself the trouble to get private Lodgings for one Night or two, for that *Chester* being a great Place, I made no doubt but there would be very good Inns and Accommodation enough; so we lodg'd at an Inn in the West Street, not far from the Cathedral,[1] I forget what Sign it was at.

Here my Spouse talking of my going to *Ireland*, ask'd me if I had no Affairs to settle at *London* before we went off; I told him no not of any great Consequence, but what might be done as well by Letter from *Dublin*: Madam, says he very respectfully, I suppose the greatest part of your Estate, which my Sister tells me is most of it in Money in the Bank of *England*, lies secure enough, but in case it requir'd Transferring, or any way altering its Property, it might be necessary to go up to *London*, and settle those things before we went over.

I SEEMED to look strange at it, and told him I knew not what he meant; that I had no Effects in the Bank of *England* that I knew of; and I hoped he could not say that I had ever told him I had: No, he said, I had not told him so, but his Sister had said the greatest part of my Estate lay there, and *I only mention'd it my Dear*, said he, *that if there was any occasion to settle it, or order any thing about it, we might not be oblig'd to the hazard and trouble of another Voyage back again*, for he added, that he did not care to venture me too much upon the Sea.

I WAS surpriz'd at this talk, and began to consider very seriously, what the meaning of it must be? and it presently occurr'd to me that my Friend, who call'd him Brother, had represented me in Colours which were not my due; and I thought, since it was come to that pitch, that I would know the bottom of it before I went out of *England*, and before I should put my self into I knew not whose Hands, in a strange Country.

UPON this I call'd his Sister into my Chamber the next Morning, and letting her know the Discourse her Brother and I had been upon, the Evening before, I conjur'd her to tell me, what she had said to him, and upon what Foot it was that she had made this Marriage? She own'd that she had told him that I was a great Fortune, and said, that she was told so at *London: Told so*, says I warmly, *did I ever tell you so*? No, she said, it was true I did not tell her so, but I had said several times, that what I had, was in my own disposal: I did so, *return'd I very quickly and hastily*, but I never told you I had any thing call'd a Fortune; no not that I had one Hundred Pounds, or the value of an Hundred Pounds in the World; and how did it consist with my being a Fortune, *said I*, that I should come here into the North of *England* with you, only upon the account of living cheap? At these words which I spoke warm and high, my Husband, and her Brother as she call'd him, came into the Room; and I desir'd him to come and sit down, for I had something of moment to say before them both, which it was absolutely necessary he should hear.

He look'd a little disturb'd at the assurance with which I seem'd to speak it, and came and sat down by me, having first shut the Door; upon which I began, for I was very much provok'd, and turning my self to him, I am afraid, says I, *my Dear*, for I spoke with kindness on his side, that you have a very great abuse put upon you, and an Injury done you never to be repair'd in your marrying me, which however as I have had no hand in it, I desire I may be fairly acquitted of it; and that the blame may lie where it ought to lie, and no where else, for I wash my Hands of every part of it.

WHAT Injury can be done me, *my Dear*, says he, in marrying you? I hope it is to my Honour and Advantage every way; I will soon explain it to you, says I, and I fear you will have no reason to think your self well us'd, but I will convince you, *my Dear*, *says I again*, that I have had no hand in it, and there I stop'd a while.

HE look'd now scar'd and wild, and began, I believ'd, to suspect what follow'd; however, looking towards me, and saying only *go on*, he sat silent, as if to hear what I had more to say; so I went on; I ask'd you last Night, said I, speaking to him, if ever I made any boast to you of my Estate, or ever told you I had any Estate in the Bank of *England*, or any where else, and you own'd I had not, as is most true; and I desire you will tell me here, before your Sister, if ever I gave you any Reason from me to think so, or that ever we had any Discourse about it, and he own'd again I had not; *but said*, I had appeared always as a Woman of Fortune, and he depended on it that I was so, and hoped he was not deceiv'd. I am not enquiring yet whether you have been deceiv'd or not, *said I*, I fear you have, *and I too*; but I am clearing my self from the unjust Charge of being concern'd in deceiving you.[1]

I have been now asking your Sister if ever I told her of any Fortune or Estate I had, or gave her any Particulars of it; and she owns I never did: And pray, Madam, *said I, turning my self to her*, be so just to me, before your Brother, to charge me, if you can, if ever I pretended to you that I had an Estate; and why, if I had, should I come down into this Country with you on purpose to spare *that little I had*, and live cheap? She could not deny one word, but said she had been told in *London* that I had a very great Fortune, and that it lay in the Bank of *England*.

AND now, *Dear Sir*, said I, *turning my self to my new Spouse again*, be so just to me as to tell me who has abus'd both you and me so much, as to make you believe I was a Fortune, and prompt you to court me to this Marriage? He cou'd not speak a word, but pointed to her; and after some more pause, flew out in the most furious Passion that ever I saw a Man in my Life; cursing her, and calling her all the Whores and hard Names he could think of; and that she had ruin'd him, declaring that she had told him I had Fifteen Thousand Pounds, and that she was to have Five Hundred Pounds of him for procuring this Match for him: He then added, directing his Speech to me, that she was none of his Sister, but had been his Whore for two Years before, that she had had One Hundred Pound of him in part of this Bargain, and that he was utterly undone if things were as I said; and in his raving *he swore* he would let her Heart's Blood out immediately, which frighted her and me too; *she cried*, said she had been told so in the House where I Lodg'd; but this aggravated him more than before, that she should put so far upon him, and run things such a length upon no other Authority than *a hear-say*; and then turning to me again, said very honestly, he was afraid we were both undone; for to be plain, *my Dear*, I have no Estate, *says he*, what little I had, this Devil has made me run out in waiting on you, and putting me into this Equipage; she took the opportunity of his being earnest in talking with me, and got out of the Room, and I never saw her more.

I WAS confounded now as much as he, and knew not what to say: I thought many ways that I had the worst of it, but his saying he was undone, and that he had no Estate neither, put me into a meer distraction; why, *says I to him*, this has been a hellish Juggle, for we are married here upon the foot of a double Fraud, you are undone by the Disappointment it seems, and if I had had a Fortune I had been cheated too, for you say you have nothing.

YOU would indeed have been cheated, my Dear, *says he*, but you would not have been undone, for Fifteen Thousand Pound would have maintain'd us both very handsomly in this Country; and I assure you, *added he*, I had resolv'd to have dedicated every Groat of it to you; I would not have wrong'd you of a Shilling, and the rest I would have made up in my Affection to you, and Tenderness of you as long as I liv'd.

THIS was very honest indeed, and I really believe he spoke as he intended, and that he was a Man that was as well qualified to make me happy, as to his Temper and Behaviour, as any Man ever was; but his having no Estate, and being run into Debt on this ridiculous account in the Country, made all the Prospect dismal and dreadful, and I knew not what to say, or what to think of my self.

I TOLD him it was very unhappy, that so much Love, and so much Good-nature, as I discovered in him, should be thus precipitated into Misery; that I saw nothing before us but Ruin, for as to me, it was my unhappiness, that what little I had was not able to relieve us a Week, and with that I pull'd out a Bank Bill of 20 *l.* and eleven Guineas, which I told him I had saved out of my little Income; and that by the account that Creature had given me of the way of living in that Country, I expected it would maintain me three or four Year; that if it was taken from me I was left destitute, and he knew what the Condition of a Woman among strangers must be, if she had no Money in her Pocket; however, I told him if he would take it, there it was.

HE told me with a great concern, and I thought I saw Tears stand in his Eyes, that he would not touch it, that he abhorr'd the thoughts of stripping me, and making me miserable; that on the contrary, he had Fifty Guineas left, which was all he had in the World, and he pull'd it out and threw it down on the Table, bidding me take it, tho' he were to starve for want of it.

I RETURN'D, with the same concern for him, that I could not bear to hear him talk so; that on the contrary, if he could propose any probable method of living, I would do any thing that became me on my part, and that I would live as close and as narrow as he cou'd desire.

HE beg'd of me to talk no more at that rate, for it would make him Distracted; he said he was bred a Gentleman, tho' he was reduced to a low Fortune; and that there was but one way left which he cou'd think of, and that would not do, unless I cou'd answer him one Question, which however he said he would not press me to; I told him I would answer it honestly, whether it would be to his Satisfaction or no, that I could not tell.

WHY then, my Dear, tell me plainly, *says he* will the little you have keep us together in any Figure, or in any Station or Place, or will it not?

IT was my happiness hitherto that I had not discovered myself, or my Circumstances at all; no not so much as my Name; and seeing there was nothing to be expected from him, however good Humoured, and however honest he seem'd to be, but to live on what I knew would soon be wasted, I resolv'd to conceal everything, but the *Bank Bill*, and the Eleven Guineas, which I had own'd; and I would have been very glad to have lost that, and have been set down where he took me up; I had indeed another *Bank Bill* about me of 30 *l.* which was the whole of what I brought with me, as well to Subsist on in the Country, as not knowing what might offer; because this Creature, the *go-between* that had thus betray'd us both, had made me believe strange things of my Marrying to my Advantage in the Country, and

I was not willing to be without Money whatever might happen. This Bill I concealed, and that made me the freer of the rest, in Consideration of his Circumstances, for I really pittied him heartily.

BUT to return to his Question, I told him I never willingly Deceiv'd him, and I never would: I was very sorry to tell him that the little I had would not Subsist us; that it was not sufficient to Subsist me alone in the *South* Country; and that this was the Reason that made me put my self into the Hands of that Woman, who call'd him Brother, she having assur'd me that I might Board very handsomely at a Town call'd *Manchester*,[1] where I had not yet been, for about six Pound a Year,[2] and my whole Income not being above 15 *l.* a Year, I thought I might live easie upon it, and wait for better things.

HE shook his Head, and remain'd Silent, and a very melancholly Evening we had; however we Supped together, and lay together that Night, and when we had almost Supp'd he look'd a little better and more chearful, and call'd for a Bottle of Wine; *come* my Dear, *says he*, tho' the Case is bad, it is to no purpose to be dejected, come be as easie as you can, I will endeavour, to find out some way or other to live; if you can but Subsist your self, that is better than nothing, I must try the World again; a Man ought to think like a Man: To be Discourag'd, is to yield to the Misfortune; with this he fill'd a Glass, and Drank to me, holding my Hand, and pressing it hard in his Hand all the while the Wine went down, and Protesting afterward his main concern was for me.

IT was really a truly gallant Spirit he was of, and it was the more Grievous to me: 'Tis something of Relief even to be undone by a Man of Honour, rather than by a Scoundrel; but here the greatest Disappointment was on his side, for he had really spent a great deal of Money, deluded by this Madam the Procuress; and it was very remarkable on what poor Terms she proceeded; first the baseness of the Creature herself is to be observ'd, who for the getting One Hundred Pound herself, could be content to let him spend Three or

Four more, tho' perhaps it was all he had in the World, and
more than all; when she had not the least Ground, more than
a little Tea-Table Chat, to say that I had any Estate, or was
a Fortune, *or the like*: It is true the Design of deluding a
Woman of a Fortune, if I had been so, was base enough; the
putting the Face of great Things upon poor Circumstances
was a Fraud, and bad enough; but the Case a little differ'd
too, and that in his Favour, for he was not a Rake that made
a Trade to delude Women, and as some have done get six or
seven Fortunes after one another, and then riffle[1] and run
away from them; but he was really a Gentleman, unfortunate
and low, but had liv'd well; and tho' if I had had a Fortune
I should have been enrag'd at the Slut for betraying me; yet
really for the Man, a Fortune would not have been ill
bestow'd on him, for he was a lovely Person indeed; of
generous Principles, good Sense, and of abundance of good
Humour.

WE had a great deal of close Conversation that Night, for
we neither of us Slept much; he was as Penitent, for having
put all those Cheats upon me as if it had been Felony, and
that he was going to Execution; he offer'd me again every
Shilling of the Money he had about him, and said, he would
go into the Army and seek the World for more.

I ask'd him, why he would be so unkind to carry me into
Ireland, when I might suppose he cou'd not have Subsisted
me there? He took me in his Arms, my Dear, *said he*, depend
upon it, I never design'd to go to *Ireland* at all, much less to
have carried you thither; but came hither to be out of the
Observation of the People, who had heard what I pretended
to, and withal, that No Body might ask me for Money
before I was furnish'd to supply them.

BUT where then, *said I*, were we to have gone next?

WHY my Dear, *said he*, I'll confess the whole Scheme to
you as I had laid it; I purpos'd here to ask you something
about your Estate, as you see I did, and when you, as I
expected you would had enter'd into some Account with me
of the particular, I would have made an excuse to you, to

have put off our Voyage to *Ireland* for some time, and to have gone first towards *London*.

THEN my Dear, *said he*, I resolv'd to have confess'd all the Circumstances of my own Affairs to you, and let you know I had indeed made use of these Artifices to obtain your Consent to marry me, but had now nothing to do but to ask you Pardon, and to tell you how abundantly, *as I have said above*, I would endeavour to make you forget what was past, by the felicity of the Days to come.

TRULY, *said I to him*, I find you would soon have conquer'd me; and it is my Affliction now, that I am not in a Condition to let you see how easily I should have been reconcil'd to you; and have pass'd by all the Tricks you had put upon me, in Recompence of so much good Humour; but my Dear, *said I*, what can we do now? We are both undone, and what better are we for our being reconcil'd together, seeing we have nothing to live on.

WE propos'd a great many things, but nothing could offer, where there was nothing to begin with: He beg'd me at last to talk no more of it, for *he said*, I would break his Heart; so we talk'd of other things a little, till at last he took a Husbands leave[1] of me, and so we went to Sleep.

HE rise before me in the Morning, and indeed having lain Awake almost all Night, I was very sleepy, and lay till near Eleven a-Clock, in this time he took his Horses, and three Servants, and all his Linnen and Bagage, and away he went, leaving a short, but moving Letter for me on the Table, as follows.

MY DEAR,

I AM a Dog; I have abus'd you; but I have been drawn in to do it by a base Creature, contrary to my Principle, and the general Practice of my Life: Forgive me, my Dear! I ask you Pardon with the greatest Sincerity; I am the most miserable of Men, in having deluded you: I have been so happy to Possess you, and am now so wretch'd as to be forc'd to fly from you: Forgive me, my Dear; once more I say forgive me! I am not able to see you Ruin'd by me, and myself unable to Support you: Our Marriage is nothing, I shall never be able to see you again: I here discharge you from it; if you can Marry to your Advantage do not decline it on my Account; I here swear to you on my Faith, and on the Word of a Man of Honour, I will never disturb your Repose if I should know of it, which however is not likely: On the other Hand, if you should not Marry, and if good Fortune should befall me, it shall be all yours where ever you are.

I HAVE put some of the Stock of Money I have left, into your Pocket; take Places for your self and your Maid in the Stage-Coach, and go for London; *I hope it will bear your Charges thither, without breaking into your own: Again I sincerely ask your Pardon, and will do so, as often as I shall ever think of you.*

Adieu my Dear for Ever,

I am yours most Affectionatly,

A. E.

NOTHING that ever befel me in my Life, sunk so deep into my Heart as this Farewel: I reproach'd him a Thousand times in my Thoughts for leaving me, for I would have gone with him thro' the World, if I had beg'd my Bread. I felt in my Pocket, and there I found ten Guineas, his Gold Watch, and two little Rings, one a small Diamond Ring, worth only about six Pound, and the other a plain Gold Ring.

I SAT me down and look'd upon these Things two Hours together, and scarce spoke a Word, till my Maid interrupted me, by telling me my Dinner was ready: I eat but little, and after Dinner I fell into a vehement Fit of crying, every now and then, calling him by his Name, which was *James, O Jemy!* said I, *come back, come back*, I'll give you all I have; I'll beg, I'll starve with you, and thus I run Raving about the Room several times, and then sat down between whiles, and then walking about again, call'd upon him to *come back*, and then cry'd again; and thus I pass'd the Afternoon; till about seven a-Clock when it was near Dusk in the Evening, being

August, when to my unspeakable Surprize he comes back into the Inn, but without a Servant, and comes directly up into my Chamber.

I WAS in the greatest Confusion imaginable, and so was he too: I could not imagine what should be the Occasion of it; and began to be at odds with myself whether to be glad or sorry; but my Affection byass'd all the rest, and it was impossible to conceal my Joy, which was too great for Smiles, for it burst out into Tears. He was no sooner entered the Room, but he run to me and took me in his Arms, holding me fast and almost stopping my Breath with his Kisses, but spoke not a Word; at length I began, my Dear, *said I*, how could you go away from me? To which he gave no Answer, for it was impossible for him to speak.

WHEN our Extasies were a little over, he told me he was gone about 15 Mile, but it was not in his Power to go any farther, without coming back to see me again, and to take his Leave of me once more.

I TOLD him how I had pass'd my time, and how loud I had call'd him to *come back* again; he told me he heard me very plain upon *Delamere Forest*, at a Place about 12 Miles off:[1] *I smil'd; Nay says he*, do not think I am in Jest, for if ever I heard your Voice in my Life, I heard you call me aloud, and sometimes I thought I saw you running after me; why said I, what did I say? for I had not nam'd the Words to him, you call'd aloud, says he, and said, *O Jemy! O Jemy! come back*, *come back*.

I Laught at him; *my Dear says he*, do not Laugh, for depend upon it, I heard your Voice as plain as you hear mine now; if you please, I'll go before a Magistrate and make Oath of it; I then began to be amaz'd and surpriz'd, and indeed frighted, and told him what I had really done, and how I had call'd after him, as above.

WHEN we had amus'd ourselves a while about this, I said to him, well, you shall go away from me no more, I'll go all over the World with you rather: *He told me*, it would be a very difficult thing for him to leave me, but since it must be, he hoped I would make it as easie to me as I could; but as for him, it would be his Destruction, that he foresaw.

HOWEVER he told me, that he Consider'd he had left me to Travel to *London* alone, which was too long a Journey; and that as he might as well go that way, as any way else, he was resolv'd to see me safe thither, or near it; and if he did go away then without taking his leave, I should not take it ill of him, and this he made me promise.

HE told me how he had dismiss'd his three Servants, sold their Horses, and sent the Fellows away to seek their Fortunes, and all in a little time, at a Town on the Road, I know not where; and *says he*, it cost me some Tears all alone by myself, to think how much happier they were than their Master, for they could go to the next Gentleman's House to see for a Service, whereas, *said he*, I knew not whither to go, or what to do with myself.

I TOLD him, I was so compleatly miserable in parting with him, that I could not be worse; and that now he was come again, I would not go from him, if he would take me with him, let him go whither he would, or do what he would; and in the mean time I agreed that we would go together to *London*; but I could not be brought to Consent he should go away at last, and not take his leave of me, as he propos'd to do; but told him Jesting, that if he did, I would call him back again as loud as I did before; Then I pull'd out his Watch and gave it him back, and his two Rings, and his Ten Guineas; but he would not take them, which made me very much suspect that he resolv'd to go off upon the Road, and leave me.

THE truth is, the Circumstances he was in, the passionate Expressions of his Letter, the kind Gentlemanly Treatment I had from him in all the Affair, with the Concern he show'd for me in it, his manner of Parting with that large Share which he gave me of his little Stock left; all these had joyn'd to make such Impressions on me, that I really lov'd him most tenderly, and could not bear the Thoughts of parting with him.

Two Days after this we quitted *Chester*, I in the Stage Coach, and he on Horseback; I dismiss'd my Maid at *Chester*; he was very much against my being without a Maid, but she being a Servant hired in the Country, and I resolving to keep no Servant at *London*, I told him it would have been barbarous to have taken the poor Wench, and have turn'd her away as soon as I came to Town; and it would also have been a needless Charge on the Road, so I satisfy'd him, and he was easie enough on that Score.

He came with me as far as *Dunstable*, within 30 Miles of *London*, and then he told me Fate and his own Misfortunes oblig'd him to leave me, and that it was not Convenient for him to go to *London* for Reasons, which it was of no value to me to know, and I saw him preparing to go. The Stage Coach we were in, did not usually stop at *Dunstable*, but I desiring it but for a Quarter of an Hour, they were content to stand at an Inn-Door a while, and we went into the House.

Being in the Inn, I told him I had but one Favour more to ask of him, and that was, that since he could not go any farther, he would give me leave to stay a Week or two in the Town with him, that we might in that time think of something to prevent such a ruinous thing to us both, as a final Separation would be; and that I had something of Moment to offer to him, that I had never said yet, and which perhaps he might find Practicable to our mutual Advantage.

This was too reasonable a Proposal to be denied, so he call'd the Landlady of the House *and told her*, his Wife was taken ill, and so ill that she cou'd not think of going any farther in the Stage Coach, which had tyr'd her almost to Death, and ask'd if she cou'd not get us a Lodging for two or three Days in a private House, where I might rest me a little, for the Journey had been too much for me? The Landlady, a good sort of Woman, well bred, and very obliging, came immediately to see me; *told me*, she had two or three very good Rooms in a part of the House quite out of the noise, and if I saw them, she did not doubt but I would like them, and I should have one of her Maids, that should do nothing else but be appointed to wait on me; this was so very kind, that I could not but accept of it and thank her; so I went to look on the Rooms, and lik'd them very well, and indeed they were extraordinarily Furnish'd, and very pleasant Lodgings; so we paid the Stage Coach, took out our Baggage, and resolv'd to stay here a while.

HERE *I told him* I would live with him now till all my Money was spent, but would not let him spend a Shilling of his own: We had some kind squabble about that, but *I told him* it was the last time I was like to enjoy his Company, and I desir'd he would let me be Master in that thing only, and he should govern in every thing else, so he acquiesc'd.

HERE one Evening taking a Walk into the Fields, *I told him* I would now make the Proposal to him I had told him of; accordingly I related to him how I had liv'd in *Virginia*, that I had a Mother, I believ'd, was alive there still, tho' my Husband was dead some Years; *I told him*, that had not my Effects miscarry'd, which by the way I magnify'd pretty much, I might have been Fortune good enough to him to have kept us from being parted in this manner: Then I entered into the manner of Peoples going over to those Countries to settle, how they had a quantity of Land given them by the Constitution of the Place; and if not, that it might be purchased at so easie a Rate that it was not worth naming.

I THEN gave him a full and distinct account of the nature of Planting, how with carrying over but two or three Hundred Pounds value in *English* Goods, with some Servants and Tools, a Man of Application would presently lay a Foundation for a Family, and in a very few Years be certain to raise an Estate.

I LET him into the nature of the Product of the Earth, how the Ground was Cur'd and Prepared, and what the usual encrease of it was; and demonstrated to him, that in a very few Years, with such a beginning, we should be as certain of being Rich, as we were now certain of being Poor.

HE was surpriz'd at my Discourse; for we made it the

whole Subject of our Conversation for near a Week together, in which time I laid it down in black and white, *as we say*, that it was morally impossible, with a supposition of any reasonable good Conduct, but that we must thrive there and do very well.

THEN I told him what measures I would take to raise such a Sum as 300 *l.* or thereabouts; and I argued with him how good a Method it would be to put an end to our Misfortunes, and restore our Circumstances in the World, to what we had both expected, and I added, that after seven Years, if we liv'd, we might be in a Posture to leave our Plantation in good Hands, and come over again and receive the Income of it, and live here and enjoy it; and I gave him Examples of some that had done so, and liv'd now in very good Circumstances in *London*.

IN short, I press'd him so to it, that he almost agreed to it, but still something or other broke it off again; till at last he turn'd the Tables, and he began to talk almost to the same purpose of *Ireland*.

HE told me that a Man that could confine himself to a Country Life, and that cou'd but find Stock to enter upon any Land, should have Farms there for 50 *l.* a Year, as good as were here let for 200 *l.* a Year; that the Produce was such, and so Rich the Land, that if much was not laid up, we were sure to live as handsomely upon it as a Gentleman of 3000 *l.* a Year could do in *England*; and that he had laid a Scheme to leave me in *London*, and go over and try; and if he found he could lay a handsome Foundation of living suitable to the Respect he had for me, as he doubted not he should do, he would come over and fetch me.

I WAS dreadfully afraid that upon such a Proposal he would have taken me at my Word, (*viz.*) to sell my little Income, as I call'd it, and turn it into Money, and let him carry it over into *Ireland* and try his Experiment with it; but he was too just to desire it, or to have accepted it if I had offered it; and he anticipated me in that, for he added, that he would go and try his Fortune that way, and if he found he cou'd do any thing at it to live, then, by adding mine to it when I went over, we should live like our selves; but that he would not hazard a Shilling of mine till he had made the Experiment with a little, and he assur'd me that if he found nothing to be done in *Ireland*, he would then come to me and join in my Project for *Virginia*.

HE was so earnest upon his Project being to be try'd first, that I cou'd not withstand him; how ever, he promis'd to let me hear from him in a very little time after his arriving there, to let me know whether his prospect answer'd his Design, that if there was not a probability of Success, I might take the Occasion to prepare for our other Voyage, and then, he assur'd me, he would go with me to *America* with all his Heart.

I COULD bring him to nothing farther than this: However, those Consultations entertain'd us near a Month, during which I enjoy'd his Company, which indeed was the most entertaining that ever I met with in my life before. In this time he let me into the whole Story of his own Life, which was indeed surprizing, and full of an infinite Variety sufficient to fill up a much brighter History for its Adventures and Incidents, that any I ever saw in Print: But I shall have occasion to say more of him hereafter.

WE parted at last, tho' with the utmost reluctance on my side, and indeed he took his leave very unwillingly too, but Necessity oblig'd him, for his Reasons were very good why he would not come to *London*, as I understood more fully some time afterwards.

I GAVE him a Direction how to write to me, tho' still I reserv'd the grand Secret, and never broke my Resolution, which was not to let him ever know my true Name, who I was, or where to be found; he likewise let me know how to write a Letter to him, so that he said he wou'd be sure to receive it.

I CAME to *London* the next Day after we parted, but did not go directly to my old Lodgings; but for another nameless Reason took a private Lodging in St. *John's-street*, or as it is vulgarly call'd St. *Jones's* near *Clarkenwell*; and here being perfectly alone, I had leisure to sit down and reflect seriously upon the last seven Months Ramble I had made, for I had been abroad no less; the pleasant Hours I had with my last Husband I look'd back on with an infinite deal of Pleasure; but that Pleasure was very much lessen'd, when I found some time after that I was really with Child.

THIS was a perplexing thing because of the Difficulty which was before me, where I should get leave to Lye Inn; it being one of the nicest things in the World at that time of Day, for a Woman that was a Stranger, and had no Friends, to be entertain'd in that Circumstance without Security,[1] which by the way I had not, neither could I procure any.

I HAD taken care all this while to preserve a Correspondence with my honest Friend at the Bank, or rather he took care to Correspond with me, for he wrote to me once a Week; and tho' I had not spent my Money so fast as to want any from him, yet I often wrote also to let him know I was alive; I had left Directions in *Lancashire*, so that I had these Letters, which he sent, convey'd to me; and during my Recess at St. *Jones's* I receiv'd a very obliging Letter from him, assuring me that his Process for a Divorce from his Wife went on with Success, tho' he met with some Difficulties in it that he did not expect.

I WAS not displeas'd with the News, that his Process was more tedious than he expected; for tho' I was in no condition to have had him yet, not being so foolish to marry him when I knew my self to be with Child by another Man, as some I know have ventur'd to do; yet I was not willing to lose him, and in a word, resolv'd to have him if he continu'd in the same mind, as soon as I was up again; for I saw apparently I should hear no more from my other Husband; and as he had all along press'd me to Marry, and had assur'd me he would not be at all disgusted at it, or ever offer to claim me again, so I made no scruple to resolve to do it if I could, and if my other Friend stood to his Bargain; and I had a great deal of Reason to be assur'd that he would stand to it, by the

Letters he wrote to me, which were the kindest and most obliging that could be.

I Now grew Big, and the People where I Lodg'd perceiv'd it, and began to take notice of it to me, and as far as Civility would allow, intimated that I must think of removing; this put me to extreme perplexity, and I grew very melancholy, for indeed I knew not what Course to take, I had Money, but no Friends, and was like now to have a Child upon my Hands to keep, which was a difficulty I had never had upon me yet, as the Particulars of my Story hitherto makes appear.

IN the course of this Affair I fell very ill, and my Melancholy really encreas'd my Distemper; my illness prov'd at length to be only an Ague, but my Apprehensions were really that I should Miscarry; I should not say Apprehensions, for indeed I would have been glad to miscarry, but I cou'd never be brought to entertain so much as a thought of endeavouring to Miscarry, or of taking any thing to make me Miscarry, I abhorr'd, I say so much as the thought of it.

HOWEVER, speaking of it in the House, the Gentlewoman who kept the House propos'd to me to send for a Midwife; I scrupled it at first, but after some time consented to it, but told her I had no particular Acquaintance with any Midwife, and so left it to her.

IT seems the Mistress of the House was not so great a Stranger to such Cases as mine was, as I thought at first she had been, as will appear presently, and she sent for a Midwife of the right sort, that is to say, the right sort for me.

THE Woman appear'd to be an experienc'd Woman in her Business, I mean as a Midwife, but she had another Calling too, in which she was as expert as most Women, if not more: My Landlady had told her I was very Melancholy, and that she believ'd that had done me harm; and once, *before me*, said to her, Mrs. *B——— meaning the Midwife*, I believe this Lady's Trouble is of a kind that is pretty much in your way, and therefore if you can do any thing for her, pray do, for she is a very civil Gentlewoman, and so she went out of the Room.

I REALLY did not understand her, but my Mother Midnight[1] began very seriously to explain what she meant, as soon as she was gone: Madam, *says she*, you seem not to understand what your Landlady means, and when you do understand it, you need not let her know at all that you do so.

SHE means that you are under some Circumstances that may render your Lying-Inn difficult to you, and that you are not willing to be expos'd; I need say no more, but to tell you, that if you think fit to communicate so much of your Case to me, *if it be so*, as is necessary; for I do not desire to pry into those things, I perhaps may be in a Condition to assist you, and to make you perfectly easie, and remove all your dull Thoughts upon that Subject.

EVERY word this Creature said was a Cordial to me, and put new Life and new Spirit into my very Heart; my Blood began to circulate immediately, and I was quite another Body; I eat my Victuals again, and grew better presently after it: She said a great deal more to the same purpose, and then having press'd me to be free with her, and promis'd in the solemnest manner to be secret, she stop'd a little, as if waiting to see what Impression it made on me, and what I would say.

I WAS too sensible of the want I was in of such a Woman, not to accept her offer; *I told her* my Case was partly as she guess'd, and partly not, for I was really married, and had a Husband, tho' he was in such Circumstances, and so remote at that time, as that he cou'd not appear publickly.

SHE took me short, *and told me*, that was none of her Business, all the Ladies that came under her Care were married Women to her; every Woman, *says she*, that is with Child has a Father for it, and whether that Father was a Husband or no Husband, was no Business of hers; her Business was to assist me in my present Circumstances, whether I had a Husband or no; for, *Madam*, *says she*, to have a Husband that cannot appear, is to have no Husband in the sense of the Case, and therefore whether you are a Wife or a Mistress is all one to me.

I Found presently, that whether I was a Whore or a Wife, I was to pass for a Whore here, so I let that go; *I told her*, it was true as she said, but that however, if I must tell her my Case, I must tell it her as it was: So I related it to her as short as I could, and I concluded it to her thus, *I trouble you with all this*, Madam, said I, *not that, as you said before, it is much to the purpose* in your Affair, but this is to the purpose, *namely, that I am not in any pain about being seen, or being publick or conceal'd, for 'tis perfectly indifferent to me ; but my difficulty is, that I have no Acquaintance in this part of the Nation.*

I Understand you, Madam, *says she*, you have no Security to bring to prevent the Parish Impertinences usual in such Cases;[1] and perhaps, *says she*, do not know very well how to dispose of the Child when it comes; the last, *says I*, is not so much my concern as the first: Well, Madam, *answers the Midwife*, dare you put your self into my Hands, I live in such a place, tho' I do not enquire after you, you may enquire after me, my Name is *B*——— I live in such a Street, naming the Street, at the Sign of the *Cradle*, my Profession is a Midwife,[2] and I have many Ladies that come to my House to Lye-Inn; I have given Security to the Parish[3] in General Terms to secure them from any Charge, from whatsoever shall come into the World under my Roof; I have but one Question to ask in the whole Affair, Madam, *says she*, and if that be answer'd, you shall be entirely easie for all the rest.

I presently understood what she meant, and told her, Madam, *I believe I understand you*; I thank God, *tho' I want Friends in this Part of the World, I do not want Money, so far as may be Necessary, tho' I do not abound in that neither :* This I added, because I would not make her expect great things; well Madam, *says she*, that is the thing indeed, without which nothing can be done in these Cases, and yet, *says she*, you shall see that I will not impose upon you, or offer any thing that is unkind to you, and if you desire it, you shall know every thing before hand, that you may suit your self to the Occasion, and be either costly or sparing as you see fit.

I told her, she seem'd to be so perfectly sensible of my Condition, that I had nothing to ask of her but this, that as I had told her that I had Money sufficient, but not a great Quantity, she would order it so, that I might be at as little superfluous Charge as possible.

SHE replyed, that she would bring in an Account of the Expences of it, in two or three Shapes, and like a *Bill of Fare*, I should chuse as I pleas'd, and I desir'd her to do so.

THE next Day she brought it, and the Copy of her three Bills was as follows.

		l.	*s.*	*d.*
1.	For Three Months Lodging in her House, including my Dyet at 10s. a Week　　.. 　　..	06	00	0
2.	For a Nurse for the Month, and Use of Child-bed Linnen　.. 　　.. 　　.. 　　.. 　　..	01	10	0
3.	For a Minister to Christen the Child, and to the Godfathers and Clark 　　.. 　　.. 　　..	01	10	0
4.	For a Supper at the Christening if I had five Friends at it .. 　　.. 　　.. 　　.. 　　..	01	00	0
	For her Fees as a Midwife, and the taking off the Trouble of the Parish 　.. 　　.. 　　..	03	03	0
	To her Maid-Servant attending.. 　　.. 　　..	00	10	0
		13	13	0

THIS was the first Bill, the second was in the same Terms.

1.	For Three Months Lodging and Diet, &c. at 20s. *per* Week .. 　　.. 　　.. 　　.. 　　..	13	00	0
2.	For a Nurse for the Month, and the Use of Linnen and Lace 　.. 　　.. 　　.. 　　..	02	10	0
3.	For the Minister to Christen the Child, &c. as above 　　.. 　　.. 　　.. 　　..	02	00	0
4.	For a Supper, and for Sweetmeats　..	03	03	0
	For her Fees, as above 　.. 　　.. 　　.. 　　..	05	05	0
	For a Servant-Maid 　　..	01	00	0
		26	18	0

THIS was the second rate Bill, the third, *she said*, was for a degree Higher, and when the Father, or Friends appeared.

	l.	*s.*	*d.*
1. For Three Months Lodging and Diet, having two Rooms and a Garret for a Servant	30	00	0
2. For a Nurse for the Month, and the finest Suit of Child-bed Linnen	04	04	0
3. For the Minister to Christen the Child, &c.	02	10	0
4. For a Supper, the Gentlemen to send in the Wine	06	00	0
For my Fees, &c.	10	10	0
The Maid, besides their own Maid only	00	10	0
	53	14	0

I LOOK'D upon all the three Bills, and smil'd, *and told her* I did not see but that she was very reasonable in her Demands,[1] all things Consider'd, and for that I did not doubt but her Accommodations were good.

SHE told me, I should be Judge of that, when I saw them: *I told her*, I was sorry to tell her that I fear'd I must be her lowest rated Customer, and *perhaps Madam*, said I, *you will make me the less Welcome upon that Account*. No not at all, *said she*, for where I have One of the third Sort, I have Two of the Second, and Four to One of the First, and I get as much by them in Proportion, as by any; but if you doubt my Care of you, I will allow any Friend you have to overlook, and see if you are well waited on, or no.

THEN she explain'd the particulars of her Bill; in the first Place, Madam, *said she*, I would have you Observe, that here is three Months Keeping, you are but 10*s.* a Week, I undertake to say you will not complain of my Table: I suppose, *says she*, you do not live Cheaper where you are now; no indeed, *said I*, nor so Cheap, for I give six Shillings *per* Week for my Chamber, and find my own Diet as well as I can, which costs me a great deal more.

THEN Madam, *says she*, If the Child should not live, or

should be dead Born, as you know sometime happens, then there is the Minister's Article saved; and if you have no Friends to come to you, you may save the Expence of a Supper; so that take those Articles out Madam, *says she*, your Lying-In will not cost you above 5*l*. 3*s*. in all, more than your ordinary Charge of Living.

THIS was the most reasonable thing that I ever heard of; so I smil'd, and told her I would come and be her Customer; but *I told her also*, that as I had two Months, and more to go, I might perhaps be oblig'd to stay longer with her than three Months, and desir'd to know if she would not be oblig'd to remove me before it was proper; no, *she said*, her House was large, and besides, she never put any Body to remove, that had lain Inn, till they were willing to go; and if she had more Ladies offer'd, she was not so ill belov'd among her Neighbours, but she could provide Accommodation for Twenty, if there was occasion.

I FOUND she was an eminent Lady in her way, and *in short*, I agreed to put myself into her Hands, and promis'd her: She then talk'd of other things, look'd about into my Accommodations, where was found fault with my wanting Attendance, and Conveniencies, and that I should not be us'd so at her House: *I told her*, I was shy of speaking, for the Woman of the House look'd stranger, or at least I thought so since I had been Ill, because I was with Child; and I was afraid she would put some Affront or other upon me, supposing that I had been able to give but a slight Account of myself.

O DEAR, *said she*, her Ladyship is no stranger to these things; she has try'd to entertain Ladies in your Condition several times, but could not secure the Parish; and besides, she is not such a nice Lady as you take her to be; however, since you are agoing you shall not meddle with her, but I'll see you are a little better look'd after while you are here, than I think you are, and it shall not cost you the more neither.

I DID not understand her at all; however I thank'd her, and so we parted; the next Morning she sent me a Chicken roasted and hot, and a pint Bottle of Sherry, and order'd the Maid to tell me that she was to wait on me every Day as long as I stay'd there.

THIS was surprisingly good and kind, and I accepted it very willingly: At Night she sent to me again, to know if I wanted any thing, and how I did, and to order the Maid to come to her in the morning for my Dinner; the Maid had order to make me some Chocolat in the Morning before she came away, and did so, and at Noon she brought me the Sweetbread of a Breast of Veal whole, and a Dish of Soup for my Dinner, and after this manner she Nurs'd me up at a distance, so that I was mightily well pleas'd, and quickly well, for indeed my Dejections before were the principal Part of my Illness.

I expected as usually is the Case among such People, that the Servant she sent me would have been some impudent brazen Wench of *Drury-Lane* Breeding[1] and I was very uneasie at having her with me, upon that Account, so I would not let her lie in that House, the first Night by any means, but had my Eyes about me as narrowly as if she had been a publick Thief.

MY Gentlewoman guess'd presently what was the matter, and sent her back with a short Note, that I might depend upon the honesty of her Maid; that she would be answerable for her upon all Accounts; and that she took no Servants into her House, without very good Security for their Fidelity: I was then perfectly easie, and indeed the Maids behaviour spoke for its self, for a modester, quieter, soberer Girl never came into any bodies Family, and I found her so afterwards.

As soon as I was well enough to go Abroad, I went with the Maid to see the House, and to see the Apartment I was to have; and every thing was so handsome and so clean, and well; that in short, I had nothing to say, but was wonderfully pleas'd, and satisfy'd with what I had met with, which considering the melancholy Circumstances I was in, was far beyond what I look'd for.

IT might be expected that I should give some Account of

the Nature of the wicked Practice of this Woman, in whose Hands I was now fallen; but it would be but too much Encouragement to the Vice, to let the World see, what easie Measures were here taken[1] to rid the Women's unwelcome Burthen of a Child clandestinely gotten: This grave Matron had several sorts of Practise, and this was one particular, that if a Child was born, tho' not in her House, for she had the occasion to be call'd to many private Labours, she had People at Hand, who for a Peice of Money would take the Child off their Hands, and off from the Hands of the Parish too; and those Children, as she said were honestly provided for, and taken care of: What should become of them all, Considering so many, as by her Account she was concern'd with, I cannot conceive.

I HAD many times Discourses upon that Subject with her; but she was full of this Argument, that she sav'd the Life of many an innocent Lamb, as she call'd them, which would otherwise perhaps have been Murder'd; and of many a Woman, who made Desperate by the Misfortune, would otherwise be tempted to Destroy their Children, and bring themselves to the Gallows:[2] I granted her that this was true, and a very commendable thing, provided the poor Children fell into good Hands afterwards, and were not abus'd, starv'd, and neglected by the Nurses that bred them up; she answer'd, that she always took care of that, and had no Nurses in her Business, but what were very good honest People, and such as might be depended upon.

I Cou'D say nothing to the contrary, and so was oblig'd to say, Madam I do not question you do your part honestly, but what those People do afterwards, is the main Question, and she stop'd my Mouth again with saying, that she took the utmost Care about it.

THE only thing I found in all her Conversation on these Subjects, that gave me any distaste, was, that one time in Discoursing about my being so far gone with Child, and the time I expected to come, she said something that look'd as if she could help me off with my Burthen sooner, if I was willing; or in *English*, that she could give me something to make me Miscarry, if I had a desire to put an end to my Troubles that way; but I soon let her see that I abhorr'd the Thoughts of it;[1] and to do her Justice, she put it off so cleverly, that I cou'd not say she really intended it, or whether she only mentioned the practise as a horrible thing; for she couch'd her words so well, and took my meaning so quickly, that she gave her Negative before I could explain my self.

To bring this part into as narrow a Compass as possible, I quitted my Lodging at St. *Jones*'s and went to my new Governess, for so they call'd her in the House, and there I was indeed treated with so much Courtesy, so carefully look'd to, so handsomely provided, and every thing so well, that I was surpris'd at it, and cou'd not at first see what Advantage my Governess made of it; but I found afterwards that she profess'd to make no Profit of the Lodgers Diet, nor indeed cou'd she get much by it, but that her Profit lay in the other Articles of her Management, and she made enough that way, I assure you; for 'tis scarce credible what Practice she had, as well Abroad as at Home, and yet all upon the private Account, or in plain *English*, the whoring Account.

WHILE I was in her House, which was near Four Months, she had no less than Twelve Ladies of Pleasure brought to Bed within Doors, and I think she had Two and Thirty, or thereabouts, under her Conduct without Doors, whereof one, as nice as she was with me, was Lodg'd with my old Landlady at St. *Jones*'s.

THIS was a strange Testimony of the growing Vice of the Age, and such a one, that as bad as I had been my self, it shock'd my very Senses, I began to nauceate the place I was in, and above all, the wicked Practice; and yet I must say that I never saw, or do I believe there was to be seen, the least indecency in the House the whole time I was there.

NOT a Man was ever seen to come up Stairs, except to visit the Lying-Inn Ladies within their Month, nor then without the old Lady with them, who made it a piece of the

Honour of her Management, that no Man should touch a
Woman, no not his own Wife, within the Month; nor would
she permit any Man to lye in the House upon any pretence
whatever, no not tho' she was sure it was with his own Wife,
and her general saying for it was, that she car'd not how
many Children was born in her house, but she would have
none got there if she could help it.

IT might perhaps be carried farther than was needful, but
it was an Error of the right Hand if it was an Error, for by
this she kept up the Reputation, such as it was, of her
Business, and obtain'd this Character, that tho' she did take
Care of the Women when they were Debauch'd, yet she was
not Instrumental to their being Debauch'd at all, and yet it
was a wicked Trade she drove too.

WHILE I was here, and before I was brought to Bed, I
receiv'd a Letter from my Trustee at the Bank full of kind
obliging things, and earnestly pressing me to return to
London: It was near a Fortnight old when it came to me,
because it had been first sent into *Lancashire*, and then
return'd to me; he concludes with telling me that he had
obtain'd a Decree, I think he call'd it, against his Wife, and
that he would be ready to make good his Engagement to me,
if I would accept of him, adding a great many Protestations
of Kindness and Affection, such as he would have been far
from offering if he had known the Circumstances I had been
in, and which as it was I had been very far from deserving.

I RETURNED an Answer to this Letter, and dated it at
Leverpool, but sent it by a Messenger, alledging that it came
in Cover to a Friend in Town; I gave him Joy of his Deliverance, but rais'd some Scruples at the Lawfulness of his
Marrying again,[1] and told him, I suppos'd he would consider very seriously upon that Point before he resolv'd on it,
the Consequence being too great for a Man of his Judgment
to venture rashly upon a thing of that Nature; so concluded,
wishing him very well in whatever he resolv'd, without letting
him into any thing of my own Mind, or giving any Answer
to his Proposal of my coming to *London* to him, but men-

tion'd at a distance my intention to return the latter end of the Year, this being dated in *April*.

I WAS brought to Bed about the middle of *May*, and had another brave Boy, and my self in as good Condition as usual on such Occasions: My Governess did her part as a Midwife with the greatest Art and Dexterity imaginable, and far beyond all that ever I had had any Experience of before.

HER Care of me in my Travail, and after in my Lying-Inn, was such, that if she had been my own Mother it cou'd not have been better; let none be encourag'd in their loose Practises from this Dexterous Lady's Management; for she is gone to her place, and I dare say has left nothing behind her that can or will come up to it.

I THINK I had been brought to Bed about twenty two Days when I receiv'd another Letter from my Friend at the Bank, with the surprizing News that he had obtain'd a final Sentence of Divorce against his Wife, and had serv'd her with it on such a Day, and that he had such an Answer to give to all my Scruples about his Marrying again, as I could not expect, and as he had no Desire of; for that his wife, who had been under some Remorse before for her usage of him, as soon as she had the account that he had gain'd his Point, had very unhappily destroy'd her self that same Evening.

HE express'd himself very handsomly as to his being concern'd at her Disaster, but clear'd himself of having any hand in it, and that he had only done himself Justice in a Case in which he was notoriously Injur'd and Abus'd: However, he said that he was extremely afflicted at it, and had no view of any Satisfaction left in this World, but only in the hope that I wou'd come and relieve him by my Company; and then he press'd me violently indeed to give him some hopes, that I would at least come up to Town and let him see me, when he would farther enter into Discourse about it.

I WAS exceedingly surpriz'd at the News, and began now seriously to reflect on my present Circumstances, and the inexpressible Misfortune it was to me to have a Child upon my Hands, and what to do in it I knew not; at last I open'd

my Case at a distance to my Governess, I appear'd melancholy and uneasie for several Days, and she lay at me
continually to know what troubl'd me; I could not for my
life tell her that I had an offer of Marriage, after I had so
often told her that I had a Husband, so that I really knew
not what to say to her; I own'd I had something which very
much troubl'd me, but at the same time told her I cou'd not
speak of it to any one alive.

SHE continued importuning me several Days, but it was
impossible, *I told her*, for me to commit the Secret to any
Body; this, instead of being an Answer to her, encreas'd her
Importunities; she urg'd her having been trusted with the
greatest Secrets of this Nature, that it was her business to
Conceal every thing, and that to Discover things of that
Nature would be her Ruin; she ask'd me if ever I had found
her Tatling of other People's Affairs, and how could I
suspect her? *she told me* to unfold my self to her, was telling
it to no Body; that she was silent as Death; that it must be
a very strange Case indeed, that she could not help me out
of; but to conceal it, was to deprive myself of all possible
Help, or means of Help, and to deprive her of the Opportunity of Serving me. *In short*, she had such a bewitching
Eloquence, and so great a power of Perswasion, that there
was no concealing any thing from her.

So I resolv'd to unbosome myself to her, I told her the
History of my *Lancashire* Marriage, and how both of us had
been Disappointed; how we came together, and how we
parted: How he absolutely Discharg'd me, as far as lay in
him, and gave me free Liberty to Marry again,[1] protesting
that if he knew it he would never Claim me, or Disturb, or
Expose me; that I thought I was free, but was dreadfully
afraid to venture, for fear of the Consequences that might
follow in case of a Discovery.

THEN I told her what a good Offer I had; show'd her my
Friends two last Letters, inviting me to come to *London*,
and let her see with what Affection and Earnestness they
were written, but blotted out the Name, and also the Story

about the Dissaster of his Wife, only that she was dead.

SHE fell a Laughing at my scruples about marrying, and told me the other was no Marriage, but a cheat on both Sides;[1] and that as we were parted by mutual Consent, the nature of the Contract was destroy'd, and the Obligation was mutually discharg'd:[2] She had Arguments for this at the tip of her Tongue;[3] and *in short*, reason'd me out of my Reason; not but that it was too by the help of my own Inclination.

BUT then came the great and main Difficulty, and that was the Child; this she told me in so many Words must be remov'd, and that so, as that it should never be possible for any one to discover it: I knew there was no Marrying without entirely concealing that I had had a Child, for he would soon have discover'd by the Age of it, that it was born, nay and gotten too, since my Parly with him, and that would have destroy'd all the Affair.

BUT it touch'd my Heart so forcibly to think of Parting entirely with the Child, and for ought I knew, of having it murther'd, or starv'd by Neglect and Ill-usuage,[4] (which was much the same) that I could not think of it, without Horror; I wish all those Women who consent to the disposing their Children out of the way, *as it is call'd* for Decency sake, would consider that 'tis only a contriv'd Method for Murther; that is to say, a killing their Children with safety.

IT is manifest to all that understand any thing of Children, that we are born into the World helpless and uncapable, either to supply our own Wants, or so much as make them known; and that without help, we must Perish; and this help requires not only an assisting Hand, whether of the Mother, or some Body else; but there are two Things necessary in that assisting Hand, that is, Care and Skill, without both which, half the Children that are born would die; nay, tho' they were not to be deny'd Food; and one half more of those that remain'd would be Cripples or Fools, loose their Limbs, and perhaps their Sense: I Question not, but that these are partly the Reasons why Affection was plac'd by Nature in the Hearts of Mothers to their Children; without which they would never be able to give themselves up, as 'tis necessary they should, to the Care and waking Pains needful to the Support of their Children.

SINCE this Care is needful to the Life of Children, to neglect them is to Murther them; again to give them up to be Manag'd by those People, who have none of that needful Affection, plac'd by Nature in them, is to Neglect them in the highest Degree; nay, in some it goes farther, and is a Neglect in order to their being Lost; so that 'tis even an intentional Murther,[1] whether the Child lives or dies.

ALL those things represented themselves to my View, and that in the blackest and most frightful Form; and as I was very free with my Governness, who I had now learn'd to call Mother; I represented to her all the dark Thoughts which I had upon me about it, and told her what distress I was in: She seem'd graver by much at this Part than at the other; but as she was harden'd in these things beyond all possibility of being touch'd with the Religious part, and the Scruples about the Murther; so she was equally impenetrable in that Part, which related to Affection: She ask'd me if she had not been Careful, and Tender of me in my Lying-Inn, as if I had been her own Child? I told her I own'd she had. Well my Dear, *says she*, and when you are gone, what are you to me? and what would it be to me if you were to be Hang'd? Do you think there are not Women, who as it is their Trade, and they get their Bread by it, value themselves upon their being as careful of Children, as their own Mothers can be, and understand it rather better? Yes, yes, Child, *says she*, fear it not, How were we Nurs'd ourselves? Are you sure, you was Nurs'd up by your own Mother? and yet you look fat, and fair Child, says the old Beldam, and with that she stroak'd me over the Face; never be concern'd Child, *says she*, going on in her drolling way; I have no Murtherers about me; I employ the best, and the honestest Nurses that can be had; and have as few Children miscarry under their Hands, as there would, if they were all Nurs'd by Mothers; we want neither Care nor Skill.

SHE touch'd me to the Quick, when she ask'd if I was sure that I was Nurs'd by my own Mother; on the contrary I was sure I was not; and I trembled, and look'd pale at the very Expression; sure said I, to myself, this Creature cannot be a Witch, or have any Conversation with a Spirit that can inform her what was done with me before I was able to know it myself; and I look'd at her as if I had been frighted; but reflecting that it cou'd not be possible for her to know any thing about me, that Disorder went off, and I began to be easie, but it was not presently.

SHE perceiv'd the Disorder I was in, but did not know the meaning of it; so she run on in her wild Talk upon the weakness of my supposing, that Children were murther'd, because they were not all Nurs'd by the Mother; and to perswade me that the Children she dispos'd of, were as well us'd as if the Mothers had the Nursing of them themselves.

IT may be true Mother, *says I*, for ought I know, but my Doubts are very strongly grounded, indeed; come then, *says she*, lets hear some of them: Why first, *says I*, you give a Piece of Money to these People to take the Child off the Parents Hands, and to take Care of it as long as it lives; now we know Mother, *said I*, that those are poor People, and their Gain consists in being quit of the Charge as soon as they can; how can I doubt but that, as it is best for them to have the Child die, they are not over Solicitous about its Life.

THIS is all Vapours and Fancy, *says the old Woman*, I tell you their Credit depends upon the Child's Life,[1] and they are as careful as any Mother of you all.

O Mother, *says I*, if I was but sure my little Baby would be carefully look'd to, and have Justice done it, I should be happy indeed; but it is impossible I can be satisfy'd in that Point, unless I saw it, and to see it, would be Ruin and Destruction to me, as now my Case stands, so what to do I know not.

A FINE Story! *says the Governess*, you would see the Child, and you would not see the Child; you would be Conceal'd and Discover'd both together; these are things impossible my Dear, so you must e'n do as other conscientious Mothers have done before you; and be contented with things as they must be, tho' they are not as you wish them to be.

I understood what she meant by conscientious Mothers, she would have said conscientious Whores; but she was not willing to disoblige me, for really in this Case I was not a Whore, because legally Married, the force of my former Marriage excepted.

HOWEVER let me be what I would, I was not come up to that pitch of Hardness, common to the Profession; I mean to be unnatural, and regardless of the Safety of my Child, and I preserv'd this honest Affection so long, that I was upon the Point of giving up my Friend at the *Bank*, who lay so hard at me to come to him, and Marry him, that *in short*, there was hardly any room to deny him.

AT last my old Governness came to me, with her usual Assurance. Come my Dear, *says she*, I have found out a way how you shall be at a certainty, that your Child shall be used well, and yet the People that take Care of it shall never know you, or who the Mother of the Child is.

O Mother, *says I*, If you can do so, you will engage me to you for ever: Well, *says she*, are you willing to be at some small Annual Expence, more than what we usually give to the People we Contract with? Ay, *says I*, with all my Heart, provided I may be conceal'd; as to that, says *the Governness*, you shall be Secure, for the Nurse shall never so much as dare to Enquire about you, and you shall once or twice a Year go with me and see your Child, and see how 'tis used, and be satisfy'd that it is in good Hands, no Body knowing who you are.

WHY, *said I*, do you think Mother, that when I come to see my Child, I shall be able to conceal my being the Mother of it, do you think that possible?

WELL, well, *says my Governess*, if you discover it, the Nurse shall be never the wiser; for she shall be forbid to ask any Questions about you, or to take any Notice; if she offers it she shall lose the Money which you are to be suppos'd to give her, and the Child be taken from her too.

I Was very well pleas'd with this; so the next Week a Country Woman was brought from *Hertford*, or thereabouts,[1] who was to take the Child off our Hands entirely, for 10 *l.* in Money; but if I would allow 5 *l.* a Year more to her, she would be obliged to bring the Child to my Governesses House as often as we desired, or we should come down and look at it, and see how well she us'd it.

The Woman was a very wholesome look'd likely Woman, a Cottager's Wife, but she had very good Cloaths and Linnen, and every thing well about her, and with a heavy Heart and many a Tear I let her have my Child: I had been down at *Hertford* and look'd at her and at her Dwelling, which I lik'd well enough; and I promis'd her great Things if she would be kind to the Child, so she knew at first word that I was the Child's Mother; but she seem'd to be so much out of the way, and to have no room to enquire after me, that I thought I was safe enough, so in short I consented to let her have the Child, and I gave her Ten Pound, that is to say I gave it to my Governess, who gave it the poor Woman before my Face, she agreeing never to return the Child back to me, or to claim any thing more for its keeping or bringing up; only that I promised, if she took a great deal of Care of it, I would give her something more as often as I came to see it; so that I was not bound to pay the Five Pound, only that I promised my Governess I would do it: And thus my great Care was over, after a manner, which tho' it did not at all satisfie my Mind, yet was the most convenient for me, as my Affairs then stood, of any that cou'd be thought of at that time.

I Then began to write to my Friend at the Bank in a more kindly Style, and particularly about the beginning of *July* I sent him a Letter, that I purpos'd to be in Town sometime in *August*; he return'd me an Answer in the most Passionate Terms imaginable, and desir'd me to let him have timely Notice, and he would come and meet me two Days Journey: This puzzl'd me scurvily, and I did not know what Answer to make to it; once I was resolv'd to take the Stage Coach to

West-chester on purpose only, to have the satisfaction of coming back, that he might see me really come in the same Coach; for I had a jealous thought, though I had no Ground for it at all, least he should think I was not really in the Country, and it was no ill-grounded Thought,[1] as you shall hear presently.

I endeavour'd to Reason my self out of it, but it was in vain, the Impression lay so strong on my Mind, that it was not to be resisted; at last it came as an Addition to my new Design of going in the Country, that it would be an excellent Blind to my old Governess, and would cover entirely all my other Affairs, for she did not know in the least whether my new Lover liv'd in *London* or in *Lancashire*, and when I told her my Resolution, she was fully perswaded it was in *Lancashire*.

HAVING taken my Measures for this Journey, I let her know it, and sent the Maid that tended me from the beginning, to take a Place for me in the Coach; she would have had me let the Maid have waited on me down to the last Stage, and come up again in the Waggon, but I convinc'd her it wou'd not be convenient; when I went away she told me, she would enter into no Measures for Correspondence, for she saw evidently that my Affection to my Child would cause me to write to her, and to visit her too when I came to Town again; I assur'd her it would, and so took my leave, well satisfied to have been freed from such a House, however good my Accommodations there had been, as I have related above.

I took the Place in the Coach not to its full Extent, but to a place call'd *Stone* in *Cheshire*, I think it is,[2] where I not only had no manner of Business, but not so much as the least Acquaintance with any Person in the Town or near it: But I knew that with Money in the Pocket one is at home any where, so I Lodg'd there two or three Days, till watching my opportunity, I found room in another Stage Coach, and took Passage back again for *London*, sending a Letter to my Gentleman, that I should be such a certain Day at *Stony-Stratford*, where the Coachman told me he was to Lodge.

I⊤ happen'd to be a Chance Coach that I had taken up, which having been hired on purpose to carry some Gentlemen to *West Chester* who were going for *Ireland*, was now returning, and did not tye it self up to exact Times or Places as the Stages did, so that having been oblig'd to lye still a *Sunday*,[1] he had time to get himself ready to come out, which otherwise he cou'd not have done.

HOWEVER, his warning was so short, that he could not reach to *Stony-Stratford* time enough to be with me at Night, but he met me at a Place call'd *Brickill*[2] the next Morning, as we were just coming into the Town.

I CONFESS I was very glad to see him, for I had thought my self a little disappointed over Night, seeing I had gone so far to contrive my coming on purpose: He pleas'd me doubly too by the Figure he came in, for he brought a very handsome (Gentleman's) Coach and four Horses with a Servant to attend him.

HE took me out of the Stage Coach immediately, which stop'd at an Inn in *Brickill*, and putting in to the same Inn he set up his own Coach, and bespoke his Dinner; I ask'd him what he meant by that, for I was for going forward with the Journey; he said no, I had need of a little Rest upon the Road, and that was a very good sort of a House, tho' it was but a little Town; so we would go no farther that Night, whatever came of it.

I DID not press him much, for since he had come so far to meet me, and put himself to so much Expence, it was but reasonable I should oblige him a little too, so I was easy as to that Point.

AFTER Dinner we walk'd to see the Town, to see the Church, and to view the Fields, and the Country as is usual for Strangers to do, and our Landlord was our Guide in going to see the Church; I observ'd my Gentleman enquir'd pretty much about the Parson, and I took the hint immediately, that he certainly would propose to be married; and tho' it was a sudden thought, it follow'd presently, that in short I would not refuse him; for to be plain with my

Circumstances, I was in no condition now to say NO, I had no reason now to run any more such hazards.

BUT while these Thoughts run round in my Head, which was the work but of a few Moments, I observ'd my Landlord took him aside and whisper'd to him, tho' not very softly neither, for so much I over-heard, *Sir, if you shall have occasion . . .* the rest I cou'd not hear, but it seems it was to this purpose, *Sir, if you shall have occasion for a Minister, I have a Friend a little way off that will serve you, and be as private as you please;* my Gentleman answer'd loud enough for me to hear, *very well, I believe I shall.*

I WAS no sooner come back to the Inn, but he fell upon me with irresistable Words, that since he had had the good Fortune to meet me, and every thing concurr'd, it wou'd be hastening his Felicity if I would put an end to the matter just there; what do you mean, *says I,* colouring a little, what in an Inn, and upon the Road! Bless us all, *said I,* as if I had been surpriz'd, how can you talk so! O I can talk so very well, *says he,* I came a purpose to talk so, and I'll show you that I did, and with that he pulls out a great Bundle of Papers; you fright me, *said I,* what are all these; don't be frighted, my Dear, *said he,* and kiss'd me, *this was the first time that he had been so free to call me my Dear;* then he repeated it, don't be frighted, you shall see what it is all, then he laid them all abroad; there was first the Deed or Sentence of Divorce from his Wife, and the full Evidence of her playing the Whore; then there was the Certificates of the Minister and Church-wardens of the Parish where she liv'd, proving that she was buried, and intimating the manner of her Death; the Copy of the Coroner's Warrant for a Jury to sit upon her, and the Verdict of the Jury, who brought it in *Non Compos Mentis;*[1] all this was indeed to the purpose, and to give me Satisfaction, tho', by the way, I was not so scrupulous, had he known all, but that I might have taken him without it: However, I look'd them all over as well as I cou'd, and told him, that this was all very clear indeed, but that he need not have given himself the Trouble to have brought them out with him, for it was time enough: Well *he said*, it might be time enough for me, but no time but the present time was time enough for him.

THERE were other Papers roll'd up, and I ask'd him, what they were? Why, Ay, *says he*, that's the Question I wanted to have you ask me; so he unrolls them, and takes out a little Chagreen Case,[1] and gives me out of it a very fine Diamond Ring; I could not refuse it, if I had a mind to do so, for he put it upon my Finger; so I made him a Curtsy, and accepted it; then he takes out another Ring, and this, *says he*, is for another Occasion, so he puts that in his Pocket. Well, but let me see it tho', *says I*, and smil'd, I guess what it is, I think you are Mad: I should have been Mad if I had done less, *says he*, and still he did not show it me, and I had a great mind to see it; so I says, well but let me see it; hold, *says he*, first look here, then he took up the Roll again, and read it, and behold! it was a License for us to be married: Why, *says I*, are you Distracted? why you were fully satisfy'd that I would comply, and yield at first Word, or resolv'd to take no denial; the last is certainly the Case, *said he*; but you may be mistaken, *said I*, no, no, *says he*, how can you think so? I must not be denied, I can't be denied, and with that he fell to Kissing me so violently, I could not get rid of him.

THERE was a Bed in the Room, and we were walking too and again, eager in the Discourse, at last he takes me by surprize in his Arms, and threw me on the Bed and himself with me, and holding me fast in his Arms, but without the least offer of any Undecency, Courted me to Consent with such repeated Entreaties and Arguments; protesting his Affection and vowing he would not let me go, till I had promised him, that at last I said, why you resolve not to be deny'd indeed, I think: No, no, *says he*, I must not be denyed, I won't be deny'd, I can't be deny'd: Well, well, *said I*, and giving him a slight Kiss, then you shan't be deny'd, *said I*, let me get up.

HE was so Transported with my Consent, and the kind manner of it, that I began to think Once, he took it for a

Marriage, and would not stay for the Form, but I wrong'd
him, for he gave over Kissing me, took me by the Hand,
pull'd me up again, and then giving me two or three Kisses
again, thank'd me for my kind yielding to him; and was so
overcome with the Satisfaction and Joy of it, that I saw
Tears stand in his Eyes.

I TURN'D from him, for it fill'd my Eyes with Tears too;
and I ask'd him leave to retire a little to my Chamber: If ever
I had a Grain of true Repentance for a vitious and abominable
Life for 24 Years past, it was then. O! what a felicity is it to
Mankind, *said I*, to myself, that they cannot see into the
Hearts of one another![1] How happy had it been for me, if I
had been Wife to a Man of so much honesty, and so much
Affection from the Beginning?

THEN it occurr'd to me what an abominable Creature am
I! and how is this innocent Gentleman going to be abus'd by
me! How little does he think, that having Divorc'd a Whore,
he is throwing himself into the Arms of another! that he is
going to Marry one that has lain with two Brothers, and has
had three Children by her own Brother! one that was born
in *Newgate*, whose Mother was a Whore, and is now a transported Thief; one that has lain with thirteen Men, and has
had a Child since he saw me! poor Gentleman! *said I*, What
is he going to do? After this reproaching my self was over, it
followed thus: Well, if I must be his Wife, if it please God to
give me Grace, I'll be a true Wife to him, and love him
suitably to the strange Excess of his Passion for me; I will
make him amends, if possible, by what he shall see, for the
Cheats and Abuses I put upon him, which he does not see.

HE was impatient for my coming out of my Chamber, but
finding me long, he went down Stairs, and talk'd with my
Landlord about the Parson.

MY Landlord, an Officious, tho' well-meaning Fellow, had
sent away for the Neighbouring Clergy Man; and when my
Gentleman began to speak of it to him, and talk of sending
for him, Sir, says he to him, my Friend is in the House; so
without any more words he brought them together: When

he came to the Minister, he ask'd him if he would venture to marry a couple of Strangers that were both willing? The Parson said that Mr. ———— had said something to him of it; that he hop'd it was no Clandestine Business;[1] that he seem'd to be a grave Gentleman, and he suppos'd Madam was not a Girl, so that the consent of Friends should be wanted; to put you out of doubt of that, says my Gentleman, read this Paper, and out he pulls the License; I am satisfied, says the Minister, where is the Lady? you shall see her presently, says my Gentleman.

WHEN he had said thus, he comes up Stairs, and I was by that time come out of my Room, so he tells me the Minister was below, and that he had talk'd with him, and that upon showing him the License, he was free to marry us with all his Heart, but he asks to see you, so he ask'd if I would let him come up.

'Tis time enough, *said I*, in the Morning, is it not? Why, *said he*, my Dear, he seem'd to scruple whether it was not some young Girl stolen from her Parents, and I assur'd him we were both of Age to command our own Consent; and that made him ask to see you; well, *said I*, do as you please; so up they brings the Parson, and a merry good sort of Gentleman he was; he had been told, it seems, that we had met there by accident, that I came in the *Chester* Coach, and my Gentleman in his own Coach to meet me; that we were to have met last Night at *Stony-Stratford*, but that he could not reach so far: Well, Sir, *says the Parson*, every ill turn has some good in it; the Disappointment, Sir, *says he to my Gentleman*, was yours, and the good Turn is mine, for if you had met at *Stony-Stratford* I had not had the Honour to Marry you: LANDLORD *have you a Common-Prayer Book*.

I started as if I had been frighted, Lord, Sir, *says I*, what do you mean, what to marry in an Inn, and at Night too: Madam, *says the Minister*, if you will have it be in the Church you shall; but I assure you your Marriage will be as firm here as in the Church; we are not tyed by the Canons to Marry no where but in the Church; and if you will have it in the

Church it will be as publick as a Country Fair; and as for the time of Day[1] it does not at all weigh in this Case, our Princes are married in their Chambers, and at Eight or Ten a Clock at Night.

I WAS a great while before I could be perswaded, and pretended not to be willing at all to be married but in the Church; but it was all Grimace;[2] so I seem'd at last to be prevail'd on, and my Landlord, and his Wife, and Daughter, were call'd up: My Landlord was Father and Clark and all together, and we were married, and very Merry we were; tho' I confess the self-reproaches which I had upon me before, lay close to me, and extorted every now and then a deep sigh from me, which my Bridegroom took notice of, and endeavour'd to encourage me, thinking, poor Man, that I had some little hesitations at the Step I had taken so hastily.

WE enjoy'd our selves that Evening compleatly, and yet all was kept so private in the Inn, that not a Servant in the House knew of it, for my Landlady and her Daughter waited on me, and would not let any of the Maids come up Stairs, except while we were at Supper: My Landlady's Daughter I call'd my Bride-maid, and sending for a Shop-keeper the next Morning, I gave the young Woman a good Suit of Knots,[3] as good as the Town would afford, and finding it was a Lace-making Town,[4] I gave her Mother a piece of Bone-lace[5] for a Head.

ONE Reason that my Landlord was so close was, that he was unwilling the Minister of the Parish should hear of it; but for all that somebody heard of it, so as that we had the Bells set a Ringing the next Morning early, and the Musick, such as the Town would afford, under our Window;[6] but my Landlord brazen'd it out, that we were marry'd before we came thither, only that being his former Guests, we would have our Wedding Supper at his House.

WE cou'd not find in our Hearts to stir the next Day; for in short having been disturb'd by the Bells in the Morning, and having perhaps not slept over much Before, we were so sleepy afterwards that we lay in Bed till almost Twelve a Clock.

I BEG'D my Landlady that we might not have any more Musick in the Town, nor Ringing of Bells, and she manag'd it so well that we were very quiet: But an odd Passage interrupted all my Mirth for a good while; the great Room of the House look'd into the Street, and my new Spouse being below Stairs, I had walk'd to the end of the Room, and it being a pleasant warm Day, I had opened the Window, and was standing at it for some Air, when I saw three Gentlemen come by on Horseback and go into an Inn just against us.

IT was not to be conceal'd, nor was it so doubtful as to leave me any room to question it, but the second of the three was my *Lancashire* Husband: I was frighted to Death, I never was in such a Consternation in my Life, I thought I should have sunk into the Ground, my Blood run Chill in my Veins,[1] and I trembl'd as if I had been in a cold Fit of an Ague: I say there was no room to question the Truth of it, I knew his Cloaths, I knew his Horse, and I knew his Face.

THE first sensible Reflection I made was, that my Husband was not by to see my Disorder, and that I was very glad of: The Gentlemen had not been long in the House but they came to the Window of their Room, as is usual; but my Window was shut you may be sure: However, I cou'd not keep from peeping at them, and there I saw him again, heard him call out to one of the Servants of the House for something he wanted, and receiv'd all the terryfying Confirmations of its being the same Person, that were possible to be had.

MY next concern was to know, if possible, what was his Business there; but that was impossible; sometimes my Imagination form'd an Idea of one frightful thing, sometimes of another; sometimes I thought he had discover'd me, and was come to upbraid me with Ingratitude and Breach of Honour; and every Moment I fancied he was coming up the Stairs to Insult me; and innumerable fancies came into my Head of what was never in his Head, nor ever could be, unless the Devil had reveal'd it to him.

I REMAIN'D in this fright near two Hours, and scarce ever kept my Eye from the Window or Door of the Inn, where they were: At last hearing a great clutter in the Passage of their Inn, I run to the Window, and, to my great Satisfaction, see them all three go out again and Travel on Westward; had they gone towards *London*, I should have been still in a fright, least I should meet him on the Road again, and that he should know me; but he went the contrary way, and so I was eas'd of that Disorder.

WE resolv'd to be going the next Day, but about six a Clock at Night we were alarm'd with a great uproar in the Street, and People riding as if they had been out of their Wits, and what was it but a Hue and Cry[1] after three Highway Men, that had rob'd two Coaches, and some other Travellers near *Dunstable* Hill, and notice had, it seems, been given, that they had been seen at *Brickill* at such a House, meaning the House where those Gentlemen had been.

THE House was immediately beset and search'd, but there were witnesses enough that the Gentlemen had been gone above three Hours; the Crowd having gathered about, we had the News presently; and I was heartily concern'd now another way: I presently told the People of the House, that I durst to say those were not the Persons, for that I knew one of the Gentlemen to be a very honest Person, and of a good Estate in *Lancashire*.

THE Constable, who came with the Hue and Cry, was immediately inform'd of this, and came over to me to be satisfy'd from my own Mouth, and I assur'd him that I saw the three Gentlemen as I was at the Window, that I saw them afterwards at the Windows of the Room they din'd in; that I saw them afterwards take Horse, and I could assure him I knew one of them to be such a Man, that he was a Gentleman of a very good Estate, and an undoubted Character in *Lancashire*, from whence I was just now upon my Journey.

THE assurance with which I deliver'd this, gave the Mob Gentry[2] a Check, and gave the Constable such Satisfaction, that he immediately sounded a Retreat, told his People these were not the Men, but that he had an account they were very honest Gentlemen, and so they went all back again; what the Truth of the matter was I knew not, but certain it was that the Coaches were rob'd at *Dunstable* Hill, and 560 *l.* in Money taken, besides some of the Lace Merchants that always Travel that way had been visited too; as to the three Gentlemen, that remains to be explain'd hereafter.

WELL, this Allarm stop'd us another Day, tho' my Spouse was for Travelling, and told me that it was always safest Travelling after a Robbery, for that the Thieves were sure to be gone far enough off when they had allarm'd the Country; but I was afraid and uneasy, and indeed principally least my old Acquaintance should be upon the Road still, and should chance to see me.

I NEVER liv'd four pleasanter Days together in my life, I was a meer Bride all this while, and my new Spouse strove to make me entirely easie in every thing; O could this State of Life have continued! how had all my past Troubles been forgot, and my future Sorrows been avoided? but I had a past life of a most wretched kind to account for, some of it in this World as well as in another.

WE came away the fifth Day; and my Landlord, because he saw me uneasie, mounted himself, his Son, and three honest Country Fellows with good Fire-Arms, and, without telling us of it, follow'd the Coach, and would see us safe into *Dunstable*; we could do no less than treat them very handsomely at *Dunstable*, which Cost my Spouse about Ten or Twelve Shillings, and something he gave the Men for their Time too, but my Landlord would take nothing for himself.

THIS was the most happy Contrivance for me that could have fallen out, for had I come to *London* unmarried, I must either have come to him for the first Night's Entertainment, or have discovered to him that I had not one Acquaintance in the whole City of *London* that could receive a poor Bride for the first Night's Lodging with her Spouse: But now being an old married Woman, I made no scruple of going directly

home with him, and there I took Possession at once of a
House well Furnish'd, and a Husband in very good Circumstances, so that I had a prospect of a very happy Life, if I
knew how to manage it; and I had leisure to consider of the
real Value of the Life I was likely to live; how different it
was to be from the loose ungovern'd part I had acted before,
and how much happier a Life of Virtue and Sobriety is, than
that which we call a Life of Pleasure.

O HAD this particular Scene of Life lasted, or had I learnt
from that time I enjoy'd it, to have tasted the true sweetness
of it, and had I not fallen into the Poverty which is the sure
Bane of Virtue, how happy had I been, not only here, but
perhaps for ever? for while I liv'd thus, I was really a
Penitent for all my Life pass'd, I look'd back on it with
Abhorrence, and might truly be said to hate my self for it;
I often reflected how my Lover at the *Bath*, strook by the
Hand of God, repented and abandon'd me, and refus'd to
see me any more, tho' he lov'd me to an extreme; but I,
prompted by that worst of Devils, Poverty, return'd to the
vile Practice, and made the Advantage of what they call a
handsome Face, be the Relief to my Necessities, and Beauty
be a Pimp to Vice.

NOW I seem'd landed in a safe Harbour, after the Stormy
Voyage of Life past was at an end; and I began to be thankful
for my Deliverance; I sat many an Hour by my self, and
wept over the Remembrance of past Follies, and the dreadful
Extravagances of a wicked Life, and sometimes I flatter'd my
self that I had sincerely repented.

BUT there are Temptations which it is not in the Power of
Human Nature to resist,[1] and few know what would be their
Case, if driven to the same Exigences: As Covetousness is
the Root of all Evil,[2] so Poverty is, I believe, the worst of all
Snares: But I wave that Discourse till I come to the
Experiment.

I LIV'D with this Husband in the utmost Tranquility; he
was a Quiet, Sensible, Sober Man, Virtuous, Modest,
Sincere, and in his Business Diligent and Just: His Business

was in a narrow Compass, and his Income sufficient to a plentiful way of Living in the ordinary way; I do not say to keep an Equipage,[1] and make a Figure as the World calls it, nor did I expect it, or desire it; for as I abhorr'd the Levity and Extravagance of my former Life, so I chose now to live retir'd, frugal, and within our selves; I kept no Company, made no Visits; minded my Family, and oblig'd my Husband; and this kind of Life became a Pleasure to me.

WE liv'd in an uninterrupted course of Ease and Content for Five Years, when a sudden Blow from an almost invisible Hand, blasted all my Happiness, and turn'd me out into the World in a Condition the reverse of all that had been before it.

MY Husband having trusted one of his Fellow Clarks with a Sum of Money too much for our Fortunes to bear the Loss of, the Clark fail'd, and the Loss fell very heavy on my Husband, yet it was not so great neither, but that if he had had Spirit and Courage to have look'd his Misfortunes in the Face, his Credit was so good, that as I told him, he would easily recover it; for to sink under Trouble is to double the Weight,[2] and he that will Die in it shall Die in it.

IT was in vain to speak comfortably to him, the Wound had sunk too deep, it was a Stab that touch'd the Vitals, he grew Melancholy and Disconsolate, and from thence Lethargick, and died;[3] I foresaw the Blow, and was extremely oppress'd in my Mind, for I saw evidently that if he died I was undone.

I HAD had two Children by him and no more, for to tell the Truth, it began to be time for me to leave bearing Children, for I was now Eight and Forty, and I suppose if he had liv'd I should have had no more.

I WAS now left in a dismal and disconsolate Case indeed, and in several things worse than ever: First it was past the flourishing time with me when I might expect to be courted for a Mistress; that agreeable part had declin'd some time, and the Ruins only appear'd of what had been; and that which was worse than all was this, that I was the most

dejected, disconsolate Creature alive; I that had encourag'd
my Husband, and endeavour'd to support his Spirits under
his Trouble, could not support my own; I wanted that
Spirit in Trouble which I told him was so necessary to him
for bearing the burthen.

But my Case was indeed Deplorable, for I was left
perfectly Friendless and Helpless, and the Loss my Husband
had sustain'd had reduc'd his Circumstances so low, that
tho' indeed I was not in Debt, yet I could easily foresee that
what was left would not support me long; that while it
wasted daily for Subsistence, I had no way to encrease it one
Shilling, so that it would be soon all spent, and then I saw
nothing before me but the utmost Distress, and this represented it self so lively to my Thoughts, that it seem'd as if it
was come, before it was really very near; also my very
Apprehensions doubl'd the Misery, for I fancied every
Sixpence that I paid but for a Loaf of Bread, was the last
that I had in the World, and that To-morrow I was to fast,
and be starv'd to Death.

In this Distress I had no Assistant, no Friend to comfort
or advise me, I sat and cried and tormented my self Night
and Day; wringing my Hands, and sometimes raving like a
distracted Woman; and indeed I have often wonder'd it had
not affected my Reason, for I had the Vapours[1] to such a
degree, that my Understanding was sometimes quite lost in
Fancies and Imaginations.

I Liv'd Two Years in this dismal Condition wasting that
little I had, weeping continually over my dismal Circumstances, and as it were only bleeding to Death, without the
least hope or prospect of help from God or Man; and now I
had cried so long, and so often, that Tears were, as I might
say, exhausted, and I began to be Desperate, for I grew Poor
apace.

For a little Relief I had put off my House and took
Lodgings, and as I was reducing my Living so I sold off
most of my Goods, which put a little Money in my Pocket,
and I liv'd near a Year upon that, spending very sparingly,

and eeking things out to the utmost; but still when I look'd
before me, my very Heart would sink within me at the
inevitable approach of Misery and Want: O let none read
this part without seriously reflecting on the Circumstances
of a desolate State, and how they would grapple with meer
want of Friends and want of Bread; it will certainly make
them think not of sparing what they have only, but of looking
up to Heaven for support, and of the wise Man's Prayer,[1]
Give me not Poverty least I Steal.

LET 'em remember that a time of Distress is a time of
dreadful Temptation, and all the Strength to resist is taken
away; Poverty presses, the Soul is made Desperate by
Distress, and what can be done? It was one Evening, when
being brought, as I may say, to the last Gasp, I think I may
truly say I was Distracted and Raving, when prompted by I
know not what Spirit, and as it were, doing I did not know
what, or why; I dress'd me, for I had still pretty good
Cloaths, and went out: I am very sure I had no manner of
Design in my Head, when I went out, I neither knew or
considered where to go, or on what Business; but as the
Devil carried me out and laid his Bait for me, so he brought
me to be sure to the place, for I knew not whither I was
going or what I did.

WANDRING thus about I knew not whither, I pass'd by
an Apothecary's Shop in *Leadenhall-street*,[2] where I saw lye
on a Stool just before the Counter a little Bundle wrapt in a
white Cloth; beyond it, stood a Maid Servant with her Back
to it, looking up towards the top of the Shop, where the
Apothecary's Apprentice, as I suppose, was standing up on
the Counter, with his Back also to the Door, and a Candle in
his Hand, looking and reaching up to the upper Shelf for
something he wanted, so that both were engag'd mighty
earnestly, and no Body else in the Shop.

THIS was the Bait; and the Devil who I said laid the Snare,
as readily prompted me,[3] as if he had spoke, for I remember,
and shall never forget it, 'twas like a Voice spoken to me over
my Shoulder, take the Bundle; be quick; do it this Moment;

it was no sooner said but I step'd into the Shop, and with my Back to the Wench, as if I had stood up for a Cart that was going by, I put my Hand behind me and took the Bundle, and went off with it, the Maid or the Fellow not perceiving me, or any one else.

IT is impossible to express the Horror of my Soul all the while I did it: When I went away I had no Heart to run, or scarce to mend my pace; I cross'd the Street indeed, and went down the first turning I came to, and I think it was a Street that went thro' into *Fenchurch-street*,[1] from thence I cross'd and turn'd thro' so many ways and turnings that I could never tell which way it was, nor where I went, for I felt not the Ground, I stept on, and the farther I was out of Danger, the faster I went, till tyr'd and out of Breath, I was forc'd to sit down on a little Bench at a Door, and then I began to recover, and found I was got into *Thames-street* near *Billinsgate*:[2] I rested me a little and went on, my Blood was all in a Fire, my Heart beat as if I was in a sudden Fright: In short, I was under such a Surprize that I still knew not whither I was a going, or what to do.

AFTER I had tyr'd my self thus with walking a long way about, and so eagerly, I began to consider and make home to my Lodging, where I came about Nine a Clock at Night.

WHAT the Bundle was made up for, or on what Occasion laid where I found it, I knew not, but when I came to open it I found there was a Suit of Child-bed Linnen in it, very good and almost new, the Lace very fine; there was a Silver Porringer of a Pint, a small Silver Mug and Six Spoons, some other Linnen, a good Smock, and Three Silk Handkerchiefs, and in the Mug wrap'd up in a Paper Eighteen Shillings and Six-pence in Money.

ALL the while I was opening these things I was under such dreadful Impressions of Fear, and in such Terror of Mind, tho' I was perfectly safe, that I cannot express the manner of it; I sat me down and cried most vehemently; Lord, *said I*, what am I now? a Thief! why I shall be taken next time and be carry'd to *Newgate* and be Try'd for my Life![3] and with that I cry'd again a long time, and I am sure, as poor as I was, if I had durst for fear, I would certainly have carried the things back again; but that went off after a while: Well, I went to Bed for that Night, but slept little, the Horror of the Fact was upon my Mind, and I knew not what I said or did all Night, and all the next Day: Then I was impatient to hear some News of the Loss; and would fain know how it was, whether they were a Poor Bodies Goods, or a Rich; perhaps, *said I*, it may be some poor Widow like me, that had pack'd up these Goods to go and sell them for a little Bread for herself and a poor Child, and are now starving and breaking their Hearts, for want of that little they would have fetch'd, and this Thought tormented me worse than all the rest, for three or four Days time.

But my own Distresses silenc'd all these Reflections, and the prospect of my own Starving, which grew every Day more frightful to me, harden'd my Heart by degrees; it was then particularly heavy upon my Mind, that I had been reform'd, and had, as I hop'd, repented of all my pass'd wickednesses; that I had liv'd a sober, grave, retir'd Life for several Years, but now I should be driven by the dreadful Necessity of my Circumstances to the Gates of Destruction, Soul and Body; and two or three times I fell upon my Knees, praying to God, as well as I could, for Deliverance; but I cannot but say my Prayers had no hope in them; I knew not what to do, it was all Fear without, and Dark within; and I reflected on my pass'd Life as not sincerely repented of, that Heaven was now beginning to punish me on this side the Grave, and would make me as miserable as I had been wicked.

Had I gone on here I had perhaps been a true Penitent; but I had an evil Counsellor within, and he was continually prompting me to relieve my self by the worst means; so one Evening he tempted me again by the same wicked Impulse that had said, *take that Bundle*, to go out again and seek for what might happen.

I Went out now by Day-light, and wandred about I knew

not whither, and in search of I knew not what, when the Devil put a Snare in my way of a dreadful Nature indeed, and such a one as I have never had before or since; going thro' *Aldersgate-street* there was a pretty little Child had been at a Dancing-School, and was going home, all alone, and my Prompter, like a true Devil, set me upon this innocent Creature; I talk'd to it, and it prattl'd to me again, and I took it by the Hand and led it a long till I came to a pav'd Alley that goes into *Bartholomew Close*,[1] and I led it in there; the Child said that was not its way home; I said, yes, my Dear it is, I'll show you the way home; the Child had a little Necklace on of Gold Beads, and I had my Eye upon that, and in the dark of the Alley I stoop'd, pretending to mend the Child's Clog that was loose, and took off her Necklace and the Child never felt it, and so led the Child on again: Here, I say, the Devil put me upon killing the Child in the dark Alley, that it might not Cry; but the very thought frighted me so that I was ready to drop down, but I turn'd the Child about and bad it go back again, for that was not its way home; the Child said so she would, and I went thro' into *Bartholomew Close*, and then turn'd round to another Passage that goes into *Long-lane*, so away into *Charterhouse-Yard* and out into *St. John's-street*, then crossing into *Smithfield*, went down *Chick-lane* and into *Field-lane* to *Holbourn-bridge*,[2] when mixing with the Crowd of People usually passing there, it was not possible to have been found out; and thus I enterpriz'd my second Sally into the World.[3]

THE thoughts of this Booty put out all the thoughts of the first, and the Reflections I had made wore quickly off; Poverty, as I have said, harden'd my Heart, and my own Necessities made me regardless of any thing: The last Affair left no great Concern upon me, for as I did the poor Child no harm, I only said to my self, I had given the Parents a just Reproof for their Negligence in leaving the poor little Lamb to come home by it self, and it would teach them to take more Care of it another time.

THIS String of Beads was worth about Twelve or Fourteen

Pounds, I suppose it might have been formerly the Mother's, for it was too big for the Child's wear, but that, perhaps, the Vanity of the Mother to have her Child look Fine at the Dancing School, had made her let the Child wear it, and no doubt the Child had a Maid sent to take care of it, but she, like a careless Jade, was taken up perhaps with some Fellow that had met her by the way, and so the poor Baby wandred till it fell into my Hands.

HOWEVER, I did the Child no harm, I did not so much as fright it, for I had a great many tender Thoughts about me yet, and did nothing but what, as I may say, meer Necessity drove me to.

I HAD a great many Adventures after this, but I was young in the Business, and did not know how to manage, otherwise than as the Devil put things into my Head; and indeed he was seldom backward to me: One Adventure I had which was very lucky to me; I was going thro' *Lombard-street* in the dusk of the Evening, just by the end of *Three King Court*,[1] when on a sudden comes a Fellow running by me as swift as Lightning, and throws a Bundle that was in his Hand just behind me, as I stood up against the corner of the House at the turning into the Alley; just as he threw it in he said, God bless you Mistress let it lie there a little, and away he runs swift as the Wind: After him comes two more, and immediately a young Fellow without his Hat, crying stop Thief, and after him two or three more, they pursued the two last Fellows so close, that they were forced to drop what they had got, and one of them was taken into the bargain, the other got off free.

I STOOD stock still all this while till they came back, dragging the poor Fellow they had taken, and luging the things they had found, extremely well satisfied that they had recovered the Booty, and taken the Thief; and thus they pass'd by me, for I look'd only like one who stood up while the Crowd was gone.

ONCE or twice I ask'd what was the matter, but the People neglected answering me, and I was not very importunate;

but after the Crowd was wholly pass'd, I took my opportunity to turn about and take up what was behind me and
walk away: This indeed I did with less Disturbance than I
had done formerly, for these things I did not steal, but they
were stolen to my Hand: I got safe to my Lodgings with this
Cargo, which was a Peice of fine black Lustring Silk,[1] and a
Peice of Velvet; the latter was but part of a Peice of about a
11 Yards; the former was a whole Peice of near 50 Yards; it
seems it was a *Mercer's* Shop that they had rifled, I say
rifled, because the Goods were so considerable that they had
Lost; for the Goods that they Recover'd were pretty many,
and I believe came to about six or seven several Peices of
Silk: How they came to get so many I could not tell; but as
I had only robb'd the Thief I made no scruple at taking these
Goods, and being very glad of them too.

I HAD pretty good Luck thus far, and I made several
Adventures more, tho' with but small Purchase, yet with
good Success, but I went in daily dread that some mischief
would befal me, and that I should certainly come to be
hang'd at last: The impression this made on me was too
strong to be slighted, and it kept me from making attempts
that for ought I know might have been very safely perform'd; but one thing I cannot omit, which was a Bait to me
many a Day. I walk'd frequently out into the Villages round
the Town to see if nothing would fall in my Way there; and
going by a House near *Stepney*, I saw on the Window-board
two Rings, one a small Diamond Ring, and the other a plain
Gold Ring, to be sure laid there by some thoughtless Lady,
that had more Money than Forecast, perhaps only till she
wash'd her Hands.

I WALK'D several times by the Window to observe if I
could see whether there was any Body in the Room or no,
and I could see no Body, but still I was not sure; it came
presently into my Thoughts to rap at the Glass, as if I
wanted to speak with some Body, and if any Body was there
they would be sure to come to the Window, and then I
would tell them to remove those Rings, for that I had seen

two suspicious Fellows take notice of them: This was a ready Thought, I rapt once or twice and no Body came, when seeing the Coast clear, I thrust hard against the Square of Glass, and broke it with very little Noise, and took out the two Rings, and walk'd away with them very safe, the Diamond Ring was worth about 3*l*. and the other about 9*s*.

I WAS now at a loss for a Market for my Goods, and especially for my two Peices of Silk, I was very loth to dispose of them for a Trifle; as the poor unhappy Theives in general do, who after they have ventured their Lives for perhaps a thing of Value, are fain to sell it for a Song when they have done; but I was resolv'd I would not do thus whatever shift I made, unless I was driven to the last Extremity; however I did not well know what Course to take: At last I resolv'd to go to my old Governness, and acquaint myself with her again: I had punctually supply'd the 5*l*. a Year to her for my little Boy as long as I was able; but at last was oblig'd to put a stop to it: However I had written a Letter to her, wherein I had told her that my Circumstances were reduc'd very low; that I had lost my Husband, and that I was not able to do it any longer, and so beg'd that the poor Child might not suffer too much for its Mother's Misfortunes.

I Now made her a Visit, and I found that she drove something of the old Trade still, but that she was not in such flourishing Circumstances as before; for she had been Sued by a certain Gentleman, who had had his Daughter stolen from him; and who it seems she had helped to convey away; and it was very narrowly that she escap'd the Gallows; the Expence also had ravag'd her, and she was become very poor; her House was but meanly Furnished, and she was not in such repute for her Practice as before; however she stood upon her Legs, as they say, and as she was a stirring bustling Woman, and had some Stock left, she was turn'd *Pawn Broker, and liv'd pretty well.*

SHE receiv'd me very civilly, and with her usual obliging manner told me, she would not have the less respect for me, for my being reduc'd; that she had taken Care my Boy was very well look'd after, tho' I could not pay for him, and that the Woman that had him was easie, so that I needed not to Trouble myself about him, till I might be better able to do it effectually.

I TOLD her I had not much Money left, but that I had some things that were Monies worth, if she could tell me how I might turn them into Money; she ask'd me what it was I had, I pull'd out the string of gold Beads, and told her it was one of my Husbands Presents to me; then I show'd her the two Parcels of Silk which I told her I had from *Ireland*, and brought up to Town with me; and the little Diamond Ring; as to the small Parcel of Plate and Spoons, I had found means to dispose of them myself before; and as for the Childbed Linnen I had, she offer'd me to take it herself, believing it to have been my own; she told me that she was turn'd *Pawn-Broker*, and that she would sell those things for me as pawn'd to her, and so she sent presently for proper Agents that bought them, being in her Hands, without any scruple, and gave good Prizes too.

I NOW began to think this necessary Woman might help me a little in my low Condition to some Business; for I would gladly have turn'd my Hand to any honest Employment if I could have got it; but here she was defficient; honest Business did not come within her reach; if I had been younger, perhaps she might have helped me to a Spark, but my Thoughts were off of that kind of Livelihood, as being quite out of the way after 50, which was my Case, and so I told her.

SHE invited me at last to come, and be at her House till I could find something to do, and it should cost me very little, and this I gladly accepted of, and now living a little easier, I enter'd into some Measures to have my little Son by my last Husband taken off; and this she made easie too, reserving a Payment only of 5*l.* a Year, if I could pay it. This was such a help to me, that for a good while I left off the wicked Trade that I had so newly taken up; and gladly I would have got my Bread by the help of my Needle if I cou'd have got Work, but that was very hard to do for one that had no manner of Acquaintance in the World.

HOWEVER at last I got some Quilting-Work for Ladies Beds, Peticoats, and the like; and this I lik'd very well and work'd very hard, and with this I began to live; but the diligent Devil who resolv'd I should continue in his Service, continually prompted me to go out and take a Walk, that is to say, to see if any thing would offer in the old Way.

ONE Evening I blindly obeyed his Summons, and fetch'd a long Circuit thro' the Streets, but met with no purchase and came Home very weary, and empty; but not content with that, I went out the next Evening too, when going by an Alehouse I saw the Door of a little room open, next the very Street, and on the Table a silver Tankard, things much in use in publick Houses at that time;[1] it seems some Company had been drinking there, and the careless Boys had forgot to take it away.

I WENT into the Box frankly, and setting the silver Tankard on the Corner of the Bench, I sat down before it, and knock'd with my Foot, a Boy came presently, and I bad him fetch me a pint of warm Ale, for it was cold Weather; the Boy run, and I heard him go down the Sellar to draw the Ale; while the Boy was gone, another Boy come into the Room, and cried, *d' ye call*, I spoke with a melancholly Air, and said, no Child, the Boy is gone for a Pint of Ale for me.

WHILE I sat here, I heard the Woman in the Bar say are they all gone in the Five, which was the Box I sat in, and the Boy said *yes*; who fetch'd the Tankard away? *says the Woman*, I did, *says another Boy*, that's it, pointing it seems to another Tankard, which he had fetch'd from another Box by Mistake; or else it must be, that the Rogue forgot that he had not brought it in, which certainly he had not.

I HEARD all this, much to my satisfaction, for I found plainly that the Tankard was not mist, and yet they concluded it was fetch'd away; so I drank my Ale, call'd to Pay, and as I went away, *I said*, take care of your Plate Child, meaning a silver pint Mug, which he brought me Drink in; the

Boy said, *yes Madam*, *very welcome*, and away I came.

I CAME Home to my Governess, and now I thought it was a time to try her, that if I might be put to the Necessity of being expos'd, she might offer me some assistance; when I had been at Home some time, and had an opportunity of Talking to her, I told her I had a Secret of the greatest Consequence in the World to commit to her if she had respect enough for me to keep it a Secret: She told me she had kept one of my Secrets faithfully; why should I doubt her keeping another? I told her the strangest thing in the World had befallen me, and that it had made a Thief of me, even without any design; and so told her the whole Story of the Tankard: And have you brought it away with you my Dear, *says she*, to be sure I have, *says I*, and shew'd it her. But what shall I do now, *says I*, must not I carry it again?

CARRY it again! *says she*, Ay, if you are minded to be sent to *Newgate* for stealing it; why, *says I*, they can't be so base to stop me, when I carry it to them again? You don't know those Sort of People Child, *says she*, they'll not only carry you to *Newgate*, but hang you too without any regard to the honesty of returning it; or bring in an Account of all the other Tankards they have lost for you to pay for: What must I do then? *says I*; Nay, *says she*, as you have plaid the cunning part and stole it, you must e'n keep it, there's no going back now; besides Child, *says she*, Don't you want it more than they do? I wish you cou'd light of such a Bargain once a Week.

THIS gave me a new Notion of my *Governess*, and that since she was turn'd *Pawn Broker*, she had a Sort of People about her, that were none of the honest ones that I had met with there before.

I HAD not been long there, but I discover'd it more plainly than before, for every now and then I saw Hilts of Swords, Spoons, Forks, Tankards, and all such kind of Ware brought in, not to be Pawn'd, but to be sold down right; and she bought every thing that came without asking any Questions, but had very good Bargains as I found by her Discourse.

I FOUND also that in the following this Trade, she always

melted down the Plate she bought, that it might not be challeng'd; and she came to me and told me one Morning that she was going to Melt, and if I would, she would put my Tankard in, that it might not be seen by any Body; I told her with all my Heart; so she weigh'd it, and allow'd me the full value in Silver again; but I found she did not do the same to the rest of her Customers.

SOMETIME after this, as I was at Work, and very melancholly, she begins to ask me what the Matter was? as she was us'd to do; I told her my Heart was heavy, I had little Work, and nothing to live on, and knew not what Course to take; she Laugh'd and told me I must go out again and try my Fortune; it might be that I might meet with another Peice of Plate. O, Mother! *says I*, that is a Trade I have no skill in, and if I should be taken I am undone at once; *says she*, I cou'd help you to a School-Mistress, that shall make you as dexterous as her self: I trembled at that Proposal for hitherto I had had no Confederates, nor any Acquaintance among that Tribe; but she conquer'd all my Modesty, and all my Fears; and in a little time, by the help of this Confederate I grew as impudent a Thief, and as dexterous as ever *Moll Cut-Purse* was, tho' if Fame does not belie her, not half so Handsome.[1]

THE Comrade she helped me to, dealt in three sorts of Craft, (*viz.*) Shop-lifting, stealing of Shop-Books, and Pocket-Books, and taking off Gold Watches from the Ladies Sides, and this last she did so dexteriously that no Woman ever arriv'd to the Perfection of that Art, so as to do it like her: I lik'd the first and the last of these things very well, and I attended her some time in the Practise, just as a Deputy attends a Midwife without any Pay.

AT length she put me to Practise, she had shewn me her Art, and I had several times unhook'd a Watch from her own side with great dexterity; at last she show'd me a Prize, and this was a young Lady big with Child who had a charming Watch, the thing was to be done as she came out of Church; she goes on one side of the Lady, and pretends, just as she came to the Steps, to fall, and fell against the Lady with so

much violence as put her into a great fright, and both cry'd
out terribly; in the very moment that she jostl'd the Lady,
I had hold of the Watch, and holding it the right way, the
start she gave drew the Hook out and she never felt it; I
made off immediately, and left my Schoolmistress to come
out of her pretended Fright gradually, and the Lady too;
and presently the Watch was miss'd; ay, *says my Comrade*,
then it was those Rogues that thrust me down, I warrant ye;
I wonder the Gentlewoman did not miss her Watch before,
then we might have taken them.

SHE humour'd the thing so well that no Body suspected
her, and I was got home a full Hour before her: This was
my first Adventure in Company; the Watch was indeed a
very fine one, and had a great many Trinkets about it, and
my Governess allow'd us 20*l*. for it, of which I had half, and
thus I was enter'd a compleat Thief, harden'd to a Pitch
above all the Reflections of Conscience or Modesty, and to a
Degree which I must acknowledge I never thought possible
in me.

THUS the Devil who began, by the help of an irresistable
Poverty, to push me into this Wickedness, brought me on to
a height beyond the common Rate, even when my Necessities
were not so great, or the prospect of my Misery so terrifying;
for I had now got into a little Vein of Work, and as I was not
at a loss to handle my Needle, it was very probable, as
Acquaintance came in, I might have got my Bread honestly
enough.

I must say, that if such a prospect of Work had presented
it self at first, when I began to feel the approach of my
miserable Circumstances; I say, had such a prospect of
getting my Bread by working presented it self then, I had
never fallen into this wicked Trade, or into such a wicked
Gang as I was now embark'd with; but practise had hardened
me, and I grew audacious to the last degree; and the more so,
because I had carried it on so long, and had never been taken;
for in a word, my new Partner in Wickedness *and I* went on
together so long, without being ever detected, that we not

only grew Bold, but we grew Rich, and we had at one time One and Twenty Gold Watches in our Hands.

I REMEMBER that one Day being a little more serious than ordinary, and finding I had so good a Stock before-hand as I had, for I had near 200*l.* in Money for my Share; it came strongly into my Mind, no doubt from some kind Spirit, if such there be; that as at first Poverty excited me, and my Distresses drove me to these dreadful Shifts; so seeing those Distresses were now relieved, and I could also get something towards a Maintenance by working, and had so good a Bank to support me, why should I not now leave off, as they say, while I was well; that I could not expect to go always free; and if I was once surpris'd, and miscarry'd, I was undone.

THIS was doubtless the happy Minute, when if I had hearken'd to the blessed hint from whatsoever hand it came,[1] I had still a cast for an easie Life; but my Fate was otherwise determin'd, the busie Devil that so industriously drew me in, had too fast hold of me to let me go back; but as Poverty brought me into the Mire, so Avarice kept me in,[2] till there was no going back; as to the Arguments which my Reason dictated for perswading me to lay down, Avarice stept in and said, go on, go on; you have had very good luck, go on till you have gotten Four or Five Hundred Pound, and then you shall leave off, and then you may live easie without working at all.

THUS I that was once in the Devil's Clutches, was held fast there as with a Charm, and had no Power to go without the Circle, till I was ingulph'd in Labyrinths of Trouble too great to get out at all.

HOWEVER, these Thoughts left some Impression upon me, and made me act with some more caution than before, and more than my Directors us'd for themselves. My Comerade, as I call'd her, but rather she should have been called my Teacher, with another of her Scholars, was the first in the Misfortune, for happening to be upon the hunt for Purchase, they made an attempt upon a Linnen-Draper in *Cheapside*,[3] but were snap'd by a Hawks-ey'd Journey-man, and seiz'd[4] with two pieces of Cambrick, which were taken also upon them.

THIS was enough to Lodge them both in *Newgate*, where they had the Misfortune to have some of their former Sins brought to remembrance; two other Indictments being brought against them, and the Facts being prov'd upon them, they were both condemned to Die; they both pleaded their Bellies, and were both voted Quick with Child; tho' my Tutress was no more with Child than I was.

I WENT frequently to see them, and Condole with them, expecting that it would be my turn next; but the place gave me so much Horror, reflecting that it was the place of my unhappy Birth, and of my Mother's Misfortunes, that I could not bear it, so I was forc'd to leave off going to see them.

AND O! cou'd I have but taken warning by their Disasters, I had been happy still, for I was yet free, and had nothing brought against me; but it could not be, my Measure was not yet fill'd up.[1]

MY Comerade having the Brand of an old Offender, was Executed;[2] the young Offender was spar'd, having obtain'd a Reprieve; but lay starving a long while in Prison, till at last she got her Name into what they call a Circuit Pardon,[3] and so came off.

THIS terrible Example of my Comerade frighted me heartily, and for a good while I made no Excursions; but one Night, in the Neighbourhood of my Governesses House, they cryed Fire; my Governess look'd out, for we were all up, and cryed immediately that such a Gentlewoman's House was all of a light Fire a top, and so indeed it was: Here she gives me a jog, now, Child, says she, there is a rare opportunity, the Fire being so near that you may go to it before the Street is block'd up with the Crowd; she presently gave me my Cue, go, Child, *says she*, to the House, and run in and tell the Lady, or any Body you see, that you come to help them, and that you came from such a Gentlewoman (that is one of her Acquaintance farther up the Street); she gave me the like Cue to the next House, naming another Name that was also an Acquaintance of the Gentlewoman of the House.

Away I went, and coming to the House I found them all in Confusion, you may be sure; I run in, and finding one of the Maids, Lord! Sweetheart, *said I*, how came this dismal Accident? Where is your Mistress? And how does she do? Is she safe? And where are the Children? I come from Madam —————— to help you; away runs the Maid, Madam, Madam, *says she*, screaming as loud as she cou'd yell, *here is a Gentlewoman come from Madam* —————— *to help us*. The poor Woman half out of her Wits, with a Bundle under her Arm, and two little Children, comes towards me, *Lord, Madam, says I*, let me carry the poor Children to Madam —————, she desires you to send them; she'll take care of the poor Lambs, and immediately I takes one of them out of her Hand, and she lifts the tother up into my Arms; *ay, do, for God sake*, says she, *carry them to her; O thank her for her kindness*: Have you *any thing else to secure*, Madam? says I, *she will take care of it*: O dear! ay, says she, *God bless her, and thank her, take this bundle of Plate and carry it to her too; O she is a good Woman; O Lord, we are utterly ruin'd, utterly undone*; and away she runs from me out of her Wits, and the Maids after her, and away comes I with the two Children and the Bundle.[1]

I Was no sooner got into the Street, but I saw another Woman come to me, O! *says she*, Mistress, in a piteous Tone, you will let fall the Child; come, this is a sad time, let me help you, and immediately lays hold of my Bundle to carry it for me; no, *says I*, if you will help me, take the Child by the Hand, and lead it for me but to the upper end of the Street, I'll go with you and satisfie you for your pains.

She cou'd not avoid going, after what I said, but the Creature, in short, was one of the same Business with me, and wanted nothing but the Bundle; however, she went with me to the Door, for she cou'd not help it; when we were come there I whisper'd her, *go Child*, said I, *I understand your Trade*, you may meet with Purchase enough.

She understood me and walk'd off; I thunder'd at the

Door with the Children, and as the People were rais'd before
by the noise of the Fire, I was soon let in, and I said, *is
Madam awake, pray tell her* Mrs. ———— *desires the favour
of her to take the two Children in*; poor Lady, *she will be
undone, their House is all of a Flame*; they took the Children
in very civily, pitied the Family in Distress, and away came
I with my Bundle; one of the Maids ask'd me, if I was not to
leave the Bundle too? I said no, Sweetheart, 'tis to go to
another place, it does not belong to them.

I WAS a great way out of the hurry now, and so I went on,
clear of any Body's enquiry, and brought the bundle of
Plate, which was very considerable, strait home, and gave it
to my old Governess; she told me she would not look into it,
but bad me go out again to look for more.

SHE gave me the like Cue to the Gentlewoman of the next
House to that which was on Fire, and I did my endeavour to
go, but by this time the allarm of Fire was so great, and so
many Engines playing,[1] and the Street so throng'd with
People, that I cou'd not get near the House, whatever I
cou'd do; so I came back again to my Governesses, and
taking the Bundle up into my Chamber, I began to examine
it: It is with Horror that I tell what a Treasure I found there;
'tis enough to say, that besides most of the Family Plate,
which was considerable, I found a Gold Chain, an old
fashion'd thing, the Locket of which was broken, so that I
suppose it had not been us'd some Years, but the Gold was
not the worse for that; also a little Box of burying Rings,[2]
the Lady's Wedding-Ring, and some broken bits of old
Lockets of Gold, a Gold Watch, and a Purse with about 24*l.*
value in old pieces of Gold Coin, and several other things of
Value.

THIS was the greatest and the worst Prize that ever I was
concern'd in, for indeed, tho' as I have said above, I was
harden'd now beyond the Power of all Reflection in other
Cases, yet it really touch'd me to the very Soul, when I
look'd into this Treasure, to think of the poor disconsolate
Gentlewoman who had lost so much by the Fire besides; and

who would think to be sure that she had sav'd her Plate and best things; how she wou'd be surpriz'd and afflicted when she should find that she had been deceiv'd, and should find that the Person that took her Children and her Goods, had not come, as was pretended, from the Gentlewoman in the next Street, but that the Children had been put upon her without her own knowledge.

I SAY I confess the inhumanity of this Action mov'd me very much, and made me relent exceedingly, and Tears stood in my Eyes upon that Subject: But with all my Sense of its being cruel and Inhuman, I cou'd never find in my Heart to make any Restitution: The Reflection wore off, and I began quickly to forget the Circumstances that attended the taking them.

NOR was this all, for tho' by this jobb I was become considerably Richer than before, yet the Resolution I had formerly taken of leaving off this horrid Trade, when I had gotten a little more, did not return; but I must still get farther, and more; and the Avarice join'd so with the Success, that I had no more thoughts of coming to a timely Alteration of Life; tho' without it I cou'd expect no Safety, no Tranquility in the Possession of what I had so wickedly gain'd; but a little more, and a little more, was the Case still.

AT length yielding to the Importunities of my Crime, I cast off all Remorse and Repentance; and all the Reflections on that Head, turn'd to no more than this, that I might perhaps come to have one Booty more that might compleat my Desires; but tho' I certainly had that one Booty, yet every hit look'd towards another, and was so encouraging to me to go on with the Trade, that I had no Gust to the Thought of laying it down.

IN this Condition, harden'd by Success, and resolving to go on, I fell into the Snare in which I was appointed to meet with my last Reward for this kind of Life: But even this was not yet, for I met with several successful Adventures more in this way of being undone.

I remain'd still with my Governess, who was for a while

really concern'd for the Misfortune of my Comerade that had been hang'd, and who it seems knew enough of my Governess to have sent her the same way, and which made her very uneasy; indeed she was in a very great fright.

It is true, that when she was gone, and had not open'd her Mouth to tell what she knew, my Governess was easy as to that Point, and perhaps glad she was hang'd; for it was in her power to have obtain'd a Pardon at the Expence of her Friends;[1] But on the other Hand, the loss of her, and the Sense of her Kindness in not making her Market of what she knew, mov'd my Governess to Mourn very sincerely for her: I comforted her as well as I cou'd, and she in return harden'd me to Merit more compleatly the same Fate.

However as I have said it made me the more wary, and particularly I was very shie of Shoplifting, especially among the *Mercers*, and *Drapers* who are a Set of Fellows, that have their Eyes very much about them: I made a Venture or two among the Lace Folks, and the Mileners, and particularly at one Shop, where I got Notice of two young Women who were newly set up, and had not been bred to the Trade: There, I think I carried off a Peice of Bonelace, worth six or seven pound, and a Paper of Thread; but this was but once, it was a Trick that would not serve again.

It was always reckon'd a safe Job when we heard of a new Shop, and especially when the People were such as were not bred to Shops; such may depend upon it, that they will be visited once or twice at their beginning, and they must be very Sharp indeed if they can prevent it.

I Made another Adventure or two, but they were but Trifles too, tho' sufficient to live on; after this nothing considerable offering for a good while, I began to think that I must give over the Trade in Earnest; but my Governess, who was not willing to lose me, and expected great Things of me, brought me one Day into Company with a young Woman and a Fellow that went for her Husband, tho' as it appear'd afterwards she was not his Wife, but they were Partners it seems in the Trade they carried on; and Partners in something else too. *In short*, they robb'd together, lay together, were taken together, and at last were hang'd together.

I CAME into a kind of League with these two, by the help of my Governess, and they carried me out into three or four Adventures, where I rather saw them commit some Course and unhandy Robberies, in which nothing but a great Stock of impudence on their Side, and gross Negligence on the Peoples Side who were robb'd, could have made them Successful; so I resolv'd from that time forward to be very Cautious how I Adventur'd upon any thing with them; and indeed when two or three unlucky Projects were propos'd by them, I declin'd the offer, and perswaded them against it: One time they particularly propos'd Robbing a Watchmaker of 3 Gold Watches, which they had Ey'd in the Day time, and found the Place where he laid them; one of them had so many Keys of all kinds, that he made no Question to open the Place, where the Watchmaker had laid them; and so we made a kind of an Appointment; but when I came to look narrowly into the Thing, I found they propos'd breaking open the House; and this as a thing out of my Way, I would not Embark in; so they went without me: They did get into the House by main Force, and broke up the lock'd Place where the Watches were, but found but one of the Gold Watches, and a Silver one, which they took, and got out of the House again very clear, but the Family being alarm'd cried out Thieves, and the Man was pursued and taken, the young Woman had got off too, but unhappily was stop'd at a Distance, and the Watches found upon her; and thus I had a second Escape, for they were convicted, and both hang'd, being old Offenders, tho' but young People; as *I said before*, that they robbed together, and lay together, so now they hang'd together, and there ended my new Partnership.

I BEGAN now to be very wary, having so narrowly escap'd a Scouring,[1] and having such an Example before me; but I had a new Tempter, who prompted me every Day, I mean my Governess; and now a Prize presented, which as it came by her Management, so she expected a good Share of the

Booty; there was a good Quantity of Flanders-Lace Lodg'd in a private House, where she had gotten Intelligence of it; and Flanders-Lace, being then Prohibited,[1] it was a good Booty to any Custom-House Officer that could come at it: I had a full Account from my Governess, as well of the Quantity as of the very Place where it was conceal'd, and I went to a Custom-House Officer, and told him I had such a Discovery to make to him, of such a Quantity of Lace, if he would assure me that I should have my due Share of the Reward: This was so just an offer, that nothing could be fairer; so he agreed, and taking a Constable, and me with him, we beset the House; as I told him, I could go directly to the Place, He left it to me, and the Hole being very dark, I squeez'd myself into it with a Candle in my Hand, and so reach'd the Peices out to him, taking care as I gave him some, so to secure as much about myself as I could conveniently Dispose of: There was near 300*l*. worth of Lace in the whole; and I secur'd about 50*l*. worth of it to myself: The People of the House were not owners of the Lace, but a Merchant who had entrusted them with it; so that they were not so surpriz'd as I thought they would be.

I LEFT the Officer overjoy'd with his Prize, and fully satisfy'd with what he had got; and appointed to meet him at a House of his own directing, where I came after I had dispos'd of the Cargo I had about me, of which he had not the least Suspicion; when I came to him, he began to Capitulate with me, believing I did not understand the right I had to a Share in the Prize, and would fain have put me off with Twenty Pound, but I let him know that I was not so ignorant as he suppos'd I was; and yet I was glad too, that he offer'd to bring me to a certainty;[2] I ask'd 100*l*. and he rise up to 30*l*. I fell to 80*l*. and he rise again to 40*l*. in a Word, he offer'd 50*l*. and I consented, only demanding a Peice of Lace, which I thought came to about 8 or 9 Pound, as if it had been for my own Wear, and he agreed to it, so I got 50*l*. in Money paid me that same Night, and made an End of the Bargain; nor did he ever know who I was, or where to enquire for me; so that if it had been discover'd, that part of the Goods were embezzel'd; he could have made no Challenge upon me for it.

I VERY punctually divided this Spoil with my Governess, and I pass'd with her from this time for a very dextcrous Manager in the nicest Cases; I found that this last was the best, and easiest sort of Work that was in my way, and I made it my business to enquire out prohibited Goods; and after buying some usually betray'd them, but none of these Discoveries amounted to any thing Considerable; not like that I related just now; but I was willing to act safe, and was still Cautious of running the great Risques which I found others did, and in which they Miscarried every Day.

THE next thing of Moment, was an attempt at a Gentlewoman's gold Watch, it happen'd in a Crowd, at a Meeting-House, where I was in very great Danger of being taken; I had full hold of her Watch, but giving a great Jostle, as if some body had thrust me against her, and in the Juncture giving the Watch a fair pull, I found it would not come, so I let it go that Moment, and cried out as if I had been kill'd, that some body had Trod upon my Foot, and that there was certainly *Pick-pockets* there; for some body or other had given a pull at my Watch, for you are to observe, that on these Adventures we always went very well Dress'd, and I had very good Cloaths on, and a Gold Watch by my Side, as like a Lady as other Folks.

I HAD no sooner said so, but the tother Gentlewoman cried out *a Pick-pocket* too, for some body, *she said*, had try'd to pull her Watch away.

WHEN I touch'd her Watch, I was close to her, but when I cry'd out, I stop'd as it were short, and the Crowd bearing her forward a little, she made a Noise too, but it was at some Distance from me, so that she did not in the least suspect me; but when she cried out *a Pick-pocket*, some body cried Ay, and here has been another, this Gentlewoman has been attempted too.

AT that very instant, a little farther in the Crowd, and very

Luckily too, they cried out *a Pick-pocket* again, and really seiz'd a young Fellow in the very Fact. This, tho' unhappy for the Wretch was very opportunely for my Case, tho' I had carried it off handsomely enough before, but now it was out of Doubt, and all the loose part of the Crowd run that way, and the poor Boy was deliver'd up to the Rage of the Street,[1] which is a Cruelty I need not describe, and which however they are always glad of, rather than to be sent to *Newgate*, where they lie often a long time, till they are almost perish'd, and sometimes they are hang'd, and the best they can look for, if they are Convicted, is to be Transported.

THIS was a narrow Escape to me, and I was so frighted, that I ventur'd no more at Gold Watches a great while; there was indeed a great many concurring Circumstances in this Adventure, which assisted to my Escape; but the chief was, that the Woman whose Watch I had pull'd at was a Fool; that is to say, she was Ignorant of the nature of the Attempt, which one would have thought she should not have been, seeing she was wise enough to fasten her Watch, so, that it could not be slipt up; but she was in such a Fright, that she had no thought about her proper for the Discovery; for she, when she felt the pull scream'd out, and push'd herself forward, and put all the People about her into disorder, but said not a Word of her Watch, or of a *Pick-pocket*, for at least two Minutes time; which was time enough for me, and to spare; for as I had cried out behind her, *as I have said*, and bore myself back in the Crowd as she bore forward; there were several People, at least seven or eight, the Throng being still moving on, that were got between me and her in that time, and then I crying out *a Pick-pocket*, rather sooner than she, or at least as soon, she might as well be the Person suspected as I, and the People were confus'd in their Enquiry; whereas, had she with a Presence of Mind needful on such an Occasion, as soon as she felt the pull, not skream'd out as she did, but turn'd immediately round, and seiz'd the next Body that was behind her, she had infallibly taken me.

THIS is a Direction not of the kindest Sort to the Fraternity; but 'tis certainly a Key to the Clue of *a Pick-pockets Motions*,[1] and whoever can follow it, will as certainly catch the Thief as he will be sure to miss if he does not.

I HAD another Adventure, which puts this Matter out of doubt, and which may be an Instruction for Posterity in the Case of *a Pick-pocket*, my good old Governess to give a short touch at her History, tho' she had left off the Trade, was as I may say, born *a Pick-pocket*, and as I understood afterward had run thro' all the several Degrees of that Art, and yet had never been taken but once; when she was so grossly detected, that she was convicted and orderd to be Transported; but being a Woman of a rare Tongue, and withal having Money in her Pocket; she found Means, the Ship putting into *Ireland* for Provisions, to get on Shore there, where she liv'd and practis'd her old Trade for some Years; when falling into another sort of bad Company, she turn'd Midwife and Procuress,[2] and play'd a Hundred Pranks there, which she gave me a little History of in Confidence between us as we grew more intimate; and it was to this wicked Creature that I ow'd all the Art and Dexterity I arriv'd to, in which there were few that ever went beyond me, or that practis'd so long without any Misfortune.

IT was after those Adventures in *Ireland*, and when she was pretty well known in that Country, that she left *Dublin*, and came over to *England*, where the time of her Transportation being not expir'd, she left her former Trade, for fear of falling into bad Hands again, for then she was sure to have gone to Wreck: Here she set up the same Trade she had followed in *Ireland*, in which she soon by her admirable Management, and a good Tongue, arriv'd to the Height, which I have already describ'd, and indeed began to be Rich tho' her Trade fell off again afterwards; as I have hinted before.

I mention thus much of the History of this Woman here, the better to account for the concern she had in the wicked Life I was now leading; into all the particulars of which she led me as it were by the Hand, and gave me such Directions, and I so well follow'd them, that I grew the greatest Artist of my time, and work'd myself out of every Danger with such Dexterity, that when several more of my Comrades run themselves into *Newgate* presently, and by that time they had been Half a Year at the Trade, I had now Practis'd upwards of five Year, and the People at *Newgate*, did not so much as know me; they had heard much of me indeed, and often expected me there; but I always got off, tho' many times in the extreamest Danger.

ONE of the greatest Dangers I was now in, was that I was too well known among the Trade, and some of them whose hatred was owing rather to Envy, than any Injury I had done them began to be Angry, that I should always Escape when they were always catch'd and hurried to *Newgate*. These were they that gave me the Name of *Moll Flanders*: For it was no more of Affinity with my real Name, or with any of the Names I had ever gone by, than black is of Kin to white, except that once, as before I call'd my self Mrs. *Flanders*, when I sheltered myself in the *Mint*; but that these Rogues never knew, nor could I ever learn how they came to give me the Name, or what the Occasion of it was.

I WAS soon inform'd that some of these who were gotten fast into *Newgate*, had vowed to Impeach me;[1] and as I knew that two or three of them were but too able to do it, I was under a great concern about it, and kept within Doors for a good while; but my Governess who I always made Partner in my Success, and who now plaid a sure Game with me, for that she had a Share of the Gain, and no Share in the hazard, *I say*, my Governess was something impatient of my leading such a useless unprofitable Life, as she call'd it; and she laid a new Contrivance for my going Abroad, and this was to Dress me up in Mens Cloths, and so put me into a new kind of Practise.

I WAS Tall and Personable, but a little too smooth Fac'd for a Man; however as I seldom went Abroad but in the Night, it did well enough; but it was a long time before I could behave in my new Cloths: I mean, as to my Craft; it was impossible to be so Nimble, so Ready, so Dexterous at these things, in a Dress so contrary to Nature; and as I did every thing Clumsily, so I had neither the success, or the easiness of Escape that I had before, and I resolv'd to leave it off; but that Resolution was confirm'd soon after by the following Accident.

As my Governess had disguis'd me like a Man, so she joyn'd me with a Man, a young Fellow that was Nimble enough at his Business, and for about three Weeks we did very well together. Our principal Trade was watching Shop-Keepers Compters, and Slipping off any kind of Goods we could see carelesly laid any where, and we made several very good Bargains as we call'd them at this Work: And as we kept always together, so we grew very intimate, yet he never knew that I was not a Man; nay, tho' I several times went home with him to his Lodgings, according as our business directed, and four or five times lay with him all Night: But our Design lay another way, and it was absolutely necessary to me to conceal my Sex from him, as appear'd afterwards: The Circumstances of our Living, coming in late, and having such and such Business to do as requir'd that no Body should be trusted with coming into our Lodgings, were such as made it impossible to me to refuse lying with him, unless I would have own'd my Sex, and as it was I effectually conceal'd my self.

But his ill, and my good Fortune, soon put an end to this Life, which I must own I was sick of too, on several other Accounts: We had made several Prizes in this new way of Business, but the last would have been extraordinary; there was a Shop in a certain Street which had a Warehouse behind it that look'd into another Street, the House making the corner of the turning.

Through the Window of the Warehouse we saw lying on the Counter or Show-board which was just before it, Five pieces of Silks, besides other Stuffs; and tho' it was almost dark, yet the People being busie in the fore shop with

Customers, had not had time to shut up those Windows, or
else had forgot it.

THIS the young Fellow was so overjoy'd with, that he
could not restrain himself, it lay all within his reach he said,
and he swore violently to me that he would have it, if he
broke down the House for it; I disswaded him a little, but
saw there was no remedy, so he run rashly upon it, slipt out
a Square out of the Sash Window dexterously enough, and
without noise, and got out four pieces of the Silks, and came
with them towards me, but was immediately pursued with a
terrible Clutter and Noise; we were standing together indeed,
but I had not taken any of the Goods out of his Hand, when
I said to him hastily, you are undone, fly for God sake; he
run like Lightning, and I too, but the pursuit was hotter after
him because he had the Goods, than after me; he dropt two
of the Pieces which stop'd them a little, but the Crowd
encreas'd and pursued us both; they took him soon after
with the other two pieces upon him, and then the rest
followed me; I run for it and got into my Governesses House,
whither some quick-eyed People follow'd me so warmly as
to fix me there; they did not immediately knock at the Door,
by which I got time to throw off my Disguise, and dress me
in my own Cloths; besides, when they came there, my
Governess, who had her Tale ready, kept her Door shut, and
call'd out to them and told them there was no Man came in
there; the People affirm'd there did a Man come in there,
and swore they would break open the Door.

MY Governess, not at all surpriz'd, spoke calmly to them,
told them they should very freely come and search her
House, if they would bring a Constable, and let in none but
such as the Constable would admit, for it was unreasonable
to let in a whole Crowd; this they could not refuse, tho' they
were a Crowd; so a Constable was fetch'd immediately, and
she very freely open'd the Door, and the Constable kept the
Door, and the Men he appointed search'd the House, my
Governess going with them from Room to Room; when she
came to my Room she call'd to me, and said aloud; Cousin,

pray open the Door, here's some Gentlemen that must come and look into your Room.

I HAD a little Girl with me, which was my Governesses Grand-child, as she call'd her; and I bad her open the Door, and there sat I at work with a great litter of things about me, as if I had been at Work all Day, being my self quite undress'd, with only Night-cloaths on my Head, and a loose Morning Gown wrapt about me: My Governess made a kind of excuse for their disturbing me, telling me partly the occasion of it, and that she had no Remedy but to open the Doors to them, and let them satisfie themselves, for all she could say to them would not satisfie them: I sat still, and bid them search the Room if they pleas'd, for if there was any Body in the House, I was sure they was not in my Room; and as for the rest of the House I had nothing to say to that, I did not understand what they look'd for.

EVERY thing look'd so innocent and so honest about me, that they treated me civiller than I expected, but it was not till they had search'd the Room to a nicety, even under the Bed, in the Bed, and every where else, where it was possible any thing cou'd be hid; when they had done this, and cou'd find nothing, they ask'd my Pardon for troubling me, and went down.

WHEN they had thus searched the House from Bottom to Top, and then from Top to Bottom, and cou'd find nothing, they appeas'd the Mob pretty well; but they carried my Governess before the Justice: Two Men swore that they see the Man, who they pursued, go into her House: My Governess rattled and made a great noise that her House should be insulted, and that she should be used thus for nothing; that if a Man did come in, he might go out again presently for ought she knew, for she was ready to make Oath that no Man had been within her Doors all that Day as she knew of, and that was very true indeed; that it might be indeed that as she was above Stairs, any Fellow in a Fright might find the Door open, and run in for shelter when he was pursued, but that she knew nothing of it; and if it had been so, he certainly went out again, perhaps at the other Door, for she had another Door into an Alley, and so had made his escape and cheated them all.

THIS was indeed probable enough, and the Justice satisfied himself with giving her an Oath, that she had not receiv'd or admitted any Man into her House to conceal him, or protect or hide him from Justice: This Oath she might justly take, and did so, and so she was dismiss'd.

IT is easie to judge what a fright I was in upon this occasion, and it was impossible for my Governess ever to bring me to Dress in that Disguise again; for, as I told her, I should certainly betray my self.

MY poor Partner in this Mischief was now in a bad Case, for he was carried away before my Lord Mayor, and by his Worship committed to *Newgate*, and the People that took him were so willing, as well as able, to Prosecute him, that they offer'd themselves to enter into Recognisances to appear at the Sessions,[1] and persue the Charge against him.

HOWEVER, he got his Indictment deferr'd, upon promise to discover his Accomplices, and particularly, the Man that was concern'd with him in this Robbery, and he fail'd not to do his endeavour, for he gave in my Name who he call'd *Gabriel Spencer*,[2] which was the Name I went by to him, and here appear'd the Wisdom of my concealing my Name and Sex from him, which if he had ever known I had been undone.

HE did all he cou'd to discover this *Gabriel Spencer*; he describ'd me, he discover'd the place where he said I Lodg'd, and in a word, all the Particulars that he cou'd of my Dwelling; but having conceal'd the main Circumstances of my Sex from him, I had a vast Advantage, and he never cou'd hear of me; he brought two or three Families into Trouble by his endeavouring to find me out, but they knew nothing of me, any more than that he had a Fellow with him that they had seen, but knew nothing of; and as for my Governess, tho' she was the means of his coming to me, yet it was done at second hand, and he knew nothing of her.

THIS turn'd to his Disadvantage, for having promis'd Discoveries, but not being able to make it good, it was look'd upon as a trifling with the Justice of the City, and he was the more fiercely persued by the Shopkeepers who took him.

I WAS however terribly uneasie all this while, and that I might be quite out of the way, I went away from my Governesses for a while; but not knowing whither to wander, I took a Maid Servant with me, and took the Stage Coach to *Dunstable* to my old Landlord and Landlady, where I had liv'd so handsomly with my *Lancashire* Husband: Here I told her a formal Story, that I expected my Husband every Day from *Ireland*, and that I had sent a Letter to him that I would meet him at *Dunstable* at her House, and that he would certainly Land, if the Wind was fair, in a few Days, so that I was come to spend a few Days with them till he should come, for he would either come Post, or in the *West-Chester* Coach,[1] I knew not which, but which soever it was, he would be sure to come to that House to meet me.

MY Landlady was mighty glad to see me, and my Landlord made such a stir with me, that if I had been a Princess I cou'd not have been better used, and here I might have been welcome a Month or two if I had thought fit.

BUT my Business was of another Nature, I was very uneasie (tho' so well Disguis'd that it was scarce possible to Detect me) least this Fellow should some how or other find me out; and tho' he cou'd not charge me with this Robbery, having perswaded him not to venture, and having also done nothing in it my self but run away, yet he might have charg'd me with other things, and have bought his own Life at the Expence of mine.

THIS fill'd me with horrible Apprehensions: I had no Recourse, no Friend, no Confident but my old Governess, and I knew no Remedy but to put my Life in her Hands, and so I did, for I let her know where to send to me, and had several Letters from her while I stayed here, some of them almost scar'd me out of my Wits; but at last she sent me the joyful News that he was hang'd, which was the best News to me that I had heard a great while.

I HAD stay'd here five Weeks, and liv'd very comfortably indeed, (the secret Anxiety of my Mind excepted) but when I receiv'd this Letter I look'd pleasantly again, and told my Landlady that I had receiv'd a Letter from my Spouse in *Ireland*, that I had the good News of his being very well, but had the bad News that his business would not permit him to come away so soon as he expected, and so I was like to go back again without him.

MY Landlady complemented me upon the good News however, that I had heard he was well, for I have observ'd, Madam, *says she*, you han't been so pleasant as you us'd to be; you have been over Head and Ears in Care for him, I dare say, *says the good Woman*; 'tis easie to be seen there's an alteration in you for the better, *says she*: Well, I am sorry the Esquire can't come yet, *says my Landlord*, I should have been heartily glad to have seen him, but I hope, when you have certain News of his coming, you'll take a step hither again, Madam; *says he*, you shall be very welcome whenever you please to come.

WITH all these fine Complements we parted, and I came merry enough to *London*, and found my Governess as well pleas'd as I was; and now she told me she would never recommend any Partner to me again, for she always found, *she said*, that I had the best luck when I ventur'd by my self; and so indeed I had, for I was seldom in any Danger when I was by my self, or if I was, I got out of it with more Dexterity than when I was entangled with the dull Measures of other People, who had perhaps less forecast, and were more rash and impatient than I; for tho' I had as much Courage to venture as any of them, yet I used more caution before I undertook a thing, and had more Presence of Mind when I was to bring my self off.

I HAVE often wondered even at my own hardiness another way, that when all my Companions were surpriz'd, and fell so suddainly into the Hand of Justice, and that I so narrowly

escap'd, yet I could not all that while enter into one serious
Resolution to leave off this Trade; and especially Considering
that I was now very far from being poor, that the Temptation
of Necessity, which is generally the Introduction of all such
Wickedness was now remov'd; for I had near 500*l.* by me in
ready Money, on which I might have liv'd very well, if I had
thought fit to have retir'd; but *I say*, I had not so much as
the least inclination to leave off; no not so much as I had
before when I had but 200*l.* before-hand, and when I had
no such frightful Examples before my Eyes as these were;
From hence 'tis Evident to me, that when once we are
harden'd in Crime, no Fear can affect us, no Example give
us any warning.

I HAD indeed one Comrade, whose Fate went very near me
for a good while, tho' I wore it off too in time, that Case was
indeed very unhappy; I had made a Prize of a Piece of very
good Damask in a *Mercers* Shop, and went clear off myself;
but had convey'd the Peice to this Companion of mine, when
we went out of the Shop; and she went one way, and I went
another: We had not been long out of the Shop, but the
Mercer mist his Peice of Stuff, and sent his Messengers, one,
one way, and one another, and they presently seiz'd her that
had the Peice, with the Damask upon her; as for me, I had
very Luckily step'd into a House where there was a Lace
Chamber, up one Pair of Stairs, and had the Satisfaction, or
the Terror indeed of looking out of the Window upon the
Noise they made, and seeing the poor Creature drag'd away
in Triumph to the Justice, who immediately committed her
to *Newgate*.

I WAS careful to attempt nothing in the Lace-Chamber,
but tumbl'd their Goods pretty much to spend time; then
bought a few Yards of Edging, and paid for it, and came
away very sad Hearted indeed; for the poor Woman, who
was in Tribulation for what I only had stolen.

HERE again my old Caution stood me in good stead;
Namely, that tho' I often robb'd with these People, yet I
never let them know who I was, or where I Lodg'd; nor

could they ever find out my Lodging, tho' they often endeavour'd to Watch me to it. They all knew me by the Name of *Moll Flanders*, tho' even some of them rather believ'd I was she, than knew me to be so; my Name was publick among them indeed; but how to find me out they knew not, nor so much as how to guess at my Quarters, whether they were at the East-End of the Town, or the West; and this wariness was my safety upon all these Occasions.

I KEPT close a great while upon the Occasion of this Womans disaster; I knew that if I should do any thing that should Miscarry, and should be carried to Prison she would be there, and ready to Witness against me, and perhaps save her Life at my Expence; I consider'd that I began to be very well known by Name at the *Old Baily*, tho' they did not know my Face; and that if I should fall into their Hands, I should be treated as an old Offender; and for this Reason, I was resolv'd to see what this poor Creatures Fate should be before I stirr'd Abroad, tho' several times in her Distress I convey'd Money to her for her Relief.

AT length she came to her Tryal, she pleaded she did not steal the Things; but that one Mrs. *Flanders*, as she heard her call'd, (for she did not know her) gave the Bundle to her after they came out of the Shop, and bad her carry it Home to her Lodging. They ask'd her where this Mrs. *Flanders* was? but she could not produce her, neither could she give the least Account of me; and the *Mercers* Men swearing positively that she was in the Shop when the Goods were stolen; that they immediately miss'd them, and pursu'd her, and found them upon her; Thereupon the Jury brought her in Guilty; but the Court considering that she really was not the Person that stole the Goods, an inferiour Assistant, and that it was very possible she could not find out this Mrs. *Flanders*, *meaning me*, tho' it would save her Life, which indeed was true; I say considering all this, they allow'd her to be Transported, which was the utmost Favour she could obtain, only that the Court told her, that if she could in the mean time produce the said Mrs. *Flanders*, they would intercede for her Pardon, that is to say, if she could find me out, and hang me, she should not be Transported: This I took care to make impossible to her, and so she was Shipp'd off in pursuance of her Sentence a little while after.

I MUST repeat it again, that the Fate of this poor Woman troubl'd me exceedingly; and I began to be very pensive, knowing that I was really the Instrument of her disaster; but the Preservation of my own Life, which was so evidently in Danger, took off all my tenderness; and seeing she was not put to Death, I was very easie at her Transportation, because she was then out of the way of doing me any Mischief whatever should happen.

THE Disaster of this Woman was some Months before that of the last recited Story, and was indeed partly the Occasion of my Governess proposing to Dress me up in Mens Cloths, that I might go about unobserv'd, as indeed I did; but I was soon tir'd of that Disguise, as *I have said*, for indeed it expos'd me to too many Difficulties.

I WAS now easie, as to all Fear of Witnesses against me, for all those, that had either been concern'd with me, or that knew me by the Name of *Moll Flanders*, were either hang'd or Transported; and if I should have had the Misfortune to be taken, I might call myself any thing else, as well as *Moll Flanders*, and no old Sins could be plac'd to my Account; so I began to run a Tick[1] again, with the more freedom, and several successful Adventures I made, tho' not such as I had made before.

WE had at that time another Fire happen'd not a great way off from the Place where my Governess liv'd, and I made an attempt there, as before, but as I was not soon enough before the Crowd of People came in, and could not get to the House I aim'd at; instead of a Prize, I got a mischief, which had almost put a Period to my Life, and all my wicked doings together; for the Fire being very furious, and the People in a great Fright in removing their Goods, and throwing them out of Window; a Wench from out of a Window threw a

Featherbed just upon me; it is true, the Bed being soft it broke no Bones; but as the weight was great, and made greater by the Fall, it beat me down, and laid me dead for a while; nor did the People concern themselves much to deliver me from it, or to recover me at all; but I lay like one Dead and neglected a good while; till some body going to remove the Bed out of the way, helped me up; it was indeed a wonder the People in the House had not thrown other Goods out after it, and which might have fallen upon it, and then I had been inevitably kill'd; but I was reserved for further Afflictions.

THIS Accident however spoil'd my Market for that time, and I came Home to my Governess very much hurt, and Bruised, and Frighted to the last degree, and it was a good while before she could set me upon my Feet again.

IT was now a Merry time of the Year, and *Bartholomew* Fair[1] was begun; I had never made any Walks that Way, nor was the common Part of the Fair of much Advantage to me; but I took a turn this Year into the Cloisters,[2] and among the rest, I fell into one of the Raffling Shops:[3] It was a thing of no great Consequence to me, nor did I expect to make much of it; but there came a Gentleman extreamly well Dress'd, and very Rich, and as 'tis frequent to talk to every Body in those Shops he singl'd me out, and was very particular with me; first told he me he would put in for me to Raffle, and did so; and some small matter coming to his Lot, he presented it to me,[4] I think it was a Feather Muff: Then he continu'd to keep talking to me with a more than common Appearance of Respect; but still very civil and much like a Gentleman.

HE held me in talk so long till at last he drew me out of the Raffling Place to the Shop-Door, and then to take a walk in the Cloister, still talking of a Thousand things Cursorily without any thing to the purpose; at last he told me that without Complement he was charm'd with my Company, and ask'd me if I durst trust myself in a Coach with him; he told me he was a Man of Honour, and would not offer any thing to me unbecoming him as such: I seem'd to decline it a while, but suffer'd myself to be importun'd a little, and then yielded.

I WAS at a loss in my Thoughts to conclude at first what this Gentleman design'd; but I found afterward he had had some drink in his Head; and that he was not very unwilling to have some more: He carried me in the Coach to the *Spring-Garden*, at *Knight's-Bridge*,[1] where we walk'd in the Gardens, and he Treated me very handsomely; but I found he drank very freely, he press'd me also to drink, but I declin'd it.

HITHERTO he kept his Word with me, and offer'd me nothing amiss; we came away in the Coach again, and he brought me into the Streets and by this time it was near Ten a Clock at Night, and he stop'd the Coach at a House, where it seems he was acquainted, and where they made no scruple to show us up Stairs into a Room with a Bed in it; at first I seem'd to be unwilling to go up, but after a few Words, I yielded to that too, being indeed willing to see the End of it, and in Hopes to make something of it at last; as for the Bed, &c. I was not much concern'd about that Part.

HERE he began to be a little freer with me than he had promis'd; and I by little and little yielded to every thing, so that in a Word, he did what he pleas'd with me; I need say no more; all this while he drank freely too, and about One in the Morning we went into the Coach again; the Air, and the shaking of the Coach made the Drink he had get more up in his Head than it was before, and he grew uneasy in the Coach, and was for acting over again, what he had been doing before; but as I thought my Game now secure, I resisted him, and brought him to be a little still, which had not lasted five Minutes, but he fell fast asleep.

I TOOK this opportunity to search him to a Nicety; I took a gold Watch, with a silk Purse of Gold, his fine full bottom Perrewig, and silver fring'd Gloves, his Sword, and fine Snuff-box, and gently opening the Coach-door, stood ready to jump out while the Coach was going on; but the Coach stopping in the narrow Street beyond *Temple-Bar*[2] to let another Coach pass, I got softly out, fasten'd the Door again, and gave my Gentleman and the Coach the slip both together, and never heard more of them.[1]

THIS was an Adventure indeed unlook'd for, and perfectly undesign'd by me; tho' I was not so past the Merry part of Life, as to forget how to behave, when a Fop so blinded by his Appetite should not know an old Woman from a young: I did not indeed look so old as I was by ten or twelve Year; yet I was not a young Wench of Seventeen, and it was easie enough to be distinguish'd: There is nothing so absurd, so surfeiting, so ridiculous as a Man heated by Wine in his Head, and a wicked Gust in his Inclination together; he is in the possession of two Devils at once, and can no more govern himself by his Reason than a Mill can Grind without Water; His Vice tramples upon all that was in him that had any good in it, if any such thing there was; nay, his very Sense is blinded by its own Rage, and he acts Absurdities even in his View; such is Drinking more, when he is Drunk already; picking up a common Woman, without regard to what she is, or who she is; whether Sound or rotten, Clean or Unclean; whether Ugly or Handsome, whether Old or Young, and so blinded, as not really to distinguish; such a Man is worse than Lunatick; prompted by his vicious corrupted Head he no more knows what he is doing, than this Wretch of mine knew when I pick'd his Pocket of his Watch and his Purse of Gold.

THESE are the Men of whom *Solomon* says, *they go like an Ox to the slaughter, till a Dart strikes through their Liver*;[2] an admirable Description, *by the way*, of the foul Disease, which is a poisonous deadly Contagion mingling with the Blood, whose Center or Fountain is in the Liver; from whence, by the swift Circulation of the whole Mass, that dreadful nauceous Plague strikes immediately thro' his Liver, and his Spirits are infected, his Vitals stab'd thro' as with a Dart.

IT is true this poor unguarded Wretch was in no Danger from me, tho' I was greatly apprehensive at first, of what Danger I might be in from him; but he was really to be

pityed in one respect, that he seem'd to be a good sort of a
Man in himself; a Gentleman that had no harm in his
Design; a Man of Sense, and of a fine Behaviour; a comely
handsome Person, a sober solid Countenance, a charming
beautiful Face, and everything that cou'd be agreeable; only
had unhappily had some Drink the Night before, had not
been in Bed, as he told me when we were together, was hot,
and his Blood fir'd with Wine, and in that Condition his
Reason *as it were* asleep, had given him up.[1]

As for me, my Business was his Money, and what I could
make of him, and after that if I could have found out any
way to have done it, I would have sent him safe home to his
House, and to his Family, for 'twas ten to one but he had an
honest virtuous Wife, and innocent Children, that were
anxious for his Safety, and would have been glad to have
gotten him Home, and have taken care of him, till he was
restor'd to himself; and then with what Shame and Regret
would he look back upon himself? how would he reproach
himself with associating himself with a Whore? pick'd up in
the worst of all Holes, the Cloister, among the Dirt and
Filth of all the Town? how would he be trembling for fear
he had got the Pox, for fear a Dart had struck through his
Liver, and hate himself every time he look'd back upon the
Madness and Brutality of his Debauch? how would he, if he
had any Principles of Honour, as I verily believe he had, I
say how would he abhor the Thought of giving any ill
Distemper, if he had it, as for ought he knew he might, to
his Modest and Virtuous Wife, and thereby sowing the
Contagion in the Life-blood of his Posterity?

WOULD such Gentlemen but consider the contemptible
Thoughts which the very Women they are concern'd with,
in such Cases as these, have of them, it wou'd be a surfeit to
them: As I said above, they value not the Pleasure, they are
rais'd by no Inclination to the Man, the passive Jade thinks
of no Pleasure but the Money; and when he is as it were
drunk in the Extasies of his wicked Pleasure, her Hands are
in his Pockets searching for what she can find there; and of

which he can no more be sensible in the Moment of his Folly, than he can fore-think of it when he goes about it.

I KNEW a Woman that was so dexterous with a Fellow, who indeed deserv'd no better usage, that while he was busie with her another way, convey'd his Purse with twenty Guineas in it out of his Fob Pocket, where he had put it for fear of her, and put another Purse with guilded Counters in it into the room of it: After he had done, he says to her, now han't you pick'd my Pocket? she jested with him, and told him she suppos'd he had not much to loose; he put his Hand to his Fob, and with his Fingers felt that his Purse was there, which fully satisfy'd him, and so she brought off his Money; and this was a Trade with her, she kept a sham Gold Watch, that is a Watch of Silver Guilt, and a purse of Counters in her Pocket to be ready on all such Occasions; and I doubt not practis'd it with Success.

I CAME home with this last Booty to my Governess, and really when I told her the Story it so affected her, that she was hardly able to forbear Tears, to think how such a Gentleman run a daily Risque of being undone, every time a Glass of Wine got into his Head.

BUT as to the Purchase I got, and how entirely I stript him, she told me it pleas'd her wonderfully; nay, Child, *says she*, the usage may, for ought I know, do more to reform him, than all the Sermons that ever he will hear in his Life, and if the remainder of the Story be true, so it did.

I FOUND the next Day she was wonderful inquisitive about this Gentleman; the description I had given her of him, his Dress, his Person, his Face, every thing concur'd to make her think of a Gentleman whose Character she knew, and Family too; she mus'd a while, and I going still on with the Particulars, she starts up, *says she*, I'll lay a Hundred Pound I know the Gentleman.

I AM sorry you do, *says I*, for I would not have him expos'd on any account in the World; he has had Injury enough already by me, and I would not be instrumental to do him any more: No, no *says she*, I will do him no Injury,

I assure you, but you may let me satisfie my Curiosity a little, for if it is he, I warrant you I find it out: I was a little startled at that, and told her with an apparent concern in my Face, that by the same Rule he might find me out, and then I was undone: *she return'd warmly,* why, do you think I will betray you, Child? No, no, *says she,* not for all he is worth in the World; I have kept your Counsel in worse things than these, sure you may trust me in this: So I said no more at that time.

SHE laid her Scheme another way, and without acquainting me of it, but she was resolv'd to find it out, if possible; so she goes to a certain Friend of hers who was acquainted in the Family, that she guess'd at, and told her Friend she had some extraordinary business with such a Gentleman (who by the way was no less than a Baronet, and of a very good Family) and that she knew not how to come at him without somebody to introduce her: Her Friend promis'd her very readily to do it, and accordingly goes to the House to see if the Gentleman was in Town.

THE next Day she comes to my Governess and tells her, that Sir ————— was at Home, but that he had met with a Disaster and was very ill, and there was no speaking with him; what Disaster, *says my Governess hastily,* as if she was surpriz'd at it? Why, *says her Friend,* he had been at *Hampstead* to Visit a Gentleman of his Acquaintance, and as he came back again he was set upon and Robb'd; and having got a little Drink too, as they suppose, the Rogues abus'd him, and he is very ill: Robb'd, *says my Governess,* and what did they take from him; why, *says her Friend,* they took his Gold Watch, and his Gold Snuff-box, his fine Perriwig, and what Money he had in his Pocket, which was considerable to be sure, for Sir ————— never goes without a Purse of Guineas about him.

Pshaw! says my old Governess jeering, I warrant you he has got drunk now and got a Whore, and she has pick'd his Pocket, and so he comes home to his Wife and tells her he has been Robb'd; that's an old sham, a thousand such tricks are put upon the poor Women every Day.

FYE, *says her Friend*, I find you don't know Sir ————,
why he is as Civil a Gentleman, there is not a finer Man, nor
a soberer grave modester Person in the whole City; he abhors
such things, there's no Body that knows him will think such
a thing of him: Well, well, *says my Governess*, that's none of
my Business, if it was, I warrant I should find there was
something of that kind in it; your Modest Men in common
Opinion are sometimes no better than other People, only
they keep a better Character, or if you please, are the better
Hypocrites.

No, no, *says her Friend*, I can assure you Sir ———— is
no Hypocrite, he is really an honest sober Gentleman, and
he has certainly been Robb'd: Nay, *says my Governess*, it may
be he has, it is no Business of mine I tell you; I only want to
speak with him, my Business is of another Nature; but, *says
her Friend*, let your Business be of what nature it will, you
cannot see him yet, for he is not fit to be seen, for he is very
ill, and bruis'd very much: Ay, *says my Governess*, nay then
he has fallen into bad Hands to be sure; and then she ask'd
gravely, pray where is he bruised? Why in his Head, *says her
Friend*, and one of his Hands, and his Face, for they us'd him
barbarously. Poor Gentleman, *says my Governess*, I must
wait then till he recovers, and adds, I hope it will not be long,
for I want very much to speak with him.

AWAY she comes to me and tells me this Story, I have
found out your fine Gentleman, and a fine Gentleman he was,
says she, but Mercy on him, he is in a sad pickle now, I
wonder what the D————l you have done to him; why you
have almost kill'd him: I look'd at her with disorder enough;
I kill'd him! *says I*, you must mistake the Person, I am sure
I did nothing to him, he was very well when I left him, *said
I*, only drunk and fast asleep; I know nothing of that, *says
she*, but he is in a sad pickle now, and so she told me all that
her Friend had said to her: Well then, *says I*, he fell into bad
Hands after I left him, for I am sure I left him safe enough.

ABOUT ten Days after, or a little more, my Governess goes
again to her Friend, to introduce her to this Gentleman; she

had enquir'd other ways in the mean time, and found that he was about again, if not abroad again, so she got leave to speak with him.

SHE was a Woman of an admirable Address, and wanted no Body to introduce her; she told her Tale much better than I shall be able to tell it for her, for she was a Mistress of her Tongue, as I have said already: She told him that she came, tho' a Stranger, with a single design of doing him a Service, and he should find she had no other End in it; that as she came purely on so Friendly an account, she beg'd a promise from him, that if he did not accept what she should officiously propose, he would not take ill, that she meddl'd with what was not her Business; she assur'd him that as what she had to say was a Secret that belong'd to him only, so whether he accepted her offer or not, it should remain a Secret to all the World, unless he expos'd it himself; nor should his refusing her Service in it, make her so little show her Respect, as to do him the least Injury, so that he should be entirely at liberty to act as he thought fit.

HE look'd very shy at first, and said he knew nothing that related to him that requir'd much secresie; that he had never done any Man any wrong, and car'd not what any Body might say of him; that it was no part of his Character to be unjust to any Body, nor could he imagine in what any Man cou'd render him any Service; but that if it was so disinterested a Service as she said, he could not take it ill from any one that they should endeavour to serve him; and so, as it were, left her at liberty either to tell him, or not to tell him, as she thought fit.

SHE found him so perfectly indifferent, that she was almost afraid to enter into the point with him; but however, after some other Circumlocutions, she told him, that by a strange and unaccountable Accident she came to have a particular knowledge of the late unhappy Adventure he had fallen into; and that in such a manner, that there was no Body in the World but herself and him that were acquainted with it, no not the very Person that was with him.

HE look'd a little angrily at first, what Adventure? *said he*; why, Sir, *said she*, of your being Robb'd coming from *Knightsbr*———, *Hampstead*, Sir, I should say, *says she*; be not surpris'd, Sir, *says she*, that I am able to tell you every step you took that Day from the *Cloyster* in *Smithfield*, to the *Spring-Garden* at *Knightsbridge*, and thence to the ——— in the *Strand*, and how you were left asleep in the Coach afterwards; I say let not this surprize you, for Sir I do not come to make a Booty of you, I ask nothing of you, and I assure you the Woman that was with you knows nothing who you are, and never shall; and yet perhaps I may serve you farther still, for I did not come barely to let you know, that I was inform'd of these things, as if I wanted a Bribe to conceal them; assure your self, Sir, *said she*, that whatever you think fit to do or say to me, it shall be all a secret as it is, as much as if I were in my Grave.

HE was astonish'd at her Discourse, and said gravely to her, Madam, you are a Stranger to me, but it is very unfortunate, that you should be let into the Secret of the worst action of my Life, and a thing that I am so justly asham'd of, that the only satisfaction of it to me was, that I thought it was known only to God and my own Conscience: Pray, Sir, *says she*, do not reckon the Discovery of it to me, to be any part of your Misfortune; it was a thing, I believe, you were surprised into, and perhaps the Woman us'd some Art to prompt you to it; however, you will never find any just Cause, *said she*, to repent that I came to hear of it; nor can your own Mouth be more silent in it than I have been, and ever shall be.

WELL, *says he*, but let me do some Justice to the Woman too, whoever she is, I do assure you she prompted me to nothing, she rather declin'd me, it was my own Folly and Madness that brought me into it all, ay and brought her into it too; I must give her her due so far: As to what she took from me, I cou'd expect no less from her in the condition I was in, and to this Hour I know not whether she Robb'd me or the Coachman; if she did it I forgive her, and I think all Gentlemen that do so, should be us'd in the same manner;

but I am more concern'd for some other things than I am
for all that she took from me.

MY Governess now began to come into the whole matter,
and he open'd himself freely to her; first, she said to him, in
answer to what he had said about me, I am glad Sir you are
so just to the Person that you were with; I assure you she is
a Gentlewoman, and no Woman of the Town; and however
you prevail'd with her so far as you did, I am sure 'tis not her
Practise; you run a great venture indeed, Sir, but if that be
any part of your Care, I am perswaded you may be perfectly
easie, for I dare assure you no Man has touch'd her, before
you, since her Husband, and he has been dead now almost
eight Year.

IT appear'd that this was his Grievance, and that he was in
a very great fright about it; however, when my Governess
said this to him he appeared very well pleased; and said,
well, Madam, to be plain with you, if I was satisfy'd of that,
I should not so much value what I lost; for as to that, the
Temptation was great, and perhaps she was poor and wanted
it: If she had not been poor Sir ———, *says my Governess*, I
assure you she would never have yielded to you; and as her
Poverty first prevailed with her to let you do as you did, so
the same Poverty prevail'd with her to pay her self at last,
when she saw you was in such a Condition, that if she had
not done it, perhaps the next Coach-man or Chair-man might
have done it.

WELL, *says he*, much good may it do her; I say again, all
the Gentlemen that do so, ought to be us'd in the same
manner, and then they would be cautious of themselves; I
have no more concern about it, but on the score which you
hinted at before, Madam: Here he entered into some freedoms with her on the Subject of what pass'd between us,
which are not so proper for a Woman to write, and the great
Terror that was upon his Mind with relation to his Wife,
for fear he should have receiv'd any Injury from me, and
should communicate it farther; and ask'd her at last if she
cou'd not procure him an opportunity to speak with me; my

Governess gave him farther assurances of my being a Woman clear from any such thing, and that he was as entirely safe in that respect, as he was with his own Lady; but as for seeing me, she said it might be of dangerous consequence; but however, that she would talk with me, and let him know my Answer; using at the same time some Arguments to perswade him not to desire it, and that it cou'd be of no Service to him; seeing she hop'd he had no desire to renew a Correspondence with me, and that on my account it was a kind of putting my Life in his Hands.

HE told her, he had a great desire to see me, that he would give her any assurances that were in his Power, not to take any Advantages of me, and that in the first place he would give me a general release from all Demands of any kind; she insisted how it might tend to a farther divulging the Secret, and might in the end be injurious to him, entreating him not to press for it, so at length he desisted.

THEY had some Discourse upon the Subject of the things he had lost, and he seem'd to be very desirous of his Gold Watch, and told her if she cou'd procure that for him, he would willingly give as much for it as it was worth, she told him she would endeavour to procure it for him and leave the valuing it to himself.

ACCORDINGLY the next Day she carried the Watch, and he gave her 30 Guineas for it, which was more than I should have been able to make of it, tho' it seems it cost much more; he spoke something of his Perriwig, which it seems cost him threescore Guineas, and his Snuff-box, and in a few Days more, she carried them too; which oblig'd him very much, and he gave her Thirty more, the next Day I sent him his fine Sword, and Cane *Gratis*, and demanded nothing of him, but I had no mind to see him, unless it had been so, that he might be satisfy'd I knew who he was, which he was not willing to.

THEN he entered into a long Tale with her of the manner how she came to know all this matter; she form'd a long Talk of that part; how she had it from one, that I had told the whole Story to, and that was to help me dispose of the Goods, and this Confident brought the Things to her, she being by Profession a *Pawn-Broker*; and she hearing of his Worship's dissaster, guess'd at the thing in general; that having gotten the Things into her Hands, she had resolv'd to come and try as she had done: She then gave him repeated Assurances that it should never go out of her Mouth, and tho' she knew the Woman very well, yet she had not let her know, *meaning me*, any thing of it; *that is to say*, who the Person was, which by the way was false; but however it was not to his Damage, for I never open'd my Mouth of it to any Body.

I HAD a great many Thoughts in my Head about my seeing him again, and was often sorry that I had refus'd it; I was perswaded that if I had seen him, and let him know that I knew him, I should have made some Advantage of him, and perhaps have had some Maintenance from him; and tho' it was a Life wicked enough, yet it was not so full of Danger as this I was engag'd in. However those Thoughts wore off, and I declin'd seeing him again, for that time; but my Governess saw him often, and he was very kind to her, giving her something almost every time he saw her; one time in particular she found him very Merry, and as she thought he had some Wine in his Head, and he press'd her again very earnestly to let him see that Woman, that *as he said*, had Bewitch'd him so that Night; my Governess, who was from the beginning for my seeing him, told him, he was so desirous of it, that she could almost yield to it, if she cou'd prevail upon me; adding that if he would please to come to her House in the Evening she would endeavour it, upon his repeated Assurances of forgetting what was pass'd.

ACCORDINGLY she came to me and told me all the Discourse; *in short*, she soon byass'd me to consent, in a Case which I had some regret in my mind for declining before: so I prepar'd to see him: I dress'd me to all the Advantage possible I assure you, and for the first time us'd a little Art; I say for the first time, for I had never yielded to the baseness of Paint before, having always had vanity enough to believe I had no need of it.

AT the Hour appointed he came; and as she observ'd before, so it was plain still, that he had been drinking, tho' very far from what we call being in drink: He appear'd exceeding pleas'd to see me, and enter'd into a long Discourse with me, upon the old Affair, I beg'd his pardon very often, for my share of it; protested I had not any such design when first I met him; that I had not gone out with him, but that I took him for a very civil Gentleman; and that he made me so many promises of offering no uncivility to me.

HE alledg'd the Wine he drank, and that he scarce knew what he did, and that if it had not been so, I should never have let him take the freedom with me that he had done: He protested to me that he never touch'd any Woman but me since he was married to his Wife, and it was a surprise upon him; Complimented me upon being so particularly agreeable to him, and the like, and talk'd so much of that kind, till I found he had talk'd himself almost into a temper to do the same thing over again: But I took him up short, I protested I had never suffer'd any Man to touch me since my Husband died, which was near eight Year; he said he believed it to be so truly; and added that Madam, had intimated as much to him, and that it was his Opinion of that part which made him desire to see me again; and that since he had once broke in upon his Vertue with me, and found no ill Consequences, he cou'd be safe in venturing there again; and so in short it went on to what I expected, and to what will not bear relating.

MY old Governess had foreseen it, as well as I, and therefore led him into a Room which had not a Bed in it, and yet had a Chamber within it, which had a Bed, whither we withdrew for the rest of the Night, and in short, after some time being together, he went to Bed, and lay there all Night, I withdrew, but came again undress'd in the Morning before it was Day, and lay with him the rest of the time.

THUS you see having committed a Crime once, is a sad

Handle to the committing of it again; whereas all the Regret, and Reflections wear off when the Temptation renews it self; had I not yielded to see him again, the Corrupt desire in him had worn off, and 'tis very probable he had never fallen into it, with any Body else, as I really believe he had not done before.

WHEN he went away, I told him I hop'd he was satisfy'd he had not been robb'd again; he told me he was satisfy'd in that Point, and cou'd trust me again; and putting his Hand in his Pocket gave me five Guineas, which was the first Money I had gain'd that way for many Years.

I HAD several Visits of the like kind from him, but he never came into a settled way of Maintenance, which was what I would have been best pleas'd with: Once indeed he ask'd me how I did to live, I answer'd him pretty quick, that I assur'd him I had never taken that Course that I took with him; but that indeed I work'd at my Needle, and could just Maintain myself, that sometimes it was as much as I was able to do, and I shifted hard enough.

HE seem'd to reflect upon himself, that he should be the first Person to lead me into that, which he assur'd me he never intended to do himself; and it touch'd him a little, *he said*, that he should be the Cause of his own Sin, and mine too: He would often make just Reflections also upon the Crime itself, and upon the particular Circumstances of it, with respect to himself; how Wine introduc'd the Inclinations, how the Devil led him to the Place, and found out an Object to tempt him, and he made the Moral always himself.

WHEN these thoughts were upon him he would go away, and perhaps not come again in a Months time or longer; but then as the serious part wore off, the lewd Part would wear in, and then he came prepar'd for the wick'd Part;[1] thus we liv'd for sometime; tho' he did not KEEP, as they call it, yet he never fail'd doing things that were Handsome, and sufficient to Maintain me without working, and which was better, without following my old Trade.

BUT this Affair had its End too; for after about a Year, I found that he did not come so often as usual, and at last he left

it off altogether without any dislike, or bidding adieu; and so
there was an End of that short Scene of Life, which added no
great Store to me, only to make more Work for Repentance.

HOWEVER during this interval, I confin'd my self pretty
much at Home; at least being thus provided for, I made no
Adventures, no not for a Quarter of a Year after he left me;
but then finding the Fund fail, and being loth to spend upon
the main Stock, I began to think of my old Trade, and to
look Abroad into the Street again; and my first Step was
lucky enough.

I HAD dress'd myself up in a very mean Habit, for as I
had several Shapes to appear in I was now in an ordinary
Stuff-Gown, a blue Apron and a Straw-Hat; and I plac'd
myself at the Door of the three Cups Inn[1] in St. *John Street*:
There were several Carriers us'd the Inn, and the Stage
Coaches for *Barnet*, for *Toteridge*, and other Towns that way,
stood always in the Street, in the Evening, when they
prepar'd to set out; so that I was ready for any thing that
offer'd for either one or other: The meaning was this, People
come frequently with Bundles and small Parcels to those
Inns, and call for such Carriers, or Coaches as they want, to
carry them into the Country; and there generally attends
Women, Porters Wives, or Daughters, ready to take in such
things for their respective People that employ them.

IT happen'd very oddly that I was standing at the Inn-Gate,
and a Woman that had stood there before, and which was the
Porter's Wife belonging to the *Barnet* Stage Coach, having
observ'd me, ask'd if I waited for any of the Coaches; I told
her yes, I waited for my Mistress, that was coming to go to
Barnet; she ask'd me who was my Mistress, and I told her
any Madam's Name that came next me; but as it seem'd I
happen'd upon a Name, a Family of which Name liv'd at
Hadly just beyond *Barnet*.[2]

I SAID no more to her, or she to me a good while, but by
and by, some body calling her at a Door a little way off,
she desir'd me that if any body call'd for the *Barnet* Coach,
I would step and call her at the House, which it seems was

an Ale-house; I said yes very readily, and away she went.

SHE was no sooner gone; but comes a Wench and a Child, puffing and sweating, and asks for the *Barnet* Coach, I answer'd presently *Here*, do you belong to the *Barnet* Coach, *says she*? yes Sweetheart, *said I*, what do ye want? I want Room, for two Passengers *says she*, Where are they Sweetheart, *said I*? Here's this Girl, pray let her go into the Coach, *says she*, and I'll go and fetch my Mistress, make hast then Sweetheart, *says I*, for we may be full else; the Maid had a great Bundle under Arm; so she put the Child into the Coach, and *I said*, you had best put your Bundle into the Coach too; No, *says she*, I am afraid some body should slip it away from the Child, give it me then, *said I*, and I'll take care of it; do then, *says she*, and be sure you take care of it, I'll answer for it, *said I*, if it were for Twenty Pound value. There take it then, *says she*, and away she goes.

As soon as I had got the Bundle, and the Maid was out of Sight, I goes on towards the Ale-house, where the Porter's Wife was, so that if I had met her, I had then only been going to give her the Bundle, and to call her to her Business, as if I was going away, and cou'd stay no longer; but as I did not meet her I walk'd away, and turning into *Charter-house-Lane*, made off thro' *Charter-house-Yard*, into *Long-Lane*, then cross'd into *Bartholomew-Close*, so into *Little Britain*, and thro' the *Blue-Coat-Hospital* into *Newgate-Street*.[1]

To prevent my being known, I pull'd off my blue Apron, and wrapt the Bundle in it, which before was made up in a Piece of painted Callico, and very Remarkable; I also wrapt up my Straw-Hat in it, and so put the Bundle upon my Head; and it was very well, that I did thus, for coming thro' the *Blue-Coat-Hospital*, who should I meet but the Wench, that had given me the Bundle to hold; it seems she was going with her Mistress, who she had been gone to fetch to the *Barnet* Coaches.

I SAW she was in hast, and I had no Business to stop her: so away she went, and I brought my Bundle safe Home to my Governess; there was no Money, nor Plate, or Jewels in the Bundle; but a very good Suit of *Indian* Damask, a Gown and Petticoat, a lac'd Head and Ruffles of very good Flanders-Lace, and some Linnen, and other things, such as I knew very well the value of.

THIS was not indeed my own Invention, but was given me by one that had practis'd it with Success, and my Governess lik'd it extreamly; and indeed I try'd it again several times, tho' never twice near the same Place; for the next time I try'd it in *White-Chappel* just by the Corner of *Petty-Coat-Lane*, where the Coaches stand that go out to *Stratford* and *Bow*[1] and that Side of the Country, and another time at the *Flying-Horse*, without *Bishops-gate*, where the *Chester* Coaches then lay,[2] and I had always the good Luck to come off with some Booty.

ANOTHER time I plac'd myself at a Warehouse by the Waterside, where the Coasting Vessels from the *North* come, such as from *New-Castle* upon *Tyne*, *Sunderland*, and other Places; here the Warehouse, being shut, comes a young Fellow with a Letter; and he wanted a Box, and a Hamper that was come from *New-Castle* upon *Tyne*, I ask'd him if he had the Marks of it, so he shows me the Letter, by Vertue of which he was to ask for it, and which gave an Account of the Contents, the Box being full of Linnen, and the Hamper full of Glass-Ware; I read the Letter, and took care to see the Name, and the Marks, the Name of the Person that sent the Goods, the Name of the Person that they were sent to, then I bad the Messenger come in the Morning, for that the Warehouse Keeper, would not be there any more that Night.

AWAY went I, and getting Materials in a publick House, I wrote a Letter from Mr. *John Richardson* of *New-Castle* to his Dear Cousin *Jemey Cole*, in *London*, with an Account that he had sent by such a Vessel, (for I remember'd all the Particulars to a tittle,) so many pieces of Huckaback Linnen,[3] so many Ells[4] of *Dutch* Holland and the like, in a Box, and a Hamper of Flint Glasses[5] from Mr. *Henzill's* Glass-house,[6] and that the Box was mark'd IC. No I. and the Hamper was directed by a Label on the Cording.

ABOUT an Hour after I came to the Warehouse, found the Warehouse-keeper, and had the Goods deliver'd me without any scruple; the value of the Linnen being about 22 Pound.

I COULD fill up this whole Discourse with the variety of such Adventures which daily Invention directed to, and which I manag'd with the utmost Dexterity, and always with Success.

AT length, as when does the Pitcher come safe home that goes so very often to the Well,[1] I fell into some finall Broils, which tho' they cou'd not affect me fatally, yet made me known, which was the worst thing next to being found Guilty, that cou'd befall me.

I HAD taken up the Disguise of a Widow's Dress; it was without any real design in view, but only waiting for any thing that might offer, as I often did: It happen'd that while I was going along the Street in *Covent Garden*, there was a great Cry of stop Thief, stop Thief; some Artists had it seems put a trick upon a Shop-keeper, and being pursued, some of them fled one way, and some another; and one of them was, they said, dress'd up in Widow's Weeds, upon which the Mob gathered about me, and some said I was the Person, others said no, immediately came the Mercer's Journey-man, and he swore aloud I was the Person, and so seiz'd on me; however, when I was brought back by the Mob to the Mercer's Shop, the Master of the House said freely that I was not the Woman that was in his Shop, and would have let me go immediately; but another Fellow said gravely, pray stay till Mr. ————, *meaning the Journeyman*, comes back for he knows her; so they kept me by force near half an Hour; they had call'd a Constable, and he stood in the Shop as my Jayler; and in talking with the Constable I enquir'd where he liv'd, and what Trade he was; the Man not apprehending in the least what happened afterwards, readily told me his Name, and Trade, and where he liv'd; and told me as a Jest, that I might be sure to hear of his Name when I came to the *Old Bayley*.

SOME of the Servants likewise us'd me saucily, and had

much ado to keep their Hands off of me, the Master indeed
was civiler to me than they; but he would not yet let me go,
tho' he owned he could not say I was in his Shop before.

I BEGAN to be a little surly with him, and told him I hop'd
he would not take it ill, if I made my self amends upon him
in a more legal way another time; and desir'd I might send
for Friends to see me have right done me: No, *he said*, he
could give no such liberty, I might ask it when I came before
the Justice of Peace, and seeing I threaten'd him, he would
take care of me in the mean time, and would lodge me safe
in *Newgate*: I told him it was his time now, but it would be
mine by and by, and govern'd my Passion as well as I was
able; however, I spoke to the Constable to call me a Porter,
which he did, and then I call'd for Pen, Ink, and Paper, but
they would let me have none; I ask'd the Porter his Name,
and where he liv'd, and the poor Man told it me very
willingly; I bad him observe and remember how I was
treated there; that he saw I was detain'd there by Force; I
told him I should want his Evidence in another place, and it
should not be the worse for him to speak; the Porter said he
would serve me with all his Heart; but, Madam, *says he*, let
me hear them refuse to let you go, then I may be able to
speak the plainer.

WITH that I spoke aloud to the Master of the Shop, and
said, Sir, you know in your own Conscience that I am not
the Person you look for, and that I was not in your Shop
before, therefore I demand that you detain me here no
longer, or tell me the reason of your stopping me; the Fellow
grew surlier upon this than before, and said he would do
neither till he thought fit; very well, said I to the Constable
and to the Porter, you will be pleas'd to remember this,
Gentlemen, another time; the Porter said, *yes*, *Madam*, and
the Constable began not to like it, and would have perswaded
the Mercer to dismiss him, and let me go, since, as he said,
he own'd I was not the Person; Good Sir, *says the Mercer to
him Tauntingly*, are you a Justice of Peace, or a Constable? I
charg'd you with her, pray do you do your Duty: The

Constable told him a little mov'd, but very handsomely, *I know my Duty, and what I am, Sir, I doubt you hardly know what you are doing*; they had some other hard words, and in the mean time the Journey-men, impudent and unmanly to the last degree, used me barbarously, and one of them, the same that first scized upon me, pretended he would search me, and began to lay Hands on me: I spit in his Face, call'd out to the Constable, and bad him take notice of my usage; and pray, Mr. Constable, *said I*, ask that Villain's Name, pointing to the Man; the Constable reprov'd him decently, told him that he did not know what he did, for he knew that his Master acknowledg'd I was not the Person that was in his Shop; and, says the Constable, I am afraid your Master is bringing himself and me too into Trouble, if this Gentle-woman comes to prove who she is, and where she was, and it appears that she is not the Woman you pretend to; *Dam her, says the Fellow again*, with an impudent harden'd Face, she is the Lady you may depend upon it, I'll swear she is the same Body that was in the Shop, and that I gave the pieces of Satin that is lost into her own hand, you shall hear more of it when Mr. *William* and *Anthony, those were other Journeymen*, come back, they will know her again as well as I.

JUST as the insolent Rogue was talking thus to the Con-stable, comes back Mr. *William* and Mr. *Anthony*, as he call'd them, and a great Rabble with them, bringing along with them the true Widow that I was pretended to be; and they came sweating and blowing into the Shop, and with a great deal of Triumph dragging the poor Creature in a most butcherly manner up towards their Master, who was in the back Shop, and cryed out aloud, here's the Widow, Sir, we have catch'd her at last; what do ye mean by that, *says the Master*, why we have her already, there she sits, *says he*, and Mr. ———— *says he*, can swear this is she: The other Man who they call'd Mr. *Anthony* replyed, Mr. ———— may say what he will, and swear what he will, but this is the Woman, and there's the Remnant of Sattin she stole, I took it out of her Cloaths with my own Hand.

I SAT still now, and began to take a better Heart, but smil'd and said nothing; the Master look'd Pale; the Constable turn'd about and look'd at me; *let 'em alone Mr. Constable*, said I, *let 'em go on*; the Case was plain and could not be denied, so the Constable was charg'd with the right Thief, and the Mercer told me very civily he was sorry for the mistake, and hoped I would not take it ill; that they had so many things of this nature put upon them every Day, that they cou'd not be blam'd for being very sharp in doing themselves Justice; Not take it ill, Sir! *said I*, how can I take it well? if you had dismiss'd me when your insolent Fellow seiz'd on me in the Street, and brought me to you; and when you your self acknowledg'd I was not the Person, I would have put it by, and not taken it ill, because of the many ill things I believe you have put upon you daily; but your Treatment of me since has been unsufferable, and especially that of your Servant, I must and will have Reparation for that.

THEN he began to parly with me, said he would make me any reasonable Satisfaction, and would fain have had me told him what it was I expected; I told him I should not be my own Judge, the Law should decide it for me, and as I was to be carried before a Magistrate, I should let him hear there what I had to say; he told me there was no occasion to go before the Justice now, I was at liberty to go where I pleased, and so calling to the Constable told him, he might let me go, for I was discharg'd; the Constable said calmly to him, Sir, you ask'd me just now, if I knew whether I was a Constable or a Justice, and bad me do my Duty, and charg'd me with this Gentlewoman as a Prisoner; now, Sir, I find you do not understand what is my Duty, for you would make me a Justice indeed; but I must tell you it is not in my Power: I may keep a Prisoner when I am charg'd with him, but 'tis the Law and the Magistrate alone that can discharge that Prisoner;[1] therefore 'tis a mistake, Sir, I must carry her before a Justice now, whether you think well of it or not: The Mercer was very high with the Constable at first; but the

Constable happening to be not a hir'd Officer,[1] but a good
Substantial kind of Man, I think he was a Corn-chandler,
and a Man of good Sense, stood to his Business, would not
discharge me without going to a Justice of the Peace; and I
insisted upon it too: When the Mercer see that, well, *says
he to the Constable*, you may carry her where you please, I
have nothing to say to her; but Sir, *says the Constable*, you
will go with us, I hope, for 'tis you that charg'd me with her;
no not I, *says the Mercer*, I tell you I have nothing to say to
her: But pray Sir do, *says the Constable*, I desire it of you for
your own sake, for the Justice can do nothing without you:
Prithee Fellow, *says the Mercer*, go about your Business, I
tell you I have nothing to say to the Gentlewoman, I charge
you in the King's Name to dismiss her: Sir, *says the Constable*, I find you don't know what it is to be a Constable, I
beg of you don't oblige me to be rude to you; I think I need
not, you are rude enough already, *says the Mercer*: No, Sir,
says the Constable, I am not rude, you have broken the Peace
in bringing an honest Woman out of the Street, when she
was about her lawful Occasion, confining her in your Shop,
and ill using her here by your Servants; and now can you
say I am rude to you? I think I am civil to you in not com-
manding or charging you in the King's Name to go with me,
and charging every Man I see, that passes your Door, to aid
and assist me in carrying you by Force, this you cannot but
know I have power to do, and yet I forbear it, and once more
entreat you to go with me: Well, he would not for all this,
and gave the Constable ill Language: However, the Constable kept his Temper, and would not be provoked; and then
I put in and said, come, Mr. Constable, let him alone, I
shall find ways enough to fetch him before a Magistrate, I
don't fear that; but there's the Fellow, *says I*, he was the Man
that seized on me, as I was innocently going along the Street,
and you are a Witness of his Violence with me since, give me
leave to charge you with him, and carry him before the
Justice; yes, Madam, *says the Constable*; and turning to the
Fellow, come young Gentleman, *says he to the Journey-man*,

you must go along with us, I hope you are not above the Constable's Power, tho' your Master is.

THE Fellow look'd like a condemn'd Thief, and hung back, then look'd at his Master, as if he cou'd help him; and he, like a Fool, encourag'd the Fellow to be rude, and he truly resisted the Constable, and push'd him back with a good Force when he went to lay hold on him, at which the Constable knock'd him down, and call'd out for help, and immediately the Shop was fill'd with People, and the Constable seiz'd the Master and Man, and all his Servants.

THE first ill Consequence of this Fray was, that the Woman they had taken, who was really the Thief, made off, and got clear away in the Crowd; and two others that they had stop'd also, whether they were really Guilty or not, that I can say nothing to.

BY this time some of his Neighbours having come in, and, upon inquiry, seeing how things went, had endeavour'd to bring the hot-brain'd Mercer to his Senses; and he began to be convinc'd that he was in the wrong; and so at length we went all very quietly before the Justice, with a Mob of about 500 People at our Heels; and all the way I went I could hear the People ask what was the matter? and others reply and say, a Mercer had stop'd a Gentlewoman instead of a Thief, and had afterwards taken the Thief, and now the Gentlewoman had taken the Mercer, and was carrying him before the Justice; this pleas'd the People strangely, and made the Crowd encrease, and they cry'd out as they went, which is the Rogue? which is the Mercer? and especially the Women, then when they saw him they cryed out, *that's he, that's he;* and every now and then came a good dab of Dirt at him; and thus we march'd a good while, till the Mercer thought fit to desire the Constable to call a Coach to protect himself from the Rabble; so we Rode the rest of the way, the Constable and I, and the Mercer and his Man.

WHEN we came to the Justice, which was an ancient Gentleman in *Bloomsbury*, the Constable giving first a summary account of the Matter the Justice bad me speak, and tell what I had to say; and first he asked my Name, which I was very loath to give, but there was no remedy, so I told him my Name was *Mary Flanders*, that I was a Widow, my Husband being a Sea Captain, dyed on a Voyage to *Virginia*; and some other Circumstances I told, which he cou'd never contradict, and that I lodg'd at present in Town with such a Person, naming my Governess; but that I was preparing to go over to *America*, where my Husband's Effects lay, and that I was going that Day to buy some Cloaths to put my self into second Mourning, but had not yet been in any Shop, when that Fellow, pointing to the Mercer's Journeyman came rushing upon me with such fury, as very much frighted me, and carried me back to his Masters Shop; where tho' his Master acknowledg'd I was not the Person; yet he would not dismiss me, but charg'd a Constable with me.

THEN I proceeded to tell how the Journeyman treated me; how they would not suffer me to send for any of my Friends; how afterwards they found the real Thief, and took the very Goods they had Lost upon her, and all the particulars as before.

THEN the Constable related his Case; his Dialogue with the *Mercer* about Discharging me, and at last his Servants refusing to go with him, when I had Charg'd him with him,[1] and his Master encouraging him to do so; and at last his striking the Constable, and the like, all as I have told it already.

THE Justice then heard, the *Mercer* and his Man; the *Mercer* indeed made a long Harangue of the great loss they have daily by Lifters and Thieves;[2] that it was easy for them to Mistake, and that when he found it, he would have dismiss'd me, &c. as above, as to the Journeyman he had very little to say, but that he pretended other of the Servants told him, that I was really the Person.

UPON the whole, the Justice first of all told me very courteously I was Discharg'd; that he was very sorry that the *Mercers* Man should in his eager pursuit have so little Discretion, as to take up an innocent Person for a guilty Person; that if he had not been so unjust as to detain me afterward, he believ'd I would have forgiven the first Affront; that however it was not in his Power to award me any Reparation for any thing, other, than by openly reproving them, which he should do; but he suppos'd I would apply to such Methods as the Law directed; in the mean time he would bind him over.

BUT as to the Breach of the Peace committed by the Journeyman, he told me he should give me some satisfaction for that, for he should commit him to *Newgate* for Assaulting the Constable, and for Assaulting of me also.

ACCORDINGLY he sent the Fellow to *Newgate*, for that Assault, and his Master gave Bail, and so we came away; but I had the satisfaction of seeing the Mob wait upon them both as they came out, Holooing, and throwing Stones and Dirt at the Coaches they rod in, and so I came Home to my Governess.

AFTER this hustle, coming home, and telling my Governess the Story, she falls a Laughing at me; Why are you merry, *says I?* the Story has not so much Laughing room in it, as you imagine; I am sure I have had a great deal of Hurry and Fright too, with a Pack of ugly Rogues. *Laugh*, says my Governess, I laugh Child to see what a lucky Creature you are; why this Jobb will be the best Bargain to you, that ever you made in your Life, if you manage it well: I warrant you, *says she*, you shall make the *Mercer* pay you 500 *l.* for Damages, besides what you shall get of the Journeyman.

I HAD other Thoughts of the Matter than she had; and especially, because I had given in my Name to the Justice of Peace; and I knew that my Name was so well known among the People at *Hicks's Hall*, the *Old Baily*,[1] and such Places, that if this Cause came to be tryed openly, and my Name came to be enquir'd into, no Court would give much Damages, for the Reputation of a Person of such a Character; however, I was oblig'd to begin a Prosecution in Form, and accordingly my Governess found me out a very creditable sort of a Man to manage it, being an Attorney of very good Business, and of good Reputation, and she was certainly in the right of this; for had she employ'd a petty Fogging hedge Soliciter,[1] or a Man not known, and not in good Reputation, I should have brought it to but little.

I MET this Attorney, and gave him all the particulars at large, as they are recited above; and he assur'd me, it was a Case, *as he said*, that would very well support itself, and that he did not Question, but that a Jury would give very considerable Damages on such an Occasion; so taking his full Instructions, he began the Prosecution, and the *Mercer* being Arrested, gave Bail; a few Days after his giving Bail, he Comes with his Attorney to my Attorney, to let him know, that he desir'd to Accommodate the matter; that it was all carried on in the Heat of an unhappy Passion; that his Client, *meaning me*, had a sharp provoking Tongue, that I us'd them ill, gibbing at them, and jeering them, even while they believed me to be the very Person, and that I had provok'd them, and the like.

MY Attorney manag'd as well on my Side; made them believe I was a Widow of Fortune, that I was able to do myself Justice, and had great Friends to stand by me too, who had all made me promise to Sue to the utmost, and that if it cost me a Thousand Pound, I would be sure to have satisfaction, for that the Affronts I had receiv'd were unsufferable.

HOWEVER they brought my Attorney to this, that he promis'd he would not blow the Coals, that if I enclin'd to an Accommodation, he would not hinder me, and that he would rather perswade me to Peace than to War; for which they told him he should be no looser, all which he told me very honestly, and told me that if they offer'd him any Bribe, I should certainly know it; but upon the whole he told me very honestly that if I would take his Opinion, he would Advise me to make it up with them; for that as they were in a great Fright, and were desirous above all things to make it up, and knew that let it be what it would, they would be alotted to bear all the Costs of the Suit; he believ'd they would give me freely more than any Jury or Court of Justice would give upon a Trial: I ask'd him what he thought they would be brought to; he told me he could not tell, as to that; but he would tell me more when I saw him again.

SOME time after this, they came again to know if he had talk'd with me: He told them he had, that he found me not so Averse to an Accommodation as some of my Friends were, who resented the Disgrace offer'd me, and set me on; that they blow'd the Coals in secret, prompting me to Revenge, or to do myself Justice, as they call'd it; so that he could not tell what to say to it; he told them he would do his endeavour to persuade me, but he ought to be able to tell me what Proposal they made: They pretended they could not make any Proposal, because it might be made use of against them; and he told them, that by the same Rule he could not make any offers, for that might be pleaded in Abatement of what Damages a Jury might be inclin'd to give: However after some Discourse and mutual Promises that no Advantage should be taken on either Side, by what was transacted then, or at any other of those Meetings, they came to a kind of a Treaty; but so remote, and so wide from one another, that nothing could be expected from it; for my Attorney demanded 500 *l.* and Charges, and they offer'd 50 *l.* without Charges; so they broke off, and the *Mercer* propos'd to have a Meeting with me myself; and my Attorney agreed to that very readily.

MY Attorney gave me Notice to come to this Meeting in good Cloaths, and with some State, that the *Mercer* might see I was something more than I seem'd to be that time they had me: Accordingly I came in a new Suit of second Mourning,[1] according to what I had said at the Justices; I set myself out too, as well as a Widows dress in second Mourning would admit; my Governess, also furnish'd me with a good Pearl Neck-lace, that shut in behind with a Locket of Diamonds, which she had in Pawn; and I had a very good gold Watch by my Side; so that in a Word, I made a very good Figure, and as I stay'd, till I was sure they were come, I came in a Coach to the Door with my Maid with me.

WHEN I came into the Room, the *Mercer* was surpriz'd, he stood up and made his Bow, which I took a little Notice of, and but a little, and went and Sat down, where my own Attorney had pointed to me to sit, for it was his House; after a little while, the *Mercer* said, he did not know me again, and began to make some Compliments his way; I told him, I believ'd he did not know me at first, and that if he had, I believ'd he would not have treated me as he did.

HE told me he was very sorry for what had happen'd, and that it was to testifie the willingness he had to make all possible Reparation, that he had appointed this Meeting; that he hop'd I would not carry things to extremity, which might be not only too great a Loss to him, but might be the ruin of his Business and Shop, in which Case I might have the satisfaction of repaying an Injury with an Injury ten times greater; but that I would then get nothing, whereas he was willing to do me any Justice that was in his Power, without putting himself, or me to the Trouble or Charge of a Suit at Law.

I TOLD him I was glad to hear him talk so much more like a Man of Sense than he did before; that it was true, acknowledgement in most Cases of Affronts was counted Reparation sufficient; but this had gone too far to be made up so; that I was not Revengeful, nor did I seek his Ruin, or any Mans else, but that all my Friends were unanimous not to let me so far neglect my Character, as to adjust a thing of this kind without a sufficient Reparation of Honour: That to be taken up for a Thief was such an Indignity as could not be put up, that my Character was above being treated so by any that knew me; but because in my Condition of a Widow, I had been for sometime Careless of myself, and Negligent of myself, I might be taken for such a Creature, but that for the particular usage I had from him afterward, and then I repeated all as before, it was so provoking I had scarce Patience to repeat it.

WELL he acknowledg'd all, and was mighty humble indeed; he made Proposals very handsome; he came up to a Hundred Pounds, and to pay all the Law Charges, and added that he would make me a Present of a very good Suit of Cloths; I came down to three Hundred Pounds, and I demanded that I should publish an Advertisement of the particulars in the common News Papers.

THIS was a Clause he never could comply with; however at last he came up by good Management of my Attorney to 150 *l.* and a Suit of black silk Coaths, and there I agreed and as it were at my Attornies request complied with it; he paying my Attornies Bill and Charges, and gave us a good Supper into the Bargain.

WHEN I came to receive the Money, I brought my Governess with me, dress'd like an old Dutchess, and a Gentleman very well dress'd, who we pretended Courted me, but I call'd him Cousin, and the Lawyer was only to hint privately to him,[1] that this Gentleman Courted the Widow.

HE treated us handsomely indeed, and paid the Money chearfully enough; so that it cost him 200 *l.* in all, or rather more: At our last Meeting when all was agreed, the Case of the Journeyman came up, and the *Mercer* beg'd very hard for him, told me he was a Man that had kept a Shop of his own, and been in good Business, had a Wife and several Children, and was very poor, that he had nothing to make satisfaction with, but he should come to beg my pardon on his Knees, if I desir'd it as openly as I pleas'd: I had no Spleen at the sawcy Rogue, nor were his Submissions any thing to me, since there was nothing to be got by him; so I thought it was as good to throw that in generously as not, so I told him I did not desire the Ruin of any Man, and therefore at his Request I would forgive the Wretch, it was below me to seek any Revenge.

WHEN we were at Supper he brought the poor Fellow in to make acknowledgement, which he would have done with as much mean Humility, as his Offence was with insulting

Haughtiness and Pride, in which he was an Instance of a compleat baseness of Spirit,[1] imperious, cruel, and relentless when Uppermost, and in Prosperity; abject and low Spirited when Down in Affliction: However I abated his Cringes, told him I forgave him, and desir'd he might withdraw, as if I did not care for the sight of him, tho' I had forgiven him.

I WAS now in good Circumstances indeed, if I could have known my time for leaving off, and my Governess often said I was the richest of the Trade in *England*, and so I believe I was; for I had 700 *l.* by me in Money, besides Cloaths, Rings, some Plate, and two gold Watches, and all of them stol'n, for I had innumerable Jobbs, besides these I have mention'd; O! had I even now had the Grace of Repentance, I had still leisure to have look'd back upon my Follies, and have made some Reparation; but the satisfaction I was to make for the publick Mischiefs I had done, was yet left behind; and I could not forbear going Abroad again, *as I call'd it now*, any more than I could when my Extremity really drove me out for Bread.

IT was not long after the Affair with the *Mercer* was made up, that I went out in an Equipage quite different from any I had ever appear'd in before; I dress'd myself like a Beggar Woman, in the coursest and most despicable Rags I could get, and I walk'd about peering, and peeping into every Door and Window I came near; and indeed I was in such a Plight now, that I knew as ill how to behave in as ever I did in any; I naturally abhorr'd Dirt and Rags; I had been bred up Tite and Cleanly, and could be no other, whatever Condition I was in; so that this was the most uneasie Disguise to me that ever I put on: I said presently to myself that this would not do, for this was a Dress that every body was shy, and afraid of; and I thought every body look'd at me, as if they were afraid I should come near them, least I should take something from them, or afraid to come near me, least they should get something from me: I wandered about all the Evening the first time I went out, and made nothing of it, but came home again wet, draggl'd and tired; However I

went out again, the next Night, and then I met with a little
Adventure, which had like to have cost me dear; as I was
standing near a Tavern Door, there comes a Gentleman on
Horse back, and lights at the Door, and wanting to go into
the Tavern, he calls one of the Drawers to hold his Horse;
he stay'd prety long in the Tavern, and the Drawer heard
his Master call, and thought he would be angry with him;
seeing me stand by him, when he call'd to me, here Woman,
says he, hold this Horse a while, till I go in, if the Gentleman
comes, he'll give you something; *yes says I*, and takes the
Horse, and walks off with him very soberly, and carri'd him
to my Governess.

THIS had been a Booty to those that had understood it;
but never was poor Thief more at a loss to know what to do
with any thing that was stolen; for when I came home, my
Governess was quite confounded, and what to do with the
Creature, we neither of us knew; to send him to a Stable
was doing nothing, for it was certain that publick Notice
would be given in the *Gazette*,[1] and the Horse describ'd, so
that we durst not go to fetch it again.

ALL the remedy we had for this unlucky Adventure was to
go and set up the Horse at an Inn, and send a Note by a
Porter to the Tavern, that the Gentleman's Horse that was
lost such a time, was left at such an Inn, and that he might
be had there; that the poor Woman that held him, having
led him about the Street, not being able to lead him back
again, had left him there; we might have waited till the
owner had publish'd, and offer'd a Reward, but we did not
care to venture the receiving the Reward.

So this was a Robbery and no Robbery, for little was lost
by it, and nothing was got by it, and I was quite Sick of
going out in a Beggar's dress, it did not answer at all, and
besides I thought it was Ominous and Threatning.

WHILE I was in this Disguise, I fell in with a parcel of
Folks of a worse kind than any I ever sorted with, and I saw
a little into their ways too, these were Coiners of Money,
and they made some very good offers to me, as to profit; but

the part they would have had me have embark'd in, was the
most dangerous Part; I mean that of the very working the
Dye, as they call it, which had I been taken, had been
certain Death, and that at a Stake, *I say*, to be burnt to
Death at a Stake;[1] so that tho' I was to Appearance, but a
Beggar; and they promis'd Mountains of Gold and Silver to
me, to engage; yet it would not do; it is True if I had been
really a Beggar, or had been desperate as when I began, I
might perhaps have clos'd with it, for what care they to Die,
that can't tell how to Live? But at present this was not my
Condition, at least I was for no such terrible Risques as
those; besides the very Thoughts of being burnt at a Stake,
struck terror into my very Soul, chill'd my Blood, and gave
me the Vapours to such a degree as I could not think of it
without trembling.

THIS put an End to my Disguise too, for as I did not like
the Proposal, so I did not tell them so; but seem'd to relish
it, and promis'd to meet again; but I durst see them no more,
for if I had seen them, and not complied, tho' I had declin'd
it with the greatest assurances of Secresy in the World, they
would have gone near to have murther'd me to make sure
Work, and make themselves easy, *as they call it*; what kind
of easiness that is, they may best Judge that understand how
easy Men are, that can Murther People to prevent Danger.

THIS and Horse stealing were things quite out of my way,
and I might easily resolve I would have no more to say to
them; my business seem'd to lye another way, and tho' it
had hazard enough in it too, yet it was more suitable to me,
and what had more of Art in it, more room to Escape, and
more Chances for a coming off, if a Surprize should happen.

I HAD several Proposals made also to me about that time,
to come into a Gang of House-Breakers; but that was a
thing I had no mind to venture at neither, any more than I
had at the Coining Trade; I offer'd to go along with two
Men, and a Woman, that made it their Business to get into
Houses by Stratagem, and with them I was willing enough
to venture; but there was three of them already, and they did

not care to part, nor I to have too many in a Gang, so I did
not close with them, but declin'd them, and they paid dear
for their next Attempt.

BUT at length I met with a Woman that had ofen told me
what Adventures she had made, and with Success at the
Water-side, and I clos'd with her, and we drove on our
Business pretty well: One Day we came among some *Dutch*
People at St. *Catherines*,[1] where we went on pretence to buy
Goods that were privately got on Shore: I was two or three
times in a House, where we saw a good Quantity of prohibited
Goods, and my Companion once brought away three Peices
of *Dutch* black Silk that turn'd to good Account, and I had
my Share of it; but in all the Journeys I made by myself, I
could not get an Opportunity to do any thing, so I laid it
aside; for I had been so often, that they began to suspect
something, and were so shy, that I saw nothing was to be
done.

THIS baulk'd me a little, and I resolv'd to push at something or other, for I was not us'd to come back so often
without Purchase; so the next Day I dress'd myself up fine,
and took a Walk to the other End of the Town, I pass'd thro'
the *Exchange* in the *Strand*,[2] but had no Notion of finding
any thing to do there, when on a sudden I saw a great Clutter
in the Place, and all the People, Shop-keepers as well as
others, standing up, and staring, and what should it be? but
some great Dutchess come into the *Exchange*; and they said
the Queen was coming; I set myself close up to a Shop-side
with my back to the Compter, as if to let the Crowd pass by,
when keeping my Eye upon a parcel of Lace, which the
Shop-keeper was showing to some Ladies that stood by me;
the Shop-keeper and her Maid were so taken up with looking
to see who was a coming, and what Shop they would go to,
that I found means to slip a Paper of Lace into my Pocket,
and come clear off with it, so the Lady Millener paid dear
enough for her gaping after the Queen.

I WENT off from the Shop, as if driven along by the
Throng, and mingling myself with the Crowd, went out at

the other Door of the *Exchange*, and so got away before they miss'd their Lace; and because I would not be follow'd, I call'd a Coach and shut myself up in it; I had scarse shut the Coach Doors up, but I saw the Milleners Maid, and five or six more come running out into the Street, and crying out as if they were frighted; they did not cry stop Thief, because no body ran away, but I cou'd hear the Word robb'd, and Lace, two or three times, and saw the Wench wringing her Hands, and run staring, too, and again, like one scar'd; the Coachman that had taken me up, was getting up into the Box, but was not quite up, so that the Horses had not begun to move, so that I was terrible uneasy; and I took the Packet of Lace and laid it ready to have dropt it out at the Flap of the Coach, which opens before just behind the Coachman; but to my great satisfaction in less than a Minute, the Coach began to move, that is to say, as soon as the Coachman had got up, and spoken to his Horses; so he drove away without any interruption, and I brought off my Purchase, which was worth near twenty Pound.

THE next Day I dress'd me up again, but in quite different Cloths, and walk'd the same way again; but nothing offer'd till I came into St. *James*'s *Park*, where I saw abundance of fine Ladies in the *Park*, walking in the *Mall*,[1] and among the rest, there was a little Miss, a young Lady of about 12 or 13 Years old, and she had a Sister, as I suppose it was, with her, that might be about Nine Year old: I observ'd the biggest had a fine gold Watch on, and a good Necklace of Pearl, and they had a Footman in Livery with them; but as it is not usual for the Footmen to go behind the Ladies in the *Mall*; so I observ'd the Footman stop'd at their going into the *Mall*, and the biggest of the Sisters spoke to him, which I perceiv'd was to bid him be just there when they came back.

WHEN I heard her dismiss the Footman, I step'd up to him, and ask'd him, what little Lady that was? and held a little Chat with him, about what a pretty Child it was with her, and how Genteel, and well Carriag'd the Lady, the eldest would be; how Womanish, and how Grave; and the

Fool of a Fellow told me presently who she was, that she was Sir *Thomas* ————'s eldest Daughter of *Essex*, and that she was a great Fortune, that her Mother was not come to Town yet; but she was with Sir *William* ————'s Lady of *Suffolk*, at her Lodgings in *Suffolk-Street*, and a great deal more; that they had a Maid and a Woman to wait on them, besides, Sir *Thomas*'s Coach, the Coachman and himself, and that young Lady was Governess to the whole Family as well here, as at Home too; and in short, told me abundance of things enough for my business.

I WAS very well dress'd, and had my gold Watch, as well as she; so I left the Footman, and I puts myself in a Rank with this young Lady, having stay'd till she had taken one double Turn in the *Mall*, and was going forward again, by and by, I saluted her by her Name, with the Title of Lady *Betty*: I ask'd her when she heard from her Father? when my Lady her Mother would be in Town and how she did?

I TALK'D so familiarly to her of her whole Family that she cou'd not suspect, but that I knew them all intimately: I ask'd her why she would come Abroad without Mrs. *Chime* with her (that was the Name of her Woman) to take care of Mrs. *Judith* that was her Sister. Then I enter'd into a long Chat with her about her Sister, what a fine little Lady she was, and ask'd her if she had learn'd *French*, and a Thousand such little things to entertain her, when on a sudden we see the Guards come, and the Crowd run to see the King go by to the Parliament-House.

THE Ladies run all to the Side of the *Mall*, and I help'd my Lady to stand upon the edge of the Boards on the side of the *Mall*, that she might be high enough to see; and took the little one and lifted her quite up; during which, I took care to convey the gold Watch so clean away from the Lady *Betty*, that she never felt it, nor miss'd it, till all the Crowd was gone, and she was gotten into the middle of the *Mall* among the other Ladies.

I TOOK my leave of her in the very Crowd, and said to her, as if in hast, dear Lady *Betty* take care of your little Sister, and so the Crowd did, as it were Thrust me away from her, and that I was oblig'd unwillingly to take my leave.

THE hurry in such Cases is immediately over, and the Place clear as soon as the King is gone by; but as there is always a great running and clutter just as the King passes; so having drop'd the two little Ladies, and done my Business with them, without any Miscarriage, I kept hurrying on among the Crowd, as if I run to see the King, and so I got before the Crowd and kept so, till I came to the End of the *Mall*, when the King going on toward the Horse-Guards; I went forward to the Passage, which went then thro' against the lower End of the *Hay-Market*, and there I bestow'd a coach upon myself, and made off; and I confess I have not yet been so good as my word (*viz.*) to go and visit my Lady *Betty*.

I WAS once of the mind to venture staying with Lady *Betty*, till she mist the Watch, and so have made a great Out-cry about it with her, and have got her into her Coach, and put my self in the Coach with her, and have gone Home with her; for she appear'd so fond of me, and so perfectly deceiv'd by my so readily talking to her of all her Relations and Family, that I thought it was very easy to push the thing farther, and to have got at least the Neck-lace of Pearl; but when I consider'd that tho' the Child would not perhaps have suspected me, other People might, and that if I was search'd I should be discover'd; I thought it was best to go off with what I had got, and be satisfy'd.

I CAME accidentally afterwards to hear, that when the young Lady miss'd her Watch, she made a great Out-cry in the *Park*, and sent her Footman up and down, to see if he could find me out, she having describ'd me so perfectly, that he knew presently that it was the same Person that had stood and talked so long with him, and ask'd him so many Questions about them; but I was gone far enough out of their reach before she could come at her Footman to tell him the Story.

I MADE another Adventure after this, of a Nature different

from all I had been concern'd in yet, and this was at a Gaming-House near *Covent-Garden*.

I SAW several People go in and out; and I stood in the Passage a good while with another Woman with me, and seeing a Gentleman go up that seem'd to be of more than ordinary Fashion, I said to him, Sir, pray don't they give Women leave to go up? *yes Madam, says he*, and to play too if they please; I mean so Sir, *said I*; and with that, he said he would introduce me if I had a mind; so I follow'd him to the Door, and he looking in, there, Madam, *says he*, are the Gamesters, if you have a mind to venture; I look'd in and said to my Comrade, aloud, here's nothing but Men, I won't venture among them; at which one of the Gentlemen cry'd out, you need not be afraid Madam, here's none but fair Gamesters, you are very welcome to come and Set what you please; so I went a little nearer and look'd on, and some of them brought me a Chair, and I sat down and see the Box and Dice go round a pace;[1] then I said to my Comrade, the Gentlemen play too high for us, come let us go.

THE People were all very civil, and one Gentleman in particular encourag'd me, and said, come Madam, if you please to Venture, if you dare Trust me I'll answer for it; you shall have nothing put upon you here; no Sir, *said I*, smiling, I hope the Gentlemen wou'd not Cheat a Woman; but still I declin'd venturing, tho' I pull'd out a Purse with Money in it, that they might see I did not want Money.

AFTER I had sat a while, one Gentleman said to me Jeering, come Madam, I see you are afraid to venture for yourself; I always had good luck with the Ladies, you shall Set for me, if you won't Set for yourself; I told him, Sir I should be very loth to loose your Money, tho' I added, I am pretty lucky too; but the Gentlemen play so high, that I dare not indeed venture my own.

WELL, well, *says he*, there's ten Guineas Madam, Set them for me; so I took his Money and set, himself looking on; I run out Nine of the Guineas by One and Two at a Time, and then the Box coming to the next Man to me, my Gentle-

man gave me Ten Guineas more, and made me Set Five of
them at once, and the Gentleman who had the Box threw
out, so there was Five Guineas of his Money again; he was
encourag'd at this, and made me take the Box, which was a
bold Venture: However, I held the Box so long that I had
gain'd him his whole Money, and had a good handful of
Guineas in my Lap, and which was the better Luck, when I
threw out, I threw but at One or Two of those that had Set
me, and so went off easie.

WHEN I was come this length, I offer'd the Gentleman all
the Gold, for it was his own; and so would have had him
play for himself, pretending I did not understand the Game
well enough: He laugh'd, and said if I had but good Luck,
it was no matter whether I understood the Game or no; but
I should not leave off: However he took out the 15 Guineas
that he had put in at first, and bad me play with the rest: I
would have told them to see how much I had got,[1] but he
said no, no, don't tell them, I believe you are very honest,
and 'tis bad Luck to tell them, so I play'd on.

I Understood the Game well enough, tho' I pretended I
did not, and play'd cautiously; it was to keep a good Stock in
my Lap, out of which I every now and then convey'd some
into my Pocket; but in such a manner, and at such convenient times, as I was sure he cou'd not see it.

I PLAY'D a great while, and had very good Luck for him,
but the last time I held the Box, they Set me high, and I
threw boldly at all; I held the Box till I gain'd near Fourscore
Guineas, but lost above half of it back at the last throw; so I
got up, for I was afraid I should lose it all back again, and
said to him, pray come Sir now and take it and play for your
self, I think I have done pretty well for you; he would have
had me play'd on, but it grew late, and I desir'd to be
excus'd. When I gave it up to him, I told him I hop'd he
would give me leave to tell it now, that I might see what I
had gain'd, and how lucky I had been for him; when I told
them, there was Threescore, and Three Guineas. Ay, *says I*,
if it had not been for that unlucky Throw I had got you a

Hundred Guineas; so I gave him all the Money, but he would not take it till I had put my Hand into it, and taken some for myself, and bid me please myself; I refus'd it, and was positive I would not take it myself, if he had a mind to any thing of that kind it should be all his own doings.

THE rest of the Gentlemen seeing us striving, cry'd give it her all; but I absolutely refus'd that; then one of them said, D———n ye *Jack*, half it with her, don't you know you should be always upon even Terms with the Ladies; so in short, he divided it with me, and I brought away 30 Guineas, besides about 43, which I had stole privately, which I was sorry for afterwards, because he was so generous.

THUS I brought Home 73 Guineas, and let my old Governess see what good Luck I had at Play: However, it was her Advice that I should not venture again, and I took her Council, for I never went there any more; for I knew as well as she, if the Itch of Play[1] came in, I might soon lose that, and all the rest of what I had got.

FORTUNE had smil'd upon me to that degree, and I had Thriven so much, and my Governess too, for she always had a Share with me, that really the old Gentlewoman began to talk of leaving off while we were well, and being satisfy'd with what we had got; but, I know not what Fate guided me, I was as backward to it now as she was when I propos'd it to her before, and so in an ill Hour we gave over the Thoughts of it for the present, and in a Word, I grew more hardn'd and audacious than ever, and the Success I had, made my Name as famous as any Thief of my sort ever had been at *Newgate*, and in the *Old-Bayly*.

I HAD sometimes taken the liberty to Play the same Game over again, which is not according to Practice, which however succeeded not amiss; but generally I took up new Figures, and contriv'd to appear in new Shapes every time I went abroad.

IT was now a rumbling time of the Year, and the Gentlemen being most of them gone out of Town, *Tunbridge*, and *Epsom*, and such Places were full of People, but the City was Thin,[2] and I thought our Trade felt it a little, as well as others; so that at the latter End of the Year I joyn'd myself with a Gang, who usually go every Year to *Sturbridge* Fair, and from thence to *Bury* Fair,[1] in *Suffolk :* We promis'd our selves great things here, but when I came to see how things were, I was weary of it presently; for except meer Picking of Pockets, there was little worth meddling with; neither if a Booty had been made, was it so easy carrying it off, nor was there such a variety of occasion for Business in our way, as in *London*; all that I made of the whole Journey, was a gold Watch at *Bury* Fair, and a small parcel of Linnen at *Cambridge*, which gave me an occasion to take leave of the Place: It was an old Bite,[2] and I thought might do with a Country Shop keeper, tho' in *London* it would not.

I Bought at a Linnen Draper's Shop, not in the Fair, but in the Town of *Cambridge*, as much fine Holland and other things as came to about seven Pound; when I had done, I bad them be sent to such an Inn, where I had purposely taken up my being the same Morning, as if I was to Lodge there that Night.

I Order'd the Draper to send them Home to me, about such an Hour to the Inn where I lay, and I would pay him his Money; at the time appointed the Draper sends the Goods, and I plac'd one of our Gang at the Chamber Door, and when the Innkeeper's Maid brought the Messenger to the Door, who was a young Fellow, an Apprentice, almost a Man; she tells him her Mistress was a sleep, but if he would leave the things, and call in about an Hour, I should be awake, and he might have the Money; he left the Parcel very readily, and goes his way, and in about half an Hour my Maid and I walk'd off, and that very Evening I hired a Horse, and a Man to ride before me, and went to *Newmarket*, and from thence got my Passage in a Coach that was not quite full to St. *Edmund's Bury*; Where as I told you I could make but little of my Trade, only at a little Country *Opera*-House,[3] made a shift to carry off a gold Watch from a Ladies side, who was not only intollerably Merry, but as I thought a little Fuddled, which made my Work much easier.

I MADE off with this little Booty to *Ipswich*, and from thence to *Harwich*; where I went into an Inn, as if I had newly arriv'd from *Holland*, not doubting but I should make some Purchase among the Foreigners that came on shore there; but I found them generally empty of things of value, except what was in their Portmanteuas, and *Dutch* Hampers, which were generally guarded by Footmen; however, I fairly¹ got one of their Portmanteuas one Evening out of the Chamber where the Gentleman lay, the Footman being fast a sleep on the Bed, and I suppose very Drunk.

THE Room in which I Lodg'd, lay next to the *Dutchman*'s, and having dragg'd the heavy thing with much a-do out of the Chamber into mine; I went out into the Street, to see if I could find any possibility of carrying it off; I walk'd about a great while but could see no probability, either of getting out the thing, or of conveying away the Goods that was in it if I had open'd it, the Town being so small, and I a perfect Stranger in it; so I was returning with a resolution to carry it back again, and leave it where I found it: Just in that very Moment I heard a Man make a Noise to some People to make hast, for the Boat was going to put off, and the Tide would be spent; I call'd to the Fellow, What Boat is it Friend, *says I*, that you belong to? the *Ipswich* Wherry, Madam, *says he*: When do you go.off, *says I*? this Moment Madam, *says he*, do you want to go thither? yes, *said I*, if you can stay till I fetch my things: Where are your things Madam, *says he*? At such an Inn, *said I*: Well I'll go with you Madam, *says he*, very civilly, and bring them for you; come away then, *says I*, and takes him with me.

THE People of the Inn were in great hurry, the Packet-Boat from *Holland*, being just come in, and two Coaches just come also with Passengers from *London*, for another Packet-Boat that was going off for *Holland*, which Coaches were to go back next Day with the Passengers that were just Landed: In this hurry it was not much minded, that I came to the Bar, and paid my Reckoning, telling my Landlady I had gotten my Passage by Sea in a Wherry.

THESE Wherries are large Vessels, with good Accommodation for carrying Passengers from *Harwich* to *London*; and tho' they are call'd Wherries, which is a word us'd in the *Thames* for a small Boat, Row'd with one or two Men; yet these are Vessels able to carry twenty Passengers, and ten or fifteen Ton of Goods, and fitted to bear the Sea; all this I had found out by enquiring the Night before into the several ways of going to *London*.

MY Landlady was very Courteous, took my Money for my Reckoning, but was call'd away, all the House being in a hurry; so I left her, took the Fellow up to my Chamber, gave him the Trunk, or Portmanteua, for it was like a Trunk, and wrapt it about with an old Apron, and he went directly to his Boat with it, and I after him, no Body asking us the least Question about it; as for the drunken *Dutch* Footman he was still a sleep, and his Master with other Foreign Gentlemen at Supper, and very Merry below; so I went clean off with it to *Ipswich*, and going in the Night, the People of the House knew nothing, but that I was gone to *London*, by the *Harwich* Wherry as I had told my Landlady.

I WAS plagu'd at *Ipswich* with the Custom-House Officers, who stopt my Trunk, *as I call'd it*, and would open, and search it; I was willing I told them, they should search it, but my Husband had the Key, and he was not yet come from *Harwich*; this I said, that if upon searching it, they should find all the things be such, as properly belong'd to a Man rather than a Woman, it should not seem strange to them; however, they being possitive to open the Trunk, I consented to have it be broken open, that is to say, to have the Lock taken off, which was not difficult.

THEY found nothing for their turn, for the Trunk had been search'd before, but they discover'd several things very much to my satisfaction, as particularly a parcel of Money in *French* Pistoles, and some *Dutch* Ducatoons, or *Rix* Dollars,[1] and the rest was chiefly two Perriwigs, wearing Linnen, and Razors, Wash-balls,[2] Perfumes and other useful things, Necessaries for a Gentleman;[1] which all pass'd for my Husband's, and so I was quit of them.

IT was now very early in the Morning, and not Light, and I knew not well what Course to take; for I made no doubt but I should be pursued in the Morning, and perhaps be taken with the things about me; so I resolv'd upon taking new Measures; I went publickly to an Inn in the Town with my Trunk, *as I call'd it*, and having taken the Substance out, I did not think the Lumber of it worth my concern; however, I gave it the Landlady of the House with a Charge to take great Care of it, and lay it up safe till I should come again, and away I walk'd into the Street.

WHEN I was got into the Town a great way from the Inn, I met with an antient Woman who had just open'd her Door, and I fell into Chat with her, and ask'd her a great many wild Questions of things all remote to my Purpose and Design, but in my Discourse I found by her how the Town was situated, that I was in a Street which went out towards *Hadly*; but that such a Street went towards the Water-side, such a Street went into the Heart of the Town; and at last such a Street went towards *Colchester*, and so the *London* Road lay there.

I HAD soon my Ends of this old Woman; for I only wanted to know which was *London* Road, and away I walk'd as fast as I could; not that I intended to go on Foot, either to *London* or to *Colchester*, but I wanted to get quietly away from *Ipswich*.

I WALK'D about two or three Mile, and then I met a plain Countryman, who was busy about some Husbandry work I did not know what; and I ask'd him a great many Questions first, not much to the purpose; but at last told him I was going for *London*, and the Coach was full, and I cou'd not get a Passage, and ask'd him if he cou'd not tell me where to hire a Horse that would carry double, and an honest Man to ride before me to *Colchester*, so that I might get a Place there in the Coaches; the honest Clown look'd earnestly at me, and said nothing for above half a Minute; when scratching his

Pole,[1] a Horse say you, and to *Colchester* to carry double; why yes Mistress, alack-a-day, you may have Horses enough for Money; well Friend, *says I*, that I take for granted, I don't expect it without Money: Why but Mistress, *says he*, how much are you willing to give; nay, says I again, Friend, I don't know what your Rates are in the Country here, for I am a Stranger; but if you can get one for me, get it as Cheap as you can, and I'll give you somewhat for your Pains.

WHY that's honestly said too, says the Countryman; *not so honest neither*, said I, to myself, *if thou knewest all*; why Mistress, *says he*, I have a Horse that will carry Double, and I don't much care if I go my self with you; *and the like*: Will you, *says I*? well I believe you are an honest Man, if you will, I shall be glad of it, I'll pay you in Reason; why look ye Mistress, *says he*, I won't be out of Reason with you then, if I carry you to *Colechester*, it will be worth five Shillings for myself and my Horse, for I shall hardly come back to Night.

IN short, I hir'd the honest Man and his Horse; but when we came to a Town upon the Road, I do not remember the Name of it, but it stands upon a River,[2] I pretended myself very ill, and I could go no farther that Night, but if he would stay there with me, because I was a Stranger I would pay him for himself and his Horse with all my Heart.

THIS I did because I knew the *Dutch* Gentlemen and their Servants would be upon the Road that Day, either in the Stage Coaches, or riding Post, and I did not know but the drunken Fellow, or some body else that might have seen me at *Harwich*, might see me again, and so I thought that in one Days stop they would be all gone by.

WE lay all that Night there, and the next Morning it was not very early when I set out, so that it was near Ten a-Clock by that time I got to *Colechester*: It was no little Pleasure that I saw the Town, where I had so many pleasant Days, and I made many Enquiries after the good old Friends, I had once had there, but could make little out, they were all dead or remov'd: The young Ladies had been all married or gone to *London*; the old Gentleman, and the old Lady that had been my early Benefactress all dead; and which troubled me most the young Gentleman my first Lover, and afterwards my Brother-in-Law was dead; but two Sons Men grown, were left of him, but they too were Transplanted to *London*.

I DISMISS'D my old Man here, and stay'd incognito for three or four Days in *Colechester*, and then took a Passage in a Waggon, because I would not venture being seen in the *Harwich* Coaches; but I needed not have used so much Caution, for there was no Body in *Harwich* but the Woman of the House, could have known me; nor was it rational to think that she, considering the hurry she was in, and that she never saw me but once, and that by Candle light, should have ever discover'd me.

I WAS now return'd to *London*, and tho' by the Accident of the last Adventure, I got something considerable, yet I was not fond of any more Country rambles, nor should I have ventur'd Abroad again if I had carried the Trade on to the End of my Days; I gave my Governess a History of my Travels, she lik'd the *Harwich* Journey well enough, and in Discoursing of these things between our selves she observ'd, that a Theif being a Creature that Watches the Advantages of other Peoples mistakes, 'tis impossible but that to one that is vigilant and industrious many Opportunities must happen, and therefore she thought that one so exquisitely keen in the Trade as I was, would scarce fail of something extraordinary where ever I went.

ON the other hand, every Branch of my Story, if duly consider'd, may be useful to honest People, and afford a due Caution to People of some sort, or other to Guard against the like Surprizes, and to have their Eyes about them when they have to do with Strangers of any kind, for 'tis very seldom that some Snare or other is not in their way. The Moral indeed of all my History is left to be gather'd by the Senses and Judgment of the Reader; I am not Qualified to preach to them, let the Experience of one Creature compleatly Wicked, and compleatly Miserable be a Storehouse of useful warning to those that read.

I AM drawing now towards a new Variety of the Scenes of Life: Upon my return, being hardened by a long Race of Crime, and Success unparalell'd, at least in the reach of my own Knowledge, I had, as I have said, no thoughts of laying down a Trade, which if I was to judge by the Example of others, must however End at last in Misery and Sorrow.

IT was on the *Christmas-day* following in the Evening, that to finish a long Train of Wickedness, I went Abroad to see what might offer in my way; when going by a Working Silver-Smiths in *Foster-lane*,[1] I saw a tempting Bait indeed, and not to be resisted by one of my Occupation; for the Shop had no Body in it, as I could see, and a great deal of loose Plate lay in the Window, and at the Seat of the Man, who usually as I suppose Work'd at one side of the Shop.

I WENT boldly in and was just going to lay my Hand upon a peice of Plate, and might have done it, and carried it clear off, for any care that the Men who belong'd to the Shop had taken of it; but an officious Fellow in a House, not a Shop, on the other side of the Way, seeing me go in, and observing that there was no Body in the Shop, comes running over the Street, and into the Shop, and without asking me what I was, or who, seizes upon me, and cries out for the People of the House.

I HAD not as I said above, touch'd any thing in the Shop, and seeing a glimpse of some Body running over to the Shop, I had so much presence of Mind, as to knock very hard with my Foot on the Floor of the House, and was just calling out too, when the Fellow laid Hands on me.

HOWEVER as I had always most Courage, when I was in most danger; so when the Fellow laid Hands on me, I stood very high upon it, that I came in, to buy half a Dozen of silver Spoons, and to my good Fortune, it was a Silver-smith's that sold Plate, as well as work'd Plate, for other Shops: The Fellow laugh'd at that Part, and put such a value upon the Service that he had done his Neighbour, that he would have it be that I came not to buy, but to steal, and raising a great Crowd, I said to the Master of the Shop, who by this time was fetch'd Home from some Neighbouring

Place, that it was in vain to make Noise, and enter into Talk there of the Case; the Fellow had insisted, that I came to steal, and he must prove it, and I desir'd we might go before a Magistrate without any more Words; for I began to see I should be too hard for the Man that had seiz'd me.

THE Master and Mistress of the Shop were really not so violent, as the Man from tother side of the Way, and the Man said, Mistress you might come into the Shop with a good Design for ought I know, but it seem'd a dangerous thing for you to come into such a Shop as mine is, when you see no Body there, and I cannot do so little Justice to my Neighbour, who was so kind to me, as not to acknowledge he had reason on his Side; tho' upon the whole I do not find you attempt'd to take any thing, and I really know not what to do in it: I press'd him to go before a Magistrate with me, and if any thing cou'd be prov'd on me, that was like a design of Robbery, I should willingly submit, but if not I expected reparation.

JUST while we were in this Debate, and a Crowd of People gather'd about the Door came by Sir *T. B.* an Alderman of the City, and Justice of the Peace, and the Goldsmith hearing of it goes out, and entreated his Worship to come in and decide the Case.

GIVE the Goldsmith his due, he told his Story with a great deal of Justice and Moderation, and the Fellow that had come over, and seiz'd upon me, told his with as much Heat, and foollish Passion, which did me good still, rather than Harm: It came then to my turn to speak, and I told his Worship that I was a Stranger in *London*, being newly come out of the *North*, that I Lodg'd in such a Place, that I was passing this Street, and went into the Goldsmiths Shop to buy half a Dozen of Spoons, by great good Luck I had an old silver Spoon in my Pocket, which I pull'd out, and told him I had carried that Spoon to match it with half a Dozen of new ones, that it might match some I had in the Country.

THAT seeing no Body in the Shop, I knock'd with my Foot very hard to make the People hear, and had also call'd aloud with my Voice: Tis true, there was loose Plate in the

Shop, but that no Body cou'd say I had touch'd any of it, or gone near it; that a Fellow came running into the Shop out of the Street, and laid Hands on me in a furious manner, in the very Moments, while I was calling, for the People of the House; that if he had really had a mind to have done his Neighbour any Service, he should have stood at a distance, and silently watch'd to see whether I had touch'd any thing, or no, and then have clap'd in upon me,[1] and taken me in the Fact: That is very true, *says Mr. Alderman*, and turning to the Fellow that stopt me, he ask'd him if it was true that I knock'd with my Foot, he said yes I had knock'd, but that might be because of his coming; Nay, says *the Alderman*, taking him short, now you contradict yourself, for just now you said, she was in the Shop with her back to you, and did not see you till you came upon her; now it was true, that my back was partly to the Street, but yet as my Business was of a kind that requir'd me to have my Eyes every way, so I really had a glance of him running over, as I said before, tho' he did not perceive it.

AFTER a full Hearing, the Alderman gave it as his Opinion, that his Neighbour was under a mistake, and that I was Innocent, and the Goldsmith acquiesc'd in it too, and his Wife, and so I was dismiss'd; but as I was going to depart, Mr. *Alderman* said, but *hold Madam*, if you were designing to buy Spoons I hope you will not let my Friend here lose his Customer by the Mistake: I readily answer'd, no Sir, I'll buy the Spoons still if he can Match my odd Spoon, which I brought for a Pattern, and the Goldsmith shew'd me some of the very same Fashion; so he weigh'd the Spoons, and they came to five and thirty Shillings, so I pulls out my Purse to pay him, in which I had near 20 Guineas, for I never went without such a Sum about me, what ever might happen, and I found it of use at other times as well as now.

WHEN Mr. *Alderman* saw my Money, *he said*, well Madam, now I am satisfy'd you were wrong'd, and it was for this Reason, that I mov'd you should buy the Spoons, and staid till you had bought them, for if you had not had Money to pay for them, I should have suspected that you did not come into the Shop with an intent to buy, for indeed the sort of People who come upon those Designs that you have been Charg'd with, are seldom troubl'd with much Gold in their Pockets, as I see you are.

I SMIL'D, and told his Worship, that then I ow'd something of his Favour to my Money, but I hop'd he saw reason also in the Justice he had done me before; he said, yes he had, but this had confirm'd his Opinion, and he was fully satisfy'd now of my having been injur'd; so I came off with flying Colours, tho' from an Affair, in which I was at the very brink of Destruction.

IT was but three Days after this, that not at all made Cautious by my former Danger as I us'd to be, and still pursuing the Art which I had so long been employ'd in, I ventur'd into a House where I saw the Doors open, and furnish'd myself as I thought verily without being perceiv'd, with two Peices of flower'd Silks, such as they call Brocaded Silk, very rich; it was not a Mercers Shop, nor a Warehouse of a Mercer, but look'd like a private Dwelling-House, and was it seems Inhabited by a Man that sold Goods for the Weavers to the Mercers, like a Broker or Factor.

THAT I may make short of this black Part of this Story, I was attack'd by two Wenches that came open Mouth'd at me just as I was going out at the Door, and one of them pull'd me back into the Room, while the other shut the Door upon me; I would have given them good Words, but there was no room for it; two fiery Dragons cou'd not have been more furious than they were; they tore my Cloths, bully'd and roar'd as if they would have murther'd me; the Mistress of the House came next, and then the Master, and all outrageous, for a while especially.

I GAVE the Master very good Words, told him the Door was open, and things were a Temptation to me, that I was poor, and distress'd, and Poverty was what many could not resist, and beg'd him with Tears to have pity on me; the Mistress of the House was mov'd with Compassion, and

enclin'd to have let me go, and had almost perswaded her
Husband to it also, but the sawcy Wenches were run even
before they were sent, and had fetch'd a Constable, and then
the Master said, he could not go back, I must go before a
Justice, and answer'd his Wife that he might come into
Trouble himself if he should let me go.

THE sight of the Constable indeed struck me with terror,
and I thought I should have sunk into the Ground; I fell
into faintings, and indeed the People themselves thought I
would have died, when the Woman argued again for me, and
entreated her Husband, seeing they had lost nothing to let
me go: I offer'd him to pay for the two Peices whatever the
value was, tho' I had not got them, and argued that as he had
his Goods, and had really lost nothing, it would be cruel to
pursue me to Death, and have my Blood for the bare Attempt
of taking them; I put the Constable in mind that I had broke
no Doors, nor carried any thing away; and when I came to
the Justice, and pleaded there that I had neither broken any
thing to get in, nor carried any thing out, the Justice was
enclin'd to have releas'd me; but the first sawcy Jade that
stop'd me, affirming that I was going out with the Goods,
but that she stop'd me and pull'd me back as I was upon the
Threshold, the Justice upon that point committed me, and I
was carried to *Newgate*; that horrid Place! my very Blood
chills at the mention of its Name; the Place, where so many
of my Comrades had been lock'd up, and from whence they
went to the fatal Tree;[1] the Place where my Mother suffered
so deeply, where I was brought into the World, and from
whence I expected no Redemption, but by an infamous
Death: To conclude, the Place that had so long expected me,
and which with so much Art and Success I had so long
avoided.

I WAS now fix'd indeed; 'tis impossible to describe the
terror of my mind, when I was first brought in, and when I
look'd round upon all the horrors of that dismal Place: I
look'd on myself as lost, and that I had nothing to think of,
but of going out of the World, and that with the utmost

Infamy; the hellish Noise,[1] the Roaring, Swearing and Clamour, the Stench and Nastiness, and all the dreadful croud of Afflicting things that I saw there; joyn'd together to make the Place seem an Emblem of Hell itself,[2] and a kind of an Entrance into it.

Now I reproach'd myself with the many hints I had had, *as I have mentioned above*, from my own Reason, from the Sense of my good Circumstances, and of the many Dangers I had escap'd to leave off while I was well, and how I had withstood them all, and hardened my Thoughts against all Fear; it seem'd to me that I was hurried on by an inevitable and unseen Fate to this Day of Misery, and that now I was to Expiate all my Offences at the Gallows, that I was now to give satisfaction to Justice with my Blood, and that I was come to the last Hour of my Life, and of my Wickedness together: These things pour'd themselves in upon my Thoughts in a confus'd manner, and left me overwhelm'd with Melancholly and Despair.

THEN I repented heartily of all my Life past, but that Repentance yielded me no Satisfaction, no Peace, no not in the least, because, *as I said to myself*, it was repenting after the Power of farther Sinning was taken away: I seem'd not to Mourn that I had committed such Crimes, and for the Fact, as it was an Offence against God and my Neighbour; but I mourn'd that I was to be punish'd for it;[3] I was a Penitent as I thought, not that I had sinn'd, but that I was to suffer, and this took away all the Comfort, and even the hope of my Repentance in my own Thoughts.

I GOT no sleep for several Nights or Days after I came into that wretch'd Place, and glad I wou'd have been for some time to have died there, tho' I did not consider dying as it ought to be consider'd neither, indeed nothing could be fill'd with more horror to my Imagination than the very Place, nothing was more odious to me than the Company that was there: O! if I had but been sent to any Place in the World, and not to *Newgate*, I should have thought myself happy.

In the next Place, how did the harden'd Wretches that were there before me Triumph over me? what! Mrs. *Flanders* come to *Newgate* at last? what Mrs. *Mary*, Mrs. *Molly*, and after that plain *Moll Flanders*? They thought the Devil had help'd me they said, that I had reign'd so long, they expected me there many Years ago, and was I come at last? then they flouted me with my Dejections, welcom'd me to the Place, wish'd me Joy, bid me have a good Heart, not to be cast down, things might not be so bad as I fear'd, and the like; then call'd for Brandy, and drank to me; but put it all up to my Score,[1] for they told me I was but just come to the College, *as they call'd it*,[2] and sure I had Money in my Pocket, tho' they had none.

I Ask'd one of this Crew how long she had been there? she said four Months; I ask'd her, how the Place look'd to her when she first came into it? just as it did now to me, *says she*, dreadful and frightful, that she thought she was in Hell, and I believe so still, *adds she*, *but it is natural to me now*, *I don't disturb myself about it*: I suppose says I, you are in no danger of what is to follow: Nay, *says she*, for you are mistaken there I assure you, for I am under Sentence, only I pleaded my Belly, but I am no more with Child, than the Judge that try'd me, and I expect to be call'd down next Sessions; *this* Calling Down, is calling down *to their former Judgement*, *when a Woman has been respited for her Belly*, *but proves not to be with Child*, *or if she has been with Child*, *and has been brought to Bed*. Well says I, and are you thus easy? ay, *says she*, I can't help myself, what signifyes being sad? If I am hang'd there's an End of me, *says she*, and away she turns Dancing, and Sings as she goes the following Peice of *Newgate* Wit,

* The Bell at St.
Sepulcher's[3] which Tolls
upon Execution Day.
If I swing by the String,
I shall hear the *Bell ring*.

And then there's an End of poor *Jenny*.

I MENTION this, because it would be worth the Observation of any Prisoner, who shall hereafter fall into the same Misfortune and come to that dreadful Place of *Newgate*; how Time, Necessity, and Conversing with the Wretches that are there Familiarizes the Place to them; how at last they become reconcil'd to that which at first was the greatest Dread upon their Spirits in the World, and are as impudently Chearful and Merry in their Misery, as they were when out of it.

I CAN not say, as some do, this Devil is not so black, as he is painted;[1] for indeed no Colours can represent the Place to the Life; nor any Soul conceive aright of it, but those who have been Sufferers there: But how Hell should become by degrees so natural, and not only tollerable, but even agreeable, is a thing Unintelligible, but by those who have Experienc'd it, as I have.

THE same Night that I was sent to *Newgate*, I sent the News of it to my old Governess, who was surpriz'd at it you may be sure, and spent the Night almost as ill out of *Newgate*, as I did in it.

THE next Morning, she came to see me, she did what she cou'd to Comfort me, but she saw that was to no purpose; however, as she said, to sink under the Weight, was but to encrease the Weight, she immediately applied her self to all the proper Methods to prevent the Effects of it, which we fear'd; and first she found out the two fiery Jades that had surpriz'd me; she tamper'd with them, persuad'd them, offer'd them Money, and in a Word, try'd all imaginable ways to prevent a Prosecution; she offer'd one of the Wenches 100 *l.* to go away from her Mistress, and not to appear against me; but she was so resolute, that tho' she was but a Servant-Maid, at 3 *l.* a Year Wages or thereabouts, she refus'd it, and would have refus'd it, as my Governess said she believ'd, if she had offer'd her 500 *l.* Then she attack'd the tother Maid, she was not so hard Hearted in appearance as the other; and sometimes seem'd inclin'd to be merciful; but the first Wench kept her up, and chang'd her Mind, and would not so much as let my Governess talk with her, but threatn'd to have her up for Tampering with the Evidence.[1]

THEN she apply'd to the Master, that is to say, the Man whose Goods had been stol'n, and particularly to his Wife, who as I told you was enclin'd at first to have some Compassion for me; she found the Woman the same still, but the Man alledg'd he was bound by the Justice that committed me, to Prosecute, and that he should forfeit his Recognizance.[2]

MY Governess offer'd to find Friends that should get his Recognizances off of the File, as they call it, and that he should not suffer; but it was not possible to Convince him, that could be done, or that he could be safe any way in the World, but by appearing against me; so I was to have three Witnesses of Fact against me, the Master and his two Maids, that is to say, I was as certain to be cast for my Life, as I was certain that I was alive, and I had nothing to do, but to think of dying, and prepare for it: I had but a sad foundation to build upon, as I said before, for all my Repentance appear'd to me to be only the Effect of my fear of Death, not a sincere regret for the wicked Life that I had liv'd, and which had brought this Misery upon me, or for the offending my Creator, who was now suddenly to be my Judge.

I LIV'D many Days here under the utmost horror of Soul; I had Death as it were in view, and thought of nothing Night and Day, but of Gibbets and Halters, evil Spirits and Devils; it is not to be express'd by Words how I was harrass'd, between the dreadful Apprehensions of Death, and the Terror of my Conscience reproaching me with my past horrible Life.

THE Ordinary of *Newgate*[3] came to me, and talk'd a little in his way, but all his Divinity run upon Confessing my Crime,[4] as he call'd it, (tho' he knew not what I was in for) making a full Discovery, and the like, without which he told me God would never forgive me;[5] and he said so little to the purpose, that I had no manner of Consolation from him; and then to observe the poor Creature preaching Confession and Repentance to me in the Morning, and find him drunk with Brandy and Spirits by Noon; this had something in it so

shocking, that I began to Nauseate the Man more, than his
Work, and his Work too by degrees for the sake of the Man;
so that I desir'd him to trouble me no more.

I KNOW not how it was, but by the indefatigable Application of my diligent Governess I had no Bill preferr'd against
me the first Sessions, I mean to the Grand Jury, at *Guild-
Hall*; so I had another Month, or five Weeks before me, and
without doubt this ought to have been accepted by me, as
so much time given me for Reflection upon what was past,
and preparation for what was to come, or in a Word, I
ought to have esteem'd it, as a space given me for Repentance,
and have employ'd it as such; but it was not in me, I was
sorry (*as before*) for being in *Newgate*, but had very few
Signs of Repentance about me.

ON the contrary, like the Waters in the Caveties, and
Hollows of Mountains, which petrifies and turns into Stone
whatever they are suffer'd to drop upon;[1] so the continual
Conversing with such a Crew of Hell-Hounds as I was with
had the same common Operation upon me, as upon other
People, I degenerated into Stone; I turn'd first Stupid and
Senseless, then Brutish and thoughtless, and at last raving
Mad as any of them were; and in short, I became as naturally
pleas'd and easie with the Place, as if indeed I had been
Born there.

IT is scarce possible to imagine that our Natures should be
capable of so much Degeneracy, as to make that pleasant and
agreeable that in it self is the most compleat Misery. Here
was a Circumstance, that I think it is scarce possible to
mention a worse; I was as exquisitely miserable as speaking
of common Cases, it was possible for any one to be that had
Life and Health, and Money to help them as I had.

I HAD a weight of Guilt upon me enough to sink any
Creature who had the least power of Reflection left, and had
any Sense upon them of the Happiness of this Life, or the
Misery of another; then I had at first remorse indeed, but
no Repentance; I had now neither Remorse or Repentance:
I had a Crime charg'd on me, the Punishment of which was

Death by our Law; the Proof so evident, that there was no room for me so much as to plead not Guilty; I had the Name of old Offender, so that I had nothing to expect but Death in a few Weeks time, neither had I myself any thoughts of Escaping, and yet a certain strange Lethargy of Soul possess'd me, I had no Trouble, no Apprehensions, no Sorrow about me, the first Surprize was gone; I was, I may well say I know not how; my Senses, my Reason, nay, my Conscience were all a-sleep; my Course of Life for forty Years had been a horrid Complication of Wickedness, Whoredom, Adultery, Incest, Lying, Theft, and in a Word, every thing but Murther and Treason had been my Practice from the Age of Eighteen, or thereabouts to Threescore; and now I was ingulph'd in the misery of Punishment, and had an infamous Death just at the Door, and yet I had no Sense of my Condition, no Thought of Heaven or Hell at least, that went any farther than a bare flying Touch, like the Stich or Pain that gives a Hint and goes off; I neither had a Heart to ask God's Mercy, or indeed to think of it, and in this I think I have given a brief Description of the compleatest Misery on Earth.

ALL my terrifying Thoughts were past, the Horrors of the Place, were become Familiar, and I felt no more uneasinesses at the Noise and Clamours of the Prison, than they did who made that Noise; in a Word, I was become a meer *Newgate-Bird*, as Wicked and as Outragious as any of them; nay, I scarce retain'd the Habit and Custom of good Breeding, and Manners, which all along till now run thro' my Conversation; so thoro' a Degeneracy had possess'd me, that I was no more the same thing that I had been, than if I had never been otherwise than what I was now.

IN the middle of this harden'd Part of my Life, I had another sudden Surprize, which call'd me back a little to that thing call'd Sorrow, which indeed I began to be past the Sense of before: They told me one Night, that there was brought into the Prison late the Night before three Highway-Men, who had committed a Robbery somewhere on the

Road to *Windsor*, *Hounslow-Heath*, I think it was, and were pursu'd to *Uxbridge* by the Country, and were taken there after a gallant Resistance, in which I know not how many of the Country People were wounded, and some kill'd.

IT is not to be wonder'd that we Prisoners, were all desirous enough to see these brave topping Gentlemen[1] that were talk'd up to be such, as their Fellows had not been known, and especially because it was said they would in the Morning be remov'd into the Press-Yard,[2] having given Money to the Head-Master of the Prison, to be allow'd the liberty of that better Part of the Prison: So we that were Women plac'd ourselves in the way that we would be sure to see them; but nothing cou'd express the Amazement and Surprize I was in, when the very first Man that came out I knew to be my *Lancashire* Husband, the same with whom I liv'd so well at *Dunstable*, and the same who I afterwards saw at *Brickill*, when I was married to my last Husband, as has been related.

I WAS struck Dumb at the Sight, and knew neither what to say, or what to do, he did not know me, and that was all the present Relief I had, I quitted my Company, and retir'd as much as that dreadful Place suffers any Body to retire, and I cry'd vehemently for a great while; dreadful Creature, that I am, *said I*, How many poor People have I made Miserable? How many desperate Wretches have I sent to the Devil; This Gentleman's Misfortunes I plac'd all to my own Account: He had told me at *Chester*, he was ruin'd by that Match, and that his Fortunes were made desperate on my Account; for that thinking I had been a Fortune he was run into Debt more than he was able to pay, and that he knew not what Course to take; that he would go into the Army, and carry a Musquet, or buy a Horse and take a Tour, as he call'd it; and tho' I never told him that I was a Fortune, and so did not actually Deceive him myself, yet I did encourage the having it thought that I was so, and by that means I was the occasion originally of his Mischief.

THE Surprize of this thing only, struck deeper into my

Thoughts, and gave me stronger Reflections than all that had befallen me before; I griev'd Day and Night for him, and the more, for that they told me, he was the Captain of the Gang, and that he had committed so many Robberies, that *Hind*, or *Whitney*, or the *Golden Farmer*[1] were Fools to him; that he would surely be hang'd if there were no more Men left in the Country he was born in; and that there would abundance of People come in against him.

I WAS overwhelm'd with grief for him; my own Case gave me no disturbance compar'd to this, and I loaded my self with Reproaches on his Account; I bewail'd his Misfortunes, and the ruin he was now come to, at such a Rate, that I relish'd nothing now, as I did before, and the first Reflections I made upon the horrid detestable Life I had liv'd, began to return upon me, and as these things return'd my abhorrance of the Place I was in, and of the way of living in it, return'd also; in a word, I was perfectly chang'd, and become another Body.

WHILE I was under these influences of sorrow for him, came Notice to me that the next Sessions approaching, there would be a Bill preferr'd to the Grand Jury against me, and that I should be certainly try'd for my Life at the *Old-Baily*: My Temper was touch'd before, the harden'd wretch'd boldness of Spirit, which I had acquir'd in the Prison abated, and conscious Guilt began to flow in upon my Mind: In short, I began to think, and to think is one real Advance from Hell to Heaven; all that Hellish harden'd state and temper of Soul, which I have said so much of before, is but a deprivation of Thought; he that is restor'd to his Power of thinking, is restor'd to himself.

As soon as I began, I say to Think, the first thing that occurr'd to me broke out thus; Lord! what will become of me, I shall certainly die! I shall be cast[2] to be sure, and there is nothing beyond that but Death! I have no Friends, what shall I do? I shall be certainly cast; Lord, have Mercy upon me, what will become of me? This was a sad Thought, you will say, to be the first after so long time that had started into my Soul of that kind, and yet even this was nothing but fright, at what was to come; there was not a Word of sincere Repentance in it all: However, I was indeed dreadfully dejected, and disconsolate to the last degree; and as I had no Friend in the World to communicate my distress'd Thoughts to, it lay so heavy upon me, that it threw me into Fits, and Swoonings several times a-Day: I sent for my old Governess, and she, *give her her due*, acted the Part of a true Friend, she left me no Stone unturn'd to prevent the Grand Jury finding [the Bill, and finding] out one or two of the Jury Men, talk'd with them, and endeavour'd to possess them with favourable Dispositions,[1] on Account that nothing was taken away, and no House broken, &c. but all would not do, they were over-ruled by the rest, the two Wenches swore home to the Fact, and the Jury found the Bill against me[2] for Robbery and Housebreaking, that is for Felony and Burglary.[3]

I Sunk down when they brought me News of it, and after I came to myself again, I thought I should have died with the weight of it: My Governess acted a true Mother to me, she pittied me, she cryed with me, and for me; but she cou'd not help me; and to add to the Terror of it, 'twas the Discourse all over the House, that I should die for it; I cou'd hear them talk it among themselves very often; and see them shake their Heads, and say they were sorry for it, and the like, as is usual in the Place; but still no Body came to tell me their Thoughts, till at last one of the Keepers came to me privately, and said with a Sigh, well Mrs. *Flanders*, you will be tried a *Friday*, (this was but a *Wednesday*,) what do you intend to do? I turn'd as white as a Clout,[4] and said, God knows what I shall do, for my part I know not what to do; why, *says he*, I won't flatter you, I would have you prepare for Death, for I doubt you will be Cast, and as they say, you are an old Offender, I doubt you will find but little Mercy; They say, *added he*, your Case is very plain, and that the Witnesses swear so home against you, there will be no standing it.

This was a stab into the very Vitals of one under such a

Burthen as I was oppress'd with before, and I cou'd not speak to him a Word good or bad, for a great while, but at last I burst out into Tears, and said to him, Lord! Mr. ———— What must I do? Do, *says he*, send for the Ordinary send for a Minister, and talk with him, for indeed Mrs. *Flanders*, unless you have very good Friends, you are no Woman for this World.

THIS was plain dealing indeed, but it was very harsh to me, at least I thought it so: He left me in the greatest Confusion imaginable, and all that Night I lay awake; and now I began to say my Prayers, which I had scarce done before since my last Husband's Death, or from a little while after; and truly I may well call it, saying my Prayers; for I was in such a Confusion, and had such horrour upon my Mind, that tho' I cry'd, and repeated several times the Ordinary Expression of, *Lord have Mercy upon me*; I never brought my self to any Sense of my being a miserable Sinner, as indeed I was, and of Confessing my Sins to God, and begging Pardon for the sake of Jesus Christ; I was overwhelm'd with the Sense of my Condition, being try'd for my Life, and being sure to be Condemn'd, and then I was as sure to be Executed, and on this Account, I cry'd out all Night, Lord! what will become of me? Lord! what shall I do? Lord! I shall be hang'd, Lord have mercy upon me, and the like.

MY poor afflicted Governess was now as much concern'd as I, and a great deal more truly Penitent; tho' she had no prospect of being brought to Tryal and Sentence, not but that she deserv'd it as much as I, and so she said herself; but she had not done any thing herself for many Years, other than receiving what I, and others stole, and encouraging[1] us to steal it: But she cry'd and took on, like a distracted Body, wringing her Hands, and crying out that she was undone, that she believ'd there was a Curse from Heaven upon her, that she should be damn'd, that she had been the Destruction of all her Friends, that she had brought such a one, and such a one, and such one to the Gallows; and there she reckon'd

up ten or eleven People, some of which I have given an
Account of that came to untimely Ends, and that now she
was the occasion of my Ruin, for she had persuaded me to
go on, when I would have left off: I interrupted her there;
no Mother, no, *said I*, don't speak of that, for you would
have had me left off when I got the Mercer's Money again,
and when I came home from *Harwich*, and I would not
hearken to you, therefore you have not been to blame, it is
I only have ruin'd myself, I have brought myself to this
Misery, and thus we spent many Hours together.

WELL there was no Remedy, the Prosecution went on,
and on the *Thursday* I was carried down to the Sessions-
House, where I was arraign'd, as they call'd it, and the next
Day I was appointed to be Try'd. At the Arraignment I
pleaded not Guilty, and well I might, for I was indicted for
Felony and Burglary; that is for feloniously stealing two
Pieces of Brocaded Silk, value 46 *l.* the Goods of *Anthony
Johnson*, and for breaking open his Doors; whereas I knew
very well they could not pretend to prove I had broken up
the Doors, or so much as lifted up a Latch.[1]

ON the *Friday* I was brought to my Tryal, I had exhausted my Spirits with Crying for two or three Days before,
that I slept better the *Thursday* Night than I expected, and
had more Courage for my Tryal, than indeed I thought
possible for me to have.

WHEN the Tryal began, and the Indictment was read, I
would have spoke, but they told me the Witnesses must be
heard first, and then I should have time to be heard. The
Witnesses were the two Wenches, a Couple of hard Mouth'd
Jades indeed, for tho' the thing was Truth in the main, yet
they aggravated it to the utmost extremity, and swore I had
the Goods wholly in my possession, that I had hid them
among my Cloaths, that I was going off with them, that I
had one Foot over the Threshold when they discovered
themselves, and then I put tother over, so that I was quite
out of the House in the Street with the Goods before they
took hold of me, and then they seiz'd me, and brought me

back again, and they took the Goods upon me: The Fact in
general was all true, but I believe, and insisted upon it, that
they stop'd me before I had set my Foot clear of the Threshold of the House; but that did not argue much, for certain
it was, that I had taken the Goods, and that I was bringing
them away, if I had not been taken.

BUT I pleaded that I had stole nothing, they had lost
nothing, that the Door was open, and I went in seeing the
Goods lye there, and with Design to buy, if seeing no Body
in the House, I had taken any of them up in my Hand, it
cou'd not be concluded that I intended to steal them, for
that I never carried them farther then the Door to look on
them with the better Light.

THE Court would not allow that by any means, and made
a kind of a Jest of my intending to buy the Goods, that
being no Shop for the Selling of any thing, and as to carrying
them to the Door to look at them, the Maids made their
impudent Mocks upon that, and spent their Wit upon it
very much; told the Court I had look'd at them sufficiently,
and approv'd them very well, for I had pack'd them up
under my Cloaths, and was a going with them.

IN short, I was found Guilty of Felony, but acquited of
the Burglary, which was but small Comfort[1] to me, the first
bringing me to a Sentence of Death, and the last would have
done no more: The next Day, I was carried down to receive
the dreadful Sentence, and when they came to ask me what
I had to say, why Sentence should not pass, I stood mute a
while, but some Body that stood behind me, prompted me
aloud to speak to the Judges, for that they cou'd represent
things favourably for me: This encourag'd me to speak, and
I told them I had nothing to say to stop the Sentence; but
that I had much to say, to bespeak the Mercy of the Court,
that I hop'd they would allow something in such a Case, for
the Circumstances of it, that I had broken no Doors, had
carried nothing off, that no Body had lost any thing; that the
Person whose Goods they were was pleas'd to say, he desir'd
Mercy might be shown, which indeed he very honestly did,

that at the worst it was the first Offence, and that I had
never been before any Court of Justice before: And in a
Word, I spoke with more Courage than I thought I cou'd
have done, and in such a moving Tone, and tho' with Tears,
yet not so many Tears as to obstruct my Speech, that I
cou'd see it mov'd others to Tears that heard me.

THE Judges sat Grave and Mute, gave me an easy Hearing,
and time to say all that I would, but saying neither Yes, or
No to it, Pronounc'd the Sentence of Death upon me; a
Sentence that was to me like Death itself, which after it was
read confounded me; I had no more Spirit left in me, I had
no Tongue to speak, or Eyes to look up either to God or Man.

MY poor Governess was utterly Disconsolate, and she
that was my Comforter before, wanted Comfort now herself,
and sometimes Mourning, sometimes Raging, was as much
out of herself (as to all outward Appearance) as any mad
Woman in *Bedlam*:[1] Nor was she only Disconsolate as to me,
but she was struck with Horror at the Sense of her own
wicked Life, and began to look back upon it with a Taste
quite different from mine; for she was Penitent to the highest
Degree for her Sins, as well as Sorrowful for the Misfortune:
She sent for a Minister too, a serious pious good Man, and
apply'd herself with such earnestness by his assistance to the
Work of a sincere Repentance, that I believe, and so did the
Minister too, that she was a true Penitent, and which is still
more, she was not only so for the Occasion, and at that
Juncture, but she continu'd so, as I was inform'd to the Day
of her Death.

IT is rather to be thought of, than express'd what was now
my Condition; I had nothing before me but present Death;
and as I had no Friends to assist me, or to stir for me, I
expected nothing but to find my Name in the Dead Warrant,
which was to come down for the Execution the *Friday*
afterward, of five more and myself.

IN the mean time my poor distress'd Governess sent me a
Minister, who at her request first, and at my own afterwards
came to visit me: He exhorted me seriously to repent of all

my Sins, and to dally no longer with my Soul; not flattering myself with hopes of Life, which he said, he was inform'd there was no room to expect, but unfeignedly to look up to God with my whole Soul, and to cry for Pardon in the Name of Jesus Christ. He back'd his Discourses with proper Quotations of Scripture, encouraging the greatest Sinner to Repent, and turn from their Evil way, and when he had done, he kneel'd down and pray'd with me.

It was now, that for the first time I felt any real signs of Repentance; I now began to look back upon my past Life with abhorrence, and having a kind of view into the other Side of time, the things of Life, as I believe they do with every Body at such a time, began to look with a different Aspect, and quite another Shape, than they did before; the greatest and best things, the views of felicity, the joy, the griefs of Life were quite other things; and I had nothing in my Thoughts, but what was so infinitely Superior to what I had known in Life, that it appear'd to me to be the greatest stupidity in Nature to lay any weight upon any thing tho' the most valuable in this World.[1]

THE Word Eternity represented itself with all its incomprehensible Additions, and I had such extended Notions of it, that I know not how to express them: Among the rest, how vile, how gross, how absurd did every pleasant thing look? I mean, that we had counted pleasant before; especially when I reflected that these sordid Trifles were the things for which we forfeited eternal Felicity.

WITH these Reflections came in, of meer Course, severe Reproaches of my own Mind for my wretched Behaviour in my past Life; that I had forfeited all hope of any Happiness in the Eternity that I was just going to enter into, and on the contrary was entitul'd to all that was miserable, or had been conceiv'd of Misery; and all this with the frightful Addition of its being also Eternal.

I AM not capable of reading Lectures of Instruction to any Body, but I relate this in the very manner in which things then appear'd to me, as far as I am able; but infinitely short of the lively impressions which they made on my Soul at that time; indeed those Impressions are not to be explain'd by words, or if they are, I am not Mistress of Words enough to express them; It must be the Work of every sober Reader to make just Reflections on them, as their own Circumstances may direct; and without Question, this is what every one at sometime or other may feel something of; I mean a clearer Sight into things to come, than they had here, and a dark view of their own Concern in them.

But I go back to my own Case; the Minister press'd me to tell him, as far as I thought convenient, in what State I found myself as to the Sight I had of things beyond Life; he told me he did not come as Ordinary of the Place, whose business it is to extort Confessions from Prisoners, for private Ends,[1] or for the farther detecting of other Offenders; that his business was to move me to such freedom of Discourse as might serve to disburthen my own Mind, and furnish him to administer Comfort to me as far as was in his Power; and assur'd me, that whatever I said to him should remain with him, and be as much a Secret as if it was known only to God and myself; and that he desir'd to know nothing of me, but as above, to qualifie him to apply proper Advice and Assistance to me, and to pray to God for me.

This honest friendly way of treating me, unlock'd all the Sluces of my Passions: He broke into my very Soul by it; and I unravell'd all the Wickedness of my Life to him: In a word, I gave him an Abridgement of this whole History; I gave him the Picture of my Conduct for 50 Years in Miniature.

I Hid nothing from him, and he in return exhorted me to a sincere Repentance, explain'd to me what he meant by Repentance, and then drew out such a Scheme of infinite Mercy, proclaim'd from Heaven to Sinners of the greatest Magnitude, that he left me nothing to say, that look'd like despair or doubting of being accepted, and in this Condition he left me the first Night.

He visited me again the next Morning, and went on with his Method of explaining the Terms of Divine Mercy, which according to him consisted of nothing more, or more Difficult than that of being sincerely desirous of it, and willing to accept it; only a sincere Regret for, and hatred of those things I had done, which render'd me so just an Object of divine Vengeance: I am not able to repeat the excellent Discourses of this extraordinary Man; 'tis all that I am able to do to say, that he reviv'd my Heart, and brought me into such a Condition, that I never knew any thing of in my Life before: I was cover'd with Shame and Tears for things past, and yet had at the same time a secret surprizing Joy[1] at the Prospect of being a true Penitent, and obtaining the Comfort of a Penitent, I mean the hope of being forgiven; and so swift did Thoughts circulate, and so high did the impressions they had made upon me run, that I thought I cou'd freely have gone out that Minute to Execution, without any un-easiness at all, casting my Soul entirely into the Arms of infinite Mercy as a Penitent.

THE good Gentleman was so mov'd also in my behalf, with a view of the influence, which he saw these things had on me, that he blessed God he had come to visit me, and resolv'd not to leave me till the last Moment, that is not to leave visiting me.

IT was no less than 12 Days after our receiving Sentence, before any were order'd for Execution, and then upon a *Wednesday* the Dead Warrant, *as they call it*, came down, and I found my Name was among them; a terrible blow this was to my new Resolutions, indeed my Heart sunk within me, and I swoon'd away twice, one after another, but spoke not a word: The good Minister was sorely Afflicted for me, and did what he could to comfort me with the same Argu-ments, and the same moving Eloquence that he did before, and left me not that Evening so long as the Prison-keepers would suffer him to stay in the Prison, unless he wou'd be lock'd up with me all Night, which he was not willing to be.

I WONDER'D much that I did not see him all the next Day, *it being but the Day before the time appointed for Execution*; and I was greatly discouraged, and dejected in my Mind,

and indeed almost sunk for want of that Comfort, which he
had so often, and with such Success yeilded me on his
former Visits; I waited with great impatience, and under the
greatest oppressions of Spirits imaginable; till about four
a-Clock he came to my Apartment, for I had obtain'd the
Favour by the help of Money, nothing being to be done in
that Place without it, not to be kept in the Condemn'd Hole,
as they call it, among the rest of the Prisoners, who were to
die, but to have a little dirty Chamber to my self.

MY Heart leap'd within me for Joy, when I heard his
Voice at the Door even before I saw him; but let any one
Judge what kind of Motion I found in my Soul, when after
having made a short excuse for his not coming, he shew'd
me that his time had been employ'd on my Account; that he
had obtain'd a favourable Report from the Recorder to the
Secretary of State[1] in my particular Case, and in short that
he had brought me a Reprieve.

HE us'd all the Caution that he was able in letting me know
a thing, which it would have been a double Cruelty to have
conceal'd; and yet it was too much for me; for as Grief had
overset me before, so did Joy overset[2] now, and I fell into a
much more dangerous Swooning than I did at first, and it
was not without a great Difficulty that I was recover'd at all.

THE good Man having made a very Christian Exhortation
to me, not to let the Joy of my Reprieve, put the Remembrance of my past Sorrow out of my Mind; and having told
me that he must leave me, to go and enter the Reprieve in
the Books, and show it to the Sheriffs, stood up just before
his going away, and in a very earnest manner pray'd to God
for me, that my Repentance might be made Unfeign'd and
Sincere; and that my coming back as it were into Life again,
might not be a returning to the Follies of Life, which I had
made such solemn Resolutions to forsake, and to repent of
them; I joyn'd heartily in the Petition, and must needs say,
I had deeper Impressions upon my Mind all that Night, of
the Mercy of God in sparing my Life; and a greater
Detestation of my past Sins, from a Sense of the goodness

which I had tasted in this Case, than I had in all my Sorrow before.

THIS may be thought inconsistent in it self, and wide from the Business of this Book; Particularly, I reflect that many of those who may be pleas'd and diverted with the Relation of the wild and wicked part of my Story, may not relish this, which is really the best part of my Life, the most Advantageous to myself, and the most instructive to others; such however will I hope allow me the liberty to make my Story compleat: It would be a severe Satyr on such, to say they do not relish the Repentance as much as they do the Crime; and that they had rather the History were a compleat Tragedy, as it was very likely to have been.

BUT I go on with my Relation, the next Morning there was a sad Scene indeed in the Prison; the first thing I was saluted with in the Morning, was the Tolling of the great Bell at St. *Sepulchres*, as they call it, which usher'd in the Day: As soon as it began to Toll, a dismal groaning and crying was heard from the Condemn'd Hole, where there lay six poor Souls, who were to be Executed that Day, some for one Crime, some for another, and two of them for Murther.

THIS was follow'd by a confus'd Clamour in the House; among the several sorts of Prisoners, expressing their awkward Sorrows for the poor Creatures that were to die, but in a manner extreamly differing one from another; some cried for them; some huzza'd, and wish'd them a good Journey; some damn'd and curst those that had brought them to it, that is meaning the Evidence, or Prosecutors; many pittying them; and some few, but very few praying for them.

THERE was hardly room for so much Composure of Mind, as was requir'd for me to bless the merciful Providence that had as it were snatch'd me out of the Jaws of this Destruction: I remained as it were Dumb and Silent, overcome with the Sense of it, and not able to express what I had in my Heart; for the Passions on such Occasions as these, are certainly so agitated as not to be able presently to regulate their own Motions.

ALL the while the poor condemn'd Creatures were preparing to their Death, and the Ordinary *as they call him*, was busy with them, disposing them to submit to their Sentence: I say all this while I was seiz'd with a fit of trembling, as much as I cou'd have been, if I had been in the same Condition, as to be sure the Day before I expected to be; I was so violently agitated by this Surprising Fit, that I shook as if it had been in the cold Fit of an Ague; so that I could not speak or look, but like one Distracted: As soon as they were all put into the Carts and gone, which however I had not Courage enough to see, *I say*, as soon as they were gone, I fell into a fit of crying involuntarily, and without Design, but as a meer Distemper, and yet so violent, and it held me so long, that I knew not what Course to take, nor could I stop, or put a Checque to it, no not with all the Strength and Courage I had.

THIS fit of crying held me near two Hours and as I believe held me till they were all out of the World, and then a most humble Penitent serious kind of Joy succeeded; a real transport it was, or Passion of Joy, and Thankfulness, but still unable to give vent to it by Words,[1] and in this I continued most part of the Day.

IN the Evening the Good Minister visited me again, and then fell to his usual good Discourses, he Congratulated my having a space yet allow'd me for Repentance, whereas the state of those six poor Creatures was determin'd, and they were now pass'd the offers of Salvation; he earnestly press'd me to retain the same Sentiments of the things of Life, that I had when I had a view of Eternity; and at the End of all, told me I should not conclude that all was over, that a Reprieve was not a Pardon, that he could not yet answer for the Effects of it; however, I had this Mercy, that I had more time given me, and that it was my business to improve that time.

THIS Discourse, tho' very seasonable, left a kind of sadness on my Heart, as if I might expect the Affair would have a tragical Issue still, which however he had no certainty of, and I did not indeed at that time question him about it, he having said that he would do his utmost to bring it to a good End, and that he hoped he might, but he would not have me secure; and the Consequence prov'd that he had Reason for what he said.

It was about a Fortnight after this, that I had some just Apprehensions that I should be included in the next dead Warrant at the ensuing Sessions; and it was not without great difficulty, and at last an humble Petition for Transportation,[1] that I avoided it, so ill was I beholding to Fame, and so prevailing was the fatal Report of being an old Offender, tho' in that they did not do me strict Justice, for I was not in the Sense of the Law an old Offender, whatever I was in the Eye of the Judge; for I had never been before them in a judicial way before, so the Judges could not Charge me with being an old Offender, but the Recorder was pleas'd to represent my Case as he thought fit.

I Had now a certainty of Life indeed, but with the hard Conditions of being order'd for Transportation, which indeed was a hard Condition in it self, but not when comparatively considered; and therefore I shall make no Comments upon the Sentence, nor upon the Choice I was put to; we shall all choose any thing rather than Death, especially when 'tis attended with an uncomfortable prospect beyond it, which was my Case.

The good Minister whose interest, tho' *a Stranger to me*, had obtain'd me the Reprieve, mourn'd sincerely for this part; he was in hopes, *he said*, that I should have ended my Days under the Influence of good Instruction, that I might not have forgot my former Distresses, and that I should not have been turned loose again among such a wretched a Crew as they generally are, who are thus sent Abroad where, *as he said*, I must have more than ordinary secret Assistance from the Grace of God, if I did not turn as wicked again as ever.

I Have not for a good while mentioned my Governess,

who had during most, if not all of this part been dangerously Sick, and being in as near a view of Death, by her Disease, as I was by my Sentence, was a very great Penitent; I say, I have not mention'd her, nor indeed did I see her in all this time, but being now recovering, and just able to come Abroad, she came to see me.

I TOLD her my Condition, and what a different flux and reflux of Fears, and Hopes I had been agitated with; I told her, what I had escap'd, and upon what Terms, and she was present, when the Minister express'd his fears of my relapsing into wickedness upon my falling into the wretch'd Companies, that are generally Transported: Indeed I had a melancholly Reflection upon it in my own Mind, for I knew what a dreadful Gang was always sent away together, and I said to my Governess, that the good Minister's fears were not without Cause: Well, well, *says she*, but I hope you will not be tempted with such a horrid Example as that, and as soon as the Minister was gone, she told me, she would not have me discourag'd, for perhaps ways and means might be found out to dispose of me in a particular way, by my self, of which she would talk farther to me afterward.

I LOOK'D earnestly at her, and I thought she look'd more chearful than she usually had done, and I entertain'd immediately a Thousand Notions of being deliver'd, but could not for my Life imagine the Methods, or think of one that was in the least feizible; but I was too much concerned in it, to let her go from me without explaining herself, which tho' she was very loth to do, yet my importunity prevail'd, and while I was still pressing, she answer'd me in few Words, thus, Why, *you have Money, have you not*? did you ever know one in your Life that was Transported, and had a Hundred Pound in his Pocket, I'll warrant you Child,[1] *says she*.

I UNDERSTOOD her presently, but told her I would leave all that to her, but I saw no room to hope for any thing, but a strict Execution of the order, and as it was a severity that was esteem'd a Mercy, there was no doubt but it would be strictly observ'd; she said no more, but this, *we will try what can be done*, and so we parted for that Night.

I LAY in the Prison near fifteen Weeks after this order for Transportation was sign'd; what the Reason of it was, I know not, but at the end of this time I was put on Board of a Ship in the *Thames*, and with me a Gang of Thirteen, as harden'd vile Creatures as ever *Newgate* produc'd in my time; and it would really well take up a History longer than mine to describe the degrees of Impudence, and audacious Villany that those Thirteen were arriv'd to; and the manner of their behaviour in the Voyage; of which I have a very diverting Account by me, which the Captain of the Ship, who carried them over gave me the Minutes of, and which he caus'd his Mate to write down at large.

IT may perhaps be thought Trifling to enter here into a Relation of all the little incidents which attended me in this interval of my Circumstances; I mean between the final order for my Transportation, and the time of my going on board the Ship, and I am too near the End of my Story, to allow room for it, but something relating to me, *and my Lancashire Husband*, I must not omit.

HE had, *as I have observ'd already* been carried from the Master's side of the ordinary Prison,[1] into the Press-Yard, with three of his Comrades, for they found another to add to them after some time; here for what Reason I knew not, they were kept in Custody without being brought to Tryal almost three Months, it seems they found means to Bribe or buy off some of those who were expected to come in against them, and they wanted Evidence for some time to Convict them: After some puzzle on this Account at first, they made a shift to get proof enough against two of them, to carry them off; but the other two, of which my *Lancashire* Husband was one, lay still in Suspence: They had I think one positive Evidence against each of them; but the Law strictly obliging them to have two Witnesses,[2] they cou'd make nothing of it; yet it seems they were resolv'd not to part with the Men neither, not doubting but a farther

Evidence would at last come in; and in order to this, I think Publication was made, that such Prisoners being taken, any one that had been robb'd by them might come to the Prison and see them.

I Took this opportunity to satisfy my Curiosity, pretending that I had been robb'd in the *Dunstable* Coach, and that I would go to see the two Highway-Men; but when I came into the Press-Yard, I so disguis'd myself, and muffled my Face up so, that he cou'd see little of me, and consequently knew nothing of who I was, and when I came back, I said publickly that I knew them very well.

IMMEDIATELY it was Rumour'd all over the Prison, that *Moll Flanders* would turn Evidence against one of the Highway Men, and that I was to come off by it from the Sentence of Transportation.

THEY heard of it, and immediately my Husband desir'd to see this Mrs. *Flanders* that knew him so well, and was to be an Evidence against him, and accordingly, I had leave given to go to him. I dress'd myself up as well as the best Cloths that I suffer'd myself ever to appear in there, would allow me, and went to the Press-yard, but had for some time a Hood over my Face; he said little to me at first, but ask'd me if I knew him; I told him, yes, very well; but as I conceal'd my Face, so I Counterfeited my Voice, that he had not the least guess at who I was: He ask'd me where I had seen him, I told him between *Dunstable* and *Brickhill*, but turning to the Keeper that stood by, I ask'd if I might not be admitted to talk with him alone, he said, yes, yes, as much as I pleas'd, and so very civilly withdrew.

As soon as he was gone, and I had shut the Door, I threw off my Hood, and bursting out into Tears, *my Dear*, says I, *do you not know me?* He turn'd pale and stood Speechless, like one Thunder struck, and not able to conquer the Surprize, said no more but this, *let me sit down*; and sitting down by a Table, he laid his Elbow upon the Table, and leaning his Head on his Hand, fix'd his Eyes on the Ground as one stupid: I cry'd so vehemently on the other Hand, that it was a good while e'er I could speak any more; but after I had given some vent to my Passion by Tears, I repeated the same Words: MY DEAR, *do you not know me?* at which he answer'd YES, and said no more a good while.

AFTER some time continuing in the Surprize, *as above*, he cast up his Eyes towards me and said, *How could you be so cruel?* I did not readily understand what he meant; and I answer'd, How can you call me Cruel? What have I been Cruel to you in? *To come to me*, says he, *in such a Place as this, is it not to insult me? I have not robb'd* you, *at least not on* the Highway?

I PERCEIV'D by this, that he knew nothing of the miserable Circumstances I was in, and thought that having got some Intelligence of his being there, I had come to upbraid him with his leaving me; but I had too much to say to him to be affronted, and told him in few Words, that I was far from coming to Insult him, but at best I came to Condole mutually, that he would be easily satisfy'd, that I had no such View, when I should tell him that *my Condition was worse than his, and that many ways*: He look'd a little concern'd at the general Expression of my Condition being worse than his; but with a kind of a smile, look'd a little wildly, and said, How can that be? when you see me Fetter'd, and in *Newgate*, and two of my Companions Executed already; can you say your Condition is worse than Mine?

COME my Dear, *says I*, we have a long peice of Work to do, if I should be to relate, or you to hear my unfortunate History; but if you are dispos'd to hear it, you will soon conclude with me that my Condition is worse than yours: How is that possible, *says he again*, when I expect to be cast for my Life the very next Sessions? Yes *says I*, 'tis very possible when I shall tell you that I have been cast for my Life three Sessions ago, and am under Sentence of Death, is not my Case worse than yours?

THEN indeed he stood silent again, like one struck Dumb, and after a little while he starts up, unhappy Couple! *says he*, How can this be possible? I took him by the Hand,

come MY DEAR, *said I*, sit down, and let us compare our
Sorrows: I am a Prisoner in this very House, and in a much
worse Circumstance than you, and you will be satisfy'd I do
not come to Insult you, when I tell you the particulars; and
with this we sat down together, and I told him so much of
my Story as I thought was convenient, bringing it at last to
my being reduc'd to great Poverty, and representing myself
as fallen into some Company that led me to relieve my
Distresses by a way that I had been utterly unacquainted
with, and that they making an attempt at a Tradesman's
House I was seiz'd upon, for having been but just at the
Door, the Maid-Servant pulling me in; that I neither had
broke any Lock, or taken any thing away, and that notwithstanding that I was brought in Guilty, and Sentenc'd to
Die; but that the Judges having been made sensible of the
Hardship of my Circumstances, had obtain'd leave to remit
the Sentence upon my consenting to be transported.

I TOLD him I far'd the worse for being taken in the Prison
for one *Moll Flanders*, who was a famous successful Thief,
that all of them had heard of, but none of them had ever seen,
but that *as he knew well* was none of my Name; but I plac'd
all to the account of my ill Fortune, and that under this
Name I was dealt with as an old Offender, tho' this was the
first thing they had ever known of me. I gave him a long
particular of things that had befallen me, since I saw him;
but I told him that I had seen him since he might think I
had, and then gave him an Account how I had seen him at
Brickhill; how furiously he was pursued, and how by giving
an Account that I knew him, and that he was a very honest
Gentleman, one Mr. ———— the *Hew and Cry* was stopp'd,
and the High Constable went back again.

HE listen'd most attentively to all my Story, and smil'd at
most of the particulars, being all of them petty Matters, and
infinitely below what he had been at the Head of; but when
I came to the Story of little *Brickill*, he was surpriz'd, *and
was it you my Dear*, said he, *that gave the Check to the Mob
that was at our Heels there, at Brickill:* Yes *said I*, it was I

indeed, and then I told him the particulars which I had observ'd of him there. *Why then*, said he, *it was you that sav'd my Life at that time*, and I am glad I owe my Life to you, for I will pay the Debt to you now, and I'll deliver you from the present Condition you are in, or I will die in the attempt.

I Told him by no means; it was a Risque too great, not worth his running the hazard of, and for a Life not worth his saving; 'twas no matter for that he said, it was a Life worth all the World to him; a Life that had given him a new Life; for *says he*, I was never in real Danger of being taken, but that time; till the last Minute when I was taken: Indeed *he told* me his Danger then lay in his believing he had not been pursued that way; for they had gone off from *Hockly* quite another way, and had come over the enclos'd Country into *Brickill*, not by the Road and were sure they had not been seen by any Body.

Here he gave a long History of his Life, which indeed would make a very strange History, and be infinitely diverting. He told me he took to the Road about twelve Year before he marry'd me; that the Woman which call'd him Brother, was not really his Sister, or any Kin to him; but one that belong'd to their Gang, and who keeping Correspondence with them, liv'd always in Town, having good store of Acquaintance, that she gave them a perfect Intelligence of Persons going out of Town, and that they had made several good Booties by her Correspondence; that she thought she had fix'd a Fortune for him, when she brought me to him, but happen'd to be Disappointed, which he really could not blame her for: That, if it had been his good Luck, that I had had the Estate, which she was inform'd I had, he had resolv'd to leave off the Road, and live a retired sober Life, but never to appear in publick till some general Pardon had been pass'd, or till he could, for Money have got his Name into some particular Pardon, that so he might have been perfectly easy, but that as it had proved otherwise he was oblig'd to put off his Equipage, and take up the old Trade again.

HE gave me a long Account of some of his Adventures, and particularly one, when he robb'd the *West Chester* Coaches, near *Lichfield*, when he got a very great Booty; and after that, how he robb'd five Grasiers, in the *West*, going to *Burford* Fair in *Wiltshire* to buy Sheep;[1] he told me he got so much Money on those two Occasions, that if he had known where to have found me, he would certainly have embrac'd my Proposal of going with me to *Virginia*; or to have settled in a Plantation, on some other Parts of the *English* Colonies in *America*.

HE told me he wrote two or three Letters to me, directed according to my Order, but heard nothing from me: This I indeed knew to be true, but the Letters coming to my Hand in the time of my latter Husband, I could do nothing in it, and therefore chose to give no answer, that so he might rather believe they had miscarried.

BEING thus Disappointed, *he said*, he carried on the old Trade ever since, tho' when he had gotten so much Money, *he said*, he did not run such desperate Risques as he did before; then he gave me some Account of several hard and desperate Encounters which he had with Gentlemen on the Road, who parted too hardly with their Money; and shew'd me some Wounds he had receiv'd, and he had one or two very terrible Wounds indeed, as particularly one by a Pistol Bullet which broke his Arm; and another with a Sword, which ran him quite thro' the Body, but that missing his Vitals he was cur'd again; one of his Comrades having kept with him so faithfully, and so Friendly, as that he assisted him in riding near 80 Miles before his Arm was Set, and then got a Surgeon in a considerable City, remote from that Place where it was done, pretending they were Gentlemen Traveling towards *Carlisle*, and that they had been attack'd on the Road by Highway-Men, and that one of them had shot him into the Arm, and broke the Bone.[2]

THIS *he said*, his Friend manag'd so well, that they were not suspected at all, but lay still till he was perfectly cur'd: He gave me so many distinct Accounts of his Adventures, that it is with great reluctance, that I decline the relating them; but I consider that this is my own Story, not his.

I THEN enquir'd into the Circumstances of his present Case at that time, and what it was he expected when he came to be try'd; he told me that they had no Evidence against him, or but very little; for that of three Robberies, which they were all Charg'd with, it was his good Fortune, that he was but in one of them, and that there was but one Witness to be had for that Fact, which was not sufficient; but that it was expected some others would come in against him; that he thought indeed, when he first see me, that I had been one that came of that Errand; but that if no Body came in against him, he hop'd he should be clear'd; that he had had some intimation, that if he would submit to Transport himself, he might be admitted to it without a Tryal, but that he could not think of it with any Temper, and thought he could much easier submit to be Hang'd.

I BLAM'D him for that, and told him I blam'd him on two Accounts; first because, if he was Transported, there might be an Hundred ways for him that was a Gentleman, and a bold enterprizing Man to find his way back again, and perhaps some Ways and Means to come back before he went. He smil'd at that Part, and said he should like the last the best of the two, for he had a kind of Horror upon his Mind at his being sent over to the Plantations as *Romans* sent condemn'd Slaves to Work in the Mines; that he thought the Passage into another State, let it be what it would, much more tolerable at the Gallows, and that this was the general Notion of all the Gentlemen, who were driven by the Exigence of their Fortunes to take the Road; that at the Place of Execution there was at least an End of all the Miseries of the present State, and as for what was to follow, a Man was in his Opinion, as likely to Repent sincerely in the last Fortnight of his Life under the Pressures and Agonies of a Jayl, and the condemn'd Hole, as he would ever be in the Woods and Wildernesses of *America*; that Servitude and hard Labour were things Gentlemen could never stoop to,

that it was but the way to force them to be their own Execu-
tioners afterwards, which was much worse, and that therefore he could not have any Patience when he did but think
of being Transported.[1]

I USED the utmost of my endeavour to perswade him, and
joyn'd that known Womans Rhetorick to it, I mean that of
Tears: I told him the Infamy of a publick Execution was
certainly a greater pressure upon the Spirits of a Gentleman,
than any of the Mortifications that he could meet with
Abroad could be; that he had at least in the other a Chance
for his Life, whereas here he had none at all; that it was the
easiest thing in the World for him to manage the Captain of
the Ship, who were generally speaking, Men of good
Humour, and some Gallantry; and a small matter of Conduct,
especially if there was any Money to be had, would make
way for him to buy himself off, when he came to *Virginia*.

HE look'd wishfully at me, and I thought I guess'd at what
he meant, *that is to say*, that he had no Money, but I was
mistaken, his meaning was another way; *you hinted just now,
my Dear said he, that there might be a way of coming back
before I went, by which I understood you, that it might be
possible to buy it off here; I had rather give* 200 *l. to prevent
going, than* 100 *l. to be set at Liberty when I came there.* That is
my Dear, said I, *because you do not know the Place so well as
I do*: that may be, said he, *and yet I believe as well as you
know it, you would do the same unless it is because*, as you told
me, *you have a Mother there.*

I TOLD him, as to my Mother, it was next to impossible,
but that she must be dead many Years before; and as for
any other Relations that I might have there, I knew them
not now: That since the Misfortunes I had been under, had
reduc'd me to the Condition I had been in for some Years, I
had not kept up any Correspondence with them, and that he
would easily believe, I should find but a cold Reception from
them, if I should be put to make my first visit in the Condition of a Transported Felon; that therefore if I went
thither, I resolv'd not to see them; But that I had many

Views in going there, if it should be my Fate, which took off all the uneasy Part of it; and if he found himself oblig'd to go also, I should easily Instruct him how to manage himself, so as never to go a Servant at all, especially since I found he was not destitute of Money, which was the only Friend in such a Condition.

HE smil'd, and said, he did not tell me he had Money; I took him up short, and told him I hop'd he did not understand by my speaking, that I should expect any supply from him if he had Money; that on the other Hand, tho' I had not a great deal, yet I did not want, and while I had any I would rather add to him, than weaken him in that Article, seeing what ever he had, I knew in the Case of Transportation he would have Occasion of it all.

HE express'd himself in a most tender manner upon that Head: he told me what Money he had was not a great deal, but that he would never hide any of it from me if I wanted it; and that he assur'd me he did not speak with any such Apprehensions; that he was only intent upon what I had hinted to him before he went; that here he knew what to do with himself, but there he should be the most ignorant helpless Wretch alive.

I TOLD him he frighted and terify'd himself with that which had no Terror in it; that if he had Money, as I was glad to hear he had, he might not only avoid the Servitude, suppos'd to be the Consequence of Transportation; but begin the World upon a new Foundation, and that such a one as he cou'd not fail of Success in, with but the common Application usual in such Cases; that he could not but call to Mind, that it was what I had recommended to him many Years before, and had propos'd it for our mutual Subsistence, and restoring our Fortunes in the World; and I would tell him now, that to convince him both of the certainty of it, and of my being fully acquainted with the Method, and also fully satisfy'd in the probability of Success, he should first see me deliver myself from the Necessity of going over at all, and then that I would go with him freely, and of my own

Choice, and perhaps carry enough with me to satisfy him that I did not offer it, for want of being able to live without Assistance from him; but that I thought our mutual Misfortunes had been such, as were sufficient to Reconcile us both to quitting this part of the World, and living where no Body could upbraid us with what was past, or we be in any dread of a Prison; and without the Agonies of a condemn'd Hole to drive us to it, where we should look back on all our past Disasters with infinite Satisfaction, when we should consider that our Enemies should entirely forget us, and that we should live as new People in a new World, no Body having any thing to say to us, or we to them.

I PRESS'D this Home to him with so many Arguments, and answer'd all his own passionate Objections so effectually, that he embrac'd me, and told me, I treated him with such a Sincerity, and Affection as overcame him; that he would take my Advice, and would strive to submit to his Fate, in hope of having the comfort of my Assistance, and of so faithful a Counsellor, and such a Companion in his Misery; but still he put me in mind of what I had mention'd before; Namely, that there might be some way to get off, before he went, and that it might be possible to avoid going at all, which he said would be much better. I told him he should see, and be fully satisfy'd that I would do my utmost in that Part too, and if it did not succeed, yet that I would make good the rest.

WE parted after this long Conference, with such Testimonies of Kindness and Affection as I thought were Equal, if not Superior to that at our parting at *Dunstable*; and now I saw more plainly than before, the Reason why he declin'd coming at that time any farther with me toward *London* than *Dunstable*; and why when we parted there, he told me it was not convenient for him to come part of the way to *London* to bring me going, as he would otherwise have done: I have observ'd that the Account of his Life, would have made a much more pleasing History, than this of mine; and indeed nothing in it, was more strange than this Part, (*viz.*) that he had carried on that desperate Trade full five and Twenty

Year, and had never been taken, the Success he had met with, had been so very uncommon, and such, that sometimes he had liv'd handsomely and retir'd, in one Place for a Year or two at a time, keeping himself and a Man-Servant to wait on him, and has often sat in the Coffee-Houses, and heard the very People who he had robb'd give Accounts of their being robb'd, and of the Places and Circumstances, so that he cou'd easily remember that it was the same.

IN this manner it seems he liv'd near *Leverpool* at the time, he unluckily married me for a Fortune: Had I been the Fortune he expected, I verily believe, as he said, that he would have taken up and liv'd honestly all his Days.

HE had with the rest of his Misfortunes the good luck not to be actually upon the spot, when the Robbery was done, which he was committed for; and so none of the Persons robb'd cou'd swear to him, or had any thing to Charge upon him; but it seems as he was taken, with the Gang, one hard-mouth'd Countryman swore home to him; and they were like to have others come in according to the Publication they had made, so that they expected more Evidence against him, and for that Reason he was kept in hold.

HOWEVER, the offer which was made to him of admitting him to Transportation was made, as I understood upon the intercession of some great Person who press'd him hard to accept of it before a Tryal; and indeed as he knew there were several that might come in against him, I thought his Friend was in the Right, and I lay at him Night and Day to delay it no longer.

AT last, with much difficulty he gave his consent, and as he was not therefore admitted to Transportation in Court, and on his Petition as I was, so he found himself under a difficulty to avoid embarking himself as I had said he might have done; his great Friend, who was his Intercessor for the Favour of that Grant, having given Security for him that he should Transport himself, and not return within the Term.[1]

THIS hardship broke all my Measures, for the steps I took afterwards for my own deliverance, were hereby render'd wholly ineffectual, unless I would abandon him, and leave him to go to *America* by himself; than which he protested he would much rather venture,[1] altho' he were certain to go directly to the Gallows.

I MUST now return to my own Case, the time of my being Transported according to my Sentence was near at Hand; my Governess who continu'd my fast Friend, had try'd to obtain a Pardon, but it could not be done unless with an Expence too heavy for my Purse, considering that to be left naked and empty, unless I had resolv'd to return to my old Trade again, had been worse than my Transportation, because there I knew I could live, here I could not. The good Minister stood very hard on another Account to prevent my being Transported also; but he was answer'd, that indeed my Life had been given me at his first Solicitations, and therefore he ought to ask no more; he was sensibly griev'd at my going, because, *as he said*, he fear'd I should lose the good impressions, which a prospect of Death had at first made on me, and which were since encreas'd by his Instructions, and the pious Gentleman was exceedingly concern'd about me on that Account.

ON the other Hand, I really was not so sollicitous about it, as I was before, but I industriously conceal'd my Reasons for it from the Minister, and to the last he did not know, but that I went with the utmost reluctance and affliction.

IT was in the Month of *February* that I was with seven other Convicts, *as they call'd us*, deliver'd to a Merchant that Traded to *Virginia*, on board a Ship, riding, as they call'd it, in *Deptford* Reach: The Officer of the Prison deliver'd us on board, and the Master of the Vessel gave a Discharge for us.

WE were for that Night clapt under Hatches, and kept so close, that I thought I should have been suffocated for want of Air, and the next Morning the Ship weigh'd, and fell down the River to a Place they call *Bugby's Hole*, which was done, as they told us by the agreement of the Merchant, that all opportunity of Escape should be taken from us: However when the Ship came thither, and cast Anchor, we were allow'd more Liberty, and particularly were permitted to come upon the Deck, but not upon the Quarter-Deck, that being kept particularly for the Captain, and for Passengers.

WHEN by the Noise of the Men over my Head, and the Motion of the Ship, I perceiv'd that they were under Sail, I was at first greatly surpriz'd, fearing we should go away directly, and that our Friends would not be admitted to see us any more; but I was easy soon after when I found they had come to an Anchor again, and soon after that we had Notice given by some of the Men where we were, that the next Morning we should have the Liberty to come upon Deck, and to have our Friends come and see us if we had any.

ALL that Night I lay upon the hard Boards of the Deck, as the other Prisoners did, but we had afterwards the Liberty of little Cabins for such of us as had any Bedding to lay in them; and room to stow any Box or Trunk for Cloths, and Linnen, if we had it, (which might well be put in) for some of them had neither Shirt or Shift, or a Rag of Linnen or Woollen, but what was on their Backs, or a Farthing of Money to help themselves; and yet I did not find but they far'd well enough in the Ship, especially the Women, who got Money of the Seamen for washing their Cloths sufficient to purchase any common things that they wanted.

WHEN the next Morning we had the liberty to come upon the Deck, I ask'd one of the Officers of the Ship, whether I might not have the liberty to send a Letter on Shore to let my Friends know where the Ship lay, and to get some necessary things sent to me. This was it seems the Boatswain, a very civil courteous sort of Man, who told me I should have that, or any other liberty that I desir'd, that he could allow me with Safety; I told him I desir'd no other; and he answer'd that the Ships Boat would go up to *London* the next Tide, and he would order my Letter to be carried.

ACCORDINGLY when the Boat went off, the Boatswain came to me, and told me the Boat was going off, and that he went in it himself, and ask'd me if my Letter was ready, he would take care of it; I had prepared myself you may be sure, Pen,

Ink and Paper beforehand, and I had gotten a Letter ready directed to my Governess, and enclos'd another for my fellow Prisoner, which however I did not let her know was my Husband, not to the last; in that to my Governess, I let her know where the Ship lay, and press'd her earnestly to send me what things I knew she had got ready for me, for my Voyage.

WHEN I gave the Boatswain the Letter, I gave him a Shilling with it, which I told him was for the Charge of a Messenger or Porter, which I entreated him to send with the Letter, as soon as he came on Shore, that if possible I might have an Answer brought back by the same Hand, that I might know what was become of my things, for SIR, *says I*, if the Ship should go away before I have them on Board I am undone.

I TOOK care when I gave him the Shilling, to let him see that I had a little better Furniture about me, than the ordinary Prisoners, for he saw that I had a Purse, and in it a pretty deal of Money, and I found that the very sight of it, immediately furnish'd me with very different Treatment from what I should otherwise have met with in the Ship; for tho' he was very Courteous indeed before, in a kind of natural Compassion to me, as a Woman in distress; yet he was more than ordinarily so, afterwards, and procur'd me to be better treated in the Ship, than, *I say*, I might otherwise have been; as shall appear in its Place.

HE very honestly had my Letter deliver'd to my Governess own Hands, and brought me back an Answer from her in writing; and when he gave me the Answer, gave me the Shilling again, *there*, says he, there's your Shilling again too, for I deliver'd the Letter my self; I could not tell what to say, I was so surpris'd at the thing; but after some Pause, *I said*, Sir you are too kind, it had been but Reasonable that you had paid yourself Coach hire then.

No, no, *says he*, I am over paid: What is the Gentle-woman, your Sister?

No, SIR, *said I*, she is no Relation to me, but she is a dear

Friend, and all the Friends I have in the World: well, *says he*, there are few such Friends in the World: why she cryes after you like a Child, Ay, *says I again*, she would give a Hundred Pound, I believe, to deliver me from this dreadful Condition I am in.

WOULD she so? *says he*, for half the Money I believe, I cou'd put you in a way how to deliver yourself, but this he spoke softly that no Body cou'd hear.

Alas! SIR, *said I*, but then that must be such a Deliverance as if I should be taken again, would cost me my Life; Nay, *said he*, if you were once out of the Ship you must look to yourself afterwards, that I can say nothing to; so we drop'd the Discourse for that time.

IN the mean time my Governess faithful to the last Moment, convey'd my Letter to the Prison to my Husband, and got an Answer to it, and the next Day came down herself to the Ship, bringing me in the first Place a *Sea-Bed* as they call it, and all its Furniture, such as was convenient, but not to let the People think it was extraordinary; she brought with her a *Sea-Chest*, that is a Chest, such as are made for Seamen with all the Conveniencies in it, and fill'd with every thing almost that I could want; and in one of the corners of the Chest, where there was a Private Drawer was my Bank of Money, *that is to say*, so much of it as I had resolv'd to carry with me; for I order'd a part of my Stock to be left behind me, to be sent afterwards in such Goods as I should want when I came to settle; for Money in that Country is not of much use where all things are bought for Tobacco,[1] much more is it a great loss to carry it from Hence.

BUT my Case was particular; it was by no Means proper to me to go thither without Money or Goods, and for a poor Convict that was to be sold as soon as I came on Shore, to carry with me a Cargo of Goods would be to have Notice taken of it, and perhaps to have them seiz'd by the Publick; so I took part of my Stock with me thus, and left the other part with my Governess.

MY Governess brought me a great many other things, but

it was not proper for me to look too well provided in the Ship, at least, till I knew what kind of a Captain we should have. When she came into the Ship, I thought she would have died indeed; her Heart sunk at the sight of me, and at the thoughts of parting with me in that Condition, and she cry'd so intolerably, I cou'd not for a long time have any talk with her.

I Took that time to read my fellow Prisoners Letter, which however greatly perplex'd me; he told me he was determin'd to go, but found it would be impossible for him to be Discharg'd time enough for going in the same Ship, and which was more than all, he began to question whether they would give him leave to go in what Ship he pleas'd, tho' he did voluntarily Transport himself; but that they would see him put on Board such a Ship as they should direct, and that he would be charg'd upon the Captain as other convict Prisoners were; so that he began to be in dispair of seeing me till he came to *Virginia*, which made him almost desperate; seeing that on the other Hand, if I should not be there, if any Accident of the Sea, or of Mortality should take me away, he should be the most undone Creature there in the World.

This was very perplexing, and I knew not what Course to take; I told my Governess the Story of the Boatswain, and she was mighty eager with me to treat with him; but I had no mind to it, till I heard whether my Husband, or fellow Prisoner, *so she call'd him*, cou'd be at liberty to go with me or no; at last I was forc'd to let her into the whole matter, except only, that of his being my Husband; I told her I had made a positive Bargain or Agreement with him to go, if he could get the liberty of going in the same Ship, and that I found he had Money.

Then I read a long Lecture to her of what I propos'd to do when we came there, how we could Plant, Settle, and in short, grow Rich without any more Adventures, and as a great Secret, I told her that we were to Marry as soon as he came on Board.

She soon agreed chearfully to my going, when she heard

this, and she made it her business from that time to get him out of the Prison in time, so that he might go in the same Ship with me, which at last was brought to pass tho' with great difficulty, and not without all the Forms of a Transported Prisoner *Convict*, which he really was not yet, for he had not been try'd, and which was a great Mortification to him. As our Fate was now determin'd, and we were both on Board, actually bound to *Virginia*, in the despicable Quality of Transported Convicts destin'd to be sold for Slaves, I for five Year, and he under Bonds and Security not to return to *England* any more, as long as he liv'd; he was very much dejected and cast down; the Mortification of being brought on Board as he was, like a Prisoner, piqu'd him very much, since it was first told him he should Transport himself, and so that he might go as a Gentleman at liberty; it is true he was not order'd to be sold when he came there, as we were, and for that Reason he was oblig'd to pay for his Passage to the Captain, which we were not; as to the rest, he was as much at a loss as a Child what to do with himself, or with what he had, but by Directions.

OUR first business was to compare our Stock: He was very honest to me, and told me his Stock was pretty good when he came into the Prison, but the living there as he did in a Figure like a Gentleman, *and which was ten times as much*, the making of Friends, and soliciting his Case, had been very Expensive; and in a Word, all his Stock that he had left was an Hundred and Eight Pounds, which he had about him all in Gold.

I GAVE him an Account of my Stock as faithfully, that is to say of what I had taken to carry with me, for I was resolv'd what ever should happen, to keep what I had left with my Governess, in Reserve; that in case I should die, what I had with me was enough to give him, and that which was left in my Governess Hands would be her own, which she had well deserv'd of me indeed.

MY Stock which I had with me was two Hundred forty six Pounds, some odd Shillings; so that we had three

Hundred and fifty four Pound between us, but a worse gotten Estate was scarce ever put together to begin the World with.

OUR greatest Misfortune as to our Stock, was that it was all in Money, which every one knows is an unprofitable Cargoe to be carryed to the Plantations; I believe his was really all he had left in the World, as he told me it was; but I who had between seven and eight Hundred Pounds in Bank when this Disaster befel me, and who had one of the faithfulest Friends in the World to manage it for me, considering she was a Woman of no manner of Religious Principles, had still Three Hundred Pounds left in her Hand, which I reserv'd, as above, besides some very valuable things, as particularly two gold Watches, some small Peices of Plate, and some Rings; all stolen Goods; the Plate, Rings and Watches were put up in my Chest with the Money, and with this Fortune, and in the Sixty first Year of my Age, I launch'd out into a new World, as I may call it, in the Condition (as to what appear'd) only of a poor nak'd Convict, order'd to be Transported in respite from the Gallows; my Cloaths were poor and mean, but not ragged or dirty, and none knew in the whole Ship that I had any thing of value about me.

HOWEVER, as I had a great many very good Cloaths, and Linnen in abundance, which I had order'd to be pack'd up in two great Boxes, I had them Shipp'd on Board, not as my Goods, but as consign'd to my real Name in *Virginia*; and had the Bills of Loading sign'd by a Captain in my Pocket; and in these Boxes was my Plate and Watches, and every thing of value except my Money, which I kept by itself in a private Drawer in my Chest, which cou'd not be found, or open'd if found, without splitting the Chest to peices.

IN this Condition I lay for three Weeks in the Ship, not knowing whether I should have my Husband with me or no; and therefore not resolving how, or in what manner to receive the honest Boatswain's proposal, which indeed he thought a little strange at first.

AT the End of this time, behold my Husband came on

Board; he look'd with a dejected angry Countenance, his great Heart was swell'd with Rage and Disdain; to be drag'd along with three Keepers of *Newgate*, and put on Board like a Convict, when he had not so much as been brought to a Tryal; he made loud complaints of it by his Friends, for it seems he had some interest; but his Friends got some Checque in their Application, and were told he had had *Favour enough*, and that they had receiv'd such an Account of him since the last Grant of his Transportation, that he ought to think himself very well treated that he was not prosecuted a new. This answer quieted him at once, for he knew too much what might have happen'd, and what he had room to expect; and now he saw the goodness of the Advice to him, which prevail'd with him to accept of the offer of a voluntary Transportation, and after his chagrine at these Hell Hounds, *as he call'd them*, was a little over; he look'd a little compos'd, began to be chearful, and as I was telling him how glad I was to have him once more out of their Hands, took me in his Arms, and acknowledg'd with great Tenderness, that I had given him the best Advice possible, *My Dear*, says he, *Thou hast twice sav'd my Life, from hence forward it shall be all employ'd for you, and I'll always take your Advice*.

THE Ship began now to fill, several Passengers came on Board, who were embark'd on no Criminal account, and these had Accommodations assign'd them in the great Cabbin, and other Parts of the Ship, whereas we *as Convicts* were thrust down below, I know not where; but when my Husband came on Board, I spoke to the Boatswain, who had so early given me Hints of his Friendship in carrying my Letter; I told him he had befriended me in many things, and I had not made any suitable Return to him, and with that I put a Guinea into his Hands; I told him that my Husband was now come on Board, that tho' we were both under the present Misfortunes, yet we had been Persons of a differing Character from the wretched Crew that we came with, and desir'd to know of him, whether the Captain might not be

mov'd, to admit us to some Conveniences in the Ship, for
which we would make him what Satisfaction he pleas'd, and
that we would gratifie him for his Pains in procuring this for
us. He took the Guinea as I cou'd see with great Satisfaction,
and assur'd me of his Assistance.

THEN he told us, he did not doubt but that the Captain
who was one of the best humour'd Gentlemen in the World,
would be easily brought to Accommodate us, as well as we
cou'd desire, and to make me easie, told me he would go up
the next Tide on purpose to speak to the Captain about it.
The next Morning happening to sleep a little longer than
ordinary, when I got up, and began to look Abroad, I saw
the Boatswain among the Men in his ordinary Business; I
was a little melancholly at seeing him there, and going
forwards to speak to him, he saw me, and came towards me,
but not giving him time to speak first, I said smiling, *I doubt,
Sir, you have forgot us*, for I see you are very busy; he
return'd presently, come along with me, and you shall see,
so he took me into the great Cabbin, and there sat a good
sort of a Gentlemanly Man for a Seaman writing, and with
a great many Papers before him.

HERE says the Boatswain to him that was a writing, is the
Gentlewoman that the Captain spoke to you of, and turning
to me, he said, I have been so far from forgetting your
Business, that I have been up at the Captain's House, and
have represented faithfully to the Captain what you said,
relating to your being furnished with better Conveniences
for your self, and your Husband; and the Captain has sent
this Gentleman, who is Mate of the Ship down with me, on
purpose to show you every thing, and to Accommodate you
fully to your Content, and bid me assure you that you shall
not be treated like what you were at first expected to be, but
with the same respect as other Passengers are treated.

THE Mate then spoke to me, and not giving me time to
thank the Boatswain for his kindness confirm'd what the
Boatswain had said, and added that it was the Captain's
delight to show himself Kind, and Charitable, especially, to

those that were under any Misfortunes, and with that he shew'd me several Cabbins built up, some in the Great Cabbin, and some partition'd off, out of the Steerage, but opening into the great Cabbin on purpose for the Accommodation of Passengers, and gave me leave to choose where I would; however I chose a Cabbin, which open'd into the Steerage, in which was very good Conveniencies to set our Chest, and Boxes, and a Table to eat on.

THE Mate then told me, that the Boatswain had given so good a Character of me, and of my Husband, as to our civil Behaviour, that he had orders to tell me, we should eat with him, if we thought fit, during the whole Voyage on the common Terms of Passengers; that we might lay in some fresh Provisions, if we pleas'd; or if not, he should lay in his usual Store, and we should have Share with him: This was very reviving News to me, after so many Hardships, and Afflictions as I had gone thro' of late; I thank'd him, and told him, the Captain should make his own Terms with us, and ask'd him leave to go and tell my Husband of it who was not very well, and was not yet out of his Cabbin: Accordingly I went, and my Husband whose Spirits were still so much sunk with the Indignity (as he understood it) offered him, that he was scarce yet himself, was so reviv'd with the Account I gave him of the Reception we were like to have in the Ship, that he was quite another Man, and new vigour and Courage appear'd in his very Countenance; so true is it, that the greatest of Spirits, when overwhelm'd by their Afflictions, are subject to the greatest Dejections, and are the most apt to Despair and give themselves up.

AFTER some little Pause to recover himself, my Husband come up with me, and gave the Mate thanks for the kindness, which he had express'd to us, and sent suitable acknowledgement by him to the Captain, offering to pay him by Advance, what ever he demanded for our Passage, and for the Conveniences he had help'd us to; the Mate told him, that the Captain would be on Board in the Afternoon, and that he would leave all that till he came; accordingly in the Afternoon the Captain came, and we found him the same courteous obliging Man, that the Boatswain had represented him to be; and he was so well pleas'd with my Husband's Conversation, that in short, he would not let us keep the Cabbin we had chosen, but gave us one, that as I said before, open'd into the great Cabbin.

NOR were his Conditions exorbitant, or the Man craving and eager to make a Prey of us, but for fifteen Guineas we had our whole Passage and Provisions, and Cabbin, eat at the Captain's Table, and were very handsomely Entertain'd.

THE Captain lay himself in the other part of the Great Cabbin, having let his round House, *as they call it*,[1] to a rich Planter, who went over, with his Wife, and three Children, who eat by themselves; he had some other ordinary Passengers, who Quarter'd in the Steerage,[2] and as for our old Fraternity, they were kept under the Hatches while the Ship lay there, and came very little on the Deck.

I COULD not refrain acquainting my Governess with what had happen'd, it was but just that she, who was so really concern'd for me, should have part in my good Fortune; besides I wanted her Assistance to supply me with several Necessaries, which before I was shy of letting any Body see me have, that it might not be publick; but now I had a Cabbin and room to set things in; I order'd abundance of good things for our Comfort in the Voyage, as Brandy, Sugar, Lemons, &c. to make Punch, and Treat our Benefactor, the Captain; and abundance of things for eating and drinking in the Voyage; also a larger Bed, and Bedding proportion'd to it; so that in a Word, we resolv'd to want for nothing in the Voyage.

ALL this while I had provided nothing for our Assistance, when we should come to the Place, and begin to call ourselves Planters; and I was far from being ignorant of what was needful on that Occasion; particularly all sorts of Tools for the Planters-Work, and for building; and all kinds of Furniture for our Dwelling, which if to be bought in the Country, must necessarily cost double the Price.

So I discours'd that Point with my Governess, and she went and waited upon the Captain, and told him, that she hop'd ways might be found out, for her two unfortunate Cousins, *as she call'd us*, to obtain our Freedom when we came into the Country, and so enter'd into a Discourse with him about the Means and Terms also, of which I shall say more in its Place; and after thus sounding the Captain, she let him know, tho' we were unhappy in the Circumstance that occasion'd our going, yet that we were not unfurnish'd to set our selves to Work in the Country; and were resolv'd to settle, and live there as Planters, if we might be put in a way how to do it: The Captain readily offer'd his Assistance, told her the Method of entering upon such Business, and how easy, nay, how certain it was for industrious People to recover their Fortunes in such a manner: Madam, *says he*, 'tis no Reproach to any Man in that Country to have been sent over in worse Circumstances than I perceive your Cousins are in, provided they do but apply with diligence and good Judgment to the Business of that Place when they come there.

She then enquir'd of him what things it was Necessary we should carry over with us, and he like a very honest as well as knowing Man, told her thus: Madam, your Cousins in the first Place must procure some Body to buy them as Servants, in Conformity to the Conditions of their Transportation, and then in the Name of that Person, they may go about what they will; they may either Purchase some Plantations already begun, or they may purchase Land of the Government of the Country, and begin where they please, and both will be done reasonably; she bespoke his Favour in the first Article, which he promis'd to her to take upon himself, and indeed faithfull perform'd it; and as to the rest, he promis'd to recommend us to such as should give us the best Advice, and not to impose upon us, which was as much as could be desir'd.

She then ask'd him, if it would not be Necessary to furnish us with a Stock of Tools and Materials for the

Business of Planting, and he said, yes, by all means, and then she begg'd his Assistance in it; she told him she would furnish us with every thing that was Convenient whatever it cost her; he accordingly gave her a long particular of things Necessary for a Planter, which by his Account came to about fourscore, or an Hundred Pounds; and in short, she went about as dexterously to buy them, as if she had been an old *Virginia* Merchant; only that she bought by my Direction above twice as much of every thing as he had given her a List of.

THESE she put on Board in her own Name, took his Bills of Loading for them, and Endorst those Bills of Loading to my Husband, Ensuring the Cargo afterwards in her own Name, by our order; so that we were provided for all Events, and for all Disasters.

I SHOULD have told you that my Husband gave her all his whole Stock of 180 *l.* which as I have said, he had about him in Gold, to lay out thus, and I gave her a good Sum besides; so that I did not break into the Stock, which I had left in her Hands at all, but after we had sorted out our whole Cargo, we had yet near 200 *l.* in Money, which was more than enough for our purpose.

IN this Condition very chearful, and indeed joyful at being so happily Accommodated as we were; we set Sail from *Bugby's-Hole* to *Gravesend*, where the Ship lay about ten Days more, and where the Captain came on Board for good and all. Here the Captain offer'd us a civility, which indeed we had no Reason to expect. Namely, to let us go on Shore, and refresh ourselves, upon giving our Words in a solemn manner, that we would not go from him, and that we would return peaceably on Board again: This was such an Evidence of his Confidence in us, that it overcome my Husband, who in a meer Principle of Gratitude, told him as he could not be in any Capacity to make a suitable return for such a Favour, so he could not think of accepting of it; nor could he be easy that the Captain should run such a Risque: After some mutual Civilities, I gave my Husband a Purse, in which was 80 Guineas, and he puts it into the Captain's hand: There

Captain, *says he*, there's part of a Pledge for our Fidelity, if we deal dishonestly with you on any Account, 'tis your own, and on this we went on Shore.

INDEED the Captain had assurance enough of our Resolutions to go, for that having made such Provision to Settle there, it did not seem Rational that we would chuse to remain here at the Expence and Peril of Life, for such it must have been, if we had been taken again. In a Word, we went all on Shore with the Captain, and Supp'd together in *Gravesend*; where we were very Merry, staid all Night, lay at the House where we Supp'd, and came all very honestly on Board again with him in the Morning. Here we bought ten dozen Bottles of good Beer, some Wine, some Fowls, and such things as we thought might be acceptable on Board.

MY Governess was with us all this while, and went with us Round into the *Downs*, as did also the Captain's Wife with whom she went back; I was never so sorrowful at parting with my own Mother as I was at parting with her, and I never saw her more: We had a fair Easterly Wind sprung up the third Day after we came to the *Downs*, and we sail'd from thence the 10th of *April*; nor did we touch any more at any Place, till being driven on the Coast of *Ireland* by a very hard Gale of Wind, the Ship came to an Anchor in a little *Bay*, near the Mouth of a River, whose Name I remember not, but they said the River came down from *Limerick*, and that it was the largest River in *Ireland*.[1]

HERE being detain'd by bad Weather for some time, the Captain who continu'd the same kind good humour'd Man as at first, took us two on Shore with him again: He did it now in kindness to my Husband indeed, who bore the Sea very ill, and was very Sick, especially when it blew so hard: Here we bought in again, store of fresh Provisions, especially Beef, Pork, Mutton and Fowls, and the Captain stay'd to Pickle up five or six Barrels of Beef to lengthen out the Ships Store. We were here not above five Days, when the Weather turning mild, and a fair Wind; we set Sail again and in two and Forty Days came safe to the Coast of *Virginia*.

WHEN we drew near to the Shore, the Captain call'd me to him, and told me that he found by my Discourse, I had some Relations in the Place, and that I had been there before, and so he suppos'd I understood the Custom, in their disposing the convict Prisoners when they arriv'd; I told him I did not, and that as to what Relations I had in the Place, he might be sure I would make my self known to none of them while I was in the Circumstances of a Prisoner, and that as to the rest, we left ourselves entirely to him to Assist us, as he was pleas'd to promise us he wou'd do. He told me I must get some Body in the Place to come and buy us as Servants, and who must answer for us to the Governor of the Country, if he demanded us; I told him we should do as he should direct; so he brought a Planter to treat with him, as it were for the Purchase of these two Servants, my Husband and me, and there we were formally sold to him, and went a Shore with him: The Captain went with us, and carried us to a certain House whether it was to be call'd a Tavern or not, I know not, but we had a Bowl of Punch there made of Rum, &c. and were very Merry. After some time the Planter gave us a Certificate of Discharge, and an Acknowledgement of having serv'd him faithfully, and we were free from him the next Morning, to go whither we would.[1]

FOR this Peice of Service the Captain demanded of us 6000 weight of Tobacco, which he said he was Accountable for to his Freighter, and which we immediately bought for him, and made him a present of 20 Guineas, besides, with which he was abundantly satisfy'd.

IT is not proper to Enter here into the particulars of what Part of the Colony of *Virginia* we Settled in, for divers Reasons; it may suffice to mention that we went into the great River of *Potomack*, the Ship being bound thither; and there we intended to have Settled at first, tho' afterwards we altered our Minds.

THE first thing I did of Moment after having gotten all our Goods on Shore, and plac'd them in a Storehouse, or

Warehouse, which with a Lodging we hir'd at the small Place or Village, where we Landed; I say the first thing was to enquire after my Mother, and after my Brother, (that fatal Person who I married as a Husband, as I have related at large;) a little enquiry furnish'd me with Information that Mrs. ————, that is my Mother was Dead; that my Brother (or Husband) was alive, which I confess I was not very glad to hear; but which was worse, I found he was remov'd from the Plantation where he liv'd formerly, and where I liv'd with him, and liv'd with one of his Sons in a Plantation just by the Place where we Landed, and where we had hir'd a Warehouse.

I WAS a little surpriz'd at first, but as I ventured, to satisfy my self, that he could not know me, I was not only perfectly easy, but had a great mind to see him, if it was possible to do so without his seeing me; in order to that I found out by enquiry the Plantation where he liv'd, and with a Woman of that Place, who I got to help me, like what we call a *Chairwoman*,[1] I rambl'd about towards the Place, as if I had only a mind to see the Country, and look about me; at last I came so near that I saw the Dwelling-house: *I ask'd the Woman* whose Plantation that was, *she said*, it belong'd to such a Man, and looking out a little to our right Hands, there says she, is the Gentleman that owns the Plantation, and his Father with him: What are their Christian Names? said I, I know not *said she*, what the old Gentlemans Name is, but his Sons Name is *Humphry*, and I believe, *says she*, the Fathers is so too; you may guess, if you can, what a confus'd mixture of Joy and Fright possest my Thoughts upon this Occasion, for I immediately knew that this was no Body else, but my own Son, by that Father she shewed me, who was my own Brother: I had no Mask, but I ruffled my Hoods so about my Face, that I depended upon it, that after above 20 Years absence, and withal not expecting any thing of me in that part of the World, he would not be able to know any thing of me; but I need not have us'd all that Caution, for the old Gentleman was grown dim Sighted, by some Distemper, which had fallen upon his Eyes, and could but just see well enough to walk about, and not run against a Tree, or into a Ditch. The Woman that was with me, had told me that, by a meer Accident, knowing nothing of what importance it was to me: As they drew near to us, *I said*, does he know you Mrs. *Owen*? so they call'd the Woman, yes, *said she*, if he hears me speak, he will know me; but he can't see well enough to know me, or any Body else; and so she told me the Story of his Sight, as I have related: This made me secure, and so I threw open my Hoods again, and let them pass by me: It was a wretched thing for a Mother thus to see her own Son, a handsome comely young Gentleman in flourishing Circumstances, and durst not make herself known to him; and durst not take any notice of him; let any Mother of Children that reads this, consider it, and but think with what anguish of Mind I restrain'd myself; what yearnings of Soul I had in me to embrace him, and weep over him; and how I thought all my Entrails turn'd within me, that my very Bowels mov'd, and I knew not what to do; as I now know not how to express those Agonies: When he went from me I stood gazing and trembling, and looking after him as long as I could see him; then sitting down on the Grass, just at a Place I had mark'd, I made as if I lay down to rest me, but turn'd from her, and lying on my Face wept, and kiss'd the Ground that he had set his Foot on.

I COU'D not conceal my Disorder so much from the Woman, but that she perceiv'd it, and thought I was not well, which I was oblig'd to pretend was true; upon which she press'd me to rise, the Ground being damp and dangerous, which I did accordingly, and walk'd away.

As I was going back again, and still Talking of this Gentleman, and his Son, a new Occasion of melancholy offer'd itself *thus*: The Woman began, as if she would tell me a Story to divert me; there goes, *says she*, a very odd Tale among the Neighbours where this Gentleman formerly liv'd: What was that, *said I*? why, says she, that old Gentleman going to *England*, when he was a young Man, fell in Love with a young Lady there, one of the finest Women that ever was seen, and Married her, and brought her over hither to his Mother, who was then living. He liv'd here several Years with her, *continu'd she*, and had several Children by her, of which the young Gentleman that was with him now, was one, but after some time, the old Gentlewoman his Mother talking to her, of something relating to herself, when she was in *England*, and of her Circumstances in *England*, which were bad enough; the Daughter-in-Law, began to be very much surpriz'd, and uneasy, and in short, examining further into things it appear'd past all Contradiction, that she (the old Gentlewoman) was her own Mother, and that consequently, that Son was his Wives own Brother, which struck the whole Family with Horror, and put them into such Confusion, that it had almost ruin'd them all; the young Woman would not live with him, the Son, her Brother and Husband, for a time went Distracted, and at last, the young Woman went away for *England*, and has never been heard of since.

IT is easy to believe that I was strangely affected with this Story; but 'tis impossible to describe the Nature of my Disturbance: I seem'd astonish'd at the Story, and ask'd her a Thousand Questions about the particulars, which I found she was thoroughly acquainted with; at last I began to enquire into the Circumstances of the Family, how the old Gentlewoman, *I mean*, *my Mother* died, and how she left what she had; for my Mother had promis'd me very solemnly, that when she died, she would do something for me, and leave it so, as that, if I was Living, I should one way or other come at it, without its being in the Power of her Son, *my Brother and Husband* to prevent it: She told me she did not know exactly how it was order'd; but she had been told, that *my Mother* had left a Sum of Money, and had tyed her Plantation for the Payment of it, to be made good to the Daughter, if ever she could be heard of, either in *England*, or else where; and that the Trust was left with this Son, who was the Person that we saw with his Father.

THIS was News too good for me to make light of, and you

may be sure fill'd my Heart with a Thousand Thoughts, what Course I should take, how, and when, and in what manner I should make myself known, or whether I should ever make myself known, or no.

HERE was a Perplexity that I had not indeed skill to manage myself in, neither knew I what Course to take: It lay heavy upon my mind Night, and Day, I could neither Sleep or Converse, so that my Husband perceiv'd it, and wonder'd what ail'd me, strove to divert me, but it was all to no purpose; he press'd me to tell him what it was troubled me, but I put it off, till at last importuning me continually, I was forc'd to form a Story, which yet had a plain Truth to lay it upon too; I told him I was troubled because I found we must shift our Quarters, and alter our Scheme of Settling, for that I found I should be known, if I stay'd in that part of the Country, for that my Mother being dead, several of my Relations were come into that Part where we then was, and that I must either discover myself to them, which in our present Circumstances was not proper on many Accounts, or remove, and which to do I knew not, and that this it was that made me so Melancholly, and so Thoughtful.

HE joyn'd with me in this, that it was by no means proper for me to make myself known to any Body in the Circumstances, in which we then were; and therefore he told me he would be willing to remove to any other part of the Country, or even to any other Country if I thought fit; but now I had another Difficulty, which was, that if I remov'd to any other Colony, I put myself out of the way of ever making a due Search after those Effects, which my Mother had left: Again, I could never so much as think of breaking the Secret of my former Marriage to my new Husband; It was not a Story, as I thought that would bear telling, nor could I tell what might be the Consequences of it; and it was impossible to search into the bottom of the thing without making it Publick all over the Country, as well who I was, as what I now was also.

IN this perplexity I continu'd a great while, and this made my Spouse very uneasy; for he found me perplex'd, and yet thought I was not open with him, and did not let him into every part of my Grievance; and he would often say, he wondred what he had done, that I would not Trust him with what ever it was, especially if it was Grievous, and Afflicting; the Truth is, he ought to have been trusted with every thing; for no Man in the World could deserve better of a Wife; but this was a thing I knew not how to open to him, and yet having no Body to disclose any part of it to, the Burthen was too heavy for my mind; for let them say what they please of our Sex not being able to keep a Secret; my Life is a plain Conviction to me of the contrary; but be it our Sex, or the Man's Sex, a Secret of Moment should always have a Confident, a bosom Friend, to whom we may Communicate the Joy of it, or the Grief of it, be it which it will, or it will be a double weight upon the Spirits, and perhaps become even insupportable in itself; and this I appeal to all human Testimony for the Truth of.

AND this is the Cause why many times Men as well as Women, and Men of the greatest, and best Qualities other ways, yet have found themselves weak in this part, and have not been able to bear the weight of a secret Joy, or of a secret sorrow; but have been oblig'd to disclose it, even for the meer giving vent to themselves, and to unbend the Mind, opprest with the Load and Weights which attended it; nor was this any Token of Folly, or Thoughtlessness at all, but a natural Consequence of the thing; and such People had they struggl'd longer with the Oppression, would certainly have told it in their Sleep, and disclos'd the Secret, let it have been of what fatal Nature soever, without regard to the Person to whom it might be expos'd: This Necessity of Nature, is a thing which Works sometimes with such vehemence, in the Minds of those who are guilty of any atrocious Villany; such as secret Murther in particular, that they have been oblig'd to Discover it,[1] tho' the Consequence would necessarily be their own Destruction: Now tho' it may be true that the divine Justice ought to have the Glory of all those Discoveries and Confessions, yet 'tis as certain that

Providence which ordinarily Works by the Hands of Nature, makes use here of the same natural Causes to produce those extraordinary Effects.[1]

I COULD give several remarkable Instances of this in my long Conversation with Crime, and with Criminals; I knew one Fellow, that while I was a Prisoner in *Newgate*, was one of those they called then *Night-Flyers*,[2] I know not what other Word they may have understood it by since; but he was one, who by Connivance was admitted to go Abroad every Evening, when he play'd his Pranks, and furnish'd those honest People they call Thief-Catchers[3] with business to find out next Day, and restore *for a Reward*, what they had stolen the Evening before: This Fellow was as sure to tell in his sleep all that he had done, and every Step he had taken, what he had stole, and where, as sure as if he had engag'd to tell it waking, and that there was no Harm or Danger in it; and therefore he was oblig'd after he had been out to lock himself up, or be lock'd up by some of the Keepers that had him in Fee, that no Body should hear him; but on the other Hand, if he had told all the particulars, and given a full account of his Rambles and Success to any Comrade, any Brother Thief, or to his Employers, *as I may justly call them*, then all was well with him, and he slept as quietly as other People.

As the publishing this Account of my Life, is for the sake of the just Moral of every part of it, and for Instruction, Caution, Warning and Improvement to every Reader, so this will not pass I hope for an unnecessary Digression concerning some People, being oblig'd to disclose the greatest Secrets either of their own, or other Peoples Affairs.

UNDER the certain Oppression of this weight upon my Mind, I labour'd in the Case I have been Naming; and the only relief I found for it, was to let my Husband into so much of it, as I thought would convince him of the Necessity there was, for us to think of Settling, in some other Part of the World, and the next Consideration before us, was, which part of the *English* settlements we should go to; my Husband was a perfect Stranger to the Country, and had not yet so much as a Geographical knowledge of the Situation of the several Places; and I, that till I wrote this, did not know what the word Geographical signify'd, had only a general Knowledge from long Conversation with People that came from, or went to several Places; but this I knew, that *Maryland*, *Pensilvania*, East and West *Jersy*, *New York*, and *New England*, lay all North of *Virginia*, and that they were consequently all colder Climates, to which, for that very Reason, I had an Aversion; for that as I naturally lov'd warm Weather, so now I grew into Years, I had a stronger Inclination to shun a cold Climate; I therefore consider'd of going to *Carolina*,[1] which is the most Southern Colony of the *English*, on the Continent of *America*, and hither I propos'd to go; and the rather, because I might with great ease come from thence at any time, when it might be proper to enquire after my Mothers effects, and to make myself known enough to demand them.

WITH this Resolution, I propos'd to my Husband our going away from where we was, and carrying all our Effects with us to *Carolina*, where we resolv'd to Settle, for my Husband readily agreed to the first Part (*viz.*) that it was not at all proper to stay where we was, since I had assur'd him we should be known there, and the rest I effectually conceal'd from him.

BUT now I found a new Difficulty upon me: The main Affair grew heavy upon my Mind still, and I could not think of going out of the Country, without *some how or other* making enquiry into the grand Affair of what my Mother had done for me; nor cou'd I with any patience bear the thought of going away, and not make myself known to my old Husband, (*Brother*) or to my Child, his Son, only I would fain have had this done without my new Husband having any knowledge of it, or they having any knowledge of him, or that I had such a thing as a Husband.

I CAST about innumerable ways in my Thoughts how this might be done: I would gladly have sent my Husband away

to *Carolina*, with all our Goods, and have come after myself;
but this was impracticable, he would never stir without me,
being himself perfectly unacquainted with the Country, and
with the Methods of settling there, or any where else: Then
I thought we would both go first with part of our Goods,
and that when we were Settled I should come back to
Virginia, and fetch the remainder; but even then I knew he
would never part with me, and be left there to go on alone;
the Case was plain, he was bred a Gentleman, and by Consequence was not only unacquainted, but indolent,[1] and
when we did Settle, would much rather go out into the
Woods with his Gun, which they call there Hunting,[2] and
which is the ordinary Work of the *Indians*,[3] and which they
do as Servants; I say he would much rather do that, than
attend the natural Business of his Plantation.

THESE were therefore difficulties unsurmountable, and
such as I knew not what to do in, I had such strong impressions on my Mind about discovering myself to my
Brother, formerly my *Husband*, that I could not withstand
them; and the rather, because it run constantly in my
Thoughts, that if I did not do it, while he liv'd, I might in
vain endeavour to convince my Son afterward, that I was
really the same Person, and that I was his Mother, and so
might both lose the assistance and comfort of the Relation,
and the benefit of whatever it was my Mother had left me;
and yet on the other Hand, I cou'd never think it proper to
discover myself to them in the Circumstances I was in; as
well relating to the having a Husband with me, as to my
being brought over by a legal Transportation, as a Criminal;
on both which Accounts it was absolutely necessary to me to
remove from the Place where I was, and come again to him,
as from another Place, and in another Figure.

UPON those Considerations, I went on with telling my
Husband, the absolute necessity there was of our not Settling
in *Potomack* River, at least that we should be presently made
publick there, whereas if we went to any other Place in the
World, we should come in, with as much Reputation, as any

Family that came to Plant: That as it was always agreeable
to the Inhabitants to have Families come among them to
Plant, who brought Substance with them, either to purchase
Plantations, or begin New ones, so we should be sure of a
kind agreeable Reception, and that without any possibility of
a Discovery of our Circumstances.

I TOLD him in general too, that as I had several Relations
in the Place where we was, and that I durst not now let
myself be known to them, because they would soon come
into a knowledge of the Occasion and Reason of my coming
over, which would be to expose myself to the last degree; so
I had Reason to believe that my Mother who died here had
left me something, and perhaps considerable, which it might
be very well worth my while to enquire after; but that this
too could not be done without exposing us publickly, unless
we went from hence; and then where ever we Settled, I
might come as it were to visit and to see my Brother and
Nephews, make myself known to them, claim and enquire
after what was my Due, be receiv'd with Respect, and at the
the same time have justice done me with chearfulness and
good will; whereas if I did it now, I could expect nothing
but with trouble, such as exacting it by force, receiving it
with Curses and Reluctance, and with all kinds of Affronts;
which he would not perhaps bear to see; that in Case of
being oblig'd to legal Proofs of being really her Daughter, I
might be at loss, be oblig'd to have recourse to *England*, and
it may be to fail at last, and so lose it, whatever it might be:
With these Arguments, and having thus acquainted my
Husband with the whole Secret so far as was needful to him,
we resolv'd to go and seek a Settlement in some other Colony,
and at first Thoughts, *Carolina* was the Place we pitch'd
upon.

IN order to this we began to make enquiry for Vessels going
to *Carolina*, and in a very little while got information, that
on the other side the *Bay*, *as they call it*, namely, in *Maryland*
there was a Ship, which came from *Carolina*, loaden with
Rice,[1] and other Goods, and was going back again thither,

and from thence to *Jamaica*, with Provisions: On this News we hir'd a Sloop to take in our Goods, and taking as it were a final farewel of *Potowmack* River, we went with all our Cargo over to *Maryland*.

THIS was a long and unpleasant Voyage, and my Spouse said it was worse to him than all the Voyage from *England*, because the Weather was but indifferent, the Water rough, and the Vessel small and inconvenient; in the next Place we were full a hundred Miles up *Potowmack* River, in a part which they call *Westmoreland* County, and as that River is by far the greatest in *Virginia*, and I have heard say, it is the greatest River in the World that falls into another River, and not directly into the Sea; so we had base Weather in it, and were frequently in great Danger; for tho' they call it but a River, 'tis frequently so broad, that when we were in the middle, we could not see Land on either Side for many Leagues together: Then we had the great River, or Bay of *Chesapeake* to cross, which is where the River *Potowmack* falls into it, near thirty Miles broad, and we entered more great vast Waters, whose Names I know not, so that our Voyage was full two hundred Mile, in a poor sorry Sloop with all our Treasure, and if any Accident had happened to us, we might at last have been very miserable; supposing we had lost our Goods and saved our Lives only, and had then been left naked and destitute, and in a wild strange Place, not having one Friend or Acquaintance in all that part of the World? The very thoughts of it gives me some horror, even since the Danger is past.

WELL, we came to the Place in five Days sailing, I think they call it *Philips*'s *Point*,[1] and behold when we came thither, the Ship bound to *Carolina*, was loaded and gone away but three Days before. This was a Disappointment, but however, I that was to be discourag'd with nothing, told my Husband that since we could not get Passage to *Carolina*, and that the Country we was in, was very fertile and good; we would if he lik'd of it, see if we could find out any thing for our Turn where we was, and that if he lik'd things we would Settle here.

WE immediately went on Shore, but found no Conveniences just at that Place, either for our being on Shore, or preserving our Goods on Shore, but was directed by a very honest Quaker, who we found there to go to a Place, about sixty Miles East; that is to say, nearer the Mouth of the *Bay*, where he said he liv'd, and where we should be Accommodated, either to Plant, or to wait for any other Place to Plant in, that might be more Convenient, and he invited us with so much kindness and simple Honesty[1] that we agreed to go, and the Quaker himself went with us.

HERE we bought us two Servants, (*viz.*) an *English* Woman-Servant just come on Shore from a Ship of *Leverpool*, and a *Negro* Man-Servant; things absolutely necessary for all People that pretended to Settle in that Country: This honest Quaker was very helpful to us, and when we came to the Place that he propos'd to us, found us out a convenient Storehouse, for our Goods, and Lodging for ourselves, and our Servants; and about two Months, or thereabout afterwards, by his Direction we took up a large peice of Land from the Government of that Country,[1] in order to form our Plantation, and so we laid the thoughts of going to *Carolina* wholly aside, having been very well receiv'd here, and Accommodated with a convenient Lodging, till we could prepare things, and have Land enough cur'd, and Timber and Materials provid'd for building us a House, all which we manag'd by the Direction of the Quaker; so that in one Years time, we had near fifty Acres of Land clear'd, part of it enclos'd, and some of it Planted with Tobacco, tho' not much; besides, we had Garden ground, and Corn sufficient to help supply our Servants with Roots, and Herbs, and Bread.

AND now I perswaded my Husband to let me go over the *Bay* again, and enquire after my Friends; he was the willinger to consent to it now, because he had business upon his Hands sufficient to employ him, besides his Gun to divert him, which they call Hunting there, and which he greatly delighted in; and indeed we us'd to look at one another, sometimes with a great deal of Pleasure, reflecting how much better that was, not than *Newgate* only, but than the most prosperous of our Circumstances in the wicked Trade that we had been both carrying on.

OUR Affair was in a very good posture, we purchased of the Proprietors of the Colony, as much Land for 35 Pound, paid in ready Money, as would make a sufficient Plantation to employ between fifty and sixty Servants, and which being well improv'd, would be sufficient to us as long as we could either of us live; and as for Children I was past the prospect of any thing of that kind.

BUT our good Fortune did not End here, I went, *as I have said*, over the *Bay*, to the Place, where my Brother, once a Husband liv'd; but I did not go to the same Village, where I was before, but went up another great River, on the East side of the River *Potowmack*, call'd *Rapahannock* River, and by this means came on the back of his Plantation, which was large, and by the help of a Navigable Creek, or little River, that run into the *Rapahannock*, I came very near it.

I WAS now fully resolv'd to go up *Point-blank*, to my Brother (Husband) and to tell him who I was; but not knowing what Temper I might find him in, or how much out of Temper rather, I might make him by such a rash visit, I resolv'd to write a Letter to him first to let him know who I was, and that I was come not to give him any trouble upon the old Relation, which I hop'd was entirely forgot; but that I apply'd to him as a Sister to a Brother, desiring his Assistance in the Case of that Provision, which our Mother at her decease had left for my Support, and which I did not doubt but he would do me Justice in, especially considering that I was come thus far to look after it.

I said some very tender kind things in the Letter about his Son, which I told him he knew to be my own Child, and that as I was guilty of nothing in Marrying him any more than he was in Marrying me, neither of us having then known our being at all related to one another; so I hop'd he would allow me the most Passionate desire of once seeing my

one, and only Child, and of showing something of the
Infirmities of a Mother in preserving a violent Affection for
him, who had never been able to retain any thought of me
one way or other.

I did believe that having receiv'd this Letter, he would
immediately give it to his Son to Read; I having understood
his Eyes being so dim, that he cou'd not see to read it; but it
fell out better than so, for as his Sight was dim, so he had
allow'd his Son to open all Letters that came to his Hand for
him, and the old Gentleman being from Home, or out of the
way when my Messenger came, my Letter came directly to
my Sons Hand, and he open'd and read it.

HE call'd the Messenger in, after some little stay, and
ask'd him where the Person was who gave him the Letter,
the Messenger told him the Place, which was about seven
Miles off, so he bid him stay, and ordering a Horse to be
got ready, and two Servants, away he came to me with the
Messenger: Let any one judge the Consternation I was in,
when my Messenger came back, and told me the old Gentleman was not at Home, but his Son was come along with him,
and was just coming up to me: I was perfectly confounded,
for I knew not whether it was Peace or War, nor cou'd I tell
how to behave: However, I had but a very few Moments to
think, for my Son was at the Heels of the Messenger, and
coming up into my Lodgings, ask'd the Fellow at the Door
something, I suppose it was, *for I did not hear it, so as to
understand it*, which was the Gentlewoman that sent him, for
the Messenger said, *there she is Sir*, at which he comes directly
up to me, kisses me, took me in his Arms, and embrac'd me
with so much Passion, that he could not speak, but I could
feel his Breast heave and throb like a Child that Cries, but
Sobs, and cannot cry it out.

I CAN neither express or describe the Joy, that touch'd my
very Soul, when I found, *for it was easy to discover that Part*,
that he came not as a Stranger, but as a Son to a Mother,
and indeed as a Son, who had never before known what a
Mother of his own was; in short, we cryed over one another a

considerable while, when at last he broke out first, MY DEAR MOTHER, says he, *are you still alive! I never expected to have seen your Face*; as for me, I cou'd say nothing a great while.

AFTER wc had both recover'd ourselves a little, and were able to talk, he told me how things stood; as to what I had written to his Father, he told me he had not shewed my Letter to his Father, or told him any thing about it; that what his Grandmother left me, was in his Hands, and that he would do me Justice to my full Satisfaction; that as to his Father, he was old and infirm both in Body and Mind, that he was very Fretful, and Passionate, almost Blind, and capable of nothing; and he question'd whether he would know how to act in an Affair, which was of so nice a Nature as this, and that therefore he had come himself, as well to satisfy himself in seeing me, which he could not restrain himself from, as also to put it into my Power, to make a Judgement after I had seen how things were, whether I would discover myself to his Father, or no.

THIS was really so prudently, and wisely manag'd, that I found my Son was a Man of Sense, and needed no Direction from me; I told him, I did not wonder that his Father was, as he had describ'd him, for that his Head was a little touch'd before I went away; and principally his Disturbance was, because I could not be perswaded to conceal our Relation, and to live with him as my Husband, after I knew that he was my Brother: That as he knew better than I, what his Fathers present Condition was, I should readily joyn with him in such Measures as he would direct: That I was indifferent, as to seeing his Father, since I had seen him first, and he cou'd not have told me better News, than to tell me that what his Grandmother had left me, was entrusted in his Hands, who I doubted not now he knew who I was, would *as he said*, do me Justice: I enquir'd then how long my Mother had been dead, and where she died, and told so many particulars of the Family, that I left him no room to doubt the Truth of my being really and truly his Mother.

MY Son then enquir'd where I was, and how I had dispos'd myself; I told him I was on the *Maryland* side of the *Bay*, at the Plantation of a particular Friend, who came from *England* in the same Ship with me, that as for that side of the *Bay* where he was, I had no Habitation; he told me I should go Home with him, and live with him, if I pleas'd, as long as I liv'd: That as to his Father he knew no Body, and would never so much as guess at me; I consider'd of that a little, and told him, that tho' it was really no little concern to me to live at a distance from him; yet I could not say it would be the most comfortable thing in the World to me to live in the House with him; and to have that unhappy Object always before me, which had been such a blow to my Peace before; that tho' I should be glad to have his Company (my Son) or to be as near him as possible while I stay'd, yet I could not think of being in the House where I should be also under constant Restraint, for fear of betraying myself in my Discourse, nor should I be able to refrain some Expressions in my Conversing with him as my Son, that might discover the whole Affair, which would by no means be Convenient.

HE acknowledged that I was right in all this, but then DEAR MOTHER, says he, *you shall be as near me as you can*; so he took me with him on Horseback to a Plantation, next to his own, and where I was as well entertain'd as I cou'd have been in his own; having left me there he went away home, telling me we would talk of the main Business the next Day, and having first called me his Aunt, and given a Charge to the People, who it seems were his Tenants, to treat me with all possible Respect; about two Hours after he was gone, he sent me a Maid-Servant, and a *Negro* Boy to wait on me, and Provisions ready dress'd for my Supper; and thus I was as if I had been in a new World, and began secretly now to wish that I had not brought my *Lancashire* Husband from *England* at all.

HOWEVER, that wish was not hearty neither, for I lov'd my *Lancashire* Husband entirely, as indeed I had ever done from the beginning; and he merited from me as much as it was possible for a Man to do, but that by the way.

THE next Morning my Son came to visit me again almost as soon as I was up; after a little Discourse, he first of all pull'd out a Deer skin Bag, and gave it me, with five and fifty *Spanish* Pistoles[1] in it, and told me that was to supply my Expences from *England*, for tho' it was not his Business to enquire, yet he ought to think I did not bring a great deal of Money out with me; it not being usual to bring much Money into that Country: Then he pull'd out his Grandmother's Will, and read it over to me, whereby it appear'd, that she had left a small Plantation, *as he call'd it*, on *York* River, that is, where my Mother liv'd, to me, with the Stock of Servants and Cattle upon it, and given it in Trust to this Son of mine for my Use, when ever he should hear of my being alive, and to my Heirs, if I had any Children, and in default of Heirs, to whomsoever I should by Will dispose of it; but gave the Income of it, till I should be heard of, or found, to my said Son; and if I should not be living, then it was to him, and his Heirs.

THIS Plantation, tho' remote from him, he said he did not let out, but manag'd it by a head Clerk, Steward, as he did another that was his Fathers, that lay hard by it, and went over himself three or four times a Year to look after it; I ask'd him what he thought the Plantation might be worth, *he said*, if I would let it out, he would give me about sixty Pounds a Year for it; but if I would live on it, then it would be worth much more, and he believ'd would bring me in about 150 *l.* a Year; but seeing I was likely either to Settle on the other side the *Bay*, or might perhaps have a mind to go back to *England* again, if I would let him be my Steward he would manage it for me, as he had done for himself, and that he believ'd he should be able to send me as much Tobacco to *England* from it, as would yeild me about 100 *l.* a Year, sometimes more.

THIS was all strange News to me, and things I had not been us'd to; and really my Heart began to look up more seriously, than I think it ever did before, and to look with great Thankfulness to the Hand of Providence, which had

done such wonders for me, who had been myself the greatest
wonder of Wickedness, perhaps that had been suffered to
live in the World; and I must again observe, that not on this
Occasion only, but even on all other Occasions of Thankfulness, my past wicked and abominable Life never look'd so
Monstruous to me, and I never so compleatly abhorr'd it,
and reproach'd myself with it, as when I had a Sense upon
me of Providence doing good to me, while I had been making
those vile Returns on my part.

But I leave the Reader to improve these Thoughts, as no
doubt they will see Cause, and I go on to the Fact; my Sons
tender Carriage, and kind Offers fetch'd Tears from me,
almost all the while he talk'd with me; indeed I could scarce
Discourse with him, but in the intervals of my Passion;
however, at length I began, and expressing myself with
wonder at my being so happy to have the Trust of what I
had left, put into the Hands of my own Child; I told him,
that as to the Inheritance of it, I had no Child but him in
the World, and was now past having any, if I should Marry,
and therefore would desire him to get a Writing Drawn,
which I was ready to execute, by which I would after me
give it wholly to him, and to his Heirs; and in the mean time
smiling, I ask'd him, what made him continue a Batchelor so
long; his answer was kind, and ready, that *Virginia* did not
yield any great plenty of Wives, and that since I talk'd of
going back to *England*, I should send him a Wife from
London.

This was the Substance of our first days Conversation,
the pleasantest Day that ever past over my Head in my Life,
and which gave me the truest Satisfaction: He came every
Day after this, and spent great part of his time with me, and
carried me about to several of his Friends Houses, where I
was entertain'd with great Respect; also I Dined several
times at his own House, when he took care always to see his
half dead Father so out of the way, that I never saw him, or
he me: I made him one Present, and it was all I had of value,
and that was one of the gold Watches, of which I mention'd

above, that I had two in my Chest, and this I happen'd to have with me, and I gave it him at his third Visit: I told him, I had nothing of any value to bestow but that, and I desir'd he would now and then kiss it for my sake; *I did not indeed tell him* that I had stole it from a Gentlewomans side, at a Meeting-House in *London*, that's by the way.

HE stood a little while Hesitating, as if doubtful whether to take it or no; but I press'd it on him, and made him accept it, and it was not much less worth than his Leather-pouch full of *Spanish* Gold; no, tho' it were to be reckon'd, as if at *London*, whereas it was worth twice as much there, where I gave it him; at length he took it, kiss'd it, told me the Watch should be a Debt upon him, that he would be paying, as long as I liv'd.

A FEW Days after he brought the Writings of Gift, and the Scrivener with them, and I sign'd them very freely, and deliver'd them to him with a hundr'd Kisses; for sure nothing ever pass'd between a Mother, and a tender dutiful Child, with more Affection: The next Day he brings me an Obligation under his Hand and Seal, whereby he engag'd himself to Manage, and Improve the Plantation for my account, and with his utmost Skill, and to remit the Produce to my order where-ever I should be, and withal, to be oblig'd himself to make up the Produce a hundred Pound a year to me: When he had done so, he told me, that as I came to demand it before the Crop was off, I had a right to the Produce of the current Year, and so he paid me an hundred Pound in *Spanish* Peices of Eight, and desir'd me to give him a Receipt for it as in full for that Year, ending at *Christmas* following; this being about the latter End of *August*.

I STAY'D here above five Weeks, and indeed had much a do to get away then. Nay, he would have come over the *Bay* with me, but I would by no means allow him to it; however, he would send me over in a Sloop of his own, which was built like a Yatch,[1] and serv'd him as well for Pleasure as Business: This I accepted of, and so after the utmost Expressions both of Duty, and Affection, he let me come away, and I arriv'd safe in two Days at my Friends the Quakers.

I BROUGHT over with me for the use of our Plantation, three Horses with Harness, and Saddles; some Hogs, two Cows, and a thousand other things, the Gift of the kindest and tenderest Child that ever Woman had: I related to my Husband all the particulars of this Voyage, except that I called my Son my Cousin; and first I told him, that I had lost my Watch, which he seem'd to take as a Misfortune; but then I told him how kind my Cousin had been, that my Mother had left me such a Plantation, and that he had preserv'd it for me, in hopes some time or other he should hear from me; then I told him that I had left it to his Management, that he would render me a faithful Account of its Produce; and then I pull'd him out the hundred Pound in Silver, as the first Years produce, and then pulling out the Deer skin Purse, with the Pistoles, and here my Dear, *says I*, is the gold Watch. My Husband, *so is Heavens goodness sure to work the same Effects*, *in all sensible Minds*, *where Mercies touch the Heart*, lifted up both his Hands, and with an extasy of Joy, *What is God a doing* says he, *for such an ungrateful Dog as I am!* Then I let him know, what I had brought over in the Sloop, besides all this; I mean the Horses, Hogs, and Cows, and other Stores for our Plantation; all which added to his surprize, and fill'd his Heart with thankfulness; and from this time forward I believe he was as sincere a Penitent, and as thoroughly a reform'd Man,[1] as ever God's goodness brought back from a Profligate, a Highway-Man, and a Robber. I could fill a larger History than this, with the Evidences of this Truth, and but that I doubt that part of the Story will not be equally diverting as the wicked Part, I have had thoughts of making a Volume of it by itself.

As for myself, as this is to be my own Story, not my Husbands, I return to that Part which relates to myself; we went on with our Plantation, and manag'd it with the help and Direction of such Friends as we got there, by our obliging Behaviour, and especially the honest Quaker, who prov'd a faithful generous and steady Friend to us; and we had very good Success; for having a flourishing Stock to begin with, as *I have said*; and this being now encreas'd, by the Addition of a Hundred and fifty Pound *Sterling* in Money, we enlarg'd our Number of Servants, built us a very good House, and cur'd every Year a great deal of Land. The second Year I wrote to my old Governess, giving her part with us of the Joy of our Success, and order'd her how to lay out the Money I had left with her, which was 250 *l.* as above, and to send it to us in Goods, which she perform'd, with her usual Kindness and Fidelity, and all this arriv'd safe to us.

HERE we had a supply of all sorts of Cloaths, as well for my Husband, as for myself; and I took especial care to buy for him all those things that I knew he delighted to have; as two good long Wigs, two silver hilted Swords, three or four fine Fowling peices, a fine Saddle with Holsters and Pistoles very handsome, with a Scarlet Cloak; and in a Word, every thing I could think of to oblige him; and to make him appear, as he really was, a very fine Gentleman: I order'd a good Quantity of such Houshold-stuff, as we yet wanted, with Linnen of all sorts for us both; as for my self, I wanted very little of Cloths, or Linnen, being very well furnished before: The rest of my Cargo consisted in Iron-Work, of all sorts, Harness for Horses, Tools, Cloaths for Servants, and Woollen-Cloth, stuffs, Serges, Stockings, Shoes, Hats and the like, such as Servants wear, and whole Pieces[1] also, to make up for Servants, all by direction of the Quaker; and all this Cargo arriv'd safe, and in good Condition, with three Women Servants, lusty Wenches, which my old Governess had pick'd up for me, suitable enough to the Place, and to the Work we had for them to do; one of which happen'd to come double, having been got with Child by one of the Seamen in the Ship, as she own'd afterwards, before the Ship got so far as *Gravesend*; so she brought us a stout Boy, about 7 Months after her Landing.

My Husband you may suppose was a little surpriz'd at the arriving of all this Cargo from *England*, and talking with me after he saw the Account of the particular; my Dear, *says he*, what is the meaning of all this? I fear you will run us too deep in Debt: When shall we be able to make Return for it all? I smil'd, and told him that it was all paid for, and then I told him, that not knowing what might befal us in the Voyage, and considering what our Circumstances might expose us to; I had not taken my whole Stock with me, that I had reserv'd so much in my Friends Hands, which now we were come over safe, and was Settled in a way to live, I had sent for as he might see.

He was amaz'd, and stood a while telling upon his Fingers, but said nothing, at last he began thus, Hold lets see, *says he, telling upon his Fingers still*; and first on his Thumb, there's 246 *l.* in Money at first, then two gold Watches, Diamond Rings, and Plate, *says he*, upon the fore Finger, then upon the next Finger, here's a Plantation on *York* River, a 100 *l.* a Year, then 150 in Money; then a Sloop load of Horses, Cows, Hogs and Stores, and so on to the Thumb again; and now, *says he*, a Cargo cost 250 *l.* in *England*, and worth here twice the Money, well, *says I*, What do you make of all that? make of it, *says he*, why who says I was deceiv'd, when I married a Wife in *Lancashire*? I think I have married a Fortune, and a very good Fortune too, *says he*.

In a Word, we were now in very considerable Circumstances, and every Year encreasing; for our new Plantation grew upon our Hands insensibly; and in eight Year which we lived upon it, we brought it to such a pitch, that the Produce was, at least, 300 *l.* Sterling a Year; I mean, worth so much in *England*.

After I had been a Year at Home again, I went over the Bay to see my Son, and to receive another Year's Income of my Plantation; and I was surpriz'd to hear, just at my Landing there, that my old Husband was dead, and had not been bury'd above a Fortnight. This, I confess, was not disagreeable News, because now I could appear as I was in

a marry'd Condition; so I told my Son before I came from
him, that I believed I should marry a Gentleman who had a
Plantation near mine; and tho' I was legally free to marry,
as to any Obligation that was on me before, yet that I was
shye of it, least the Blot should some time or other be
reviv'd, and it might make a Husband uneasy; my Son the
same kind dutiful and obliging Creature as ever, treated me
now at his own House, paid me my hundred Pound, and
sent me Home again loadcd with Presents.

SOME time after this, I let my Son know I was marry'd,
and invited him over to see us; and my Husband wrote a very
obliging Letter to him also, inviting him to come and see him;
and he came accordingly some Months after, and happen'd
to be there just when my Cargo from *England* came in,
which I let him believe belong'd all to my Husband's
Estate, not to me.

IT must be observ'd, that when the old Wretch, my
Brother (Husband) was dead, I then freely gave my Husband
an Account of all that Affair, and of this Cousin, as I had
call'd him before, being my own Son by that mistaken
unhappy Match: He was perfectly easy in the Account, and
told me he should have been as easy if the old Man, as we
call'd him, had been alive; for, *said he*, it was no Fault of
yours, nor of his; it was a Mistake impossible to be prevented;
he only reproach'd him with desiring me to conceal it, and
to live with him as a Wife, after I knew that he was my
Brother, that, he said, was a vile part: Thus all these little
Difficulties were made easy, and we liv'd together with the
greatest Kindness and Comfort imaginable; we are now
grown Old: I am come back to *England*, being almost
seventy Years of Age, my Husband sixty eight, having
perform'd much more than the limited Terms of my Transportation: And now notwithstanding all the Fatigues, and
all the Miseries we have both gone thro', we are both in good
Heart and Health; my Husband remain'd there sometime
after me to settle our Affairs, and at first I had intended to
go back to him, but at his desire I alter'd that Resolution,

and he is come over to *England* also, where we resolve to spend the Remainder of our Years in sincere Penitence, for the wicked Lives we have lived.

Written in the Year 1683.

F I N I S.

TEXTUAL NOTES

References are to page and line. *1*: the Clark copy of the first edn.; *2*: the Cornell copy of the second edn. (see *supra*, p. xxiii, notes 1, 2.).

2. 7 is made] is to be made *add. 2.* 2. 32 other] another *2.* 3.29 first or last *2*: first and last *1.* 5. 10 Thieves purchase ... say, of] *om. 2.* 7. *title* HISTORY] FORTUNES *2.* 7. 12 Steps ... String, *ed.*: Steps, ... String *1*: Steps ... String; *2.* 7.13 knew *2*: know *1.* 8. 12 nor] but *2.* 8. 25/6 in ... again,] after which *2.* 8. 28 Favour of] Favour afterward of *add. 2.* 9. 35 had also *2*: had also had *1.* 10. 4 Religiously] Religiously also *add. 2.* 10. 28 where *2*: were *1.* 10. 31 set] had set *add. 2.* 11. 11 Service,] Service at all *add. 2.* 11. 30 get at] get a Day at *add. 2.* 12. 8 keep] find *2.* 12. 9 will] would *2.* 13. 2/3 took up] look'd upon *2.* 13. 4 any body knows,] I know; *2.* 13. 5 Gentlewoman's] Lady's *2.* 13. 16 that terrible Bug-bear] *om. 2.* 13. 27 pleas'd to be familiar [with] me *ed.*: pleas'd to be familiar me *1*: mightily pleased *2.* 13. 35 I understood by it no more *ed.*: I understood by it to no more *1*: it was no more *2.* 14. 17 myself] my self besides *add. 2.* 14. 22 and Humble;] *om. 2.* 14. 30 and always Clean;] *om. 2.* 15. 2/3 it ... say,] I was past it; for *2.* 15. 4 she ... it] was enough *2.* 15. 8/9 and ... Needle,] *om. 2.* 15. 10 of the Town] *om. 2.* 15. 28 so much] such a *2.* 16. 25 Children] Day-Children *2.* 17. 16/17 away, ... unsent] *om. 2.* 17. 23 Mistress,] Mistress had better Thoughts for me, I call her generous, *add. 2.* 17. 34/5 and had ... do,] *om. 2.* 18. 4/5 , tho' ... yet] *om. 2.* 18. 33 but they] *Viz.* that mine *2.* 19. 7/8 could ... sometimes] happened often *2.* 20. 2 begun] begin *2.* 20. 8 opener] open *2.* 20. 26 have] has *2.* 20. 27 have] has *2.* 20. 28 as *2*: has *1.* 22. 6 says] says he *2.* 22. 32 of my own Safety, or] *om. 2.* 23. 15 God knows] *om. 2.* 24. 10 had fir'd] had now fir'd *add. 2.* 24. 14 as before] just as he did before *2.* 24. 31 of *ed.*: off *1, 2.*

24. 35 come that] come to that *add. 2.* 25. 1 being both well warm'd,] *om. 2.* 25. 21/2 my Thoughts ... Necessity] I so much as think *2.* 25. 29/30 requir'd, this Gentleman had *ed.*: requir'd; this Gentleman, had *1*] requir'd, he had *2.* 25. 37 and] On the other Hand, *2.* 26. 13 indeed] and indeed *add. 2.* 26. 19 but] when but *add. 2.* 26. 26 opportunity] an Opportunity *add. 2.* 27. 3/4 which ... Meaning;] *om. 2.* 27. 4 but Brother, says *ed.*: but Brother? says *1*: but *says 2.* 27. 6/7 hear, you ... is: *2*: hear. You ... is, *1.* 27. 20 asks] ask'd *2.* 27. 23 which] all which *add. 2.* 28. 3 mighty] mightily *2.* 29. 16 ; chiefly by his contrivance;] and *2.* 29. 29/30 and that ... all] *om. 2.* 30. 21 among the Servants,] *om. 2.* 31. 2/3 agreeable ... expect;] *om. 2.* 31. 11/14 but from ... yet] for I was a stranger to those things, but *2.* 31. 15/16 but then it came] it came also *2.* 31. 34 of me, and] *om. 2.* 31. 35/6 and when ... Publick] so *2.* 32. 5 not] *om. 2.* 32. 30 not] hardly *2.* 33. 14 all] of *2.* 33. 18 the Sex] his Sex *2.* 34. 2 Countenances] Faces *2.* 34. 30 as ... been,] *om. 2.* 35. 17/18 my ... time] I was thereby *2.* 36. 2 got an Opportunity,] found Means *2.* 37. 31/2 and as ... before]

as *I told you* 2. 38. 12 What . . . said,] *om.* 2. 38. 15 for ought 2: for I ought *1*. 38. 32
, you . . . nothing] *om.* 2. 38. 35 step *ed.*] stop *1*, 2. 39. 6 and with splendor at once,]
om. 2. 40. 13/14 Remedy so . . . That] Remedy, only that 2. 41. 3/5 , or . . . them]
om. 2. 41. 29/30 to . . . Passion;] *om.* 2. 41. 35 might come] might one time or other
come *add.* 2. 42. 14/15 , or so . . . Decent] *om.* 2. 42. 20/1 ; only . . . Strugle] *om.*
2. 42. 22/3 so Melancholly,] *om.* 2. 42. 37 call'd her Maid to] bid her Maid 2. 43.
21 are not a talking] don't talk 2. 43. 29/30 one that is near . . . had too] one too
that is so near . . . had 2. 44. 34/5 with all my heart] *om.* 2. 45. 17 first:] first, *and
the like*: *add.* 2. 45. 33 me that] us 2. 46. 28/9 out of her Senses] gone 2.

47. 8/9 Mrs *Betty*, . . . *Miss*] no Mrs. 2. 47. 24 go first] go in first *add.* 2. 47. 27
come if] come in if *add.* 2. 48. 7 game at] game of 2. 48. 34/5 and . . . him,] *om.* 2.
49. 6/8; and that . . . Recovering] *om.* 2. 49. 23 another] the other 2. 49. 27 to go]
om. 2. 49. 28 without] without it *add.* 2. 49. 29 because . . . Disturb'd, and] *om.* 2.
49. 31 of,] on 2. 49. 32 gain'd] had done 2. 49. 35 with Freedom] in Freedom 2.
49. 36 Plainess 2: Plainest *1*. 50. 8 silent, dull,] *om.* 2. 50. 11 carried respectfully to
him] carried as respectfully 2. 50. 22/3 , that . . . before] *om.* 2. 51. 26 Gentlewoman,]
Lady 2. 52. 3 one has] one that has *add.* 2. 52. 27 if . . . in it;] *om.* 2. 52. 29 her; . . .
too] her presently, 2. 52. 35/6 think we can] make us 2. 53. 27 Fool enough] enough
Fool 2. 54. 3/4 me upon] me again upon *add.* 2. 54. 6/7 besides . . . all:] *om.* 2.
54. 24/5 , and that . . . carried] *om.* 2. 54. 35/6 and desir'd . . . him;] *om.* 2. 55. 5 the
Thing . . . far, that] *om.* 2. 55. 6 comply with] comply to 2. 55. 8 and Sisters] and his
Sisters *add.* 2. 55. 27 500 *l.* in Money,] *Five Hundred Pounds* 2. 55. 32/4 and with . . .
repeat, that I . . . suppose, that *ed.*] and with . . . repeat: That I . . . suppose, that *1*]
that you may suppose 2. 56. 6 , as ever] *om.* 2. 56. 7 Sense] the Sense *add.* 2. 56. 9
and] that 2. denial in] denial from me in *add.* 2. 56. 18 he entreated] and entreated 2.
56. 22 our just] our own just *add.* 2. 57. 17/18 for, should be 2: for; should he be
1. 58. 3/4 So certainly . . . Affection, and] *om.* 2. 59. 6 as was proportionable]
was suitable 2. 60. 3/4 *so* . . . *Publick*] *om.* 2. 60. 15 Men of Gallantry and Figure,]
om. 2. 60. 25 be one] like one 2. 61. 2 to keep her self] to make her self a Wife 2.
61. 12 before, . . . mentioning,] *om.* 2. 61. 16/17 , and as . . . too] *om.* 2. 62. 12 and
was . . . *Mint*, but] *om.* 2. 62. 15 *sometime*,] *something before* 2. 62. 17 , *tho'* . . . *much*]
om. 2. 63. 2/3 , and got . . . they could] *om.* 2.

63. 17 so dextrously] desperately 2. 63. 18/19 in . . . Manner,] *om.* 2. 63. 33 ,
some and some,] *om.* 2. 64. 10 one I durst] one who I could 2. 64. 26 found an]
found that an *add.* 2. 65. 1 who were overwhelm'd in] in the most 2. 65. 14/16 they
put . . . gave them;] *om.* 2. 65. 25 are] were 2. 66. 8/9 and the . . . before me,] *om.* 2.
66. 16 which . . . safe;] *om.* 2. 66. 30 accepted her] accepted of her *add.* 2. 67. 2
that is, with a good Fortune *ed.*: that is, with good a Fortune *1*: *om.* 2. 67. 8 into a
good 2] into good *1*. 67. 12/14 and that . . . Country;] *om.* 2. 67. 36 had but *ed.*:
had, but *1*: had 2. 68. 23/4 and was . . . that she] that she was . . . she 2. 68. 29/30
without . . . Character] *om.* 2. 68. 36/7 and would . . . Town;] *om.* 2. 69. 24/5 in
a . . . in was;] *om.* 2. 69. 27 as to Estate] *om.* 2. told] told too 2. 69. 36 As . . . Head,]
om. 2. 69. 37 it; immediately] all this, and immediately 2. 70. 17 I confess] *om.* 2.
70. 31 and having allarm'd . . . Water] and seeing . . . Water alarm'd 2. 70. 36/7
and his . . . side] *om.* 2. 71. 5 and was . . . Man,] *om.* 2. 71. 12 *Redriff*] Rotherhith 2.
71. 17/18 excusing . . . Rashness,] *om.* 2. 71. 19 to clear] only to clear 2. 72. 4 and in]
and another in 2. 72. 16 SHE . . . way,] *om.* 2. 72. 34/5 and . . . Part] *om.* 2. 73. 6

turning . . . and] *om. 2.* 73. 9/10 and . . . him;] *om. 2.* 73. 23 like a prudent Woman]
om. 2. 74. 11 and . . . ask'd] *om. 2.* 74. 34 a Woman] an honest Woman 2. 75. 14/15
their Thought] their own Thought 2. 75. 15/16 resolve . . . comes; that] *om. 2.*
75. 17 run 2: runs *1.* 75. 24/5 for not accepting 2: for accepting *1.* 75. 32 the Thing,]
the same thing 2. 75. 37 of which . . . itself] *om. 2.* 76. 19/20 for . . . Matrimony]
om. 2. 76. 23/4 which . . . itself] *om. 2.* 77. 13 when . . . Fortune] *om. 2.* 77. 34
after . . . Relations] *om. 2.* 78. 8/10 , because . . . Game:] *om. 2.* 78. 12/13 as scarce]
om. 2.

78. 20 bear 2: bare *1.* 78. 25/6 nay, . . . Satisfaction] *om. 2.* 79. 29 any more . . .
Affection;] *om. 2.* 80. 29 be under . . . owning my own] own my 2. 80. 34/5 after . . .
Subject] *om. 2.* 81. 4/5 and that . . . at all;] *om. 2.* 81. 7 and that . . . there,] *om. 2.*
81. 15 generally . . . tune of] of about 2. 81. 17 much; very well, 2] much very
well; *1.* 81. 18 thither as] thither then as 2. 81. 22/3 tho' . . . Plantations,] *om. 2.*
81. 36/7 more . . . Courtship;] *om. 2.* 85. 4/5 and he . . . together] *om. 2.* 85. 15
To make . . . short] *om. 2.* 86. 1 if . . . miserable] *om. 2.* 86. 3/4 old Woman . . .
old Woman] old Woman . . . so 2. 86. 13/14 such . . . Slaves] *om. 2.* 86. 15 from
Newgate . . . Prisons] *om. 2.* 86. 26 and Cloathes, and other] and 2. 87. 3/4 and
pulling . . . her Hand] *om. 2.* 87. 24 and who lay in . . . was] in . . who was 2. 87. 25/6
be Hang'd . . . dyed] dye . . perish'd 2. 88. 5 and the terrible . . . thro',] *om. 2.*
88. 11 place. *ed.*: place? *1,* 2. 88. 18 not her] not of her 2. 88. 25 and I] and that I
2. 88. 29/30 since . . . Relation] if 2. 88. 32/3 which . . . me,] *om. 2.* 89. 13/14
who . . . Brother] *om. 2.* 89. 22 as . . himself] *om. 2.* 89. 27 but . . . Children] *om. 2.*
90. 5 but . . . Fate guided] *om. 2.* 90. 13/14 I found . . ., or that] *om. 2.* 90. 31 as a
Husband] *om. 2.* 91. 1 Resolution. In] Resolution, that in 2. 91. 11/12 Work . . .
Children,] *om. 2.* 91. 30 and . . . Strangers] *om. 2.* 92. 3 knows] is acquainted with 2.
92. 7 my Husband . . . call'd)] him 2. 92. 22 breaking] bringing 2. 92. 26/7 and
took . . . *mean time*] when 2. 93. 11/12 tho' . . . . true,] *om. 2.* 93. 30/1 as . . . Night]
om. 2. 94. 7/8 which . . . true] *om. 2.* 94. 10 in Law] *om. 2.* 94. 17/18 as . . . my
Passion] *om. 2.* 96. 31/2 and expose . . . degree] *om. 2.* 96. 36/7 the Children . . .
Effects;] *om. 2.* 97. 13/14 that we might lie . . . together *both edns., although D.
probably wrote* live: *see infra, p. 100, ll. 4-5.* 97. 18 as . . . able] *om. 2.*

97. 21 not . . . destitute, but] *om. 2.* 97. 22 Justice] Justice too 2. 98. 12/14 and . . .
Secresie] *om. 2.* 98. 17 on my . . . hers] *om. 2.* 98. 26/7 tho' . . . Conscience, yet]
om. 2. 98. 33 in . . . Policy] *om. 2.* 100. 3/4 that . . . renew'd,] *om. 2.* 100. 33 and . . .
still] *om. 2.* 102. 28 bear] *both edns., although D. perhaps wrote* hear. 104. 18 and un-
easie] *om. 2.* 104. 32/3 Careful . . . heard of me] just to this 2. 105. 10/11 *for* . . .
meant] *om. 2.* 105. 13 my native Country] *om. 2.* 105. 33 4 Acquaintance . . . Acquain-
tances] Acquaintances . . . Acquaintance 2. 105. 36/7 as . . . enquire] *om. 2.* 106. 12
any thing that] what 2. 106. 13 I . . . amiss] *om. 2.* 106. 25/6 in . . . Thoughts] *om. 2.*
106. 28 now 2: none *1.* 107. 15 given] gotten 2. 107. 16/17 any of them . . . any of
them offered] any of them . . . offered 2. 107. 21 at that time 2: at time *1.* 107. 25
Bath] the Bath 2. 107. 34/5 and . . . Sea] *om. 2.* 108. 1/2 which . . . 500 *l.*] *om. 2.*
108. 8/9 where . . . Acquaintance] *om. 2.* 108. 25 and . . . same] *om. 2.* 108. 36 Bath]
the Bath 2. 109. 1 and . . . him] *om. 2.* 109. 4/5 as . . . Cases,] *om. 2.* 109. 7/8 from
the Disturbance of . . . Circumstance as that was] under . . . Circumstance 2.
109. 15 when he . . . Bed] *om. 2.* 109. 23/4 and I . . . him] *om. 2.* 110. 5/6 been a
means to make] made 2. 110. 17 or . . . so,] *om. 2.* 110. 34/5 are . . . Ships] is . . .

Ships 2. 111. 20/1 she . . . foolishly] *om. 2.* 111.25 *answering,*] *answered*; 2. 111. 28/9 which . . . Moment] *om. 2.* 112. 10/11 then reaching . . . bad me 2] reaching . . . bad then me *1*; *in the 1st edn.* (p. 133 l. 32) then *has probably been put by mistake at the end rather than the beginning of the line.* 112. 12/13 which . . ., in which] which . . .; in this 2. 112. 15 taking my Hand] taking me by the Hand 2. 112. 22 Home] *om. 2.* 113. 12 where . . . Business] *om. 2.* 113. 14 *Bath*] the *Bath* 2. 113. 19 ; however,] , so 2. 114. 3/4 abating the freedom of . . . and abating] abating . . . and 2. 114. 18 all . . . be] *om. 2.*

115. 8/9 to Bed in the Bed . . . the Room] to Bed in the other Bed 2. 115. 26 strong vigorous] vigorous 2. 115. 31 understood] saw 2. 115. 34 the Moderation] the same Moderation 2. 115. 35 and he with me] *om. 2.* 116. 7 subsist me] subsist on 2. 116. 15 Wine that Night] *om. 2.* 116. 16 either of] *om. 2.* 117. 34 about it] about that part 2. 118. 2/3 my . . . knowing] *om. 2.* 118. 8/10 and including . . . including] with . . . including 2. 118. 31 there . . . it] *om. 2.* 118. 33 a time] the time 2. 118. 37 happens . . . Bounty] *om. 2.* 119. 6/7 in . . . House, and] *om. 2.* 119. 22 the Accident of] *om. 2.* 119. 32/3 knew no . . . him than that] knew of no . . . him 2. 120. 4 I mean . . . as Bedfellows] *om. 2.* 120. 5 was as no] was no 2. 120. 6 and so . . . way] *om. 2.* 121. 8/9 a little . . . Sick] *om. 2.* 121. 34 secur'd or] *om. 2.* 122. 16/17 I waited . . . surprize and amazement I waited] I waited . . . surprize 2. 123. 4 Correspondences . . . are] Correspondences . . . is 2. 123. 14 and a religious] *om. 2.* 123. 20 can be no] cannot be 2. 123. 29 *Bath*, that] *Bath*, and that 2. 124. 17 such . . . describe] *om. 2.* 124. 20/1 and liv'd . . . Wife] *om. 2.* 124. 34 forsaken of God's Grace, and] *om. 2.* 125. 8 a Maintenance] being able 2. 125. 15 which . . . Reasons;] *om. 2.* 125. 19 or Repentance] *om. 2.* 125. 22/3 and an honest] *om. 2.* 125. 28/9 the Temptations which the Devil never fails to excite us to] Temptations 2. 126. 14/15 and receiv'd the Money] *om. 2.* 127. 7 and . . . *Bristol,*] *om. 2.* 127. 8 hard of, yet] hard, but yet 2. 127. 26 *Redriff*] *Rotherhith* 2. 127. 30/1 and had Pride . . . want it] *om. 2.* 128. 3/4 at . . . together] *om. 2.* 128. 6 my 2: any *1.* 128. 6/7 and could . . . Fidelity;] *om. 2.* 129. 17 Woman that went for a] *om. 2.* 130. 17 pack'd . . . and] *om. 2.* 130. 24/5 and . . . Day] *om. 2.* 130. 36/7 which . . . them] *om. 2.* 131. 17 I . . . good] *om. 2.* 131. 27/8 which . . . then] *om. 2.* 131. 32 and Business over] *om. 2.*

132. 32 into keeping,] *om. 2 (eliminating a possible double entendre).* 133.34 Man] a Man 2. 134. 31 as he did,] *om. 2.* 135. 6 *I hope, too,*] *om. 2.* 137. 10/11 easie . . . much easier than it is in] easier . . . than 2. 138. 21/2 but . . . in] *om. 2.* 139. 2/3 all which . . . all] and which . . . all 2 *(grammatically worse).* 139. 6/7 Conference . . . last Conference] Conference . . . last 2. 139. 22 propose] mention 2. 139. 30/1 had . . . and] *om. 2.* 139. 31 any thing] any such thing 2. 140. 7/8 , and . . . thing] *om. 2.* 140. 31/2 of Marriage] *om. 2.* 141. 9 a Divorce from his first Wife] the Divorce 2. 141. 34 their] their own 2. 142. 4/5 who . . . that] *om. 2.* 143. 19 good Land] in good Land 2. 143. 31 Romish Clergyman] Priest 2. 144. 22 the Ferry Boat] a Ferry-Boat 2. 144. 31/2 in the West street] *om. 2.* 144. 32 forget] forgot 2. 145. 9 hoped] hope 2. 145. 21 since . . . pitch,] *om. 2.* 145. 32 did not] never did 2. 145. 34 *quickly and hastily*] *quick* 2. 145. 35 no not that] No, that 2. 146. 3 high 2: sigh'd *1.* 146. 3/4 and her . . . him,] *om. 2.* 146. 5 come] come in 2. 146. 21 you will have] there will be 2. 147. 1 the unjust Charge of] *om. 2.* 147. 5/6 turning . . . her,] *om. 2.* 147. 8 should I] should I ever 2. 147. 29 frighted] frighten'd 2. 148. 24 of my self] *om. 2.* 148. 35 among strangers] *om. 2.* 149. 2 stand] *om. 2.* 149. 11/12 as close and] *om. 2.*

149. 30 which I had own'd] *om.* 2.   150. 13 15 *l.*] 5 *l.* 2 (*however*, 15 *l.* Newberry '3').
150. 27/8 and pressing . . . Hand] *om.* 2.   150. 29 truly] true 2.   150. 33/4 deluded . . .
Procuress] *om.* 2.   151. 5 of a Fortune] of Fortune 2.   151. 11 really] already 2.
151. 37 particular] Particulars 2 (*the singular is possible—for this usage see* OED
sb. 3—although the plural may better suit the context).   152. 1/2 to have gone first
towards] so have gone for 2.   152. 19 was 2: is *1*.   152. 23 rise] rose 2 (*for* rise—
rhyming with his—*as a 16-18C. past tense form, see* OED A2 γ, *citing Monmouth,
Hobbes,* &c.; *Joseph Wright*, English Dialect Dictionary, *V. 125; cf. also infra,
p. 210 l. 32*).   153. 18 *A.E.*] *J.E.* 2.   153. 30 vehement] violent 2.

154. 2 but . . . Servant] *om.* 2.   154. 16 about 15 Mile] above 15 Miles 2.   155. 26
gave it him 2: gave him *1*.   155. 35/6 really lov'd . . . and] *om.* 2.   156. 4/5 and I
resolving to keep] keeping 2 (*and I mistakenly deleted*).   158. 10/11 if we liv'd,] *om.* 2.
158. 14/15 Circumstances] Figure 2.   159. 15/16 : However, those Consultations] ,
which 2.   159. 19 the whole Story] part of the Story 2.   159. 30 and . . . Resolution,]
om. 2.   160. 36/7 stood to . . . would stand to it] stood to . . . would 2.   161. 16 be
brought to] *om.* 2.   161. 17 endeavouring . . . of] *om.* 2.   162. 26 in such Circumstances, and] *om.* 2.   162. 36 in . . . Case] *om.* 2.   164. 7 and . . . *Fare*] *om.* 2.   164. 10
follows 2: Follow *1*.   164. 30 13 00 0] 12 00 0 2 (*twelve weeks @ 20s. is indeed £12.
But each bill is obviously meant to be roughly twice the preceding one; in order to keep
this ratio, the 2nd edn. retains the 1st edn. total of £26.18.0, thus introducing a new and
more conspicuous error*).   165. 18 for that] *om.* 2.   165. 31 , you are but] you at but 2.
165. 37/166. 1 or . . . Born,] *on.* 2.   166. 21 where was found fault] where I was,
found fault 2.   166. 32 she is not] *om.* 2 (*introduces nonsense*).   167. 1 pint] *om.* 2.
168. 4 unwelcome] *om.* 2.   168. 9/10 at Hand . . . Hands] always ready . . . Hands 2.
168. 20/1 and . . . Gallows] *om.* 2.   168. 24 starv'd,] *om.* 2.   168. 26 honest] *om.* 2.
168. 29 question you] question but you 2.   168. 29 honestly] *om.* 2.   168. 35/6 and . . .
come] *om.* 2 ('it' *has perhaps been omitted after* 'expected' *in 1st edn.*).   169. 32 wicked]
om. 2.   170. 21 I . . . it] *om.* 2.   170. 34 a thing . . . Nature] *om.* 2.   171. 14 about
twenty two] about twenty 2.   172. 16 Tatling of other People's Affairs 2: Tatling to
her of other Peoples Affairs *1* (*the context demands* to me).   172. 28 absolutely] *om.* 2.
172. 36 and Earnestness they] there 2.   174. 27/8 can be . . . better] *om.* 2.   174. 34
and the honestest] *om.* 2.   175. 6 what was done with me] what I was 2.   175. 9/11 that
Disorder . . . the Disorder] that . . . the Disorder 2.   176. 20 or . . . is] *om.* 2.   176. 21
says *I* 2: says she *1* (I *is required by the context*).   176. 34/5 to ask . . . or] *om.* 2.   178. 5/6
and it . . . presently] *om.* 2.   178. 10 going in] going into 2.

178. 29 I think it is] *om.* 2.   179. 13/14 seeing . . . purpose] *om.* 2.   179. 36 tho' . . .
thought] *om.* 2.   180. 17/18 as if I had been surpriz'd] *om.* 2.   180. 19 a purpose] on
purpose 2.   181. 9 so I made] so I only made 2.   181. 9/10 and accepted it] *om.* 2.
181. 17/18 Why . . . why you] Why . . . you 2.   181. 18 fully satisfy'd that] fully
5 and Joy] *om.* 2.   182. 9 a vitious and] an 2.   182. 28 if possible,] *om.* 2.   182. 29
Cheats and] *om.* 2.   182. 34 Neighbouring] *om.* 2 (*cf. infra, p. 184, ll. 26-7*).   183. 32
Lord] *om.* 2.   183. 37/184. 1 and . . . Fair] *om.* 2.   184. 20 except . . . Supper] *om.* 2.
184. 32 Guests *ed.*: Guess *1*, 2—*an* OED-*recorded 16-17C. spelling*.   185. 5/6 my . . .
Stairs] *om.* 2.   185. 19 sensible] *om.* 2.   185. 29/30 know, if possible . . . impossible]
know . . . impossible 2.   185. 34/5 fancied . . . fancies] fancied . . . Thoughts 2.
186. 5 see them] I saw them 2.   186. 21 and I 2: I and *1*.   186. 23 durst to say] durst
say 2.   186. 23/4 not the Persons . . . honest Person] honest Persons . . . honest

Person 2. 186. 30/1 afterwards ... afterwards take] afterwards ... take 2. 187. 7
that remains] that he remains 2. 187. 36/7 being an old married Woman] om. 2.
188.6 ungovern'd] om. 2. 188. 11 the Poverty] that Poverty 2. 189. 28/9 to tell the
Truth] om. 2. 190. 10/12 that while ... Subsistence, I ... Shilling, so] that ...
Subsistence, so 2. 190. 30 from God or Man] om. 2. 191. 5 meer] om. 2 (again,
'complete'—but here liable to misinterpretation). 192. 16 began ... and] om. 2. 192. 30
wrap'd up] om. 2. 193. 27 not sincerely repented of] not repented of 2. 193. 28/9
on ... Grave] om. 2. 194. 5 was going] was a going 2. 195. 24 swift as the Wind]
om. 2. 195. 26 and after ... more] om. 2. 196. 22 know] knew 2. 197. 3 seeing ...
clear] om. 2. 197. 11 fain] forc'd 2. 197. 13 unless ... Extremity] om. 2. 197. 29
and ... poor] so that 2. 197. 32 stirring] om. 2. 198. 23 here she was defficient]
om. 2. 198. 25 to a Spark] om. 2.

198. 37 my Bread ... got] om. 2. 199. 11 and came ... empty] om. 2. 199. 25
Child] om. 2. 199. 37 me Drink] me to Drink 2. 200. 11 and that it had made a
Thief of me] om. 2. 200. 16 are minded to be sent] want to go 2. 200. 22 Tankards]
Tankards as 2. 201. 34 big with Child] with Child 2. 201. 35 Church] the church 2.
202. 6 pretended] om. 2. 202. 18 I must acknowledge] om. 2. 202. 23 so great ...
Misery] om. 2. 202. 30 miserable 2: miserables 1. 203. 13 and miscarry'd] om. 2.
203. 17 so industriously] om. 2. 203. 19 into the Mire] in 2. 204. 14 was forc'd to
leave off] left off 2. 204. 36/7/205. 1 she gave ... the House] om. 2. 205. 4 Lord!]
alas! 2. 205. 5 And how does she do?] om. 2. 205. 11 Lord,] om. 2. 205. 20 Lord] om.
2. 206. 11 clear ... enquiry] om. 2. 207. 2 and afflicted] om. 2. 207. 5 not] om. 2.
207. 13 began quickly to forget] quickly forgot 2. 207. 14 the taking them] it 2.
207. 19 join'd so with the Success] had such success 2. 207. 22 so wickedly] om. 2.
207. 25 and Repentance] om. 2. 207. 28 my Desires] all 2. 207. 36 of being undone]
om. 2. 207. 37 I remain'd still with my Governess, who] MY Governess 2. 208. 2
and who it seems] for she 2. 208. 11/12 sincerely for her 2: sincerely her 1. 208. 20
bred to the Trade] bred to Trade 2. 208. 21 I think] om. 2. 208. 29 two] two after
this 2. 208. 30 too ... this] om. 2. 209. 20 as a thing out of my Way] om. 2. 209. 31
and lay together] om. 2. 210. 3 being then Prohibited] being Prohibited 2 (see
explanatory note). 210. 7/8 had such a ... him, of such ... if] had a ... him, if 2.
212. 9 till ... perish'd] om. 2. 212. 21 proper for the Discovery] om. 2. 212. 25
Minutes time ... time] Minutes ... time 2. 212. 31 or ... soon] om. 2. 213. 21
Art and] om. 2. 214. 29 of the Gain, and no Share] om. 2 (reverses sense). 215. 1 I
mean ... Craft] om. 2. 215. 28/9 on several other Accounts] om. 2.

216. 8/9 and without noise] om. 2. 216. 13 fly for God sake] om. 2. 217. 20 Bed,
in] Bed, and in 2. 217. 33/4 and that was very true indeed ... be indeed that]
which was very true ... be that 2. 218. 18 him 2: them 1. 218. 34 he ... him 2: I
... me 1. 218. 37 her] her neither 2. 219. 29 but run away] om. 2. 219. 34 in]
into 2. 220. 37/221.1 and that ... escap'd] om. 2. 221. 26/7 upon ... made] om. 2.
221. 28 in Triumph] om. 2. 221. 37 or where I Lodg'd] om. 2. 222. 32 an inferior
Assistant] om. 2. 222. 35 I say ... this] om. 2. 223. 9 the Preservation of] om. 2.
224. 3/4 for a while 2: for while 1. 224. 18 common Part of the] om. 2. 224. 21/2
nor did ... it] om. 2. 224. 25 first told] first he told 2. 224. 34 without Comple-
ment] om. 2. 225. 17 unwilling to go 2: unwilling go 1. 225. 26 he had] om. 2. 226. 3
and ... them] om. 2 (see explanatory note). 226. 16 if any ... was] om. 2. 226. 23/4
corrupted] om. 2. 227. 4 sober solid] sober and solid 2. 227. 25/6 as I ... would he]

om. 2. 227. 37 searching] *om. 2.* 228. 14 that is . . . Guilt] *om. 2.* 228. 30/1 and Family too] *om. 2.* 230. 3 grave] *om. 2.* 230. 24 for I . . . him] *om. 2.* 231. 12 take ill] take it ill *2.* 231. 25/6 so . . . Service] *om. 2.* 232. 20/1 so justly . . . that . . . of it to me] justly . . . in which . . . I had *2.* 233. 20 Sir—, *says my Governess*] Sir *says she 2.* 233. 26 done it] done it more to your Hurt *2.* 234. 6 using . . . time some Arguments] endeavouring . . . time *2.* 234. 35/6 Tale . . . Talk] Talk . . . Tale *2* (*though 1 makes sense, 2 fits both contexts better*). 235. 24 Head] Head then *2.* 236. 13/14 I . . . let him take] he . . . taken *2.* 237. 1/2 whereas all the Regret, and] all the *2.* 237. 6/7 satisfy'd . . . satisfy'd] satisfy'd . . . fully satisfy'd *2.* 237. 8 and cou'd trust me again] *om. 2.* 238. 33 just beyond] near *2.* 239. 10 under Arm] under her Arm *2.* 239. 13/14 and I'll . . . it; do] take it *2.* 239. 24 cross'd] *om. 2.*

239. 28 and very Remarkable *ed.*: and very Remarkable *1*: *om. 2.* 240. 12 *Chester ed.*: *Cheston 1, 2.* 240. 29 getting . . . House, I] *om. 2.* 240. 33/4 Linnen, so] Linnen, and so *2.* 241. 9 finall] *om. 2.* 242. 6 in a more legal way] *om. 2.* 242. 19 his Evidence] him *2.* 242. 37 do you do your] do your *2.* 243. 21 and *Anthony*] and Mr *Anthony 2.* 243. 30 cryed] they cry'd *2.* 244. 1 I SAT still now, and] I Now *2.* 245. 20 Occasion] Occasions *2.* 246. 18 hot-brain'd] *om. 2.* 246. 21 I went] we went *2.* 247. 24 I *2*: he *1* (*see explanatory note*). 247. 30 by Lifters] by the Lifters *2.* 249. 8 that . . . itself, and] *om. 2.* 249. 16 that] and that *2.* 249. 23 and that] *om. 2.* 249. 24/5 I would . . . satisfaction] *om. 2.* 249. 37 would . . . to] must *2.* 250. 2 or . . . Justice] *om. 2.* 251. 6 pointed to] appointed *2.* 251. 8 his way] *om. 2.* 251. 9 believ'd *2*: believe *1.* 251. 9/10 I believ'd] *om. 2.* 251. 29 a sufficient Reparation of Honour] Reparation *2.* 251. 33/4 and . . myself] *om. 2.* 252. 2 he . . . handsome] *om. 2.* 252. 10 I agreed and] *om. 2.* 252. 11 complied with it] I comply'd *2.* 252. 18 him] them *2* (*see explanatory note*). 252. 28 if I . . . pleas'd] *om. 2.* 252. 36 make] make his *2.* 253. 1 Haughtiness and] *om. 2.* 253. 2 imperious, cruel *2*: impious, cruelter *1.* 253. 3 , and in Prosperity] *om. 2.* 253. 4 in Affliction] *om. 2.* 253. 17/18 any more than *2*: than any more *1.* 254. 8 when] *om. 2.* 255. 16/17 for as . . . so I] for tho' . . . yet I *2.* 255. 29 more room to Escape] *om. 2.* 256. 15 been so] been there so *2.* 256. 16/17 and were . . . be done] *om. 2.* 257. 11/12 so that . . . so that] and . . . so that *2.* 257. 18 without any interruption] *om. 2.* 257. 25 suppose it was] suppos'd *2.* 258. 4/5 of *Suffolk,*] *om. 2.* 258. 25/6 we see the Guards come] the Guards came *2.* 258. 33 felt it, nor] *om. 2.* 258. 35 among . . . Ladies] *om. 2.*

258. 36 of her] *om. 2.* 258. 36 to her] *om. 2.* 259. 1 from her] *om. 2.* 259. 2 oblig'd unwillingly] unwilling *2.* 259. 8/9 got before the Crowd and kept so] kept before the Crowd *2.* 259. 27 and be satisfy'd] *om. 2.* 260. 2 *Covent 2*: *Convent 1.* 260. 13 among them] *om. 2.* 260. 36 Nine of the *ed.*: Nine the of *1*: of the *2.* 261. 2 had the Box *2*: had at the Box *1.* 261. 17 told them to see] him to have seen *2* (*see explanatory note*). 261. 21 cautiously; it] cautiously, which *2.* 261. 23/4 and at . . . times] *om. 2.* 261. 27 I gain'd] I had gain'd *2.* 262. 4/5 to any] to do any *2.* 263. 35 made a shift to carry off] I got *2.* 265. 15 as for *2*: for as *1.* 265. 25 and he] and that he *2.* 266. 1 things, Necessaries *ed.*: things Necessaries *1*: Things Necessary *2.* 266. 15 and I *2*: I and *1.* 266. 35 so that *2*: that so *1.* 267. 12 *and the like*] *an you like 2* (*1 makes sense, although the emendation makes better sense* (=*if you like*); *the would represent a possible misreading* (*as y*ᵉ) *of a ms. abbreviation of you*). 268. 33 History is *2*: Historys *1.* 269. 3/4 at least . . . Knowledge] *om. 2.* 270. 1 make Noise] make a Noise *2.* 270. 11 so little *2*: *om. 1.* 270. 16 of Robbery] *om. 2.* 271. 1/2 or gone near

it] *om. 2*. 271. 8 clap'd in upon me, and] *om. 2*. 272. 10/11 came off with flying Colours, tho'] came well off *2*. 272. 21/2 the Weavers] a Weaver *2*. 272. 28 fiery *ed.*: firery *1, 2* (OED *records* firey, *but not* firery; *for* fiery, *cf.* infra. *p. 276 l. 25*). 273. 7 with terror] *om. 2*. 273. 16 mind that] mind too that *2*. 273. 22/3 as I was upon the Threshold] *om. 2*. 274. 12 and unseen] *om. 2*. 274. 27/8 and even the hope] *om. 2*. 275. 6 ago] ago they said *2*. 275. 18 I believe *2*: lieve *1*. 275. 20 for] *om. 2*. 276. 36 and chang'd her Mind,] *om. 2*. 277. 5 as I told you] *om. 2*. 277. 7/8 by the Justice that committed me] *om. 2*. 277. 12 that could be done, or] *om. 2*. 277. 17 and prepare for it] *om. 2*. 277. 18 upon] upon for that *2*. 277. 23 of Soul] *om. 2*. 277. 37 and Spirits] *om. 2*. 278. 1/2 more, than his work] *om. 2*. 278. 15 Caveties, and] *om. 2*. 278. 16 petrifies *ed.*: prutifies *1*: peterifies *2* (*see explanatory note*). 278. 18 as I was with *ed.*: as I was, which *1*: *om. 2* (*which probably represents a compositorial misreading of D.'s characteristic contraction* wᵗʰ *as* wᶜʰ).

278. 21 then] and then *2*. 278. 29/30 speaking of common Cases] *om. 2*. 278. 35 another; then I *ed.*: another then; I *1*: another; I *2*. 278. 35 first remorse] first, some Remorse *2*. 279. 3 of old] of an old *2*. 279. 25 become a meer *2*: became meer a *1*. 279. 29 thoro' *2*: thro' *1*. 279. 35 of before: They *2*: of, before they *1*. 279. 37/280. 1 the Road to *Windsor ed.*: the to Road *Windsor 1*: *om. 2*. 280. 5 we Prisoners, were *2*: we were Prisoners, were *1*. 280. 11 Part of the Prison] Place *2*. 280. 15 with whom I *2*: who *1*. 280. 28/9 desperate on *2*: Desperate that on *1*. 280. 30/1 and that . . . take] *om. 2*. 280. 35 the having it thought that I was so] its having it thought so *2*. 281. 2 for him] *om. 2*. 281. 3 told me, he *2*: told he *1*. 281. 11 his Misfortunes] my Misfortunes *2*. 281. 22 at the *Old-Baily*] *om. 2*. 281. 23 harden'd] *om. 2*. 281. 24/5 acquir'd in the Prison abated, and conscious Guilt *ed.*: acquir'd, abated, and conscious in the Prison Guilt *1*: acquir'd, abated, and conscious Guilt *2* (*the words* in the Prison *must have been in the MS., and somehow got shifted to their position in 1, where* (*as the corrector recognized*) *they make no sense*). 281. 26 think is] think indeed is *2*. 281. 27 Hellish] *om. 2*. 281. 29 Power of] *om. 2*. 282. 9/10 finding [the Bill, and finding] out one or two *ed.*: finding out one or two *1*: finding the Bill; she went to several *2* (*in 1, p. 347 ends with* finding: *as the corrector realized, this must have the* Bill *as its object, and the governess must be the subject of the lines that follow. In my hypothetical restoration of the MS. reading, the repetition of* finding *would help to account for its omission in the second instance: grammatically the suggested reading is within normal Defoean usage, but the emendation is offered with misgivings. Cf. World's Classics edn., p. 325:* finding the bill. She sought out one or two). 282. 13/14 they . . . rest] *om. 2*. 283. 3/4 Lord! Mr. ––––] O Sir, *2*. 283. 4 send for the Ordinary] *om. 2*. 283. 21/2 Condemn'd, . . . be] *om. 2*. 283. 24 Lord! I shall be hang'd] *om. 2*. 283. 28 Tryal and Sentence] a Sentence *2*. 283. 30 thing herself] thing *2*. 283. 31 stole] had stolen *2*. 284. 37/285. 1 brought . . . they] *om. 2*. 285. 2 believe, and] *om. 2*. 285. 3 they stop'd me *2*: they stop'd *1*. 285. 8/9 seeing . . . there, and] *om. 2*. 285. 21 under my Cloaths] *om. 2*. 286. 5 yet not . . . Speech] *om. 2*. 286. 16 (as . . . Appearance)] *om. 2*. 286. 31 or to stir for me] *om. 2*. 286. 36 first, . . . afterwards] *om. 2*. 287. 14/15 the greatest and best things] *om. 2*. 287. 19 in Nature] *om. 2*. 287. 24 how vile, how gross] *om. 2*. 287. 32/3 or . . . Misery] *om. 2*. 288. 14/15 for private Ends, or] *om. 2*.

288. 23 and Assistance] *om. 2*. 289. 1 more, or] *om. 2*. 289. 21/2 that is . . . me] *om. 2*. 289. 24/5 upon a *Wednesday*] *om. 2*. 290. 5 Clock he came] Clock; when he came *2*. 290. 15/16 to the . . . State] *om. 2*. 290. 20 and yet it was too much for me]

om. 2. 290. 28 Sheriffs, stood] Sheriffs, he stood *2.* 290. 33/4 and to repent of them]
om. 2. 290. 37/291. 1 the goodness . . . Case] that goodness *2.* 291. 6 wild and]
om. 2. 291. 27 some huzza'd] some Brutishly huzza'd *2.* 291. 29 that is . . . Pro-
secutors] *om. 2.* 292. 8 as to be . . . to be] as I was the Day before *2.* 292. 10 the
cold Fit of] *om. 2.* 292. 14/15 and without Design, but] *om. 2.* 292. 23 but still . . .
Words] *om. 2.* 292. 32 me I] me that I *2.* 292. 37 tho' very seasonable,] *om. 2.*
293. 29 this part] his part *2.* 293. 34 they generally are, who] *om. 2.* 294. 1 during
. . . part] *om. 2.* 294. 10 relapsing] relapsing again *2.* 294. 28/9 yet my . . . while]
yet, as *2.* 294. 34/5 I would . . . but] *om. 2.* 295. 3/4 order . . . sign'd] *om. 2.* 295.
13 the Minutes of] *om. 2.* 295. 29 Evidence for some time *ed.*: Evidence some time
1: Evidence *2.* 295. 30 on this Account *2*: on for this Account *1* (*probably for was
meant to be part of the preceding clause*—they wanted Evidence *for* some time—*and
got dropped one line; these words are at the beginning of the line* in 1). 296. 2 being taken
any] were taken, and any *2.* 296. 3 that . . . by them] *om. 2.* 296. 24 Voice, that] Voice
too, that *2.* 296. 35 a Table . . . the Table] the Table *2.* 297. 8/9 What . . . in?] *om. 2.*
297. 22 look'd . . . wildly, and] *om. 2.* 297. 33 am under] am now under *2.* 298.
16/17 to remit . . . consenting] for me *2.* 298. 26 told him that I had *ed.*: told him
if I had *1*: told him I had *2* (*if probably represents a misreading of the contraction* y^t
[=that] *in D.'s manuscript*). 298. 30 one Mr. -----] *om. 2.* 298. 37 that . . . there]
om. 2. 299. 16 not by the Road] *om. 2.* 299. 20 me he] me that he *2.* 299. 22 really
his Sister, or] *om. 2.* 299. 30 it had . . . Luck, that] *om. 2.* 299. 32 retired sober]
new *2.* 299. 35 that so] so that *2.* 301. 18/19 and told . . . Accounts] *om. 2.* 301.
25 as *Romans*] as the *Romans 2.* 301. 27 let . . . would,] *om. 2.*

301. 34 Pressures and] *om. 2.* 302. 14 and some Gallantry] *om. 2.* 302. 28/9 it
was . . ., but that] *om. 2.* 303. 1 if . . . Fate] *om. 2.* 303. 12 in that Article] *om. 2.*
303. 20 before he went] *om. 2* (*some such phrase as* about returning *probably preceded
this one in the MS., and was accidently omitted in* 1). 303. 21 ignorant] *om. 2.*
303. 31/2 our mutual Subsistence, and] *om. 2.* 304. 6/7 or we . . . Prison] *om. 2.*
304. 8 it, where *2*: it, this where *1.* 304. 16 and Affection] *om. 2.* 304. 18 of my
Assistance, and] *om. 2.* 304. 32/3 to bring me going] with me *2.* 305. 16/17 or had . . .
him] *om. 2.* 305. 25 before a Tryal] *om. 2.* 305. 33/4 who . . . Grant] *om. 2.* 306. 3
venture, . . . certain to] *om. 2.* 306. 6 according . . . Sentence] *om. 2.* 306. 10
naked and] *om. 2.* 306. 22/3 I really was . . . it, as I was before, but I industriously
conceal'd] I was . . . it now, but I conceal'd *2.* 306. 26 seven] thirteen *2.* 306. 27
as they call'd us] *om. 2.* 307. 1 allow'd . . . particularly were] *om. 2.* 307. 12 and see
us if we had any] to see us *2.* 307. 14/15 the Liberty of little Cabins for such of us]
little Cabins allow'd for such *2.* 307. 18 or a Rag of] *om. 2.* 307. 27 have the liberty]
be allow'd *2.* 307. 37 myself . . . sure] *om. 2.* 308. 4 not to the last] *it is worth noting
that this phrase is not cancelled in* 2: *cf.* infra, *p. 310, ll. 34–6 and following pp.* 308.
10 I entreated] I had entreated *2.* 308. 27 had my Letter deliver'd] deliver'd my
Letter *2.* 308. 35/6 the Gentlewoman, your *ed.*: the Gentlewoman your *1*: that
Gentlewoman, is she your *2.* 309. 18/19 its Furniture . . . extraordinary] its
ordinary Furniture *2.* 309. 34 by the Publick] *om. 2.* 310 1/2 look too well provided in the Ship] appear too Well *2.* 310. 9/10 he was . . . but found] *om. 2.* 310.
32 read a long Lecture to her of] told her *2.* 311. 19/20 or . . . had] *om. 2.* [*Here, in
2, appear the two paragraphs* infra, *p. 312 l. 32–p. 313 l. 23 (all of p.386 in 1)*]. 312. 5
which every one knows is] *om. 2* (*cf.* supra,
p. 286 ll. 20–8). 312. 12/13 I reserv'd] I had reserv'd *2.* 312. 13 , besides some] ;

besides I had some 2. 312. 13 things, as] things with me, as 2. 312. 15/16 the Plate . . .
Money, and] *om. 2.* 312. 19 (as to what appear'd)] *om. 2.* 312. 27 sign'd by a Captain
(*qu.* the Captain *in MS.?*)] *om. 2.*

312. 32 IN this condition I lay for three Weeks in the Ship] HOWEVER, I lay in an
uncertain condition full three Weeks 2 (*see note following p. 311 ll. 19-20* supra).
313. 19 took] he took 2. 314. 20 for a Seaman] *om. 2.* 315. 10/11 as to . . . Be-
haviour] *om 2.* 315. 15 and we] and that we 2. 315. 17 as . . . late] *om. 2.* 315.
28/9 and are . . . up] *om. 2.* 316. 16/17 while . . . there] *om. 2.* 316. 23 , that . . .
publick; *ed.:* ; that . . . publick, *1:* *om. 2.* 316. 25/28/30 Comfort in the Voyage . . .
drinking in the Voyage . . . nothing in the Voyage] Comfort in the Voyage . . .
drinking . . . nothing 2. 317. 11/12 if we . . . it] *om. 2.* 317. 18/19 diligence and]
om. 2. 317. 22/3 very honest as well as] *om. 2.* 318. 4 long particular] List 2. 318. 19
we had . . . Cargo] all 2. 319. 7 Expence and] *om. 2.* 319. 8 if . . . again] *om. 2.*
319. 13 dozen Bottles] Dozen of Bottles 2. 319. 24 the Mouth of] *om. 2.* 319. 31
and was very Sick] *om. 2.* 320. 11/12 buy us as Servants] buy me as a Servant 2.
320. 12/13 us . . . us] me . . . me 2. 320. 15 these two Servants] me for a Servant 2.
320. 15/16 my Husband and me] my Husband not being order'd to be Sold 2.
320. 16 we were] I was 2. 320. 22/3 we were] I was 2. 320. 23 we] I 2. 320. 25 us]
me 2. 321. 7/8 which I . . . hear] *om. 2.* 321. 9/10 he liv'd . . . I liv'd with him, and
liv'd] I liv'd, and liv'd 2. 321. 17 the Plantation where 2: a Plantation, where *1.*
321. 37 the old Gentleman] he 2. 322. 3-5 The Woman . . . to me] *om. 2.* 323. 2 seen]
seen here 2. 323. 7/8 when she was in *England*] *om. 2.* 323. 10 short, examining]
short, in examining 2. 323. 13 his Wives] her 2. 323. 16 the Son, her Brother and
Husband,] he 2. 324. 2 how, and when] *om. 2.* 324. 33/4 and it was impossible to . . .
thing] it was impossible too 2. 324. 37 found . . . yet] *om. 2.* 325. 33 as secret] as a
secret 2. 325. 34/5 would necessarily be] has been 2. 326. 16 and that . . . it] *om. 2.*
327. 13 most 2: only *1.* 327. 17 to make myself known enough] *om. 2.* 327. 35 or
that . . . Husband] *om. 2.* 328. 1 with all our Goods] *om. 2.*

328. 5 with part of our Goods] *om. 2.* 328. 7 and fetch the remainder] *om. 2.*
328. 9/10 by Consequence] *om. 2.* 328. 13/14 and . . . as Servants] *om. 2.* 328. 19
Brother, formerly my *Husband*] old Husband 2. 328. 25 the benefit of] lose 2. 328.
27 myself to them in] *om. 2.* 329. 3/4 either . . . ones] *om. 2.* 329. 18 claim and]
om. 2. 329. 20/1 with chearfulness and good will] *om. 2.* 329. 26 at loss] at a Loss 2.
329. 27 whatever it might be] *om. 2.* 330. 1 and from . . . Provisions] *om. 2.* 330. 17
River, or] *om. 2.* 330. 19/20 and we . . . know not] *om. 2.* 330. 35/6 if he lik'd of it]
om. 2. 331. 9 and simple Honesty] *om. 2.* 331. 20 Government 2: Governor *1*
(*Bülbring reports that in the MS. of* Comp. Eng. Gent. *a* complicated shorthand
abbreviation is used for the words *government, governor,* and *govern* (Forewords,
xviii); *see explanatory note*). 332. 8/9 to employ . . . sufficient] *om. 2.* 333. 1 one,
and only] own, and only 2. 333. 26/7 *so as to understand it*] *om. 2.* 334. 5/6 as to . . .
Father] *om. 2.* 334. 24/5 to conceal our Relation, and] *om. 2.* 335. 8 no little concern 2: no concern *1.* 335. 10 most comfortable 2: comfortabless *1.* 335. 14 while I
stay'd] *om. 2.* 335. 15 also *1, 2* (*in 1, p. 414, this word bridges ll. 13-14 as* al-/so; *I
suspect the MS. read* always *so*). 335. 31 secretly now] almost 2. 336. 6/7 deal of
Money 2: deal Money *1.* 336. 10/11 that is, . . . liv'd] *om. 2.* 336. 12 and given]
and had given 2. 338. 21 and Improve] *om. 2.* 338. 21/2 and . . . Skill] *om. 2.* 338. 32
come 2: came *1.* 339. 13 told him that 2: told that *1.* 339. 18 My husband] Says

my Husband 2 (*the 19 italicized words that follow cannot be spoken* by *the man, but are Moll's parenthetical comment* about *him.*).   339. 32/3 I have ... by itself] *om.* 2 (*for* 2 *to make sense,* and but that *(l. 30) should also have been altered to* but).   339. 34 As ... as] BUT 2.   339. 35 I return to ... myself] I return therefore to my own Part 2.   339. 36 our Plantation] our own Plantation 2.   339. 37 Direction 2: diversion *1*.   339. 37/340. 1 by our obliging Behaviour] *om.* 2.   340. 28/9 and whole Pieces also, to make up 2: and to whole peices also make up *1*.   341. 3 the Account of the particular] the Particulars 2.   342. 16 Estate, not] Estate, and not 2.   342. 34 both in 2: both of in *1*.   342. 35 remain'd 2: remain *1*.

EXPLANATORY NOTES

The following abbreviations have been used:

(1) **Works by Defoe**:

App. Jour.: *The Original Weekly Journal*, later called *Applebee's Original Weekly Journal*, reprinted in Lee, *q.v.*

Aug. Triumph.: *Augusta Triumphans*: *Or, The Way To Make London The most flourishing City in the Universe* (1728).

Col. Jack: *The History and Remarkable Life of the truly Honourable Col. Jacque* (1722), ed. Samuel Holt Monk (1965).

Coll. Misc. Lett.: *A Collection of Miscellany Letters, Selected out of Mist's Weekly Journal*, 2 Vols. (1722).

Comp. Eng. Gent.: *The Compleat English Gentleman* [1728–29], ed. Karl D. Bülbring (1890).

Comp. Eng. Trades.: *The Complete English Tradesman*, 2 Vols. (1727; Vol. 1, 2nd edn.).

Conj. Lewd.: *Conjugal Lewdness*: *Or, Matrimonial Whoredom* (1727).

Due Prep.: *Due Preparations for the Plague As well for Soul as Body* (1722), in *Rom. & Narr.*, *q.v.*

E.H.R.A.: *An Essay on the History and Reality of Apparitions* (1727).

Ess. upon Proj.: *An Essay upon Projects* (1697).

Fam. Instr.: *The Family Instructor*, 2 Vols. (1718; Vol. 1, 3rd edn.).

Far. Adv.: *The Farther Adventures of Robinson Crusoe* (1719), in *Rom. & Narr.*, *q.v.*

G.L.S.C.: *The Great Law of Subordination consider'd* (1724).

J.P.Y.: *A Journal of the Plague Year* (1722), ed. Louis A. Landa (1969).

Lee: William Lee, *Daniel Defoe: His Life and Recently Discovered Writings*, 3 Vols. (1869).

Letters: *The Letters of Daniel Defoe*, ed. George Harris Healey (1955).

Merc. Polit.: *Mercurius Politicus.*

Mist. Jour.: *The Weekly-Journal*; *or Saturday's Evening Post*, commonly called *Mist's Weekly-Journal*, reprinted in Lee, *q.v.*

Plan Eng. Comm.: *A Plan of the English Commerce* (1728; reprinted 1928).

Pol. Hist. Dev.: *The Political History of the Devil, As Well Ancient as Modern* (1726).

Rel. Court.: *Religious Courtship* (1722; 2nd edn., 1729).

Abbreviations

Rob. Cru.: *The Life and Strange Surprising Adventures of Robinson Crusoe* (1719), in *Rom. & Narr.*, *q.v.*

Rom. & Narr.: *The Romances and Narratives of Daniel Defoe*, ed. George A. Aitken, 16 Vols. (1895).

Rox.: *The Fortunate Mistress*: *Or, A History Of The Life And Vast Variety of Fortunes Of Mademoiselle de Beleau, Afterwards Call'd The Countess de Wintselsheim, in Germany. Being the Person known by the Name of the Lady Roxana, in the Time of King Charles II* (1724), ed. Jane Jack (1964).

Second Vol.: *A Second Volume of the Writings Of The Author Of The True-Born Englishman* (1705).

Ser. Refl.: *Serious Reflections During The Life And Surprising Adventures of Robinson Crusoe* (1720), in *Rom. & Narr.*, *q.v.*

Tour: *A Tour Thro' the Whole Island of Great Britain* (1724–26), ed. G. D. H. Cole and D. C. Browning, 2 Vols. (1962).

True Coll.: *A True Collection of the Writings Of The Author of the True Born English-man* (1703).

Voy. Don Man. Gon: *The Voyage of Don Manoel Gonzales*, in Vol. ii of *A General Collection of the Best and Most Interesting Voyages and Travels in All Parts of the World*, ed. John Pinkerton (1808; written [only in part by D.] ca. 1730, first printed in 1745; see J. R. Moore, *Checklist of the Writings of D. D.* (1960), No. 517, pp. 229–30).

(II) Works by other authors:

Ashton: John Ashton, *Social Life in the Reign of Queen Anne* (1911).

Ath. Merc.: John Dunton *et al.*, *The Athenian Mercury*, 20 Vols. (1691–7; cited by volume, number, and question).

Blount: Thomas Blount, *A Law-Dictionary and Glossary*, 3rd edn. (1717).

Brit. Dep.: Emman. Bowen, *Britannia Depicta or Ogilby Improv'd* (1720).

Brown, *Amusements*: Tom Brown, *Amusements Serious and Comical* (1700), ed. Arthur L. Hayward (1927).

Bruce: Philip A. Bruce, *Economic History of Virginia in the Seventeenth Century*, 2 Vols. (1896).

C.I.H.T.: John Houghton, *A Collection for the Improvement of Husbandry and Trade*, ed. Richard Bradley, 3 Vols. (1727).

Chron. Diary: *The Chronological Diary For The Year* [1714–22].

Comp. Hist. Highwaymen: Alexander Smith, *A Complete History of the Lives and Robberies of the most Notorious Highwaymen* (1719), ed. Arthur L. Hayward (1926).

Cunnington: C. Willett & Phillis Cunnington, *Handbook of English Costume in the Eighteenth Century* (1957).

Eng. Hist. Doc.: *English Historical Documents*, ed. E. C. Douglas, Vol. ix, *American Colonial Documents to 1776*, ed. Merrill Jensen (1955).

Gay, *Trivia*: John Gay, *Trivia; or, The Art of Walking the Streets of London* (1716), in *Poetical Works*, ed. G. C. Faber (1926).

Abbreviations

George: M. Dorothy George, *London Life in the XVIIIth Century* (1925).

Gloss. Anglic. Nova: *Glossographia Anglicana Nova*: *or, A Dictionary Interpreting Such Hard Words of Whatever Language, as are at present used in the English Tongue*, 2nd edn. (1719).

Goodinge: Thomas Goodinge, *The Law against Bankrupts*, 3rd edn. (1719).

Hall, *Resolutions*: Joseph Hall, *Resolutions and Decisions of Divers Practical Cases of Conscience* (1648), in Vol. vii of *Works*, ed. Philip Wynter, 10 Vols. (1863).

Hawkins: William Hawkins, *A Treatise of the Pleas of the Crown*, 2nd edn., 2 Vols. (1724–26).

Herrick: Cheesman A. Herrick, *White Servitude in Pennsylvania: Indentured and Redemption Labor in Colony and Commonwealth* (1926).

Jacob, *Mod. Just.*: Giles Jacob, *The Modern Justice: Containing the Business of a Justice of Peace, in All its Parts*, 3rd edn. (1720).

Jacob, *New Law Dict.*: Giles Jacob, *A New Law Dictionary* (1729).

Jones: M. G. Jones, *The Charity School Movement, A Study of Eighteenth Century Puritanism in Action* (1938).

Macky, *Journey*: [John Macky], *A Journey through England*, 2 Vols. (1724); Vol. i 4th edn., Vol. ii 2nd edn.

McCormac: Eugene I. McCormac, *White Servitude in Maryland, 1634–1820* (1904).

Marshall: Dorothy Marshall, *The English Poor in the Eighteenth Century* (1926).

Merch. Mag.: Edward Hatton, *The Merchant's Magazine: or, Trades Man's Treasury*, 6th edn. (1712).

New Dict. Cant. Crew: B. E., *A New Dictionary of the Terms Ancient and Modern of the Canting Crew, In its several Tribes, of Gypsies, Beggers, Thieves, Cheats, &c.* [1698].

New View: [Edward Hatton], *A New View of London*, 2 Vols. (1708).

OED: *Oxford English Dictionary*.

Oldmixon: John Oldmixon, *The British Empire in America*, 2 Vols. (1708).

Orig. & Gen. Lett.: *Original and Genuine Letters sent to the Tatler And Spectator, During the Time those Works were publishing*, ed. Charles Lillie, 2 Vols. (1725).

Phillips: *The New World of Words; Or, Universal English Dictionary . . . Compiled by Edward Phillips, The Seventh Edition, Revised, Corrected, and Improved . . . By J[ohn] K[ersey]* (1720).

Radzinowicz: Leon Radzinowicz, *A History of English Criminal Law and its Administration from 1750* [Vol. 1]: *The Movement for Reform 1750–1833* (1948).

Select Trials: *Select Trials, for Murders, Robberies, Rapes, Sodomy, Coining, Frauds, And other Offences: at the Sessions-House in the Old-Bailey. Vol. 1 From the Year 1720, to 1724, inclusive* (1734).

Abbreviations

Smith: Abbot Emerson Smith, *Colonists in Bondage: White Servitude and Convict Labor in America, 1667–1776* (1947).

Spectator: The Spectator, ed. Donald F. Bond, 5 Vols. (1965).

Strype: *A Survey of the Cities of London and Westminster . . . by John Stow . . . Corrected, Improved, and very much Enlarged . . . By John Strype . . . In Six Books*, 2 Vols. (1720).

Tatler: The Tatler, ed. George A. Aitken, 4 Vols. (1899).

Tucker: Susie I. Tucker, *Protean Shape: A Study in Eighteenth-Century Vocabulary and Usage* (1967).

Walford: George E. Thornbury and Edward Walford, *Old And New London*, 6 Vols. (1887–93).

Ward, *London-Spy*: Ned Ward, *The London-Spy* (1700), ed. Ralph Straus (1924).

Wheatley: Henry B. Wheatley, *London Past and Present*, 3 Vols. (1891).

Wood, *Institute*: Thomas Wood, *An Institute of the Laws of England*, 4th edn. (1728).

Page 1. (1) *Novels and Romances v. private History*: the formula is a commonplace in prefaces to novels and romances of the period, including D.'s own; see Arthur J. Tieje, 'A Peculiar Phase of the Theory of Realism in Pre-Richardsonian Fiction' *PMLA*, xxviii (1913), 213–52, esp. 216–7, 224–6.

(2) *pretends*: not necessarily an insincerity, affectation, or groundless presumption, a *mere* pretense. To pretend may be 'to maintain, or affirm; to use a Pretence, to make as if' (Phillips); 'pretension' may be 'a Claim or Title to any thing' (*Gloss. Anglic. Nova*); and D. frequently uses 'pretend' in the sense of 'propose,' 'aspire to,' etc.: cf. 'there I could not pretend to Stay', 'their pretended Lovers', *infra*, pp. 56, 74.

(3) *wrap it up so clean . . . vitious Readers*: in *Conj. Lewd.* D. faces a similar difficulty—'how to expose Modestly Things which 'tis hardly Modest so much as to mention, and which must require abundance of clean Linnen to wrap them up in' (p. 7). 'As to a vicious Mind forming corrupt Ideas from the most modest Expressions, . . . The Crime of that Part is wholly their own, I am no way concerned in it . . . if a vicious Mind hears the Vice reproved, and forms pleasing Ideas of the Crime, . . . the fault is in the Depravity of the Mind, not in the needful and just Reprover' (*ibid.*, pp. 8, 9).

Page 2. (1) *ALL possible Care . . . the modestest Hearer*: for similar protestations see *Rox.*, p. 2; cf. Arthur J. Tieje, 'Expressed Aim of Long Prose Fiction from 1579 to 1740', *JEGP*, xi (1912), 423–4.

(2) *IT is suggested . . . in the Reading*: elsewhere D. uses a comparison between *Paradise Lost* and *Paradise Regained* to support the contention that readers, not authors, are to blame if 'the criminal Part' pleases more

than 'the penitent Part': *Fam. Instr.* ii.[i]-ii, 230-1; *App. Jour.*, 19 June 1725 (Lee, iii. 396); cf. *infra*, p. 291.

(3) *the Gust and Palate of the Reader*: 'There is something so wicked in the Gust of Men's reading palates in this Age, that they love what is Malicious; something Wicked, in every Paper' (*App. Jour.*, 22 Feb. 1724, Lee, iii. 235). *Gust*: 'Taste, Relish' (Phillips).

(4) *Application*: D.'s use of the term reflects traditional homiletic theory, which divided sermons into 'doctrine' and 'use'; 'application' was defined as 'all the Uses that are inferred from the Doctrine', and was regarded as 'the life and soul of a Sermon', by which 'Sacred Truths are brought home to a man's particular conscience, and occasions' (John Wilkins, *Ecclesiastes: or A Discourse Concerning the Gift of Preaching*, 6th edn. [1679], p. 29). Cf. D.'s *E.H.R.A.*, p. 394; *The Storm* (1704), sig. [A5v]; *The Lay-Man's Sermon upon the Great Storm* (1704), p. 2; *App. Jour.*, 1 June 1723, Lee, iii. 141.

Page 3. (1) *garbl'd*: 'to cleanse from Dross and Dirt, as Grocers do their Spices' (Phillips). A Garbling Office had been established in London in the fifteenth century to inspect 'several Sorts of Goods, more particularly subject to Frauds, Mixtures and false Package, in order to cleanse them, and make them Merchantable' (*Review*, iv. 635, 17 Feb. 1708); cf. *Comp. Eng. Trades.*, i. 252-3, and *An Enquiry into Occasional Conformity* (1702), in *True Coll.*, p. 390.

(2) *Advocates for the Stage*: elsewhere D. usually sides with Jeremy Collier in the controversy initiated by *A Short View of the Immorality and Profaneness of the English Stage* (1698); but he holds that the blame for dramatic immorality lies chiefly with audiences, and offers economic extenuations for playwrights and actors. See *Review*, 3 May 1705, ii. 101-2; 26 Oct. 1706, iii. 511-2; 29 Oct. 1706, iii. 515-6; 1 Sept. 1709, vi. 257-60. Cf. also *Due Prep.*, in *Rom. & Narr.*, xv. 5-6.

Page 4. (1) *Warnings to honest People to beware*: D. here adopts the conventional justification of rogue biography. Typical is the motto, '*Felix quem faciunt aliena pericula cautum*' (*Comp. Hist. Highwaymen*, p. 2). D. issues similar warnings elsewhere: cf. *App. Jour.*, 28 Nov. 1724; Lee, iii. 337.

(2) *Diligence and Application . . . no Case can be so low, so despicable*: on the principle that '*no Condition is so low or so despicable in a Tradesman, but he may with Diligence and Application recover it*', see *Comp. Eng. Trades.*, ii, Part i, chap. vii; D. implicitly equates transported convicts and bankrupt tradesmen insofar as both can make fresh starts, whereas 'In all other Disasters of Life, once unhappy, ever unfortunate' (ii. 188, cf. ii. 201-2, and *infra*, p. 189 n. 2).

(3) *a new Cast for his Life*: a new throw of the dice, another chance; the image recurs during Moll's poetical courtship, when she 'ventur'd all

upon the last cast of Poetry', and when Moll says that in matrimony a woman has 'but one Cast for her Life' (*infra*, pp. 79 and 75).

Page 5. *a Midwife-keeper*: on the equivocal role of 'Mother Midnight', see *infra*, notes to pp. 163 and 213.

Page 7. (1) *Newgate* . . . *Old-Baily*: London prison and criminal court respectively; see *infra*, pp. 273-4.

(2) *where else, I know not*: D. knew of orphan asylums in several other European capitals. In *Merc. Polit.* for Feb. 1720, he mentions the Royal Hospital of Lisbon (p. 36); in *Aug. Triumph*. he says that England should 'follow the Steps of the *Venetians*, the *Hamburgers*, and other foreign States, &c, who have for Ages past prosecuted this glorious Design' (p. 15). Cf. *The Guardian*, No. 105 (11 July 1713). For earlier attempts in England to make better provision for parish children than boarding them out with nurses, see George, p. 43, and Frederic M. Eden, *The State of the Poor* (1797), iii. ccclxxiii.

Page 8. (1) *three Pieces of fine* Holland: 'Holland, or Holland-Cloth, a kind of Linnen Cloth made in that Country' (Phillips). In *Plan Eng. Comm.*, D. says hollands are used 'for Shifts and Sheets, and such like fine Uses', and come 'of all Prices and Denominations, from 1s. to 12s. *per* Ell' (p. 156). Cf. *Rox.*, p. 212, and *infra*, p. 63.

(2) *pleaded her Belly*: executions of women in a state of pregnancy were suspended until they delivered the child: see Radzinowicz, p. 12; cf. also *Street-Robberies, Consider'd* (1728), attributed—I suspect mistakenly—to D., pp. 6-8.

(3) *No Parish to have Recourse to*: by the Act of Settlement of the Poor of 1662 (14 *Car.* 11, *c.* 12), each parish was bound to find accommodation for persons born within its boundaries and to support those unable to support themselves. The difficulties and inequities in the administration of the Poor Laws are touched upon elsewhere in *M.F.*—see *infra*, pp. 117 n. 2, 163 n. 3—and in D.'s other writings; cf. *J.P.Y.*, p. 96.

Page 9. *Skin discolour'd, or blacken'd*: it was believed that most 'gypsies' were true-born Englishmen in disguise. D. says of the Elizabethan vagrancy act, 'Why those who pretended to be *Ægyptians*, were deem'd Rogues, need not be enlarg'd upon. They are upon the same level with those who call themselves Great *Poles, Protestant Churchmen, Palatines, Hugonots*, &c.'—i.e. mere imposters; see *Charity Still a Christian Virtue* (1719), p. 11. The same assumption was embodied in the law: 'By Stat. 12 *Annae, c.* 23, . . . all persons pretending to be Gypsies, or wandering in the Habit or Form of counterfeit *Egyptians* . . . shall be deemed Rogues and Vagabonds' (Jacob, *Mod. Just.*, pp. 458-9). Whatever the true ethnic status of the '*Ægyptians*', beggars of all kinds exploited and abused young children. Thomas Coram's petition to the king in 1739, to promote the

establishment of a hospital for foundlings, complains that 'some of those
Miserable Infants are Blinded or Maimed or Distorted in their Limbs in
order to move Pity and Compassion and thereby become the fitter Instruments of gain to those Vile, Mercyless Wretches' (quoted in R. H. Nichols
and F. A. Wray, *The History of the Foundling Hospital* (1935), p. 16; cf.
also Marshall, p. 226; Radzinowicz, p. 113).

Page 10. (1) *the Magistrates . . . order'd that I should go to Service*: as D.
noted elsewhere, 'a Justice of Peace may oblige young People who are
idle, and live, as 'tis call'd, at their own Hands, to go to Service, and may,
if they refuse it, send them to the House of Correction'; on the other
hand, if a young woman proves that she works and 'is able to maintain
herself without being a Charge to her Parents, or the Parish, I do not
find the Magistrate can compel such a one to go to Service' (*G.L.S.C.*, p.
87; cf. Jacob, *Mod. Just.*, who significantly limits the scope of the law to
unmarried women between the ages of 12 and 40).

(2) *could get my Living without going to Service*: in the *Tour* D. mentions
Colchester, Taunton in Somerset, and 'the eastern and middle part of
Norfolk' as places where, by spinning yarn for the flourishing manufacture
of woollens, 'the very children after four or five years of age, could every
one earn their own bread' (i. 62, 266).

(3) *Spin Worsted . . . the chief Trade of that City* [Colchester]: see
Review, 12 Apr. 1705, ii. 66; 22 Mar. 1707, iv. 71–2; *A Brief Deduction of
the Original, Progress, and Immense Greatness of the British Woollen
Manufacture* (1727), pp. 42–3 and *passim*; and the recent study by A. F. J.
Brown, 'Colchester in the Eighteenth Century', in *East Anglian Studies*,
ed. Lionel M. Munby (1968), pp. 146–73. Brown numbers the spinners
in 1700 at perhaps 10,000, of whom some 2,000 were in Colchester itself,
the rest women and girls in neighbouring villages.

Page 11. (1) *what, would you be a Gentlewoman*?: Moll's aspirations may
be contrasted with the spirit of the contemporary charity schools, which
were intended to give poor children an education proper to their rank in
life. Instructors were urged to take 'all proper measures to inure the
children to labour and industry', lest 'the advantages they received from a
pious education should incline them to put too great a value upon themselves'; the object was to make them humbly accept those 'servile offices
which are necessary in all communities and for which the wise Governor
of the World had by his Providence designed them' (S.P.C.K. Circular
Letters of 1712 and 1719, quoted in Jones, p. 92). To bring up paupers
'mannerly' and 'genteelly'—to enable them to escape their dismal lot—was
to flout the educational principles of many humane men of the day: see
George, p. 221; Dorothy Marshall, *English People in the Eighteenth Century* (1956), p. 152; *D. & Spir. Autobiog.*, pp. 128–30; and Jacob Viner,
'Man's Economic Status', in *Man Versus Society in Eighteenth-Century*

Britain, ed. James L. Clifford (1968), pp. 33–5. D. himself defended charity schools in *Charity Still a Christian Virtue* (1719); in the preface to *Col. Jack*, p. 1; and in *App. Jour.* for 13 July 1723 (Lee, iii. 157–9).

(2) *THREE-PENCE . . . when I Spin*: 'In this poor trade of spinning', children 'not above seven or eight years old' were judged 'able to get more and spin better than older people', earning 2*d*. to 4*d*. a day as early as the 1680s: see Thos. Firmin, *Proposals for the employing of the Poor* (1678), quoted in Frederic M. Eden, *The State of the Poor* (1797), i. 205. At the London Workhouse in Bishopsgate Street in 1708, children spinning wool and flax and knitting stockings could earn up to 4*d*. in a ten-hour working day (see George, p. 219). Cf. also D.'s *G.L.S.C.*, p. 83.

(3) *plain Work*: 'plain needlework or sewing, as distinct from fancy work or embroidery' (*OED*).

Page 12. *sad*: grave, solemn.

Page 14. *the Ladies Lac'd-heads*: cf. 'Heads to Dress up', *infra* p. 15. 'A "head" was the general term for a head-dress, usually indicating an indoor cap. . . . universally worn indoors and often out of doors as well . . . lace edging was usual except among the working classes' (Cunnington, p. 153). Cf. Ned Ward, *British Wonders, &c.*, in *A Collection of Historical and State Poems* (1717), p. 15.

Page 15. *a meer Mother*: mere = complete, 'nothing short of' (*OED*, citing *Rob. Cru.*); cf. *infra* p. 187, 'meer Bride'.

Page 17. *But my new generous Mistress, for she*: one of the few instances in *M.F.* of syntax becoming so elaborate that the sentence is left incomplete. Sense might be restored simply by deleting 'for she', but D. evidently intended something different, and the nine words added in the second edition have, it must be acknowledged, a plausibly Defoean ring.

Page 18. (1) *to Sing much better*: in *Aug. Triumph.*, D. says of music that 'I have been a Lover of the Science from my Infancy, and in my younger Days was accounted no despicable Performer on the Viol and Lute, then much in Vogue' (p. 16). His library contained *Choice Airs and Songs to the Theorbo-Lute or Bass-Viol*: see *Librorum . . . Danielis De Foe, Gen. Catalogus* (1731), p. 46, item 58. In *Ess. upon Proj.*, he regards music as a desirable part of the young ladies' programme in his proposed 'Academy for Women' (p. 292). And I suspect that D. may have written a letter to *The Spectator* signed 'R. T.', advocating the encouragement of English musicians (printed in *Orig. & Gen. Lett.*, i. 233–7). On the other hand, there is no evidence that he or his contemporaries thought such training was appropriate for poor orphan-girls. In a 1724 address to teachers of London charity schools, Bishop Gibson maintains that 'fine singing' has no place in schools designed to make good Christians and good servants;

such accomplishments, he feels, tend to grow by degrees 'unto a more polite kind of education', and are therefore to be avoided in the charity school curriculum (see Jones, p. 81).

(2) *Advantages of Education*: in *App. Jour.* for 8 Aug. 1724, D. condemns 'the Cruelty of denying [women] that early Erudition, which would make them Equal, if not Superior in all manner of Science, and even more capable of all possible Improvement than the Men' (Lec, iii. 291); cf. also *Ess. upon Proj*, pp. 282–304.

Page 20. (1) *baited his Hook*: this image is associated with the devil later in *M.F.* (p. 191) and elsewhere in D.'s writings; *e.g.* Col. Jack reports that 'the subtile Tempter baited his Hook for me' (p. 19). As the elder brother is to Satan, so Moll is to Eve: '*Satan* fastening upon poor, proud, ridiculous Mother *Eve* . . . made presently a true Judgment of her Capacities, and of her Temper; took her by the right Handle, and soothing her Vanity (which is to this Day the softest Place in the Head of all the Sex) wheedl'd her out of her Senses, by praising her Beauty, and promising to make her a Goddess' (*Pol. Hist. Dev.*, p. 103).

(2) *Mrs.* Betty: according to Maximillian E. Novak (*Economics and the Fiction of Daniel Defoe* (1961), p. 84) the name Betty indicates that Moll is a chambermaid. But a contemporary 'TABLE of Titles and Distinctions for the information of the women of Great-Britain' urges, 'Let every common maid-servant be plain Jane, Doll, or Sue, and let the better-born, or higher placed in servitude, be distinguish'd by Mrs. Patience, Mrs. Prue, or Mrs. Abigal' (printed in *Orig. & Gen. Lett.*, i, 223–4). Cf. also Dorothy M. Stuart, *The English Abigail* (1946), pp. 82–106.

(3) *nothing but Money now recommends a Woman*: D. frequently deplores the venality that had come to dominate match-making, and his own two years of haggling with Henry Baker over the dowry of D.'s daughter Sophia illustrate the power of 'Interest' in such negotiations: see *Letters*, p. 461f; *infra*, p. 67 n. 2.

Page 23. *discover'd that I was a Fool*: discover, 'to display (unconsciously or unintentionally); to exhibit, betray, allow to be seen or perceived' (*OED*; cf. also Tucker, pp. 272–3).

Page 25. *Capitulation*: 'the making of terms, or of a bargain or agreement; stipulation' (*OED*); cf. *Rox.*, pp. 42, 145, 184.

Page 27. *Turn-Over*: 'linen band or the like worn round the neck and turned down; a turn-down collar or neckband' (*OED*).

Page 28. (1) Mile-End: in the 1720s D. held a lease on Kingswood Heath, an estate worth about £300 per annum, in the parish of St. Michael, Mile End, Colchester; see J. R. Sutherland, 'A Note on the Last Years of Defoe', *MLR*, xxix (1934), p. 140; *Letters*, p. 463 n. 3.

(2) *to Marry me as soon as he came to his Estate*: Swift's 'Directions to the Waiting-Maid' and Eliza Haywood's *Present for a Serving Maid* both warn that the master's son will not keep promises of marriage (*Directions to Servants*, in *Prose Works*, ed. Herbert Davis (1959), xiii. 57–8; Haywood (1743), p. 43, quoted by Bernard Kreissman, *Pamela-Shamela* (1960), p. 17).

Page 30. (1) *I saw the Cloud, tho' I did not forsee the Storm*: cf. 1 Kings 18:44 f.

(2) *the Kindness . . . had got vent*: 'Of news, etc.: to become known, to be divulged or let out' (*OED*, citing *J.P.Y.*).

(3) *at a Point*: 'decided, determined, resolved' (*OED*, *obs.*); the semicolon after 'Point' becomes a comma in the second edition, altering the meaning to 'position' or 'stage'.

Page 39. *as effectual . . . as if we had been publickly Wedded*: 'Marriage being nothing but a Promise, the Ceremony is no Addition to the Contract, only a Thing exacted by the Law, to prevent Knaves doing what seems here to be attempted, and therefore . . . when the Promise was made, the Man and Woman were actually Marryed; and he can never go off from it, nor Marry any other Woman; but he must break all the Constitutions of the Marriage Contract, the Sanction of the Law excepted' (*Review*, *Supp.* [Nov. 1704], iii. 19–20; cf. *Review*, iii. 227; *Ath. Merc.*, v, ii. 4; xiii, vi. 6; and xi, xxiv. 3).

Page 43. (1) *rout*: 'fuss, clamour, noise' (*OED*).

(2) *Beauties a Portion, and good Humour with it, is a double Portion*: the *Oxford Dict. Eng. Prov.* cites several seventeenth-century variants on the first idea (p. 186), but no exact anticipations. 'Portion' = 'that Estate or Sum of Money, which a Woman brings her Husband in Marriage' (Phillips).

Page 45. *a rattling way . . . rattled and jested*: 'to talk rapidly in a thoughtless, noisy, or lively manner' (*OED*); cf. 'rattled and made a great noise', *infra* p. 217; an 'empty rattling Way' (*Rox.*, p. 9); a 'noisie rattling way' (*Comp. Eng. Gent.*, p. 191).

Page 47. (1) *sham*: 'to pass off (something) *upon* (a person) by deceit; to palm off' (*OED*). Johnson calls it 'a low word'; D. frequently uses it adjectivally (*e.g.* 'sham Messengers', *infra*, p. 122) and substantively ('Trick, Shuffle, Sham and Sharping', *A Hint to the Blackwell-Hall Factors* (1705), p. 2).

(2) *brush'd off*: 'to burst away with a rush, move off abruptly, be gone, decamp, make off' (*OED*); 'to Fly or Run away' (*New Dict. Cant. Crew*).

Page 48. (1) *to Amuse his Sister*: 'to stop or stay one with a trifling Story, to make him lose his Time, to feed with vain Expectations, to hold in Play' (Phillips); 'to beguile, delude, cheat, deceive' (*OED*, citing D.'s *System of Magic*). Cf. *The Consolidator* (1705), p. 144; *Not*[tingh]*am*

Politicks Examin'd (1713), pp. 7, 19; and Tucker, pp. 209–10.

(2) Where Love is the Case,/The *Doctor's* an Ass: cited from Taylor's *Shilling* (1622) in W. Carew Hazlitt, *Eng. Proverbs and Prov. Phrases* (1907), p. 526.

Page 52. (1) *her Jointure . . . her Portion*: on the relation at this period between the size of the dowry which the wife brought with her from her father, and the size of the jointure, 'the annual income which her husband settled on her in case she survived him', see H. J. Habakkuk, 'Marriage Settlements in the Eighteenth Century', *Trans. Roy. Hist. Soc.*, 4th Ser., xxxii (1950), pp. 20 f.

(2) *no contending with . . . a Fool*: see Prov. 29:9.

Page 53. Answer, *and* Answer not: see Prov. 26:4–5; cf. also *App. Jour.*, 5 Aug. 1721 (Lee, ii. 411).

Page 57. *to church, like a Bear to the Stake*: The *Oxford Dict. Eng. Prov.* gives several fifteenth- and sixteenth-century occurrences of this common proverb for reluctance.

Page 58. *not oblig'd to tell him, that I was his Brother's Whore*: in *Ductor Dubitantium* (1660), Jeremy Taylor had observed that '*Nemo tenetur infamare se*, is a rule universally admitted among the casuists, "no man is bound to discover his own shame" ' (*Whole Works*, ed. Reginald Heber, rev. Charles P. Eden (1850), x. 113); cf. also *Ath. Merc.*, ix. xxviii, 2.

Page 59. *as effectually Criminal . . . actually done it*: in *E.H.R.A.*, a woman is told that by loving a married man she 'had intentionally committed Whoredom with him': 'you wish'd you were a-bed with him, and you are as guilty by wishing to Sin, as if you had done it' (p. 195). D.'s Scandal Club had advised one would-be adulterer 'to reflect what *Intentional Guilt* lies on your Thoughts in this Case'; another, 'to repent of the Sin of Adultery, since according to the known Text, *Matt.* 5.28, you have as much already committed it, as if you had actually lain together' (*Review*, *Supp.*, Jan. 1705, p. 6 (misnumbered 7); Sept. 1704, p. 7).

Page 60. (1) Land-water-thing, *call'd*, a Gentleman-Tradesman: in *Rox.* (p. 7f.) the affectation of gentility on the part of a tradesman is represented as grotesque in itself and disastrous in its consequences; cf. also *Comp. Eng. Trades.*, i. 117 f.

(2) *catch'd in the very Snare . . . I laid for myself*: cf. Ps. 9:15–16, Prov. 26:27.

(3) *Trepan'd*: trepan, 'to catch in a trap; to entrap, ensnare, beguile' (*OED*); cf. *Col. Jack*, p. 112.

(4) *a* Draper *too*: Moll's situation echoes that of a woman who complains to the *Review* that she is '*fatigu'd with the Addresses of several*

importunate Suitors', including linen-drapers (*Supp.*, Jan. 1705, p.8). Like Moll, she balks at marrying a tradesman for fear of losing all claims to gentility; and she is particularly wary of linen-drapers because of the case of Tom Pitkin, who had recently defrauded his creditors by declaring bankruptcy and absconding with £70,000. The importance of Pitkin's case is indicated in D.'s *Party Tyranny* (1705), p. 11 (misnumbered 13), and by the statute (3 & 4 *Annae c.* 11) passed in 1704 to relieve his creditors, apprehend him, and recover his booty. Two years later Pitkin's and similar cases prompted further parliamentary action, in which D. took strong personal interest: see his *Remarks on the Bill To Prevent Frauds Committed by Bankrupts* (1706), p. 3 and *passim*. The subsequent behaviour of Moll's gentleman-linen-draper husband suggests that this episode owes something to the Pitkin scandal of fifteen years earlier.

Page 61. *I was hurried on* (*by my Fancy* . . .) *to Ruin my self*: on undertaking the slaving voyage, Crusoe says, 'I was hurried on, and obeyed blindly the dictates of my fancy rather than my reason' (*Rom. & Narr.*, i. 43).

Page 62 (1) *a Scarf*: a part of clerical costume, associated at this time specifically with noblemen's chaplains. See John Oldham's 'Satire Addressed to a Friend', in which the chaplain 'tho' in silken Scarf, and Cassock drest,/Wears but a gayer Livery at best' (*Works* (1722), ii. 126); cf. *The Spectator*, Nos. 21 and 539, 24 Mar. 1711 and 18 Nov. 1712 (i. 89, iv. 427); and D.'s *Comp. Eng. Gent.*, p. 46.

(2) *Vanity is the perfection of a Fop*: the theme is elaborated in *Rox.*, pp. 7–9; on the connection between folly and conceit, see also *Good Advice to the Ladies* (1702), pp. 7–8; *The Commentator*, No. xlii (27 May 1720); *Ser. Refl.*, in *Rom. & Narr.*, iii. 73; *Reformation of Manners* (1702), in *True Coll.*, pp. 55–6.

(3) *the* Mint: an area in Southwark which had long provided sanctuary for debtors; see Strype, iv. 31. Despite the removal (by 8 & 9 *W.* 3, *c.* 27, *s.* 15) of its legal status as a sanctuary, the debtors there had remained able to intimidate officers and prevent arrests by sheer force of numbers. The status of the Mint was a topical question at the time *M.F.* appeared; in 1723 Parliament was to amend the earlier act of 1697, and effectually put an end to the Mint as a debtors' sanctuary. See Adam Anderson, *Origin of Commerce* (1787), iii. 136.

(4) Spunging-House: 'a Victualling House near some Prison, where Persons newly Arrested for Debt are kept for some time, till they agree with their Adversary, or are remov'd to a closer Confinement' (Phillips); in the *Tour*, D. lists 'One hundred and nineteen Spunging Houses' among the '*Tolerated* PRISONS' of London (i. 353). Cf. also *Review*, i. 59–60.

(5) *taking care to reserve something* . . . *for myself*: the Athenian Society allowed that 'in some Cases such .secret securing one parties separate interest, without giving the other any account, may be very just, vertuous,

and prudent. As for Instance, when either the Man or the Wife run on will-fully and obstinately in an unavoidable Course of ruining themselves and their Families . . . the last Remedy is as reasonable as to lay things of value out of the way of Children and Fools' (*Ath. Merc.*, v. ix. 2; cf. ix. xiv. 9). The Jesuits went still further: see Nicolas Perrault, *La Morale des Jesuites* (1667), p. 690; Blaise Pascal, *Provincial Letters*, trans. A. J. Krail-sheimer (1966), p. 123.

(6) *in the Night take away every thing . . . of any Value and secure it*: Parliament had sought to hinder such practices by the statute 5 *Annae c.* 22. *s.* 1, which provided 'That if any . . . Bankrupt . . . or any other Person or Persons . . . shall . . . remove, carry away, conceal, destroy or embezzle any of the Goods . . . to the Value of Twenty Pounds or upwards . . . being thereof lawfully convicted, shall suffer as a Felon, without Benefit of Clergy' (Goodinge, p. 290; cf. also 3 *Geo.* 1, *c.* 12 (1716), and *supra* p. 60, n. 4).

Page 63. (1) *got over into* France: in the *Review* (1 Mar. 1709), D. speaks of 'at least 5000' debtors 'who being made desperate by the Cruelty of Creditors, the Severity of the late Acts for Bankrupts Surrenders, terrify'd with Escape-Warrants, and the Dread of perpetual Imprisonment, are fled out of the Kingdom, some with, some without their Families, and all with what Estate they can secure; by which they help both to depopulate and impoverish the Country' (v. 579–80).

(2) *three a Clock in the Morning . . . into the* Mint: in *Ess. upon Proj.*, D. had spoken of 'Men (and Carts) to be had, *whose Trade it is*, and who in One Night shall remove the greatest Warehouse of Goods . . . in the Town, and carry them off into those Nurseries of Rogues, the *Mint* and *Friars*' (p. 198).

(3) *I might have been stop'd there by the Creditors*: according to statute (21 *Jac.* 1), 'the Wife must be summon'd to come before the Commis-sioners; and if she come not, or refuse to be sworn, they may imprison her as well as the Husband: So likewise if she refuses to discover the Truth' (Goodinge, p. 61).

(4) *before they could get out the Commission*: creditors who intend to take out a commission of Bankrupt, explains Goodinge, must first make affidavit before a master in Chancery. Then there must be a petition presented to the Lord Chancellor, or Lord Keeper. Finally, commissioners must be named, and a bond entered into before the goods of the bankrupt can be seized and distributed (pp. 5–7).

(5) *some and some*: gradually or piecemeal: see D's *Tour*, i. 203, 252.

Page 64. (1) *a Widow bewitch'd*: see D.'s discussion of the similar case of a 'Widower Bewitch'd' in the 'Advice from the Scandal Club' (*Review*, 24 April 1705, ii. 86–8).

(2) *a Husband, and no Husband*: Moll will later observe of her Bath lover

that 'he had a Wife', but also that 'he had no Wife, that is to say she was as no Wife to him' (pp. 109, 120); the banker's clerk reports, 'I have a Wife and no Wife' (p. 134): thus the ambiguities of Moll's own situation are compounded by those of the men she moves among. For analogous paradoxes, cf. p. 106, where Moll calls herself 'a Woman of Fortune, tho' I was a Woman without a Fortune', and the horse-theft which Moll calls 'a Robbery and no Robbery' (p. 254).

(3) *limitted from Marriage*: 'Marrying a second Husband or Wife, the first living, is Felony. But if either of them be absent abroad above seven Years, without Notice of being living, the other may marry again; as they may likewise in Case of a Divorce. 1 *Jac.* 1' (Jacob, *Mod. Just.*, p. 183). Anglican and Puritan casuists tended to argue that if the husband was not heard of within four, seven, or ten years, the wife was free to remarry; the absences they had in mind were those caused by overseas trade, war, and the like, though fear or the malice of others were sometimes recognized as legitimate grounds for separations. See William Perkins, 'Of Christian Oeconomie', in *Workes* (1616–18), ii. 688; Richard Baxter, *Christian Directory* (1673), in *Practical Works*, ed. William Orme (1830), iv. 167; Joseph Hall, *Resolutions*, pp. 398–9; *Ath. Merc.*, iv, vii. 3.

(4) *out of my Knowledge*: outside her sphere of acquaintance; cf. Col. Jack, who feels secure because he has 'grown out of every Body's knowledge, and most of those I had known were grown out of mine' (p. 184).

(5) *Sons of Affliction*: cf. Prov. 31:5.

(6) *at the Sign of the* Bull: this inn, and its milieu prior to the parliamentary act of 1723 which cleared the Mint, are described in William Rendle, *The Inns of Old Southwark and their Associations* (1888), pp. 262–7. Not located on Strype's map (iv. 27) or mentioned in his account of the Mint (iv. 31).

(7) *my Lord* Rochester's *Mistress*: see the closing lines of Rochester's song, 'Phyllis, be gentler, I advise', which warn the coy mistress that she will 'Die with the scandal of a whore/And never know the joy' (*Complete Poems*, ed. David M. Vieth (1968), p. 32). D. had paraphrased these lines in *An Elegy on the Author of the True-Born English-Man* (1704), in *Second Vol.*, pp. 85–6.

Page 65. (1) *endeavouring to drown their Sorrow in their Wickedness*: Ned Ward says of 'The Broken Shop-Keepers Club' in the Mint that 'their Chief Business is to wear away all Sense of their Present Misfortunes, to damn their Creditors, Drink confusion to Bayliffs, & charge their Ruin on their Extravagant Wives, Faithless Servants, or Injustice of their Relations; but not a word of their own Negligence, Keeping Whores, Horses, & the like' (*The History of the London Clubs* (1709), reprinted n.d., pp. 18–9).

(2) *Sighs would interrupt their Songs*: cf. *Rox.*, p. 48; elsewhere D. says

of the mixture of sighs and songs that ' 'tis a kind of respiration natural to a stifled conviction—a hesitation that is the consequence of a captivated virtue, a little insurrection in the soul against the tyranny of profligate principles' (*Ser. Refl.*, in *Rom. & Narr.*, iii. 68); cf. also *More Reformation*, in *Second Vol.*, p. 48.

(3) *to Destruction*: the *Ath. Merc.* says of the sanctuaries for debt that 'all own 'em the greatest *Sinks of Villany* that are out of Hell, and we shou'd as soon expect a Man shou'd remain honest who joyn'd himself with a Crew of *Banditti*, as long retain any Sentiments of *Religion* and Virtue, after he once gets into these places' (xii, xxiv. 2). Cf. D.'s *Ess. upon Proj.*, p. 200: 'I have known many a man go in among them Honest . . . but I never knew one come away so again'. See also *Remarks on the Bill To Prevent Frauds Committed by Bankrupts* (1706), p. 15; *App. Jour.*, 20 Apr. 1721 (Lee, ii. 367–70); *Parochial Tyranny* (1727), p. 11.

Page 67. (1) *Marriages . . . the Consequences of politick Schemes, for forming Interests, and carrying on Business*: a common complaint of contemporary writers; *e.g.*, 'our marriages are made, just like other common bargains and sales, by the mere consideration of interest or gain, without any love or esteem, of birth or of beauty itself, which ought to be the true ingredients. . . . Yet this custom is of no ancient date in England' (Sir William Temple, *Miscellanea* (1679), quoted in H. J. Habakkuk, 'Marriage Settlements in the Eighteenth Century', *Trans. Roy. Hist. Soc.*, 4th Ser., xxxii (1950), 25).

(2) *Money only made a Woman agreeable*: see *supra*, p. 20 n. 3; *Mist's Jour.*, 30 Jan. and 19 Mar. 1720 (Lee, ii. 187, 212); cf. also *The Commentator*, No. lxi (1 Aug. 1720).

(3) *the Market run very Unhappily on the Mens side*: for this image and similar contentions, see also *Mist's Jour.*, 7 Mar. 1719, and *App. Jour.*, 20 Aug. 1720 (Lee, ii. 107, 269–70).

Page 71 Redriff: on the Surrey side of the Thames between Bermondsey and Deptford, Redriff—a corruption of Rotherhithe—has always been inhabited by seafarers, including Lemuel Gulliver; cf. Wheatley, iii. 157, 174–5; Strype, App., 87.

Page 72. *according to my Lord* Rochester: D. quotes this couplet in *Mist's Jour.*, 12 Sept. 1719 (Lee, ii. 146), and again in *G.L.S.C.*, p. 69, apropos of a woman who tricks a man into marriage by getting him drunk, after he has seduced her by the same means. There is an earlier echo in Bk. 3 of *Juro Divino* (8vo edn. (1706), sig. H2). D. quotes other passages from this poem in *Comp. Eng. Gent.*, pp. 40–1. Moll discreetly omits the next couplet: 'A woman's ne'er so ruined but she can/Be still revenged on her undoer, man;/How lost soe'er, she'll find some lover, more/A Lewd, abandoned fool than she a whore' ('A Letter from Artemisia in the Town to Chloe in the Country', *Complete Poems*, ed. David M. Vieth (1968), p. 110).

Page 73. (1) *he pretended . . . to place himself above the occasion of a Character*: here in the sense of a report *on* his character, as again at p. 75 ('the Lives of very few Men now a-Days will bear a Character') and p. 109 ('my Landlady . . . gave me an advantageous Character of him').

(2) ramble: ordinarily, disjointed or digressive talk or writing, but here perhaps simply empty, clichéd speech.

Page 74. (1) *uncomatable*: characterized by Johnson as 'a low, corrupt word', its only pre-*M.F. OED* citations are from Congreve, Ned Ward, and Steele (1694–1709), but D. had used it in *The Consolidator* (1705), p. 95, and '*Come-at-able*' in correspondence in 1707 (*Letters*, p. 213); cf. also Mandeville, *Fable of the Bees*, ed. F. B. Kaye (1966), i. 95.

(2) *the Wars . . . have carried the Men . . . away*: in *G.L.S.C.*, D. says that 'a long and fatal War of near 30 Years' has 'carried away . . . above five Hundred Thousand Men out of the three Kingdoms, first and last; either kill'd, or run into foreign Service, or dead of Diseases in the Service, or otherwise remov'd from the general Body of the People' (p. 139); cf. *Some Seasonable Queries, On . . . A General Naturalization* (1694), sig. A. But in *App. Jour.* for 10 Apr. 1725 it is suggested that 'there were so many Women more than Men that sold themselves to go over to Virginia, and our other Plantations in America, that I should find it was equal to all the great numbers of Men who went away in the time of War' (Lee, iii. 375).

Page 75. *run into Matrimony, as a Horse rushes into the Battle*: 'to run headlong upon [matrimony], is rightly compar'd to a Horse rushing into the Battle, and argues a miserable Thoughtlessness of what is before us' (*Rel. Court.*, p. 203); cf. *Conj. Lewd.*: 'to rush into Matrimony as a Horse rushes into the Battel, intimates a Fury, not a rational sober Christian Proceeding', and denotes 'a raging inflamed Appetite' (p. 339; cf. also pp. 32–3).

Page 77. *just . . . to Deceive the Deceiver*: In *Pol. Hist. Dev.*, D. cites 'the old Latin Proverb, *Fallere fallentem non est fraus . . .* 'tis no Sin to cheat the *Devil*, which for all that, upon the whole I deny' (p. 353). On the question, '*Whether it be a Sin to deceive the Deceiver?*' see *Ath. Merc.*, ii, xx. 10: 'although Circumstances may make an Action more or less sinful, yet they change not the nature of Sin; for Deceit is Deceit, though used to a Deceiver'. On the other hand, the imposter Mary Carleton had endorsed this 'received principle of justice' (Francis Kirkman, *The Counterfeit Lady Unveiled* (1673), ed. Spiro Peterson (1951), p. 23), as had the highwayman Ned Wicks (*Comp. Hist. Highwaymen*, p. 220), and a supposititious correspondent in *App. Jour.* (7 Apr. 1722, Lee, ii. 508).

Page 79. *Diamond Ring, and writes upon the Glass*: a custom frequently alluded to in the literature of the period. Two of Swift's epigrams '*On seeing Verses written upon Windows in Inns*' begin, 'The glass, by lovers nonsense blurr'd,/Dims and obscures our sight', and 'Thanks to my Stars, I once can see/A window here from scribbling free' (*Poems*, ed. Harold Williams, 2nd edn. (1958), ii. 402). Cf. also 'The Toilette', ll. 25–6, in Gay, *Poetical Works*, p. 135; *Spectator*, No. 220, 12 Nov. 1711, ii. 356.

Page 81. *I did not care to be Transported*: i.e. carried off as if she were a convicted felon; see *infra*, p. 86 f.

Page 82. *shrewdly put to it*: faced with an awkward, vexatious, or difficult challenge.

Page 83. *Composition for a Debt*: 'when a Debtor cannot pay his whole Debt, he agrees with the Person to whom he oweth the Money, to take part in lieu of the whole Debt, for which part he obtaineth a Receipt in full, as for the whole Debt; and this Money is said to be paid by Composition' (*Merch. Mag., s. v.*).

Page 86. (1) *Stories . . . of the Country* [and] . . . *of the People*: the narrative that follows is amplified in *Col. Jack*, pp. 152–3, and in *App. Jour.*, 26 Jan. 1723, where D. attempts to lessen the 'Dread and Terror' of transportation to Virginia by arguing that the convicts' 'Labour is not harder, or their Usage worse, than many hired Servants in *England* on Yearly Wages', and that by 'applying themselves with Honesty and Industry to a due Course of Business' once their 'time is out', they are 'sure of rising in the World' (Lee, iii. 95–7; cf. also *Plan Eng. Comm.*, pp. 273–4). Other colonial propagandists made similar claims: see Hugh Jones, *The Present State of Virginia* (1721), ed. R. L. Morton (1956), p. 87.

(2) *Servants . . . more properly call'd* Slaves: on this point there is some difference of opinion: one authority asserts that 'At no time in the history of Maryland was the condition of the servant that of a slave' (McCormac, p. 61); another argues that although their legal rights differed, the actual situations of servants and slave were identical (Bruce, ii. 104–5); a third cites contemporary evidence for the interchangeable use of the terms (Herrick, p. 3 n. 9 and *passim*). In fact, there were three classes of servants, not two: black slaves, whites who emigrated voluntarily and paid for their passage by binding themselves to five years or so of service, and white criminals transported judicially. The distinction between slaves and voluntary servants was fairly clear, but the status of the transported convict, while legally akin to that of the voluntary servant, tended in practice to be closer to that of the slave, and may at times have been worse. See Harrison Fairfax, 'When the Convicts Came', *Virginia Mag. of Hist. and Biog.*, xxx (1922), 257–8; cf. also Smith, pp. 233–5.

(3) *Land allotted them by the Country*: what the servant was to receive

varied at different dates and in different colonies, and might be determined either by the provisions of his indenture or by the custom of the country. One writer warns that the grant of land 'according to the custome of the Country' is 'an old delusion', and advises servants to be sure that the land is guaranteed them in their indentures (John Hammond, *Leah and Rachel* (1655), reprinted in *Narratives of Early Maryland*, ed. Clayton C. Hall (1925), p. 289). Nor did the custom of the country require any allotment of land in Virginia at the end of the century (see Bruce, ii. 40–3). Writing in 1729, Joshua Gee says that it would encourage transported convicts to 'continue their Industry' if, after they had served their terms, 'Provision was made to allow each of them, 100 Acres or more of Land free for some Time'; the implication is that this was not current practice (*The Trade and Navigation of Great Britain Consider'd*, pp. 60–1, quoted in Herrick, p. 115 n. 7).

(4) *Cure the Land*: Col. Jack has 'a large Quantity of Land Cur'd, *that is*, Freed from Timber' (p. 155).

(5) *Train Bands*: 'certain Regiments made of the Inhabitants of a City or Town, train'd up to bear Arms, and instructed in Military Discipline' (Phillips).

(6) *burnt in the Hand*: this practice was 'not so much in Nature of a Punishment, as a Mark to notify that the Person may have his *Clergy* but once' (Jacob, *New Law Dict.*, s.v. 'Benefit of Clergy'; but cf. *The Livery Man's Reasons* (1701), p. 11, where branding seems to be regarded primarily as a punishment). Benefit of clergy was a means of showing mercy to criminals convicted of certain felonies for the first time: if they could read ('*ut clericus*') they were branded and set free. 'Now even the Women . . . have . . . the benefit of their Clergy, tho not so much as put to Read; for in such Cases where the Men are allow'd it; the Women are of course fizz'd in the Fist, without running the risque of a Halter by not Reading' (*New Dict. Cant. Crew*, s.v. 'Neck-verse'). Cf. Strype, v. 385; *Col. Jack*, p. 165; Arthur L. Cross, 'Eng. Crim. Law and Benefit of Clergy During the 18th and Early 19th Centuries', *Am. Hist. Rev.*, xxii (1916), 544–65, esp. 551 f; *infra*, p. 204 n. 2.

Page 87. Newgate . . . *half Peoples this Colony*: this estimate is not as exaggerated as some recent criticism would suggest. In *Econ. and the Fiction of D. D.* (1961), M. E. Novak writes, 'In 1670 Virginia prohibited the importation of convicts into her territory, and six years later Maryland enacted a similar statute. As far as is known, this law was effective until 1718, when a new English law opened these two colonies to felons once more' (p. 146). Such laws were indeed passed in various colonies, not once but repeatedly—for they were regularly vetoed by the British government, so that the importation of convicts continued throughout this period; see

Eng. Hist. Doc., ix. 461–2; ibid., pp. 460–1 for the law of 1718 (4 *Geo.* I., *c.* 11).

Page 88. (1) *her Master married her*: to encourage women to emigrate, colonial propagandists made much of their matrimonial prospects. 'If any maid or single woman have a desire to go over, they will think themselves in the Golden Age . . . for if they be but civil and under 50 years of age, some honest man or other will purchase them for their wives' (*A Brief Description . . . of Carolina* (1666), in *Eng. Hist. Doc.*, ix. 121). Especially quick and advantageous matches were to be found in Virginia: see Bruce, ii. 51; *G.L.S.C.*, p. 140.

(2) *whether I would or no*: on the unbearable weight of secrets, see *infra*, p. 325 n.

Page 89. *what Difficulties presented to my view*: cases of conscience arising from incestuous matches contracted in ignorance had been discussed by various seventeenth-century casuists: see Jeremy Taylor, *Ductor Dubitantium*, in *Whole Works*, ix. 149; Joseph Hall, *Resolutions*, pp. 410–4; *Ath. Merc.*, xvi, xx. 1; vi, xxvi. 3. In the *Heptameron* of Margaret of Navarre, a 'council of conscience' advises the guilty mother 'never to reveal the secret to her children, who had not sinned, inasmuch as they had known nothing'—a decision endorsed by the English casuists (*The Heptameron*, ed. George Saintsbury (1903), ii. 40).

Page 91. *plung'd*: 'Plunge, Trouble, Incumbrance; as *To put to a Plunge, To be in a great Plunge*' (Phillips).

Page 92. (1) *out of my Power to stir without his Consent*: 'after Marriage the Will of the *Wife* in Judgment of Law is subject to the Will of the Husband; and it is said a *Wife* hath no Will, *sed fulget radiis Mariti*' (Jacob, *New Law Dict.*). As to 'the Constitution of the Country', I have not found any relevant provisions in 'The Acts of Assembly, and Laws, of Virginia', in *An Abridgement of the Laws in Force and Use in Her Majesty's Plantations* (1704). As Oldmixon points out, however, on all but strictly local matters, 'the Acts of Parliament and Statutes of England' and the 'Orders of the Queen and Council in *England*' have 'the Force of Laws in the Plantations' (p. 299).

(2) *a Mad House . . . to Murther me*: in the *Review* of 8 June 1706, D. had called for 'publick Regulation' of private madhouses, in which sane people could be confined by vicious relatives (iii. 274–6, misnumbered 277–80); in the *Tour* he lists 'Fifteen Private Mad-Houses' among the '*Tolerated* PRISONS' of London (i. 353); in *Aug. Triumph.* he urges that 'all private Mad-Houses should be suppress'd at once, and it should be no less than Felony to confine any Person under pretence of Madness without due Authority' (p. 34); cf. also *App. Jour.*, 28 Jan. 1721 (Lee, ii. 333). 'Certifying procedures . . . were introduced in the first instance not so much to

legalise the depriving an insane person of his liberty as to protect a sane man from unlawful confinement "as a Lunatick" ' (Richard Hunter and Ida Macalpine, *Three Hundred Years of Psychiatry 1535–1860* (1963), p. 298, commenting on *Mrs. Clark's Case, 1718*).

Page 96. (1) *Rhapsodies*: 'a tedious impertinent spinning out of a Discourse, to little or no purpose' (Phillips); or perhaps merely an extravagant and incoherent effusion.

(2) *leave me to Sue for the little Portion that I had . . . the Children . . . ruin'd too, having no legal Claim*: 'None of these Marriages are void in themselves, but voidable in the Spiritual Court. For if a Man takes his Sister to Wife, they are *Baron* and *Feme* till a Divorce, and till then the issue are not Bastard' (Wood, *Institute*, p. 58). But once divorce on grounds of consanguinity is obtained, 'Dower is gone; and . . . the Children are Bastard. . . . But in these *Divorces*, the Wife 'tis said shall receive all again that she brought with her. . . . But this is where the Goods are not spent. If she knows her Goods unspent, she may bring Action of Detinue for them; and as for Money, *etc.* which cannot be known, she must sue in the Spiritual Court' (Jacob, *New Law Dict.*).

Page 103. (1) *Rum . . . the usual Dram of the Country*: Oldmixon says of Maryland that 'Their common Drink is Cyder', but also mentions 'Wine brought from *Madera* and *Fyall*, Rum from *Barbados*' (p. 207). As to the size of a dram, D. describes in *Col. Jack* an alcoholic whose potations proceeded 'from a Drop to a Sup, from a Sup to a Dram, from a Dram to a Glass, and so on' (p. 240); cf. also *Due Prep.*, in *Rom. & Narr.*, xv. 42).

(2) [threat of suicide]: D. says of the suicide of 'that mad Fellow Cato' that 'it was Dying for fear of Shame, which was both Cowardice, and the extreme of Pride' (30 Dec. 1721; Lee, ii. 471); the question was politically topical when *M.F.* appeared, for the *London Journal* having defended suicide and the assassination of tyrants, D. attacked both in *App. Jour.* (16, 23, 30 Dec. 1721; 6, 13 Jan. 1722 (Lee, ii. 462–78 *passim*)). Also making suicide topical was 'the Mortality that has been so remarkable of late among our Great Men'—those involved in the South-Sea scandal: 'How many Self-Murders do we hear of, almost every Day, occasion'd by the violent precipitate Fall of Families in this Calamity?' (*Coll. Misc. Lett.*, i. 158; *App. Jour.*, 3 Mar. 1722 (Lee, ii. 494)).

Page 105. (1) *the Ship sprung her Main-mast*: split or cracked it.

(2) *Bristol, where my Brothers chief Correspondent liv'd*: 'either the Tobacco is bought from the Planters by the Merchants of *England*, and by them shipped, or else it is shipped by the Inhabitants of the Countrey, and consigned to their Correspondents in *England*' (*An Essay upon the Government of the English Plantations on the Continent of America* (1701), ed. Louis B. Wright (1945), p. 27). In his own early venture into the

tobacco trade, D. followed the former course, employing a factor who was to buy directly from the planters in Maryland: see James Sutherland, 'Some Early Troubles of D. D.', *RES*, ix (1938), 275–90. On the importance of Bristol to the American trade, see Oldmixon, p. 318. In a letter to Harley, D. reports that he has spent four days in Bristol (26–9 Aug. 1705), but his account in the *Tour* is perfunctory (*Letters*, p. 111; *Tour*, ii. 36–7, 115). The legend popularized by Wilson, that D. retreated to Bristol in the 1690s to escape creditors, has never been substantiated (*Memoirs of the Life and Times of D.D.* (1830), i. 221–2; cf. Sutherland, *Defoe* (1937), pp. 43–4).

(3) *Recruit*: 'Money (Expected.) *Have you rais'd the Recruits*, c[ant] is the Money come in' (*New Dict. Cant. Crew*).

Page 106. (1) *gay fine Company*: in the *Review* of 2 Oct. 1707, D. lists as Bath's 'very good Customers, the Rakes, Bullies, Gamesters, Whores, Bauds, &c.' and says that 'Sober and substantial Families . . . now shun the Place on Account of the Revelling and Rabble' (iv. 400). In the *Tour* he says that Bath, 'more like a prison than a place of diversion, scarce gives the company room to converse out of the smell of their own excrements, and . . . the very city it self may be said to stink like a general common-shore' (ii. 168).

(2) [Bath] *a Mistress sometimes, but very rarely . . . a Wife*: two decades later Richardson observes, 'Even the gentlemen, whose conduct in the general is governed by principles of virtue, . . . oftentimes give themselves airs of gallantry, and never have it in their thoughts to commence a treaty of marriage with an acquaintance begun upon that gay spot' (*Pamela*, ed. M. Kinkead-Weekes (1966), ii. 468–9). Cf. Alexander Sutherland, *Attempts to Revive antient Medical Doctrines* (1763), quoted by A. Barbeau, *Life and Letters at Bath in the XVIIIth Century* (1904), p. 103 n. 5.

Page 107. (1) *not . . . the least Slur upon my Reputation*: according to John Macky, one reason 'Common Women are not to be met with here, so much as at *Tunbridge* and *Epsom*', is that 'every thing that passes here is known on the Walks, and the Characters of Persons' (*Journey*, ii. 123). *The Guardian* speaks of 'those malignant Humours of Scandal which run throughout the Body of Men and Women there assembled' (No. 174, 30 Sept. 1713 (1714), ii. 501). 'I hear you have a Mint at the *Bath* for *Scandal*, as we have here [in London] for *Money*', writes Tom Brown in 1699 (*Works*, 5th edn. (1719), i. 195). And Capt. Charles Walker calls Bath 'that most remarkable and most remarking Place, which is more publick than any Town, or even City in all England, (I except not our dear wicked *Metropolis* it self)' (*Authentick Memoirs of the Life of the Celebrated Sally Salisbury* (1723), p. 41).

(2) *I had not given the least Reflection*: changed in second edition to 'I had not gotten the least Reflection'; the meaning is probably, 'I had not

given [rise to] "Censure, Reproach or Abuse" ' (Phillips).

(3) *melancholy Hours . . . pass'd the Winter . . . heavily*: 'In Winter *Bath* makes a very melancholy Appearance'; 'five Months in the Year 'tis as Populous as *London*, the other seven as desolate as a Wilderness' (Misson, *Memoirs and Observations* (1699), and [Ned Ward], *A Step to the Bath* (1700), both quoted in Ashton, pp. 329–32).

Page 109. *even when I was in Bed*: the incident mentioned by George A. Aitken—a case involving Richard Steele, which led to an action for breach of contract—confirms the plausibility of such behaviour in D.'s day: see *Rom. & Narr.*, vii. xii. Cf. also *Comp. Lett. of Lady Mary Wortley Montague*, ed. Robert M. Halsband (1966), ii. 14 n.; Gabriel Odingsells, *The Bath Unmask'd. A Comedy* (1725), sigs [B6ᵛ], [C6ᵛ] – [C7ʳ].

Page 112. *Huddled* [the money] *all into the Drawer again*: 'To Huddle, to confound or mingle things together after a confused manner' (Phillips).

Page 115. *away he comes to my Bed*: D.'s Scandal Club had considered the question, 'Whether the Woman that would permit a Man to set upon her Bed, after she is in it, and the whole Family before that time being gone to rest, would not, in all likelihood, admit him in some time into the same', and whether 'by the frequent permission of the Man, the Virtue of the Woman might be seduced and she thereby become a Prostitute': see *Review*, *Supp.* (Nov. 1704), pp. 20–1; cf. also *Conj. Lewd.*, p. 4; *Ath. Merc.*, ix, xvii. 4; xvi, xix. 1.

Page 116. (1) *wise Men . . . the brink of a Command*: Bishop Hall quotes William Perkins as saying, 'If a man be to choose his way, let him so cast it as that he may not approach near the brink of danger' (*Resolutions*, pp. 386–7). In *An Appeal to Honour and Justice*, D. quotes a similar proverb from Ecclus. 3:29 (*Rom. & Narr.*, vii. 169); and in *Ser. Refl.* he maintains that 'no case can be doubtful which does not border upon the frontiers of dishonesty; and he that resolves not to be drowned had best never come near the brink of the water' (*Rom. & Narr.*, iii. 30).

(2) *Penitentials*: 'utterance, demeanour, or behaviour of a penitent' (*OED*; earliest citation from *Clarissa*); cf. also *supra* p. 65.

Page 117. (1) *Sir* Walter Cleave: the introduction of well-known bankers of the late seventeenth century in *Rox.* and *Col. Jack* suggests the possibility that here too D. may have been glancing at an actual person. A goldsmith named Edward Cleave was in partnership with John Cox at the Peacock and Feathers in Cornhill between 1715 and 1720. Lady Mary Wortley Montague lost money by them when they went bankrupt in late 1720, and D. may have Cox and Cleave in mind when he speaks of the Sun-Fire directors entrusting 'their whole Darby in the hands of a brace of bankrupts' (F. G. Hilton Price, *Handbook of London Bankers* (1891),

p. 48; Montague, *Comp. Lett.*, ed. Robert M. Halsband (1966), ii. 2; *Coll. Misc. Lett.*, ii. 105). D. probably refers to Cox and Cleave in *App. Jour.* for 17 Sept. and 1 Oct. 1720 (Lee, ii. 281, 285–6). But the Christian names do not correspond, and I know of no other Defoean allusion to or connection with anyone named Cleave, so the association must remain tenuous and doubtful.

(2) *satisfied the Parish Officers*: the poor laws (see *supra*, p. 8 n. 3; *infra*, p. 163 nn. 1 & 3) obliged the parish to provide for bastards born within its bounds. A pregnant pauper who was not a settled inhabitant could be returned to her place of legal settlement, or simply (and often brutally) smuggled into another parish when the time of her confinement drew near. But anyone who could 'secure' the parish, by paying a few pounds or (as here) by providing character-references, was not further molested. 'The parish officers did everything they could to check the growth of bastardy, a thing which they abhorred, not on moral grounds, but because it was likely to cost the parish money, and so raise the rates' (Marshall, p. 221; cf. pp. 207–24 and *passim*). For legal provisions on these matters see Jacob, *Mod. Just.*, p. 51; *New Law Dict.*, *s.v.* 'Bastard'.

(3) *Travel*: i.e. 'travail', as in second edition. Roxana, incommoded by having 'a Bastard in [her] Belly', can 'get rid of it' only 'by the ordinary Method of Patience, and a hard Travel' (p. 163).

Page 118. *Chariot*: 'a light sort of Coach' (Phillips). 'We think *vehicle*—that blanket term in traffic regulations—the prose word, and *chariot* the poetic', but the reverse was true in the eighteenth century (Tucker, p. 169).

Page 119. *Inclination was not to be resisted*: throughout his writings D. maintains that 'Inclination' is sufficient to overturn 'Principle', 'Moderation', and reason itself; instances are cited in *D. & Spir. Autobiog.*, pp. 75–6, 139–41.

Page 123. *the more the Affection . . . before, the Hatred will be the more in Proportion*: although the idea is commonplace, the reiterated stress on 'hatred' may be an echo of 11 Sam. 13:15, in which Amnon, after violating Tamar, ' . . . hated her exceedingly: so that the hatred wherewith he hated her was greater than the love wherewith he had loved her'. Cf. also *Review*, 13 Apr. 1708, v. 27.

Page 124. *convincing Work*: 'In *Divinity*, the first Degree of Repentance, by which a Penitent is convinced or made apprehensive of the evil Nature of Sin, and of his own Guiltiness' (Phillips, *s.v.* 'Conviction').

Page 126. *frankly*: 'Freely, unrestrictedly' (*OED* 1), or perhaps 'Without . . . reserve' (*OED* 3).

Page 127. *a Goldsmith*: although the Bank of England was founded in

1694, the goldsmiths retained throughout this period their traditional role as the nation's bankers. 'They may very properly be call'd *Banquiers*, rather than *Goldsmiths*, for they keep all the private Cash of the Nation; and in every Shop you will see daily Receipts and Payments made as in a Bank' (Macky, *Journey*, i. 290). In *Ess. upon Proj.*, D. says 'Our Banks are indeed nothing but so many Goldsmiths Shops' (p. 40), and in *The Commentator* he again defines 'The Nature of a Bank' as 'in short a great Goldsmith's Shop, and no other' (No. lxiv, 12 Aug. 1720).

Page 128. (1) *void of Council*: see Deut. 32:28; cf. *Capt. Singleton*, in *Rom. & Narr.*, v. 62.

(2) *have it cried*: give public notice that it is found.

Page 129. *Necessity, not . . . Inclination*: to be contrasted with what the banker's clerk is soon to say of his wife: 'she is a Whore not by Necessity, which is the common Bait of your Sex, but by Inclination, and for the sake of the Vice' (p. 135); and compared with D.'s statement in *The True-Born Englishman* (1701) that Englishwomen are ' . . . Modester than other Nations are:/For where the Vice prevails, the great Temptation/Is want of Money, more than Inclination' (*True Coll.*, p. 20; cf. also *Review*, 24 Oct. 1704, i. 283.)

Page 130. *Talleys*: 'Tally, a cleft piece of Wood, to score up an Account upon by Notches; particularly such as is given by the Officers of the Exchequer, to those that pay Money there upon Loans, &c.' (Phillips).

Page 136. (1) *you may Cry her down*: i.e., have it proclaimed publicly, as through a notice in the *Gazette*, that you will no longer be responsible for any debts she contracts. D. often uses the phrase figuratively, as in *Conj. Lewd.*, p. 16.

(2) [divorce] *very tedious and expensive*: in *App. Jour.* for 12 Dec. 1724, an unhappy husband wishes Parliament would pass a law 'To make the Proofs of Adultery in Man, or Woman more certain and possible' (Lee, iii. 342); difficulties on this point—which was practically the sole basis for divorce—increased the time and expense required to obtain a divorce decree in the ecclesiastical court. See *Col. Jack*, p. 198, and *infra*, p. 170 n.

Page 140. *a Contract . . . to Marry him as soon as the Divorce was obtain'd*: contracts contingent on divorce from (or the death of) the superfluous spouse were frequently condemned in seventeenth-century casuistical manuals: see Robert Sanderson, 'The Case of Unlawful Love', *Works*, ed. Wm. Jacobson (1854), v. 88–103; cf. *Ath. Merc.*, vi, xxv. 6–8.

Page 142. (1) *all* Roman Catholicks: John Macky says of Lancashire that there are 'more of the *Roman* Catholick Religion in this County, than in any three others in *England*' (*Journey*, ii. 144). In Lancashire Col. Jack is married by a disguised '*Romish* Priest in Orders', of whom 'there are many in that Part of the Country' (p. 248). Because of their Jacobite sympathies, the Lancashire Catholics were objects of official anxiety and popular hostility during and after the Jacobite rising of 1715; see Edward Baines, *History of the County Palatine and Duchy of Lancaster* (1836), ii. 67.

(2) *little, but the prejudice of Education in all the Differences . . . about Religion*: cf. *The Protestant Jesuite Unmask'd* (1704), p. 48: 'every one is fond of the *Religion* they were bred in. *Custom* has more *Elegance* [qu. 'eloquence'?] than all the Force of *Reason*'. Cf. Locke, *Essay concerning Human Understanding*, IV, xv. 6; IV, xx. 17–8 (ed. Alexander C. Fraser (1959), ii. 367–8, 456–9).

(3) *a safe Card at home*: '*a sure Card*, a trusty Tool, or Confiding Man' (*New Dict. Cant. Crew*); but perhaps in the less cynical sense of a reliable expedient.

Page 143. (1) *the* Irishman: the Irish fortune-hunter appears frequently in the literature of the period, more often as a comic type than as a serious figure; see *The Spectator*, Nos. 282 and 311 (23 Jan., 26 Feb. 1712; ii. 598, iii. 125); Erasmus Jones, *A Trip Through London*, 2nd edn. (1728), p. 26. In *Coll. Misc. Lett.*, a fortune-hunter is described as 'the Spawn of a neighbouring Isle, noted for having great Estates abroad and none at Home' (ii. 119).

(2) *as effectually as a Church of* England *Parson*: in the *Far. Adv.*, a marriage performed by a priest is held to be 'as authentic and valid . . . as if they were married by one of our own clergymen', and in the *Review* marriage is judged 'not at all the less valid for being perform'd by a Priest of the Church of *Rome*' (*Rom. & Narr.*, ii. 127–8; *Review, Supp.* (Jan. 1705), 7–8 (misnumbered 6–7)). Giles Jacob reports that such marriages 'are deemed to have the Effects of a legal Marriage in some instances', although certain legal privileges are only obtained through C. of E. marriages, and persons defined by statute as 'Popish Recusants convict' are penalized for being '*married* otherwise than according to the Orders of the Church of England, by a Minister lawfully authorized, and in some open *Church*' (*New Law Dict.*; cf. *Chron. Diary* (1720), p. 12). According to Lecky, a later law provided that 'every marriage celebrated by a Catholic priest between a Catholic and a Protestant should be null, and that the priest who officiated should be hung' (*Hist. of Eng. in 18th C.* (1878), i. 313), but the Jacobite scares provoked no such severities under George I.

Page 144. *an Inn in the West Street, not far from the Cathedral*: Mrs. Elizabeth Berry, City Archivist of Chester, has kindly suggested to me that the phrase 'West Street' refers to Watergate Street, which was the main westward street in the city, and that the inn in question was the Yacht Inn, which until recently stood on the south side of Watergate Street adjoining Nicholas Street. The account of Chester in the *Tour* suggests that D. had been there at least twice, once about the year 1690, and again not long before the composition of the *Tour* (ii. 69–71). In a letter to Harley he reports that he was there on 12 Sept. 1705 (*Letters*, p. 112).

Page 147. the unjust Charge of being concern'd in deceiving you: Moll's defence rests on the assumption that words alone deceive, and that there is no such thing as a tacit lie. On other occasions D. challenges this assumption: see *Ser. Refl.*, in *Rom. & Narr.*, iii. 48 f.; *Comp. Eng. Trades.*, pp. 241–8; *Little Review*, v. 63. On these questions cf. also Jeremy Taylor, *Ductor Dubitantium*, in *Whole Works*, x. 128–30, 106–10; Richard Baxter, *Christian Directory*, in *Practical Works*, ed. William Orme (1830), ii. 512.

Page 150. (1) a Town called Manchester: 'It may with propriety be stiled the greatest mere village in England; for it is not so much as a town strictly speaking, the highest magistrate being a constable or headborough; yet it is more populous than York, Norwich, or most cities in England . . . for the people here . . . are reckoned at no less than fifty thousand' (*Voy. Don Man. Gon.*, p. 40). Stukeley's *Itinerarium Curiosum* of 1724 also describes Manchester as 'the largest, most rich, populous, and busy village in England' (quoted in Edward Baines, *Hist. of the County Palatine and Duchy of Lancaster* (1836), ii. 292).

(2) *six Pound a Year*: John Aikin speaks of the 'economy in living' at Manchester early in the century (*A Description of the Country . . . round Manchester* (1795), pp. 182, 187). The level of prices was presumably similar at Lancaster; in 1688–90, William Stout boarded there for £5 *p.a.*; in 1730 board and lodging cost him £12 *p.a.* (*Autobiography*, ed. J. D. Marshall, Chetham Society *Remains*, 3rd ser., Vol. xiv (1967), pp. 90, 97, 205).

Page 151. riffle: 'pillage or rob' (*OED*).

Page 152. a Husbands leave: i.e. went to sleep; like the more familiar 'French leave', proverbial for unceremonious parting.

Page 154. heard me very plain . . . about 12 Miles off: Rodney M. Baine argues that 'for Defoe and for many of his readers the incident evidently suggested angelic concern for Moll, concern based upon angelic foresight of the life in store for her after her separation from her Jemy', and cites Aubrey, Turner, Mather, and Beaumont as providing 'examples of communion with the invisible world by means of voices' (*D.D. and the Supernatural* (1968), pp. 25–6). Moll's own later ascription of a 'blessed hint' to 'some kind Spirit' (*infra*, p. 203) would seem to support the view that good spirits, acting as agents of Providence, are concerned for her welfare. Yet John Wilkins, in his influential *Mercury: The Secret and Swift Messenger* (1641), cites 'a relation in *Joach. Camerarius*, of some that have heard their friends speaking to them distinctly, when they have been many miles asunder', and concludes that 'this hee [Camerarius] justly refers to Diabolicall Magick, and the illusion of spirits' (p. 132).

Page 160. *entertain'd in that Circumstance without Security*: see *infra*, p. 163 n. 3. Elizabethan and Jacobean statutes that were still in force labelled bastardy '*a great Dishonour to almighty God*', '*an Offence against God's Law and Man's Law*', which gave '*evil Example, and encouragement of Lewd Life*'; yet the full penal provisions of these statutes came to bear only '*If the Bastard is likely to prove chargeable to the Parish*'. 'With submission, what if it is not?' asks Jeremy Collier. 'Is Wealth a Privilege for Lewdness? and, must no body be punish'd but those who have no Money in their Pocket?' (*Essays Upon Several Moral Subjects, Part III* (1705), p. 134). Moll's story bears out the fact that wealth clearly *was* 'a Privilege for Lewdness'.

Page 162. *Mother Midnight*: a cant name for midwives: see *infra*, p. 213 n. 2, '*Midwife and Procuress*'.

Page 163. (1) *the Parish Impertinences usual in such Cases*: see *supra* p. 117 n. 2. 'No sooner does any woman . . . come to dwell or lodge any where about this town, that is but suspected to be with child, but notice is carried . . . to the overseers of the poor, who thereupon immediately come in a body to make an enquiry of, who begot it? when? how? where? mixing such odious lewdnesses with their pretended authority, while the affrighted, fainting, poor creature, half dead with shame, fear, and anger, is at once become their pastime and their prisoner' (*Orig. & Gen. Lett.*, i. 48; the entire letter is a moving account of the fate of unwed mothers and their offspring at this time (46–54)). Cf. also George, p. 217, and Sidney and Beatrice Webb, *English Local Government: English Poor Law Hist.*: *Part I. The Old Poor Law* (1927), p. 342.

(2) *my Profession is a Midwife*: cf. '*Midwife and Procuress*', *infra*, p. 213 n. 2. To be 'secur'd from the Mercenary Rage of a parcel of *Parish Cormorants*', the pregnant unwed heroine of a tale by Ned Ward similarly entrusts herself to a midwife of 'Hypocritical Eloquence and Puritanical Deportment'; see *The Rise and Fall of Madam Coming-Sir: Or, An Unfortunate Slip from the Tavern Bar into the Surgeons Powdering Tub* (1703), p. 15.

(3) *Security to the Parish*: Richard Kilburn's *Choice Presidents upon all Acts of Parliament* (1700) offers samples of 'A Bond for the Discharge of a Parish from the Charge of A Bastard-Child', and 'A release (from the Overseers of the Poor) to one that paid five pounds to be freed from keeping a Bastard-Child' (pp. 42–3). In *Parochial Tyranny* [1727], D. attacks the 'hellish Commerce' of 'those Church-Wardens and Vestries who lump it with Harlots and Whore-mongers, and take Bastards from off their

Hands at so much *per* Head' at 'from two Guineas to five, according to the Circumstances' (p. 19). See also 'Nicholas Boggle's' letter to *Mist's Jour.*, 29 Mar. 1720 (Lee, iii. 214–5).

Page 165. *very reasonable in her Demands*: elsewhere in D.'s fiction, lyings-in tend to be considerably more expensive: cf. *Rox.*, p. 77, *Col. Jack*, pp. 195–6. As Mother Midnight's three bills indicate, the cost of lying in varied greatly according to social class or pretensions, and like nearly everything else, was cheaper in the country than in London: cf. *Blundell's Diary and Letter Book, 1702–1728*, ed. Margaret Blundell (1952), p. 26; Dorothy Marshall, *English Poor*, p. 210.

Page 167. Drury-Lane *Breeding*: Drury-Lane was notorious for its brothels: see *App. Jour.*, 4 Dec. 1725 (Lee, iii. 447); cf. also George, p. 83.

Page 168. (1) *too much Encouragement to the Vice, to let the World see, what easie Measures were here taken*: ironically, D. was to anticipate the same objection to the establishment of a foundling hospital: 'methinks, I hear some oversqueamish Ladies cry, *what would this Fellow be at? would not he set up a Nursery for Lewdness, and encourage Fornication? who would be afraid of sinning, if they can so easily get rid of their Bastards? we shall soon be over-run with* Foundlings *when there is such Encouragement given to* Whoredom' (*Aug. Triumph.*, p. 14).

(2) *sav'd the Life . . . of many a Woman, who . . . would other wise . . . bring themselves to the Gallows*: in *Aug. Triumph.*, D. says 'merciless Mothers' also manage to 'escape the Vengeance due to shedders of Innocent Blood' by hiring 'pretended Midwives, who . . . bring them off for three or four Guineas . . . [by] swearing the Child was not at its full Growth, for which they have a hidden Reserve, that is to say, the Child was not at Man's or Woman's Growth' (p. 9).

Page 169. *I abhorr'd the Thoughts of* [abortion]: on abortion, see *Review*, iii. *Supp.* (Jan. 1705), 14–5; *Conj. Lewd.*, Chap. 5; *Ath. Merc.*, v, *Supp.*, 12; viii, iv. 1; viii, xx. 6; xvi, xiii. 1; xvii, xxviii. 4. Cf. also Hall, *Resolutions*, pp. 300–3, and Thomas Wood, 'Seventeenth-century Moralists and the Marital Relationship', *Trivium*, i 78–80.

Page 170. *Scruples at the Lawfulness of his Marrying again*: divines had deplored 'the libertie, that in these our daies many doe take, of divorcing their wiues for adulterie and marying of others' (Edm. Bunny, *Of Divorce for Advlterie, and Marrying Againe* (1610), Pref., sig. **2; a copy listed in the Defoe/Farewell library catalogue). The 107th Canon of the C. of E. prohibits such remarriages, and negative judgements—usually founded on Matt. 5:32—are common throughout the period; cf. *Ath. Merc.*, i, iv. 2. On the other hand, the Westminster Assembly of Divines had found it 'lawful for the innocent party to sue out a divorce and, after

the divorce, to marry another, as if the offending party were dead'
(*Confession of Faith* (1643), Chap. XXIV. Par. V (Edinburgh, 1877), pp.
103–4). Richard Baxter similarly maintains that 'They that are released by
divorce upon the other's adultery, &c. may marry again' (*Christian
Directory*, in *Practical Works*, iv. 167); and Wm. Hawkins points out that
although 'those who are divorced only *a Mensa & Thoro*' are technically
separated, not fully divorced, 'such separations are taken for Divorces in
common understanding'; see *supra*, p. 136 n. 2.

Page 172. *gave me free Liberty to Marry again*: in *The Christian Directory*,
Richard Baxter says 'if all should have leave to marry others when they
consent to part, it would bring utter confusion, and it would encourage
wicked men to abuse their wives, till they forced them to consent. Therefore some must bear the trouble which their folly hath brought on themselves, rather than the common order should be confounded' (*Practical
Works*, iv. 159). D. makes a similar point in *Far. Adv.* (*Rom. & Narr.*, ii.
151).

Page 173. (1) *no Marriage, but a cheat on both Sides*: whether such deception invalidates a marriage contract had been discussed by various
seventeenth-century casuists; William Perkins is typical in arguing that
'though the deceit be very offensiue to the party deluded, & vpon his
complaint ought in equity to be punished by the Magistrates; yet it is not
of force to break the contract' (*Workes* (1616–18), ii. 683–4); cf. *Ath.
Merc.*, xiv, xxvi. 1. For more light-hearted discussions of this issue, see
also Ben Jonson's *Epicoene, or the Silent Woman*, V, iii; *Spectator*, No. 41
(17 Apr. 1711), i. 173f.

(2) *the Obligation was mutually discharg'd*: for refutations of the plea,
'*Why shou'd not a mutual Consent dissolve the Marriage Contract, since it
is the Essence, or of the Essence of it, and that which makes has power to
unmake in all other Contracts*', see *Ath. Merc.*, iv, ii. 6, and *Conj. Lewd.*,
p. 118.

(3) *Arguments . . . at the tip of her Tongue*: for such arguments, see
Locke's *Two Treatises of Government*, 11, §81, ed. Peter Laslett (1967), p.
339; *The Counseller's Plea for the Divorce of Sir G. D. and Mrs. F.* (1715),
pp. 7–9; and '*Mr. Milton's Arguments*', recapitulated in *App. Jour.* for
24 Apr. 1725 (Lee, iii. 379–80; cf. also iii. 355–6). Such arguments are
common in Restoration poetry and drama: see *e.g.* 'The Vision', ll. 122–4,
in *The Poetical Works of John Sheffield, Duke of Buckingham* (Edinburgh,
1780), p. 48.

(4) *murther'd, or starv'd by Neglect and Ill-usuage*: a parliamentary
committee investigating the problem in 1716 reported that 'a great many
parish Infants, and exposed Bastard Children, are inhumanly suffered to
die by the Barbarity of Nurses, especially Parish Nurses, who are a sort of
People void of Commiseration or Religion, hired by the Churchwardens

to take off a Burden from the Parish at the cheapest and easiest Rates they can; and these know the manner of doing it effectively as by the burial Books may evidently appear' (*House of Commons Journals*, xviii. 396 (8 Mar. 1716); see Marshall, p. 99). On 28 Feb. 1718 '*Eleanor Gallimore*, a Parish Nurse, was indicted for the Murder of an Infant of two Months old, by starving it; but she was acquitted' (*Chron. Diary* (1718), p.9). On 12 Sept. 1718 the same woman was 'indicted for the Murder of one of her Nurse-Children, by beating it with a Mop-Stick upon the Head, stamping upon it, &c., but she was acquitted' (ibid., p. 33). Cf. also *Rox.*, pp. 79–80; *Aug. Triumph.*, p. 10; *Spectator*, No. 246 (12 Dec. 1711), ii. 457; R. H. Nichols and F. A. Wray, *The Hist. of the Foundling Hospital* (1935), p. 16.

Page 174. *intentional Murther*: for the principle that '*the Intention of Murther is equally Criminal in the Eyes of God with the Act it self*', see *A New Test of the Church of England's Loyalty* (1702), in *True Coll.*, p. 405; *Far. Adv.*, in *Rom. & Narr.*, ii. 69; *Ser. Refl.*, in *Rom. & Narr.*, iii. 8, 20; *Rox.*, p. 273; *App. Jour.*, 11 Mar. and 24 June 1721 (Lee, ii. 350, 395).

Page 175. *their Credit depends upon the Child's Life*: Mother Midnight's argument, that the hired nurses' concern for their professional reputation is a stronger motive for taking good care of their charges than maternal affection or duty, echoes a doctrine propounded by several of D.'s other cynical personae. A character in *Capt. Singleton* observes that 'I would as *Evening Post*, 'Meeting House' argues that '*'Tis safer to trust those whose* principles binds himself ' (*Rom. & Narr.*, vi. 228); and in the *Whitehall Evening Post*, 'Meeting House' argues that '*'Tis safer to trust those whose Interest binds them to be honest*, than those *whose Principle binds them*, because *there are always in the World more Knaves than Fools*' (30 Dec. 1718; Lee, ii. 86).

Page 177. *Hertford, or thereabouts*: according to a satire of 1722, parish officers dispose of the chargeable children of the poor by packing them off 'To *Enfield*, or to *Hartford* Town,/Where, in a little time, in course,/ They're choak'd with Filth, or starv'd at Nurse' ([Ned Ward], *The Parish Gutt'lers: Or, The Humours of a Select Vestry*, p. 50).

Page 178. (1) *I had no Ground for it at all . . . it was no ill-grounded Thought*: the second edition eliminates the contradiction by deleting the latter phrase (see textual note); but there are other signs in the same paragraph that D. may be rapidly improvising and not quite sure of Moll's next move: *e.g.* Moll says 'once I was resolv'd to take the Stage Coach' etc., as if she later decided not to, whereas this is exactly what she does.

   (2) *Stone in* Cheshire, *I think it is*: actually in Staffs.; according to *Brit. Dep.*, Stone was on the main London-Chester road, roughly a dozen miles from Cheshire.

Page 179. (1) *oblig'd to lye still a* Sunday: cf. Stat. 29 *Car*. II. *c*. 7 (1677), 'For the better observation and keeping holy the Lords day', which obliged travellers to obtain warrants signed by a J.P. Most provisions of the Sunday Observance Act remained in effect until 1871, but were not regularly enforced; cf. Joan Parkes, *Travel in England in the Seventeenth Century* (1925), pp. 36–7.

(2) *a Place call'd* Brickill: in *J.P.Y.*, the narrator says that his brother fled from the plague 'into *Buckinghamshire*, or *Bedfordshire*, to a Retreat he had found out there for his Family' (p. 13); F. Bastian argues convincingly that this brother would have been D.'s own father, and suggests very plausibly that this retreat was at Little Brickhill, the first village reached on passing from Bedfordshire into Buckinghamshire on the great post road from London to Chester. See 'Defoe's *Journal of the Plague Year* Reconsidered', *RES*, n.s. xvi (1965), 159–60.

Page 180. Non Compos Mentis: '(*Lat. i.e.* that is not in his right Wits.) The term in Common Law signifies, . . . A Lunatick, that is sometimes sensible, and sometimes not' (Phillips).

Page 181. *Chagreen Case*: made of 'a sort of rough-grained Leather' (Phillips); the jeweller in *Rox*. also carries diamonds in 'a shagreen Case' (p. 51).

Page 182. *a felicity . . . to Mankind . . . that they cannot see into the Hearts of one another*: cf. *App. Jour.*, 31 Aug. 1723: 'How happy . . . is it for the greatest Part of Mankind, that Nature has made no Glass Beehives to the Heart; that it is not in Man to know what is in Man! What a Sink of Wickedness! What a Hell of Treachery and Falshood would be every Day the Subject of our Speculations! . . . Blessed Fate of Men! How happy are we, that we see no more than the Outsides of one another! And where is the Man who could bear an Inspection into the Inside of his Soul?' (Lee, iii. 179).

Page 183. *he hop'd it was no Clandestine Business*: cf. the clergyman's fears, two paragraphs later, that Moll may be 'some young Girl stolen from her Parents'. In response to the virtual kidnapping of young ladies for the sake of their fortunes, Parliament had passed severe laws against clandestine marriages, which made it a felony to assist in abducting, concealing, or marrying minors without consent of their fathers (29 *Car*. 2). We are told that Mother Midnight 'very narrowly . . . escap'd the Gallows' for her part in such an escapade (*infra*, p. 197), and in *G.L.S.C.*, D. says that one '*She-Devil*' convicted of this crime has been 'deservedly brought to the Gallows' (p. 285).

Page 184. (1) *not tyed by the Canons to Marry no where but in the Church* [or to] *the time of Day*: in fact, both places and times were carefully prescribed in the canons of the Church of England, but exceptions were made for people of quality in the statute 7 & 8 *W*. 3. *c*. 35, 'for enforcing Licences and Banns, places and times of Marriage'.

(2) *it was all Grimace*: 'Hypocrisy, Dissimulation, Shew' (Phillips); cf. *Coll. Misc. Lett.*, ii. 86; *Rox.*, p. 213.

(3) *Suit of Knots*: 'a set of gaily-coloured ribbon bows . . . forming an additional decoration to the gown' (Cunnington, p. 143).

(4) *it was a Lace-making Town*: in *Comp. Eng. Trades*. (p. 332), D. cites Stony-Stratford as the source of English lace; presumably Little Brickhill, less than ten miles away, was part of the same lacemaking district.

(5) *Bone-lace*: so called 'because the thread is wound about with trotter bones, which are clean, white and heavy, and with twisting these various ways, they form divers sorts of laces' (*C.I.H.T.*, ii. 404–5). Elsewhere the manufacture of bone-lace is said to have 'employed above a hundred thousand poor People in the Country' (*Coll. Misc. Lett.*, i. 84). Cf. *infra*, p. 210 n. 1.

(6) *the Musick . . . under our Window*: the sixth plate in Hogarth's series, 'Industry and Idleness', shows a band of musicians—mainly drummers—playing outside Francis Goodchild's house the morning after his marriage; by the eighteenth century this long-standing custom (known as 'charivari') had become more mercenary than honorary, and 'a general nuisance' (John Trusler, *Hogarth Moralized* (1768), pp. 83–4).

Page 185. *my Blood run Chill in my Veins*: D.'s favorite formula for expressing alarm or horror: see *Due Prep.*, *Rom. & Narr.*, xv. 105, 123; *Far. Adv.*, *Rom. & Narr.*, ii. 200; *Ser. Refl.*, *Rom. & Narr.*, iii. 243; *Fam. Instr.* ii. 106, 156; *Rel. Court.*, p. 94; *Rox.*, p. 270; cf. *infra*, pp. 255, 273.

Page 186. (1) *Hue and Cry*: '(in Common-Law) a Pursuit of one having committed Felony on the High-Way by describing the Party, and giving Notice to several Constables, from one Town to another, till the Offender be taken, or at least pursu'd to the Sea-side' (Phillips).

(2) *the Mob Gentry*: *OED*, citing this example, glosses 'Mob' as 'simple'; but 'Gentry' itself may be playful or contemptuous, in which case 'Mob' is probably being used in its ordinary sense of tumultuous, disorderly; the phrase as a whole would thus tend to reinforce the contrast between Moll's cool 'Assurance' and the 'Uproar' of people acting 'as if they had been out of their Wits'—and therefore easily duped.

Page 188. (1) *Temptations . . . not in the Power of Human Nature to resist*: 'some Distresses . . . Human Nature is not quallify'd to bear. . . . The honestest Man in the World will eat his Neighbours Loaf if it be in his Cupboard, rather than perish' (*Review*, 8 Feb. 1709, v. 543–4); 'to be reduc'd to Necessity is to be wicked; for Necessity is not only the Temptation, but is such a Temptation as human Nature is not empower'd to resist' (*Col. Jack*, p. 161); cf. *Comp. Eng. Trades.*, ii. 193; *App. Jour.*, 16 June 1722 (Lee, iii. 16–7); and esp. *Ser. Refl.*, in *Rom. & Narr.*, iii. 35, 41, 55.

(2) *Covetousness is the Root of all Evil*: cf. 1 Tim. 6:10; *App. Jour.*, 11 Mar. 1721 (Lee, ii. 348).

Page 189. (1) *an Equipage*: a French term, says the *Gloss. Anglic. Nova*, 'frequently used amongst us for a Coach and good Number of Footmen'.

(2) *to sink under Trouble is to double the Weight*: cf. *infra*, p. 276, 'to sink under the Weight, was but to encrease the Weight'. In *Far. Adv.*, a Spaniard tells Crusoe that grief is 'the most senseless insignificant passion in the world' since it looks to the past instead of the future; he clinches his argument with the proverb, 'In trouble to be troubled,/Is to have your trouble doubled' (*Rom. & Narr.*, ii. 108; cf. also *Capt. Singleton*, in *Rom. & Narr.*, vi. 14; *The Commentator*, No. xxiii, 18 Mar. 1720; *Rel. Court.*, p. 118).

(3) *Melancholy and Disconsolate . . . Lethargick, and died*: in the *Review* for 17 May 1712, D. says 'I have not more Contemptible Thoughts of a Dog, a Bear, or any Brute, than I have of a Man, whom I see . . . soon *dejected*'; such a man 'is the most Soul-less, dispirited Thing in the World, and is fit for nothing but to despair, and perhaps, at last, die for fear of Death' (viii. 722); cf. *Comp. Eng. Trades.*, ii. 183–4, and contrast D.'s admiration for William III: '*Antaeus* like, from every Fall he rose,/ Strengthen'd with double Vigour to oppose' (*The Mock Mourners*, in *True Coll.*, p. 54).

Page 190. *Vapours*: 'depression of spirits, hypochondria, hysteria, or other nervous disorder' (*OED*, citing *Rob. Cru.*).

Page 191. (1) *the wise Man's Prayer*: see Prov. 30:9. D. quotes or alludes to this text in the *Review*, iii. 110 (5 Mar. 1706); *Rob. Cru.*, in *Rom. & Narr.*, i. 3; *Ser. Refl.*, in *Rom. & Narr.*, iii. 33; *Col. Jack*, p. 163; *Comp. Eng. Gent.*, pp. 102–3; *Coll. of Misc. Lett.*, ii. 14. Other contemporary discussions of this theme are cited in *Defoe & Spir. Autobiog.*, p. 78 n.

(2) Leadenhall-street: see *infra*, p. 192 n. 1.

(3) *the Devil . . . laid the Snare . . . prompted me*: D. believed that Satan 'deludes and betrays mankind' through his 'art or capacity of insinuation, suggestion, accusation, &c.' (*Pol. Hist. Dev.*, p. 49). 'But 'tis plain', D. elsewhere remarks, 'his power is not so great as we imagine; he can only prompt to the crime—he cannot force us to commit it; so that if we sin it is all our own, the devil has only to be charged with the art of insinuation'. 'The main tempter', D. declares, is 'our own corrupt, debauched inclination, which is the first moving agent'; the devil's knack is 'to procure ensnaring things, and lay them in the way of the man whom he finds so easily to be ensnared', so that he 'ensnare[s] us by the help

of our corrupt affections' (*Ser. Refl.*, in *Rom. & Narr.*, iii. 266, 248).

Page 192. (1) Leadenhall-street . . . *a street that went through into* Fenchurch-street: Strype describes Leadenhall Street as 'a Place of great Trade, well inhabited, and a great Through-fare'; Fenchurch Street was also 'a Street of good account, being large, well built and inhabited by Merchants and others'; among the streets connecting them he mentions Lime Street and Billiter Lane (ii. 82; ii. 163; see map, ii. 83).

(2) *into* Thames-street *near* Billinsgate: the distance Moll has run is roughly half a mile: see (for the possible 'ways and turnings') Strype's maps of Lime Street, Langborne, and Billingsgate wards (ii. 83, 151, 165).

(3) *Try'd for my Life*: 10 & 11 *W.* 3, *c.* 23 (1699), known as the Shoplifting Act, declared that any theft from a shop, warehouse, coach-house or stable 'to the value of 5*s*., tho' no Body be therein, or there is no actual Breaking, is *Felony* excluded Clergy' (Jacob, *New Law Dict.*, s.v. 'felony'). 12 *Ann. c.* 7 (1713) extended these provisions to 'any *Dwelling House*, or *Out-House* thereto belonging' (Wood, *Institute*, p. 375). On the development of the law of larceny, see Radzinowicz, pp. 41–9.

Page 194. (1) *a pav'd Alley that goes* [from Aldersgate Street] *into* Bartholomew Close: Moll could have taken either of two passages, 'of which one is through *Northumberland Alley*, and the other through *Half Moon Alley*' (Strype, iii. 284; cf. map, iii. 230).

(2) Chick-lane . . . Field-lane . . . Holbourn-bridge: on this district, 'one of the best-situated to be a refuge for evil-doers', see George, p. 82; Strype, iii. 283. Until the area was razed during construction of Holborn Viaduct in the 1860s, Field Lane remained 'one of the most disreputable thoroughfares in London' (Wheatley, ii. 39).

(3) *second Sally into the World*: Alan D. McKillop has noted a reprise of this scene in D.'s *E.H.R.A.*, pp. 207–9; see *Early Masters of Eng. Fict.* (1956), p. 222 n. 39. For a still closer analogue, cf. *Pol. Hist. Dev.*, pp. 361–2. A contemporary newspaper advertisement describes 'A Child about 6 Years Old being led away by a Fat Squat Wench, . . . at 5 of the Clock in the Evening, from Brook Street in Ratcliffe to Golden Lane without Cripplegate, being robbed of a Gold Chain marked A. H. and a Silver Thimble and Purse', and offers a reward to anyone who 'can discover the wench' (quoted in Ashton, p. 418).

Page 195. Lombard-street . . . Three King Court: Strype says Lombard Street 'is throughout graced with good and lofty Buildings, amongst which are many that surpass those in other Streets, and generally is inhabited by Goldsmiths, Bankers, Mercers, and other eminent Tradesmen' (ii. 162); for Three Kings Court, see ii. 163, and map, ii. 151.

Page 196. *Lustring Silk*: lustring, 'A glossy silk fabric' (*OED*); 'A fine non-lustrous Taffeta' (Cunnington, p. 409).

Page 199. *a silver Tankard, things much in use in publick Houses at that time*: Ashton says of silver plate that 'To such an extent did its use obtain, that taverns were ordered not to have silver tankards, the temptation to steal them being so great' (p. 140). Cf. Ernest Bernbaum, *The Mary Carleton Narratives 1663–1673* (1914), p. 57.

Page 201. *as dexterous as* . . . Moll Cut-Purse . . . *tho'* . . . *not half so Handsome*: the alias of Mary Frith (1584?–1659), who 'gained great notoriety as a bully, pickpurse, fortune-teller, receiver, and forger' (*D.N.B.*). As to her looks, a spinster in *App. Jour.* says 'I have seen her Picture, an Original of Sir *Peter Lely's*, and I can Vouch she was a very comely Jade' (6 Apr. 1723; Lee, iii. 127).

Page 203. (1) *no doubt from some kind Spirit, if such there be* . . . *the blessed hint from whatsoever hand it came*: see *supra*, p. 154 n. These passages do not establish that Moll (or D.) believes in the actual existence of 'angelic concern' for her; both passages are qualified and hypothetical, specimens of a recurrent interest rather than proofs of an abiding conviction.

(2) *as Poverty brought me into the Mire, so Avarice kept me in*: the connection between poverty and avarice is implicit in the careers of several of D.'s other heroes and heroines, notably Col. Jack and Roxana. On 'the Fear of Want' leading to avarice, see *Spectator*, No. 55 (3 May 1711), i. 232. With the reason-avarice opposition in the following sentence, cf. *The Commentator*, No. xlvi (10 June 1720).

(3) *a Linnen-Draper in* Cheapside: Strype calls Cheapside 'a very stately spacious Street, adorned with lofty Buildings; well inhabited by Goldsmiths, Linnen Drapers, Haberdashers, and other great Dealers' (iii. 49; cf. map, iii. 27).

(4) *snap'd* . . . *seiz'd*: snap, 'to catch, capture, or seize quickly, suddenly, or by surprise' (*OED*, citing *Capt. Singleton*).

Page 204. (1) *my Measure was not yet fill'd up*: probably an echo of Matt. 23:32; cf. *Rox.*, p. 159, 'my Measure of Wickedness was not yet full'; *The Cartoucheans in France*, in *Rom. & Narr.*, xvi. 95; *G.L.S.C.*, Pref., p. 1.

(2) *having the Brand of an old Offender, was Executed*: on 'benefit of clergy', see *supra*, p. 86 n. 6. 'The effect was that the criminal always carried with him in his burnt hand the register of his previous conviction, and could not possibly evade the law which debarred him from enjoying the privilege a second time' (Luke O. Pike, *Hist. of Crime in England* (1873–6), ii. 281).

(3) *what they call a Circuit Pardon*: I have not found the term elsewhere, but in *Mist's Jour.* for 28 Dec. 1717, D. speaks of 'Court Pardons, Acts of Clemency, and the like', and notes that 'general Pardons are often pass'd to deliver Criminals of the worst kinds' (Lee, ii. 11; cf. *App. Jour.*, 5 Aug. 1721, Lee, ii. 412). D.'s MS. may have read 'Ct.', which the compositor

expanded to 'Circuit' rather than 'Court'.

Page 205. *away comes I with . . . the Bundle*: see D.'s description of a fire in *The Commentator*, No. xii (8 Feb. 1720): 'some in the Croud . . . had nothing to lose, and under a Pretence of assisting their Neighbours, got into their Houses to Pillage and Plunder'. Cf. also *Review*, i [ix], 105 (31 Jan. 1713).

Page 206. (1) *Engines playing*: according to Thomas Fuller, the fire engine was introduced to England in the reign of James I (*Hist. of the Worthies of England* (1662), p. 191), but it does not seem to have performed well in 1666, and D. reports in 1697 that 'After the Fire of *London*, the Contrivance of an Engine to Quench Fires, was a Project the Author was said to get well by, and we have found to be very useful' (*Ess. upon Proj.*, p. 25).

(2) *burying Rings*: rings customarily presented at funerals as mementos of the deceased; see Ashton, pp. 257–60, and Appendix.

Page 208. *a Pardon at the Expence of her Friends*: 'if any Person out of Prison, having committed any *Robbery*, discovers two or more *Robbers*, so as they are convicted, he shall be entitled to a Pardon. 4 *W.* & *M. c.* 8. And . . . by 5 *Annae c.* 31, *sect.* 7 . . . every Person who shall be guilty of Burglary, or of the felonious breaking and entering any House in the Day-time, and after shall discover two who shall have committed such Burglary or Felony, so as they be convict, *&c.* shall have 40*l.* and be entitled to a Pardon' (Wood, *Institute*, p. 662).

Page 209. *Scouring*: 'beating, drubbing, or chastising' (*OED*, citing *Mem. of a Cavalier*).

Page 210. (1) *Flanders-Lace, being then Prohibited*: it was prohibited throughout this period ('then' was omitted in the second edition): among the relevant acts are 13 & 14 *Car.* 2. *c.* 13; 9 & 10 *W.* 3. *c.* 9; 11 & 12 *W.* 3. *c.* 2. 'Altho' of long time it has been prohibited, yet being of small bulk, and much in fashion, it was still brought in, notwithstanding abundance of seisures' (*C.I.H.T.*, ii. 404–5; for the thriving trade in smuggled lace, cf. *Voy. Don Man. Gon.*, pp. 92, 95).

(2) *to bring me to a certainty*: 14 *Car.* 2. *c.* 13, 'An Act prohibiting the Importation of Foreign Bonelace', provided a penalty of £100 and forfeiture of the goods, half of which went to the crown, the other half to the informant 'that shall sue for the same in any of the Kings Courts of Record'. The method agreed on by Moll and the customs official was swifter, surer, and no doubt more lucrative to both. See Jacob, *New Law Dict.*, *s.v.* 'Customs'.

Page 212. *Rage of the Street*: See Gay, *Trivia*, iii, ll. 73–6, p. 80: 'Seiz'd by rough hands, he's dragg'd amid the rout,/ And stretch'd beneath the pump's incessant spout:/ Or plung'd in miry ponds, he gasping lies,/ Mud choaks his mouth, and plaisters o'er his eyes'. Cf. *G.L.S.C.*, p. 122; *Lives of Six Notorious Robbers*, in *Rom. & Narr.*, xvi. 354; *Col. Jack*, p. 19.

Page 213. (1) *a Key to the Clue of a* Pick-pockets *Motions*: the phrase sounds redundant today, but D. may be using 'Clue' not in the sense of 'key' but in its older sense of a thread or coil of yarn: i.e., 'a key to the obscure or tangled course of . . . '

(2) *Midwife and Procuress*: *New Dict. Cant. Crew* defines 'Mother Midnight' as 'a Midwife (often a Bawd)'; in *The Rise and Fall of Madam Coming-Sir* there is 'an *Amphebious Necessary*, between Bawd and Midwife' (p. 15); and Tom Brown ironically laments that 'bawding of late years, which used to be a trade of itself, is now grown scandalous and very much declined, by reason that midwives, like a parcel of encroaching hussies, have engrossed the whole business to themselves, to the starving of experienced old ladies who have spent their days and worn out their beauty in the service of the public' (*Amusements*, p. 445). Mother Midnight's double role has already been hinted at, *supra* p. 162, 'she had another Calling too . . . '

Page 214. *vowed to Impeach me*: 'To Impeach, (*Fr.* Law-Word) to accuse and prosecute for Felony or Treason; especially to charge another as guilty of the same Crime with one's self' (Phillips).

Page 218. (1) *to enter into Recognisances to appear at the Sessions*: 'A bond or obligation, entered into and recorded by a court or magistrate, by which a person engages himself to perform some act . . . (as to appear when called on . . .); also, a sum of money pledged as a surety for such performance and rendered forfeit by neglect of it' (*OED*). Cf. 'forfeit his Recognizance', *infra*. p. 277 n. 2.

(2) Gabriel Spencer: see *infra*, p. 255 n., 'burnt to Death at a Stake'.

Page 219. *he would either come Post, or in the* West-Chester *Coach*: i.e. on horseback, using horses hired from post-houses along the way, or by coach; cf. Joan Parkes, *Travel in England in the Seventeenth Century* (1925), pp. 52–8.

Page 223. *to run a Tick*: 'to go on the Score, or a trust' (*New Dict. Cant. Crew*).

Page 224. (1) Bartholomew *Fair*: a fair held annually in West Smithfield at Bartholomewtide (late August). It dated to the twelfth century, and had long been an important trade fair, but by D.'s time had become 'of little other Use, than for idle Youth, and loose People, to resort to, and to spend their Money in Vanity; and (that which was worse) in Debaucheries, Drunkenness, Whoredom, and in seeing and hearing Things not fit for Christian Eyes and Ears: Many of the Houses and Booths here, serving only to allure Men and Women to such Purposes of Impiety' (Strype, iii.

240). Though under attack by reformers throughout this period (see following notes), the fair survived until 1855.

(2) *the Cloisters*: 'Certainly no place sets mankind more upon a level than Smithfield does. Lords and bellows-menders, beaux and flayers of dead horses, colonels and foot-soldiers, bawds and women of virtue, walk cheek-by-jowl in the cloisters, and jostle one another by candle-light' (Brown, *Amusements*, p. 143). The *Observator* for 21 Aug. 1703 also chronicles the 'strange medley of lewdness' in the Cloisters (quoted in Wheatley, i. 114); and cf. D.'s *Reformation of Manners* (1702), pp. 15–6.

(3) *Raffling Shops*: in the *Review* (7 Sept. 1706, iii. 425–7), D. prints a Lord's Mayor's order 'for Prevention of Disorders, Tumults and Riots in *Bartholomew Fair*, and Places adjacent, especially in the Cloysters', and prohibiting '*Games, Interludes, Rafflings*, or *Musick-meetings*'; but booths for all these purposes continued to thrive despite grand jury indictments and Lord Mayors' orders; cf. *An Elegy on the Author of the True-born English Man*, in *Second Vol.*, pp. 82–3; Narcissus Luttrell, *Brief. Hist. Rel. of State Affairs 1678–1714*, v. 600 (11 Oct. 1705).

(4) *he presented it to me*: Ned Ward says of a Bartholomew Fair raffling shop that 'whatsoever the Gentlemen won, they presented to the Fair Lady that stood next, tho' . . . strangers one to another' (*London-Spy*, p. 270). On raffling in the Cloisters, see also Henry Morley, *Memoirs of Bart. Fair* (1892), pp. 262–3.

Page 225. (1) Spring Garden, *at* Knight's-Bridge: in the seventeenth and early eighteenth centuries there were at least five different retreats called 'Spring Gardens', the most fashionable of which was the 'New Spring Garden', better known as Vauxhall Gardens. Little is known about the Spring Garden in Knightsbridge, which seems to have long had a disreputable air. Strype calls Knightsbridge 'a Place of no great Account for Inns or publick Houses', and does not mention the Spring Garden (vi. 67); Walford locates it 'in the grounds of an old mansion which stood on the north side of what is now Lowndes Square', and identifies it with the 'World's End' mentioned in Pepys's Diary (v. 20; cf. Warwick Wroth, *London Pleasure Gardens of the 18 C.* (1896), p. 221). In Congreve's *Love for Love*, 11, ii, Mrs. Frail defends herself against the charge that 'to be seen with a man in a hackney-coach is scandalous', but admits that 'If I had gone to Knightsbridge . . . with a man alone, something might have been said'. The tone of the place is also suggested indirectly in *Col. Jack*, when two of the hero's fellow footpads rob a coach between Hyde Park Gate and Knightsbridge: 'there was in it, only a Gentleman and a Punk . . . that he had pick'd up . . . at the *Spring-Garden* a little farther; . . . when they come to the Slut, she Damn'd them, and curs'd them for robbing the Gentleman of his Money, and leaving him none for her' (pp. 64–5).

(2) Temple-Bar: 'a stately Gate, with two Posterns' designed by Sir

Christopher Wren, which stood at the junction of the present Strand and Fleet Street, 'where the Freedom of the City of *London*, and the Liberty of the City of *Westminster* doth part' (Strype, iii. 278).

Page 226. (1) *and never heard more of them*: omitted in the second edition, the phrase suggests that D. had not yet planned the remainder of the episode, since of course Moll does hear a great deal more of them.

(2) They go . . . their Liver: cf. Prov. 7:22–3; *App. Jour.*, 8 April 1721 (Lee, ii. 360). In the remainder of the paragraph, 'the foul Disease' is evidently venereal.

Page 227. *his Reason . . . had given him up*: in *The Commentator* No. lvi (15 July 1720), D. presents a comparable character named 'Thomas Wine Cellar'; for attacks on drunkenness, cf. also *Col. Jack*, p. 421; *G.L.S.C.*, pp. 6, 64; *The Poor Man's Plea* (1698), in *True Coll.*, p. 291. This man's situation also resembles at several points a case of conscience printed three decades earlier in the *Ath. Merc.*, xi, i. 9.

Page 237. *prepar'd for the wick'd Part*: cf. *More Reformation: A Satyr upon Himself* (1703): 'The Bottle conquers all his Reformation,/And makes Religion stoop to Inclination . . . Thank Heaven! there's few such Hypocrites as these;/That wipes his Mouth and acts without Remorse,/Sins and repents, repents and sins in course' (in *Second Vol.*, p. 42).

Page 238. (1) *three Cups Inn*: 'On the Ely side of St. John Street near Hick's Hall' (*New View*, i. 82; cf. Strype's map, iv. 61).

(2) Hadly *just beyond* Barnet: in the second edition 'just beyond' is altered to 'near', but in *Brit. Dep.*, Hadley appears just beyond High Barnet on the main Holyhead road, 12 miles from London (p. 51).

Page 239. *into* Newgate-Street: 'Though Defoe's place names may be plotted on a map, in the reading they give the impression not of an ordered map, but of a jumble, a labyrinth in both subject and object, in Moll and in the city, in the individual and in the world (Stuart Miller, *The Picaresque Novel* (1967), p. 92). By and large this is so, although Moll's route often cannot be traced on a modern map—much of her path in the present passage was obliterated when Smithfield market was expanded in the nineteenth century—and contemporary maps show that this area was in fact a maze of alleys, courts, and lanes (see Strype's maps of Cow Cross and the Charterhouse, iv. 61, and the wards of Faringdon Within and Without, iii. 231). D. exploits but does not strictly speaking create the labyrinthine jumble of Moll's London surroundings.

Page 240. (1) White-Chappel . . . Stratford *and* Bow: Strype calls Whitechapel 'a spacious fair Street for Entrance into the City Eastward'; at this corner, he says, 'ply a great Number of Stage Coaches . . . that belong to

Stratford Bow . . . and other places' (ii. 27; see map, ii. 3, and D.'s *Tour*, i. 6).

(2) *the* Flying-Horse, *without* Bishops-gate, *where the* Chester *Coaches then lay*: Hatton locates the Flying Horse 'on the E. side of *Bishopsgate str.* just without the Gate' (*New View*, i. 30); cf. Strype, ii. 109, and map, ii. 90. In the area were 'divers great Inns . . . of a considerable Trade, and resort for Waggons and Stage Coaches that go Northwards' (Strype, ii. 107). The first- and second-edition reading '*Cheston*' is almost certainly a mistake for '*Chester*'.

(3) *Huckaback Linnen*: a kind of coarse linen used for towelling, etc. Its manufacture is described in *C.I.H.T.*, ii. 400; in *Plan Eng. Comm.*, D. reports that 'at one Market in *Lancashire* . . . there is the Value of 500*l.* a Week sold in Hukabacks only; yet . . . this sort of Linen is scarce seen at *London*' (pp. 154–5).

(4) *so many Ells*: 'Ell, a Measure containing Three Foot and Nine Inches' (Phillips).

(5) *Flint Glasses*: 'A pure lustrous glass, now made from a composition of lead oxide, sand, and alkali' (*OED*); Houghton reports that 'Our glass-men for making the best flint-glass use instead of powder of flints a very white sand, such as we strow upon writing, which is commonly brought from *Maidstone* in *Kent*' (*C.I.H.T.*, ii. 50).

(6) *Mr.* Henzill'*s Glass-house*: 'Sometime in the reign of queen Elizabeth . . . came over to England from Lorraine, the Henzells . . . They were by occupation glass-makers. They settled at Newcastle, and wrought in their trade at the Close-gate on the river Tyne . . . at a place called from their abiding in it the Glass houses' (M. A. Richardson, *The Borderer's Table Book* (1846), i. 240; cf. also ii. 102). D. mentions the glass houses of Newcastle in *Col. Jack*, p. 108, and in the *Tour*, ii. 251; cf. also John Brand, *Hist. and Antiq. . . . Newcastle upon Tyne* (1899), ii. 45. There are numerous references to Newcastle in the *Letters* and the *Review*; D. was evidently well acquainted with the commercial and political life of the town.

Page 241. Pitcher . . . Well: this proverb, common in seventeenth-century rogue literature, may owe its origin to Eccles. 12:6; cf. *New Dict. Cant. Crew*; Richard Head and Francis Kirkman, *The English Rogue* (1928), p. 43; Francis Kirkman, *The Counterfeit Lady Unveiled* (1673), ed. Spiro Peterson (1951), p. 93; *Comp. Hist. Highwaymen*, p. 86.

Page 244. I may keep . . . discharge that Prisoner: 'A Constable cannot detain a Man at his Pleasure; but only stay him to bring him before a Justice, to be examined'; when a prisoner is once in custody, it is a felony for the constable voluntarily to permit his escape (Jacob, *New Law Dict.*). In practice, however, 'hired officers' (see next note) discharged prisoners on their own initiative: 'Though fortune yield thee captive, ne'er despair,/

But seek the constable's consid'rate ear;/He will reverse the watchman's harsh decree,/Moved by the rhet'rick of a silver fee' (John Gay, *Trivia*, III, ll. 315–8, p. 85).

Page 245. Constable happening to be not a hir'd Officer: constables were chosen annually by the parish vestry from among local householders. The office was irksome and unsalaried, and substantial parishioners usually paid a fine rather than serving; in 1721 D. himself gave £10 to be excused from such parish offices in Stoke Newington. On the 'insupportable hardship' of serving as constable, see his *Parochial Tyranny* [1727], p. 17. The task was thus shifted to hired deputies 'that make it a Trade, and continually take Money, to permit all manner of Lewdness and Debaucheries' (*Review, Supp.* (Sept. 1704), 26; cf. *An Effectual Scheme for the Immediate Preventing of Street Robberies* (1731), p. 14). A typical satire of the day speaks of constables, 'Who with their mercenary Staves/ Protect Night-walking Sluts and Knaves,/For Bribes, and always are as ready,/ T'oppress the Honest and the Needy'. ([Ned Ward], *The Parish Gutt'lers: Or, The Humours of a Select Vestry* (1722), pp. 18–9). The inefficiency, unpopularity, and corruption of the entire arrangement are richly documented in Sidney and Beatrice Webb, *English Local Government*, Vol. 1, *The Parish and the County*, p. 62 f.

Page 247. (1) *his Servants refusing to go with him, when I had Charg'd him with him*: i.e. the mercer's servant's refusing to go with the constable, when Moll had charged the constable with the mercer's servant. The necessary correction of first-edition 'he' to 'I' was made in the second edition; the rest of the third-person pronouns, confusing but correct, were allowed to stand.

(2) *the great loss . . . daily by Lifters and Thieves*: 'such is the slippery dealings of this age, especially in mercers and drapers business, that the shop-keeper ought never to turn his back towards his customers; and this is the reason why the mercers and drapers in particular are oblig'd to keep so many journeymen, and so many apprentices in their shops, which were it not for the danger of shop-lifting, wou'd be a needless, as it is a heavy, expence to them' (*Comp. Eng. Trades.*, i. *Supp.* p. 44).

Page 248. Hicks's Hall, *the* Old Baily: 'Hick's-hall is situated in the middle of St. John's-Street, toward the south end, and is the sessions-house for the justices of the peace of the county of Middlesex' (*Voy. Don. Man. Gon.*, p. 85; see Strype, iv. 61); the Old Bailey, also a court of justice, was 'commonly called the *Sessions House*; as well for the City and Liberty thereof, as for the County of Middlesex' (Strype, iii. 281; cf. *infra*, p. 284, 'carried down to the *Sessions-House*').

Page 249. petty Fogging hedge Soliciter: 'Born, brought up, habitually sleeping, sheltering, or plying their trade under hedges . . . hence used

generally as an attribute expressing contempt' (*OED*, s.v. 'hedge'); cf.
Ned Ward's 'Character of a Pettifogger', *London-Spy*, pp. 192–5).

Page 250. Suit of second Mourning: there were two stages of mourning; in
the second, the dress might be of silk rather than crape or bombazine,
with the linen accessories fringed rather than plain; *The Spectator* describes
a woman 'dressed in a black tabby [silk] mantua and petticoat without
ribbons . . . an agreeable second mourning' (Cunnington, pp. 317–8, 118,
139).

Page 252. the Lawyer was only to hint privately to him: changed (mistakenly) in the second edition to 'them': the antecedent is 'the Mercer', last
referred to as such five paragraphs earlier, but the subject of the four
intervening ones.

Page 253. an Instance of a compleat baseness of Spirit: cf. the account in
App. Jour., 4 Mar. 1721, of a man who had quickly made and lost a fortune
in South Sea stocks: 'as he was unmeasurably Insolent in his fancy'd
Prosperity, he is . . . in as great an extream of Abject meanness of Spirit
in his Adversity . . . he must have but a mean Share of Spirit . . . that
debases himself to the most Scandalous Submissions undesir'd; nor do
such base Cringings assist him, or recommend him to any Thing but
Contempt' (Lee, ii. 347). D. himself had more than once been compelled
to 'Submissions', but could take pride in having been above 'base Cringings' toward those who had him in their power: see his *Letters*, pp. 1–18.

Page 254. Gazette: 'An official journal containing lists of government
appointments and promotions, names of bankrupts, and other public
notices' (*OED*).

Page 255. burnt to Death at a Stake: on 5 July 1721, Barbara Spencer was
burnt at the stake at Tyburn; she had been convicted of coining, which
was punishable as high treason (*Select Trials*, pp. 32–5; cf. Luke O. Pike,
History of Crime in England, (1873–6), ii. 287–8). According to the
Newgate Calendar 'the common practice, consistent with the dictates of
humanity, is first to strangle them, so that they are dead before the fire can
touch the body' (quoted in Charles Gordon, *The Old Bailey and Newgate*,
n.d., p. 153). Moll's alias in her male disguise had been *Gabriel Spencer*
(*supra*, p. 218). Ben Jonson killed an actor of this name in a duel in 1598,
but the echo may be mere coincidence.

Page 256. (1) Dutch *People at St*. Catherines: in this neighbourhood,
immediately east of the Tower of London, there had been a sizeable
colony of Dutch and Flemings since the mid-sixteenth century; see
Strype, v. 299, and George, p. 343.

  (2) Exchange *in the* Strand: often referred to as the New Exchange, as
distinct from the Royal Exchange. In the Restoration drama its young

shopkeepers are much preyed upon by gallants rather than thieves: cf. Wheatley, ii. 581–3.

Page 257. *fine Ladies* . . . *in the* Mall: the half-mile-long Mall had been laid out by Charles II and remained the most fashionable promenade in London throughout the eighteenth century. The literature of the period is full of allusions; see William B. Boulton, *Amusements of Old London* (1901), ii. 140–55; Wheatley, ii. 457–9.

Page 260. *the Box and Dice go round a pace*: from the terminology two paragraphs later it is clear that the game is hazard, the nature and rules of which are summarized by William B. Boulton, *Amusements of Old London* (1901), i. 134–6.

Page 261. *I would have told them to see how much I had got*: i.e. counted them; the second edition unaccountably emends 'told them to see' to 'him to have seen', which spoils the sense, as does the reading 'told him to see' (World's Classics edition, p. 301).

Page 262. (1) *the Itch of Play*: in *Aug. Triumph.*, D. calls 'the Itch of gaming' 'the most pernicious of Vices' and 'a kind of avaritious Madness', from which people 'ought to be restrained by Law' if they 'have not Sense to command themselves by Reason' (p. 39); cf. *The Commentator*, No. xvii, 26 Feb. 1720.

(2) *a rumbling time of the Year* . . . *the City was Thin*: 'To Rumble, to make a hollow Noise' (Phillips), but possibly a misprint for 'rambling'. 'Towards autumn . . . the town is thin . . . the court, the nobility and gentry, the lawyers, and many of the citizens being gone into the country. . . . The west end of it appears perfectly deserted; in other parts their trade falls off ' (*Voy. Don Man. Gon.*, p. 95). Cf. also [Thomas Baker], *Tunbridge-Walks . . . A Comedy* (1703), p. 1.

Page 263. (1) Sturbridge *Fair* . . . Bury *Fair*: in the *Tour*, D. says that 'Bury-Fair, like Bartholomew-Fair, is a fair for diversion, more than for trade', whereas Sturbridge Fair is 'not only the greatest in the whole nation, but in the world'; he briefly satirizes the 'scandalous liberty' of the 'assemblées' held nightly during Bury Fair, but surveys in detail the trade carried on at Sturbridge Fair (i. 51–2, 80–5). The latter was held annually from 24 Aug. to 29 Sept. in a field near Barnwell Abbey, two miles east of Cambridge; for another contemporary impression, see Ned Ward's *A Step to Stir-Bitch Fair* (1700).

(2) *an old Bite*: 'An imposition, a deception; passing from the notion of playful imposition or hoax, to that of swindle or fraud' (*OED*). For earlier versions of this 'bite' in the literature of roguery, see *Comp. Hist. Highwaymen*, pp. 48, 71; for an actual case, committed in London on 2 May 1721, see *Select Trials*, p. 39.

(3) *a little Country* Opera-*House*: according to the Bury and West Suffolk Record Office, there is no evidence that there was a permanent theatre of any kind in Bury until 1734, when the building known as the Market Cross was fitted up as a theatre by the town authorities. Mention is made in the records of the north hall of the Guildhall being used for theatrical purposes in 1722, although there are no details as to performances. But an advertisement for 'three different Consorts, to be performed by the best Performers in the Opera, as well Vocal as Instrumental', at 'Mr. Eastlands Assembly Rooms in Bury', 'for the Diversion of the Quality and Gentry, in the Time of Bury-Fair', appeared in the *Suffolk Mercury*, Vol. viii, No. 14 (25 Sept. 1721). (This information was kindly provided by Mr. Frank Fordham, Borough Librarian of Bury St. Edmunds.) It is probably to some such concerts as these that D. refers.

Page 264. *fairly*: 'gently, peaceably, quietly, softly' (*OED* 5); or perhaps rather 'completely, fully, quite, "clean" ' (*OED* 7).

Page 265. (1) Dutch *Ducatoons, or* Rix *Dollars*: silver coins, the ducatoon varying in value from 5s. to 6s. [25p. – 30p.], the rix dollar worth 2s. 3d. to 4s. 6d. [11p. – 23p.] (*OED*).

(2) *Wash-balls*: 'A ball of soap (sometimes perfumed or medicated) used for washing the hands and face, and for shaving' (*OED*); Ashton quotes a curious 'composition for best Wash balls' from a contemporary journal: the ingredients include rice powder, flour, starch powder, white lead, orris root, and colouring (p. 97).

Page 266. *useful things, Necessaries for a Gentleman*: changed in the second edition to 'necessary', the sb. may be correct: cf. 'stores of Linnen and other Necessaries', *supra*, p. 85; 'Tools, and Cloaths, and other Necessaries', *supra* p. 86.

Page 267. (1) *scratching his Pole*: = 'poll', the top of his head.

(2) *a Town . . . upon a River*: probably Stratford St. Mary, Suffolk, on the river Stour; see *Brit. Dep.*, p. 138.

Page 269. *a Working Silver-Smiths in* Foster-lane: Strype calls Foster Lane, in Aldersgate Ward, 'a Place of a good resort for Silver Smiths, who forge and work Plate for the Goldsmiths, who sell it' (iii. 120).

Page 271. *clap'd in upon me*: 'to come or go with sudden and decisive motion, throw oneself, drop, fall, strike *in*' (*OED*, citing *Far. Adv.*); cf. *Rox*. p. 282.

Page 273. *fatal Tree*: 'a gallows' (*OED*).

Page 274. (1) *hellish Noise*: 'at the women felons' apartment in the Common-Side . . . are a troop of hell-cats lying head and tail together in a dismal, nasty, dark room, having no place to divert themselves but at the grate, adjoining to the foot passage under Newgate, where passengers may, with surprise and pity, hear them swear *extempore*, being so shamefully versed in that most odious profanation of Heaven that volleys of oaths are discharged through their detestable throats whilst asleep' (*Memoirs of the Right Villainous Jack Hall* (1717), quoted in Introduction to *Comp. Hist. Highwaymen*, p. x; cf. Strype, iii. 194).

(2) *an Emblem of Hell itself*: a commonplace in seventeenth-century 'characters' of Newgate, already fully developed in Geffray Mynshul's *Essayes and Characters of a Prison and Prisoners* (1618; reprinted 1821), p. 49 f. Cf. Head and Kirkman, *The English Rogue* (1928), pp. 67–8 (borrowing from Mynshul). A work of 1718, on one of the Southwark prisons, was entitled *The Marshalsea, or Hell in Epitome* (cf. William Rendle, *The Inns of Old Southwark* (1888), p. 55 n.). See also 'the Master's side', *infra* p. 295 n. 1.

(3) *mourn'd that I was to be punish'd for it*: during a storm, Roxana has 'only such a Repentance as a Criminal has at the Place of Execution, who is sorry, not that he has committed the Crime, as it is a Crime, but sorry *that he is to be Hang'd for it*' (p. 129). Capt. Singleton is 'afflicted at the punishment, but not at the crime; alarmed at the vengeance, but not terrified at the guilt' (*Rom. & Narr.*, vi 223). And *Col. Jack* notes that 'the Terror of Punishment works strongly upon the Mind: In view of Death, Men are fill'd with Horror of Soul, and immediately they call that Repentance which I doubt is too often mistaken; being only a kind of Anguish . . . an Amazement founded upon the dreadful View of what is to follow' (p. 166).

Page 275. (1) *put it all up to my Score*: i.e. charged it all to my account (see 'run a Tick', *supra* p. 223 n.). The sale of spirits in Newgate and other major prisons contributed greatly to the profits of the keepers and the disorders of the inmates. On the custom of 'garnish', which compelled every newcomer to pay for drink for other prisoners, see Sidney and Beatrice Webb, *English Prisons Under Local Government* (1922; reprinted 1963), p. 25 n. 1.

(2) *the College*, as they call'd it: a traditional slang term for Newgate; see *New Dict. Cant. Crew*; the *Brief Hist. Account of the . . . Six Notorious Street Robbers* (1726), reprinted [mistakenly?] as D.'s in *Rom. & Narr.*, xvi. 349; and particularly Ned Ward's account of 'that famous University', *London-Spy*, p. 112.

(3) *The Bell at* St. Sepulcher's: 'the big bell of St. Sepulchre's church was rung on the night preceding every execution of criminals confined at Newgate; at midnight the sexton would come outside the convict's cell and after ringing a hand-bell would deliver a speech. Next morning— when the procession moved toward Tyburn—it stopped at St. Sepulchre's

where a clergyman would say prayers for those to be hanged and the bell would ring again' (Radzinowicz, pp. 174–5; cf. *New View*, ii. 547, 707).

Page 276. Devil is not so black, as he is painted: see Morris P. Tilley, *Dict. of the Prov. in Eng. in 16th & 17th C.* (1950), p. 152; used again in *E.H.R.A.*, p. 364.

Page 277. (1) *have her up for Tampering with the Evidence*: 'Preventing Evidence to be given against a Criminal is punishable by Fine and Imprisonment; and a Person was fined one Thousand Marks in such a case' (Jacob, *New Law Dict.*). The law applied to those who 'but endeavour to dissuade a Witness from giving Evidence against a Person indicted', as well as those who succeeded in stifling evidence; see Hawkins, *Treatise*, p. 59.

(2) *forfeit his Recognizance*: a sample of 'A recognizance to prosecute a felon' is printed in Giles Jacob, *Mod. Just.*, p. 358. 'In these Recognizances . . . the usual Penalty is 40*l*.' (Jacob, *New Law Dict.*). Cf. 'Recognizances', *supra* p. 218 n. 1.

(3) *Ordinary of* Newgate: the chaplain, whose main duty was to prepare condemned prisoners for death. 'The Ordinary of Newgate's Place is a Cure of Souls, and such a one as upon many Accounts ought particularly to be served by a Man of the most exemplary Goodness and Holiness possible; and therefore is very far from being infamous' (*Coll. Misc. Lett.*, i. 148). In spite of this charitable distinction between the office and the men who actually filled it, D.'s picture of the Newgate Ordinary in *M.F.* reflects a more common contemporary view; it may also reflect D.'s animosity towards Paul Lorrain, Ordinary of Newgate from 1698 until his death in 1719, whom D. had attacked in 1703 in *A Hymn to the Funeral Sermon*. Cf. 'to extort Confessions . . . for Private Ends', *infra* p. 288 n.

(4) *all his Divinity run upon Confessing my Crime*: 'as the prisoner and others, his fellow-sufferers, expressed it, the Chaplain urged the confession of sins they were never guilty of, to such a degree, as put them out of temper, and hindered them from that great work which they had but so small a time to perform' (R. Mawson, *The Case of Matthias Brinsden* (1722), quoted in *The Works of Thomas Purney*, ed. H. O. White (1933), pp. xvi–xvii).

(5) *a full Discovery . . . without which . . . God would never forgive me*: 'It is a Question among Divines whether a Criminal can be a true Penitent, and may expect God's Mercy, if he does not, when he confesses his Offence, add to his Confession a full Discovery of all his Accomplices; so as that to the utmost of his Power they may be brought to Justice. I am not Casuist enough to decide this Cause, tho' in my Opinion, I incline to the Negative, namely, that he cannot' (*App. Jour.*, 29 Dec. 1722; Lee, iii. 83).

Page 278. *like the Waters . . . which petrifies . . . whatever they . . . drop upon*: cf. D.'s account of the formation of stalactites and stalagmites in the caverns of Derbyshire: this process, he says, 'is frequent and natural both to water and to stone, placed thus under ground, and seems to be the way by which even stone itself, like other vegetables, fructifies and grows' (*Tour*, ii. 170–1). Among earlier naturalists, Thomas Robinson similarly observes that 'The *active Principle* in the Generation is a *petrifying Juice*, or *Water*' (*An Essay towards a Nat. Hist. of Westmorland and Cumberland* (1709), p. 27). In the *Nat. Hist. of Oxford-Shire* (1676), Robert Plot describes '*concretions*' made of 'a cold sort of *water*, thickened with *terrene* and *petrifying* particles' (p. 96); cf. also Charles Leigh, *The Nat. Hist. of Lancashire, Cheshire, and the Peak, in Derbyshire* (1700), p. 69.

Page 280. (1) *topping Gentlemen*: 'eminent, chief, noted; as *A Topping Man*' (Phillips); Johnson calls it 'a low word'.

(2) *Press-Yard*: 'for the better sort, who have the appearance of Gentry, there are very good Rooms and other Accomodation in the *Press Yard*, a place so call'd from a Press there, used for the pressing such obstinate Criminals as will not plead to their Indictments, &c.' (*New View*, ii. 757). 'On each floor of the prison were certain apartments technically belonging to the keeper's house and known as the Press-Yard. They were let to such prisoners as could put down a handsome fee and were prepared to continue paying through the nose for every slight mitigation of their discomfort' (Arthur L. Hayward, Introduction to *Comp. Hist. Highwaymen*, p. x).

Page 281. (1) Hind, *or* Whitney, *or the* Golden Farmer: three notorious seventeenth-century highwaymen, executed in 1652, 1694, and 1689 respectively; see *Comp. Hist Highwaymen*, pp. 136–40, 42–50, 30–6. D. alludes to Whitney elsewhere: see *More Reformation* (1703), in *Second Vol.*, p. 61, and *A Hymn to the Pillory* (1703), in *Second Vol.*, p. 111.

(2) *I shall be cast*: 'to be found or declared guilty; to be convicted; to be condemned' (*OED*).

Page 282. (1) *endeavour'd to possess them with favourable Dispositions*: a bill for preventing the corrupting of juries was introduced in the Commons early in 1721: see Abel Boyer's *Political State of Great Britain* for February (xxi. 190–1). 'As for the Corruption of Juries', D. writes the following year, 'we have a Law lately pass'd, which, it is hoped, will remove all Complaints of that kind' (*App. Jour.*, 10 Mar. 1722; Lee, ii. 497). But I cannot account for D.'s optimism, since the only relevant statute passed in this session (9 *Geo*. 1. *c*. 8. *s*. 11) added no new legislation; it merely noted the problem and extended former statutes for another seven years.

(2) *the Jury found the Bill against me*: 'If the bill be found, it is brought

in *billa vera*'; 'these two words, signify . . . that the Presenter hath furnished . . . probable Evidence, and worthy further consideration. Whereupon the Party presented is said to stand *indicted* of the Crime, and tied to make answer to it, either by confessing or traversing the Indictment' (*Voy. Don Man. Gon.*, p. 132; Blount, s.v. '*Billa vera*'; cf. also Radzinowicz, pp. 91-2).

(3) *Housebreaking, that is . . . Burglary*: '*Burglary* . . . Is where a Man breaketh and entereth the House of another, wherein some Person is, in the Night-time, to the Intent to commit some Felony, whether the intent be executed or not . . . the like offence committed by Day is called *House-Breaking*' (Jacob, *New Law Dict.*, s.v. 'Burglary').

(4) *as white as a Clout*: proverbial; clout = lump, patch of cloth.

Page 283. receiving . . . and encouraging: in *The Life and Actions of Jonathan Wild*, D. refers to 'an Act passed in the reign of the late King William, making it felony to buy or receive any stolen goods, knowing them to be stolen' (*Rom. & Narr.*, xvi. 247). I have found no such Williamite act, but in the first session of Anne's reign, Parliament passed 'An Act for punishing of Accessaries to Felonies and Receivers of stolen Goods' (1 *Ann. c.* 9); and according to 4 *Geo. 1. c.* 11, 'Buyers or receivers of stolen goods *knowingly* shall be transported to *America* for 14 years' (Hawkins, p. 515). In the eyes of the law Mother Midnight is therefore no less a felon than the actual thieves.

Page 284. not . . . broken up the Doors, or so much as lifted up a Latch: 'if a Person be within a House, and Steal Goods, and then open the House on the Inside, and go out with the Goods, this is Burglary, tho' the Thief do not break the house. . . . If a Thief unlocks a Door, or draws the Latch of a Room, to rob, &c. . . . these are Breaking' (Jacob, *New Law Dict.*; cf. also *Lives of the Most Remarkable Criminals* (1735), ed. A. L. Hayward (1927), p. 6).

Page 285. small Comfort: apropos of two defendants acquitted of conspiracy, but found guilty of consulting, machinating, proposing, and intending to beat, wound, and evilly treat a man, D. says 'sure there is no great matter got to the Defendants by such Acquittal. A Man indicted at the *Old-Baily* for Fellony and Burglary, after a long Tryal, has the comfort of being acquitted of the Burglary, but must be hang'd for the Felony' (*A True State of the Difference between Sir George Rook, Knt. and William Colepepper Esq.* (1704), p. 37).

Page 286. as any mad Woman in Bedlam: Bethlehem Hospital, the lunatic asylum; Roxana similarly calls herself 'as truly craz'd and distracted . . . as most of the People in *Bedlam*' (p. 234).

Page 287. I now began . . . in this World: cf. 'A Vision of the Angelick

World', in *Rom. & Narr.*, iii. 261, where D. had anticipated this paragraph in nearly the same words. Cf. also *J.P.Y.*, pp. 175–6.

Page 288. *Ordinary . . . whose business it is to extort Confessions . . . for private Ends*: i.e., in order to obtain materials for so-called 'Newgate biographies', brief life-histories, confessions, and dying speeches of malefactors, which were sold in the streets and at the criminal's execution. These catchpenny works generally purported to be taken down by the Newgate Ordinary from the condemned man's own words. As an agent for John Applebee, a publisher who specialized in Newgate biography, D. is thought to have interviewed and written about various criminals between 1719 and 1726. The hero of *The Remarkable Life of John Sheppard* says that all the divines who visited him were 'gingerbread fellows' who came 'rather out of curiosity than charity, and to form papers and ballads out of his behaviour' (*Rom. & Narr.*, xvi. 205; cf. *Comp. Hist. Highwaymen*, Pref., p. 2; Radzinowicz, pp. 178–81).

Page 289. *Tears . . . yet . . . surprizing Joy*: the same paradoxical emotions characterize D.'s other penitents: 'his Face was ever smiling . . . and yet his Eyes had Tears standing in them, at the same time . . . for he had a delightful Sorrow, if that be a proper Expression, in speaking of [his conversion]' (*Col. Jack*, pp. 164–5); 'no tears like those that are raised by any humble sense of infinite, undeserved, forgiving grace; and no joy . . . like the joy that is founded in sorrow, founded in repentance' (*Due Prep.*, in *Rom. & Narr.*, xv. 166).

Page 290. (1) *a favourable Report from the Recorder to the Secretary of State*: on this procedure see Radzinowicz, p. 111.

(2) *Joy overset*: with Moll's account of a sudden reprieve leading to 'dangerous Swooning', cf. Crusoe's report that 'when a malefactor [at the gallows] . . . has a reprieve brought to him . . . they bring a surgeon with it, to let him blood that very moment . . . that the surprise may not drive the animal spirits from the heart, and overwhelm him: *For sudden joys, like griefs, confound at first*' (*Rom. & Narr.*, i. 50); this line is quoted again in *A New Family Instructor* (1727), p. 236. On the principle that 'Joy is as Extravagant as Grief' and just as dangerous, cf. *Col. Jack*, p. 26; *A Continuation of Letters Written by a Turkish Spy at Paris* (1718), pp. 109–11, 266–8; *J.P.Y.*, p. 245; *Rox.*, pp. 253–4; and esp. *Far. Adv.*, in *Rom & Narr.*, ii. 17–21.

Page 292. *but still unable to give vent to it by Words*: 'I was' is probably called for after 'but still'; the second edition omits the entire phrase.

Page 293. *an humble Petition for Transportation*: Moll's transportation is not strictly speaking a sentence but a form of conditional pardon. Only after the passage of 4 *Geo.* 1. *c.* 11 in 1718 could the courts themselves order transportation for non-capital offenses: until that date, 'According to the common law and the Habeas Corpus Act it was illegal to inflict a penalty of exile or transportation. But it was not illegal to pardon a felon upon the condition that he transport himself out of the country, and the term of his exile might thus be fixed as the authorities desired. From 1655 to 1718 this was the legal device by which convicts were transported' (Smith, p. 91; cf. James C. Ballagh, 'White Servitude in the Colony of Virginia', *Johns Hopkins Univ. Stud. in Hist. and Polit. Sci.*, xiii (1895), *passim*). But for 'Felony not within the Benefit of the Clergy', transportation remained a condition of royal pardon rather than a direct court sentence under the act of 1718; see Radzinowicz, pp. 108–10; A.G.L. Shaw, *Convicts and the Colonies* (1966), p. 25 f.

Page 294. *I'll warrant you Child*: the sense seems to demand 'I'll warrant you *not*, Child'—i.e. 'I'm sure you *haven't* ever known of a convict worth £100 being transported'.

Page 295. (1) *the Master's side of the ordinary Prison*: in *Memoirs of the Right Villainous Jack Hall* (1717), this part of Newgate is likened to Hell, 'for really no place has a nearer resemblance to the eternal receptacle of punishment than the Master's-Side. The Cellar, where poor relentless sinners are guzzling in the midst of debauchery and new invented oaths which rumble like thunder through their filthy throats, is a lamentable den of horror and darkness' (quoted in Introduction to *Comp. Hist. Highwaymen*, p. vii).

(2) *the Law strictly obliging them to have two Witnesses*: I cannot account for this, since 'The Testimony of one single Evidence is sufficient for the King in all Causes, except for Treason; where there must be two Witnesses to the same overt Act, &c. In all other Criminal Matters, one Evidence is enough; and to a jury one Witness is sufficient' (Jacob, *New Law Dict.*, s.v. 'Evidence'; cf. Charles Viner, 'Evidence', *A General Abridgment of Law and Equity* (1746), xii. 36 n.; [Geoffrey Gilbert], *The Law of Evidence* (1756), pp. 150, 154.).

Page 300. (1) *Grasiers . . . going to* Burford *Fair in* Wiltshire *to buy Sheep*: Burford is actually in Oxfordshire, and although D. was knowledgeable in all aspects of the wool trade, the mistake is probably his rather than Moll's or Jemmy's, for in *Plan Eng. Comm.*, he locates Burford Fair in Dorsetshire (p. 121). A grazier is 'one that deals in Cattel [i.e. livestock], that breeds or fattens them for Sale' (Phillips).

(2) *riding near 80 Miles . . . broke the Bone*: this passage may owe something to the story of 'Swift Nicks', who in 1676 had established an alibi for a highway robbery committed at Gad's Hill in Kent by riding in a single day to York, where he appeared as a gentleman of leisure 'at bowles on the publick green'; D. retells the story in the *Tour*, i. 104–5.

Page 302. *he could not have any Patience when he did but think of being*

Transported: cf. *Merc. Polit.*, Nov. 1716, for the similar story of a man, offered life on condition of transportation, who prefers hanging to what he regards as slavery (p. 520).

Page 305. *Security . . . that he should Transport himself, and not return within the Term*: 'Very often, security was required for the safe arrival of the convict in America and his non-appearance in England till his term of banishment had expired'. The result was frequently long delay, as a prisoner unable to furnish the necessary security remained in gaol. The sheriffs sometimes gave security themselves to avoid the expense of supporting the convict in prison (McCormac, pp. 94–5; cf. Smith, p. 97).

Page 306. *much rather venture*: probably an escape, possibly even a trial—in any case not the voyage to America; the second edition avoids obscurity by making him 'much rather go directly to the Gallows'.

Page 309. *all things are bought for Tobacco*: 'Tobacco is our Meat, Drink, Cloathing and Monies; not but that we have Money both *Spanish* and *English* pretty plenty, which serves only for Pocket Expenses, and not for trade, Tobacco being the Standard for Trade, not only with the Merchants, but also among ourselves' ('*Part of a Letter from the Reverend Mr.* Hugh Jones *to the Reverend Dr. Benjamin Woodroofe, F.R.S. concerning several Observables in* Maryland', in *Philosophical Transactions*, xxi (1699), p. 439). Nor in Virginia was 'any thing us'd in Traffique, but Tobacco' (Robert Beverley, *Hist. and Pres. State of Virginia* (1705), ed. Louis B. Wright (1947), p. 314).

Page 316. (1) *his round House*, as they call it: 'in merchant ships, a name given to the cabin or apartment built on the afterpart of the quarter-deck' (William Falconer, *New Univ. Dict. of the Marine*, 1815).
  (2) *Steerage*: 'That division of the after part of a ship which is immediately in front of the chief cabin; the second cabin' (*i.e. not* the usual modern meaning—an area in the bow and on a lower deck, for lowest-rate passengers) (*OED*).

Page 319. *largest River in* Ireland: the Shannon.

Page 320. *free . . . to go whither we would*: the *American Weekly Mercury* of 14 Feb. 1721, announcing the arrival of 114 convicts in Maryland, states that their term of service was avoided if they could muster enough money to pay for their passage, in which case there was 'only this part of their sentence to be answered, that they must not return to England in so many years' (quoted in Herrick, p. 121).

Page 321. *what we call a* Chairwoman: '*Chare-women*, Underdrudges, or Taskers, assistants to Servantmaids' (*New Dict. Cant. Crew*).

Page 325. *guilty . . . oblig'd to Discover it*: in an essay on the irresistible
force of conscience in *App. Jour.*, D. says 'in cases of Treason, Murther,
and the like Crimes, how often have we seen, that when the Guilty Persons
have apply'd themselves . . . to conceal their Guilt, and to make their
Escape from Justice; they have . . . by a Faltering Tongue . . . or by some
unconcealable Part of their Conduct, been their own Betrayers, discover'd
the Crime, and detected themselves' (2 Mar. 1723; Lee, iii. 110; cf. also
Review, *Supp.*, Nov. 1704, 8–10).

Page 326. (1) *extraordinary Effects*: those guilty of 'atrocious Villainy'
regularly inculpate themselves in contemporary works designed to cele-
brate divine justice. See William Turner, *A Compleat History of the Most
Remarkable Providences, both of Judgment and Mercy, Which have Hapned
in this Present Age* (1697), sigs. [Ddd2ᵛ] – [Ddd4ᵛ]; cf. *The Whole Duty
of Man* (1658), Sun. X, Par. xvi (ed. Wm. B. Hawkins, 1842, p. 181). In
Conj. Lewd., guilty secrets lead to delirium (p. 143) and to talking in sleep
(pp. 183–4).

(2) Night-Flyers: cf. Swift, 'A Description of the Morning': 'The
turnkey now his flock returning sees,/Duly let out at nights to steal for
fees' (*The Tatler*, No. 9, 30 Apr. 1709, i. 82).

(3) *those honest People they call Thief-Catchers*: two decades earlier
thief-takers are defined as those 'who make a Trade of helping People (for
a gratuity) to their lost-Goods and sometimes for Interest or Envy snaping
the Rogues themselves; being usually in fee with them, and acquainted
with their Haunts' (*New Dict. Cant. Crew*). D. often deplores thief-
catching as a 'scandalous practice', and maintains that such men as
Jonathan Wild 'deserve the gallows as richly as any of the thieves' whom
they betray (*Life and Actions of Jonathan Wild*, in *Rom. & Narr.*, xvi, 270.

Page 327. Carolina: D.'s interest in this colony dated back at least to 1706,
when he published *Party Tyranny*, and he had written in 1711 that
Carolina 'is Esteemed the Most Healthy of all Our Colonys in the North
Parts of America' (*Letters*, p. 348).

Page 328. (1) *indolent*: here apparently the consequence of having been
'bred a gentleman', but contemporary writers often deplore the indolence
of planters in the middle and southern colonies. Robert Beverley reproaches his fellow Virginians for 'a Laziness that is unpardonable', calls
them 'abominable Ill-husbands', and says, 'I should be asham'd to
publish this slothful Indolence of my Countrymen, but that I hope it will
rouse them out of their Lethargy, and excite them to make the most of all
those happy Advantages which Nature has given them' (*Hist. and Pres.
State of Virginia* (1705), ed. Louis B. Wright (1947), pp. 296, 295, 319).
Indolence was usually traced to the balminess of the climate or the rich-
ness of the land, seldom to the cheapness of labour, see John Lawson, *A*

New Voyage to Carolina (1709), ed. Hugh T. Lefler (1967), p. 90; Herrick, p. 71.

(2) *which they call there Hunting*: rather than 'shooting'; D. seems to have been struck by this Americanism (which persists), for he repeats it, *infra* p. 331.

(3) *the ordinary Work of the* Indians: George Alsop reports an 'extreme glut and plenty' of venison; deer are 'daily killed by the *Indians*, and brought in to the *English*', and some are also 'killed by the Christian Inhabitant, that doth it more for recreation, than for the benefit they reap by it', so that 'the flesh of Venison becomes (as to food) rather denyed, than any way esteemed or desired' (*A Character of the Province of Maryland* (1666), ed. John G. Shea, 1869, p. 38).

Page 329. *from* Carolina, *loaden with Rice*: discussing English imports in 1728, D. says, 'As to the Rice, it is a new Trade, being the Product of one Colony only, namely of *Carolina*, and has been brought over in Quantity but a few Years; but it is an encreasing Trade' (*Plan Eng. Comm.*, p. 182); in 1721 South Carolina produced 21,879 barrels of rice but had difficulty marketing it ([Francis Young], *A View of the Trade of South Carolina* (1722), pp. 9–14). On the necessity of importing foodstuffs into Virginia, owing to exclusive concentration on tobacco-raising and the sloth of the planters, see Oldmixon, p. 316.

Page 330. Philips's Point: 'probably the present Clay Island at the mouth of the Nanticoke River in Dorchester County' (George E. Gifford, 'D.D. and Maryland', *Maryland Hist. Mag.*, lii (1957), 308.

Page 331. (1) *a very honest Quaker . . . much kindness and simple Honesty*: for the presence of Quakers on the Eastern Shore of Maryland at this period, see George Fox's *Journal*, ed. John L. Nickalls (1952), pp. 612–64 *passim*; D. may have owed further information to William Penn, with whom he is known to have had some dealings (see *Letters*, pp. 7–8); but as George E. Gifford points out, 'The one positive source of information . . . was his tobacco factor in Maryland, Samuel Sanford' ('D.D. and Maryland', *Maryland Hist. Mag.*, lii (1957), 312). The phrase 'and simple Honesty' was omitted in the second edition; other sympathetic Quakers, more noted for kindness than for honesty—of which they observe the letter but not the spirit—appear in *Rox.* and *Capt. Singleton*.

(2) *we took up a large peice of Land from the Government of that Country*: see textual note. Tending to bear out the second edition reading 'Government' is the captain's remark, *supra* p. 317, that ex-servants 'may purchase Land of the Government of the Country'; but possible support for the first edition reading 'Governor' is to be found in Moll's report that they purchased land 'of the Proprietors of the Colony', *infra* p. 332.

Page 336. *five and fifty* Spanish *Pistoles*: Oldmixon's conversion table (p. 316) reckons the pistole at 17*s*. 6*d*. (87p.), so that Humphry's gift was worth £48.13. The actual buying power of this sum is hard to assess. Local commodities were extremely cheap, but nearly all manufactured goods had to be imported from England, and were correspondingly costly (see Oldmixon, p. 292).

Page 338. *Yatch*: mod. *yacht*; '*Yatches*, are Vessels with one Deck . . . of Burden from 30 to 160 Tun' (John Harris, *Lexicon Technicum*, ii (1710), *s.v.*).

Page 339. *Horses, Hogs, and Cows . . . a Penitent . . . a reform'd Man*: the influence of worldly prosperity on Jemmy's spiritual and moral regeneration has evoked critical scorn, but D. elsewhere defends this principle: 'In a state of life where circumstances are easy, and provision for the necessaries of life, which the best saint cannot support the want of, is quietly and plentifully made, has not the mind infinitely more room to withdraw from the world, than when at best it must wander for its daily food?' (*Ser. Refl.*, in *Rom. & Narr.*, iii. 12). Cf. *Col. Jack*, pp. 308–9.

Page 340. *whole Pieces*: 'A length (varying according to the material) in which cloth or other textile fabric is woven' (*OED*); 'a certain Number of Ells or Yards of Cloth, Stuff, Silk, &c.' (Phillips).